LUCINDA BRAYFORD

LUCINDA BRAYFORD

By

MARTIN BOYD

E. P. DUTTON & COMPANY, INC.

NEW YORK

1948

PRINTED IN THE UNITED STATES OF AMERICA
AT THE COUNTRY LIFE PRESS, GARDEN CITY, N. Y.

CONTENTS

Lucile M. Keeney

LUCINDA BRAYFORD

Part One
1858–1912
THE SHOULDER-KNOTS OF LIVERY

Ne fallait-il pas à l'amour, comme aux plantes Indiennes, des terrains preparés, une température particulière? Les soupirs au clair de lune, les longues étreintes, les larmes qui coulent sur les mains qu'on abandonne, toutes les fièvres de la chair et les langueurs de la tendresse ne se séparaient donc pas du balcon des grands châteaux qui sont pleins de loisirs, d'un boudoir à stores de soie avec un tapis bien épais, des jardinières remplies, un lit monté sur une estrade, ni du scintillement des pierres précieuses, et des aiguillettes de la livrée.

MADAME BOVARY.

CHAPTER ONE

On a November evening in the middle of the nineteenth century, Mr William Vane, an undergraduate of Clare College, Cambridge, gave a wine party in his rooms. His guests as well as himself had that day ridden to hounds. There had been two kills and they were in high spirits.

A Mr Brayford, of Trinity, while singing a roundelay, let his cigar butt fall on to a spot on the carpet where Mr Vane yesterday had dropped and broken a bottle of scented hair pomade. No one noticed the burning cigar, but Mr Brayford was still sober enough to notice the smell of smouldering wool and smoking perfume.

"Gad!" he exclaimed. "What a stench!" A few minutes later he said: "Gad! I'm going to puke."

Vane had also noticed the smell. Brayford's last remark stimulated a dormant echolalia in his confused and heated brain.

"Gad! It's the Puseyite!" he cried. "The filthy man must be burning incense. Let us wash the filthy man."

Shouting "No Popery!"—which expressed in two words the extreme limit of their religious aspiration—the party trooped down the stairs and burst open the door of the rooms below, which were kept by Aubrey Chapman, a scholarly, slightly asthmatic, mildly High Church undergraduate, who intended to take Holy Orders. Chapman had just retired to bed with a hot brick wrapped in newspaper, as he had that afternoon caught a chill while attending evensong in King's Chapel. Vane and Brayford dragged him from his cosy refuge, while the rest of the party made havoc of his rooms. Then carrying the weakly protesting Chapman and a poor print of the Sistine Madonna, the only evidence of Popery they could find, they marched across the court of that charming seventeenth-century palace out onto the bridge. Chapman clung to one of the stone balls to prevent himself being flung into the Cam, but Vane loosened his fingers, and he fell with a splash into the icy river. Brayford flung the print of the Madonna after him, and with a final shout of "No Popery!" they returned to their claret, leaving Chapman to struggle out on the far bank and, clad only in his dripping nightshirt, to climb painfully over the wrought-iron gate, back onto the bridge.

Vane, as he pulled the corks from another half-dozen bottles, said:

"Two fox and a Puseyite—a damned satisfactory day!"

However, the outcome of the day gave less satisfaction than the day itself. Aubrey Chapman developed double pneumonia and nearly died. He belonged to a family which had ramifications throughout the ecclesiastical and academic worlds. It so happened that Vane's tutor, though bearing a different name, was Chapman's cousin. He offered Vane the choice of paying all the expenses of Chapman's illness, which were considerable, or of being sent down. Vane chose the former, but it put him in financial difficulties. He was socially ambitious and would not change his style of living, nor give up the companionship of men like Brayford, who was the nephew of a viscount.

One night, when playing some gambling game in Brayford's rooms at Trinity, he saw an opportunity of retrieving his financial position. The party's attention was momentarily distracted by a new arrival. He changed a king which had been dealt to his neighbor for a two which had been dealt to himself. But he was not naturally a cheat. He might run up tailors' and wine bills he had little hope of paying, or deceive girls of a lower class, but he had never done anything he believed to be dishonorable. He hesitated as he moved the cards, and in that moment Brayford turned his head. He said with faint surprise:

"Gad, Vane, you're cheating!"

After this it was not possible for Vane to stay at Cambridge, nor, as his father, a London attorney, advised, even in England.

"You'd better go to Australia," said his father. "You like horses."

He paid his son's debts and gave him a very generous sum of capital with which to start life in the new country. For some time after this, William Vane used to say that his life was wrecked by "the damned Puseyite," and that he was in fact a martyr to religious conviction.

Aubrey Chapman, in spite of his illness, took a First and was ordained, but he did not recover from the effects of his ducking, and after two years in a curacy in the Midlands, his doctor told him it was suicide for him to remain in the English climate. His father, a country vicar, advised him to go to Australia, as there men of his connections and scholarship must be few, and he would doubtless obtain preferment, and might with regained health become a colonial bishop at an early age, which was better than a premature admission to the Kingdom of Heaven. So, a few years later than William Vane, after some tedious months in a six-hundred-

4

ton sailing ship, he landed in Melbourne, where he presented himself with letters of introduction at Bishopscourt, a bluestone building on Eastern Hill.

Meanwhile, William Vane, having spent some of his capital on cutting a dash in Melbourne, had invested the rest in a share of a station called Noorilla in the Riverina. It was owned and managed by a dour Ulsterman called McBane, with an only daughter. Vane gave McBane to understand that he was richer than he was, that his father, who actually had given him his inheritance in his lifetime, would leave him more money, and then married the daughter. She was a pretty girl who took after her mother, a lively and sensitive creature from Mayo who had died under the harsh nature of her husband and the harsh Riverina sun.

McBane was thrown from a buck-jumper and killed before he discovered the real extent of his son-in-law's finances. He had been a very careful and industrious man, and had been fortunate in his seasons. William Vane suddenly found himself, when still quite a young man, richer than his own father. He at once installed a manager at Noorilla, and brought his wife to Melbourne, where he built a house at Kew, which in reference to a Norfolk Island pine planted in the center of a circular carriage drive he called "The Pines."

While still in a state of elation with his good luck, he met Aubrey Chapman, just arrived from England, walking down Collins Street. He slapped him on the back and hailed him as his greatest benefactor. Chapman, who was weak from the voyage, who was feeling dreadfully lonely and detested the crudities of this new country, regarded Vane as the man who in all his life had done him the greatest injury. He replied with the acidity of an affronted clergyman, but Vane, who had just had a couple of whiskies, was too jovial to notice this. He invited him to come out to The Pines, and even referred lightly to the incident on Clare bridge.

"No ill feelings, I hope? Just youthful high spirits, eh?" He put his hand affectionately on Chapman's shrinking shoulder and, feeling the better for the encounter, strolled off down the street. Chapman did not take advantage of the invitation to visit The Pines until it was repeated nearly thirty years later.

The next night Chapman dined at Bishopscourt. There was a Mr Lanfranc there, a young Irish barrister. The talk was about Cambridge. Mr Lanfranc said:

"There's a man called Vane who has been put up for the club. I believe he's a Cambridge man. You didn't happen ever to run across him?" he asked Chapman.

Aubrey Chapman was tempted of the devil. He saw, not the kingdoms of the world, but the gray courts of Cambridge, the noble court of Trinity, the soaring pinnacles of King's and the lovely court of Clare, where he had once hoped to be a Fellow, and from which he was now separated by all the oceans of the world. He was possessed by intolerable nostalgia and bitterness. Tears came to his eyes, which appeared to squint, and his gentle refined face suddenly looked extraordinarily vicious and mean.

"He was sent down for cheating at cards," he exclaimed.

"Oh!" said Mr Lanfranc, and quickly changed the conversation.

The bishop noted that Chapman seemed to be an ill-natured and even ill-bred young man, to disturb with this sordid fact the urbanity of his dinner table. If he thought Mr Lanfranc should be made aware of it, he could have taken him aside afterwards. He did not mark Chapman down for preferment.

William Vane, on the other hand, was blackballed for the Melbourne Club, which inflicted on him a social disability nearly as great as that of being sent down from Cambridge. He had always been a little flamboyant; now, to counteract this disability, he increased the ostentation of his living. He made frequent trips home to England and brought back with him racehorses and expensive carriages.

The effect of his malicious disclosure on Aubrey Chapman himself was very different. He remained a curate for five years and then was appointed Vicar of Jolimont, a suburb close to Melbourne on the eastern side, which became noted some years later as the scene of a terrible railway accident. On receiving this living, Chapman married the daughter of a doctor, a very jolly, pretty girl who treated him with a motherly affection which was almost contemptuous. They had two children, a boy called Dick, and a girl five years younger, called Julie, who took after her mother.

Vane's first two children were girls. Then he had a son, Frederick, born in the same year as Dick Chapman. Fred and Dick went to the Melbourne Grammar School together, and, to Vane's amusement and Chapman's distaste, became close friends. Dick often brought Fred, on his way home to Kew, to tea at Jolimont Vicarage, to which Mr Chapman could not object without revealing the reason for his hostility to the Vanes, the incident on Clare bridge.

Julie Chapman, aged ten, thought Fred Vane, aged fifteen, next to her brother Dick, the most wonderful boy in the world. Dick, alone of the Chapmans, visited The Pines, and from him she heard glowing tales of this house, of the rich furniture and the rich cakes, the carriages, the horses and the extensive orchard. Fred's sumptuous, inaccessible background enhanced his attraction.

When Julie was eighteen and Fred twenty-three, she had only changed her opinion of him by removing the exception of Dick. They now met at occasional dances and parties, and before Julie was nineteen they were engaged to be married. Fred came to ask Aubrey Chapman's consent to the marriage. Chapman, after thirty years in the colony, had that morning received an intimation of his appointment as a Canon of St. Paul's Cathedral, Melbourne. His natural gentleness of disposition, which he had always longed to be strong enough to display, now had an opportunity to express itself without loss of dignity. He forgave himself his malicious disclosure at the bishop's dinner table, which was harder to do than to forgive Vane for throwing him over the bridge, and with a gesture of magnanimity he allowed Julie's marriage to Fred Vane. Also it was more satisfactory that she should marry the son of a rich man.

He then accepted an invitation to dine at The Pines. He was a little dismayed to find how baroque in appearance William Vane had become since they had last met. He was now a widower. He did not appear to be quite sober, and boasted of his horses and wines, forcing different vintages on the reluctant canon, and insisting in a rather curious manner on the soundness of his wealth. His two daughters, being used to it, were unconcerned at their father's behavior. They were patronizing to the canon, and particularly so in their references to Julie. They were older than Fred and neither of them married, as they had treated every suitor coldly, expecting him to be after their father's money, which was probably just, as they were not very attractive girls.

The wedding took place quite soon. The Misses Vane were bridesmaids, and believing that one wedding brought on another they were elated in their manner, which was both feline and ladylike.

Immediately after the wedding William Vane left for England. Fred and Julie, on their return from their honeymoon, were to live at The Pines. The two sisters were also to live there until they had found some suitable dwelling. William Vane had not specified what this was to be. Fred and Julie came back from their month in Tasmania to learn that he had fallen overboard from the P. and O. liner into the Great Australian Bight. The result of this was more disastrous than Aubrey Chapman's immersion in the Cam. Mr Vane was drowned.

7

CHAPTER TWO

"Apparently poor papa had outrun the constable," was the elder Miss Vane's greeting to the honeymoon couple, as they descended from the wagonette at the door of The Pines.

"What had he done?" asked Julie, wide-eyed, and looking all dewy in her dismay.

"Our father never did anything dishonorable," said Miss Vane in reproof, "but, like many a gentleman before him, he lived beyond his means. The expression I used implies that he was considerably in debt."

"Aren't we rich, then?" asked Julie, like a child who has had a sugar cake snatched from its mouth.

"We may be temporarily inconvenienced," said Miss Vane.

"Oh, well, I've always got you," said Julie, and gave Fred a hug and a kiss, which Miss Vane thought in bad taste, seeing the information they had just received.

Miss Vane's "temporarily inconvenienced" was rather more than an understatement. Fred had hitherto lived on an allowance and had little knowledge of his father's affairs. When he investigated them, in the company of Mr Blake, the family lawyer, who recently had built a house in a field adjoining The Pines, he found that Noorilla and The Pines were both heavily mortgaged, that his father had gradually sold all his other assets, and that this year's income from Noorilla had already been spent in giving a final appearance of wealth at the wedding.

Fred held a family council of himself, Julie, the three sisters and Mr Blake. William Vane had some years ago left his property in two equal parts, one to go to Fred, the other to be divided between the sisters. Fred told his sisters that if everything was sold up and they claimed their share they might not have more than a few hundred pounds each, and he himself would have to take some more or less humiliating employment. But if they would forgo their claim for the present, he would dismiss the manager and go to Noorilla, where by practicing the most rigid economies he might ultimately pay off the mortgage, and the Vanes would retain their status as pastoralists. Neither the sisters nor Julie at that time would have thought of opposing any plan of Fred's. Mr Blake demurred, but finally the arrangement was agreed to. The sisters were

8

to rent a house in Studley Park Road and open a school for girls.

Julie's reign as a bride at The Pines lasted for a month, and all that time was spent in packing, contriving to meet bills and in sorting out what furniture could be spared for the school, and what was too personal and valuable for the tenants. Julie wanted to take the heavy cut glass, a Boule writing table and some Crown Derby china up to Noorilla, but Fred said it would be unsuitable. This was the only intimation she had of what life at Noorilla was to be. She had an idea that it would be lonely, but she was too much in love to mind that. She had visited two very comfortable squatters' homes in the Western District, and imagined that the elegance of life at Noorilla would be only a degree less than that at The Pines. Fred, who was more like his maternal grandfather than his father, was only concerned with what he called "the realities of life," by which he meant hard cash, and had not troubled to disillusion her. He had not foreseen the shock it would be to Julie to arrive at Noorilla, and when she spent the first night in weeping, he thought he had married an hysterical fool.

Aubrey Chapman had come to Australia for health and preferment, William Vane had come *malgré lui*. McBane arrived twenty years before them, in search of one thing only—money. He allowed nothing to stand in the way of its accumulation. What he intended to do with it when accumulated, he had no idea. Being a strict Presbyterian, he was obliged to believe that it would not benefit him in the next world. In those last moments as he was flung from his horse, it was probably an immense satisfaction to him to know that he owned, if only for a few gasping seconds longer, property worth £100,000, which, if he had lived, he had neither the taste nor education to spend intelligently, nor the nature to spend on pleasure.

The first homestead at Noorilla had been built with his own hands of thick clay walls, whitewashed, with a bark roof. It was rather a pleasant building, what there was of it. After his wife died, McBane fixed his affections on his daughter, who coaxed him into building a more respectable house. He added four square weatherboard rooms to the original adobe, put a verandah round them, and roofed the whole with galvanized iron. The furniture remained poor and hideous.

The absence of any suggestion of luxury, even of comfort, was satisfying to Fred. He hated anything that reminded him of his father's extravagance. He had always been a little restive under idleness, and now he felt he had a real man's work to do, to face a tough contest with circumstances and to wrest his inheritance from ruin.

If Julie tried to make the homestead at Noorilla more elegant in ways that cost nothing, such as cutting up an old silk dress into cushion covers for the hot ugly little drawing-room, he was displeased. He expected her as a dutiful wife to be concerned only with his struggle, in which he was not successful. The year of his arrival at Noorilla there was a drought. The next year there was another, though not so serious. The Vanes had no money at all, after they had paid the interest on the mortgage and wages to the jackeroos. They could live on their own mutton, but they needed a little cash. Canon Chapman, wondering what strange stars bound him in affliction to William Vane, even after his death, allowed Julie a hundred pounds a year, his whole private income. This merely enabled Julie, Fred and their baby daughter, Lydia, to survive. It did not provide Julie with any comfort. She had to do all the housework unaided, cook the eternal mutton and rice pudding for their own and the jackeroos' dinner and look after the baby.

Her lot was made less bearable by the fact that Fred did not seem to think it hard. He was slaving on the station, and he assumed that a devoted wife would be glad to do her share indoors. Mrs Chapman had come back with Julie for a few months after the baby was born, but her hostility to Fred on Julie's account became so open that Julie begged her to return to Melbourne and look after the canon. Although Julie had defended Fred against her mother's attacks, when Mrs Chapman had left she began, under the extra burden of work, to admit to herself their justice. She and Fred often snapped irritably at each other. The only time that they were happy together was when he watched her give Lydia her evening bath, but even then Julie was often so tired that she could only treat it as another burdensome duty.

She wrote to her mother and said she thought she would go crazy from loneliness and exhaustion if she did not have some help, but she could not afford to pay wages to a servant, nor was one likely to come alone to such a remote place.

There had just come to stay in a boarding house at Jolimont a Miss Watson, the daughter of a country doctor who had died leaving her a tiny income. She had a high forehead, graying hair, and peered brightly through steel-rimmed glasses. She had passed matriculation at the Melbourne University and liked to be with cultured people. She was afraid that the necessity to augment her income might force her into crude associations.

Mrs Chapman, unaware of her position, told her of Julie's plight. This seemed to Miss Watson a heaven-sent opportunity to live within her means and to associate with gentlepeople. It seemed almost too good to be true, so that she asked timidly, as if begging a superlative favor:

"Do you think, Mrs Chapman, she would care for me to go and stay for a while? Although I had thought of teaching, I am very efficient at domestic work, and fond of the country, while I should adore the little baby, especially as it's a girl. I should not require a salary, as I have a small income."

This offer to Mrs Chapman also seemed too good to be true. After half-hearted warnings about the roughness of life at Noorilla, she said that she was sure Julie would be delighted. After a brief correspondence it was arranged that Miss Watson should go *au pair* to Noorilla. When this was settled, she felt that the period of ill fortune and loneliness which had followed on her father's death had come to an end. She had been obliged to sell the house that she had lived in since girlhood, and as she could not bear to live elsewhere in the valley where it was situated, she had broken all her ties of friendship and come to Melbourne where she knew no one. Or rather, she had not broken the ties of friendship, but had pulled them away from their adhesions, and they were left floating and searching blindly in the air, seeking to attach themselves to something. For the first week or two in the boarding house at Jolimont she could not believe that her old friends and haunts were inaccessible to her, and she lay at night in a state of numb pain, which might be momentarily eased by a vivid memory of some corner of her father's house or garden, only to return with increased wretchedness when the memory had passed. When in Jolimont church they sang: "If I forget thee, O Jerusalem, let my right hand forget her cunning," Miss Watson's voice broke into silent sobs.

Between the time when it was decided for her to go to Noorilla and the day of her departure, the tendrils of her affections began to sprout with new life, preparing to twine themselves round Julie, her baby and the station homestead. She was so full of happy anticipation that the other people in the boarding house treated her with unusual kindness, and some of the tendrils of her affection became attached to them, so that it was quite a wrench for her to leave. The heaviness she felt at her departure was lightened in the train by conversation with a very agreeable schoolmaster. Fred, taciturn and resentful at having to waste an extra day in the town hanging about to meet her, did not provide a pleasant contrast to her cultivated traveling companion. She experienced a slight shock of dismay when he led her out to the high cart in which they were to do the thirty-mile drive back to Noorilla.

11

Fred did not believe in making conversation. If he had nothing to say, he said nothing. He had nothing to say to Miss Watson. He was adequately polite in handing her and her belongings into the trap, which was a kind of enlarged and debased dog-cart, but after a few minutes he only replied in monosyllables to Miss Watson's eager friendliness, and they bumped along in silence for five hours over the unmade roads. It was no longer the worst heat of summer, but the roads were parched and dry. They were followed by clouds of white dust. The smaller cloud of black flies also journeyed with them, hovering over their backs.

Miss Watson consoled herself by thinking that in an hour or so this grim journey would be over, and she would be surrounded by the amenities of a station homestead. It was a pity that Mr Vane was not more cultured, but it was not really on him that she had fixed her hopes.

When at last they arrived in the station yard, where the footprints of cattle were hard-baked in the mud, and drove up to the little mud-colored house, and Julie came out to meet them, Miss Watson had a sensation of devastating loneliness. Julie had spent the last week polishing and scrubbing to make the bare and hideous little house as attractive as possible. The last thing she had tidied was herself. Although her dress was a good one, she had not had time to press it, and her exhaustion gave her the look of a poor woman in her best clothes.

Miss Watson was seeking for someone to be kind to her. She was prepared to spend herself in gratitude for this kindness. But Julie appeared as if she were only in the condition to receive, not to give kindness. She hardly looked like a lady. The house certainly was unlike a gentleman's home.

"Are you really Mrs Vane?" asked Miss Watson, who was given to speaking her thoughts.

"Yes," said Julie, smiling, "I hope you had a good journey. I expect you are tired."

Miss Watson was too unhappy to speak. Julie gave her an anxious glance, and said:

"I'll show you your room. I'm afraid it's not very luxurious here."

The room allotted to Miss Watson opened off the end of the verandah. The floor was bare except for two little red woollen mats by the bed and the washstand. The iron bedstead and the chest-of-drawers with its badly fitted mirror had been enameled white by Julie. The room smelled not unpleasantly of enamel and floor polish. There was a vase of white daisies—the only flowers available—on the dressing table, and a new cake of "Brown Windsor" soap on the washstand.

Miss Watson looked at the room, and in reply to Julie's apologies for the drawer that jammed and the corner curtain which took the place of a wardrobe, said:

"I expect I shall manage."

Julie gave a nervous smile, and went out, shutting the door behind her. On the verandah she met Fred, carrying in Miss Watson's trunk.

"I doubt whether it's worth bringing in," she said.

"Why?"

"I don't think we're up to her standard."

"If she doesn't like it, she can go," growled Fred. "I didn't want her to come, anyhow."

Julie did not reply, but went along to the kitchen to open a tin of salmon for high tea.

In her room Miss Watson sat on the bed in an almost stunned condition. When she thought of the kind people in the Jolimont boarding house, she wished she could cry, but her disappointment was too deep and her loneliness too dry for that. She could not think what to do. It would be impossible to stay in this place, and how could she leave without offending Canon and Mrs Chapman? Then she felt indignant with them for letting her come here. Indignation gave her an access of energy, and she washed and then sat down to brush her hair.

She was very proud of her magnificent head of hair, which she had encouraged by doing Harlene hair drill. It fell round her like a weeping ash, concealing the upper part of her body. Through it came her spindly arms, vigorously wielding a silver-backed brush and comb, and in the small head which sprouted this amazing growth, her thoughts darted feverishly, seeking a way of escape.

She had just done her hair again when Julie knocked on the door and said: "Tea is ready, Miss Watson."

In hot weather Fred usually sat at meals in his shirt-sleeves, but today, persuaded by Julie, he had put on a dark coat. There was a star of small creases at the back of the neck, where it had hung on the peg. Before they sat down he and Julie took their table-napkins and drove the flies down the room and out of the open window, which he immediately shut to prevent their return.

Fortunately tonight the two jackeroos were camping on outlying parts of the station, so it was easier for Julie to attempt a little elegance. In addition to the luxury of tinned salmon, the cold mutton had been sliced and decorated with parsley in a silver entrée dish, which Julie had smuggled up to Noorilla. There was also a vase of daisies on the table.

Fred was made a little self-conscious by these arrangements, and became facetious.

"I don't know," he said, "whether this parsley is meant to be eaten. I'm not a rabbit."

"Parsley is only eaten in sauce," said Miss Watson, "but it makes things nice and fresh. In the valley I always put parsley on the butter."

Fred warned Miss Watson that they could not run to tinned salmon every night. Then he asked why there was no tomato sauce.

"There is," said Julie, and handed him a little blue jug. It was usually in a bottle.

"There's a fly in it," said Fred. "Why can't you leave it in the bottle?"

Julie flushed uncomfortably. Miss Watson began to feel sorry for Julie. She was very loyal to her sex, and she thought Fred clumsy and boorish, just like a man. The hostility he had awakened in her made her feel more kindly towards Julie.

She helped her clear away the tea and to wash up. She was very good at housework, and made a few suggestions as to how things might be managed more easily.

After they had washed up, they went out to sit in deck chairs on the east verandah. The sun was setting on the other side of the house. It was pleasant here in the cool shadow, with the distant hills and the dry plains turned purple and gold beyond the green leaves of the vine.

Julie asked tentatively: "Do you think you will like it here?"

Miss Watson's deck chair creaked. Her face was red beneath the almost Fijian aureole of her hair. She was making a tremendous effort to be both straightforward and to protect herself from exploitation.

"Mrs Vane," she said, gasping a little, "I'm sorry. It's not what I expected. I can't stay." Then seeing Julie's look of dismay she added involuntarily, "At least, not for more than a month."

Julie's eyes brightened.

"Even if you stayed for a month it would be a great relief to me," she said.

Miss Watson was immediately angry with herself for agreeing to stay for so long. She at once blamed Fred and switched her anger onto him. She would tell him a few home truths before she left. He had no right to take a young lady from a nice home like Joli-

14

mont Vicarage and bring her to a place like this. How she herself was going to get through a whole month here, she could not imagine.

When at ten o'clock Julie woke Lydia to feed her, she took Miss Watson to show her the baby. This softened Miss Watson's heart so much that she became more reconciled to her visit.

In a few days the battle between herself and Fred became open. Fred was amused and called her "What-ho!," at first behind her back and then to her face. This became corrupted to Watteau, and soon Julie and the jackeroos adopted the nickname.

When the month was up, Watteau found that her floating adhesions had curled themselves round Lydia.

"I'll stay just a little longer, as the weather is cooler now," she said to Julie, "and I have always heard the winter is very pleasant in the Riverina."

Before Christmas she said:

"I wouldn't like to leave you alone to cope with the Christmas dinner. I'll stay till New Year."

In the New Year she said she would stay till the weather became too hot. When the weather became too hot, she had not the heart to leave Julie.

There was another drought. The paddocks were brown. The Vanes' situation became desperate. They had not enough money to meet the interest on the mortgages. The rent from The Pines paid part of this and hitherto the station had paid the rest. They had to sacrifice Julie's allowance to try to meet it, and Watteau gave her income to be used for household expenses.

Julie now hoped that Fred would no longer be able to carry on, and that they would have to return to Melbourne. If he took a post in a bank or some office, he would earn enough for them to live at least in simple comfort. They would have gas and main water. She consoled herself by making secret plans of what she would do when the crash came. They had about six hundred pounds in shares which Fred had kept in her name in the event of failure. She decided that with this they could buy a little double-fronted villa somewhere in Hawthorn or Armadale. They could take some good furniture from The Pines, and she would live comfortably with friends and without this ceaseless anxiety. Fred at times appeared almost crazy. He was brutally rude to herself and to Watteau, although without Watteau's help they could not have held out so long. She now felt that she hated Fred. They seldom spoke amicably to each other by day, while their reconciliations at night were infrequent and purely physical.

Julie told Watteau of her plans, and together the two women agreed that life at Noorilla was hell.

"I shall never forget what you have done for us, not till I die," Julie said tearfully to Watteau.

"I did it for you and Lydia, Mrs Vane," said Watteau.

One morning at breakfast Fred muttered:

"I believe the drought is going to break."

His blue eyes had an odd staring look in them. Outside the sun scorched down from a cloudless sky.

"I can't see any sign of it," said Watteau.

Fred darted a look of malevolent contempt at her and went off to drive into the town on business. Julie came out onto the verandah and called to him to bring back a new kettle.

"There's no money," he shouted, and jerked the horse's reins. She watched him drive away across the brown paddocks which stretched to the horizon, unbroken by any green save the scanty gray-green of gum trees. The baked ground, cracked like the glaze on old pottery, sent up heat as from an open oven door.

Julie felt a kind of satisfaction at the desolate aridity of the scene.

"We can't hold out much longer, thank Heaven," she thought.

Fred stayed the night in the town, as it was too much for the horse to return the same day. Julie and Watteau spent a pleasant evening discussing Julie's plans for the future. The six hundred pounds was mentioned several times.

Fred came back the next evening in time for tea.

"Did you buy a kettle?" asked Julie.

"No, I bought some sheep," said Fred.

"Be serious," said Julie irritably.

"I am serious."

"And I bought a herd of elephants," said Watteau.

Julie was looking curiously at Fred. She thought he really had gone out of his mind, as he had not spoken in the tone he used when joking.

"How many sheep have you bought?" she asked.

"Some thousands—all the sheep on Bostock's station."

"You don't really mean it?"

"I do mean it. The drought is going to break, so you needn't think they are green spectacles."

"They'll need green spectacles if they're going to find any grass here," said Watteau.

"You can't pay for them," said Julie.

"I bought them from Bostock for sixpence each. They'll die if he keeps them. There's just enough grass here to keep them alive for a week or two, and the drought is going to break."

"How are you going to pay for them?"

"We've got that six hundred pounds."

Julie went pale. Watteau, trembling with indignation, pushed back her chair and stood up.

"You are a wicked, cruel man!" she exclaimed. "You don't think of anyone but yourself. This is no place to keep a lady brought up like Mrs Vane was, and now you go and spend the last of the money gambling like your wicked old father. That's all it is, sinful gambling."

"Be quiet about my father," growled Fred.

"I shall not be quiet. I have a right to speak. I have lent my own money to keep us all from starvation, and I was very glad to do it for the sake of Mrs Vane and baby, but not to buy starving sheep." Watteau, when her sense of justice was affronted, was not troubled by delicate feelings.

"You'll get your money back."

"And how, I should like to know?"

"The drought's going to break."

Julie felt sick with disappointment. She cleared the dirty plates and cups from the table and took them out to the kitchen, where she began to wash up. She heard Watteau's shrill voice like that of an angry sparrow, still raging at Fred. She had passed that stage. She had a quiet hatred for Noorilla, too deep to be expressed. She hated the dishes she washed, and the grey soapy water. She began to hate parts of her own body, her coarsened hands with the skin broken round the nails.

Soon Watteau came out carrying a tray with the rest of the things from the tea-table.

"I'm not sorry I spoke as I did to Mr Vane," she said, defensively. "It's time someone opened his eyes. You've put up with enough in my opinion."

"I'm not going to put up with any more," said Julie quietly.

"What are you going to do?"

"I'm going back to Jolimont. I'll take in sewing or teach music."

"Well, I must say I'm very glad to hear it," said Watteau.

She and Julie spent the evening on the verandah, again making plans. If Canon Chapman would continue his allowance, with Watteau's little income they might take a small house and teach music together. Julie was dour and determined, but Watteau began to enjoy herself. She loved a conspiracy, especially one of two women against a man. Whenever she passed Fred in the next few days she gave him a malicious leer, as much as to say: "You don't know what's in store for you, my good man."

All through these days the huge flocks of mournful sheep were being moved from Bostock's, the adjoining station, onto the dry plains of Noorilla. A number of them, half-starved, smelly and bleating, were herded through the station yard. Round and above them clung the cloud of white dust. It came in the evening through the open doors of the house, settling in a fine film on the tables and hanging in the curtains, filling the place with the smell of sheep. While Fred was entirely preoccupied with moving the flocks, Julie was surreptitiously packing.

On the day that the last of Bostock's sheep was moved into Noorilla, she finished her preparations. In the morning she was going to ask Fred to drive her with Watteau and Lydia to the station. She would say that she was going on a visit to her parents. She would write from Jolimont to say that she was not coming back. She felt that she hated Fred so much that she could not even bear to have the intimacy of an open quarrel with him.

At night the air was heavy and the bedroom intolerably close. She lay awake, thinking of all the circumstances of her marriage. This was the last night she would spend with Fred. In the double bed she kept herself as far from him as possible. A kind of dry bitterness possessed her.

After she had been lying awake, for some hours it seemed, she felt that Fred too was awake. She was terrified that he would make some sleepy half-conscious amorous approach to her, but he lay quite still. She felt he was listening, and again she was afraid that he was listening to learn whether she was awake. She tried to regulate her breathing to make it sound as if she were asleep.

She heard something drop on the iron roof, and thought it must be the noise of some bird, though why should birds be flying at night? The noise was repeated, then again, as if someone were throwing pebbles. It was not until the sound became a steady pattering that she realized it was rain. The pattering became a drumming and she heard the water gurgling into the tanks on the verandah.

"Julie!" Fred shouted, and gripped her arm. "Wake up! It's raining!"

He leapt out of bed and lighted a candle. His hands were trembling as he shielded the flame of the match. He looked up for a moment at the ceiling and then dashed on to the verandah. She heard him patter along in his bare feet to Watteau's door. He banged on it and cried:

18

"Watteau, you old fool, wake up! The drought's broken. It's raining."

Julie sat up in bed and listened. She heard Fred out in the yard shouting: "The drought's broken. By God, it's raining!"

In a few minutes he came back into the room. He had taken off his pyjamas and had been running naked in the rain. He stood in the candlelight, the water dripping from his gleaming body. His blue eyes were dancing.

"O God, we're saved! O God, we're made!" he cried. He was laughing and crying at the same time. He began to dry himself with a towel, and as he did so, he looked so beautiful and so happy that Julie suddenly felt something break inside her. She too melted with the coming of the rain. She forgave him everything and she burst into tears. He leapt into the bed and took her in his arms, at first hugging her in wild delight, then kissing her tenderly. From this reconciliation was born the second of Julie's daughters, who was christened Lucinda.

CHAPTER THREE

FRED'S SUCCESSFUL GAMBLE, which put him for the first time since his father's death in a comparatively secure financial position, was followed by another good season at Noorilla. Julie went to Melbourne for the birth of Lucinda and Watteau remained at the station to look after Fred and the jackeroos. The house had been made more comfortable and they could now afford two servants. Watteau and Fred spent their time together in bickering, which Fred openly enjoyed and Watteau enjoyed without realizing it. She said that she would leave when Julie returned, now that her help was no longer needed. However, when Julie came back with Lydia and the baby, she found that she could still be of use, in spite of the two maids, and she postponed her departure until Lucinda was out of the cradle.

The next year there was again a good season. In the autumn the tenant of The Pines wrote saying that he wanted to give up the house at the end of November. Julie looked wistful when Fred read out this letter. Fred smiled at her across the table. A year's prosperity had already tinged his manner with pompous indulgence.

Love, driven out of the window by the years of poverty, had returned in a non-romantic form. Julie, during those years, had grown to admire success more than anything. Fred was successful, so now she admired him, especially as to have an admirable husband increased her own sense of importance. He had been desperate and sometimes brutal under failure, but he now enjoyed making an occasional generous gesture. It was evidence of his prosperity.

"Would you like to go back to The Pines?" he asked.

Julie raised her eyes expressively.

"Of course it's impossible," said Fred. "Some day, perhaps." He took up his letters and left the room. He intended to savor to the full the sense of power it gave him to make this concession. A week later he said:

"What would you do if you did go back to The Pines?"

"Oh!" cried Julie, "I should have a 'Day at Home'!"

Fred teased her for a few days longer and then announced that he had taken The Pines out of the agent's hands, and that they were to go there before Christmas. When the elation, which lasted for three or four days, had subsided, Watteau said to Julie:

"I don't suppose you'll want me any longer, Mrs Vane. I'm very glad if I've been of any help, I'm sure."

"Oh, Watteau!" exclaimed Julie, "I couldn't possibly do without you. You *must* come to The Pines with us. I never contemplated anything else. I should be dreadfully hurt if you left us."

The arrival of the Vanes at The Pines had something of the *éclat* with which a favorite musical comedy actress arrives on the stage. Kew society rustled with expectation and faint amusement. Julie was so obviously delighted with her possessions and her every prospect, that she communicated pleasure to those who met her. She had the naïve satisfaction of the *nouveau riche* in her new luxuries, and yet she was not very vulgar. Miss Lanfranc, a daughter of the Irish barrister, now a judge, with whom Canon Chapman had dined many years ago at Bishopscourt, was among the numbers of people who left cards at The Pines. When she came away she smiled and said to her sister Brigid: "There is always an element of vulgarity in success."

Fred began to collect stations as other people collect pictures or china. Julie first of all had a brougham, then a landau, and finally a private hansom. It was the private hansom which established her position as a leader of society, and compensated for the slight disability of living in Kew instead of Toorak. All these carriages were emblazoned with the dubious Vane crest.

Not only in the number of carriages but in The Pines itself there was evidence of Fred's increasing wealth. The house had been repainted before they moved in. The sisters had chosen the wallpapers, as Julie was up at Noorilla. This had been a small fly in Julie's ointment, but Fred had said firmly, "You can trust my sisters' taste." The most startling change at The Pines was when the old wooden verandah was removed and the house surrounded by a stucco balustraded balcony in emulation of the Italianate mansions which were being built in Toorak by Sir Percival Everard-Jones, one of the instigators of the land boom. He had just finished his own house, Tourella, the largest of them all and a riot of colonnades and marble.

Julie wanted to go to England. Nearly all the people "in society" had been at least once to England. She suggested it tentatively to Fred but he was quite unresponsive. He disliked the whole idea of England. It was where his father had squandered his good Australian fortune. In England, he realized, no one would know who he was. He would be thought unimportant if not actually common.

Once, when he was just off on a round of inspection of his stations, he asked Julie what she would do while he was away. He did not ask her to come with him. He knew that she did not want to see a sheep station again as long as she lived.

"Why don't you go to Colombo and back for the trip?" he suggested. "The sea air will do you good."

"By myself?" said Julie, pleased but doubtful.

"You could take Watteau."

Fred made this suggestion partly from kindness, but also because it would please him, when people in Queensland or the Riverina asked him where his wife was, to be able to say, "Oh, she's just run across to Colombo for a change," and to add something affectionately patronizing about women's whims.

The day after Fred left for Queensland, Julie and Watteau embarked on a P. and O. liner for Colombo. Watteau was very excited. She had never been on a ship before. The aunts brought Lydia to see them off, but not Lucinda who was still a baby. Lydia cried when the great wall of the ship parted from the pier, bearing Julie and Watteau away from her. This black cliff with its myriad blind eyes of portholes, its sudden spewings of dirty water, and its smells seemed as sinister to her as it was enormous. Julie waving her handkerchief from the first-class deck also wept a little and called that she would be back in a month, but Lydia was too young to measure time.

Watteau too noticed the ship's smell. It rather tempered her excitement. She and Julie shared a cabin, and as they arranged their things while the ship steamed down Port Phillip Bay she said now and then:

"I hope I shall become used to the smell."

21

They went down to dinner before the ship entered the Rip, that space of turbulent waters caused by the currents at the mouth of the bay. It was not the thing to dress for dinner on the first night out, but Watteau, perhaps determined not to be dispirited by the ship's smell, had put on a modestly low dress. Round her neck was a black velvet band with a cameo at the throat. She ate her soup and a little fish. Then they entered the Rip. As the ship rolled, Julie thought that Watteau's color was a reflection from the green wave which rose over the portholes of the saloon, but when the translucent wave subsided Watteau remained the same color.

"I'm very sorry, Mrs Vane," she said, "but I must go up for some air." She lurched from the saloon, and other passengers glanced amusedly at this lady with the festive garments and woebegone face.

When Julie came up from dinner she found Watteau in bed. Her face was still green and damp with sweat. She looked very limp. It was very rough in the Bight and she remained more or less in this condition during the week's voyage to Fremantle. The only times when she showed any spirit were when Julie suggested that she should make an effort to come out on deck into the fresh air. She was furious at the suggestion that she should leave her bunk. By the time they reached Fremantle she was really ill, and the doctor said that it would be unwise for her to continue the voyage.

Fortunately Watteau had a cousin in Perth who had come to meet the ship. At first Watteau, with that sense of duty which was her chief characteristic, insisted on continuing the voyage.

"Mr Vane has paid my fare and he expects me to go with Mrs Vane," she said. "It would be terrible to waste all that money."

Julie said it would be worse for Watteau to commit suicide. She said that they would stay in an hotel in Perth, which would be quite a pleasant change. However, as the cousin offered to have Watteau to stay, and as Watteau was so upset at the idea that Julie should be deprived of her trip to Colombo, it was agreed that she should go on alone and pick up Watteau on the return journey.

Relieved of her sea-sick companion, Julie enjoyed the rest of the voyage. She made a whist-four with a returning A.D.C. and a Mr and Mrs Bumpus, who were jolly people, well known in Melbourne. They also had left behind a little daughter who was called Clara.

She was sorry to leave the ship at Colombo, and in spite of the excitement to one who had never before left Australia, of the tropical scenery and what she felt to be the faintly exotic atmosphere of the hotel, she felt very lonely on her first evening. On the ship, freed from the encumbrance of Watteau, it had been rather easier to make agreeable associations. Now she wished that she was with her again.

All the groups at the other tables in the dining-room seemed complete. There was not one person except herself sitting alone. When she had been there three nights of her fortnight's stay, she felt that the other visitors were conscious of her presence. One or two of them eyed her curiously, possibly wondering who the pretty young woman was, and why she was staying there alone, but no one made any friendly advance, although Julie more than once, when she felt these glances on her, composed her features into an expectant half-smile. On the fourth day she felt hurt, and wished she had stayed in Perth with Watteau. After dinner she went up to her room, where she had photographs of Lydia and Lucinda on the dressing table, and she spent the evening writing a long affectionate letter to Fred, and one to Lydia to be read aloud to her by the aunts. She had to make these letters sound as if she were having a marvellous time, as she could not admit that she was not being gay and successful, but her desire to be home again was expressed so convincingly that Fred, when he read it, smiled with rather grim satisfaction. He thought this would cure Julie of wanting to gad about in foreign parts, although he had suggested it.

The next day a man with no companion appeared at luncheon. He was in the early thirties, clean-shaven, dark, and with that kind of hair which, if not kept in order, flops about and gives a boyish appearance. As with herself on arrival, the other guests seemed conscious of his presence and she saw them give him the same half-curious glances. A mother with a daughter followed him closely out of the dining-room, and at the door looked at him with that expectant smile which Julie had worn on her first days at the hotel, but the man kept his eyes lowered, and stood aside, bowing, for them to pass out before him. There was something in this aloof courtesy which made Julie sure that he was a man of some standing.

Although Julie thought herself obviously a lady, the next day at luncheon she looked at him more often than was consistent with this belief. Also in Julie's bright eyes there was a suggestion of intimacy which strangers would not regard as well-bred. Julie, all her life, especially since her return from Noorilla, had moved amongst people who knew who she was and were pleased to see her. She had had no cause, in social defense, to suppress her natural amiability.

At dinner in the evening she felt the man's eyes rest on her once or twice. He left the room before her, and she felt a slight disappointment that she would not see him till the next day, but when she came out into the lounge he was waiting there, seated by a small table.

He flashed at her the most direct and charming smile, which somehow went with his floppy hair.

"Won't you have coffee with me?" he asked.

"Oh, I'd love to," said Julie impulsively. "D'you know I've been at this hotel for nearly a week, and you're the first person who has spoken to me."

"I'm glad I have not to wait so long for some conversation." His voice thrilled Julie. She thought it extremely gentlemanly, which seemed to make it all right for her to sit with him. Her father had a gentlemanly voice, but it was harsh and staccato, whereas this man's voice was deep and perfectly produced. They talked about the hotel and the sights of Colombo. Now and then she noticed a puzzled expression in his eyes when she spoke. She seemed to have the attitude and ideas of an ordinary gentlewoman, which from her inviting glances he had not expected, but her vowels were a little flat. Also the years on the station had affected Julie. This was not always obvious, but occasionally in some gesture of the hands, in some bleakness of expression, through all her wealth and buxom prettiness could be glimpsed the woman who had spent so long at the washtubs and the saucepans of mutton at Noorilla. She mentioned her home in Melbourne.

"Oh!" he said. "I thought you weren't English." She looked a little hurt and he added: "You have a so much nicer manner than Englishwomen abroad."

They parted early and he went off smiling to his room. Julie was much more entertaining than he had thought she would be. Instead of being an adventurous widow, as he had imagined, with whom he might easily amuse himself, she was a very innocent young married woman. It was rather touching.

Julie was too excited to sleep. Having been bottled up in herself for five days, she found this conversation extremely stimulating. She lay awake wondering how long Maitland, which he had told her was his name, would be staying at the hotel, and how much time she could with propriety spend in his company. As nobody else here knew who she was nor cared to make her acquaintance, there was no reason to bother about the appearances of propriety. The idea of any actual improper conduct did not enter her head. She did not think in that fashion.

He was not present at luncheon the next day and she spent a dull and restless afternoon, wandering about looking at sights which a

24

week ago had appeared exotic and strange to her, but which were now familiar.

In the evening he was already there when she came into the dining-room. He rose as she entered and asked if he might sit at her table. Julie was a little startled, but as the other guests had not shown her any friendliness she felt indifferent to their opinion, and giving a slight toss of the head, she said:

"I should be delighted."

He ordered the waiter to move over his place.

After dinner they sat outside on the terrace, in the warm scented air of the tropical night. Julie was now proud that she was doing something "fast," and would have preferred her behavior to be noticed to its being ignored. The excitement of deliberately being "fast" tinged her manner to Maitland, which implied that there was a kind of alliance or conspiracy between them against the rest of the hotel. He told her that he was an Oxford man, an anthropologist, and that he was spending two years traveling about the world studying the marriage customs of various colored peoples. He was shortly going to the South Sea Islands, calling at Melbourne on the way.

"You must certainly let me know when you arrive," said Julie, "and come to dine with us." She gave him a card with her address at The Pines.

After a while some couples who had been sitting near them drifted away, and they sat enclosed together in the darkness. He began to tell her of some of these marriage customs which he had studied. He spoke naturally in his quiet well-modulated voice, and that made the frankness with which he mentioned these things seem proper and reasonable to her, whereas from a less cultivated man it would have been intolerable. She felt as a young girl might feel, who is being instructed in love by someone of the most sensitive intelligence and sympathy, so that she dares to unfold and reveal her emotions, confident that they will be received with no vulgarity, and will not be exploited nor harmed.

It was not very late when they said good night. He suggested that they should drive out the following evening to Mt. Lavinia, and Julie said with feeling:

"Oh, that would be lovely!"

When she had gone to bed she could not sleep, but lay awake in excited contemplation of her expanded horizons. In the respectable confines of Kew society she had never imagined that the primal impulses of life, even among "natives" (by which she meant everyone from the most highly civilized Brahmin or Chinese nobleman to a drunken aboriginal hanging round the Noorilla shearing-sheds), could be at the same time both formalized and vitalized to the degree of passionate intensity which Maitland had indicated to her. She felt that her experience of life was ridiculously inadequate for a grown woman who had had two children. By daring to be "fast" she had cracked her usual protective shell of convention. She did not foresee any further result of this, but she felt extremely restless.

The next day she came in late to luncheon and he was already seated at the table. As she crossed the room to him a subtle sprightliness in her manner made some people glance at her with faint smiles, and others with astonishment at her effrontery.

She left him immediately after luncheon to rest, and she spoke in a rather loud casual voice, so that people near by might know how matter-of-fact was their acquaintance.

They arrived at Mt. Lavinia as the evening fell with all the splendors of a tropical sunset. The drooping palm-fronds, the deep green of the forest blotted with purple shadows, the sky and the horizon green and vermilion, the excited sea breaking into a thousand shades of green and purple as it reached the shore—all these things made her pulses quicken with new anticipations, which were fulfilled when, leading her by the hand along the shore, he came to a secluded place among the rocks and turning, took her in his arms and kissed her on the lips, and drew her down beside him on a smooth place of rock. All the things he had told her seemed to be part of his love-making, and she in turn seemed to become part of the whole natural world, of the cinnamon-scented forest, the smooth rocks and the brilliant sea.

When late at night they arrived back at the hotel, he kissed her hand at the door of her room and left her. As she undressed she did not look at the photographs of Lydia and Lucinda, and even brushed her hair standing at the wardrobe mirror, so that she need not sit looking at them—and yet she could not move them.

She was about to go to bed when there was a knock at the door and Maitland, wearing a dressing-gown, came into the room.

"Oh!" she said, disconcerted. She felt that by coming into her room he was asserting some claim over her, establishing her infidelity by bringing it into contact with the civilized world. There on the shore, between the forest and the sea, it had had a different quality, wilder and more innocent. But when he put his arms round her, her resistance melted, and without protest she watched him put out the light.

In the morning Julie again had to face the photographs of her children on the dressing table. In the cold daylight, even though it was the daylight of the tropics, she had to face the fact that she was what she would call a disreputable woman. Her years at Noorilla had given her a hatred of anything sordid and she felt as if she had made a moral return to the washtubs and the boiled mutton. She spent a wretched morning in her room, afraid to go out for fear of meeting Maitland. She had her luncheon sent up to her, as now the idea of sitting in public at the same table with him was as shocking to her as the idea of walking down Collins Street with a placard round her neck on which was written, "I am a bad woman."

When she could bear her confinement no longer, and ventured out of doors, it was in the heat of the early afternoon, when most people are resting. She went to another hotel for tea, and sitting there alone, completely unknown in an utterly strange place, she had the sense of being already a waif and an outcast on the world. She pushed her chair back behind a large vase of some exotic flowers and shed a few quiet tears.

She was not, however, a morbid woman, and when she had returned to her hotel, and had a bath, and put on her most attractive evening dress—because she must not, she thought, let herself down—and when the becoming lights of the evening succeeded the glare of the day, she found that the wells of life and hope were springing up in her again, and thought that perhaps she had been making too much fuss about an incident, which delightful though it was, must not be allowed to occur again. She reconstituted herself in her own imagination as a respectable woman. She kissed the photographs of the children, and feeling now capable of behaving as a woman of the world, she went down to dinner. But when she saw Maitland waiting at their table, all her confidence melted, so that when she sat down beside him she could only murmur some inaudible reply to his greeting, and the sequence of the past twenty-four hours was repeated, with only slight variations, until the end of the week, when she took the ship back to Melbourne.

When they said good-bye Maitland referred to their soon meeting in Melbourne. Julie was terrified and made him promise that if they did meet he would not recognize her.

She was too emotionally upset to join in the social life of the ship, and kept to herself until Watteau joined her at Fremantle. Watteau was too full of the excitement of her stay with her cousin —she had attended no less than seven "days-at-home" and two meetings of a Browning Society, at one of which she had been asked, as a woman who had passed matriculation, to give her view of the poet—to question Julie very closely about her adventures, or to notice the look in her eyes of someone who has just passed through an exhausting emotional experience.

27

Julie was very nervous of her meeting with Fred, feeling that some involuntary expression might betray her guilt, but Fred greeted her with so much affection and confidence, though the confidence was more in himself than in her, that she almost wept in his embrace, which would further have dispelled his doubts, if he could ever have conceived any, as to her fidelity.

Within a few weeks Julie had persuaded herself to forget the incident. It was like a dream. Then she discovered that she was going to have a child, and she knew that only Maitland could be its father. Just at this time she heard that Maitland had arrived in Melbourne, and was staying with a Professor Jamieson at the university. She went out as little as possible during the two months he was there, for fear of meeting him, though when she did see him once or twice in the distance at large functions, she felt a painful joy. Then his engagement was announced to Miss Nellie Jamieson, and on his return to Melbourne from Fiji they were married. At this time Julie's baby was born. She had given her whole attention to deceiving the doctor and Fred. It was easy to do this, partly because it would have occurred to neither of them to be suspicious, and the doctor simply regarded it as a case of prolonged pregnancy, but also because at the time of the birth of the child, which was a boy, the Victorian land boom burst, and everyone was far too concerned about the financial ruin of their friends, and their own reduced circumstances, to bother about who was the father of Mrs Vane's baby. They had even forgotten that nine months ago she was away on a trip to Colombo. Ladies who had kept their own carriages were obliged to open tea-shops. People who had lived in the Italianate palaces sold them for a song, and went to live in hot weatherboard houses in the country. Fred said: "Every dog has his day." He had had his day of misfortune earlier, and he steered astutely through the boom and the crash with negligible loss. He was very pleased with himself, especially now that Julie had a son, who was christened William after his putative grandfather.

By the time Julie was about again the Maitlands had left for England.

CHAPTER FOUR

As THE CHILDREN grew older the Vanes went to Flinders for the summer. The same people came to stay every year. Julie took the opportunity of paying off her duty to their relatives. Dick's children, who were rather unpopular with the young Vanes, came down from Noorilla and spoiled a fortnight of the holidays. Fred's sisters came for a week, and also Canon Chapman, whose wife had died about the time Bill was born. The only visitor to Flinders who was not invited as a duty was Tony Duff, a very young dancing partner of Julie's. She called him her *"preux chevalier."* He was an only son and lived with an invalid mother. He liked being with the Vanes, where he was treated as one of the family. He felt an affection for all of them, including Watteau, though not perhaps for Fred. The children were devoted to him. He told them fantastic stories and allowed them unrestrainedly to exploit his good-nature.

Bill particularly was fond of him, and talked to him with a confidence he never gave to Fred. As Bill grew older he became almost terrified of the man whom he called his father. When Fred was away on a tour of inspection of his stations, Bill was a lively spirit about the house. He rode his pony confidently about the paddock or down to the school to see his aunts. On the morning when Fred was due to return he woke up with a sense of fear. The girls went about in a state of pleasurable excitement, saying: "Daddy's coming home today." Julie was the same, and in the midst of all this excitement he was like someone who was expected to show delight at a visit to the dentist. He developed a nervous twitching, which was most evident when Fred at last arrived and he was expected to kiss him. Fred, always seeing the boy at his worst, was bitterly disappointed in him. He called his vindictiveness towards him the duty of a stern but loving parent. He boasted that he never thrashed him, but he took him out into the paddock and made him put his pony at terrifying jumps, so that in his presence Bill always appeared a coward on horseback. He wanted to send him to a boarding-school when he was nine years old.

Julie would not hear of this, and her disagreement with Fred was in danger of developing into a quarrel when a new school was founded in Kew for the sons of people like the Vanes. Fred agreed that Bill should go as a day boy. From this on there always seemed to be a number of green-capped small boys about The Pines. Bill brought them home from school in the afternoon, and Julie would find them climbing up trees or hiding in the garden.

"They are like mice about the place," she said to Watteau, but she was amused and pleased at this access of young life. One of these boys was the youngest son of Mr Blake, the solicitor, who lived next door and had nine children. Fred called him Blake IX. He was Bill's particular friend.

The girls did not go to school, as both Fred and Julie thought it more ladylike for them to be educated at home with governesses. Their last governess was a Frenchwoman who taught them deportment and imparted to Lucinda a very good French accent. Lydia could not pick it up. All their three successive governesses impressed on them that the most important thing on earth was that they should be ladies.

Julie sometimes felt that Lydia would not be very obviously a lady, but she had no doubts about Lucinda.

From her childhood Lucinda had shown a composure and sensitive charm which had marked her as a natural aristocrat. It became a kind of superstition in the family that Lucinda was so exceptional that her future would be distinguished. Her physical texture, her hair and skin, were delicate and flowerlike. Tony Duff showed clearly that she was his favorite, but she treated him with less effusiveness than Lydia and Bill showed him.

When Lydia was nearly eighteen Julie gave a dance for the children. Lydia was to come out next year at Government House. The year after that, Julie thought, she would bring out Lucinda, rather young, and give a big ball for both the girls, probably at the St Kilda town hall.

Tony Duff's most useful function in life was to give people advice about their parties, and he came to help Julie with her children's dance. He was now thirty, but he still had a boyish air of vivacity, and, except when he was giving social advice, people treated him as if he were barely out of his teens. Fred tolerated him about the place but called him a "poodle-fakir."

He stood beside Julie, watching the young people dance round the large and generally useless vestibule at the back of the house, which had been converted into a ballroom. They were mostly the children of neighbors and not all from families which were regarded as "in society." Some of the boys in stiff-looking new suits and with plastered hair did not look very well-bred. Lydia was dancing with Roger, the eldest Blake boy with whom she had always been rather friendly.

The same thought occurred simultaneously to both Julie and Tony.

"Why don't you move to Toorak?" said Tony. "It would be better now that the girls are growing up."

"What, leave The Pines!" exclaimed Julie. "Fred wouldn't hear of it." But she knew that if she were to realize her ambitions for her daughters she would have to move to Toorak. This was the fourth dance Lydia had had with Roger, who, although he was a very nice boy, was not eligible as a husband for Lydia. Old Mr.

Blake was a gentleman—he had been educated at Winchester—but Roger was only a medical student, and it would be years, even if he were successful, before he could keep Lydia in a fitting style. Her glance fell on Lucinda who was standing alone by the door. Lucinda looked aloof and virginal, but as if she were waiting. Julie had a sudden panic that she might fall in love with one of these boys in ready-made suits.

"Go and ask Lucinda to dance," Julie said to Tony.

"I'd rather dance with you."

"Don't be silly," said Julie, pleased, and she tapped him with her fan.

As Lucinda had treated him with more reserve than the others he was not sure that she would want to dance with him. He crossed over to her and said, by way of apology: "Your mother says I'm to dance with you."

Lucinda's eyes, which had smiled up at him as he approached, became clouded, and she said in a kind of troubled voice:

"Don't you want to, then?"

"Of course I do," said Tony. "I only thought I might seem an old buffer to you."

Since his thirtieth birthday he had thought that he was middle-aged, but as he felt little different from when he was twenty he treated the fact of his age as a rather painful joke, and was inclined to talk about it too much.

"You don't seem any older than I am," said Lucinda.

As Tony put his arm round her to guide her into the dance he saw that in some way her emotions were stirred. He was a good dancer but generally spoiled his dancing by chattering. Now he was aware that she was in a state in which his chatter would be unacceptable. He kept silence and danced very well. He felt protective and tender towards her, and with a faint twinge of jealousy wondered which of these boys had brought that expression to her eyes. When the music stopped he stood beside her till the beginning of the next dance, but they did not speak much.

The music began again, and a boy of fifteen in a blue suit and white gloves came up to them, and with a shy glance at Tony, who appeared to him an intensely sophisticated middle-aged man, said to Lucinda in the same tone in which he would have said the responses in church, "May I have the pleasure of a dance?"

Lucinda smiled, and turning to Tony with a look in her eyes which said clearly, "If you don't want me I may as well go with him," she moved away with the boy.

Tony could not believe that the look was meant for him, or that he could possibly be responsible for any stirring of Lucinda's emotions, and yet as he thought about it he became convinced that it was so. He was both amused and touched.

"Why are you smiling in that smug and incredulous fashion?" asked Julie as he rejoined her.

Tony was slightly embarrassed.

"I didn't know that I was smug," he said.

"Let's go and get something to drink while the supper room is empty," said Julie.

She and Tony edged their way round the dancing children, some of them very painstaking and earnest, others hilarious, and went into the dining-room, which was arranged with a buffet along one wall. It was laden with jellies and colored sugared cakes, and oyster patties and bowls of claret cup. There was whisky for the grown-ups, but both Julie and Tony drank claret cup.

The room was empty except for the maids and Lucinda, who was still with the blue-suited boy. They were sitting in the far corner eating ice-creams. Lucinda looked across at Tony and smiled. Her smile was shy and confident and extremely young.

"You're not listening to what I am saying," said Julie with good-humored irritation.

"No, I'm sorry, what was it?" asked Tony, coming out of a trance.

"I said do you think it would be a good idea if we were to build a house in Toorak?"

Tony had a little red de Dion-Bouton motor car in which he drove home from the dance. When he had put it in the garage of his mother's house in Tintern Avenue he did not feel inclined to go to bed, and he strolled down the garden. The waning moon had risen, and he could see clearly the double-flowering peach trees and the daffodils beneath them. There were scents of spring in the garden which he did not clearly define. He was thinking about Lucinda, and yet he did not know what to think about her. He was vividly conscious of the fact of her existence, and it filled him with a tender amusement. When he thought of the shape of her nose he almost laughed, it was so delicate and so amusing. When he thought of her eyes and of the way that she had smiled at him in the supper room he almost cried. The flowering peach trees, standing so still in the breathless night, seemed to be part of her. She was only vaguely the focus of this tenderness for all young life which had newly awakened in him.

"The Vanes are charming kids," he said to himself. He was very glad that he was going down to Flinders for part of their holidays. There was a daphne in bloom by the door where he entered the house. Its scent was intoxicating. When at last he went to bed he was full of hope.

Julie, going to bed, discussed the dance with Fred.

"They were rather a mixed bunch," said Julie. "It doesn't matter while the children are young, of course, but not many of those boys will be eligible husbands. Lydia danced five times with Roger Blake."

"What's wrong with that?"

"You wouldn't like her to marry him."

"She might do a lot worse. Our daughters won't need to look for money, but they will need good husbands. Young Roger will go far. I know horses and I know men. He'll be a better match than your poodle-fakir."

"It was very good of Tony to come out to the children's party. He was most helpful."

"All right. Keep your poodle-fakir," said Fred.

"He's not *my* poodle-fakir," said Julie warmly, feeling a little guilty at her innocent affection for Tony.

"Well, if you're going to deceive me," said Fred, grinning brutally, "for God's sake do it with a man." He had no wild dreams beyond the amassing of enormous wealth, but if he had, Julie's infidelity would not have occurred in them. It amused him to chaff her like this.

"You may know men and horses, but you don't know women," said Julie.

"I knew what I was about when I married you."

Julie smiled. Fred went into his dressing-room. When he came back she said:

"It would be better for the girls if we lived in Toorak."

Fred looked at her and a slow grin spread over his face.

"So that's how the wind blows. You're not satisfied to be Mrs Vane of The Pines." He chuckled and got into bed.

"I thought we might build a house," said Julie.

"Fools build houses for wise men to live in," growled Fred and covered his head with the bedclothes.

CHAPTER FIVE

A HOUSE IN TOORAK was discussed as a possibility during the Christmas holidays at Flinders. Usually they went to Flinders after Christmas. Tony would have a midday Christmas dinner with his mother in Tintern Avenue and go over to The Pines in the afternoon, spending the rest of the day with the Vanes. This year the children clamored to go to Flinders immediately the holidays began, and Julie agreed. Tony tried to appear indifferent when she told him, but he was upset. He had bought his Christmas presents for the children. His present to Lucinda was a set of the major English poets in very good uniform binding. Each book was stamped with her initials in a medallion which he had designed himself.

Having very tentatively introduced the subject, Tony at last persuaded his mother to have their Christmas dinner on Christmas Eve, and feeling guilty and excited he left by car very early the next morning for Flinders. It was shortly before eleven when his car bumped along the wide grassy road to the gate of Strathallan, the boarding-house annex which the Vanes occupied every summer, and the family were just leaving for church. Bill and his friend, the youngest of the nine Blake brothers, dashed out to the car shouting: "Tony! Tony's arrived!" The others followed more slowly. Tony, grinning and wiping his forehead, got out of the car and joined in the babel of "Merry Christmas." Lucinda stood a little apart. He did not speak to her, but their eyes met in a faint momentary smile. He turned away and replied, laughing, to Bill's chaff.

"Mum, must we go to church now Tony's arrived?" asked Bill. There was some discussion which ended in Tony's agreement to go to church with them, though Julie said it was a shame when he must want to rest after his drive. But Tony always did what the children wanted. He said that he would follow them to church when he had brushed his clothes and washed.

"Keep a place for me," he said, and again his eyes flickered towards Lucinda.

The wide road was empty when he came out again, having washed in a primitive bathroom and changed his dusty shoes. The sun was now becoming scorchingly hot, and before leaving the shade of the sparse pine trees which sheltered Strathallan, he stood a moment and looked about him. The house was a long wooden building with an iron roof and a wide verandah, along which were drying bathing dresses and towels. Indoors there were flies and sand in the bedrooms. The main boarding-house across the road was a larger edition of Strathallan. They were both at the top of a steep grassy slope, below which was a short golden beach, protected at the end by a jutting-out cliff which the boys called "The Tarpeian Rock." Behind the house rose the dry downs, scattered with the white skeletons of gum trees, killed by the strong salt winds, a hideous arboreal graveyard. The north wind now blew over the brown paddocks like the blast from an oven. It flung itself at the brilliant green sea, flecking it with white spray as dazzling as fire.

"What a place to choose for a holiday!" thought Tony, who preferred the cool mountain glades of Macedon and Olinda. He did not know how vividly this harsh and wistful landscape was to remain photographed in his mind all the days of his life. As he opened the churchyard gate he heard the nasal voices of the choir strained to reach the high notes of "Join the triumph of the skies," and although he had only once been to England, and never at Christmas time, this shrill noise, rising thinly to the high and blazing sky, struck him as a travesty of Christmas celebration, as fantastic and remote from its original meaning as in an opposite direction Catholic rites had become in countries where they were encrusted in local superstitions, in Mexico or in Sicily, where one might commit any sin on Easter Eve as Our Lord was in the tomb and could not notice it.

In the church a place had been kept for him between the two boys. Lucinda, to whom he had not yet spoken, gave him a glance which said unmistakably that she would, if possible, have kept him a seat beside her. He could not believe that the affection he felt for her could be returned, and though his mind told him that this glance meant nothing, his heart was flooded with a tender kindliness which made him feel that this celebration of Christmas, with its worship of young and innocent life, preserved its meaning in spite of the grotesqueness of its external circumstances. His thought was hardly as articulate as this. He felt more than he reasoned.

The varnish on the pitch-pine pews had become sticky with the heat. When they stood up for the psalms their tweed suits came away with a tearing sound, leaving a thin growth of hair on the pews. Bill's suit seemed particularly adhesive, and when they stood up for the hymn before the sermon, Tony turned to smile at him. Bill did not return the smile. His face was damp and green. He felt as if his head were full of steam. Then he went cold all over and could hardly stand up. At last physical necessity overcame his boyish embarrassment at being conspicuous, and he stumbled out of the church, and lay gasping on a shady patch of dry grass.

Tony followed him out, and Julie, when she saw what had happened, came after them.

"I'm all right," Bill was saying. "The church was stuffy. I felt all hot and cold but I'm all right now."

"You'd better go home," said Julie, "and lie down till lunch time. Will you go with him, Tony?"

Tony hesitated. He wanted to be in the same place as Lucinda. Bill saw his hesitation and said:

"I'm all right, mum. I can go by myself." He stood up and walked a little shakily out of the churchyard. There was something about the shape of his shoulders and the angle of his straw hat with the green school band which awoke Julie's never very dormant impulse to protect him.

"Very well, I'll go with him," she said to Tony.

"Oh, no, I will." Tony's polite eagerness sounded forced, and Julie ignored it and went with Bill.

Tony re-entered the church. Julie had left a vacant place beside Lucinda, but Blake was sitting alone in the pew behind. Sheer nervousness made Tony go back to his seat beside Blake.

Tony managed to walk back to Strathallan with Lucinda, but they hardly spoke. Two months ago he would have kept up an amiable chatter all the way. Now he censored all his conversation in advance, to make sure that he would not say anything she would think silly. From her earliest childhood she had been used to his inconsequent talking. His reticence awakened the very criticism he had feared. Also, because now she was emotionally affected by him she wanted to think him perfect, and his new hesitating manner worried her.

The family had exchanged their presents at breakfast time, so that Tony's gifts, handed out before luncheon, received particular attention. When Lucinda opened the parcel of finely bound books she gave an exclamation, as much of protest as of pleasure, and everyone came over to look at them.

Bill picked one up and sniffed at it, and Blake exclaimed:

"Aren't they marvelous?"

Fred came in from where he had been lying in a hammock under the pine trees and appraised the books.

"I hope you will look at their contents, my dear, not only the binding," he said.

The munificence of Tony's gift to Lucinda was the main topic of conversation till lunch time, and recurred at intervals throughout the day. No one seemed surprised, as it was expected that Lucinda should always have the best of things, but Tony wished that he could have given it to her privately. He wished that they would stop talking about the books.

He was relieved when it was time to cross the road to luncheon in the main boarding-house. The Vanes had a table to themselves at the end of the long dining-room. Bill was now wearing flannel shorts and a green school blazer. As they sat down Fred noticed this and said:

"You did not go to church like that, I hope, my son."

Bill began that nervous twitching to which he was liable when Fred spoke to him in reproof. He did not seem to know what to reply.

"He wasn't very well," said Julie. "He went home before the sermon."

"If I had gone home before the sermon when I was a boy," said Fred, "I should have been thrashed." This was quite untrue, as there was nothing old William Vane would have thrashed him for, except going to confession or cheating at cards.

This incident hardly stimulated the Christmas gaiety, and Tony tried to cover it over with the bright gossip which made him popular in society, but now for the first time the note of his conversation struck him as false. Fred had brought some champagne down from The Pines for the Christmas dinner, and as this went a little to Tony's head he heard his own voice babbling on, shrill and shallow, and yet this habit was so strong that he did not quite realize what was wrong, nor immediately bring himself to be silent.

Across the table Lydia and Lucinda seemed to be enclosed in a superior world of their own. The hot room, the extremely inappropriate food—roast turkey and a brandy-soaked plum pudding, while outside the north wind scorched the paddocks and the temperature was 102 degrees in the shade—left them apparently unaffected. They were wearing white muslin dresses with stiff frills and embroidered with different colored flowers. In church their hair had hung down their backs, caught at the neck with silk bows. Now, partly because of the heat, and partly for fun, they had done it on the top of their heads. Their cheeks were a little pinker than usual from the champagne, but they appeared unruffled and cool, both physically and mentally. Everything that happened seemed to have a bearing on some private joke between themselves, and if Fred was boorish, or Tony witty, or Watteau obvious, or the boys gauche, they exchanged the same glance of amused complicity. They called each other Flip and Flop.

37

Only Julie paid any attention to Fred. The children as much as possible excluded him from their consciousness, as they regarded him as a hindrance to their enjoyment. He sat at the head of the table feeling ill-used, almost as if he had been cheated in a business deal. It was high time Bill was removed from this atmosphere of females and poodle-fakirs.

"I'm going up to Noorilla tomorrow," he said. "Would you two boys like to come with me? I may go on to Wombidgee and Churt. I would of course pay your expenses," he added to Blake.

Bill twitched and looked down at his plate. Blake's mouth fell open and he stared at Fred in dismay.

"Thank you very much, Mr Vane," he said at last, "but I don't know if my father would let me go. He wants me to have sea air," he explained, and grinned with sudden relief and pleasure in the ingenuity of this excuse.

"I should not have thought that a tour of stations, which any manly boy would jump at, would exactly injure your health," said Fred. "What about you, my son?"

Bill looked shiftily about the table. He knew that he must look cowardly and dishonest and all the things that Fred expected him to be.

"I don't want to go if Blake IX can't come," he muttered.

"Then it rests with you, young man." Fred turned again to Blake, deliberately exercising his adult will-power against the boy. Blake's face was like a small red balloon.

"It's awfully kind of you, Mr Vane," he said, and then blurted out, "but I like being here best."

"Very well," said Fred, anger showing through his affectation of indifference, "as you are not my son I cannot order you to come, but Bill must come with me tomorrow. You must get to know the stations which you'll have to control some day." He put down his table-napkin and left the room.

"Oh, what a shame!" said Watteau. "On Christmas Day too, and the boys so inseparable!"

"I won't go," said Bill, "I'd rather die. I'll fling myself from the Tarpeian Rock."

"Don't be silly," said Lydia. "You wouldn't fling yourself from anywhere. I'd go with Daddy like a shot."

"Why don't you, then? He won't put you on buckjumpers and call you a coward if you don't break your neck, and make you sleep in filthy little wooden rooms full of flies and eat filthy mutton. I hate stations. I don't want to own the damn things."

"Bill!" exclaimed Watteau. "Before the girls!"

"The girls swear too behind your back. Lydia does anyhow."

"You beastly little tell-tale. You're afraid of horses," said Lydia.

"Well, you're afraid of sharks."

"A horse doesn't bite your leg off."

"It might."

"You're ridiculous."

"I can swim farther than you anyhow. Can't I, Blake IX?"

The family row spread and spluttered, bright with irrelevant invective, round the table. Tony and Blake, not permitted by relationship to share in the rudeness, but appealed to at intervals to endorse some gross insult, smiled sheepishly. Tony until recently would not have felt this embarrassment, but now to everything connected with Lucinda he could only make the most sensitive approach. His love for her had complicated his whole attitude to the Vanes, and he found it affecting even trivial incidents, such as his refusal to return with Bill from church. Julie sat through the squabble with an air of absentminded tolerance. She did not look happy, but her resignation gave her a look of wisdom. Watteau had none of this resignation, so that in spite of her mop of greying hair she seemed younger than Julie, like an angry bird, and the children treated her as one of themselves.

Julie pushed back her chair.

"You've all eaten too much," she said. "You'd better go to your rooms and rest till it's time to bathe."

Bill and Blake dawdled to pick at a few more raisins and sweets before they left the table. The others were waiting for them in the hall, where there was a piece of mistletoe hanging over the door. Everyone had to pass under it to go out. Bill kissed Julie, who laughed and hugged him. He moved away from the door as the girls went out and Tony held it open for them. Lucinda was only a foot away from him, under the mistletoe. He could easily have kissed her. He was longing to, but she seemed to him so flawless and sacred that he could not take advantage of this vulgar custom to touch her.

He crossed the road behind Bill and Julie, who were walking arm in arm. Perhaps because deep in himself there lay the knowledge that he would never have one, he felt with sudden poignancy how wonderful it would be to have a child, a young growing human life to direct, especially when that life was an extension of one's own, but drawn from the body and colored by the soul of the person one loved most in all the world. At that moment the potential joy of human life became for him so intense that it was almost a terrible sadness.

39

His eyes were dark and wide. He glanced at Lucinda and their eyes met, but when she saw his expression she turned away.

Fred was sitting on the edge of the verandah smoking a cigar. Julie and the girls, who alone were not nervous in his presence, went up to him, but the rest of the party drifted away. Soon the girls went indoors and Julie said:

"Lydia would like to go with you instead of Bill."

"I have told Bill he is to come."

"It will spoil his holiday."

"He's got to be made a man. It seems to me that I pay to keep in luxury a crowd of people who oppose my wishes. That infernal What-ho is always shoving her oar in, Poodle-fakir Duff hangs about drinking my best wine, and my own son when I try to encourage him to have an eye to his future interests behaves as if I were doing him an injury, and you side with them all. I'm damned if I know why men marry and have families."

"Christmas dinners are dreadfully unsuitable to this climate," said Julie.

"Pah!" Fred sank into silence.

The next morning at breakfast Fred announced pontifically that he was taking Lydia instead of Bill. He made it sound as if Bill had been deprived of a treat which had been transferred to his sister. Bill's face became radiant, and when anything at all amusing happened his whole body simmered with laughter, so that it was hardly possible to keep up this pretense.

Throughout Boxing Day there was a rising tide of high spirits at Strathallan, which reached its climax when Hart, the chauffeur, brought the car round after luncheon to drive Fred and Lydia to the railway station at Bitterne. Julie drove with them to see them off at the train.

Those who were left stood by the gate, dutifully waving, until the car turned out of sight, then the high spirits burst into a spontaneous demonstration. Bill turned and began to wrestle with Blake, Tony felt as if the muscles of his face had received a tonic, while Watteau began to hum to herself as she turned towards the house. Tony was not only relieved at Fred's departure but delighted at Lydia's, as although he quite liked her, it meant that Lucinda would be thrown far more into his company, especially after tomorrow, when Canon Chapman arrived for his annual holiday and Julie would be taken up with entertaining her father.

Julie came back from Bitterne, hot and inclined to be cross. At once she sensed the happy relaxation following Fred's departure. Sometimes she felt it herself, but today it irritated her. Watteau was lying in a hammock reading a purple-bound novel by Mrs Florence Barclay. The boys came out of the house wearing shorts over their bathing suits. They had twisted their towels into turbans round their heads, and on the top of each turban they had stuck a large naval orange; their eyes had that lively expression which the young have when they exploit their own absurdity. Lucinda and Tony were sitting some way off, on the dry ground underneath a pine tree. It was a shame, Julie thought, that they had not been nicer to Fred. What rubbish Watteau read! Normally she would have thought the boys' get-up rather engaging, but Julie was herself like a child to this extent, that when she was annoyed she could not see anything as funny. What irritated her most was something in the attitude of Tony as he leant towards Lucinda. It was only a momentary instinctive irritation, and as soon as she had given way to it by going over to them and telling Lucinda that she thought it selfish of her not to have gone to Bitterne to see Daddy off, she attributed it to herself being in a bad mood and soon forgot it.

But Tony stood up quickly. He had been so happy that he felt guilty. He thought Julie was cross because he was sitting with Lucinda. He had already found that if two people showed signs of escaping into a blissful world of their own it provoked interference or at least moral indignation from their friends. He said:

"Well, I think I'll go for a swim." He called out, "Wait for me, Bill."

"I'll come too," said Lucinda. It seemed to her quite right that Tony should love her. It was something beautiful and natural that there was no need to conceal from Julie or anyone else. She had not yet taken in its full implications, and never having been to school she had not been made self-conscious about these things by sniggering and chaff.

Tony walked beside Bill until they were out of sight from the house, then he fell back and walked with Lucinda. Bill and Blake went carefully ahead, trying to walk all the way down to the beach with the oranges balanced in their turbans, and saying to each other. "I bet yours falls off at the steps."

Tony felt perfectly at ease with Lucinda when he was alone with her, or when only the boys were present, for the boys too saw no reason why Tony should not "have a crush" on Lucinda. To them it was simple phenomenon to be accepted. When they were with other people, the need to conceal his feelings made Tony speak to Lucinda with affected heartiness as he spoke to the boys, or with facetiousness, in which his real feelings were not wholly concealed.

For example he made up some verses about Flinders, in which he called her Cinders. She was puzzled and hurt by this, but like many young people, uncertain of their own knowledge of life, she accepted it as an adult peculiarity, and did not judge it as a vulgarity in Tony, partly because she knew that when they were alone together their sympathy was not spoiled by any falsity of manner, and that then he showed towards her a gentle understanding. Julie, seeing only Tony's public manner towards Lucinda, felt that some situation had arisen, but thought it was that Lucinda had a sentimental schoolgirlish attachment to him, which bored him and that he was trying to deflect it with heartiness. It was silly of him, she thought, to have given Lucinda that expensive Christmas present.

Now as they walked down to the beach they were perfectly at ease together. He had no need to force nor to conceal the expression of his love.

It was still hot, but there was a cool breeze from the sea. At the rough steps cut in the red rock, Blake's orange fell off his head and bounced down and lay like a child's ball on the deep yellow sand below. Bill shouted, "You owe me sixpence!" He was so excited that his own orange fell off and followed Blake's. They squabbled amicably about their bet.

They swam and splashed about in the sea for a while, and then came up and lay on the Tarpeian Rock. Bill and Blake shared their towels, lying on one to protect their backs from the scorching rock, and using the other to shield their eyes from the sun. At the same time they ate their oranges, which resulted in more contention as the juice squirted in their eyes.

Tony and Lucinda sat in a narrow strip of shade made by the cliff. They spoke in a lazy desultory fashion and watched the antics of Bill and Blake.

The sun, which had struck so deep into the rock that long after dark its surface would return warm breaths of air, had also possessed those who lay on it. Blake turned over and Bill rubbed cocoanut oil on his back to stop it from blistering. He fooled about as he did it, and then a darker mood troubled his spirit and he hugged his friend so violently that he gasped: "Look out, you're breaking my ribs!" The oil bottle fell over, and Bill, inconsequently forgetting the mood of a moment earlier, dashed to save it.

Lucinda looked at Tony. She recognized that behind Bill's ragging there had been an impulse of sensuality, and again that seemed to her a thing to be accepted naturally, and less consciously she felt it to be an enrichment of life, and to contain some dim promise of a deeper relationship between Tony and herself. As she looked at him her eyes were full of candid and innocent acceptance. This glance was almost more than Tony could bear. His eyes darkened. She in turn was moved so that she looked away at the scene before her, and although she made no deliberate attempt to remember it, in that moment it was printed vividly on her mind and remained there for many years—the sea with its dazzling white horses, the hot expanse of the Tarpeian Rock, and the two sprawling sunburnt boys with their oranges—and she remembered always the feel of the cool wind as it caressed her arms and lifted her hair.

Canon Chapman arrived the next afternoon. He would stay for the inside of a fortnight missing only one Sunday's duty at Jolimont, and he expected to be entertained all the time. He was not pleased when he heard that Fred had gone off on a tour of his stations.

"Ah, those stations!" he exclaimed, as if they were some form of naughty juvenile indulgence, or he may have been thinking of the days when he had to keep Fred and Julie alive at Noorilla.

When the children were younger they had welcomed him with joy and hung about him affectionately as he told them whimsical stories and gave them boiled sweets. Now they greeted him kindly but soon drifted off on their own more interesting occasions. They were embarrassed when he told them stories, and awkwardly amused when he gave them boiled sweets, as since Christmas there had been large boxes of the best chocolates lying about the house. He still behaved as if he brought an access of life and pleasure to Strathallan, and they did not like to disillusion him. They had a tacit arrangement whereby it was always someone's duty to be amused by grandpapa, and they had private squabbles if anyone thought he was having more than his fair share of this entertainment. With increasing age the canon's smile became fixed in more determined geniality, and his voice more staccato. He called Tony "Our *arbiter elegantiarum*" and Watteau "Our unfailing domestic prop, our dispenser of home truths."

In the evening he said: "Wouldn't it be nice to have some music? Perhaps Bill would put on some records?" Bill had to leave his half-finished game of halma and spend the rest of the evening by the gramophone, putting on records, while Canon Chapman leant back in his chair with his fingertips together, nodding in time to the semi-classical tunes which he had asked for. Sometimes he ignored them and discussed family matters with Julie, but if Bill then moved away from the gramophone, he said: "Don't weary in well-doing, young man. A background of music is very agreeable."

The next morning the canon walked to the township, where he

43

sent a letter-card to his housekeeper and bought three pennyworth of boiled sweets. After luncheon he said:

"Now, what about an excursion? An hour for digestion and then for the hills. We shall not be without sustenance."

He brought the bag of boiled sweets from his pocket and put it on the table. The boys could not meet each other's eyes.

"We're going to bathe this afternoon," said Bill.

"But you have already bathed this morning," said his grandfather. "Is so much bathing wise?" he asked Julie.

"It seems to agree with them," said Julie. "Still, I think one of you ought to go for a walk with grandpapa."

"Why don't you come and bathe with us, grandpapa?" asked Lucinda affectionately.

"Bathe!" exclaimed the canon. "A pagan enjoyment! I can keep adequately clean in the bath." He had not bathed since that November night in the Cam, fifty years earlier.

Julie pushed back her chair, hoping that if the party scattered the boys might make their escape. On the way back across the road she walked with Tony and Lucinda.

"Wouldn't you be an angel, Tony, and take Papa for a walk? It's hard on the boys to miss their bathe."

Tony was generally so helpful that she did not expect that he would do anything but agree. Although he was sorry for the boys having to go off for a tramp with the canon, he was delighted at the prospect of a whole afternoon's bathing alone with Lucinda. As soon as the canon had made his suggestion Tony's heart had begun to beat quickly in anxiety lest it should not be accepted.

He did not answer Julie at once. She glanced at him and was surprised at the look of wretchedness in his face. She did not think it could be caused only by the prospect of a hot walk, and that still unawakened suspicion which she had felt on her return from seeing Fred off again touched her mind.

"Mummy, it's awfully hot to go walking with Grandpa," said Lucinda. "He tears along to show how strong he is."

"Oh, very well," said Julie crossly. "The boys will have to go."

Tony had not spoken.

At three o'clock the canon, followed by the two reluctant boys, set out for the scorching hills and the shadeless skeletons of trees. The more hot and tired the boys became the more the canon appeared to be pleased. He thought: "Here am I at seventy less tired than these boys of fourteen." He took off his black alpaca coat and his clerical collar, which had a little black bib attached to it. His collarless neck was not pleasing.

44

"Grandpa," said Bill, wiping the sweat from his eyes, and whisking at the cloud of black flies which tried to settle on his back, "if we went back now we'd have time for a bathe before tea."

"Never turn back from the plough, young man," said the canon.

At this Bill abandoned all pretense of affection or respect for his grandfather. He fell behind with Blake and muttered:

"Silly old fool! Doesn't he look ghastly without his collar? Just like a hen."

The canon remembered with satisfaction that he had been delicate when young. It made his present toughness even more of an achievement. In the evening Julie said to Watteau:

"Father is really a wonderful old man."

Watteau however was rather shocked by his hard tenacity and replied:

"A gentleman of that age would be more suitably occupied in thinking of the Kingdom of Heaven than of his muscles. We are told the Lord delighteth not in any man's legs. Certainly not in an old man's legs I should say."

All the afternoon Tony and Lucinda had lain on the Tarpeian Rock. Tony in his over-sensitive condition took almost any trace of glumness or irritation in others as a sign of disapproval of his love, and any amiability as a sign of acquiescence. Because he was allowed to spend the afternoon alone with her, he imagined for the time being that Julie had practically given them her blessing.

As they lay on the rock they talked about the future. Underlying the vagueness of their talk there was an implication that they would be together in the years ahead, but this might only have been because separation, that partial death, had not yet come into either of their lives.

They talked about the house which Julie wanted to build in Toorak. Tony was very interested in houses and their decoration, and he scratched plans on the rock with the end of a piece of burnt stick. Again, beneath this conversation, there was the hint that some day they might plan a house for themselves.

They were late for tea. Canon Chapman was already back. The boys were still sullen and indignant. Julie now was beginning to feel irritation when she saw Tony and Lucinda together, primarily because she thought them selfish not to contribute to the general entertainment. Again Tony sensed this irritation and, to make the situation appear quite normal, he said with tactless heartiness to Bill:

"Well, are you still alive?"

45

"No, I'm jolly well roasted to death. I suppose you two have been spooning in the shade all the afternoon."

"Bill, don't be vulgar," said Julie sharply.

"We've been designing you a house," Tony said with a supreme effort to appear calm.

"Oh, in that case you're forgiven."

"I don't want to leave The Pines," said Bill. "There's only one place better than Kew."

"And where may that be?" asked the canon, amused.

"Heaven!" said Bill promptly, which shocked his grandfather.

Canon Chapman for the next few days monopolized as much of the boys' time as he could. He preferred their society, not only because their youth was stimulating, but because he liked giving information. He was uneasy with Tony, as he had an aesthetic knowledge that went beyond his own purely academic culture. Also as Tony spent nearly all his time at parties in rich houses, the canon somewhat mistakenly regarded him as a "man of the world."

The result of this was that Tony and Lucinda were left even more alone together, while the wretched boys were trailed, sweating and muttering expostulations, round the countryside, and rewarded with threepenny bags of boiled sweets. In the evenings Tony, Julie and Lucinda hung over a large piece of drawing paper beneath the lamp, and worked out the plan of the new Toorak house. The canon thought himself well fitted to criticize this, and where their plan showed any feeling for space and light or abandonment of the stuffy inconveniences of Victorianism, he allowed himself to be amused.

Julie was quite excited by the plan. She was sure the house would create a sensation and she could talk of nothing else. When she saw Tony and Lucinda lean back from the table and look at each other with glowing eyes, she thought that they were sharing her excitement about this beautiful house. It would be like a breath of spring, a fairy palace among all the Toorak mansions. She had already decided to call it The White House.

At the end of the week the canon made his annual visit to Mrs Talbot of Cape Furze. She was the daughter of a former Dean of Melbourne. The canon had had a very tenuous romance with her when he was still a curate at St Peter's and could not afford to marry. She had married instead Mr Talbot of Cape Furze, a station owner, but she kept up a correspondence with Canon Chapman, and since Julie had been coming to Flinders he drove out once a year to visit her, generally taking Julie and two of the children. At breakfast he said:

"We have a different treat for my two acolytes today. A motor drive and luncheon with Mrs Talbot of Cape Furze."

"Aren't we going to walk?" said Billy acidly. Blake sniggered and looked self-conscious.

"It is a little far for walking. We have the car and the services of the excellent Hart."

"May we bathe before we go, mum?" asked Bill.

"I fear this inordinate passion for the sea needs disciplining," said his grandfather. "My two acolytes must learn that there are two voices, one of the sea, one of the mountains."

Julie was moved by what might have appeared a whim, but what was in reality the sum of three or four subtle apprehensions, all taken in at the same moment, each separate one too slight to be formulated in her mind. She saw a glance exchanged between Tony and Lucinda, she saw the look of disgust on Bill's face, but she was most influenced by a sudden uneasy recognition that her father took pleasure in making the two boys uncomfortable.

"It's too hot for the boys to go to Cape Furze," she said decidedly. "Tony and Lucinda will come. You may go and spend the day at the Tarpeian Rock, and Watteau will bring you down a picnic lunch, won't you, Watteau?"

Tony and Lucinda exchanged a grimace, but as they would be together they did not think the trip to Cape Furze a very great hardship.

The canon, deprived of his power over the boys, wore a fixed but unpleasant smile all the way to Cape Furze. He gave short replies to Julie's occasional pleasant remarks. Tony and Lucinda sat in the small seats facing them. When her father sulked, Tony noticed on Julie's face that same look of absent-minded tolerance which she had during the squabble at their Christmas dinner. He felt a sudden affection for her, a sort of extension of his love for Lucinda, and to please her he began to talk about the plan for the Toorak house, at which she at once became animated, while the canon grew more sulky. At last he became tired of his self-exclusion from the conversation and said:

"You may find some architectural inspiration at Cape Furze. It has more the atmosphere of a country home in the old world than any place I have seen in Australia."

The car turned left down a wide road more rutted and bumpy than any they had yet traveled. Hart drove slowly, and every now and then after a bad bump he turned and said:

"Sorry, ma'am, but this ain't Collins Street."

On either side of the road the paddocks stretched for miles in the pale brown honeycomb of a vast rabbit warren. There was no proper wire-fencing, no trapping, and the rabbits had eaten the grass to the roots. The scorching sun had done the rest. Mrs Talbot, faithful to every memory of her late husband, even kept on his drunken and incompetent manager.

"Mrs Talbot," said Tony, "must be like the enchanted princess protected by these waste lands instead of by brambles."

This remark, though in doubtful taste, did not displease the canon as much as might have been expected.

"It is indeed an Ultima Thule," he said.

When it seemed that they had put a whole desert between themselves and civilization, they came to a white gate and a tiny Gothic lodge set in a small clump of pine trees. Three children were seated on the hard earth at the door, playing with bones. At the sight of the motor car two jumped up eagerly, but the third ran screaming with terror into the lodge.

An unusually dirty, gray-haired woman came out and opened the gate. The canon gave her twopence.

"Here," he said genially, "feudal customs prevail."

The car bumped on for another mile, still through the pale brown honeycomb. They turned round a low hill and came in sight of Cape Furze House. Set amidst those parched, distorted paddocks on the edge of an arid coast, protected only by a few pines, almond trees and eucalyptus, it had no resemblance to an English country house. Its white stone gables and twin gothic towers had shed all association with the north. They had been bleached of its influence by the salt and the sun, and brought into affinity with the twisted white stems of the gumtrees. They shone chalkily above the sombre pines. The only bright green was the harsh splash of some sea shrub down the cliff to the right of the house which blazed against the expanse of the sea itself, today wine-dark and vivid.

When they were admitted to the house through a massive but blistered door, which the elderly parlormaid shut quickly behind them to keep out the noontide heat, they found it difficult at first to see in an interior which was as cool and dark as the outside was dazzling. Two frightening suits of Japanese armor loomed in the darkness. These flanked the drawing-room door, which suddenly opened between them, framing in an oblong of light the tiny hobbling figure of Mrs Talbot, who in Australian fashion had come out to meet her guests instead of waiting for them to be shown in to her.

Mrs Talbot led them back into the drawing-room, where nothing had been changed since the last century, and where the chintz covers, though freshly glazed, were fifty years old. Mrs Talbot had pale blue eyes which danced with excitement. Her frail old body seemed to be bubbling and shaking with quiet silvery laughter. She used to love parties but now she never left her home, and any visitor was an excitement at Cape Furze. She was delighted with Lucinda and stroked her hand and said:

"Oh what a lovely creature! She's prettier than I was, and I was the beautiful Miss Dermot. Your grandfather was one of my beaux." She shook again with almost soundless laughter and wiped the tears from the corners of her eyes.

When she said that Canon Chapman was one of her beaux, he said "Ahem! Ahem!"

The luncheon table in the bogus baronial dining-room was like an illustration from an early edition of Mrs Beeton. It was crowded with ruby glass and a great many objects of ornate silver filigree. An epergne was filled with yellow roses and surmounted by a pineapple. There were quantities of very good food. The delicate garfish had been caught by the gardener that morning in the sea below the house. There were three roast ducklings between the five of them, and, surprisingly in this outpost of civilization, an iced pudding with strawberries in it. The claret was some of the last that had been laid down by Mr Talbot.

Because she was their hostess and also a unique survival, they were all prepared to be as agreeable as possible to Mrs Talbot, even if she had turned out to be disagreeable, but she enjoyed her own party so much that it was impossible not to be charming to her, and to laugh at everything she said. Her chaff of the canon, together with the good claret, of which he drank more than half a bottle, had a stimulating effect on him, and there was a light in his eye more benign than its usual tenacious glint. Tony's and Lucinda's ages were both so far removed from her own that she placed them together as "the young people," and the smiles which she gave them from time to time had an amused approval. Tony was surprised to find that the canon, following Mrs Talbot's lead, gave him what might almost be described as "a knowing wink." Julie alone felt rather out of the party, as if she were with children. She thought Mrs Talbot a nice, rather silly old thing, unable to take an interest in the only thing that mattered outside one's private affairs, the activities of Toorak society.

Back in the drawing-room they were brought, instead of coffee, huge breakfast cups of very strong Indian tea. Julie again tried to bring the conversation back to Toorak, and to make Mrs Talbot grasp the important fact that she intended to build a house there.

When Mrs Talbot at last began to talk of Toorak, it was the Toorak of fifty years ago. Julie's father-in-law was mentioned.

"We did not know him," said Mrs Talbot, forgetting the relationship, "but I believe he was a man of quite respectable origins."

"Oh, quite, quite!" said the canon, delighted to hear the baneful influence of his life referred to as if he were a gardener or a groom whose character had been doubted.

Julie tapped her foot on the floor and looked out of the window.

"I expect the young people would like to go and look at the garden," said Mrs Talbot.

Julie stood up, not that she thought herself a young person, though she was nearly the same generation as Tony, but she did think herself as capable as he was of walking round a garden. Mrs Talbot by "look at the garden" meant "be alone together." She was not going to have her little plot thwarted. Also she did not want to be left alone with the canon. She only found it possible in company to treat him as one of her beaux. Alone they were embarrassed with one another.

"I want to show you my Rockingham tea service which belonged to my grandmother," she said to Julie. "It will be preferable to walking in the heat." Julie could not very well refuse.

Mrs Talbot led Tony and Lucinda down a long stone passage and let them out by a door in which there were panes of red glass, which made the outside world, already sufficiently hot, appear as if it were on fire. Although the terraces were crumbling, and half the garden abandoned to gorse and brambles, she still behaved as if Cape Furze were a show place, and directed them to what had been its finest pleasances.

"Let's find somewhere cool," said Lucinda. They were in a little square court of hard earth, in the center of which was a loquat tree. They went down some steps and along a stony path between gnarled hedges of rosemary and came into an orchard of old unpruned trees.

"I like this place," said Lucinda, "everything is old. I've never seen so many old things together—Mrs Talbot and the house and the furniture and even the trees. There's nothing young at all."

"Only you," said Tony.

"You needn't rub it in."

"Rub it in? Surely you don't mind being young?"

"Don't you mind, then?"

Accepting as natural his love for her, she saw no reason why it should not be an implication of their talk. Tony had not accepted it as natural. To him, although it colored all his thoughts and directed all his actions, its recognition was like an acceptance of the miraculous. Now he could hardly believe that Lucinda's question allowed him the right to expect certain things in her as the object of his love. He was too emotionally affected to reply. They walked on through the orchard in silence. Lucinda thought she had been gauche.

They came to a gate in a hedge of hawthorn, bramble and a common white rose which was in full flower. Beyond the hedge the ground sloped steeply to a narrow cove. To the right loomed the great chunk of the cape, its red bluffs glowing in the full face of the sun, its sides spread with the harsh green sea-shrub, and below it the flat purple sea.

"Shall we go down there?" asked Tony.

"If you would like to?"

"I'd like to go anywhere that you want to go."

She gave a faint awkward smile. Sometimes he was inclined to be offhand, even facetious; then he said things that were almost too much. He opened the gate. As she passed through it, close to him, he had a waft of the clean smell of her hot young skin. Somehow this made him more sensible in his manner, not facetious nor over-flattering. They talked quietly as they made their way down the steep path, and laughed as they slipped on the dry grass. The path ended at the top of a low cliff. Although the sea was calm there was a slow swell which made a perpetual movement of breaking waters among the rocks at the foot of the cliff and under the bluff. The gate through which they had come was out of sight, and there was nowhere within the range of their eyes any evidence of the work of man. One felt that among that heavy and slowly swirling seaweed lurked dangerous fish, shark and octopus and stingray. At first they threw pieces of loose rock into the water, to enjoy the brilliance of the spray as it shot into the air, but then they found a shaded space of grass a little way along the cliff, and they sat there looking out to sea.

Since they had come through the gate it seemed that they had shed all misunderstanding, and that a truth had been showed to them. They did not speak much, but after a while Lucinda said:

"You seem different from what you were before."

"That's because I love you." The words which he had been trying for so long to say, the fact which he had been trying to convey by all kinds of foolish oblique methods, came out in perfect simplicity.

"I love you too," said Lucinda.

Tony's heart sang. He put out his hand and touched her. They sat there for a long time, looking at the sea, and they hardly spoke.

They were out of sound of call from the house, and no one there, neither the canon nor the elderly domestics nor even Julie could have negotiated the steep path to find them. It was only when Tony saw how far the shadow had crept round the face of the bluff that he exclaimed that it must be late. He pulled her to her feet and kissed her once on the cheek. She smiled gently.

When they came back in to the drawing-room their eyes were very bright. Whatever their appearance Julie would have been cross with them, as tea had been in for half an hour. On the heavy silver tray the florid kettle had ceased to boil. The three different sorts of cake had been cut, but Julie and the canon had made little impression on them.

"Are we late? I'm most awfully sorry," said Tony. He looked intensely happy.

"I've been looking for you everywhere," said Julie.

"We went down to the sea," explained Lucinda.

"It's quite all right. There's still plenty to eat," said Mrs Talbot. "Will you ring and we'll have some fresh tea?" she said to Tony.

"Oh no," said Julie, "that will do quite well for them."

Tony thought that Julie was too much inclined to treat him as a humble accessory of her household. He was feeling elated, and he thought, "Why should Julie decide that I am to have cold tea?" Also he could not endure that anything but the best should be offered to Lucinda. He crossed over and gave the bell pull a good tug. It came away and fell like an embroidered snake among the polished steel fire-irons.

"How clumsy of you!" said Julie crossly.

Tony suddenly disliked Julie. Now that he knew that Lucinda loved him he felt that his inclusive love for all the Vanes was no longer necessary.

"I'm most awfully sorry," he said to Mrs Talbot.

"It doesn't matter. It's always coming down," she replied, but she sounded a little plaintive, which justified Julie in looking more annoyed. Tony thought, "All old people are impossible."

When he and Lucinda had drunk two breakfast cups of the fresh brew of tea, and had eaten large chunks of an iced sponge cake, filled with passion fruit and cream, a message was sent to Hart to bring round the car.

When they were taking their places in the car Julie said to Lucinda:

"You're looking tired, dear. You had better sit in front. You'll be more comfortable than on that tip-up seat." She wanted to separate her from Tony.

"Oh," said the canon, who disliked to think that he was missing any advantage, "I should like to sit in front. One would have a better view of the countryside. Lucinda may have my seat." He climbed in beside Hart.

The result of all this was that Tony and Lucinda sat facing each other all the way back to Flinders. Their eyes were the eyes of young people in love, and when their glances met, which they did frequently, it seemed that their souls were exchanged.

Julie, now that she was free from her afternoon's irksome restraint in Mrs Talbot's drawing-room, was no longer cross. This attachment between Tony and Lucinda of which she had only hitherto been half aware, had become obvious to her, and it was something far too serious for her to be merely cross about. She did not talk much after they had turned the corner, out of sight of the house and of Mrs Talbot standing waving in the Gothic doorway. She had that expression, wise and kind and a little worried, which she had worn during the children's squabble at the Christmas dinner table.

Tony saw the expression, and his dislike of her which he had felt when he broke the bell-pull faded, and his love for Lucinda seemed to extend to include all things within her radius. He thought that Julie had accepted the fact of his love for her daughter, which was true. She had accepted the fact, but she had not yet thought what she was going to do about it. It was this consideration which made her appear kind and worried as she turned her head away, so as not to intercept those adoring messages between their eyes, and watch instead the pale brown honeycomb through which they jolted homewards.

After their evening meal, instead of returning to Strathallan, Julie went down the wide grassy road to the sea. She wanted to be alone to think over the situation. In all the twelve or more years she had known Tony she had never known him seriously attached to any girl. He had flirted with dozens, but always with that hint of facetiousness which was too obviously assumed for self-protection. If this really was his first experience of falling in love it was most unfortunate, as their refusal to allow it would be such a blow to him that it would break his friendship with the family, and he was most useful socially, and about the house. Also she was fond of him.

For a moment Julie considered whether it might not after all be allowable. Was thirteen years such a difference in age when the man was older? Tony was of a quite good family. She dismissed the idea almost as soon as she had thought of it. Everyone, not only her immediate family but all their friends, expected Lucinda to make a brilliant marriage. She was recognized to be unique in her loveliness, her graceful manners and her quick but not unkind intelligence. It would be simply preposterous, an impossible anti-climax, for her to marry Tony, and before Lydia her elder sister was even engaged. Of course on Lucinda's part it was only a schoolgirl's infatuation, and she would soon get over it. Still, when Julie thought of those exchanged glances on the drive back from Cape Furze, she was uneasy.

She sat on the grassy cliff above the sea and watched the sunset. Its green and orange glories faded from the sky, but a large yellow moon came up behind her to keep away the darkness.

"Hullo, mummy."

She turned. Lucinda and Tony were behind her, standing close together and smiling. Lucinda's voice was musical with happiness.

"Darling," said Julie gently, "you ought to be in bed. You've had a long and tiring day."

"Oh no, it's been heavenly," said Lucinda.

"Still, it's time you were in bed. Go back now. Tony can stay and talk to me."

They both looked disappointed, but she thought it as well that they should not be alone to say good night.

"Shall I take Lucie home and then come back here?" suggested Tony. Sometimes the family called her Lucie, and Tony had followed their example. Julie had always thought this natural, but now it irritated her.

"No," she said, "she can go quite well alone."

Tony and Lucinda touched hands. As she moved away she turned again and smiled at him. He followed her with his eyes.

"Sit down, Tony," said Julie. Her voice was serious but friendly.

He sat beside her on the grass and asked if she minded his smoking. They were silent while he lighted his cigarette.

"I have a bone to pick with you," said Julie. "No, not quite that."

"What is it, then?"

"I don't think you ought to play on Lucinda's emotions."

"No." He could think of nothing else to say. "I didn't intend to," he added. He meant, although he could not say so, that he had not deliberately begun the affair. It was Lucinda who had done that, in innocent directness.

"You could make her be sensible."

"Isn't she being sensible?"

"Don't pretend. You know she has an absurd infatuation for you. It's not your fault, but you could tactfully cool it off—not play up to it to amuse yourself."

"I'm not doing it to amuse myself."

"You can't be serious."

"What if I were?"

"You'd be sillier than I think you are."

54

"Why?"

"You're thirty-two, aren't you, and Lucinda is barely seventeen."

"I'm only just thirty-one," said Tony. He spoke in a husky and awkward voice, as his age was the thing he was most ashamed of.

"It's the same thing," said Julie.

They were silent, both remembering that Julie, ten years ago, had had a rather more than maternal feeling for Tony. Julie wanted to say: "You're a good deal nearer my age than Lucinda's," but it would have reminded them too sharply of this. She had unfortunately only yesterday read that Tolstoy at the age of seven fell in love with a little girl who was destined to be his mother-in-law.

"Well—will you help me?" she said at last.

"How?"

"By persuading Lucinda to be sensible. You could easily do it—in a kind brotherly sort of way—and for Heaven's sake don't look at her like that," she snapped suddenly.

"Like what?"

"Like you did in the car coming home."

"Oh!" Tony's blush was visible in the moonlight. He stood up. "I'm a bit tired of being treated as a nincompoop," he said, "a sort of tame dog about the house that can arrange the flowers."

Julie thought she had gone too far. She did not want to quarrel with Tony.

"Dogs don't arrange flowers," she said, taking refuge in flippancy.

He ignored her remark and went on in an even accusing tone. "Apparently I am to have the disabilities of both youth and age—to be bossed about like a boy, and told in a strange house that cold tea is good enough for me, but when it comes to exercising any of the privileges of a boy I am told I'm an old man. I'm sick of it. I'm sick of holding dowagers' opera cloaks. They can go to the devil."

"Tony, don't be unreasonable. You know I'm most awfully grateful for all you've done for us. I value your friendship enormously and the children adore you—I only don't want you to spoil it all with foolishness. It isn't even your foolishness I'm talking about. I only want you to help me with Lucinda. Be a good boy and sit down again." She patted the grass beside her. When the logic of a man became too much for her she had two methods of dealing with it. One was to become plaintive, the other to pretend that the man was after all only a little boy. She employed them both with Tony.

If Tony thought that anyone had friendly intentions towards him he found it almost impossible not to be amiable, and he was very easily deceived about friendly intentions. He hesitated, murmured something and sat down again on the grass.

"I don't want you not to be friendly with Lucinda," said Julie. "I only want you both to be sensible. She's much too young to think of anything of that kind yet."

"I'd better go on to Portsea tomorrow," said Tony.

"That wouldn't be sensible, to run away."

"The aunts are coming on Friday. I'd be leaving anyhow before then." Actually he had intended to endure Fred's sisters for the sake of being near Lucinda.

"Why not stay till Thursday?"

"No, I'll go tomorrow. The Lanfrancs said I could come when I liked."

The fact that he had this casual entrée to the Lanfrancs household reminded Julie that Tony was still a social asset. She stood up, took his arm, gave it a little squeeze and said:

"Come on—we'd better go indoors."

At breakfast Lucinda looked so beautiful that Tony could hardly bear to let his glance rest on her. Her eyes were so clear, her skin blooming and perfect with the morning air.

He walked back with her across the road.

"I'm going on to Portsea this afternoon," he said.

"Are you?" She showed surprise and a touch of disappointment.

"Julie says we must be sensible." He said this with an uneasy smile. He wanted to ally Lucinda with himself against the rest of the world, including her mother.

"Oh!" She seemed uninterested, perhaps mildly puzzled.

"D'you think we ought to be?"

"I don't know." She laughed, that clear silvery laugh which was so musical and yet had a hint of emptiness in it. "I don't know really what being sensible means."

Suddenly it all seemed easy to him. He had lain awake throughout the night building up an agonizing situation out of nothing.

He told Julie that he was leaving after luncheon.

"Oh, very well," she said. She looked wise and kind again.

Tony and Lucinda spent the morning with the boys at the Tarpeian Rock. The canon had a slight headache from yesterday's jaunt and did not require their company. With much diplomacy Tony managed things so that the boys left the beach first. When they had climbed the steps and their voices were no longer audible from above the cliff, he turned to Lucinda and said:

"Let's say good-bye now."

She acquiesced in this, but he saw that she did not feel that a secret quasi-dramatic farewell was necessary. She had not his urge to make of their love a plot against the world. So again he only kissed her on the cheek. She smiled, but looked faintly troubled, and he was not certain whether this troubled look was because he was going away, or because she did not see the necessity of a private farewell. He was not absolutely happy as they climbed up the rough steps in the rock, but when she said, "We'll be back at The Pines in a fortnight," and he knew from her voice that it was a promise, to herself as much as to him, of their soon meeting again, his uneasiness completely evaporated.

Before he arrived at Portsea in the evening he stopped his car on the top of a hill overlooking Port Phillip Bay. The fact of Lucinda's existence had suddenly overwhelmed him with delight. He had to stop to experience this happiness. Odd moments of the last few days became so vivid in his mind that he almost felt as if he were living them again. He heard the funny, husky sound of her voice when she asked him if he did not mind her being young, and this morning when she said they would be back at The Pines in a fortnight. He saw her standing above the rocks of Cape Furze, saying: "I love you too." He felt as if he were blest by heaven. He had never known anything like this feeling before, and he sat perfectly still in his car. Then he remembered her at the breakfast table that morning, looking, he thought, so absolutely lovely, so young as if she had only that moment been created, and her eyes seemed as if she had just looked on something so innocent and beautiful that he could hardly bear to meet them for the stab of delight it gave him. Sometimes too, her youthfulness was funny. He laughed aloud and banged his hand down on the wheel of the car.

"O God, it's marvelous!" he exclaimed. It was marvelous to be alive. He had not known what it was to live before. Now life was clear ahead. It had direction. It had meaning. He had only to wait a year, till Lucinda was eighteen. He was so full of life and confidence that he was sure no one would be able to oppose his wishes.

The Lanfrancs were a witty, legal family. Their *summum bonum* was a smart repartee. They were accustomed to amuse themselves by scoring off Tony. This evening they were piqued to find him more than their match. Mr Justice Lanfranc went up to bed chuckling at his daughters' discomfiture. Tony went to his room and sat up in bed writing a long letter to Lucinda. It was in the Lanfranc idiom, lively and erudite, but full of implied tenderness.

He remained pleased with this composition for two days, but when there was no reply from Lucinda by the first possible post, he was filled with misgiving. Would she think it a silly letter? When by the end of his week at Portsea he had not heard from her he was filled with panic. What a complete fool he had been to write to her in that strain.

When he returned to Tintern Avenue he found a letter from her waiting for him. It had been written by return of post but had not been forwarded. She had not known how long he was staying at Portsea.

It was a simple and friendly letter and made no attempt to reply to his discursive wit. There were only two things in it which indicated her feeling for him. One was the brief sentence, "We miss you here." The other was the signature, "With love from Lucinda." She also wrote, "I never thanked you enough for the lovely books you gave me at Christmas." She said at some length how beautiful they were and how good it was of him to have given them to her. He was not very pleased at this. It sounded as if there was something exceptional in his giving her a nice present.

CHAPTER SIX

JULIE RANG UP TONY on the afternoon they returned from Flinders and asked him to come over to dinner.

Tony was delighted. Although he did not change into a dinner suit, he shaved again and put on a clean shirt. His idea was that if he came in day clothes, but looking fresh and immaculate, he would give the impression that he was always fresh and immaculate. From now on he observed innumerable tortuous subtleties of this kind in his relations with the Vanes. He even formed superstitions about his clothes. Certain colored handkerchiefs and ties he associated with happy days, with Lucinda, and on days when he was most anxious that all should go well he wore those colors.

When he arrived at The Pines, Florrie the parlormaid told him that Julie was out in the garden. He had expected to find them waiting to welcome him. Before he had fallen in love with Lucinda he would not have minded if Florrie had told him that they were down at the river. Now he felt absurdly hurt. He went through the house, instead of walking round, so that he could look at himself in a mirror in the hall.

Julie was with Watteau choosing ripe peaches, and trying to find some early grapes on a vine which was tangled with the peach trees at the side of the house, and which was laden with more green than purple bunches. In some the green was fusing into purple and suggested a semi-precious stone. Julie was very hearty.

58

"Oh, Tony," she said, holding out her left hand, "come and help us find some ripe peaches. Fred is coming back tomorrow, and it would be a good thing if we could show him a completed plan of the house. I have a drawing board and some proper paper and things, and I thought we might draw it out to scale this evening."

"Right-ho!" said Tony cheerfully.

He looked for ripe peaches and tried to conceal his impatience for Lucinda's appearance.

"Lucie and Bill," said Watteau, speaking apparently, as she so often did, with suppressed indignation, "have gone to play tennis at the school and are staying to supper with the aunts."

"Oh!" said Tony, trying to appear indifferent, but his voice was high and strained. He was furious with Julie.

"They did not know you were coming," volunteered Watteau.

"No, they'd gone when I rang up," said Julie.

"Oh!" said Tony again. He could see that Julie felt guilty. This did not prevent her from offering him only a choice between beer and cider at dinner. He refused both and she had to open some wine.

They pored over the plan until ten o'clock. They became so absorbed in it that they forgot their mutual resentment. At ten o'clock Bill and Lucinda came in, having been playing "Pit" with the aunts.

Bill said "Hello, Tony," and greeted him effusively. Lucinda stood smiling, looking very pleased. Julie sent Bill off to bed and went up a little later to tuck him in. Watteau immediately said she would go and make some tea, and she left the room.

"Thank you for your letter," said Tony.

"Oh—thank you for yours."

"Did you think it was idiotic?"

"No, why? It was amusing. I liked it."

"Lucinda, if I do write idiotic letters, don't judge me by them ever, will you? Sometimes when I begin to write, my pen and everything else runs away with me. You understand, don't you?"

She did not understand but she said, "All right!"

He kissed her on the cheek. She smiled. Julie came into the room and had an odd expression at finding them alone together—not exactly cross and not exactly suspicious. It was the look of someone who grudgingly pays a bill.

Fred did not really like going for a tour of his stations in the hottest weather, but he disliked more being at Flinders in the company of his father-in-law, his sisters and Tony. Lydia met some school friends in Sydney and went off to visit them for a week. Fred stayed on alone at the Wentworth and enjoyed himself.

When he returned to Melbourne he felt rather guilty, so that Julie had not much difficulty in persuading him to build the house in Toorak. Three acres of land in St George's Road had just come into the market. Fred, having beaten down the price to two-thirds, bought it, and he and Julie took Tony's plan in to Mr Buxton, the most fashionable Melbourne architect at that time. Mr Buxton was very impressed by the plan and said, "Tony Duff would have made a splendid architect. He has a remarkable sense of design."

Fred was pleased by this, as he felt that he was getting some return for all his food and wine that Tony had consumed, and for all the hours he had endured in his company.

He also made Julie, as a condition of his building the house, agree to Bill's leaving Trinity and going to Geelong. Julie was slightly confused in her own mind as to the object of all her social ambition. She had an instinctive belief that the most desirable thing was to be rich and important. She had a vague idea that Fred pursued riches and herself importance for the benefit of their children. She was hardly prepared to sacrifice one of the children to social importance, though at this stage she believed that everything must be done for the girls. Bill was happy as a day-boy and she did not want to send him away from home yet. Most of the rich squatters' sons went to Geelong. It was understood that Bill would have to go there eventually, but Julie wanted to put it off for another year.

She drove down to discuss the matter with the headmaster, who was urbane but faintly ironical. He said that if they wanted Bill to mix now with the boys who would be his friends in later life, that was the very rich, it might be wiser to send him to Geelong, but if they thought in terms of educational value, and the development of a sensitive character, as it was his duty to think, there was no doubt that for the present Bill would do better to stay where he was. He walked out with her to where her hansom, flecked with yellow spots of sunlight, was waiting under the elm trees. For short journeys Julie still preferred a carriage to a motor car.

"It is, of course, a problem," said the headmaster with a faint smile which irritated Julie, and made her think that after all Bill would be better at Geelong. At dinner she told Fred of this conversation.

"Of course he wants to keep a Vane at the school," said Fred. "He has a Vane on the council. That should satisfy him."

"I'm sure," exclaimed Watteau, "that the canon would never be guided by self-interest."

"Everybody is guided by self-interest. You don't know the world," said Fred contemptuously.

Julie looked worried.

60

Bill was full of indignation when he heard that he was to be sent off as a boarder. His nerves twitchings became worse. During his first term he wrote five times to Blake IX. In his second term only once, and after that not at all. At the end of his first term he came home with blue rings under his eyes, though after that he seemed happy enough.

Julie was too busy to give much thought to Bill. She and Tony and Mr Buxton had at last brought the plan of the new house to as near perfection as possible. Externally the lines were long and low, with white columned loggias at either end. Inside were to be vistas of polished floors, plain cool archways, a library paneled in native wood, and a ballroom with a little *art nouveau* plaster work on the ceiling.

Fred was brought in to inspect the completed plan.

"H'm!" he said. "I expect that will cost a pretty penny." He said it with a twinkle in his eye, as a father fingering a sovereign in his pocket might ask his son if five shillings were enough.

"Well," he said, having examined it thoroughly, "you must give me a door out the other side of my den. I can't be mobbed by women. Otherwise it looks all right to me. Let me know how much I'm to be ruined." He gave a rich laugh.

On the way out to Kew he stopped the car to buy a *Herald* from a boy in the street.

"Hullo!" he said, glancing through it, "Miss Everard-Jones of Tourella has died."

"Oh, has she?" said Julie. "Poor old thing!"

"I don't expect she's left much."

"No. It's a pity it takes so long to make a garden. Still it's a good thing that those trees are already grown on the site."

"Yes," said Fred absently. He did not pay much attention to her talk about the new house for the rest of the way home.

Tony, during the months when he was evolving the plans of The White House, was moved all the time by the thought of Lucinda. On many days he went over to The Pines and worked for hours on the plan, simply in the hope of seeing her and spending a short time in her company. He gave infinite care to every detail of the plan, trying to create a house which would be a fitting dwelling place for her. He spent a whole day on working out the proper width for three steps which were to lead up from the hall to the ballroom, and as he did so he imagined her standing at the top of them. He spent a week designing the delicate plaster work for the ceiling with its pattern of lilies which was a play upon her name. It may have been a trifle *art nouveau*, but even that gave it a youthful

61

freshness after the pompous Italianate mansions of the boom, and the glaring red so-called "Queen Anne" houses which had followed them. When the whole thing was finished Tony seemed to come out of a trance. The design had been literally inspired, and he knew it. Mr Buxton's admiration he took as a matter of course.

Julie too had known, but not quite admitted to herself, that Tony's work was inspired, and also the source of its inspiration. If, when he had several engagements he was unable to do much work on the plan, she would ring him up and say:

"Do come over to dinner and bring the plan. Lucinda will be here."

Once or twice she offered this bait and Tony arrived to find that after all Lucinda had gone out. Then Tony refused to bring the plan in from the car, saying, "I really haven't done any more to it."

The happiest evening he spent at this time was one when he brought over the completed design for the ballroom ceiling. After dinner Canon Chapman's housekeeper rang up to say that he was unwell and would like Julie to go over. It was Hart's evening off, and Fred drove her over in the car. Roger, the eldest Blake boy from next door, came in and took Lydia for a walk down to the river. Watteau disappeared.

Tony went out to his car and brought in his design and unrolled it on a card table in the drawing-room. He had drawn it with meticulous care, and had painted it in the intended colors.

"You see they are lilies," he said, smiling at her. "That's because of your name. The ceiling is to be a faint creamy-pink and the lilies are to be silver. I have tried to get it as near as possible but the silver paint wasn't very good."

"Oh, it'll be lovely! How well you've drawn it. I'd no idea you could draw so well, Tony. You're awfully clever."

"I didn't know I could, either." He laughed, then said more seriously, "I did it for you."

"Why should you take so much trouble for us?" She sounded almost anxious.

"It's not for *us*, it's for *you*, Lucinda."

"Oh!" She lifted her head and smiled, but her eyes were moist. It seemed as if it were too much, more than she could accept. He took her hand and they sat together on the sofa, talking with serious friendliness until it was quite late, and they heard the car return with Fred and Julie.

Lucinda went over and switched on the lights. This pleased Tony, as it implied that it would not do for Julie to find them sitting alone in the dark room.

62

Julie came in and said, "Papa only had an attack of indigestion. Where are the others?"

"I don't know," said Lucinda.

Julie eyed them sharply, but she sensed that the atmosphere was more one of quiet friendliness than of emotion, and at the same time she saw the design on the table.

"Oh, good! More plans!" she exclaimed, and with her plump jewelled fingers she smoothed it out and held down the curling edges.

"How pretty! But why have you painted it like that?"

"Those are the colors it's to be."

"But surely a ceiling must be white. I couldn't have a pink and silver ceiling. It would be freakish."

"If you won't have it pink and silver I shan't use this design," said Tony.

"Mummy, it must be pink and silver," said Lucinda.

Again Tony was pleased, and he had a sense of security. He thought that Lucinda, who at first had felt that all this was more than she could accept, had now brought herself to accept it, and that by agreeing to this plan which was the symbol of his love and refusing to have it altered, she was accepting his love itself.

As he drove home he was again possessed by the feeling of complete love, which had come to him on the hill above Portsea. He was troubled neither by the criticism nor the anxiety which so often make a torment of love. He sang quietly to himself all the love songs that he knew.

It was a week after this that the plans were taken to Mr Buxton, who had to prepare duplicates for the builders, and make a few technical corrections.

Two weeks later than this Tony was dining at The Pines. Julie as usual began talking about the new house.

"Oh, do let us talk of something else," said Lydia. "Sorry, Tony, but there are other things to talk about, aren't there?"

Fred, who had been in town all the afternoon, had returned in one of those withdrawn and silent moods, which Julie knew came upon him when he was doing a big business deal of some kind. It was as if he had withdrawn all his energies into himself and had concentrated them in the center of his being where he had conceived an idea. When he was in the mood nothing could touch him, nothing could move him, and he appeared completely indifferent to anyone else's comfort or feelings.

"The house will not be built," he said, "not by me."

There was a moment of incredulous silence. Florrie, who was

63

taking away the soup plates, and who had heard the house discussed at every meal for months past, hurried out to the kitchen to tell the other servants.

There had been dreadful moments in Julie's life, some connected with Bill's birth, others before that at Noorilla, when she had thought that she faced the ruin of all she valued in life. They had given her reserves of strength and dignity, and because of them she sometimes had that kind and worried look which made people feel most affection for her.

"Have you lost money?" she asked quietly.

"On the contrary, I have never been better off."

"I don't understand."

"I have bought Tourella," said Fred. "I shall not need to build a house."

Again there was silence. Florrie came in with a dish of fried flounder. Fred had a grim smile, but the rest of the party looked bewildered.

Watteau's frail and frizzy head shook with indignation.

"And what is to happen to Mr Duff's plan, that he's made such a labor of love?" she asked, voicing a question which everyone else thought too dreadful to utter.

"As I have said before," explained Fred, "fools build houses for wise men to live in. I have bought Tourella, including its furniture, for exactly one quarter of what it cost to build, and for one half of what the new house would have cost. I have managed to sell the site in St George's Road for nearly twice what I paid for it. Am I to forgo these advantages because Mr Duff has amused himself for some months at a drawing board. Will you answer that, Miss What-ho?"

"Money isn't everything," said Watteau with temerity.

The rudeness to Tony was hideous.

"What about Mr Buxton?" asked Julie to turn attention away from it.

"I shall make a proper arrangement with him," said Fred. He paid Mr Buxton a few pounds for the duplicate plans he had made. A few months later Mr Buxton had to design a house for the Radcliffes, a Western District family. He wrote to Fred and asked if he might use the plan for The White House. Fred agreed on the condition that Mr Buxton paid him. Fortunately Fred believed that the creative artist's work should receive the lowest monetary reward of any, and he fixed a price for the use of the plan which Mr Buxton thought it worth while to pay. He thought it was the property of the Vanes, and had no idea that it was Tony's exclusive creation, though he was a little uneasy about the deal. He told Tony that he was using the plan, and did not happen to mention that he had paid Fred for it. Tony was so pleased that his labor was not to be wasted, and that his ideas would be expressed in bricks and mortar, that the financial aspect of it did not occur to him. He was very friendly with the Radcliffes, and he gave them the same advice about detail that he would have given to Julie if the Vanes had built the house. Julie, when she heard of it, was a little jealous, but by then she was involved in such tremendous social activity that the affair of the plan had become unimportant.

"Did you say you had bought the furniture?" she asked Fred, when she had absorbed the fact that Mr Buxton would be paid off.

"I have, and it is not the least part of the bargain. Sir Percival Everard-Jones brought it from all over Europe. Some of it is magnificent work from the Great Exhibition. There are two large cloisonné vases in the hall, nearly five feet high, which I am told are worth £500 each."

"My God!" muttered Tony savagely.

"What a terrible disappointment to everybody!" exclaimed Watteau.

"I fail to see how it can be a disappointment to live in the largest and finest private house in Melbourne. The windows, the doors and all the fittings are of the best quality and in perfect condition, and if you want 'art' the marble pavement in the hall was brought from Italy."

He did not wait for dessert, but taking the decanter of port from the sideboard he went off to his study.

Julie looked more worried than Tony had ever seen her. She was at the moment more ashamed of Fred than disappointed about the house.

"I'm awfully sorry, Tony," she said, after a pause.

"It doesn't matter. Anyhow it was fun designing it," said Tony weakly. He felt like one of those Italians mentioned by Samuel Butler, who, when they have been unfortunate, say, *"Sono disgrazio."* He felt that his situation was too pitiful to be endured publicly. He tried to talk easily about something else, but he could not keep the strained note out of his voice.

When the dessert was put on the table Julie asked Florrie where the port was.

"The master took the decanter into his study, ma'am."

"Go and get it, darling," Julie said to Lucinda. She was afraid to send anyone else lest Fred should refuse to let it go, and put a further insult on Tony.

After dinner it was almost as if there had been a death in the family. The main topic of conversation of recent months had been removed, or rather had become taboo. Tony sat on the sofa, scraping the unmelted sugar from the bottom of his coffee-cup, a childish habit which he had not abandoned.

Roger Blake came in to look for Lydia.

"You don't look very lively in here," he said.

"Daddy's bought Tourella," said Lydia.

"What! Not Buckingham Palace?"

"Sort of."

"What about the White House?"

"Gone down the drain," said Lydia laconically.

"Whew!" Roger gave a faint whistle of sympathy. "Coming down to the river?"

"Right-oh!"

"You don't mind, do you, Mrs Vane?" He turned with a confident smile to Julie. Julie did not like Lydia's going so often down to the river with him in the evening, but at the moment she was too distracted to stop them. She had asked Fred to discourage Roger from coming so much to the house, saying he was hardly an eligible fiancé for Lydia. Fred to her surprise had refused.

"That boy is doing brilliantly at the university," he said, "and he will make a better husband for Lydia, if he wants her, than some poodle-fakir in society. I intend to put his foot on the ladder, and after that you'll see him race to the top." He had already told Mr Blake that if any money were needed for Roger's education he would be glad to advance it. Julie liked Roger, but she thought that his engaging urchin's manner made him utterly unsuitable as a husband for one of the girls.

Roger turned at the door and nodded to Tony, a gesture in which he summed up the whole situation.

"You know," said Tony, "you'll be able to do a lot with Tourella. It has a fine staircase, and some of the rooms are magnificent. The snag is the furniture. Those cloisonné vases."

"I must go and look over it," said Julie. "I don't suppose you'd come," she added tentatively.

"Oh yes, it would be fun."

"You are an angel, Tony. Really, I don't know how you can forgive us."

Now that the thing had come out into the open, and they no longer pretended that Tony had not been treated with gross rudeness and ingratitude, they were more at ease with each other. They

66

smiled a little tearfully and sat on quietly discussing the aesthetic potentialities of Tourella.

Tony left early, before Lydia and Roger came back from the river. Lucinda went out with him to his car and Julie left them alone together.

"I'm most awfully sorry about the house," said Lucinda.

"It's all right," said Tony.

She repeated it with a kind of urgency, as if he must take in what she said, and yet there was no criticism of Fred in her attitude. She was very fond of her father, and accepted his more unpleasant acts as phenomena of nature, like a thunderstorm.

Tony was holding her hand. He kissed the tips of her fingers and got into his car. She stood and waved to him as he drove out of the gate. He had a curious feeling of emptiness. His love for Lucinda and his design for the house had been so interwoven in his mind that the evening's events had left him bewildered.

The purchase of Tourella meant that the Vanes moved to Toorak very much sooner than if they had waited for a house to be built for them. They moved in before the spring race meetings. Julie would have liked to give a ball in Cup Week, but all the dates were booked with other big dances, and she satisfied herself with a garden party. She brought Lydia out at Government House and intended to give a ball for Lucinda the following year.

For some time Fred had disliked his sisters keeping a school, and yet, although he could easily have afforded it, he also disliked the idea of compensating them financially if they gave it up. However, now he offered them The Pines, the brougham, which was very seldom used, and to bring their income up to an adequate level if they would sell the school. These two women still thought in terms of Victorian gentility, and the idea of returning to their old home and being "carriage ladies" appealed to them so strongly that they sold the school, to their astonishment, at a profit of £10,000. Fred managed the deal for them. Having been fully occupied for a number of years, and having developed the resistance and drive and organizing ability which are necessary in a school, they suddenly found themselves with little outlet for their energies. Their two maids had a dreadful life, enduring all the organization and instruction which formerly had been diffused amongst one hundred and eighty children.

Tony still spent a good deal of time at the Vanes. Julie wanted his help in choosing curtains and covers, and colors for redecoration for Tourella. Fred would allow almost nothing to be replaced on the grounds of taste, but Julie complained that most of the stuffs were faded. Electric lights had not been installed at Tourella, so all the ponderous gas fittings had to be changed for new light fittings. Fred would not hear of the removal of the two cloisonné vases.

Julie and Tony were seen about together more than usual, in Buckley and Nunn's and the Mutual Store and other shops. Even a little scandal began to breathe about them. One or two of her closer friends chaffed Julie about this, but she was not displeased, partly because it was flattering to herself, but more because it showed how absurd was Tony's attachment to Lucinda, if that still existed.

Tony modified the expression of his love for Lucinda for the time being, as this was part of his plan of action. Having told himself that he must make no further declaration of his feelings until she was eighteen, he experienced a time of calm and security. He had no wish other than to see her often, to be left alone with her sometimes, and to give her occasionally an almost fraternal kiss. Because he was so moderate in his demands, and because she saw no signs of that tortured anguish which accompanies a frustrated love, Julie began to think that it was nothing but a harmless sentimentality which would end when Lucinda came out and met numbers of other young men at dances. She continued, half-consciously, to use Lucinda as a bait when she particularly wanted Tony at The Pines or Tourella. Sometimes, as before, he would arrive to find Lucinda not there. His behavior then was the only thing that made Julie think that his feeling for Lucinda was more than a sentimentality. He would be irritable, almost rude, and leave early.

CHAPTER SEVEN

THE MOVE TO TOURELLA was effected with the maximum of comfort. The Vanes did not leave The Pines until their new home was in complete working order. The servants were sent over immediately after breakfast, the family lunched with the aunts, and drove over in the afternoon to Tourella, where Colman the new butler was waiting under the *porte cochère* to open the door of the car.

"Dear me!" said Watteau, standing in the hall and looking up at the Corinthian columns, "isn't it different from Noorilla?"

"Shall I bring tea into the drawing-room, madam?" asked Colman.

"Oh yes," said Julie, almost emotionally, "in ten minutes."

Julie, although she had visited Tourella nearly every day since Fred had bought it, had hardly been able to believe that she was really to live in such magnificence, but now when she knew that her trunks were waiting to be unpacked in her bedroom upstairs, and when her own butler, the first she had ever had, was about to bring in the tea, the realization that she was mistress of this mansion produced a moment of mild intoxication. She felt as if importance were actually inflating her body. She took in a deep breath, and when she breathed out it seemed to have left her a little heavier, as if that slight layer of fat which made her a plump and jolly matron had become a little thicker.

Julie, emerging from the middle classes into grandeur, was not quite sure how grand she ought to be. The decision was more difficult as money fixed no limit. She wished to go as far as possible towards an aristocratic ménage, but to stop short of the theatrical or ridiculous. An English duke might have fourteen powdered footmen in crimson liveries. A simple squire might have a butler and only one footman in brass buttons and a striped waistcoat, while some Irish landowner who could just manage to pay the interest on his mortgages, on occasions when he entertained, might drag in the stable-boy, who also acted as the village postman, and fitting him with a pair of white cotton gloves, cause him to announce, "Your honor is served." All these styles of living were rather more distinguished, more dynastic, than the parlormaid at Kew. Julie would have liked a footman, but she felt rather timid about employing one. She felt that if an occasion arose in society when she was obliged to say "my footman" her body would give an involuntary wriggle, her voice would go rather high and sound at the same time apologetic and prim. As it was, Florrie had cried when she heard that a butler was to be put over her. She would have left if she had been banished altogether from the dining-room, and she was invaluable as a personal maid.

Although Julie had acquired an added sense of importance on occupying Tourella, it was the naïve importance which a child feels on its birthday. As they passed on a tour of inspection from Fred's library with its heavy leather armchairs to the morning room, where the new cretonne covers were very fashionable, black and white striped and spotted with pink roses, and thence through the billiard-room and the dining-room smelling faintly of sherry and pineapple, back past the cloisonné vases and the Corinthian columns to the drawing-room where Miss Everard-Jones's lavender brocade curtains had been too good to replace, Julie's smile was saved from smugness by a hint of amusement. But this disappeared when she found that Watteau also was amused. They were only a family party at dinner including Watteau and Tony, but Julie had ordered a very good meal as it was their first night at Tourella. There was champagne, and when Colman handed Watteau a quail she said:

"Dear me, we are grand. Do you remember my first night at Noorilla? We didn't have quail then—tinned salmon, and that was a treat."

Fred grinned, but Julie was angry, and looked nervously at the butler to see what effect this disclosure might have on him. Nor did she care for Tony to know of the extreme privation of her early married life.

"It was very hard to get provisions up there," she said.

"Hard to pay for 'em," said Fred. He liked to exaggerate, if this were possible, the poverty of those days, as it made his present success a more remarkable witness of his own ability.

Julie began to find Watteau less of an asset. Her whole effort was directed towards making Tourella homely. She said and did things which caused Julie social embarrassment. In the middle of a large dinner party she would get up and fetch something for herself from the sideboard. She appeared suddenly to have remembered, after a lapse of eighteen years, all the more sordid details of life at Noorilla, and she referred to them frequently. There was a touch of stupidity in the lines of her mouth and chin, but the look of intelligence in the bright beady eyes which peered out from beneath her mop of hair made one doubt that her tactlessness was unintentional. Watteau was inclined to be rationalistic in her belief, or unbelief, but she retained from the religion she had mostly discarded the conviction that riches destroyed virtue, and that it was one's duty to humble pride.

Julie began to wonder if it would not be possible to pension off Watteau. She had always said that she wanted to return to her home in the Valley. She thought of asking Fred if he would buy back the little house and give it to Watteau. He had always complained about her; he might be glad to be rid of her at the price. She found that it was always difficult to speak to Fred about money. If she were to say, "I would like a diamond tiara," he would probably answer, "Certainly, my dear. You shall have the best that money can buy." But when she said, "I am sending poor old Miss Crick (a former governess of the girls, who was ill and penniless) five pounds for Christmas," he retorted, "You know, my dear, my money is not inexhaustible."

However, an incident occurred which gave Watteau the deeds of her old home, but did not remove her from Tourella.

Only a fortnight after they had moved in, and a week before the garden party, Fred awoke one night and thought he heard someone moving. The door was open into Julie's room and he called out, "Are you all right, my dear?" She did not reply. More from curiosity than any clearly defined motive he went into her room and switched on the light. Immediately a masked man, standing at the dressing table, fired at him but missed. Fred leapt at the man and grabbed at the revolver, which went off again. By a curious chance the bullet hit a hanging electric light bulb, which made a third explosion. Julie awoke and cried out. Fred and the man, struggling together, reached the landing. Julie, calling for help, followed them. Watteau, her hair hanging in two thick plaits down her back, appeared like a female Samson. She at once joined in the fray. She bit the burglar's hand so that he dropped the revolver. Then she snatched off his mask and, pulling his legs, upset him. He and Fred rolled down the stairs on to the half landing.

Lydia came out of her room along the gallery and growled sleepily, "What's the row?"

"Fetch Colman! Fetch Hart!" gasped Watteau, clinging desperately to one of the burglar's kicking feet. Julie was too distraught to do anything but ring bells and exclaim, "Oh dear! Oh dear!"

By this time the noise had brought Colman. He and Fred managed to hold the heaving body of the burglar, while Watteau and Lydia tied him up with some old skipping ropes of the girls. Lucinda slept through the whole incident.

Fred was not seriously hurt, but the burglar had stamped on his bare feet, and he stayed in bed for two days. When he came down again he said:

"You're a sensible woman, What-ho! You're not such a fool as you look."

A month later he handed her the deeds of her old home. It was let on a long lease. "I will take the rent and see to the repairs for you," he said. For once Watteau was unable to speak.

Tony was disgusted that he had not been given the opportunity of saving Fred from the burglar. Since they had moved into Tourella, although they were living much closer to him, he had seen less of the family. Julie was occupied with social activities, and his help was no longer necessary for interior decoration. Not seeing Lucinda so frequently, he became anxious about their relationship. The kind of love he had shown her ever since the return from Flinders, which made no demands and apparently had no expectations, and so was accepted by her as little more than part of the general family affection, now became troubled and more urgent. In a few months she would be eighteen, and then Tony was going

71

to ask her to marry him, and to ask Fred to allow it. At times he felt confident, but sometimes he lay awake at night, his body taut at the contemplation of his temerity. If only he had saved Fred from the burglar he would have been unable to refuse him anything, and to do Fred justice, when he did not feel himself under a moral obligation to swindle somebody, he could be extremely generous. Or, he thought sardonically, if the burglar had killed Fred his way might have been clear. Watteau, although sometimes useful, was like a piece of grit in the Vane machine, interfering with the works at critical moments.

The day before the garden party Julie rang him up and asked him to come and help her to supervise the arrangements. Tony rang the bell and waited in the shadow of the *porte cochère*. The front doors were open. Before a servant answered the bell Lucinda, wearing a print dress and carrying a basket, appeared in the hall. She stood a moment and hesitated, as someone does who, just going out, wonders if she has forgotten something. He stood watching her. For a moment he thought, "Is she as beautiful as I think she is? Am I enduring all these anxieties for someone who is not unique, but only one of millions in the world?" But it seemed to him, looking at her with detached appraisement, that she was perfect, and that his reason endorsed what his heart felt. He had a moment of shame that he had allowed himself to think like this. It was immediately succeeded by an intense emotion when his mind and his heart together seemed to be galvanized by his love.

Lucinda turned and saw him. Her face lighted up with joy. She ran out to him and exclaimed: "Tony, what are you doing? You don't have to ring here. Why didn't you walk in and call out: 'Anybody at home?' "

They stood smiling at each other. Tony thought, "She must love me or she would not be so delighted to see me." He did not take into account that young people who are happy show pleasure at meeting almost anyone whom they like.

"I'm going to pick flowers for the party. We can't leave everything till tomorrow morning. There's so much to do. Come and help me."

He did not attempt to kiss her, but he took her hand as they walked across the crunching white gravel of the drive, and down a lawn to a part of the garden where flowers were grown for picking. They did not at once begin to pick flowers but walked about between the borders, discussing which were the most suitable to pick.

"What you ought really to do," said Tony, "is to pick great

boughs of oranges and put them in those cloisonné vases." Below the garden was an orange grove, and they strolled down there between the trees. They gathered oranges and sat on the ground and ate them. All the time they talked together in the easy fashion of people who have reached complete understanding, and as on the day at Cape Furze, they were unconscious of the passage of time. It was nearly six o'clock when they returned to the house laden with boughs from the orange trees, bearing their golden fruit and dark glossy leaves. They dumped them on the marble floor of the hall and went into the drawing-room to look for tea.

"Tony, you are late," complained Julie. She thought that he had just arrived. "Where have you been, Lucie? I was looking for you everywhere."

"I was down in the garden. Isn't there any tea?"

"It's gone out long ago. If you want some you must go and make it in the pantry. Are you going to help me, Tony?"

"If you want me to. We've brought up some orange branches for the hall. They'll look marvelous in that Italian setting."

Julie came out to look at them. She was a little startled at their treatment of the orange trees, but pleased at the original decoration. She and Tony arranged them while Lucinda went along to make tea. Tony said he would put some water in the vases—it would be impossible to fill them—to keep the branches fresh. He went along to fetch it from the pantry, and stayed there, drinking tea with Lucinda. The butler came in to put out the glass and silver for dinner.

"Oh, Colman, I hope we're not in the way," said Lucinda, "but we forgot the time." They went on drinking more tea and talking in an amusing, friendly way to the butler.

Tony stayed on so late that Julie asked him to stay to dinner. After dinner they all sat in the morning-room, discussing the arrangements for tomorrow. Julie, unaware that Tony and Lucinda had spent three hours in the orange grove in the afternoon, in that confused state of mind in which she occasionally threw a sop to Tony, thinking it did not matter, left them alone together to say good night.

Lucinda walked down with him to the gate. Because of thugs and burglars, he said, he walked back with her to the house.

"It's been a most perfect day," he said.

"Yes, it has," Lucinda agreed.

Neither of them could speak. Tony tried to, but he only made an odd sound in his throat. They stood quite still for a moment. Their fingers touched and he turned away down the drive.

"I know now that it's all right," he told himself. "I know now that she loves me. We have only to spend our time together for life to be heaven. When we are left alone together we have complete understanding."

Normally, walking home in the dark, along these wide deserted Toorak roads, where the tree trunks provided ambush for the footpads who came from the slums across the river, as vermin creeps out at night in a dirty inn, he was nervous. Tonight he had no trace of fear.

Early the following afternoon, heralded by the aunts from The Pines in their brougham, a steady stream of carriages and motor cars began to disturb the finely raked gravel of the drive. The archbishop and his wife, four judges and a party from Government House were amongst those directed by Hart down the garden to where Julie, wearing long white gloves and diamonds in her hat, stood with Fred at the top of some wide stone steps to receive them.

All over the wide lawns of Tourella the women's dresses were brighter than the flowers in the borders. The babble of people enjoying themselves was pleasant in the open air. The men seemed to put on an extra urbanity with their top hats. Conspicuous among the black coats were those of the archbishop and Canon Chapman, the former showing unusual courtesy to his hostess's father. The canon, enjoying this reflected importance and looking up at the colonnades of the house which rose arrogantly above the extensive gardens, had an odd moment of doubt, not of his religious faith, but whether after all it had been his supreme misfortune when William Vane had flung him over Clare bridge. The archbishop left him, and the canon stood slightly dazed. Lucinda and Tony were crossing the lawn, near where he stood.

"Hullo, grandpa," said Lucinda. "Isn't anyone looking after you?"

"I don't need looking after, my dear," said the canon testily.

"You'll want some tea."

"I shall find it. I shall find it. Ah, the *arbiter elegantiarum*," he said, turning to Tony. "I very much doubt, young man, whether the plan you evolved would have approached this in magnificence." He waved his hand at the house. "I very much doubt it."

Lucinda looked troubled, but Tony smiled and said:

"It wasn't meant to be magnificent, sir."

"Oh! Not so?" said the canon. "Well, I must pass on." He bowed stiffly and went over to speak to a thin lady in black.

The mention of the plans for the White House awoke a kind of sadness in Tony and Lucinda.

"I wish we *had* built it," said Lucinda.

Tony, looking up appraisingly at the colonnades of Tourella, had very different feelings from Canon Chapman. It was amazing how little of the real spirit of the Renaissance the architect had managed to put into the house. Every pillar and every piece of carved stone was nothing but an advertisement of wealth. The house seemed to assert the height of the barriers between himself and Lucinda. He wanted to be alone with her, and was just going to suggest that they should go down to the orange grove when Lucinda said:

"Look. There's Melba."

The famous prima donna was shaking hands with Julie and Fred, and introducing a young man who accompanied her. Julie and Melba, followed by Fred and the young man, walked slowly across the lawn towards the house. Melba stopped now and then to speak to friends. The news spread that she was going to sing in the ballroom. The guests strolling about the garden turned, as if a tide had changed and were moving them, and converged on the open French windows. There was a crush at the windows, and a girl named Clara Bumpus tore her dress on the catch, while Mr Justice Lanfranc squashed his silk hat. When the ballroom was full there were still people outside crowded round the open windows. Tony and Lucinda squeezed through the window nearest the piano and stood against the wall. The crowd pushed them closer together and their fingers entwined. Fred and Julie were sitting near them in the front row of chairs.

Melba sang two or three songs, *Down in the Forest*, Musetta's song from *Bohême*, and finally *Home, Sweet Home*. As the notes of this last song dropped like so many pure and perfect jewels into the afternoon air, everybody was moved except the Misses Lanfranc, who cast their eyes about the ostentatious room and smiled ironically. Tony squeezed Lucinda's fingers. Fred at this moment noticed their hands and looked up and saw the expression on their faces. His satisfaction that Melba should have so graciously given this sentimental endorsement to his occupation of Tourella was forgotten.

The loveliest voice in the world stopped singing. There was a felt silence, then a burst of applause in which three ladies split their white kid gloves. One of these ladies put her glove away in a drawer of keepsakes and told her great-nieces that she split it clapping Melba.

The party moved in to tea, which was served at buffets in the dining-room and in the billiard-room. Fred conducted a small and distinguished group to see where he had grappled with the burglar. Melba admired the orange boughs in the cloisonné vases. This was the first time Fred had noticed them. He was angry at the damage to the trees, and at the danger to the vases, but said nothing before his guests.

Soon the carriages and the cars began to roll away as thickly as they had come. Fred looked sullenly at the churned-up gravel, while Julie, flushed with triumph, bade lively and affectionate farewells. At last there was no one left but the aunts from The Pines.

"It has been quite a success," said Gladys Vane, "though it was a pity people pushed so to enter the ballroom."

"I heard Nellie Mitchell sing when she was a young girl," said Norah, "and I said at the time that she would probably achieve success."

"Where's your brougham?" growled Fred.

"In the drive."

"Well, get into it."

He led Julie back into the hall, leaving his sisters only slightly dispirited as they were accustomed to his rudeness.

"Who put those there?" he demanded, looking at the orange boughs.

"Tony," said Julie. "They look very chic. Melba admired them."

"They didn't come off Melba's orange trees. Does that young poodle-fakir know that these vases are worth £500 each?"

"I expect he has heard you say so," said Julie, rather reckless with the excitement of her party.

"Well, if I meet him he'll hear me say something else. He's not coming into my house again."

"Oh, Fred, don't be absurd," protested Julie. "I let him put the orange boughs there."

"When I say a thing I mean it. He's not coming inside my house again."

He went through into the dining-room where the hired waiters were taking down the buffets. Julie followed him.

"Bring me a whisky," he said to one of the men. He took the glass and went out with Julie into the garden to see if the crowd had spoilt the lawns.

"You can't mean that about Tony," Julie protested. "He's our oldest friend. He's most helpful."

"If you think I'm going to allow a poodle-fakir old enough to be her father to make sheep's eyes at my daughter, and squeeze her hand in public, you're mistaken, my dear."

"Lucinda, you mean?" asked Julie.

"Yes, I do mean Lucinda. So you've noticed it?" He gave her the scrutiny he generally turned on a man with whom he was doing a deal. Julie looked worried.

"I thought that was over," she said.

"I didn't know it had begun."

"Lucie was rather silly about Tony last summer holidays at Flinders. I suppose he found it amusing."

"He's not going to amuse himself with my daughter."

They walked about the garden for half an hour or more talking about Lucinda and Tony. Julie no more than Fred approved of the attachment, but she was fond of Tony. Also she knew that if they offended him he was capable, more from a desire to entertain than from malice, of making Tourella appear ridiculous and themselves figures of fun in all the more exclusive families in Melbourne. She did not dare tell Fred this, as the idea that he could be threatened by Tony would have made him furious and vindictive.

They went down to look at the damage to the orange trees, which fortunately was so slight that they were unable to find the trees from which the boughs had been taken. Julie managed to persuade Fred to agree to a compromise. Tony was not to be invited to the house when he was at home, except to large parties. They would not go to Flinders for the holidays, but to Tasmania. This would anyhow be more suitable for the girls than the primitive conditions at Strathallan, and Tony would not have to be invited.

A few days later Tony met Lucinda in Collin's Street. They went off to have tea together at the Wattle Tea-rooms, a cheerful place where there were good cakes and the tables were always decorated with iceland poppies.

"We're going to Tasmania for the holidays," announced Lucinda, with the pleasure which young people show at any new adventure.

Tony caught his breath. "Oh!" he said. "Not to Flinders?"

"No. Why don't you come too?"

"Shall I? Would you like me to?"

She laughed. "Of course I would."

She told him that they were going first to Hadley's Hotel in Hobart, and then to The Bower for the strawberry fête, and up to New Norfolk and down to the Huon and all over the place. They were taking two cars. Fred would drive one and Hart the other. There would be sure to be room for him. They talked excitedly about the places they would visit. They were so obviously happy together that one or two people turned to watch them.

It did not occur to Tony, who had for years spent part of every

Christmas holiday with the Vanes, and who for as long had put himself at Julie's beck and call, that he would not be welcome on this trip. He and Lucinda went out to Toorak together, sitting on the front of the dummy of the cable tram. They looked amused and very pleased with each other.

Julie was accustomed to spend the half-hour before changing for dinner at the telephone gossiping, and fixing minor social engagements. The friend whom she first rang up said, "I saw Lucinda and Tony Duff having tea at The Wattle this afternoon. They were evidently enjoying themselves."

The next friend whom she rang up said, "I saw Tony and Lucinda coming out on the tram this afternoon. They were full of high spirits."

Mrs Bumpus, whom she rang up a little later, was worried about her daughter Clara. "She's such a hoyden," she said. "I'm thinking of taking her home next year and sending her to a finishing school in Paris."

Sometimes Lucinda seemed to be so full of happiness, to be so perfectly poised that she commanded instinctive respect. She was like that this evening at dinner.

"Tony's coming to Tasmania with us," she said.

Julie glanced sharply at Fred, who however merely growled: "And who asked him?"

"I did," said Lucinda, smiling at what she thought was her father's affected grumpiness.

"And are you going to pay his hotel bills?"

Lucinda laughed. "No, Daddy. I haven't enough money. I expect he can pay them himself."

"And how is he going to travel?"

"There'll be plenty of room if we take two cars."

"There will be no room for Mr Tony Duff in one of my motor cars," said Fred.

"Oh, Daddy, there will be," said Lydia in her husky, booming voice.

"If Mr Tony Duff wants to go to Tasmania he can go in his own motorcar," said Fred. He took up the decanter of port and left the dining-room. Julie followed him.

Before she went to bed she wrote to Tony saying that she would love to have him with them in Tasmania, but as Fred was coming she really thought it would be better not.

"I know you will understand," she wrote. "You are such an understanding person. It is no use pretending that you and Fred get on well together, and you would be at such close quarters all the time. It was different at Flinders when Fred only came for a day or two. You must come to our Christmas party at Tourella before we go."

Tony resigned himself to a miserable January. He bought another expensive present for Lucinda and quite enjoyed the Christmas party, at which he kissed her twice. If he had one criticism of Lucinda it was that she did not seem to feel the sorrow of parting. When he said that they would not meet again for six weeks her eyes remained serene and unclouded and she said simply, "No."

From Tasmania she sent him three picture postcards and two letters. He read these letters several times, giving them as much attention as a scholar gives to an ancient manuscript or to a great poem, trying to arrive at the exact inflection of meaning in every word.

Lucinda would be eighteen in March. Tony spoke to his mother about his allowance and the possibility of its being increased should he want to marry. When he mentioned marriage his mother was so upset that he had to pretend for the time being that he had no such intention.

The Vanes returned to Melbourne at the beginning of February. Julie at once rang up Tony and said, "Have you heard the news?" He wished that she would not always ring him up on arrival, as he longed for Lucinda to do it, and to hear from her that they were home.

"No. What news?" he asked.

"We're all going to England in a fortnight. Come along to dinner and we'll tell you about it. Fred's dining at the club."

He listened in a dazed condition to Julie's excited plans for the next six months. The girls were to go to a finishing school in Paris. Watteau was to look after Tourella and Bill, but he was expected to spend most of his holidays up at Noorilla with his cousins the young Chapmans, the children of Julie's brother, Dick, who was managing the station. Tony did not know that the wish to separate him from Lucinda had originally put the idea of this trip into Julie's head, but he was sufficiently wretched. The only thing that awoke a moment's vague suspicion was a false heartiness in Julie's voice when she said:

"You must write to us regularly, Tony, and tell us all the gossip. We rely on you. You must come here often and cheer up Watteau and Bill."

As he walked home, as indifferent to the menace of thugs as he had been in his joy, this suspicion recurred to him, but in the morning he thought it impossible that the whole Vane family, except

79

Bill, should travel ten thousand miles to be free of his company.

He saw very little of Lucinda before they sailed, as Julie and the girls were in the throes of preparation for departure. He went down to see them off, and on the pretext of going to look at the dining saloon he managed to lead her away from the chattering crowds on the deck of the P. and O. liner. They stood rather shyly together in the quasi-palatial saloon, where the atmosphere of luxury was pervaded with that horrible smell which is inseparable from the most splendid ships. A few stewards were arranging tables, but after the decks the room seemed empty.

He gave her the presents he had brought her, an anthology of French poetry, bound to match the set he had given her at Flinders, and the best box of sweets he could find in Melbourne. He had sent flowers to her cabin. He had become reckless now and gave no presents at all to Julie nor to Lydia.

"You're too kind to me, Tony," she said.

"That's impossible."

"Well, I'm very grateful. I don't think I ever thank you enough."

"I don't want you to thank me, Lucie. I only want you to be pleased with what I give you. Not that I give you anything."

"You do. You give me lovely things. I shall always treasure them."

"I wish I could give you a lot more—everything."

They stood silent for a while, not knowing what to say.

"I wish you weren't going away," he said.

"Still, it's not for very long, is it? We'll be back in a few months."

"It'll seem a very long time to me—a century."

She smiled at him. She began to say something but the siren went to warn the visitors to leave the ship, and they were deafened. When it stopped she said:

"I expect we'd better go up to the deck again."

"Yes." He longed to kiss her but did not, partly because of the stewards. As they went up the companionway he took her hand and kissed it and she smiled at him again.

In the first weeks after she had gone he spent hours analyzing their relationship. He came to certain conclusions, and then the next day remembering some other incident would come to different conclusions.

He waited anxiously for the first letters from her. He thought she might write or at least send a picture postcard from Adelaide or Fremantle. When at last a letter did arrive a month later, posted at Colombo, although he was delighted to receive it, it was too late to assuage the first acute pain of their parting. He read this and every letter she sent him from Europe with the same anxious scrutiny which he had given to her letters from Tasmania.

He went often to Tourella, especially in the school holidays, and dined with Watteau and Bill. There were cadences in Bill's voice which reminded him of Lucinda's. He went also to get material for his letters to her, and he thought it a good thing to keep his place there as *persona grata*. Bill when he left always asked, "When are you coming again? Can't you come tomorrow?" Tony liked Bill and was always easily amused by young people, but he thought too that it was wise to establish a friendship wherever possible with one of the Vanes.

Bill was adequately fed, clothed, sent to a good school, and when he needed anything, a cricket bat or a saddle, was given the best obtainable. Otherwise his family took little account of him. At present everything was being done for the girls. When he tried to tell Julie about some doubt he had, or some half-formulated ambition, she did not listen, but said, "Yes, darling" and kissed him. Fred still was capable of bringing on her nervous twitching. Watteau was kindest to him, and though he thought her rather silly he was very fond of her. He was happier alone at Tourella with Watteau and Tony than when the family were at home. He only went once up to Noorilla and hated it. Not only did he dislike the flies and the heat and the smell of sour milk which permeated the house, but his cousins thought that because he had good clothes he must be a coward and to amuse themselves they put him on dangerous horses. When he killed a six-foot snake from which they had run away they pretended that it had been already dead.

Even so, he was not completely happy at Tourella, as although he would face any reasonable peril of the noonday, he was afraid at night. Now that the family were away his bedroom was isolated. No one was sleeping in the adjoining rooms and he could shout at the top of his voice without being heard. When he was told of Fred's encounter with the burglar he was secretly terrified, and pictured to himself what he would have done if he had been at home and the man had happened to be in his room. Of course he would have had to attack him, but undoubtedly the man would have killed him. Every night he went to bed prepared to meet a desperate situation. He took his double-barreled gun out of its case, loaded it and put it by his bed. In the morning he put it back again so that the housemaid would not know of this precaution. He was ashamed to lock his door, and sometimes as he lay awake, hardly daring to breathe, he would stare for so long at its dim outline that it seemed to move, and some faint midnight creaking would be magnified to a step in the room. On moonlight nights he would stare out of the window, expecting to see murderers hiding in the shadows of the huge garden. So when Tony came to dine he begged him to stay as late as possible, to put off the hour of going to bed, and so that he might at least begin the night with the courage from recent companionship.

Fred returned from England earlier than Julie and the girls. He hated being there, as apart from a few Australians whom he met, no one knew how important he was. He was involved in a slight motor accident in Regent Street. In reporting it only one of the evening papers gave his name, and this one referred to him as "an Australian farmer named Vane." He returned home in disgust, leaving Julie and the girls to be presented at the last court of the season by the wife of the High Commissioner for Australia. He never left Australia again. "England," he said, "is a country of poodle-fakirs and popinjays."

Bill tried to summon up some feelings of pleasure at Fred's return, but the only satisfaction it gave him was that he was less afraid at nights, as Fred's bedroom was close to his own. It meant also that Tony's visits were less frequent, although as Fred usually dined at the club they did not stop altogether.

The Radcliffes' new house, built to Tony's plan but on a different site in Kooyong Road, was nearly finished, and he spent a good deal of time there, supervising the details of decoration and the choice of fittings. Everything was the same as he had designed it for the Vanes except the ballroom ceiling. For this he did a new design of stars and the background was sky blue. It was pretty but less inspired.

Tony did not think much about money. He had heard from Watteau that Fred would settle two thousand a year each on the girls when they married. His mother kept control of their own finances, but from his present allowance and their general way of living he imagined that ultimately he would have about fifteen hundred a year. He did not want his mother to die, but he knew her health was precarious. If and when he married Lucinda they would not be able to afford a place the size of the White House, but he could in a smaller house build a replica of the ballroom, and he intended to use there the design he had made for Lucinda.

CHAPTER EIGHT

JULIE AND THE GIRLS arrived back in Melbourne well before the
spring race meetings. Tony and Watteau went to meet them at
Port Melbourne. Bill was at school. On the pier they found Canon
Chapman and the aunts. Fred arrived by car and Hart brought the
second car for the overflow. Fred shook hands with Canon Chapman and nodded to the others. He stood a little apart from them
as he thought it unsuitable that Mr Vane of Tourella should be
seen in public with people as insignificant as Tony and Watteau,
or even with his own sisters, though people for whom Fred had a
sneaking veneration, like the Lanfrancs and the Radcliffes would,
if they thought about it, prefer to be seen with Tony rather than
with himself.

After a confused and excited reunion on the ship, they all went
back to Tourella for luncheon, during which Julie monopolized
the conversation with a description of Buckingham Palace. She now
appeared to think that only what advanced the social importance
of the Vanes was of any account. Tony said little to Lucinda, expecting her, as so infinitely his superior, to show the first signs of
regard. But Lucinda had become more adult to this extent, that
she expected Tony, as a man, to pay her attention. As not only at
luncheon but throughout the afternoon he seemed to hold himself
aloof from her, and even to have some cause of grievance against her,
she thought that he must have ceased to care for her. She was a little
sorry but it did not distress her very much. Her attitude towards
him had been more an acceptance than a return of love. When he
no longer showed her these tokens of particular feelings she thought
it was probably because he liked children and she was no longer
a child.

Julie talked steadily till tea-time. It was impossible for Tony or
Watteau to leave her, though Roger was able, without giving
offense, to take Lydia down to the orange grove. This was not because Julie approved of his going out with Lydia, but because he
would be an unappreciative and undiscerning audience for her
grand experiences. Lucinda hung about the morning room where
they were sitting, and once or twice she gave Tony a tentative
friendly smile.

Julie had written from the Hyde Park Hotel to the Dean of Ilchester, who was a cousin of her father's. She had mentioned the relationship and hoped that they might meet if he came to London. The Dean invited her and the girls to stay, and they had a marvelous week, of which the most exciting event had been tea at Crittenden.

"It's a most wonderful historic house," said Julie, "with a beautiful avenue of chestnuts. The Brayford family have been there since the Middle Ages, but the house was rebuilt in 1670 when they got the title. Lord Crittenden is a twelfth viscount. There are seven reception rooms and an enormous room with a painted ceiling that they call the saloon."

"It sounds like a public house to me," said Watteau.

"Nonsense, you don't understand English customs," said Julie. "But the most exciting thing is that Lord Crittenden's youngest brother, Hugo Brayford, is coming out to Melbourne as an A.D.C. He arrives next month. Lady Crittenden was very simple and asked us to be nice to him."

"If he's like the other aides," growled Lydia, who with Roger had just returned for tea, "it's all we'll be able to do to get him to be civil to us."

"The Brayfords are *very* nice people," said Julie crossly. "We saw the second brother, Paul. I must say I didn't care for him so much, but they say Hugo is quite different."

After tea Julie's voice gave out and she went to her room to rest. She shook hands with Tony and said, "Come and see us again soon, Tony. I'll ring up and fix a date for dinner. It's been awfully good of you to keep an eye on Bill."

Tony supposed that he was expected to leave. He nodded a general good-bye and turned to the door. Lucinda looked at him and made a slight movement in her chair, as if to rise and come with him. Because he had not until now been given an opportunity to be alone with her, he was too embittered to respond. She looked hurt and sat back again in her chair.

Tony walked home in a state of acute wretchedness. He was going along to his room to mope when the maid told him that his mother was in the drawing-room and wanted to see him. Although it was not a cold day she was lying on a sofa close to the fire. She wanted to hear about the Vanes and their trip. It was painful to Tony to recount it all, but there was a close bond between him and his mother, and though at times he was thoughtless, and even hard when it came to a choice between her and Lucinda, at other times, when he remembered her invalid state and her generosity to him, he put himself out to please her. It was understood between them that he should recount to her all his experiences in society, and in that way give her a little vicarious pleasure. When he had finished telling her about the Vanes' presentation at court and their luncheon at Crittenden, she said:

"Why don't you marry one of those girls?"

He turned sharply.

"Wouldn't you mind?" he asked.

"I think it would be a very good thing."

He leaned forward and kissed her with more affection than he had shown since he was a boy.

Julie at once set about making Tourella as much like her idea of an English house as possible. Watteau had allowed a few middle-class arrangements to creep into the ménage. Julie readjusted these and had now acquired sufficient assurance to employ a footman. Florrie, shedding a few tears, was banished from the dining-room and the pantry, and became exclusively a ladies' maid.

For the next few months the Vanes seemed to spend all their time at parties. Tony saw a good deal of Lucinda, but it was mostly on a tennis court, or watching races or polo, or at a dinner table, or in a ballroom. Here he had more opportunity of advancing their intimacy, but at that time it would have been thought extraordinary if he had asked her for more than two dances. He would spend a whole day in anticipation of these two dances, and if for some reason the atmosphere had not been quite right, the following day in a wretched analysis of what had been wrong. He was waiting for the moment when he had restored that emotional flow between them, that complete understanding which he had felt at Cape Furze, to ask her to marry him. Every day he was certain that this would happen tomorrow.

CHAPTER NINE

THE RADCLIFFES, HAVING MOVED into the White House, gave a ball there in Cup Week. Julie gave a dinner party for this ball. As everyone knew that Tony really had designed the White House, she thought it would give a *cachet* to her party to have him there, and also for him to arrive at the ball with her.

Tony had made up his mind that whatever happened he was going to propose to Lucinda this evening. Roger's engagement to Lydia had already been agreed to, willingly by Fred, reluctantly by Julie, but it was to be kept secret until he had graduated. Only

Roger and the family were collected in the drawing-room when Tony arrived at Tourella. Julie was in her presentation dress. She was still putting on weight, and there was almost a suggestion of brutality, something feline, in the smooth heavy shoulders and arms which protruded from the gold brocade. Fred, whose evening clothes never seemed quite to fit him, stood smiling tolerantly beside her. Curiously, it was the slight misfit of Fred's clothes which made him look like a gentleman. They gave him a hand-made appearance, without which he would have been too much the sleek business man, though he always remained lean and scraggy. He shook hands quite heartily with Tony. Apparently Tony was to be in a small way the lion of the evening, and as Fred had made a few hundred pounds on Tony's plan, he saw no reason to be ill-natured towards him. Julie squeezed his hand and said:

"At last we are to see *our* house. I'm sure I shall feel that it ought to belong to me. Still, I'd much rather live here," she added, looking up at the heavy cornices. "You don't mind my saying that?" She squeezed his hand again.

Lucinda came up to Tony with more natural, unselfconscious friendliness than she had shown since her return from Europe.

"Oh, Tony, it will be marvelous to see the house," she said. "I'm so glad it was built after all."

Colman began to announce other guests. Tony and Lucinda stood away from the group round the fireplace. He was amazed and delighted at the sudden return of easy friendliness between them. She was wearing a dress of pale pink filmy stuff which made her look like some warm and living flower. Her eyes were bright with happiness. He was sure that this was the appointed night for his proposal. Everything had worked up to reach its climax this evening. His house had been built. Everyone who had seen it admitted that it was the most delightful house in Melbourne. People could no longer regard him as an idler with no ability in any direction.

"Where's Watteau?" he asked, for something to say.

"She's gone to see some friends in Kew. She would have made the table uneven." Lucinda laughed her silvery, airy laugh. She had a more detached attitude towards her family's efflorescence of grandeur than any of the others, treating it as enjoyable but rather funny. Tony laughed too.

"Poor Watteau," he said.

"Oh, she didn't mind. She suggested it."

"What have you been doing today?"

"I played tennis at Government House."

"Did you win?"

86

"I don't remember." She laughed again.

"Was the earl there?" This was Lord Wendale, whose appointment as Military Secretary had excited Melbourne.

"Yes, and his . . ." Her voice faded as she turned to wave to Miss Lanfranc who had just been announced with her father.

"And his what?" asked Tony.

"Who's what?"

"The earl's what."

"Oh, his wife." They laughed at the idiocy of their conversation.

"You're taking me in. I'm glad," said Lucinda.

"Why are you glad?"

"Well, you're the hero of the evening, aren't you? And you're my oldest friend."

Tony felt on the verge of intoxication.

"Do you remember the garden party here?" he asked.

"Of course. It was only a year ago, though it seems ages since then," she added thoughtfully.

"D'you remember Melba singing in the ballroom?"

"Yes." She was smiling across at Miss Lanfranc.

"You're not listening to me," he said.

"I was, but you've gone all reminiscent. We're not old people."

"Don't you think I'm an old person?" he asked.

"You, Tony! Why, I don't feel that you're any older than Bill." She was now smiling into his eyes and giving him her full attention. This is the moment, thought Tony. It was even more exciting, more impudent to propose in a roof full of people, under the very noses of Fred and Julie.

"Then would you—" he began.

"Dinner is served, madam," said Colman loudly from the door.

"Come on," said Lucinda, "we'll have to go in at the tail as I'm the least important."

"I think you're the most important," said Tony.

"This is the first dinner party we've had with the new footman," she said. "His name's Albert." She seemed to think that this too was a bit of a joke.

The Radcliffes' dance did not begin till ten o'clock. Fred made this the excuse to keep the men in the dining-room, listening to his opinion on current affairs. When at last they moved to the drawing-room it was time to leave. The Lanfrancs offered Tony a lift in their car, and he felt obliged to take it, though he hated being separated from Lucinda, even for a five minutes' drive.

"It beats me," said Mr Justice Lanfranc, recalling the conversation over the port, "how a man as stupid as Vane can have made so much money. Perhaps one needs a lower form of intelligence to understand the general low intelligence of the business world. When I was a young man a business man was not considered a gentleman. Most of the time Vane says, 'I'm a plain business man,' but after a few glasses of port he says, 'I'm only a simple farmer.' That place don't strike me as much like a farmhouse. What the deuce is he? Damn good port, anyhow."

"Papa, you are shocking," said Miss Lanfranc.

"That's because I associate so much with criminals. Never you become a judge, Tony, my boy. You'll go to the dogs if you do." He chuckled comfortably. He was a little drunk.

The Vanes' car had passed them and gone on ahead, but Julie waited for them on the Radcliffes' steps. In spite of her satisfaction in Tourella she did feel a pang of envy as she stood in the cool arcade of the hall with its ivory-colored walls. At the end, on either side of the low steps leading up to the ballroom, was an austere alcove in which was an alabaster urn, filled with spring flowers. The only other decorations were little double-flowering peach trees, set in tubs full of violets. Through all the smells of the ball—the predominating women's scent and the Turkish and Egyptian cigarettes, the smells as the evening progressed of roast snipe and champagne coming from the dining-room, the smell of hot if well-washed bodies which the perfume did not always hide—through it all crept in elusive whiffs the woodland fragrance of violets.

"This is really my house, you know," said Julie, laughing, as she shook hands with Mr Radcliffe, but there was an edge to her voice.

"I thought it was really Tony's house," said Mrs Radcliffe, turning to him.

"Yes, it is Tony's," said Lucinda.

"A house belongs to the man who pays for it," declared Fred.

"In that case I expect it belongs to me," said Mr Radcliffe quietly.

"Whosoever it is, it's charming," said Julie, feeling that she had been undignified in showing envy.

They passed through into the ballroom. Tony was beside Lucinda.

"Oh, you've done a different ceiling," she said.

"Yes, I kept the other one for you."

"But I shall never have a house like this."

"You might have a room like this."

When she said anything which he could fit to his own thoughts, he imagined that she shared those thoughts.

"How many dances are you going to give me?" he asked.

"The usual two, I suppose."

"Won't you give me three tonight—because of the house?"

"All right—but I expect it will cause a scandal." She laughed. He was pleased at the remark.

"May I have the supper dance?"

Her brow puckered. "I'm sorry, not that."

"Have you given it to someone?"

"Well, I did really."

He filled in one dance early in the program and two towards the end.

There was a stir at the door. The Government House party had arrived.

A tall young man, rather heavily built, with a sanguine face, light blue eyes and crisp golden hair, detached himself from the group and came over to Lucinda. He had blue lapels and gilt buttons on his dress coat. He looked extraordinarily clean. He gave a barely perceptible glance of apology to Tony and said to Lucinda:

"Have you kept those dances for me?"

"Yes, I have." She handed him her program eagerly. For a moment she had returned to that ingenuous adolescence which, before she went to England, had enchanted Tony. The aide-de-camp wrote on the program and handed it back to her.

"Oh, you've taken three," she said. Her voice and her smile showed that she was pleased, but also that she thought him rather dreadful. He gave another indifferent glance at Tony and moved away.

"Who's the professional pig-sticker?" asked Tony.

"Captain Brayford, the new A.D.C. He's Lord Wendale's cousin," she said coldly.

"The earl's cousin. You didn't tell me you'd met him."

"I told you in the drawing-room before dinner."

"You said the earl's wife. You didn't say his cousin."

"Oh, well," said Lucinda. She wished Tony would not go on calling Lord Wendale "the earl." It sounded silly and provincial to her. Then she was ashamed of being cold to Tony. She made an attempt at explanation.

"Captain Brayford's awfully funny," she said. "This afternoon he said to me, 'D'you jump wahhead?' I thought 'wahhead' must be a New Zealand dance, so I said we weren't New Zealanders. He said, 'Do they jump wah in New Zealand?' So then I knew he meant did we jump wire out hunting. I was terribly embarrassed, but I couldn't help laughing, and he said I must give him two dances to make up for it, and show that I didn't dance like a Maori. But he's taken three. Still, it doesn't matter."

"Oh, I see," said Tony. Some young man came up to ask Lucinda to dance. Feeling vaguely disturbed he went off to fill up his own program.

He heard Lady Wendale say to Mrs Radcliffe, "Your house is really delightful. It's the most·charming new house I have ever seen."

His confidence was restored. He knew that he was oversensitive and apt to magnify trivial incidents into a situation. The incident of her keeping the supper dance for Brayford meant nothing. Any girl would do that for a newly arrived A.D.C. She had been obviously affectionate to himself the whole evening, and Lucinda was not fickle nor a humbug.

After Lucinda's first dance with Hugo Brayford he asked her for three dances at the Government House ball the next night.

"Oh no, two," she said, laughing.

"Well, two more at the Williams's on Thursday."

"Very well."

"And two more at the Australian Club on Friday."

"You must ask me for those on Thursday."

Lucinda enjoyed this conversation, his boldness, her denial and the element of flirtation. Julie, standing near, watched them with satisfaction, but also with a degree of impatience. She had told everyone that they had visited Crittenden and lunched with Hugo Brayford's brother, and had given as much as possible the impression that they were friends, but so far no one had introduced Captain Brayford to her. She thought the Wendales, to whom Fred had lent hunters, might have done this. At last she bustled rather defiantly up to where Hugo and Lucinda were arranging their dances ahead.

"Oh, this is my mother," said Lucinda, not actually criticizing Julie, but feeling embarrassed.

"You must excuse my breaking in like this," said Julie, her voice a little high and excited, "but I feel I must make myself known to you. I know your brother and Lady Crittenden, and they asked me to—well, they said to be kind to you, but I don't expect you'll need that! We went to tea at Crittenden House. What a glorious home that is! Anyhow, I do hope you'll dine with us. Could you manage one night this week? Perhaps you'll arrange it with Lucinda. Or could you come on Saturday? There's no big party that night, but we're having a few friends, about fifty people, to dance till twelve o'clock. Won't you come and dine with us first? Now I shan't keep you any longer."

Brayford gravely thanked her and said he would like to come. Julie, just restraining herself from tapping his arm with her fan, said, "Don't forget," and went over to explain to Mrs Radcliffe how Lady

Crittenden had particularly asked her to be kind to Captain Brayford.

"You didn't tell me you knew Marian," said Brayford to Lucinda.

"We don't really," said Lucinda. "A cousin we were staying with
took us to visit Crittenden."

"Marian's a bit of a Tartar. Well, now that we're family friends
you'll have to give me three dances tomorrow."

Tony, from across the room, watched this scene with anxiety.
"Julie is flinging Lucinda at his head," he thought. "It'll probably
put him off."

Still, Brayford did not look put off, as, leaving Lucinda to fill the
rest of her program, his pale blue eyes surveyed the room in search
of other partners. He looked even more pleased with himself than
when he had come in.

However, Tony's first dance with Lucinda restored his confidence.
He felt that they had recovered that happy sympathy which had
begun at Tourella before dinner, but when they sat out after the
dance he did not think that the mood was quite right for him to
propose to her. It would be better later in the evening when the
emotional condition was heightened. He was glad he had been interrupted by Colman's announcing dinner. Then he was only speaking
from excitement. He wanted to speak from love. During this first
interval he hoped further to win her confidence by his fraternal
manner. He was sure that this was right as she was so affectionate
towards him.

Before he danced with her again she had danced with Hugo Brayford. In the interval after the dance he led her along to the library,
which had not yet been discovered as a sitting-out place. When
Lucinda danced with him she felt as if her bones were melting. She
had never before experienced anything like this sensation. In the
library, designed by Tony to create an atmosphere of studious
tranquillity, he sat on the arm of her chair. In spite of his height he
managed to do this gracefully and without any suggestion of impertinence. She answered his questions and laughed that silvery,
empty laugh, but she really did not know what she was saying. She
looked at him occasionally as if she were trying to make sure of the
reality of this phenomenon which had suddenly appeared in her life.

When Tony danced with her the second time he did not seem to
be able to gain her full attention. Through some perversity of the
band they had hardly any time to sit out, and he had to leave her
before he could extract any explanation of her changed mood. The
unfortunate girls who were his partners between this and his third
dance with Lucinda wondered what they had done to offend him.

When at last the time came for his third dance with Lucinda he was more in a state of grim determination than of tenderness. Whatever happened he was going to ask her to marry him during the interval. If he did not do so tonight, or rather this morning, as it was now nearly two o'clock, he knew that he would never do it. He was full of a sense of ill-usage at his treatment by the Vanes. This resentment was mostly directed against Julie and Fred, but Lucinda too was its partial object, as she had caused him so much suffering. He was angry with her for being so beautiful, and for having become more self-confident than the shy and friendly adolescent of The Pines and Flinders. He did not speak while they were dancing, and before the music stopped he said:

"Let us go and sit down."

There was more chance of finding a quiet room while everyone was dancing. Only the young people were left now. Fred and Julie and the older married people had gone home at about midnight. Tony, unconsciously following Brayford's example, took Lucinda to the library. Clara Bumpus was sitting with a bull-necked young squatter on the edge of the heavy library table.

"Oh, damn!" muttered Tony.

Lucinda smiled serenely. She merely thought that Tony disliked Clara Bumpus.

"Don't let us embarrass you," said Clara Bumpus cheerfully. "We're just going anyhow." She slid to the floor. "Good Heavens! I've sat on the table. I shan't be married for seven years. I shall have to go to India." She went out with the young squatter.

"That girl's like a footballer in a ball dress," growled Tony.

"But a good-natured footballer, I think," said Lucinda.

He looked at her quickly. Interpreting everything she said in the light of his infatuation for her, he thought she meant that it was good-natured of Clara to leave them alone together.

"How would you like not to be married for seven years?" he asked. His manner was brittle and nervous. There was even a trace of a sneer in his voice.

"Not much. This is an awfully nice room, Tony. I haven't really said how much I like the house." She was feeling so happy and he seemed a little depressed. She wanted to cheer him up.

"Would you marry me?" he asked.

"Don't be silly. Is this paneling Queensland maple?"

"Yes. Would you?"

"Would I what?"

"Marry me." His voice went thick with the effort of repetition. She turned to find Tony staring at her with a strange and disagreeable expression. He looked resentfully greedy and abject all at once. Her embarrassment was almost a physical sensation.

"I do mean it." He heard his own voice sounding harsh and angry. He knew that it would be impossible for anyone, even if she wanted to, to accept a proposal made in this way. But if he had not spoken tonight something would have happened to his will. He would have been afflicted with moral paralysis.

"But it's ridiculous. We've known each other for so long," she stammered.

"Is that disability?"

"But I mean we're . . . we're like relatives." She avoided mentioning his age, of which she had become conscious this evening for the first time.

"But we're no relation," he snapped. Now the words came pouring out, irresistible, automatic, but they were not caressing words, fountains of love and worship. They were more like a counsel's speech, full of accusation and proof. He dragged from the quiet and shaded corners of memory into the shriveling glare of his argument incidents at The Pines and on the Tarpeian Rock, and the day at Cape Furze. Feelings which at the time had been too elusive and tender for words he now stated bluntly in support of his argument.

She was horrified. Her dismay soon turned to anger at the violation he was inflicting on her, the operation he was performing upon her emotional being.

"If you don't stop," she said, "you'll make me say something dreadful."

He looked at her and saw that he had no hope. The plans and dreams that had given his life direction for the past three years had collapsed. He ran his finger along the beading at the edge of the library table. Lucinda had a feeling of pity for him, but her anger remained too strong for her to give it expression. She was more angry because she knew that if she had not played tennis with Hugo Brayford yesterday afternoon she might have accepted Tony. He would in a way have exploited her ignorance of life. Then she thought this was unfair.

"We mustn't quarrel, Tony," she said after a while.

"It doesn't matter now."

"That's a horrid thing to say."

He shrugged his shoulders. The music stopped in the ballroom. They heard the chatter of people crossing the hall to the dining-room. Lucinda hoped some of them would come along to put an end to this painful tête-à-tête. Tony, although it was causing him acute misery, did not want it to end. No one came and she turned to leave the room. With that twisted smile which formerly had attracted her as whimsical, and which now irritated her beyond endurance, he watched her go. As the door clicked smoothly behind her he crossed to the mantelpiece which he himself had designed, and with a gesture of despair leaned his head against it. The gesture gave him no satisfaction. He did not feel despair, merely an emptiness as when an aching tooth has been pulled out. His tension was released, but not into rapture, only into nothingness.

"O God!" he said flatly, and pushed back the boyish lock of dark hair which flopped over his forehead, and which, like his whimsical smile, was one of his recognized attractions.

The butler put his head round the door. When he saw Tony he came into the room and said:

"Mr Duff, sir, you're wanted on the telephone."

"At this hour!" exclaimed Tony. "All right. Thank you, Bates."

His mother's nurse was speaking. She said that Mrs Duff had taken a turn for the worse and that he ought to come home.

As he crossed the hall to the cloakroom he passed Clara Bumpus, who yapped cheerfully, "Marvelous dance!"

Mrs Duff was barely conscious when Tony came into her room. She could not speak, but her eyes gave a glimmer of recognition. He kissed her gently and sat down by the bed. His love which was frustrated in every other direction now turned exclusively on his mother.

He sat watching her pale and fleshless face, the tired lines of her closed eyes, and recalled a thousand memories of care and tenderness. Even so he fell asleep, as the effects of the champagne he had drunk at the dance began to wear off.

He was awakened in the morning by the sunlight glaring on his white shirt-front. His mother appeared to be asleep, so he went off to bed. He had hardly flung his dress coat on a chair when the nurse came to tell him that his mother was dead.

CHAPTER TEN

ON THE MORNING AFTER the Radcliffes' dance Lady Wendale and Hugo Brayford were riding on horses lent by Fred to Lord Wendale along the Alexandra Avenue. The Wendales' son, a boy of ten, cantered beside them on his pony. On their right the Yarra, swollen with recent rains, was yellow beneath the high blue sky. The air was full of that stimulating radiance which so often marks an Australian spring morning.

At the end of the avenue they turned and walked their horses slowly back towards Anderson Street. The boy, who was nicknamed Baa, partly from his courtesy title of Castlebar, and partly because his father jokingly called him a black sheep, rode on ahead.

"Is that Vane girl rich?" asked Hugo casually.

Lady Wendale laughed.

"Her father is—quite."

Hugo appeared to digest this. Then he asked, "What is her family?"

"Quantity or quality?"

"Well—er—both."

"She has a brother at Geelong—that's the sort of Eton here—and a sister who has just become engaged to a young doctor, though it's not public yet. When they marry they are to be allowed two thousand a year, which is I suppose what you want to know."

"H'm! It's not colossal."

"There are no colossal fortunes in Australia."

"And quality? Are the parents very vulgar or anything? Mama seemed a bit breezy at the dance last night."

"No. They're not exactly vulgar. I believe Mrs Vane has quite good English connections."

"Apparently she's been to Crittenden."

"Her cousin is Dean of Ilchester. He took them there. You know Marian is obsessed with the clergy. I should say the Vanes are rather like rich manufacturing people at home, but with worse voices and better horses, which amply makes up for it."

"Never met any," said Hugo. "Not a bad name, Vane."

"I believe Vane *grandpère* was a bit of a rip. He died full of debt, and the son accidentally made himself a millionaire in the effort to retrieve the situation. Both the grandfathers were at Cambridge—at Clare, Mrs Vane tells me. In fact she's told me three times."

"Which is Clare?"

"It's the college by King's Chapel. It has a lovely bridge."

"Don't remember it. Only been there once. Was Vane himself at Cambridge?"

"No. He's a bit grim. I shouldn't think he'd part with any money without an obvious return."

"I see," said Hugo thoughtfully.

Dolly Wendale was amused, but also faintly disgusted.

"Listen to me, Hugo," she said, "I don't disapprove of men marrying rich girls. Someone has to marry them, and it's better that it should be someone nice, and that the money should come into the good families. I often tell Jack that he shouldn't have married me, but a soap or a cotton queen. But after all you have two elder brothers and you won't have to keep up Crittenden. You only want money for your own pleasure. I don't even blame you for that. But Lucinda Vane is one of the most charming girls I know. She's absolutely free from whatever slight vulgarities may afflict her parents, and her nature's as good as her looks. Any young man worth his salt who wanted her ought to lose his head so completely that if he thought about her money at all it would only be as an obstacle. I tell you straight, now, that if I think you are only after her money I shall go to Papa Vane and tell him so—and that would cook your goose, my boy."

Hugo looked at her in astonishment.

"Good Lord Dolly," he exclaimed. "You couldn't do that. It would be a shocking thing to do."

"I don't agree. You know I generally do what I say. You must promise me here and now that you won't ask Lucinda to marry you unless you're really in love with her, and that if you do marry her, you'll play fair."

"All right," he grumbled.

"Say, I promise."

"All right. I promise."

Baa trotted up to them.

"Are you talking about Cousin Hugo's rich wife?" he asked.

"What d'you mean?" said his mother severely.

"I heard Daddy tell Captain Murray that Cousin Hugo had come out to find a rich wife. When I grow up I'm going to have a wife who's terribly rich. Then I shan't have to borrow my horses."

"Daddy was only joking, and you're a mercenary little pig. You're not to talk like that."

Baa laughed. He was a rosy-cheeked boy, and everyone was charming to him from the governor down to the grooms. He cantered off again along the Avenue.

"That boy of yours wants takin' in hand," said Hugo.

"I know, but it's so difficult here. He must go to school as soon as we return to England. We thought of leaving him behind, but it would have meant his spending the holidays at Crittenden, rather too much at Marian's mercy."

"Why don't you send him to school here?"

"My dear, I couldn't. He might come home talking about a riney die."

"They don't all talk like that."

"Oh, no. Lucinda doesn't, for one."

"What d'you think Paul would say to it?"

"I shouldn't worry. Paul's ridiculous, but all you Brayfords treat him as a sort of infallible pope. Even Marian treats him as a protestant treats the pope, instead of as just a conceited young man. Why doesn't he get married?"

"He seems to think that women are only there to talk to. Funny." Hugo chuckled.

The Vanes took a house at Macedon for the summer. Julie complained that they had no country house, though actually they had five country houses—Noorilla, Wombidgee, Churt, Mathieson and Willawonga—but they were all in remote burning plains, blasted by the January sun. They were all built of weatherboard and corrugated iron, and they all smelt of sheep. At Noorilla they were forced into contact with Julie's whining sister-in-law and her nasal children, to be reminded of whose existence was intolerable. When Fred pointed out that they had all these stations to go to, she said that if he would pull down the house at Noorilla and build a new one, and send Dick and his wife to manage Wombidgee or Churt, she would be glad to go there. She felt that if the house at Noorilla were pulled down, one of the chief witnesses to her years of humiliation would be gone. While if she were able to invite people up to a fine country mansion at Noorilla, Watteau's occasional references to that place would lose their sting.

Fred, however, was superstitious about spending anything on luxury, or even comfort at the stations. Their function was to produce money, not to absorb it. He would pay two hundred pounds more easily to rent a house at Macedon than two pounds for a new kitchen sink at Noorilla.

Hugo Brayford was staying at Government Cottage. He played tennis nearly every day with Lucinda and danced with her in the evenings. They went for picnics, driving in Fred's four-in-hand drag along dusty roads to some cool gully, scented with sassafras and fern, and dangerous with snakes.

When the Vanes returned to Melbourne in March, Lucinda's engagement to Hugo Brayford was announced. At times during the holidays, in the intervals between the peaks of her happiness, she had felt uneasy about Tony. She thought it unkind of Julie not to have invited him to Macedon, though in a way she was glad he was not there. Perhaps anyhow he could not have come owing to his being in mourning for his mother. She heard that he was staying with the Radcliffes in the Western District. He had not written to her— not even sent a card at Christmas, nor an answer to her letter of sympathy about his mother.

On the morning after they arrived back in Melbourne—this was the day on which her engagement was to be made public—she walked down to Tintern Avenue to see him, and tell him of it personally. She was so happy that she could not bear the idea of doing anything unkind to, or of having a misunderstanding with anyone of whom she was so fond. She wanted also to establish, and to have acknowledged by Tony, the pretense which she made to herself, that her feelings for him had not differed greatly from those which she had for Bill or Lydia, and this pretense was partly true.

There was a builders' dray outside Tony's house. Some lime and cement were spilt on the path, and a daphne bush by the door had been trampled and broken. She rang the bell, half expecting to hear that Tony had already sold the house and left, but he answered it himself. When he saw her he gave a slight start, but he lifted one corner of his mouth in a smile and asked her to come in. He led her into the dining-room, which was the only downstairs room untouched by the builders.

"What are you doing to the house, Tony?" she asked.

"Turning it into flats. Didn't you know I was broke?"

"No. Seriously?"

"Yes. Apparently we've been living on capital for years. Poor mother lost a lot in the boom, and she didn't know how to retrench. She had to have a permanent nurse and she gave me far too much. Well, there it is. How's everybody?"

"We're very well. I'm awfully sorry, Tony."

"That's all right. Would you like to see the flats?"

"Yes, I would." She could not bring herself to tell him yet of her engagement.

The house, he explained, would make three flats, two of four rooms each, and one of three rooms, but the three-roomed flat would contain the big drawing-room and he was keeping that for himself.

"Then I shan't have to live in utter squalor," he said with his whimsical smile.

At first she had been struck by his old appearance. She thought she saw one or two grey hairs above his ears. He no longer took such minute care of himself, now that he had no motive for it, and he was not naturally vain. She felt sorry for him, but at the same time, stirred by Hugo's caresses as by the resplendent noonday sun, she realized how grotesque and dim would have been her marriage to Tony. But as he explained to her the arrangement of the flats, his animation returned to him, and she had a comfortable feeling that they had re-established their old friendly relationship, without any of what she now chose to call "silliness." He was having a new window put in the drawing-room.

"All the woodwork is to be ivory-white and the walls pearl-gray. The pictures will look splendid against it. I'm only keeping the best ones—Streeton's 'Purple Noon' and Walter Wither's 'Sunlit River' and a couple of water-colors. The curtains are to be corn-color. One should always have curtains that take the light—never cold colors, never blue or green."

He was so enthusiastic that Lucinda smiled. All this preoccupation with stuffs and colors, which formerly she had accepted as natural, now seemed to her curious in a man. She could not imagine Hugo fussing about drawing-room curtains. He saw her smile.

"I'm going to be a decorator, you know," he said.

"A what?"

"A decorator. The rent of the flats will keep me from starvation, but I must earn some money. Mr Radcliffe is backing me. They've been most extraordinarily kind. They've helped me through the whole of this ghastly business. I'm going to advise people on arranging and decorating their interiors. The interiors of their houses, I mean, of course."

"I'm sure you'll do it awfully well."

"I'm going to do parties too—do the decorations and see to all the arrangements."

"Oh, you must do my wedding!" exclaimed Lucinda, and then blushed.

"What, are you going to be married?"

"Yes. The engagement's being announced today. I came to tell you first."

"That was nice of you. Whom are you marrying?" he asked as an afterthought.

"Hugo Brayford." She looked a little confused. The name recalled the incident of the Radcliffe dance, which they both wished to forget.

"Congratulations. I suppose Julie's pleased."

"She doesn't seem to mind." Lucinda laughed.

"You'll go to live in England, I suppose," said Tony, in a studied, even voice.

"Not immediately. Hugo's going to stay as A.D.C. for a year."

"Will you live at Government House?"

"No. It's rather full with the other aides and the Wendales. We may take a house—or one of your flats perhaps."

"Hardly grand enough for you."

"We're not going to be grand. Hugo's quite poor really, apart from his pay."

"I expect your father will alleviate his distress." He found some satisfaction in saying this. Lucinda did not take offense.

"I hope he does," she said, smiling candidly. "Though I don't mind being poor."

"No. I hope I shan't mind either. But I shan't have your consolations." He said this in such a gentle and natural voice, without self-pity, that she was deeply moved. She wanted to express her feeling in some way but could not think of the right words. She put out her hands towards him. At that moment a man covered with white dust, and with his trousers tied with string below the knees, came in and said:

"D'you want the opening of that there fireplace two foot six or two foot nine from the floor?"

"I gave you the plan," said Tony.

"It's left behind at the office."

"I can't possibly tell you off-hand. I worked it out carefully on the plan."

"We can't get on till we know."

"Really, it's too tiresome. This is the second time this has happened. I'll let you know in ten minutes."

"We can't do anything till you do," said the man. He lighted his pipe and went out of the room.

"These men are hopeless," said Tony fussily, "and can't an Australian workman ever manage to call one 'sir'?"

"Well, I'd better go," said Lucinda.

He walked with her to the gate, talking about the height of the fireplace, but when she held out her hand to say good-bye he put aside his irritable manner. He watched her walk away up Tintern Avenue. At the corner of Toorak Road she turned and waved. He was smiling whimsically.

As Lucinda walked back to Tourella she felt ashamed that the Vanes had done nothing to help Tony, beyond sending a wreath and a carriage to his mother's funeral.

She mentioned it at luncheon. Hugo was not present. There was to be a dinner party in the evening at which the engagement would be announced. Tony had not been invited to this, partly owing to the mourning for his mother, which Julie found very convenient at this juncture.

"Tony's going to be a decorator," said Lucinda. Julie frowned and indicated the men at the sideboard. When they had left the room she said:

"Do you mean he's going to be a tradesman, dear?"

"I bet he'll be a dear tradesman," said Fred.

"Is it being a tradesman?" asked Lucinda. "He's going to show people how to furnish their houses, and he will take on the arrangements for parties. Couldn't he do my wedding?"

"If you think, my dear," said Fred, "that I'm going to pay good money to a young man to arrange my drawing-room chairs, when I have a wife, two daughters and seven servants, not to mention our factotal What-ho, you are mistaken."

"Mr Duff has done ever so much for nothing. It's high time he was paid for something," said Watteau.

"He has been adequately paid in kind. If you were to put all the bottles of my wine he has drunk in a row it would stretch from here to Tintern Avenue."

"Oh, Fred, that's an exaggeration," said Julie. She too was uneasy at not having shown more friendliness to Tony at the time of his mother's death, but it had happened in the middle of Cup Week. She knew, though she did not like to admit it even to herself, that she owed a great deal of her social success to Tony. It was he who had asked the Lanfrancs and the Radcliffes to call on her, and it was through him, so varied were the apron strings to which he was tied, that the archbishop had come to the Tourella garden party. Now that there was no longer any chance of his being troublesome with Lucinda, she felt an unqualified affection for him.

"Couldn't you find him a more suitable position?" she asked Fred.

"What qualifications has he? I could send him up to Mathieson as a jackeroo." He chuckled.

"That's absurd. Couldn't he work in an office?" This was a faint echo from the days when Julie had thought it would be the height of genteel security to have Fred working in an office. "Then at any rate he wouldn't be a tradesman," she added.

"It's better to be an honest tradesman than a poodle-fakir."

"I don't think it is," said Lucinda, laughing a little at her own temerity. "I like people who live for pleasure."

They all looked at her in astonishment, as they all believed that Fred's relentless acquisition of money, and Julie's resolute social activities, her dinners, her balls, her bridge, her expensive and careful dressing, had almost nothing to do with pleasure, but served some deep if obscure moral purpose, that they were almost a reflection of the Divine Will.

"I hope, my dear," said Fred pompously, "that you have some more serious aim in life than the pursuit of pleasure."

"I don't really know," said Lucinda and laughed again.

The men came in with the pudding. Julie pursed her lips and changed the subject.

CHAPTER ELEVEN

JULIE DID ASK TONY to do the decorations for Lucinda's wedding. If Fred made a fuss she intended to pay for them out of her own allowance. She asked him to luncheon to discuss the arrangements. She was a little doubtful about asking him, as she was still uncertain as to whether he was a tradesman, and Hugo was arriving at Tourella to stay for a week. Tony did not go any more to big parties. She thought this must be due to sensitiveness about his altered position, but she heard that he still dined privately with the Lanfrancs.

This was the first time Tony had been to Tourella since the night of the Radcliffes' dance. As he came into the drawing-room, Julie had just come down from inspecting Hugo's room. His luggage, a large quantity for a short visit, had arrived before him in a Government House car.

"Oh, Albert," said Julie to the footman who had just shown in Tony, "who unpacked Captain Brayford's things?"

"I did madam."

"The socks are put in the same drawer as the handkerchiefs. Captain Brayford is an English aristocrat, and he's accustomed to having things done correctly. Will you please put them in separate drawers?"

"Very good, madam." Albert blushed and withdrew.

"Oh, Mummy," said Lucinda, "Hugo won't mind that."

"We mustn't let our country down, Lucie dear," said Julie and then turned to greet Tony.

"Well, Tony," she said cheerfully, "we haven't seen you for ages."

Tony's smile was more twisted than usual. A year ago Julie would not have ignored him while she staged a scene with the footman. She was wearing a hat for luncheon in her own house, which she never used to do.

"We must go thoroughly into the business of the wedding after lunch. It must be very well done as it's a brilliant match." She put her arm round Lucinda and gave her a hug. "I suppose you've heard all about the Brayfords. You hear about everything and everyone."

"I haven't been about lately."

"Hugo's father was the eleventh Viscount Crittenden. He was married twice."

"Tony doesn't want to hear all that, Mummy," said Lucinda.

"Of course he must know whom you're marrying," said Julie.

"His first wife was a daughter of the Prince de Mireval. She had two sons, the present Lord Crittenden and his brother Paul. His second wife, whom they all call Susannah, is an aunt of Lord Wendale's. She's Hugo's mother."

"Oh, Mummy," protested Lucinda. "Anyone would think I was marrying all Hugo's family."

"Well, you are marrying into his family, darling."

The only thing that Tony had heard about the Brayfords was that for people of their sort they were far from being well-off. It was odd that Julie should think this a brilliant match, but she was impressed by any title, and it was of course very satisfactory for any Vane to marry a peer's son. Here, too, Hugo had the glory of being attached to a miniature court, of driving in a motor car that bore a crown instead of a number, and of moving in a group whose arrival was always heralded by *God Save the King*.

One of these motor cars was heard drawing up under the *porte cochère*. Colman announced Captain Bradford, and Hugo came into the room. He was so resplendent with health and well-being, so immaculate in appearance, that Tony could easily understand Lucinda's being swept off her feet, and yet, when they were introduced, he felt such a dislike for the man that he could hardly bring himself to shake hands. He thought it outrageous that anyone who was going to marry Lucinda should appear so complacent, so completely self-possessed. In fact he looked as if he possessed everything. The rest of the household appeared and they all went in to luncheon. Hugo treated everyone with the same cheerful geniality, which Tony felt expressed a quite unconscious contempt. He had the air of a man who, having found the softest cushion available, was about to sit on it, and being in this enviable position could afford to be amiable. Lucinda was radiant, and though this was a little painful to Tony he accepted it as natural, and it was less painful to him than the obvious difference which Julie, and even Fred, paid to their future son-in-law. Julie gave an excessive number of orders to the servants, mostly with a view to his comfort. Only Roger's manner was unaffected by his presence, though Roger had some cause for complaint, as his marriage to Lydia had been postponed for some months owing to Lucinda's coming first.

Watteau also appeared to preserve her integrity. She and Tony found themselves alone together for a few minutes.

"Lucie and the Captain make a lovely pair," she said. "She's a very lucky girl, but it wouldn't have been my choice."

Julie fixed the date of Lucinda's wedding as early as she decently could. It had to come before Lydia's, as Roger would not graduate for nearly another year, just before Hugo was due to return to England, and it was not desirable to have the weddings too close together.

Tony was at Tourella nearly every day for the few weeks preceding the wedding, but he did not see much of Lucinda, as she spent most of her time with Hugo. When they did meet she was very affectionate towards him. One of Julie's minor worries was whether she could properly invite Tony to the wedding, seeing that she was employing him in this capacity. However, when he came to her one day and said that if she would like it, he could get the archbishop to perform the ceremony—a thing Canon Chapman, who seemed fated to be unpopular with bishops, had failed to do—she was reassured about his status, and that evening she posted him an invitation with a little note pretending that she had not done so before because it was assumed he was coming, and it seemed like asking for a present, but he was not to think of giving one.

Tony, when he next saw Julie, said that he was doing the decorations as a present to Lucinda. Julie was very pleased at this, as it would avoid her having to make explanations to Fred, and Tony would not be spending any of his scarce money.

It was still autumn on the day of the wedding, and the dahlias which lined the Tourella drive hung in heavy static bloom. About the garden the leaves of ornamental trees had turned to a brilliant crimson.

A crowd began to collect outside the Cathedral an hour before the bride arrived. They watched the stream of motor cars and carriages disgorging the guests, and with Australian frankness commented on any fashion which they thought extreme, or personality which was either well known or peculiar.

Julie drove in with Lydia and Canon Chapman in their second largest car. She was still on the Cathedral steps when the Governor arrived with the Wendales and another A.D.C. They greeted her affably, and she stood there for a few intoxicating minutes, elevated in this open place, talking on a plane of equality with the highest in the land. She felt as if she had at last reached her proper level, and confused with her pleasurable excitement was the vague imagination that she would spend the rest of her life moving conspicuously in exalted circles.

She stood aside to let the vice-regal party go into the Cathedral, but she followed them closely up the aisle, past the crowd of rustling and whispering guests.

Mr Justice Lanfranc was Lieutenant-Governor. He invited Tony into his pew, and also reserved a place for Julie and Lydia. Julie's satisfaction at this honor was dimmed when she saw Tony at the other end of the pew. She thought it extraordinary of the Lanfrancs to have invited Tony into the State Governor's pew. She complained about it to Fred in the evening. He said, "My dear, the Lanfranc family is so old that they're nearly idiotic. If they were horses I wouldn't have 'em near my stud."

The decorations were jars of creamy-colored spotted lilies, placed at the entrance to the choir and on the altar steps. Lucinda's dress was of creamy satin with an old lace veil lent by Lady Wendale. As she came up the aisle on Fred's arm, followed by six bridesmaids in primrose-colored tulle, she was in fact whiter than her dress. When she was with Hugo she was suffused with an intense physical well-being, which continued in a state of blissful happiness for hours after he had left her. The excitement and rush of the last few days had left her so tired and strung up that she could hardly recapture even the memory of this happiness. When she was alone with him it was strongest. The presence of other people seemed to forbid this intimate emotion. A street full of sightseers, a Cathedral full of people, the presence of Governors and bishops inhibited it altogether. When she saw Hugo waiting for her in his unfamiliar scarlet tunic and tight braided trousers, and Captain Murray beside him in the dark uniform of the Rifle Brigade, even his confident smile failed to convince her that she was not embarking on some fantastic adventure. She had a moment of panic and she gave an involuntary sideways glance at Julie, and when, farther along the pew, she saw Tony watching her with wide and wistful eyes, she held his glance for a moment and turned quickly away.

Hugo, who told her afterwards when they were driving out to Tourella that he had "swotted up his drill," spoke his part without diffidence, and his voice was heard clearly half-way down the long cathedral. When he said: "With all my worldly goods I thee endow," Miss Lanfranc whispered to Tony: "Surely Lucinda should say that?" and Tony gave a twisted smile. Lucinda's responses were inaudible.

Within an hour the spotted lilies had been collected from the jars and sent off to the Austin Hospital for Incurables, and the stream of motor cars was speeding back to Toorak. The carriage horses trotted briskly, but their Edwardian owners suffered the disadvantage of arriving late for the reception.

The Governor-General, forbidden by etiquette to attend parties in private houses, drove back to Government House, but Mr Justice Lanfranc did not feel called upon to observe such lonely splendor.

"I am a democratic monarch," he said to Tony, who beside the younger Miss Lanfranc sat with his back to the pair of spanking bays, "and I have no objection to drinking a pint or two of Fred Vane's champagne. In fact, as doubtless he brought it somewhere at half-price, I am not unwilling to drink a quart."

With agreeable malice they poked fun at Julie's grandeur and Fred's astuteness.

"We mustn't talk like this about the Vanes. They're Tony's oldest friends," said Miss Lanfranc.

"I don't mind," said Tony. It gave him a feeling of intense relief to hear them ridiculing the Vanes. It made his love for Lucinda less painful. He stayed with the Lanfrancs all the afternoon.

Fred and Julie, with Lucinda and Hugo, were receiving the guests in the drawing-room at Tourella. They passed on through a lobby into the ballroom, where the wedding breakfast was arranged. The presents were on view in the dining-room.

When Colman announced the Lanfrancs, Hugo, who had been shaking hands with everyone with impartial geniality, showed an unusual flicker of interest.

"There was a Lanfranc in my regiment, sir," he said as he shook hands with the judge. "Pat Lanfranc, a great friend of mine."

"You astonish me!" said Mr Justice Lanfranc. "Is he already grown up? He's my cousin's boy. When I last saw him he was seven. He was a fine boy, a great charmer."

Julie was delighted that a cousin of the Lanfrancs was a friend of Hugo's. It somehow made the marriage more natural. She turned eagerly to join in the conversation.

"Which Lanfrancs are those?" she asked.

Lucinda and Tony were left on the outside of the group. She had recovered from the dread she had felt in the Cathedral. All her friends had streamed past her paying the most affectionate and delightful compliments. She could not help returning emotionally the goodwill she received.

"Tony, you are a darling," she said. "It's wonderful, all that you've done. I shall write to you when we're away. And I'll send you a postcard as well."

"Then at least I have something to look forward to."

Perhaps for the first time a note of flirtation had entered into their conversation. There was a sort of light admission that he had wanted to marry her, and that she was no longer angry about it, but flattered and pleased. Tony's smile was less twisted.

They were interrupted by the aunts, whose brougham was the last to arrive from the Cathedral.

"This is a great day for the House of Vane," said Gladys, kissing everyone but Hugo and Fred. Julie looked cross. Although she agreed, she would prefer Gladys not to say that sort of thing before Hugo.

"It was quite a royal ceremony," said Norah. The richer Fred became, the more his sisters were apt to talk of the Vanes as if they were some ancient European dynasty.

"Only *vice*-regal, dear," said Gladys.

Hugo continued to smile imperturbably. He was prepared for the Australians to be even more peculiar than the aunts, and he did not object to the implication of flattery in all this.

They moved into the ballroom. There was a long table at the end of the room reserved for the bride and bridegroom and their near relatives. On it towered a huge cake, decorated with the usual white pilasters, cupids, silver horseshoes and orange blossoms. Mr Justice Lanfranc, as State Governor, was invited to sit at this table. He insisted on having Tony to sit with him. Canon Chapman sat between Miss Lanfranc and Lady Wendale. When he had drunk several toasts he again had that curious feeling of doubt about old William Vane, whether after all he had not been his benefactor when he threw him over Clare Bridge.

"I hate water," he confided with a giggle to Lady Wendale.

Lucinda stood up, and with difficulty thrust with Hugo's sword through the hard icing of the mammoth cake. There were speeches. Hugo's was confident and brief.

"Anyone would think he was opening a bazaar," muttered Tony to Miss Lanfranc.

Fred replied to the toast of the bride's parents. He spoke at some length. He mentioned his several stations, and also that the families of the bride and bridegroom had already been acquainted in England, his wife's cousin the Dean of Ilchester being a frequent visitor to Crittenden. He ended with a reference to "my daughter, the Honorable Mrs Brayford."

The Misses Lanfranc exchanged a glance, but the guests were not as embarrassed as they would have been before the champagne was opened. Julie sat beside Lord Wendale, who was *in loco parentis* to Hugo. The dignity with which Lord Wendale bore his admitted comparative poverty gave an added distinction to his extremely gentlemanly appearance. Julie at the height of her success more than ever expressed her power in her physique, in the set of her shoulders and the swing of her arms. The contrast between her and Lord Wendale was almost grotesque, thought Tony, as he let an appraising intelligent eye rest on them for a moment. Julie intercepted this glance and returned it with a dark malevolence which shocked him. She was sufficiently annoyed with him for sitting at that table. As a result of this glance, she was not really friendly with him again until more than five years later.

Lucinda and Hugo left the table to go and change. Other people drifted away from the ballroom into the garden or to have another look at the presents. Lucinda in a blue coat and skirt and Hugo in a gray suit appeared on the staircase. The news that they were going away spread almost telepathically through the house and garden, and everyone made a dash for the front door. A car was waiting for them, not under the *porte cochère* but on the far side of the drive, as Fred had said that they must have a run for their money. Some young men had tied old shoes to the back of the car.

Lucinda hesitated when she saw the lane through which they had to run the gauntlet, but Hugo took her arm and walked unruffled through the laughter and showers of confetti, as if it had been as impersonal as a shower of rain. A handful of confetti missed him and hit Clara Bumpus in the face. She shouted, "Oh, you dirty dog!"

Without hurry Hugo handed Lucinda into the car. When they were comfortably settled he nodded to Hart, raised his hand to the crowd, and without looking back disappeared round the bend of the drive. At the corner of Albany Road another car, piled with their luggage and free of old shoes and confetti, was waiting for them.

"That's fooled 'em," said Hugo cheerfully as they changed into this.

Suddenly the wedding seemed to be over. Some of the more thirsty and greedy guests returned to the ballroom, but within half an hour they had all gone, excepting Canon Chapman, who, very flushed and complaining of fatigue, had gone up to rest on Bill's bed. Bill had come up from Geelong for the day, and had to leave soon after the bride and bridegroom to catch his train back to school. He had grown rather lanky. He took Julie aside and said shyly, "Mum, I'm in the crew." At that moment the Wendales came up to say good-bye, and Julie did not properly assimilate the information.

She did not recall it until they were seated at a family dinner in the evening. She was trying to hurry the dinner as she had taken a box for a musical comedy. She thought it socially advantageous to appear in public on the night of the wedding. It somehow extended her importance as the hostess of the afternoon. Fred was assessing the damage done to the drive.

"It'll cost me ten pounds to get it right again," he said. "The confetti's trodden into the gravel."

Julie, searching for some more lively topic of conversation, remembered about Bill.

"Oh, Bill's in the Geelong crew," she exclaimed.

"Good," said Fred. "I expect my son to do well. Open another bottle of champagne, Colman."

"If we drink any more champagne, we shan't get to the theatre," growled Lydia. "I'm half under the table already."

Julie looked prim.

"Perhaps a little claret would be more wholesome," said the canon, who had stayed on to dinner.

"If you mix your drinks, grandpa, you'll have another headache," said Lydia.

"My headache was entirely due to the heat of the sun and the unaccustomed crowd," explained the canon.

"I've drunk nothing but lemonade all day and I'm sure I'm as cheerful as anyone," said Watteau acidly.

"We must drink my son's health," said Fred.

There was another loud pop at the sideboard.

"A joyful sound," said the canon.

When they had drunk Bill's health, Fred announced pompously:

"I propose the health of my daughter, the Honorable Mrs Brayford."

Roger looked very uncomfortable. It was painful to him to modify his hero-worship of Fred.

Fred noticed his sullen expression and put it down to the preferential treatment given to Lucinda and Hugo.

"You must not be hurt, my boy," he said, "because I am giving Lucinda a more generous settlement than Lydia. She will have a high position to keep up, and Hugo is a soldier serving his country and will not earn much. What I give them I give partly for the defense of our Empire. But I have every confidence in you. I am proud of both my sons-in-law. Fill up your glass. Colman, fill up Mr Blake's glass."

"We'll have coffee here, Colman, straight away," said Julie. "Otherwise we shall be late."

"I do not wish to go to the theatre," said Fred. "The canon and I shall stay and discuss my port and my daughter's wedding."

Julie stood up. "You'd much better go home, papa," she said.

"No. I wish to discuss the wedding," said Fred. "By the way, I did not notice any present from Mr Tony Duff. Was he too broke to buy one?"

"He arranged all the decorations," said Watteau indignantly. "I should think that was a good enough present for anybody."

"It was a very cheap present," declared Fred, "and my daughter is not anybody. She is somebody. Colman, fill the glasses. We must drink the health of my daughter, the Honorable Mrs Brayford."

While Fred was so assiduously drinking her health, Lucinda was sitting with Hugo under the ti-tree on the cliffs at Sandringham, about ten miles away. They had been lent a bungalow here for the first few days of their honeymoon. It was a wide-verandahed place built of jarrah with a bright-red roof. Ever since they had arrived there she had been surprised and reassured by Hugo's composure. When they had gone along to their rooms they had found Hugo's soldier servant unpacking his luggage.

"Out of here, Wilson," said Hugo, bland but authoritative, as one might speak to a faithful dog. No one in Australia would dare to speak to a servant in that tone.

One of the housemaids sent by Julie from Tourella came in with Lucinda's dresses on her arm. These familiar faces made Lucinda feel that somehow it was improper for her to be here alone with Hugo. When the bride and bridegroom had gone off from other weddings she had imagined them as somehow lost in a mysterious and intoxicating unknown. She had been nervous about her own disappearance into this region, but the commonplace business of settling into a bungalow at Sandringham, and Hugo's matter-of-fact manner were both an anti-climax and a relief from her fear. He was now seated beside her, reading semi-facetiously an account of their wedding from the late edition of *The Herald*.

"A beautiful bride and a handsome husband," he quoted. "That's you and me, m'dear. Well, gettin' dark. Time to turn in."

He pulled her to her feet, gave her a warm hug and they strolled back under the stars to the outer-suburban bungalow.

"Might have a round of golf tomorrow," said Hugo.

Lucinda was a little hurt at his manner, but when they came indoors he amply made up for it. As the days of their honeymoon passed she became grateful for his lack of sentimentality. He showed an excellent sense of how life should be arranged. She had thought that he would be incapable of bothering about the colors of furnishings, but she found that he hated rooms that were in bad taste. He never became ruffled, and that also pleased her, so that by the time they returned to Melbourne she not only loved him with her body and soul, but her mind also approved him, so there was none of that discord which comes when the mind and the heart disagree.

There was one occasion when he did show anger. They were

in the Sydney express, and were the first to come into the restaurant car. Hugo stayed by the door to ask the waiter about a table. This waiter was a curious-looking man with a massive and powerful forehead, though the lower part of his face was unpleasant and slightly negroid. Lucinda saw him take something from his pocket and show it rather furtively to Hugo. Hugo's eyes blazed, and he barked, "Get out of here!" with such compressed fury that she thought he was going to strike the man, who smirked and backed away.

"What happened?" she asked, when Hugo rejoined her.

"Nothing."

"What did he show you?"

"Postcards."

"Oh, I wanted some postcards. I promised to send one to Tony."

"They weren't fit to be seen. Please don't refer to it again."

When they returned to Melbourne they took a furnished house in Acland Street, South Yarra, so that Hugo would be close to Government House. Lucinda was very much sought after, and they spent most of the first ten months of their married life at parties. She only saw Tony two or three times during these months, as he no longer went to these functions, many of which he had himself arranged, and he was now seldom at Tourella. She asked him one night to dinner, just themselves with Miss Lanfranc to make a fourth, but it was not a success. He did not get on very well with Hugo when they were left together in the dining-room. There was no feeling of hostility between them, but before going to bed Hugo said to Lucinda, "That old beau of yours don't seem to have much to say for himself."

They left for England at the end of March 1912. Just before they sailed the parties became thicker than ever. Lucinda said one day that she would like a rest from it all, and suggested that she and Hugo should take a picnic lunch and drive off into the country for the day. She wanted not only a rest from people, but also to have a last look at the Australian countryside which had formed the close and natural world of her childhood, and which, when in later years she tried to recapture the sensations of infancy, she would first have to evoke, the shabby white stems of the gums, the fern trees, the thin army of ants crossing a wooden verandah, the smell of these insects, and of dry sticks, and of burning eucalyptus trees.

They drove out through Eltham up to the Christmas Hills, where they picnicked by the roadside. They went for water to a tiny clay-built cottage with a bark roof and tangled passion fruit and grape vines sprawling over it. There was something eternal about this cottage, utterly different from the average Australian shack with its weather-board and galvanized iron roof. A toothless old woman charged them threepence for the water, but gave them three pounds of large purple grapes and several passion fruit for the same sum. They made a fire of sticks on a clearing by the wayside and boiled billy tea. The idea had been established at The Pines and Tourella that any young man who was careful of his appearance, and who had taste and good manners, must necessarily be a milksop, afraid of horses and useless at any practical job. This view was implied in most of Fred's talk. Lucinda did not question it but she said with that smile with which she admitted her own failings, "All the same I prefer milksops."

Hugo built the fire, made a tripod of forked sticks to hold his billy, and cleared a space of dry earth so the fire would not spread, as efficiently as any Australian. Although he was so fastidious, this efficiency, his skill with horses, the simplicity with which he accepted what came his way, made Lucinda feel that in marrying him she had the best of both worlds. He had talked to the old woman at the cottage with far more natural friendliness than many Australian young men would have shown. As he stooped to put the muslin bag of tea into the billy, again she felt that complete happiness which comes when the heart and mind are in agreement. He turned his head quickly and saw the expression in her eyes.

After luncheon they climbed the hill above the road. From its summit they had a view for many miles to the Black Spur and the mountains of Healesville, which were blue and gold and splashed with deep purple shadows. The hill was covered with gum saplings. The sun drew out the fragrance from their aromatic leaves. The earth was baked hard from the long summer. Strips of fallen bark and red sugar-ants seemed to add to the hot dry smell of the place. In the clear space where they rested on the hilltop were some small prickly shrubs. Here the land seemed terribly ancient, wistful and yet harsh, and nowhere as far as they could see was any sign of human life, except a thin line of smoke which rose from the vine-covered cottage concealed below the hill.

They sat down to rest after the climb. Lucinda lay back and closed her eyes against the sun, white and blinding in the mid-heaven. Hugo began to make love to her. At first she tried to restrain him, because of the time and place. But then the time and place, the high and piercing sun, the stark earth, seemed to fuse in her body in a wild desire. A kind of ferocity seized them, a joy passed beyond endurance to pain. She felt that she was consumed by the sun itself, by some first principle of life that immolated her body in an act of new creation.

They never referred to this day again, nor mentioned this hilltop as long as they lived. They were both too conventional to care to think that they might be the passive instruments of forces outside themselves.

Part *Two*

1912–1917

INVOKING THE STORM

Et lui, l'insensé invoquait la tempête,
Comme si dans la tempête pouvait régner la paix.

LERMONTOFF.

CHAPTER ONE

WHEN THE P. AND O. LINER in which Hugo and Lucinda were traveling had left Colombo Lucinda became certain that she was going to have a child. She did not tell Hugo immediately, being shy about it, but on the night before they arrived at Marseilles she decided to tell him at bedtime. After dinner he played poker with some men in the smoke-room.

"How did you get on?" she asked.

"Lost a bit."

"How much?" She was not particularly interested, but she found that by showing interest in his affairs she could focus his attention on herself, which was what she wanted at the moment.

"About twenty pounds," he said indifferently.

She started. "Isn't that rather a lot, darling?"

"Good Lord, no. Nothing out of the way."

"It's a third of our week's income."

"Don't be mercenary." He seemed annoyed, and while he was in this mood she did not care to tell him about the child. She was not really worried about the money, as she had never known it to be a serious consideration.

They left the ship at Marseilles and crossed France by train. By the time they arrived at Victoria Station she had still not found a suitable opportunity to tell him.

They were met at the station by Hugo's mother. Lucinda was nervous at the prospect of this meeting, and the little she had heard about her mother-in-law had not reassured her. She knew that Marian, the present Lady Crittenden, did not get on well with her, and she had thought Marian so simple and friendly on the day they had gone to Crittenden that she felt that anyone who did not get on with her must be in some way ill-natured. Dolly Wendale had said, "Susannah Crittenden? Oh, she's a very grand lady," and she had laughed. Lucinda was not sure what she had meant by that laugh. Hugo had only said, "You don't want to be afraid of Mama," which suggested that she was someone to be afraid of.

Lucinda, as the train drew in to Victoria Station, had a glimpse through the plate-glass window of the Pullman of a festive-looking hat towards which Hugo waved. Their carriage stopped some way down the platform and Lucinda could see the plumes on the hat hurrying towards them, before its wearer could be seen through the crowd. When Susannah reached them she embraced Hugo and demanded:

"Where is she? Where is she?"

She turned to Lucinda and said, "Oh, you're much better even than the photographs," and kissed her. "Did you have a good crossing?"

When Lucinda replied Susannah's expression changed subtly to complete satisfaction. She had been afraid of an Australian accent. She led Lucinda over to her car while Hugo saw to the luggage. It was a large car but Susannah seemed to fill it; not that she was physically large but she was expansive. She had come to the station from a party and she seemed to be all pearls and feathers. When Hugo rejoined them, they drove to Susannah's house in Bryanston Square. Lucinda had never felt so immediately at ease with anyone as she did with Susannah. She was almost tearful with gratitude at being accepted so quickly and naturally as one of the family.

Susannah took her up to her room and fussed over her.

"Are you sure you'll be comfortable?" she said. "This house is horribly poky, and there are only two bathrooms. I'm sure you're used to superlative luxuries. When I went to America I thought I was in Paradise."

"Australia is not like that," said Lucinda. "Some of the places I've stayed at in the country have only one tin bath."

"Oh!" Susannah apparently did not care to hear this. "Well, come down as soon as you're ready, my dear."

The drawing-room astonished Lucinda. She did not know that people furnished their houses like this. Everything possible was Italian baroque—the mirrors, the chandeliers, the high chairs were all of carved and gilded wood. A Canaletto hung over the mantel-piece. On the writing table was a pair of altar candlesticks filled with large pink candles. The curtains were of old rose brocade, and a seventeenth-century chasuble was flung over the piano, on which stood a number of signed photographs of European royalties.

After tea Susannah showed Lucinda these photographs.

"This is dear Margharita of Italy," she said. "Here is the Kaiser. He gave it to me at Kiel last year. I dined on his yacht and he opened some of his special pink champagne for me."

Lucinda smiled. She felt somehow that pink champagne was appropriate to her mother-in-law.

"Here is our own beloved Alexandra."

"Have you a photograph of Queen Mary?" asked Lucinda when she had admired this.

"No." Susannah turned away from the piano. "You will want to rest after your journey. I'll send my maid to help you dress."

Before they went down to dinner Lucinda said to Hugo, "Why didn't you tell me that your mother was so charming?"

"Best to find out for yourself," said Hugo, who was fixing his white tie. "You'd better go on down. She doesn't like to be the first in the drawing-room."

However, when Lucinda came into the drawing-room Susannah was not there, but a young man was standing examining the Canaletto. He turned as she came into the room, and giving a slightly exaggerated bow, said, "May I introduce myself? I am Paul Brayford. Perhaps you remember meeting me at Crittenden?"

"Of course I do," said Lucinda and shook hands. Paul bowed again. Lucinda was not sure that she liked him. He was utterly unlike Hugo, being short and dark, with a large nose. He reminded her of the famous drawing of Dante. She felt that there was some uneasiness or irony in his bow. She had not remembered him like this at Crittenden. He had not appeared so formal.

"I was examining Susannah's new Canaletto," he said, and went on to make some technical criticisms of the painting. "Do you like it?" he asked.

"Yes, I think I do," she said.

It seemed to her strange that he should embark at once on such an impersonal subject—almost a little inhuman, and yet in a way she found it rather flattering. He spoke to her as if she knew as much about painting as himself, whereas on her last trip to England she had not only been treated rather as a schoolgirl, but when she had been spoken to as an adult it was often in a patronizing manner, implying that as an Australian she must be devoid of any cultivated taste.

They were some time together in the drawing-room before Susannah and Hugo joined them. Just as Lucinda had seldom felt as immediately at ease with anyone as with Susannah, so she had seldom felt so immediately ill-at-ease with anyone as with Paul. He imparted a kind of nervousness to her, and yet he interested her. He had very expressive eyes. After he had given her a glance of almost affectionate friendliness, he would suddenly turn away and speak abruptly.

He talked about the ballet with an enthusiasm which surprised her. He said that it was the most complete form of art which had yet been evolved—that it included painting and music and that it also had a literary element—that it expressed a new and vital spirit of which the influence would be to make life more passionate. "I don't mean literary in the Edmund Gosse sense of the word," Paul explained, "but literary in the sense of the poems of Anacreon." They were going to Covent Garden after dinner to see Nijinsky in *Scheherazade*. They were going into Rosie's box.

"Rosie is one of Susannah's gutter millionaires," Paul explained contemptuously. "He gave her that Canaletto."

Lucinda smiled uncertainly. She did not know whether Paul meant to be funny. No one whom she had known in Melbourne would have talked of a "gutter millionaire," nor of life being made more passionate by art.

Susannah came in, gave a quick, critical glance at Lucinda's dress, and then said to Paul, "Isn't she lovely? You should go to Australia too."

Hugo came in and said, "Hullo, Paul, how's modern art?"

"I don't think you would understand if I explained it to you," said Paul.

Lucinda looked anxiously from her husband to his half-brother, but there seemed to be no animosity behind this hardly affectionate greeting.

During dinner they discussed members of the family, how they were and what they were doing. There was so much mention of Crittenden that Lucinda had the feeling that if this place were taken away from them, the Brayford family would fall apart and cease to exist.

"All this family talk must be rather dull for you," said Susannah.

"Still, she has to learn about us," said Paul.

Hugo seemed to be different in the company of his family. He unconsciously adopted a family idiom and manner. His father had been imbued with the culture of the 'nineties and had admired everything French. The viscounty had come to him from a cousin, and as a young man he had not expected to inherit. He had gone to Paris to study painting. He had wanted to marry the daughter of a law lord, but he had not been considered a good enough match. His pride was hurt as well as his affection. When he inherited Crittenden he married Amélie de Mireval, partly because he loved her, partly because she was French, and partly because her father was a prince. When she died he married Susannah Boyne, and so proved to the law lord that he was considered eligible for far more important people than his daughter, who ended up with an Indian Army officer. But this original snub had made him insist on his nobility and culture. Paul had been most susceptible to his father's influence, but even Hugo had odd cultural streaks in his sporting, military make-up, and as a boy he had been forced to acquire a Parisian accent.

Susannah appeared so kind and friendly that when Lucinda went back with her to the baroque drawing-room she felt sufficiently confident to say:

"I hope I shall be able to live up to you."

Susannah did not appear pleased. She made an odd little sound and Lucinda felt that she had blundered. However a moment later she was as friendly and cheerful as before, and when they entered the car to go to Covent Garden she fussed about Lucinda's comfort.

They arrived at the opera house in the thick of the crowd. Lucinda had been used to crowded parties in Melbourne, and to edging her way into a ballroom through a crush of well-dressed people, but there was something far more exciting about this place and this crowd There seemed to her to be more beautiful faces among the women. Some of them wore magnificent jewels. Now and then she caught sight of a man's face that impressed her with its look of sagacity, or of one which, more than she remembered seeing elsewhere, seemed the embodiment in flesh and bone of an idea, or of one which was surprising in its look of tired wickedness. As Hugo had taken on the color of his family, so Lucinda felt herself taking on the color of this society in which she found herself. Susannah looked at her with approval and introduced her to three or four people whom they met in the foyer. They spoke to her with kindly interest. One of them was a duchess. When they were in the box Susannah bowed and smiled to several people in the stalls and in other boxes.

Lucinda had not expected to enjoy the performance very much. From what Paul had said she imagined that it would be rather over her head. The first chords of *Scheherazade* startled her. When the curtain went up and revealed the amazing interior of the Léon Bakst harem, she felt a quite extraordinary increase of excitement. The sinister green and purple canopy, the splendid arabesques of the ceiling, the silver lamps and the blood-colored floor were unlike anything in her previous experience, as was also the wild and plaintive Russian music. The eunuch let out the slaves and Nijinsky leapt across the stage in one superb bound. His high cheek bones, his long, obliquely set eyes, intensified the savage life which he expressed in every gesture. The impersonal music continued to weave its remote and liquid pattern, like a stream disturbed increasingly by the gusty passion of a storm. Lucinda happened to glance at Paul. He was staring at Nijinsky, his eyes wide, his pupils dilated, his mouth half open beneath his beaky nose. The ballet reached its high point of passion and its climax of death. Lucinda had an involuntary bewildered vision of the hill-top where she had picnicked with Hugo, on the day before they left Melbourne. She shut it from her mind and looked again at Paul. He was crushing a program in his tightly clenched hand, and his heavy eyelids were half closed.

When the curtain fell and the lights went up he showed no trace of this rapt expression. He turned to Lucinda and said:

"If you watch Nijinsky you won't see him at any moment when his body does not form a perfect pattern. If you were to freeze him into stone at any second, even during the most rapid movement, you would have a perfect statue."

"Nijinsky is not in the last ballet," said Susannah. "Shall we go?"

"He won't dance to an emptying house," said Paul. "If we're going, we'd better go now. There's no need to be rude to Leontiev and Lepoukhava. The last ballet at Covent Garden makes one doubt whether there's such a thing as an English gentleman."

Susannah dropped Lucinda and Hugo at Bryanston Square, and went on with Paul to some function.

They went into the baroque drawing-room where there was a tray of drinks. Hugo poured himself out a whisky-and-soda.

"Well, it's good to be home again," he said. "Paul seems to have taken to you. That's a good thing. So has Mama."

Lucinda laughed. Hugo looked at her questioningly. She did not know why she laughed. It was partly that the events of this, to her, extraordinary evening should give him a sense of home-coming. She had had a conventional idea of Hugo as the simple, straightforward soldier, but now she felt that it was herself who was simple. Or was he so simple that he took this exotic room with its old chasubles and florid gilt, and all the fantastic splendors of Covent Garden as just part of the comfortable world to which he was accustomed. She also laughed because he was only concerned as to what Paul and Susannah thought of her, not what she might think of them. Suddenly she blurted out:

"I'm going to have a baby."

"Good girl," said Hugo imperturbably, "the fifteenth viscount."

She laughed again, to see her sentimental ideas evaporate. She had imagined that this sacred fact should be whispered shyly in a moment of exquisite tenderness.

Still, Hugo kissed her.

CHAPTER TWO

THE NEXT DAY THEY went down to Crittenden, arriving in time for tea. The station for Crittenden was a halt on a branch line. The only person waiting on the narrow wooden platform was a footman. A top-heavy old-fashioned motor car, with much polished brass and coronets on the panels, was in the lane outside. To be met in such a place and such a fashion—the train stopped specially for them to alight—seemed very "English" to Lucinda. She said so to Hugo, and he made a curt reply. She found that he disliked her to take a detached attitude towards English things, and this began the long process in which she forgot that she was Australian. She was a little piqued that Marian had not come to meet them. She had expected her to be at the station, especially as Susannah had come to Victoria.

It was not far to the house from Crittenden Halt. They drove through deep lanes, shaded by leafy banks. The lanes were so narrow that Lucinda wondered what would happen if they met another vehicle. They came out onto a road, opposite some fine wrought-iron gates beyond which was a magnificent avenue of chestnuts. At the end of the avenue the mellow brick and stone façade of the house was rose-red in the afternoon sunlight. Suddenly Lucinda had a curious feeling, it was hardly emotional but more as if her skin had reacted to a change, a sleeply warmth in the atmosphere.

"Oh! That's Crittenden," she said. "I'd forgotten it was so lovely."

She was surprised when she had said this as she had not remembered it as particularly lovely.

"Not a bad old place," said Hugo. "Wants a lot spent on it."

The car did not go through the iron gates but turned along the road until they came to a white wooden gate.

"Those gates are only opened for royalty," Hugo explained, "and as royalties never come here, they're never opened. There's no made road up the avenue."

Inside the park, in the shadow of some tall elms, and about a hundred yards from the road, was a picturesque house, also of red brick. Behind it was the church.

"Is that the vicarage?" asked Lucinda.

"No, that's the dower house. It's called the End House," said

Hugo. "It's empty at the moment. Mama won't live there. She says it has a jinx on it."

"What's a jinx?"

"A sort of blight—brings you bad luck."

The car stopped at a door on the north side of Crittenden House, not at the main portico which looked down the avenue. Lucinda on the day they had come to luncheon with Dean Chapman, had been so glutted with sightseeing that she had noticed very little. Crittenden had seemed to her merely very large and rather shabby. But now the feeling she had had when she glimpsed it from the road came upon her more strongly. It seemed to breathe out age and peace in warm waves on the afternoon air. While they waited for the footman to open the door of the car she happened to glance up at the house. In that brief glance she received an impression which she hardly noticed at the time. It was made by the doorway with its two flat pilasters of Bath stone, surmounted by a curved pediment with a coat-of-arms. Till now she had always thought that only the gothic past had interest and poetic appeal, partly because she had assimilated this Victorian idea with her education, and partly because the classical motives were repeated with mechanical hardness in Tourella and the Melbourne Town Hall. But in this doorway, formal and yet sensitive, with its delicate carving softened by two and a half centuries of sun and frost, she had an impression of a different attitude towards life from that she had known hitherto. It was vague and hasty, and was dispelled almost immediately by Lord Crittenden's appearing in the doorway, coming out to greet them, but it recurred to her later in the day and once or twice in the distant future when again she entered this door. It was linked up with the impression made on her by Susannah's drawing-room and by the Russian Ballet, although the doorway was as unrelated to them as they were to each other. When she came to know him better she mentioned this feeling she had had to Paul.

"It was the excitement of finding yourself in the living stream of culture," he said. "I imagine that Australia is rather out of it. It must be imported, not inherited and continuous."

Arthur came down the steps and shook her warmly by the hand. He appeared a good deal older than either Hugo or Paul and was a little gray at the temples. He did not say a great deal but he beamed with pleasure, and his eyes twinkled as he looked at Lucinda. His manner was almost paternal, so that she found it hard not to call him Lord Crittenden, but she felt immediately that she liked him very much. It evidently gave him great satisfaction to have Hugo home again. He took him by the arm as they turned to go indoors.

"I can't think where Marian's gone," he said, with a touch of vexation that she was not there to meet them. "I suppose she's with her fowls. She has some prize fowls," he explained, "that she is training to lay a prodigious quantity of eggs. She spends half the day with them. Ah, there she is."

Marian, wearing a linen dress and carrying a basket of eggs, came along the side of the house. She was tall, long-faced and had an indefinable air of importance.

"Well, Hugo, my dear," she said, "how nice to see you—and your bride." She turned and shook hands with Lucinda. "I hope you don't feel it's too much like going to the dentist, meeting so many new relatives."

"Oh, no!" said Lucinda, "everyone's so nice, and I've never been to the dentist." But she thought that if all the relatives were like Marian she might feel a little nervous. Julie often said that English people were stiff and Lucinda now realized what she meant.

"I got twenty eggs again this afternoon," Marian said to Arthur.

"I hope you like omelettes," said Arthur, to keep Lucinda the center of attention. "If so you've come to the right place. Now I expect you want your tea after all that traveling."

They had tea in the saloon, a very large room with a seventeenth-century painted ceiling and a row of windows looking down the avenue. Marian put the basket of eggs on a yellow damask chair, and when the tea came in gave a footman instructions what to do with them.

Lucinda felt that Marian was reserving her judgment of her, though she did not appear exactly critical. She thought that possibly her very simple dress and the basket of eggs were not accidental, but intended to convey some lesson to herself. She had a little of the same kind of uneasiness with Marian that she had felt with Paul, as if they were behaving in some particular way especially for her benefit. She also had the feeling, which like the impression made by the doorway was stronger in recollection than at the moment, that Marian did not fit the house she ruled, that she was a foreign element beneath this ceiling of rosy nymphs and these splendid chandeliers. Crittenden had been built to be flooded by the sunlight of a summer afternoon, and it was now fulfilling its purpose. It had been built too for a people who lived for pride and graceful pleasure. The sunlight which streamed in between the yellow damask curtains, picked out here and there a scroll of gilded carving, a piece of fine and faded petit-point of which the subject was entirely frivolous. It made rainbows in the prisms of the chandeliers, and illuminated the distance in a Poussin *Bacchanal* which hung between portraits of past viscounts on the far wall. It made a broad band of golden light across a kingwood writing table at which it would only be seemly to write letters of assignation, or to a monarch, but on this writing table Marian had put a clumsy silver inkstand, an inscribed presentation to her father who had been a housemaster at Paul's public school. About the room were other attempts of a respectable and strong-minded woman to assert her personality amid this frivolous Restoration grandeur.

Marian's conversation, mostly with Hugo, seemed to be for Lucinda's benefit. She spoke to her directly so little as to be almost rude, though the undivided attention which Arthur gave her made this less obvious. Marian talked to Hugo about the estate and about horses. She conveyed the impression that English gentlepeople did not live in houses with gorgeous ceilings and gilded chairs for pleasure, but only from a stern sense of duty to the lower orders. At last, with the air of fulfilling every obligation in due course, she turned to Lucinda.

"I believe you met my husband's cousins, the Wendales, in Australia."

"Yes, we did."

"Did you see their little boy?"

"See him!" interjected Hugo. "He spent half the day sliding down our banisters."

"It's absurd of Dolly not to have left him behind at a prep school. He could have spent his holidays here. He could have shared the Greene-James's cricket coach."

"I told her she ought to send him to school in Melbourne."

"Would that be desirable?"

Lucinda laughed. Marian looked irritated.

"Of course I realize there must be very good schools in Australia," she said, and added, changing the subject, "and are you glad to be back in England or do you think you will miss your home?"

"I'm glad to be on any land after the ship," said Lucinda. "But of course I'm glad to be here. I've been longing to see Crittenden again. It's much lovelier than I remembered it."

"I expect you will see things from rather a different angle this time."

"Well, you must look on this as your home now, mustn't she, Hugo?" said Arthur. "That's right, isn't it, Marian?"

"Of course," said Marian, taking some needlework from behind a cushion and beginning to match wools.

After tea Marian took them up to their rooms, which were at the south-west corner of the house and scented with sweet peas of which there were bowls on the dressing table.

"I've given you the Peacock room for a sitting-room," said Marian. "We don't use it in the summer."

When they were alone Lucinda said to Hugo: "I don't think Marian likes me very much."

"She's not a gusher," said Hugo, "but she's all right. You'll get used to her."

"She was awfully nice that day we came to lunch," said Lucinda. "I suppose she thought there was no danger of my marrying one of the family."

"You're a better match than she was, old girl, so you don't need to worry," said Hugo complacently.

Lucinda laughed again. She was beginning to think that these Brayfords were not only impressive but amusing.

"What is the Peacock room?" she asked.

"It's next door," said Hugo. "My father painted it. Susannah says there's a jinx on it because it's peacocks."

They went to look at it. The walls were stretched with canvas on which the eleventh viscount had painted, rather in the manner of Conder, a design of white peacocks against cypresses and mysterious gray-green trees. The woodwork was ivory-white.

"How pretty!" exclaimed Lucinda. "Did your father really paint this?" She was surprised. She thought it very funny that a peer should decorate a room, but Hugo appeared to see nothing unusual in it.

"Yes, he was a clever old boy," he said in simple appreciation. "You must get Paul to take you round the place. He knows the history of every stick and stone in Crittenden."

Later, when Lucinda had just finished dressing for dinner, Marian came to her room. She asked her if she was sure that she had everything she wanted, and apologized for the house being old-fashioned and uncomfortable. Lucinda thought that Hugo must have told Arthur that she had complained of her sister-in-law's manner, and that now she was trying to make up for it. Actually Hugo had told Arthur that Lucinda was going to have a child. Till she heard this, Marian had imagined that Lucinda was one of these selfish "modern" young women who only married for social advantage and to have a good time. As she had herself been unable to provide an heir, and as Paul showed no signs of marrying, she thought for another woman to marry a Brayford and to refuse to have children was a form of cheating.

At dinner Arthur had up a bottle of his best port, ostensibly in honor of their arrival, but really to celebrate the beginning of a new generation of Brayfords. There was a subtle difference in his manner towards Lucinda, while Marian's friendliness was very different from her attitude of the afternoon. She still spoke rather as if the life of a peeress was grim and earnest, but when her eyes met Lucinda's they had a look of genuine friendliness. Round the walls of the dining-room were more portraits of past Brayfords. The latest was a portrait of Arthur's mother by his father. The draperies and jewels were painted more sensitively than the face, to which Paul bore a strong likeness. Arthur explained to Lucinda who these people were, and she felt that she had been completely accepted as one of the family. She was very happy all the evening with a quiet sort of happiness which was new to her. When they came back to the saloon from the dining-room she found that four standard oil lamps with yellow silk shades had been placed about the room. It was not till then that she realized the house had no electricity. It was not installed till a year after the war. The curtains were still undrawn as Marian would not shut out any daylight. Out in the park the long shadows were spreading till the last touch of sunset vanished from the grass, and the long English twilight began. In the saloon, with the fading twilight, the yellow shaded lamps grew steadily brighter. In their gentle glow the room appeared even more beautiful than in the afternoon. The old English gilt, the paintings, the ceiling and the damasks, blended in softer and richer harmonies than by day, and the fine proportions of the room were evident. The atmosphere of the place was more powerful than ever. Lucinda felt it almost like a drug. She felt that she could stay here forever, where against a background of such dignity, life was lived with a natural simplicity which could only be described by the German word *gemütlich*.

Paul came down to Crittenden for the week-end, arriving in time for dinner on Friday. He talked steadily the whole evening, and in fact for the whole week-end. He put forward extreme views on art and other subjects to which Arthur and Hugo listened with an odd mixture of ridicule and respect. They thought Paul slightly absurd, but recognized that he had more brain than either of them. It was clear that Paul and Marian had little liking for one another. Marian's manner during his visit became once more defensive and aloof. The implication of all that she said was a repudiation of Paul's views, which in turn almost denied her the right to existence.

"The artist and the aristocrat are the only people worthy of consideration," he said, "the rest of mankind should function merely to make their existence tolerable."

Marian in turn talked about the success of her relatives in the Services and at the Universities.

"I can't understand," she said, referring to one of her cousins, "why Enid doesn't send Tom to Oxford. Even if he is going into the City, does it mean he must cease to be a gentleman?"

"Of course it does," said Paul. "It would be very confusing if it didn't. And if he weren't one, Oxford wouldn't make him one. The idea that education makes a gentleman is bourgeois and poisonous."

He said things of this kind with savage relish, and Lucinda was not sure that she liked him. Yet he was charming to her, which seemed hardly consistent with his arrogant ideas, and after he had left on Tuesday instead of Monday, a delay for which he let her know she was responsible, the house was dull for a day or two. He conducted her all over Crittenden, showed her the room where Caroline Brayford's fiancé had been stabbed during the Monmouth rebellion, and gave her the family history from its twelfth-century origin, with its few scandals and romances which he exaggerated. On Saturday, Dean Chapman dined at Crittenden and invited them all to luncheon on Monday and to see over the cathedral, but only Paul and Lucinda were able to go.

During the week-end, Paul, who was far from reticent, half intentionally explained himself to her.

He was to have followed Arthur to Eton, but at the age when he should have gone he had an illness. When he recovered, his father was going through one of those occasional periods of financial difficulty into which his extravagance led him, and Paul, partly because of his health, was sent to a smaller and much less famous public school. Marian was the daughter of his housemaster. When he was sixteen years old she called him "a little squit," in retaliation for a boast he had made about his ancestry. Although this had happened twelve years ago he had not forgiven her. Arthur came down to visit him at his mediocre school and fell in love with her. She committed an even worse crime by marrying him. Old Lord Crittenden, who had shown the world that only the highest aristocracy were fitting brides for the Brayfords, died from the shock. Paul went about saying cheerfully, "Of course Marian killed my father."

Also, at sixteen, he happened to find the *Memoirs* of the Duc de Saint-Simon in the library at Crittenden. He soaked himself in these volumes, with their obsession with birth and precedence, in which some of his maternal ancestors were mentioned. They gave him an intense satisfaction in his own nobility, which was, with his tongue, the only weapon he had against the world. He was not physically strong, he disliked games, his cleverness was not academic, and he had not even, like his brothers, been to Eton. He pretended to believe—he did half believe it—that birth alone claimed respect. At this time the master of an Oxford college, a man of humble origins but of world-wide reputation as a counselor of future prime ministers, came to stay at Crittenden. He did not much care for the look of Paul but addressed a few affable words to the son of his host, whose sour, staccato replies he put down to a schoolboy's nervousness in the presence of a great scholar. He would have been astonished to learn that Paul was behaving as he imagined that a peer of France would have behaved towards a presumptuous inferior in the reign of Louis Quatorze.

Influenced by Saint-Simon to believe that the army was the only possible career for a man of his birth, he went to Sandhurst, but the smallness of his allowance and his boredom and consequent inefficiency at soldiering obliged him to join a not very distinguished line regiment. On his father's death, when he inherited his portion as a younger son, he resigned his commission and devoted himself to a belated but enthusiastic pursuit of culture.

When he was talking for effect, or dismissing people as unimportant by some arbitrary standard of his own, although at these times he was often amusing, Lucinda did not feel very much at ease with him, but at other times, when he was talking naturally on some subject of which he had knowledge, she felt that she really liked him.

As well as the history of Crittenden he told her about the local families who were their neighbors. The nearest of these were the Greene-Jameses at Cary and Miss Fitzauncell of Fitzauncell Castle. Miss Fitzauncell who was nearly ninety was the last direct descendant of the son of an eleventh-century bishop of Bayeux, and Paul regarded her almost as a social equal. The Greene-Jameses were originally London merchants and had only been at Cary since the Regency.

"They're exactly like horses," said Paul. "They neigh when they are introduced, and when I see Mrs Greene-James in Bond Street I am always surprised that she is up on the footpath."

When Paul left Lucinda knew a great deal more not only of the history and geography of Crittenden and its neighborhood, but also of the ramifications of affection and antipathy throughout the family and the county. It was useful information to have, but it marred slightly her first whole-hearted response to the tranquil beauty of the place. The dullness she felt when he had left was due as much to this as to the cessation of his stimulating but too often destructive talk.

Towards the end of the week she and Hugo went up to London

for a month. They stayed at Claridges as it was too crowded for Susannah if they stayed long at Bryanston Square. Through Susannah they had innumerable invitations, and Lucinda spent the month in such a continuous succession of gaieties that she hardly had time to think.

One afternoon she went with Susannah and Mr Rosenfeld, her "gutter millionaire," to watch Hugo play polo at Hurlingham. They went to have tea on the lawn while Hugo was changing. On his way to join them he stopped to speak to a woman who was sitting with some friends at another table. She had black hair and the kind of skin which used to be compared with camellias. She was striking in appearance if not absolutely beautiful.

"Who is Hugo talking to?" asked Lucinda.

"Mrs Fabian Parker," said Susannah indifferently. "She's one of the three Lavenham sisters. They have a reputation for looks."

"Only for looks?" said Rosie, and lifted one eyebrow.

Susannah showed a complete lack of response to this innuendo, and Hugo joined them.

At a ball they went to in the evening Lucinda noticed that Hugo danced twice with Mrs Fabian Parker, but after that she only saw her once again in a crowd at some function, before they returned to Crittenden in July.

Although she had enjoyed herself very much, Lucinda was so tired after the London racket that she was delighted to come back to the peace of Crittenden. Marian with her baskets of eggs and her simple clothes awoke a real affection in her, and she forgot the slight taint which Paul had left behind. Arthur and Marian pressed her to stay at Crittenden until her baby was born, which would be some time in December. She was very happy to do so and Hugo seemed pleased at the idea.

They spent the drowsy July days in agreeable idleness. There were a few tennis parties and Lucinda met most of the county neighbors. Old Miss Fitzauncell called and in the quavering voice of old age talked all the time about herself and her castle, very conscious of the fact that she was a museum piece. She asked Lucinda to tea and entertained her in vaulted rooms filled with the treasures and dusty junk of centuries. When a drab gray curtain was drawn, its hidden folds revealed that it was of rose and silver Carolean brocade. Lucinda remembered with a pang of faint amusement the day she had spent at Cape Furze, and thought how small, bright and modern that house was in comparison with this authentic antiquity.

Some of the Greene-Jameses came to play tennis, and she was surprised to find that Paul had not exaggerated their resemblance to horses. Winnie Greene-James, who reminded her of Clara Bumpus, attempted a flirtation with Hugo. He made a chaffing but indifferent response. They had known each other since childhood. She told him of the marvelous time she had been having while he had been "out in the wilds." When she had said this she apparently remembered that Lucinda was Australian, and gave her a glance of careless apology.

"You'll have your work cut out to keep Hugo in order," she said, laughing loudly.

Lucinda found that she liked Marian more the better she knew her, and that a real friendship was growing between them, whereas Susannah seemed to have advanced at once to the degree of friendliness she wanted between them, and their relationship remained static at that point. Nevertheless she did feel a slight restraint with Marian, who seemed to think it presumptuous of her to make any kind of comment on English things or people. When Lucinda ventured a mild criticism of Winnie Greene-James, Marian replied coldly:

"She's a nice wholesome English country girl."

One morning Hugo stopped Lucinda as she was going down to the garden to help Marian pick sweet peas. If there were no county or ecclesiastical activity which demanded her attention Marian did small jobs about the place. She could not bear to see anyone idle nor to be idle herself.

"You like it here all right, don't you, darling?" asked Hugo.

"Of course, I simply love it," said Lucinda.

"You know we're asked to Lochaber for the twelfth?"

"Yes." She looked doubtful and fiddled with the scissors in her basket.

"You're not keen on coming?"

"Marian doesn't think I ought to go."

"No. Would you mind if I went?"

"Would you be away long?"

"A week or two, I suppose."

Lucinda rather thought that Hugo should not want to go away without her, but she told herself that it would be too much to ask him to miss the grouse-shooting. She answered slowly:

"Of course you must go, darling. I shall miss you dreadfully, but I can't expect you to stay with me all the time. Anyhow, won't you have to rejoin your regiment soon? We haven't made any plans really, but we've been having such a lovely time."

"I've resigned my commission," said Hugo. "I meant to tell you before. You wouldn't like trailing round after a regiment."

She was surprised that he had not discussed this step with her, but delighted that he taken it. Her pleasure showed in her face and she exclaimed:

"Oh, then we can have our own house?"

"Well, yes, I suppose we can. But we can stay here as long as we like, you know. Arthur's glad to have us." He was relieved at the way she had taken his announcement. He had thought she might have been critical, as she knew that Fred had given her a larger allowance than Lydia, seeing that Hugo was a soldier and could not be expected to make money.

"Yes, but we'll have to have our own house some day."

"It's not a bad idea. We must ask Susannah to find one for us. You're sure that you don't mind about Lochaber?"

"Not now that I know you won't be joining your regiment."

"Good girl." He kissed her and went off to try a new hunter over a brushwood jump in the park. He thought it might not be a bad idea to have a small house in London. They could come to Crittenden for the hunting.

Lucinda joined Marian at the sweet peas. She told her that Hugo had resigned his commission.

"Gosh!" said Marian.

"Why?"

"What on earth's he going to do with himself?"

"He always finds plenty to do."

"So does Satan."

Lucinda thought Marian went too far.

"We're going to take a house," she said coldly.

Marian saw a pie in which she might put a finger.

"Why don't you take the End House?" she said.

"I think Hugo wants to live in London."

"I expect he does. He'd be much better in the country. The country's the only place to bring up children. Arthur would do up the End House if anyone were going to live in it."

When they had finished stripping the sweet peas, Marian suggested that they should walk across the park and inspect the End House. On the way she explained that Susannah had the right to occupy it for life but did not want to. It could not be let in its present condition, and Arthur did not feel obliged to modernize it for Susannah to draw the rent.

"Couldn't she pay him out of the rent what it cost to do it up?"

"Of course, but they pride themselves on not being business people," said Marian, turning a huge key in the blistered front door of the End House. They came into a flagged hall which had the same smell of damp stone that a church has.

"These flags must come up," said Marian.

"But they're so picturesque."

"They'll give you rheumatic fever. You must have a wooden floor in here—thick carpets and an anthracite stove."

They went upstairs and down long dreary passages to the kitchen regions, where old stone sinks were chipped and brown, and the huge range was rusty. The rooms were all paneled in painted wood, upstairs white faded to ivory and downstairs in imitation grained oak. They were beautifully proportioned with fine fireplaces and big windows, but Lucinda felt slightly depressed by the air of long neglect.

However, Marian helped to dispel this by her efficient cheerfulness.

"The kitchen's too far from the dining-room," she said. "We must knock down a few walls and make a new kitchen where those pantries are. You must cut down those laurels in the garden and that hideous monkey-puzzle that darkens the dining-room."

By the time they returned to Crittenden House, Marian had arranged everything. Arthur should pay for the alterations and repairs as it was estate property, but Hugo and Lucinda should pay as rent interest on the amount they cost. As Susannah did not use the house she might as well let Hugo and Lucinda have it. They sought out Arthur and informed him of these plans. He was very pleased at the idea of having them so close and readily agreed. At luncheon they faced Hugo with the *fait accompli*. He was not very pleased, but as Arthur was so delighted with the plan he did not like to oppose it, and after all they would have the house for practically nothing. Arthur had no idea that Hugo had not been consulted, and Marian did not enlighten him.

A few days later Hugo left for Scotland, and on the same morning the workmen began pulling up the flags in the End House.

At breakfast one day Marian read out the names of the Lochaber house party from the *Morning Post*. When she came to the name Mrs Fabian Parker, she stopped and gave a meaning glance at Arthur, which he ignored. Lucinda had an uneasy feeling.

"Is there anyone else?" she asked.

"Only Hugo and Mr Westby," said Marian.

"Westby's a rum old boy," said Arthur, and told some anecdote of this wealthy bachelor, who, born a Quaker, lived, moved and had his being amid the highest social influences. Lucinda was amused and forgot about Mrs Fabian Parker.

During the autumn she was busy buying furniture for the End House. Two or three times a week she drove with Marian into the county town and they poked about in antique shops. She also made a few excursions to London where she stayed with Susannah, to buy glass and china, curtains and carpets. She was not yet certain of her own taste and deferred to their judgment. Marian liked simple, well-made mahogany and was fond of a bargain. Susannah liked splendor and color and did not bother about the cost. The result was that the furniture at the End House was plain, while the curtains and chintzes were either magnificent or *chic*, and on the austere Georgian dining table blossomed gold-powdered filigree Venetian glass.

The Peacock room was still nominally Lucinda's sitting-room, but Marian spent a good deal of time there with her, especially on cold days. One rainy afternoon they were having tea there together when the post was brought in.

There was only one letter for Lucinda. She gave an exclamation as she read it. Marian looked up from her own letters and said:

"What's the matter?"

"Nothing. It must be some mistake."

"Who has made a mistake?" Marian was hot after the authors of mistakes.

"The bank."

"Banks don't generally make mistakes. What sort of mistake have they made?"

"They say I'm overdrawn, but I can't be. It's impossible."

"You've been spending a good deal on furniture, my dear."

"I know, but Daddy gave me a thousand pounds extra for that. I haven't nearly spent it, and Hugo can't have spent much in Scotland. He won't have any hotel bills."

"Hugo!" said Marian sharply. "Does he draw on your account?"

"We share the account. He . . . we thought it would be nicer."

"Much nicer for Hugo, no doubt."

"Marian, you mustn't talk to me like that about Hugo," said Lucinda, quietly but nervously.

"It's no good living in a fool's paradise, my dear," said Marian. "Hugo is not economical in his habits. He went to Australia to recover from a financial crisis."

Arthur came in to tea. He saw Lucinda looking rather white and Marian rather grim. He made some genial, commonplace remark to ease the tension.

"Hugo has overdrawn Lucinda's account," said Marian.

Arthur puckered his forehead. Lucinda felt sorry for him, and for herself and for Hugo—in fact for everyone except Marian.

"It's nothing. Please don't bother about it," she said. "I'll write to the manager. My next quarter's money comes soon."

"What does the Bank want you to do?" asked Marian.

"They've met the check, but they ask me to make it up as soon as possible. I've written three more checks since that one, but not for very much."

"I should think it would be advisable to ask for your passbook," said Arthur.

A man came in with some more hot water for Arthur's tea and the subject was dropped.

The next morning Lucinda had a letter from Hugo, informing her as usual of his bag since he last wrote, and telling her to look after her health, but with a postscript saying he had been unlucky at baccarat and advising her not to spend much until next quarter. She did not mention this to Marian. However, on the morning after, her passbook lay conspicuously by her plate at the breakfast table, and Marian was unable to restrain her curiosity and her genuine wish to be helpful. Hugo had written checks for over five hundred pounds, which could only be to pay his losses at cards.

After breakfast Arthur and Marian retired to the library for a consultation. Lucinda took some baby-linen she was embroidering and sat in a cane chaise-longue under a cedar tree at the far end of the terrace. She began to feel that the End House was a burden she had undertaken. How could she run a house like that if Hugo went away and lost their money? If they had no house, but just stayed about with people, at Crittenden, at Bryanston Square with Susannah, or in hotels, and went back to Tourella for six months every other year, money would not matter so much. She made excuses in her mind for Hugo. Once when she went to dinner with some people in Domain Road she had lost an awful lot at poker. She did not want to go on playing, but she did not see very well how she could stop. She had lost nearly three pounds. It had seemed dreadful to her at the time, and she did not tell Julie or Fred. She supposed that Hugo was playing with people accustomed to much higher stakes, and he could not stop either. And he *had* warned her that he had lost the money, so that she should not overdraw. It would be absurd to let money come between them, or houses and furniture. Still, when she had a baby she would have to have a house. She wished Hugo would come back. His presence gave her a sense of security. And yet he had caused this feeling of insecurity. She was bewildered and wretched.

Arthur came along the terrace and sat beside her. He had a folded slip of paper in his hand.

"You must let me help you over this," he said with a sort of gruff diffidence. "I've calculated that this will pay off your overdraft and give you a hundred pounds to go on with. You can pay me back when it's convenient. I think you and Hugo should have separate accounts. Marian and I have. A joint account never works. I've written to Hugo." He handed her a check.

Lucinda thanked him very gratefully, but said: "I don't want money to come between us."

"You don't want lack of money to come between you, either," said Arthur, smiling.

She felt that the incident had upset him a great deal. She knew that he was very fond of Hugo and would hate to have any cause for disagreement with him. She did not know that with the added expense of restoring the End House, it was extremely inconvenient for him to have to part with two hundred pounds at that moment. She was accustomed to regard the head of the family as controlling inexhaustible supplies of wealth. If Fred had this auriferous quality, surely it would be more highly developed in a peer of the realm.

Arthur had written:

> "DEAR HUGO,
>
> Lucinda is somewhat distressed to find her banking account overdrawn. Apparently you are responsible. I have lent her some money to tide her over, and have advised her to have a separate account of her own. I expect you agree to this. Looking forward to seeing you back here soon.
>
> Your affectionate brother,
ARTHUR."

At the end of the week Lucinda had a letter from Hugo. He demanded why on earth she thought it necessary "to blurt out our private affairs to Marian." In a postscript he added that he would not be back at Crittenden till mid-October as he had accepted some further shooting invitations. She took it that he meant this as a punishment for her. She went up to her bedroom and wept, partly because, although she longed for him to come back, she had been made to realize that he had failings.

In the meantime Paul came down to Crittenden and stayed for some months. He spent most of his time talking to Lucinda. He gave her advice about the End House, much as Tony might have done. She was surprised to find, under his cynical manner and malicious gossip, how extraordinarily kind he was. He seemed ashamed of this kindness and was liable to follow an affectionate glance from his expressive eyes with some rather cruel witticism. The End House was now nearly ready, but they were not to move in until the New Year, after the baby was born. By Marian's direction the anthracite stove and the boiler were kept alight all through the autumn so that the house would be thoroughly aired.

Paul was very concerned about the baby. He was horrified when he heard that Hugo had upset Lucinda by overdrawing her account, and tried to compensate this by sheltering her from everything but beautiful and soothing influences. He chose her books to read, arranged charming and original bunches of flowers in the Peacock room, and played the chapel organ to her twice daily, at eleven in the morning and before it was time to change in the evening.

The chapel at Crittenden was one of the eleventh viscount's extravagances. Amélie de Mireval had been horrified, on social rather than religious grounds, at the idea of a nobleman's château without its own chapel, especially with no Roman Catholic church near. Lord Crittenden was pleased at the excuse for bringing something of the Italian renaissance into his house. He knocked two large rooms into one, painted the ceiling blue with gold stars, brought an altar-piece from Venice, brocades from Florence and baroque silver ornaments from various places abroad. When Amélie died and he married the protestant Susannah, she left the chapel as it was, except that she took one of the chasubles for her grand piano, but Marian thought a reformation necessary, though not an extensive one as she was high church. She removed a monstrance, a triangular candlestick before an image, and replaced the altarcards by the English prayer book. With no further ceremony than the flick of her duster, the chapel became Anglican. It was only used when Paul played the organ, or in very cold and wet weather, when Arthur read prayers to the household instead of their going to church.

Although Paul made extreme and sometimes apparently outrageous statements, Lucinda came to think him more serious than the other Brayfords. It was because he seemed at all costs anxious to know the truth and what was of value. He played to her only Bach, Handel and sixteenth-century church music. When they were singing Palestrina in the cathedral he rang up the dean, asked him to reserve two choir stalls and took Lucinda in to hear it. He implied that as her child might occupy a dynastic position he should from the beginning be subjected to traditional influences.

"You look at so many things from a completely fresh and dis-

138

interested point of view," said Lucinda, "and yet you accept other things simply because they are traditional."

"I don't accept them because they are traditional," said Paul, "but because they are clearly beautiful, true and highly civilized."

As Lucinda sat on a rush-seated *prie-dieu*, listening to his playing, while her eye wandered from the gold stars on the ceiling to the shepherd in the altar-piece, it seemed to her that this curious impersonal music lifted her on to another plane, not only far removed from the social life of Toorak, but even from life at Crittenden itself. She felt that she was subject to some power beyond herself and beyond the temporary advantages of men. In Melbourne she had not felt that at all—she had not felt that there was any power beyond Fred's check book. On that first afternoon when she arrived at Crittenden she had had a hint of this feeling, but nothing to the extent which it came upon her in the chapel while she listened to Paul. It seemed to her that only when one's life was linked to the beauties and tragedies of the past, as in this music and in this house, did it have any richness of texture, that only when one had accepted a background of pessimism did one's pleasures become civilized. She was surprised to find herself thinking in these terms. It was, she supposed, through talking so much to Paul, through having so much time to think, and most probably because she was bearing a child. But it was also, she had no doubt, due to the kind of music chosen by Paul. She wondered if these aloof melodies of Palestrina, so tranquil and yet so disturbing, could really have any influence on the nature of her child.

CHAPTER THREE

HUGO'S RETURN TO CRITTENDEN in the middle of October did not much interfere with Lucinda's hours in Paul's company. She was almost painfully delighted to see him again. He greeted her affectionately and neither of them referred to the overdraft. He had none of the air of a returned prodigal. She was surprised that he was not at all jealous of her intimate friendship with Paul. Once when she was feeling particularly at ease with him she chaffed him about this.

"I'd trust any woman anywhere with Paul," he said, "apart from the fact that you're his sister-in-law."

"Then why does Marian always talk of him as if he were slightly disreputable?"

"God knows," said Hugo indifferently.

He at once began to shoot and hunt. Occasionally he went up to London for the day and sometimes stayed a night or two at his club. Lucinda's figure was now such that she did not care to appear in public.

Once when Hugo had gone up for the day, she was helping Marian to strip dried lavender from its stalks. Marian had a bedroom cleared for this purpose and the floor covered with newspapers. Where Lucinda was working was a copy of *The Times* of the day before. While she half listened to Marian's attack on the Asquith government, her eye glanced down the columns of the newspaper, and was arrested by the announcement: "Mrs Fabian Parker has arrived at the Ritz from Scotland."

"Who is Mrs Fabian Parker?" she asked.

Marian looked up sharply.

"Why d'you want to know?"

"I just wondered," said Lucinda. "You read out her name as one of the people at Lochaber. It says here that she has returned to London."

"The less you know of Mrs Fabian Parker the better," said Marian. "She's not our sort."

When Lucinda went down to the chapel for music, she asked Paul:

"Who is Mrs Fabian Parker?"

Paul shrugged his shoulders. "*Une femme fatale.* Have you met her?"

"No. There seems to be some mystery about her."

"Who is making it?"

"Marian."

"Marian is often led astray by righteousness," said Paul.

In the evening when Hugo returned from London she asked him about his day, and said:

"Where did you lunch?"

"At the Ritz."

"Oh, I thought you said you were going to the Cavalry Club."

"Well, I didn't," he said shortly.

She became uneasy about Hugo's frequent visits to London, but at times she put down her suspicions to a distorted imagination due to her condition. She grew to think that Paul was a more reliable character than Hugo, which seemed absurd. Hugo, steady-eyed, strongly built, not over-talkative, was the type she had been taught to regard as the acme of reliability, whereas Paul with his sensitive wavering glances, his exotic tastes, his malicious chatter, his small limbs, was what Fred would have judged the very embodiment of irresponsibility if not of downright shiftiness, even more so than Tony. It was odd, she thought, that she should have two close friends of the "poodle-fakir" type.

At the end of October she had a cable from Julie, saying that she was coming to England for the birth of the baby. She was of course invited to Crittenden, where she arrived on a cold December afternoon, bringing with her all the social bustle of a Toorak matron, cheerfully affectionate in her greeting to Lucinda, which she interrupted to exclaim, "Oh, my keys for the maid!" as she fumbled for them in her bag, almost ogling Arthur as she shook him warmly by the hand, and then suddenly shy and prim with Marian. To Hugo she gave a kind of grin of complicity, as much as to say, "You are a naughty boy."

Everybody at Crittenden liked Julie. She enjoyed herself so thoroughly, admired everything enthusiastically, while her own pretensions were so naïve. Susannah, when she met her later, was the only one of the family who did not take to her. If people attempted to be mondaine Susannah expected them to be of the real world or not at all. She may have felt that Julie was a slight caricature of herself.

They were all so nice to Julie that by dinner-time the nervousness which underlay her bustling arrival had disappeared. She told them about the Cup Week ball she had given on the night before she sailed.

"My dear, I simply walked out of my ball-dress into my traveling clothes. My cabin was full of sweets and flowers. It was just like a continuation of the party."

Lucinda, in spite of the plum-colored liveries and the dim portraits beyond the candlelight, felt as if she were dining in Toorak.

Julie went on to tell them about two new stations Fred had bought.

"You must forgive all this family gossip. It's dreadful of me," she said to Marian.

"No. It's most interesting," said Marian, but without conviction.

"Your father has made over two stations to me," said Julie to Lucinda. "Wombidgee and Churt."

"Then you are Baroness Wombidgee," said Paul.

Paul's manners were normally so good that no one could believe that he had been impertinent. There was a moment's awkward silence.

"What a nice name for you, Mummy," said Lucinda. The silence broke into laughter. For the rest of her time at Crittenden Julie was known as Baroness Wombidgee, and although she rather suspected Paul, she liked the name. It showed friendliness on the Brayford's part, and better than she knew it suited her plump figure, her expensive clothes, her jewels, her arch and genial manner. Paul called her *Madame la baronne* and she half felt herself to be one of the old nobility.

On Christmas Day the vicar came up at half-past nine and held a service in the chapel for the benefit of Lucinda, which the family and some of the servants attended. The next day the baby was born, just after sunset. It was a boy, which everyone in conversation had assumed it would be, though they had all secretly mistrusted this confidence and expected it to be a girl. Everything went fairly well and there were two days of discussion over its name. Marian said it must be called Stephen because of its birthday. Hugo wanted it called Arthur. Lucinda wanted it called Hugo. Finally it was registered as Stephen with six other family names insisted on by Paul. The christening was postponed until Susannah returned from Monte Carlo, where Rosie had lent her a villa.

Marian invited Julie to stay at Crittenden till the christening, but Julie was afraid she might outstay her welcome. As soon as Lucinda was up and about she went to visit a Melbourne friend who had taken a flat in Mount Street, and on from there to Paris to buy clothes.

Lucinda moved into the End House at the beginning of March. Fires had been burning in every room for ten days beforehand. Hugo said that moving was a woman's business and went off to London till it was over, though the house had long been quite ready for them, and the only moving necessary was of themselves and their clothes. Lucinda walked down to the End House before tea, beside the nurse who was wheeling Stephen in his perambulator. She thought it a little unkind of Hugo not to be with her on the first night in their new home, but he was not sentimental about that sort of thing. He was to come down the following afternoon, and Julie, who had returned from Paris and was spending a day or two in London, was to arrive soon after him.

Julie was staying at the Ritz. On the day before Lucinda's move she came in from a morning's shopping to find Hugo sitting waiting for someone. When he saw her he rose and greeted her politely, but without enthusiasm.

"I thought you always stayed at the Hyde Park Hotel," he said.

"I used to," said Julie, "when I had the family with me, but now I'm on the loose. What are you doing, you naughty man? Why aren't you helping with the move?"

"Marian's managing it efficiently. I came up to be out of the way."

Julie made a few more bright remarks, but Hugo seemed absentminded. Suddenly, with an air of decision he gave her his full attention.

"I'm lunching here with two friends," he said. "Would you care to join us?"

Julie was delighted.

"I have to telephone," said Hugo, "would you excuse me for a moment?"

"Oh, yes. I'll go up to my room. I shan't be long."

When she came down again Hugo was seated on a sofa beside a striking-looking woman with dark hair and a beautiful pale skin. He was apparently making some explanation to her and she did not look very pleased. When they saw Julie, Hugo stood up, and the woman, when she was introduced, spoke to her with great charm. Her name was Mrs Fabian Parker.

A tall, soldierly man of about thirty came in from Arlington Street, looked about and walked quickly across to them. He apologized for being late, shook hands with Mrs Parker and turned to be introduced to Julie.

"This is Major Pat Lanfranc," said Hugo.

"Oh," said Julie, "how very interesting. Your uncle the judge is one of our oldest friends."

They went in to luncheon. The two men stood aside and Julie overheard Pat murmur, "you didn't give me much time, old boy." She was too excited at entering the restaurant in the company of someone so utterly smart as Mrs Fabian Parker to take any inference from this remark.

The first letter that Lucinda received at the End House was a note the following morning from Julie, saying what train she would come by the next day, and what a delightful lunch she had just had with Hugo, one of the Lanfrancs and the most charming woman she had ever met, a Mrs Fabian Parker.

Lucinda had been looking forward to going in their own new car to meet Hugo at the station. That again was to be a sentimental occasion. When she had read Julie's letter she felt that she could not go. She was distrait all the morning. She felt that she was being absurd, as really she had no clear reason for jealousy. After all there were four people at the luncheon, including her own mother. If there had been any reason to evade Julie, Hugo would have managed it. She knew him well enough by now to know that. All the same she sent Wilson, Hugo's former soldier servant who had become a sort of chauffeur-valet, to the station to meet him.

In spite of this, Hugo was quite jovial when he arrived at the End House. He kissed her affectionately, and putting his arm round her waist said, "now let's see the grand result." They made a tour of inspection of the house and he praised everything, but first they visited the heir-presumptive of Crittenden, who slept, pink and placid, waiting for his grandmother to return from Monte Carlo to sponsor his renunciation of the world, the flesh and the devil. Lucinda felt that all her fears and jealousies had been contemptible, yet she could not bring herself to ask Hugo straight out, "who is Mrs Fabian Parker?"

At last *The Times*, the *Morning Post* and the *Daily Telegraph* announced that Susannah Viscountess Crittenden had arrived at Crittenden from Bryanston Square. Marian thought all this vulgar self-advertisement. Although Susannah was only the dowager, Marian suffered a continual eclipse from her, and once at some function an American woman to whom she was talking, on discovering her identity said, "Oh, I thought you were the other Lady Crittenden," and turned away.

Now everyone fussed, from Arthur down to the gardeners, because Susannah was coming to Crittenden. The head-gardener sent in the most magnificent hyacinths for her room. Marian sent them back saying they were too strongly scented, and he then sent in some even more remarkable early tulips.

Susannah had an idea of what Marian had to endure, and her manner was that of some charming child which deprecates punishment. She told Marian how wonderfully she ran the house, and to make up for having delayed Stephen's christening, as soon as she had drunk her tea she went down to the End House to see him. She raved over Stephen who gurgled back at her, and she was affable to Julie, but when she was alone with Hugo she said:

"Your mother-in-law is very *bourgeoise*."

"Paul says she's not as *bourgeoise* as Marian. He says she's the aristocracy of her own country. Anyhow, what's Rosie?" asked Hugo.

"A guttersnipe," said Susannah. "I like the tops and the bottoms. At least they're real, but I can't stand the middles."

The christening took place next day in the chapel at Crittenden House, which was strongly scented with the hyacinths rejected from Susannah's room. Dean Chapman performed the ceremony. Marian and Lydia by proxy were the godmothers, but there were six godfathers, three of whom were peers and one a German Serene Highness, an old flame of Susannah's. The others were Pat Lanfranc and Paul. Fred sent his grandson a thousand pounds.

All the county were present, including Miss Fitzauncell whose father had been a page to George III. She insisted on holding Stephen in her arms, so that when he was an old man at the end of the century he could say he had been held by someone whose father had known George III. As she held the child, dimly remembering some Bible story or some Highland legend, she saw herself as an ancient prophetess.

"I am the last of an ancient line, and so are you," she said to the whimpering baby, "but before you die you will make the name of Brayford famous." With a smile of evil satisfaction she handed the child back to his nurse.

"He's not the last of the Brayfords—not by a long chalk," said Hugo.

"The Brayfords don't need to be made famous," muttered Paul.

When the dean sprinkled the tepid water on the baby's forehead he did not cry, but gave a gurgle of laughter. When they were drinking champagne and eating christening cake afterwards in the saloon there was some reference to this.

"He can't have any original sin," said Paul.

"I hope to God he has," said Hugo, and Winnie Greene-James heartily agreed with him.

Since the shooting had ended Hugo had been restless at Crittenden. This became more noticeable after the christening. He wanted to go up to London for part of the season, but, as Lucinda pointed out, they could not afford it now that they had to keep up the End House. Hugo's expression when she said this suggested that he had a grudge against the house, but Lucinda was delighted to have a home of her own, and she enjoyed this country life with its pleasant domestic duties, and helping Marian in her various social and charitable works. However, Julie invited them for a fortnight to the Ritz before she left for Australia, and Susannah after that for three weeks to Bryanston Square.

Paul suggested that they should go with him to Paris to see the first performance of Le Coq d'Or. Susannah would be there too. When Julie heard this she asked Hugo and Lucinda to come as far as Paris with her to go to Le Coq d'Or, and to see her off at the Gare de Lyon. On the night before she caught the boat train Julie made her first and last appearance in the European beau monde. She sat in a box with Susannah, and Paul's cousin, the prince and princesse de Mireval, and there, half-intoxicated by her company and by the bewildering Russian spectacle, she forgot that her smooth plump hands had ever known the wash-tubs of Noorilla, or even the feather duster with which she used to keep their sitting-room tidy at Flinders.

The next day they saw Julie off at the train for Marseilles.

"In the autumn you must bring Stephen out to see his grandfather," she said. "You'll avoid the English winter."

Lucinda and Hugo agreed, but Lucinda knew that the English winter, with the shooting and hunting, was the very thing that Hugo did not want to avoid. They accepted Julie's invitation, but she felt that when the time came to go he would make some excuse. Julie said to Paul:

"Why don't you come too? We'd give you a marvelous time in Melbourne."

Paul smiled. "I'd love to come," he said. "Would you entertain me at the Château de Wombidgee?"

Although Paul joked it was evident that he intended to go and Julie realized it. She was tremendously flattered and pleased. Her misgivings about Paul evaporated.

"You are all darlings," she said, and the tears brimmed in her eyes. She kissed Lucinda and Hugo, and Paul, as he was in France, kissed her hand.

In the taxi, going back to the hotel, Lucinda said to Paul:

"I'm surprised that you got along so well with my mother."

"Why?"

"Well, Mummy's a darling but she's not an exponent of culture."

"She has the necessary foundation of culture," said Paul. "She lives for pleasure."

Back in London Lucinda found herself in that whirl of activity, exhausting and enjoyable, in which everything seemed to be in a state of flux, and it was impossible to control one's finances. After their three weeks with Susannah they were invited to a house near Arundel which Rosie had taken for Goodwood. At the end of the week Hugo balanced his betting book and found he was down nearly two hundred pounds.

Lucinda returned to the End House with relief. She dashed upstairs to see Stephen, and then hurried across the park to Marian, whose London season had consisted of a fortnight at Brown's Hotel.

"Oh, it's marvelous to be back," she cried. "I never want to leave Crittenden again. Where is Arthur?"

"He's telephoning to London for the latest news."

"Oh, yes, isn't it dreadful? Is there going to be a war?"

"I don't know. Willy Greene-James is afraid Asquith may back out of it. I can't think why we don't annex the Balkans and teach them sense."

CHAPTER FOUR

HUGO immediately rejoined his regiment, which was stationed near Crowborough. Paul also rejoined the line regiment to which he had originally gone from Sandhurst. He came down to Crittenden on leave once or twice during the autumn of 1914, and Lucinda saw a good deal of him. He detested soldiering more than ever, and complained that the war would have a blighting influence on literature and painting.

Marian wanted to turn Crittenden into a hospital, but as it had no electric light and few bathrooms, the authorities, to Arthur's great relief, refused the offer. The footmen were dismissed to go into the army. Half the house was shut up with dust sheets over the furniture, and for a while they lived in the other half, with the butler, who was too old to enlist, and three maids. Marian thoroughly enjoyed this retrenchment. She instinctively chose the more drab rooms to occupy, and there was a touch of vindictive pleasure in the efficiency with which she turned Crittenden into a middle-class establishment. Arthur was colonel of the local territorials and was in charge of the depot in the county town. He motored in every day to his duties. He did not like bringing back officers from his mess to dine in a poky little room behind the library. It was a new and disagreeable idea to him that a war should interfere with a country gentleman's style of living.

"Even the poorest people have a proper dining-room," he protested inaccurately.

However, early in 1915 he was given an appointment at the War Office. They took a house in Cadogan Place which was too small for Marian to practice any further economies of space, and Crittenden was shut up till after the war.

Lucinda was very dull when Arthur and Marian had left. Hugo wrote that he seemed to be fixed for some time at Crowborough, and suggested that they should take a furnished house there. So the End House too was shut up, and Lucinda with Stephen, his two nurses and two maids, settled in a bright, "artistic" modern villa on the edge of a pinewood. She found that her life had suddenly changed its pattern. As a soldier's wife she was no longer a private individual, but had new and peculiar duties. She found them amusing. Hugo was fully occupied and had no time to be discontented. He was very affectionate towards her, and she thought that she was happier than she had been since the first days of their marriage. Hugo had his pay, they were living economically, and he could not play for high stakes with his fellow officers. Her bank balance, instead of always being on the verge of an overdraft, swelled comfortably, and she lost the secret dread of having sooner or later to appeal to Fred, who had already been so generous, to get them out of a scrape.

Hugo's second-in-command at Crowborough was Pat Lanfranc, of whom Lucinda had heard a good deal, but had only met at Stephen's christening. He often came back with Hugo to dinner. She grew to like him very much, and Hugo, who also was fond of him, looked with indulgence on their friendship and their occasional semi-flirtatious passages. That his wife and his best friend should like each other he took as an endorsement of his own taste.

In the autumn the regiment was dismounted, and early in the New Year was ordered abroad. Pat, who was an expert on horses, was kept in England and given an appointment in the remount department. He lived in London, from whence he made excursions all over the country—sometimes crossing to Ireland.

Lucinda was depressed at the thought of returning alone to the End House. Hugo suggested that she should take a house in London. Marian thought this an excellent idea, and wrote that she had already found a suitable house, just off Knightsbridge, on the Park side, so that Stephen could be wheeled into the park without having to cross the road.

Two days before the regiment embarked Pat came to say goodbye to Lucinda.

"You'll come and see me in London, won't you?" she said. "In Wellington Court. I'll send you the address."

Saying good-bye to him marked the beginning of the breaking up of the pleasant association of the past months. It was a little bit like saying good-bye to Hugo, which she would have to do in two days. The awareness of all this, and the background of the war heightened the emotion of their parting. Pat held her hand longer than usual, and she felt that her eyes were moist.

Three days later, feeling lifeless and empty, she arrived with Stephen and three taxis full of maids, nurses, perambulators and luggage at the little house in Wellington Court. She wondered how they were to fit into it, and thought she must have mistaken the number, when Marian, wearing a dark blue uniform and a tricorne hat, appeared like some sort of commissionaire in the doorway.

"Well, my dear," said Marian, hearty but kind, "how are you?"

"I'm all right. I'm a little tired," said Lucinda.

"Well, everything's ready for you."

Marian had brought two of her own servants to prepare for Lucinda's arrival. The beds were made, the fires lighted, and in the kitchen even the chicken for dinner was ready to go into the oven, and the brussels sprouts were prepared and left in a bowl of water. When they returned to the tiny drawing-room, tea had appeared with hot scones and a white Fuller's walnut cake.

"Marian, you are marvelous," said Lucinda. "I was simply dreading all the business of settling in and getting food, and then finding that some essential thing like salt was missing. I'm really terribly grateful. Susannah did offer to send some things from Fortnum's."

"I told her not to bother and that I'd see to everything. If I'd left it to Susannah there would have been a bunch of outsize lilies and nothing to eat. I hate that messy Irish way of living."

Lucinda smiled. She thought how really kind and good Marian was beneath her brusque manner. Although Susannah had always been charming to her, she felt that she was hard and worldly at the core.

"What war work are you going to do?" asked Marian.

"I don't know. I hadn't really thought of it."

"Everyone should do something, and it will keep your mind occupied."

The door opened and the maid announced, "Lady Crittenden."

Susannah came in carrying a pot of *foie gras* and a large bunch of outsize lilies.

"My dear," she said kissing Lucinda affectionately, "how are you? Forgive these feeble gifts, but Marian assured me she was providing all the necessaries. That uniform *is* becoming, Marian. You are fortunate, I should look frightful in a uniform."

"Thank you so much," said Lucinda self-consciously. "The flowers are lovely. I'll put them in water now."

"What a darling little house!" exclaimed Susannah, "those grey *boiseries* and the Fragonard engravings—a perfect little French salon. A view over the park too. How did you find it?"

"Marian found it. I'll go and arrange the flowers."

Lucinda, feeling embarrassed and a little cowardly, took the lilies down to the pantry. She thought that Susannah must know that they had been criticizing her. Lucinda hated not to be straightforward, and as she had just decided that she was absolutely pro-Marian in the suppressed discord between the two women, she did not feel able to make an adequate response to Susannah's display of affection.

149

She returned carrying the lilies in a seventeenth-century French pottery vase. It was true, as Susannah had pointed out, that the house was subtly in very good taste, but that, she knew, as far as Marian was concerned was an accident. When she came into the drawing-room Marian was saying:

"Arthur saw him two nights ago rattling the door handle at the bar of a theatre after the closing hour. It's not what one expects from the Prime Minister of England."

"Then Arthur must have been wanting to get into the bar too. Still, I can forgive anyone for wanting a drink at any time nowadays," said Susannah. "What a wonderful vase you've got those flowers in, darling. How clever of you to find this house, Marian."

Marian did not respond but continued to talk about the failings of the Asquith family, who she said were pro-German and addicted to every possible vice. She knew that Susannah was quite well acquainted with them, but that did not stop her tirade. Susannah sat looking patient and tired, letting her eyes wander from the engravings to the little jeweled clock on the mantelpiece, and thence to the aubusson carpet.

"This carpet ought to be in a museum," she said, when she had an opportunity to speak.

"There's one something like it in the Peacock room at Crittenden," said Lucinda, who also was anxious to change the subject.

"They've found filthy postcards in the pockets of German prisoners," said Marian.

"Poor things!" said Susannah.

Marian snorted.

"By the way," she asked Lucinda, "do you know Mr Straker?" She referred to an Australian who had recently arrived in England. He had bought one of the big London dailies, in which he was conducting, in American journalistic style, a campaign for the replacement of worn-out ministers by efficient business men, and for the more vigorous prosecution of the war.

"No," said Lucinda, "I've never heard the name."

"He seems to be a leading Australian."

"I don't remember meeting any Strakers."

"He's on the right tack, whoever he is," said Marian. "He wants to hang the Kaiser. I hope they do it publicly. If so I'll book a seat."

She knew too that Susannah was rather proud of having dined with the Kaiser on his yacht at Kiel.

"I'm not enthusiastic about butchery as a spectacle," said Susannah. "I once saw a bullfight at Seville. It wasn't very enjoyable."

"I have General and Mrs Fraser dining," said Marian. "I must go home."

"Is it dinner-time already?" asked Susannah.

"No, but my new cook's an idiot."

Lucinda went down with Marian to the door. If she showed particular friendliness to either Marian or Susannah in the other's presence she felt that it was an offense, especially now, when Marian had just been so rude to Susannah. She was uneasy at the things Marian had said, and hoped they weren't true. Somehow Marian made her feel guilty for not wanting to believe them true, but she had to thank her adequately for finding the house, and she could do this more easily on the doorstep. Marian was too ruffled to respond, and saying something about "Susannah's pro-German friends," she marched off towards Knightsbridge.

When Lucinda came back into the drawing-room Susannah said:

"How Marian does enjoy the idea of punishment! Paul says that there is no more terrible strain one can have in one's blood than that of the schoolmaster."

"I don't think she means everything she says," said Lucinda, mildly defensive. "She's been marvelous about the house. Even the vegetables are ready for dinner." She laughed and Susannah laughed too.

"It's dreadful of me to laugh, when she has been amazingly kind," said Lucinda, but with the relaxing of the tension she went on laughing until she had to wipe her eyes.

"The house is charming," said Susannah; "but I'm sure Marian only chose it because it has good drains. And one would think you had been here a month. I expected to have tea on a box in the kitchen."

She did not look as if she expected to sit in the kitchen. She pulled off a hat trimmed with paradise feathers and put it beside her on the sofa. Round her neck were ropes of pearls, and her handbag had a monogram and coronet in diamonds. She had of course been to a party.

"Do you mind, darling?" she said, kicking off her shoes and putting her feet up on the sofa, "and could your wonderfully efficient servants make me some fresh Indian tea?"

"The poor old Kaiser," said Susannah when Lucinda had rung for the tea. "He is not a very agreeable man and he loved playing soldiers, but I'm sure that a real war horrifies him far more than it does Marian. I don't believe anyone wanted the war except some generals—and Austen and Winston perhaps."

Susannah lay back drinking her Indian tea, and talking about the war and international relationships in a way that struck Lucinda as far more well-informed and intelligent than anything she had heard at Crittenden or at Crowborough. Neither Hugo nor Pat Lanfranc mentioned the political considerations of the war. If they spoke of it at all it was only as a soldier's job. Although she hardly referred to it, it was clear that Susannah felt deeply Hugo's departure for the Front. Lucinda had never before had a serious and intimate conversation with her. She went on to talk about her own affairs. Rosie had been interned.

"He used to help me with my investments," said Susannah. "Some of the things have given up paying since the war. I expect people to say that he did much more than that, but it's not true. He did lend me his box at Covent Garden and a few things like that. Perhaps I shouldn't have accepted them, but I hate being dull. Anyhow, I shall have to give up Bryanston Square and move to a smaller house."

"Why don't you take a house near here?" suggested Lucinda.

"My dear, I'm not the Knightsbridge type. I'd always be meeting Marian on her way to Harrods."

Susannah put on her hat and adjusted it before the Louis Quinze mirror above the mantelpiece. She kissed Lucinda on both cheeks and said: "Now that you're in London we must see more of each other."

When she had gone Lucinda sat alone for a while, thinking about Susannah and Marian. Only an hour or so ago she had thought Marian much the nicer. Now she had changed her opinion. She wondered if she herself suffered from some inherent instability of character. She went on to wonder if she could ever possibly change her opinion of Hugo, and come to care more for some other man. She had to admit to herself that it was a possibility. She was ashamed to admit this on the very day after Hugo had left to face the dangers and hardships of war. For perhaps about the first time in her life she tried to make a serious estimate of her own character. She thought that the best thing about her might be her readiness to accept anything that appeared to be true. Yet this might almost be a weakness, as it gave her no tenacity to any fixed opinion. She knew that her laugh had a silvery musical quality, but also that it sounded a little empty, which might be because she was so easily disillusioned.

She had not changed when the parlormaid announced dinner. At the door she turned and looked back at the little salon. The wall lights made a soft rosy glow on the gray *boiseries*, which must have been brought from France and fitted here. The delicate grace of the room, combined with the logical precision of its decoration, gave her a sense of freedom of mind after the sentimental pretentiousness of the villa at Crowborough. She suddenly felt that she liked this little house very much indeed. Apart from its attractiveness, it was the first home that she had had which was really her own and not an adjunct of the regiment or of Crittenden.

Besides the mysterious Mr Straker, Bill arrived from Australia about this time. On the same ship were the two Misses Lanfranc. Mr Justice Lanfranc had died earlier in the year, and his daughters decided that they would prefer the society of South Kensington to that of South Yarra. They took a little house in Trevor Square, which was quite close to Wellington Court.

Bill had wanted to enlist but Fred sent him to England, where he would be certain of obtaining a commission straight away, with the influence of the Brayfords behind him. Fred saw no reason why he should not have some return for the allowance he made Hugo and Lucinda.

Bill disliked the idea of this, and was determined to preserve his own identity apart from the Brayfords. Marian very kindly asked him to stay at Cadogan Place, as there was hardly room for him in Lucinda's house. He refused and went to a hotel at the bottom of Queen's Gate, inhabited mostly by old ladies, for which Lucinda chaffed him. He did however dine at Cadogan Place, after which Arthur secured him a commission in an infantry regiment stationed near Oxford. He went to stay with their Chapman relatives and also to visit some cousins of Watteau's at Richmond.

"I didn't know that Watteau had any cousins at Richmond," said Lucinda.

"I suppose she thought that you were too grand for them," said Bill.

Pat Lanfranc did not call at Wellington Court as he had promised. Lucinda was a little hurt and disappointed. She would in any case have called on the Misses Lanfranc, but she went rather sooner than she would have if they had not been relatives of Pat's. She thought she might hear some news of him from them.

Paul, when he had the opportunity, was continuing her musical education, which he had begun during those months at Crittenden before Stephen was born, and he took her once or twice to Benediction at Brompton Oratory on Sunday afternoons. She formed the habit of going there when she had nothing else to do. She found the religious atmosphere a soothing contrast to the war, and the beautiful singing was not interrupted by a sermon, nor was she bothered by any explicit dogma which she could understand. Once or twice she bought a candle and lighted it for Hugo. She thought this action silly, but it gave her a faint satisfaction.

One afternoon on the way back from the Oratory she called on the Misses Lanfranc. A babel of voices came from the drawing-room windows. When Lucinda was shown in both the Misses Lanfranc greeted her with affectionate delight, and Lucinda was very glad she had come. For a minute she felt an almost embarrassing emotion, as, although three quarters of the people in the room were English, the Lanfrancs brought back so vividly the atmosphere of home. One of the Australians was a Mrs Maitland, the widow of an Oxford professor. She had been a Miss Nellie Jamieson of Melbourne.

"I knew your mother years ago in Melbourne," she told Lucinda, "but not very well." She explained that she now lived in Oxford. She had a house in St. Giles's.

"My brother is stationed near Oxford," said Lucinda.

"Would he like to come and see us?" asked Mrs Maitland. "We can provide a meal or a bath, which is what most subalterns seem to want when they come on leave."

"I'm sure he'd love to," said Lucinda. She glanced involuntarily at Mrs Maitland's daughter, a dark pretty girl called Anne whom she had brought with her. It struck her that she was not unlike Bill. She had the same full-lipped mouth and wide-set eyes. Lucinda did not doubt that Bill would be glad to visit the Maitlands and she gave Mrs Maitland his address.

At last she had an opportunity to talk alone with Miss Lanfranc. She asked her about Melbourne, but for some reason found it difficult to mention Pat. However, Miss Lanfranc said:

"I believe our cousin Pat is in your husband's regiment. Mrs Vane told us she lunched with him—at the Ritz." Miss Lanfranc gave a faintly malicious smile, and Lucinda could see Julie telling her Melbourne friends that she had lunched with Pat and Hugo and Mrs Fabian Parker at the Ritz.

"Oh yes, we know him quite well," said Lucinda. "Where is he?" she added, and hoped that her voice sounded quite natural.

"He has been away in Ireland for over a month."

"Oh, has he?" Lucinda suddenly felt very pleased. That explained why he had not called. Everything had combined to make this a delightful afternoon, the music she had heard, the crocuses in the park, with their bright promise of spring, meeting these old friends, and then this welcome explanation.

Miss Lanfranc said that they were doing some war work, tying up parcels for prisoners at a house in Wilton Crescent. Lucinda said she was looking for something to do, and it was arranged that she too should come to Wilton Crescent. It was light work and conveniently close.

She left fairly early as she wanted to go back to see Stephen have his bath. At the door a tall soldier was paying off a taxi. When he turned she saw that it was Pat.

"Good Lord, Lucinda!" he exclaimed. "I've just been to call on you, but as you were out I thought I'd come and see the cousins."

Lucinda felt a warm comfortable tingling at the sound of his deep, friendly voice.

"Oh, I'm just leaving. What a nuisance!" she said.

"Come back again." He took her hand to draw her back towards the house.

"No. I can't do that. Will you have dinner with me?"

"Certainly I will."

"I'm just going to see Stephen bathed. Come along in about an hour."

"Marvelous," said Pat. "My luck's in after all."

Stephen gurgled happily in his bath and kicked and splashed with spasmodic delight at being alive. She became so lost in the satisfactions of motherhood that when she left him she had nearly forgotten that Pat was coming to dine. She went down to ask the cook how the dinner could be made more interesting, and to see about opening some wine, but these things did not now seem so important to her. By the time Pat arrived she had become a little nervous at the prospect of dining alone with him. Hitherto, except at odd moments, they had always met in Hugo's company. However, when he arrived, his manner was so naturally friendly that she thought she had been silly, or even vulgar, to feel nervous about their being alone together. They talked about Crowborough and the Brayfords. He was older than Hugo, and as a small child he had known Susannah in Dublin.

"She was a great beauty. There were all kinds of tales about the daring things she did. She drove alone in a hansom cab with a German naval officer."

She had not realized until this evening that the Lanfrancs were an Irish family. They talked a little about the war situation. He asked her who was the Australian called Straker whom everyone was hailing as a "strong man."

"I don't know. I've never heard of him," said Lucinda.

When he left he asked her if she would have lunch with him on Tuesday. He suggested a French restaurant in Soho, saying that the food was very good there, but they both knew that the real reason for his choice was that it was wiser not to show themselves together at one of the fashionable restaurants.

Lucinda did not feel inclined to go immediately to bed and she sat down to write to Hugo. She told him what a pleasant day she had had, that she had called on the Misses Lanfranc and had met Pat as she was leaving and invited him back to dinner. Hugo replied that he was glad she was enjoying herself.

When Lucinda came back from lunching with Pat she found Susannah waiting in the little gray-paneled drawing-room.

"They said you'd be back to tea, so I waited," she said.

Lucinda explained that she had been lunching with Pat.

"I suppose it was all right?" she asked.

Susannah raised her eyebrows. She showed a faint vexation, a barely perceptible hardening of expression. Lucinda did not know whether it was caused by her having lunched with Pat or by her having been so provincial as to question its propriety.

Pat formed the habit of coming to dine at Wellington Court on every Sunday evening when he was in London. It seemed merely an extension of his habit of frequently dropping in to dinner when they were at Crowborough.

CHAPTER FIVE

BILL when he was first at Oxford came up nearly every weekend to see Lucinda, but when he had made the acquaintance of the Maitlands he did not come so frequently. After a gap of six weeks he wrote that he would be up on the following week-end, but on Thursday he wrote to suggest that Lucinda should come to Oxford instead. By the same post came a note from Mrs Maitland asking her to stay at her house. As Pat was to be away from London on that week-end, Lucinda accepted the invitation.

Bill, with Anne Maitland, met her at Oxford railway station. He had the happy but slightly anxious appearance of someone watching the meeting of two people both of whom he likes very much. Lucinda had met Anne before at the Lanfrancs', but they had hardly spoken to one another.

They arrived at St. Giles's in time for tea. Bill and Anne were both very attentive to Lucinda, but as soon as they decently could, they slipped out through the open French windows into the garden. It was a sunny spring afternoon, and at intervals the bells of Oxford made desultory music.

Mrs Maitland looked after the young people, and exchanged an involuntary smile with Lucinda.

"They took to each other at once," she said.

"They're very alike," said Lucinda. "It can't be the attraction of opposites."

"No, it isn't, but I'm afraid it's serious."

"Why afraid?"

"Well, they're very young."

"Will they be engaged?" Lucinda asked diffidently.

"They want to be. That was one reason—not the only reason, of course—why I hoped you would come down. I wanted to ask if your people would agree."

"Why shouldn't they agree? Anne is charming. I am sure they will be delighted, and it is nice your being an Australian."

"Bill, I gather, will be very rich," said Mrs Maitland. "It's best to be frank. We are not at all well off."

"He won't want any *more* money," said Lucinda, smiling.

"People don't always see it in that light. You approve, at any rate. I'm very pleased about that, but we shan't announce the engagement till I hear what your parents say."

"I don't think there is any doubt about that. They'll say that Bill is very lucky."

On Sunday afternoon Bill and Anne took a canoe up the Cher. Mrs Maitland and Lucinda went to evensong at Christ Church. The college was full of Flying Corps cadets.

"I do miss the undergraduates," said Mrs Maitland. "You must come down after the war, when Oxford is its real self again. I suppose I shall still be here. I don't want to leave Oxford, but I do want to go to Australia, more than ever if Anne should be there. It's dreadful to be drawn by two countries on opposite sides of the world. Do you feel that?"

"Of course I want to go back to Australia—quite often," said Lucinda. "If I am able to do that I think I prefer to live in England."

They had just come out of the cathedral. Mrs Maitland took Lucinda aside to see the fine stone staircase leading up to the hall. Lucinda felt, as she had on her first arrival at Crittenden, the influence of the past almost like a drug, and she knew that she could never live contentedly if she were to be entirely separated from it.

"If I had to choose," she said, "I think I would choose England." Perhaps, she thought, as they walked back to St. Giles's, it was the people as much as the place which made her want to stay here—friends like Marian and Paul and, of course, Pat Lanfranc.

When they returned to the house Bill and Anne were still out on the river, but they came in just before dinner, walking hand-in-hand into the drawing-room. Their faces were so illuminated that they seemed to bring into the room with them all the pastoral happiness of a summer afternoon. Their happiness seemed to affect the household. Throughout the evening it bubbled up into laughter at the slightest excuse. At last Bill had to return to his camp, setting off up the Woodstock Road on a rickety bicycle he had hired from a village shop. Before he left he had a few words alone with Lucinda. He told her that he and Anne were engaged.

"I expect it's a bit of a surprise to you," he said.

"It's not a surprise at all," said Lucinda, smiling.

"You'll tell the family what she's like, won't you? They might think my description exaggerated."

"All right. I shan't exaggerate."

"There's no need to," said Bill, his face clouding.

"No. That's what I meant."

Bill smiled again. His dark eyes were swimming with emotion. He looked the very picture of a sensitive and romantic young man. Lucinda thought what a good thing it was that he had found so early a girl as well suited to him as Anne. Otherwise he might take some hard knocks from girls like Winnie Greene-James, or be grabbed by some little vulgarian for his money. She said to Mrs Maitland:

"They both seem very vulnerable."

"Everyone is vulnerable nowadays," said Mrs Maitland.

"Oh yes, but I didn't quite mean it in that sense."

The next morning in the train she reviewed the events of the week-end, and thought what a pleasant interlude it had been. But it was true that now everyone was vulnerable, not only because of their own peculiar sensibility. How dreadful it would be for Anne when Bill was sent to the Front, as was bound to happen soon, or for herself if Pat's appointment ended and he were ordered abroad. The thought came involuntarily into her mind. She had been dwelling on Bill's and Anne's problems, and while her attention was directed away from her own they had arranged themselves in their true pattern, to face her when she turned to them again. The train was passing through Pangbourne when she realized that her major anxiety was not lest Hugo should be wounded or killed, but lest Pat should be ordered abroad. She was almost dazed as she took in the implications of this, and felt at the same time both happy and miserable. It seemed to her so important that no happiness should be lost where it was possible, that when she arrived at Padington she went straight to a post office and cabled to Fred and Julie: "Bill engaged to Anne Maitland, daughter of late Oxford professor. Mrs Maitland formerly Nellie Jameson, Melbourne. Anne entirely delightful. Waiting your consent. Please cable immediately. Love. Lucinda."

Pat was dining with her that evening as they had both been away on the Sunday. She stopped the taxi at a florist's and with a new kind of attention she bought yellow irises and some expensive forced strawberries in case Marian had not sent along any of the fruit and flowers she had regularly from Crittenden.

When she arrived at Wellington Court, Kate the parlor-maid greeted her with an air of pleased excitement, and announced that the major had come home suddenly on leave.

"Oh!" exclaimed Lucinda. "Where is he?"

"He's gone to see her ladyship in Queen Street," said Kate. To the servants Susannah and Marian were distinguished by the streets they lived in. Susannah had moved from Bryanston Square to a little house in Queen Street.

"When did he arrive?" Lucinda asked any question to give herself time to think.

"Last night, madam. I told him that you were at Oxford, and said should I send a wire, but the major said it was too late to disturb you."

"I wish you had. I would have come up by an earlier train." She said this because she was sure that she must appear more bewildered than delighted. "I'll go to Queen Street now."

"The major will be back to lunch, madam."

"Oh. What a good thing I bought these strawberries."

Kate took the suitcase upstairs and Lucinda went into the dining-room and put the strawberries on the sideboard. Kate had laid the table for two with the best glasses. She had also been out and bought some pink carnations. Lucinda took the irises up to the drawing-room, where they looked charming against the grey walls. To find that the preparations she had intended for Pat were to be for Hugo disturbed her so that she sat down for a moment to try to calm herself, but she found that she could not order her confused thoughts. All kinds of wild ideas suggested themselves to her. She hated not to be straightforward with anyone, in even the most trivial relationship. She had now, far more acutely, the sensations she had experienced when she was with Susannah and Marian in this room. She had then tried to escape them by going off to arrange Susannah's lilies—in the same French pottery vase, she noted with a tiny detached corner of her mind, in which she had just put the yellow irises, which she also noted looked far better in here than the lilies.

Should she say at once to Hugo: "I love Pat"? Would that be the straightforward thing to do? But how could she do that when it would involve Pat, and she did not know whether he returned her love. She had a moment of further confusion when she feared that he might not, and yet part of her felt certain that he did. Or did he dine every Sunday night out of friendship for Hugo? That was ridiculous. New aspects of the situation, new considerations arising from the admission she had made to herself in the train at Pangbourne, presented themselves every moment. She had come to no conclusion when she heard the bang of a taxi door, and the click of the front door opening. She went out on to the landing and saw down the tiny staircase the top of Hugo's head, and the short thick wavy hair through which she had so often run her fingers.

Before she knew what had happened she was in his arms. This physical contact, without any further effort on her part, helped to settle her mind for her. It engulfed thought in sensation and sensation seemed the only reality. The current was switched again along neglected wires. All that she had thought about loving Pat more than Hugo appeared only a figment of the imagination. Pat was only a very good friend. She exclaimed more than once to Hugo within the next ten minutes, as if her relief were really inexpressible:

"Oh, I am so glad you are back." To which he replied affectionately:

"Good old girl."

There are some misunderstandings which one conceives about another's feelings which, if they were revealed, would make one wish to die of shame. Lucinda believed that her idea that Pat loved her was one of these misconceptions. She was so convinced of this that she was able to announce quite naturally to Hugo that Pat was dining with them that evening.

"Good," said Hugo. "Has he been looking after you?"

"He has dined here occasionally—generally on Sundays. I lunched with him one day at a restaurant."

She felt a great relief that she was able to tell all this so calmly to Hugo. She put all the fears and ecstatic hopes of the earlier part of the day down to the state of her nerves. They were dispelled by the sane happiness of having Hugo with her again. Yet she was a little uneasy at her own instability—that she was able to change so quickly, even if the whole process had only occurred in her imagination.

They sat talking through the early part of the afternoon. He was reticent about his experiences and only related a few comic happenings. She told him the family gossip, what there was of it. The most interesting item was the story about Paul, who had returned wounded from France some weeks earlier and was in a hospital in Norfolk. Arthur had been down to see him. Apparently he had been wounded, not at the Front, but, characteristically, in a duel with his company commander, who had insulted a subaltern, fresh from Sandhurst, whom Paul had befriended. The company commander had fired at the ground, but in his nervousness had shot Paul in the foot. Paul had fired over his opponent's head. The affair was hushed up and Paul's name went into the ordinary casualty lists. Paul thought his wound very honorable.

Hugo laughed at this story.

"They say it will leave him with a limp," said Lucinda.

"Bad luck," said Hugo. "Still, it'll keep him at home for a bit. Paul's not the sort of feller to be at a war."

She also told Hugo about Bill's engagement.

"Professor's daughter—spectacles and straight hair, eh?"

"Oh no, she's lovely," Lucinda protested.

"Good," said Hugo.

Before dinner they walked down to Cadogan Place to see Arthur and Marian, who catechised Hugo about the conduct of the war from the angle of the serving soldier. Arthur, who was talking to Lucinda, stopped to listen to his replies with that deference which he always showed to the opinion of anybody he thought competent to give one.

Pat was barely in time for dinner. He came in uniform, straight from the War Office. As he came into the little gray and yellow drawing-room at Wellington Court he was eager and apologetic, but when he saw Hugo standing pink and clean in his boiled shirt and black tie the expression was wiped off his face.

"Well, I'm blowed!" he exclaimed and shook hands with Hugo.

Lucinda had the feeling that Hugo's presence had somehow resolved Pat's attitude, as it had, earlier in the day, her own. The relationship between them at Crowborough, Pat's friendship for both of them, tinged with innocent gallantry towards herself, seemed to have been re-established. Hugo said:

"I hear you've been looking after my wife. Not too well I hope."

Lucinda and Pat smiled without embarrassment, and Kate announced dinner. Later when Lucinda left the two men with their port, she said to Pat:

"Don't let him stay too long. I've just got him back."

As soon as she had said this she thought it sounded false and affected. She waited rather uneasily in the drawing-room, with the sensations of a person who has made a gaff. These feelings were aggravated when Pat and Hugo came up, as Pat's mood had quite changed. He appeared preoccupied and almost fidgety. He suggested that they should go to a play or a night club, but Hugo said they could go tomorrow night. He wanted to experience first the comforts of home. He pulled out a card table and they played poker.

Once when Hugo turned to reach the cigarette box Pat gave her a look so penetrating and expressive that her heart began to beat more rapidly, though she could not make out what he wanted to convey. He had very bad luck with his cards and lost steadily. Hugo put his mood down to this and said jocularly:

"You haven't got a poker face, my boy."

Lucinda knew that it was not his cards that disturbed him. While Hugo was dealing he took out an engagement book and made a note in it. Then he tore out the page.

"There are so many things I have to remember," he explained.

As he was leaving he slipped the folded paper from his book into her hand. She was afraid, and bothered what to do with it. While Hugo was showing him out she glanced at it hurriedly.

"I must see you *alone* as soon as possible," she read. She puckered her forehead, and then slipped it with the money which she had won at poker into her handbag.

"Well, old girl, bedtime," said Hugo, as he came back into the drawing-room. He gave her a hearty hug. She was not as happy as she had expected to be.

The next morning they went shopping. Hugo had an appointment with his tailor, and Lucinda left him in Conduit Street, arranging to meet in twenty minutes at Aspreys, where she was to buy a present for Susannah's birthday on Friday. She at once looked about for a public telephone, and when she found one she rang up Pat at the War Office. When she heard his voice answering she said:

"It's Lucinda. I'm ringing up from a public telephone. What did you want to say to me?"

"I can't tell you over the telephone. When can we meet?"

"I thought we were going to dance somewhere this evening. Hugo said that you were going to bring a partner."

"I'm not," he answered gruffly. "The present situation is intolerable."

She did not reply at once. This was the first admission that there was a situation between them. She knew for certain that she had not imagined it all. When she spoke again the tone of her voice had changed. It was lower and softer.

"I don't see how we can meet alone while Hugo is on leave."

She heard some interruption at the other end, and Pat said:

"The general wants me. Take care of yourself, my dear."

The tenderness with which he spoke was unmistakable, even over the telephone. When she came out into the street she was so disturbed by the implications of this conversation that for a moment she could not think what she was doing. When an attendant spoke to her in Aspreys she seemed to come out of a trance, as she said vaguely:

"Oh, I want a birthday present."

She gave almost senseless replies to the man, who brought out some little enamel stamp-boxes for her inspection. She had made no choice by the time Hugo joined her.

"Have you got what you want?" he asked.

"Yes. I'll have this one." She pushed a blue and silver box towards the shopman. "I'll take it with me." The box was rather expensive. Hugo, with that satisfaction which he showed at the evidences of her having money, watched her count out the notes to pay for the box.

"We're doing Susannah proud," he said.

In Bond Street he suggested that they should go to some public place for tea.

"I want to see people all dressed up, after months of khaki and French tarts in widows' weeds."

They turned in the direction of Claridges. At the corner of Brook Street they ran into Winnie Greene-James wearing uniform.

"Good God!" exclaimed Hugo. "What are you, a female field marshal?"

"I'm a W.A.A.C.," said Winnie, "having a marvelous time." She nodded to Lucinda and said, "How are you?"

"Come and have tea with us," said Hugo. "Though I prefer women in pretty clothes."

"That's very unpatriotic of you, and not very gallant either."

Hugo and Winnie continued their crude adolescent badinage down Brook Street. Lucinda walked in silence, glad to have time to compose herself.

In Claridges they sat under a suspended basket of hydrangeas. Hugo and Winnie still held the conversation, such as it was. A woman whose pearls and paradise feathers were if anything more festive than Susannah's passed their table. Her eyes rested a moment on Lucinda, who recognized her as a Mrs Galway, a rich Melbourne woman who had come to live in London a few years before the war, where, through the ruthless exercise of wealth, wit and impudence, helped by slight aristocratic connections, she had inserted herself into the highest society and even entertained minor royalties. She had also a beautiful voice, and a charm of manner which she put on when she addressed people of importance. She stopped and said to Lucinda:

"You must excuse me, but aren't you Lucinda Vane? I knew you in Melbourne, though I don't suppose you remember me."

"Yes. You are Mrs Galway."

"How clever of you to remember."

"Won't you have tea with us? This is my husband, Major Brayford—Miss Greene-James."

It appeared that Mrs Galway knew a number of Hugo's friends. She was also acquainted with Susannah and had known Rosie. Winnie was surprised that anyone so *mondaine* as Mrs Galway should have come from Melbourne, and practically said as much. Mrs Galway's retort was to ask her with appalling insolence, "Do you work in a stable?" and then to ignore her, while to Hugo she gave a rather scurrilous résumé of the morals of their mutual friends. Hugo enjoyed this conversation, and when Mrs Galway invited them to dinner, on an evening later in the week, he accepted at once. Mrs Galway rose to go. She said to Hugo and Lucinda, "Then I'll see you on Friday." To Winnie she gave a malicious grin and wished her "Good huntin'!"

Lucinda disliked intensely the tone of Mrs Galway's conversation. It made what might be innocent friendship appear an intrigue, and what was not innocent appear sordid. She imagined what Mrs Galway might say about herself and Pat. On the way back to Wellington Court she wondered how innocent it was, and gave distracted replies to Hugo's observations. When they arrived home Kate gave them a telephone message from Colonel Lanfranc, saying that he could not dine tonight as he had to leave suddenly for Northumberland on duty, and would not be back for a week. Hugo was annoyed. She had only twice before known him to show so much vexation—once with the man who had offered him postcards in the Sydney express, and when she had let Arthur and Marian discover his gambling debts, but that had been by letter.

"How in the devil are we going to make up another party at the last minute?" he demanded. "He said he'd bring a partner."

Hugo wanted to cram as much pleasure as possible into his week's leave. They went to plays or danced every evening, and lunched and dined out more often than at home. Lucinda quite enjoyed this sudden burst of liveliness, and it did not give her much time to think about Pat. Towards the end of the week she had a cable from Julie:

"You must keep this cable entirely secret. You must stop Bill's and Anne's marriage by any means. It is a matter of life and death. Please believe me. Do anything. Please trust your loving mother. It must not happen. Reply to Watteau. Am staying with her."

Lucinda stared at the cable and turned it over, examining it as if she expected to find it a silly hoax. She had just dressed for the dinner with Mrs Galway, and was waiting for Hugo to come down when the cable arrived. Apart from the injunction of secrecy, she would not have wanted to show it to Hugo, as she was afraid it disclosed some idiotic snobbery of Julie's, for which he could only have contempt. She slipped it into her handbag, where it lay beside Pat's note, asking to see her alone.

In the taxi on the way to Claridges she was conscious of these two pieces of paper in her bag. They seemed to her like two bulky and guilty documents. She tried to think what Julie's cable could possibly mean. Why on earth was she staying with Watteau? At the beginning of the war Watteau had left Tourella and had returned to her home in the valley, of which she had recovered the tenancy. It was unlikely that Julie would visit her for more than a patronizing cup of tea, and yet she said she was staying there. Lucinda was determined that she would in no way interfere between Bill and Anne. It would be a crime. But what could Julie mean?

Mrs Galway's other guests were a young guardee and his wife and an oldish duke, a widower who had not remarried. At first the conversation was conventionally well-bred, but, towards the end of dinner the duke began to tell *risqué* stories in a rather sniggeringly adolescent manner. The guardee, with an almost expressionless face, capped the duke's stories with others in the same genre. Mrs Galway evidently thought the party a great success. Hugo did not appear to enjoy the stories very much, but he had fixed ideas about the respect due to one's hostess and to a duke, and he smiled adequately, but when possible he talked of other things to the wife of the guardee.

They went on to a night club. Mrs Galway danced with the duke. Lucinda thought they were horrible together. When they were all at the supper table she opened her bag to take out her handkerchief and saw the two pieces of paper side by side. Mrs Galway remarked on the fine needlework of the bag and asked to see it. Lucinda snapped it shut before handing it to her.

"It's all right," said Mrs Galway with her malicious smile, "I shan't pry into your secrets."

"My wife has no secrets," said Hugo confidently.

"Every woman has secrets," retorted Mrs Galway.

It was after midnight. Lucinda was so tired and overwrought

that she thought Mrs Galway must have seen the two notes in her bag and sensed their significance. Mrs Galway again began her scurrilous gossip. Hugo, although he did not care for the *risqué* stories, appeared to enjoy this. They had all drunk a good deal of champagne, and were willing to accept the most fantastic tales—at least they sounded fantastic to Lucinda. She did not believe that people in good society could have the vices Mrs Galway attributed to them. Yet because she could not believe this, she felt middle-class and provincial. When she returned home she had the uneasiness of a person whose view of life has been clouded.

In the morning she read Julie's cable again, trying to discover what lay behind it, but she was unable to do so. She could only think that either Julie was intoxicated with snobbery, and would only be content for Bill to marry into the aristocracy, or else she had some ancient quarrel with Mrs Maitland—but it was very unlike Julie to keep up a quarrel. She was far more given to emotional reconciliations. She put the cable back in her bag, beside Pat's note. She would think what to do about it next week.

Bill and Anne came to London for the week-end. Bill was staying at the Hyde Park Hotel and Anne in Trevor Square with the Misses Lanfranc. They all lunched with Arthur and Marian on Sunday. Bill was ridiculously happy. Before luncheon he stood talking to Lucinda, and glancing across every now and then to where Arthur was paying compliments to Anne.

"Everybody's behaving marvelously," he said. "It's ripping of Lady Crittenden to ask us to lunch. Your cable to the family worked all right. Look." He took a folded paper from his mammoth cigarette case and handed it to Lucinda. It was a cable form similar to the one in her bag, but on it was written:

"All delighted. Congratulations and best love from Mum and Dad. Go to Mr Davis for money."

Lucinda was more than ever bewildered by Julie's cable. She decided to burn it at the first opportunity and then to forget it. The kindest thing was to treat it as an aberration. She knew that Julie was not very sensible nor very scrupulous where her social ambitions were concerned.

"I've bought the ring," said Bill. "Come and look at it." He took her across to Anne and said to Arthur, "Do you mind, sir, if I show Lucinda Anne's ring?"

Arthur laughed and said, "I see I must not monopolize all the beauty."

At luncheon Bill, even more than Anne, was the focus of attention. He said, "I think I'm the luckiest man in the world," and everybody laughed. He joined in the laughter and added, "Well, I am, all the same." Hugo chaffed him mildly, and even Marian was so affected by the general good spirits that she forgot to talk about the Asquiths and the war.

Lucinda could not help comparing the atmosphere of this luncheon with that of Mrs Galway's dinner. Here everything was open and friendly and fundamentally decent. She resolved that she would have no further contact with Mrs Galway and her kind. Then she remembered the two notes in her handbag. About Julie's she had made up her mind—but what was she to do about Pat's? An anxious look came into her eyes. Marian noticed it as they went back to the drawing-room, and she asked her if she were quite well. Marian was not over-imaginative, but to her Lucinda had for that brief moment appeared as might someone who recognizes the first faint twinge of the disease from which he will die.

In the afternoon the Brayfords went back with Bill and Anne to Miss Lanfranc's Sunday afternoon party. There were a number of Australians there, and it was rather like walking suddenly out of Knightsbridge into Toorak. They all congratulated Bill, and some old friends who had not seen her since her marriage were particularly nice to Lucinda. Although no one could be simpler in themselves than Arthur and Marian, the circumstances of their life complicated their approach to the outside world. These Australians seemed to Lucinda to have a delightful simplicity, a natural friendliness, to which for a moment she longed to return. Someone asked after Julie, and spoke of her affectionately. These were the people with whom Lucinda had so often seen her mother, bustling and a little self-important, but fundamentally kind and generous.

"She's very well, I think," said Lucinda. "She's staying with Miss Watson." Bill overheard this and exclaimed:

"Mum's staying with Watteau?"

"I mean she's been to see her," said Lucinda, annoyed at her own indiscretion.

"She didn't tell me," said Bill.

Lucinda again remembered the two notes in her bag. An explanation of the cable suddenly occurred to her. Old maids often became peculiar, and Watteau, although she was a dear, did occasionally have a malignant glint in her eye. Was it possible that she had made up the cable herself? She adored Bill and might have been moved by some preposterous jealousy. Living alone in that remote country place after all the social activity of Tourella, her brain might easily become fertile with miasmatic plots. Lucinda seized on this explanation with relief, and was ashamed that she had ever thought that

Julie had sent it. To make up a little for this she spoke of her mother with the greatest admiration and affection, and said that she hoped to see her as soon as the war was over. When they rose to go Lucinda said to Miss Lanfranc:

"Hugo's leave ends on Tuesday, so I shall be back at the Red Cross on Wednesday morning."

Hugo looked a little solemn and said:

"As a matter of fact, Lucie, I find I have to return tomorrow."

"Oh!" said Lucinda flatly, "I didn't know. Then I'll come on Tuesday."

The Brayfords as they left were the center of attention. It was thought rather brutal of Hugo to make this announcement to Lucinda in public. When they arrived back at Wellington Court, before they went up to change—they were going to dine with Susannah—Lucinda tore the cable up into little pieces and put it in the basket. She had decided that the Watteau explanation was the correct one, and that she need give it no more thought. Pat's note she kept in her bag.

Hugo left the next afternoon. He asked Lucinda not to come to see him off at the train, and they said good-bye in the little gray and yellow drawing-room, while he was waiting for the taxi. Hugo held her in his arms and said, "Take care of yourself, old girl. Get about a bit. Don't sit at home moping."

Lucinda could not speak. Hugo's presence gave her the same sense of security which she had felt in the early days of their marriage before the incident of the overdraft. The matter-of-fact way in which he returned to the terrible dangers of the Front filled her with admiration for him, and she felt that when he was gone she would be exposed to the uncertainties and weakness of her own nature.

"Oh, I wish you didn't have to go," she cried.

"I'd be a poor soldier if I didn't," he replied. This was the only time she ever heard him make any reference to his duty and she thought how extraordinarily well-bred he was, and was thankful that she was married to a man who observed so punctiliously the code of a gentleman, so that she knew, for example, that she could leave her handbag lying about containing any secret notes and he would not dream of opening it. She repeated:

"Still I wish you didn't have to go."

She watched the taxi turn into Knightsbridge, and then went back to the drawing-room. Although there was no visible sign of his occupation, the room for her had a strong feeling of Hugo's recent presence. By tomorrow, she knew, this would have faded, and in a few days it would be gone. She stood by the open window, looking across Rotten Row—where some Australian soldiers were riding—to the leafy shades of the park.

She heard Stephen's cheerful prattle on the stairs as he was being taken down for his afternoon walk. She went out on to the landing, and called down to where he was being strapped into his go-cart:

"Wait a minute, Nannie. I'll take him today."

Stephen was delighted to have Lucinda wheeling him. He was always a sweet-tempered child, but today a new kind of high spirits descended on him, or welled up in him. It was hard to say which it was. A leaf fell from a tree and blew lightly into his face. He started, but went into fits of laughter when he saw what had touched him. This happy innocence of his spirit filled her with compassionate love. She wondered whether it was a positive thing, brought "not in entire forgetfulness" from some other world, or whether it was merely an absence of knowledge of the sordid griefs and doubts of this world. While she was alone with him she felt that Wordsworth's ode was true, and that walking beneath the trees and across the sunlit grass of the park they were enclosed in some space where their spirits moved freely together in light. Long afterwards she remembered this afternoon as itself a space of light in a long stretch of shadow, like one of those pools of light which they traversed as they walked beneath the trees.

CHAPTER SIX

WHEN SHE CAME back to the house she found a message for her to ring up Pat at the War Office. At once all the feeling of tranquil love left her. The expression of her face as Kate gave her this message somehow upset Stephen, and he cried as he was taken upstairs. Her heart beat rapidly as she asked for Pat's number. When he heard Lucinda's voice he said, "Can I see you soon?"

"When?" She hoped he would not say tonight. She did not feel prepared to meet him, and she thought it would be unwise for him to dine the very night Hugo left. "Hugo went back today," she added.

"Yes, I know. I saw him," said Pat. His voice sounded grim. "Tonight I have to dine with the general. Are you free tomorrow evening?"

"Very well. Where shall we dine?"

"Can you give me dinner there? I want to talk."

"All right."

"Till tomorrow then. Good-bye, my dear."

"Good-bye," she said, and clicked down the receiver.

All the next day she was in a state of nervous tension. She went to the Red Cross in the afternoon and tied up parcels, but she gave hardly intelligible replies to Miss Lanfranc's conversation. This was put down to her depression at Hugo's return to France, but she was wondering what Pat wanted to say to her when they were alone. If he wanted to make love to her she would not know how to respond. She knew that tacitly, almost unconsciously, she had encouraged him, but Hugo's visit had made the whole idea even of a sentimental friendship with Pat unwelcome to her. But she felt that he had something to tell her more serious, and even more unwelcome, than a declaration of love.

Pat again came in uniform, straight from the War Office. He apologized to Lucinda for not having changed.

"I would have had time, but I wanted to see you as soon as possible," he said.

"What is it that you want to tell me?"

"We'll wait till after dinner. Then we shan't be interrupted."

During dinner her tension relaxed, and talking about ordinary things they dropped into their former easy relationship. Lucinda felt that the discussion ahead would be no more awkward than if it had to do with some ordinary domestic problem.

When they were back in the drawing-room, and Kate had taken away the coffee-cups, he came over and sat beside her on the sofa. He took her hands and said quietly:

"Lucinda, you know that I love you."

She hesitated before she replied, "I don't think you ought to tell me just as Hugo has gone back to France."

"That's what's brought it to a head—Hugo's coming on leave, I mean. That's why I had to see you. How much do you care for Hugo?"

"Quite a lot. I wish he hadn't gone back. I don't mean because he's gone into danger. I mean because I didn't want him to go away."

"Would you feel the same about him if you knew that he was unfaithful to you?"

"It's difficult to say. Of course it would affect my feelings for him very much."

"Would you be prepared to let him go?"

"I don't suppose that I should try to hold anyone against his will."

"If you were free, do you think you would accept my love?"

"Yes, I think I would."

"Good."

He stood up and went over to the fireplace, where he examined the little French clock. Then he turned and looked down at her.

"They say all's fair in love and war," he said. "I don't believe it, but if the other side doesn't play fair it makes one's own course more difficult. The trouble is that Hugo is not really 'the other side' to me. We've been friends for years."

"Yes. Go on," said Lucinda as he hesitated.

"Have you ever met Mrs Fabian Parker?"

"I've seen her once or twice, at Burlingham and other places."

"She was Hugo's mistress before he went to Australia." He looked at her with an odd mixture of ruthlessness and concern to see how she took this disclosure. "I wouldn't tell you this if he had given her up. He saw a good deal of her before Stephen was born. He was with her once at the Ritz when he ran into your mother. He at once fetched me round to pretend she was my friend and to get him out of a hole. When he found you were at Oxford he spent the first night of his leave with her. He wanted me to bring her last Tuesday to make up a *partie carrée* to go to dance somewhere, so that he could associate respectably with her under your nose. He asked me here, after dinner. That was why I wrote you that note. I wanted to stop it at once. As I couldn't I went away till Hugo had gone back to France. Yesterday afternoon, just before I rang you up, I was at Victoria Station. I saw Mrs Fabian Parker in a pullman in the Brighton train. She was obviously looking out for somebody, and then Hugo came and joined her. He did not go back to France yesterday. He went to Brighton for the last night of his ten days' leave."

There was a long silence. Pat continued to stand by the mantelpiece. Now and then he gave her an anxious glance.

"I didn't want to hurt you, telling you this, Lucinda my dear," he said, "but it was a necessary operation, and afterwards you'll be happier with me."

"Why didn't he marry her in the first place?" Lucinda asked in a calm but puzzled voice. "She must have far more money than I have."

"Fabian Parker was a flinty old devil. She loses the lot if she marries again."

They exchanged a few almost disinterested comments on the

relationship between Hugo and Mrs Fabian Parker. Lucinda stood up.

"I'm sorry, Pat," she said. "I can't take it in properly—all the implications. I'm really terribly tired. I can't say anything to you—not while I'm in this state. You see, yesterday I thought I loved Hugo as much as ever. I can't suddenly turn round in a day. It is too unstable. And yet what you've told me hasn't hurt me very much. I think because really I knew it all the time. I must try to get some sleep, and let all the things that are boiling in my mind settle down. Perhaps in the morning they'll seem clearer. I've been worried for days, but my worries have been intangible. Now at least one of them is clearly stated. Could we meet again in a day or two—say on Thursday?"

She held out her hand to him. He kissed it and they exchanged a glance which satisfied him.

The morning light clarified, but did not alter Lucinda's view of the situation. It convinced her that she had known for a long time that Hugo was unfaithful to her—ever since that morning at Crittenden when she had been helping Marian strip the lavender, and seeing the name in *The Times* had asked, "Who is Mrs Fabian Parker?" She doubted whether Hugo had ever felt for her more than mild affection and physical attraction, and her own feeling for him, after her first infatuation for this resplendent young creature with his almost princely background—it would be humbug to pretend that she had not been influenced by that, just as it would be to pretend that Hugo had not been influenced by her money—had died down to the same thing. She felt an intense relief as she admitted these things to herself. She was also indignant, and the more she reviewed her marriage the stronger became her indignation. Hugo had simply used her as a banker and a bedfellow. In this ruthless mood of tearing the cobwebs from her eyes, she saw everything in hard lines which were as unreal as her former misty vision. Even the times when she had thought they were happy together, as in the house in South Yarra and at Crowborough, she now saw in retrospect as a fool's paradise, while when one of those moments of extreme happiness, of almost ecstasy, such as that noonday on the Christmas Hills, flickered in her memory, she shut it out, so that her ruthless honesty was not complete, like that of so many people who pride themselves on clarity of vision, but who shut out from their sight all that is not brutal, vindictive and coarse.

On Thursday afternoon she had a second cable from Julie:

"Did you get my cable? Reply to Watteau. Urgent. Love. Mother."

The effect of this was to increase Lucinda's indignation. She had to abandon the explanation that it was all a plot of Watteau's. For one thing Watteau would never put "Love" in a cable. She did not now try to think of any explanation, except that Julie did not consider Anne grand enough. She quite unjustly blamed Julie for her own marriage. She saw Julie in the Radcliffes' ballroom, talking excitedly to Hugo and inviting him to Tourella, and she had taken a house at Macedon to be near Government Cottage where Hugo was staying. Lucinda did not remember her own state at the time, that she would have been upset if Julie had not done these things, and that if her parents had objected to Hugo she would readily have run off with him.

It was wicked, she told herself, of old people to interfere with the love affairs of their children. Anyhow, this time she was not going to be fooled. She was going to manage her own life. As for the cable, she replied:

"Had your cable. Interference impossible. Have done nothing. Anne entirely eligible and delightful."

She had an impulse to send this to Tourella and risk exposing the whole plot, whatever it was, but her natural kindness and a latent feeling that there might be some serious reason for sending it to Watteau prevented her. Relenting a little more, she thought it sounded too abrupt, and she added, "Love, Lucinda."

She was in an excited and rather reckless state when Pat arrived on Thursday evening. She told him all she had been thinking since she saw him last.

"I see it now. Hugo has simply exploited me," she said. "I have no obligation towards him."

They spent the evening discussing the technicalities of divorce. At last they decided that Lucinda should write to Hugo, and they composed the letter together. She told him that she knew of his relationship with Mrs Fabian Parker, and that he had not returned to France on Monday, but had gone away with Mrs Parker. Presumably he would not wish to return to her and she would institute divorce proceedings.

While they talked of these things they had a sense of being close together, of their fates being identified, but they displayed no tenderness nor emotion. When the letter had been composed, addressed and stamped, they turned and looked at each other with faintly troubled smiles. They sat for a little while silently holding hands, and then he left. He knew that she wanted to be free of the idea of herself as Hugo's wife before he spoke of his own feelings, and she was grateful for his restraint.

The next day Mrs Galway rang her up and invited her to luncheon on Sunday. Lucinda said that she was very sorry, but she was engaged on Sunday. Mrs Galway suggested Tuesday.

"I go to work at the Red Cross immediately after lunch on Tuesday," said Lucinda. The excuse was so feeble that she hoped Mrs Galway would be put off, but over-sensitiveness was not one of this lady's failings.

"Which day can you come? You mustn't mope just because that handsome husband of yours has gone away."

"Well, I could manage Tuesday if I could leave early."

"We'll see about that when you come. Tuesday then," said Mrs Galway.

Lucinda was annoyed with herself for accepting the invitation. She could not think why Mrs Galway should be so persistent. Lucinda had found that women seemed to like her, but they were mostly older women like Marian and Miss Lanfranc. She had no close friend of her own age. Perhaps it was because she had never been to school.

She hoped that Mrs Galway was not going to seek her out. Her friends, though exalted in rank, seemed to be a little tarnished and she might want, through Lucinda, to become intimate with solidly respectable country people like Arthur and Marian. When Mrs Galway discovered that Lucinda was divorcing Hugo she would drop her again. Lucinda did not give much thought to that sort of thing, but she did not care for the idea of being dropped by Mrs Galway. She would feel rather as Paul might feel if he were cut by a business man, if he ever allowed himself to know one.

There were six people at the luncheon. Mrs Galway appeared to prefer those who were either very grand or very young. There were the duke, a Melbourne boy of nineteen who was a subaltern in an English regiment, and a Scottish viscount and his wife. Only a few months ago, while these two were entertaining a large house party in the Highlands, the viscount had been cited as corespondent by a middle-class husband, and the case had been given some publicity. Lucinda remembered marveling at the sang-froid necessary to carry off such a situation, when his guests came down and opened their newspapers. She had also wondered what had happened to the unfortunate wife. Now, meeting this man gave her a qualm. Pat had said that Hugo would not refuse her a divorce, but this viscount illustrated the fact that where people's position or class security was concerned they did not always behave, nor would their associates expect them to behave, with the strictest honor.

Lucinda apologized and, explaining that she had to go to the Red

Cross, left early. Mrs Galway was annoyed and said good-bye with a rudeness which startled her other guests. She did not mind salacious scandals, but she was genuinely shocked at Lucinda's leaving before a viscountess. Also Lucinda, although her clothes were very good, was at this time not always smartly dressed. When she was happy she was apt to buy things just because they were pretty, and with these would impair the otherwise perfect taste of her turn-out. When she was unhappy, for some reason she gave far more attention to her clothing, and appeared unmistakably a *femme du monde*. Today, being reluctant to lunch with Mrs Galway, she had not changed from the dress in which she had been shopping at Harrods. Then, feeling she was too dowdy to lunch at Claridges, she had pinned in her hat one of those unfortunate brooches which she had bought in a happy moment. She knew it looked wrong, but she was already late, and she was too disturbed about more important things to care.

The subaltern left with her, and asked if he might walk with her as far as Park Lane. While she waited for him to go down to fetch his hat and stick she thought, with a mixture of chagrin and relief, "Well, that's finished me with Mrs Galway."

The subaltern appeared to be extremely pleased at having lunched in the company of a duke. All the way along Brook Street he praised the manners of the aristocracy. He did not leave Lucinda at Park Lane, but walked with her to Knightsbridge, continuing the theme with variations and expressing naïve delight with everything English. She was faintly amused and did not give very attentive replies, but when at last he left her he said with an anxious friendliness which she found touching:

"Shall we meet again?"

He was looking at her eagerly, and she recognized in his eyes all that wonder at a new world, all that hopefulness which she had felt when she first came to England. She realized that she was no longer very young. She was at any rate past the age at which people found naïveté amusing.

This realization had a curious effect on her. She had a sense of loss, of being to some extent defenseless, now that she had not the excuse and protection of absolute youth. She invited the subaltern to call, and gave him her address in Wellington Court. It turned out that he knew Miss Lanfranc, and, hardly knowing what she was doing, she said she would be there next Sunday.

In Knightsbridge she met Susannah, who greeted her affectionately. Lucinda was reserved in her response, as she thought if she were not, Susannah, when she discovered that she was divorcing

Hugo, would think her a humbug. For something to say she asked: "Does this brooch look awful in my hat?"

"No. It's quite pretty," said Susannah. "Where have you been?"

"I've been lunching with Mrs Galway at Claridges."

"Oh!" Susannah looked doubtful.

"I thought I wasn't smart enough," said Lucinda, smiling.

"One should always be smart," said Susannah. "It's a great protection. But the war makes everything so difficult."

"I may need protection," said Lucinda.

"What do you mean?" asked Susannah. "Oh, there's a taxi. I never thought I should have to use taxis. This horrible war."

She hailed the cab, which drew up to the curb.

"Good-bye, my dear. Come and see me soon. And don't forget, always be smart."

Lucinda went into a large shop, and in a deserted corner she took the brooch out of her hat. She then went to Wilton Crescent to tie up parcels for the prisoners of war. It was possible, she thought, that this odd, disjointed encounter with Susannah might be the last time she would see her to speak to. While she tied up the parcels of tinned food and tobacco, the sense of a kind of disintegration in her life possessed her. She gave absent-minded replies to Miss Lanfranc, who was discussing Mr Straker, explaining that he could not possibly be a gentleman.

The next morning, on Lucinda's early tea-tray was a letter from Hugo. Her heart beat violently, and she was afraid to raise herself to pour out the tea lest the maid should notice her agitation. She waited until Kate had left the room before opening the envelope. She had been unable to foresee what Hugo would say, but its contents amazed her. He described the Channel crossing, told her to look after herself and said that he expected to be "pretty busy" for the next week or two, and only referred to her letter in a postscript:

"P.S. With regard to your request I have no intention of making it possible for you to divorce me. I very much regret the incident of which you complain, and cannot understand how you know of it. I think it would be better if we did not refer to this matter again."

Lucinda was bewildered by this effrontery. She had not thought it possible that people could behave in this fashion, and yet she had had an inkling of it, and not only from Hugo. The Scottish viscount whom she had met yesterday must have said something of the kind to his wife, when he was cited as corespondent. The world was entirely different from what she had imagined it to be. Hugo was like some tough leather surface against which one beat one's hands without scratching them or breaking any bones, but without evoking any response.

Lucinda, when she had drunk a cup of tea, immediately rang up Pat, to catch him at his rooms before he left for the War Office. When she told him that Hugo would not agree to a divorce he did not answer at once. Then he asked:

"How soon can I see you? This evening?"

"This evening I'm dining with Arthur and Marian."

"Could I come round afterwards? Or would that be too late?"

"I suppose it would rather," said Lucinda doubtfully. "But I must see you soon. Could we lunch together?"

"I'm lunching with the general. Why don't you come round here? We could talk undisturbed."

"When?"

"Tonight when you leave the Crittendens'."

Lucinda did not answer for a moment. Then she said, "Very well. I'll come at about half-past ten."

When Marian had asked her to dine this evening Lucinda had tried to excuse herself. She did not think it likely that Hugo had mentioned when writing to Arthur her request for a divorce, but she felt it best to make sure. It would be dreadful to turn up for dinner at Cadogan Place and be greeted with chilly politeness. She felt in some way a humbug for going there at all, especially now, when she had made this appointment with Pat. Or was it an assignation? If Marian knew that she was going on to Pat's rooms, that was the name she would give it. Pat's voice had sounded quite natural when he suggested it, but she wondered if he too intended it as an assignation. She now felt so at sea in trying to estimate what people thought or how they would behave, that she had no idea how the Brayfords would react to her attempt at divorce, if it were known. She was most concerned about Marian. Susannah would still probably drop in occasionally before dinner to tell her the family gossip, while Marian, if they came face to face in Sloane Street, would think that every word they exchanged was an extension of adultery, or a betrayal of Crittenden solidarity. It was strange that the maintenance of an artificial enmity could be a sign of virtue. She rang up Marian, who at the other end of the telephone said crossly:

"Don't tell me that you can't dine this evening. The Bassingbournes are coming, and I have a pair of fowls up from Crittenden."

"No. I just rang up to make sure that you were expecting me."

"Of course. Didn't you write it down?"

"No."

"If I didn't write down my engagements I should be in chaos."

"Has Arthur heard from Hugo?"

"No. Why? Have you?"

"Yes. I had a letter this morning."

"Is he all right?"

"Yes—quite, I think."

"You sound doubtful. Well, my dear, I'll see you this evening—eight fifteen or half-past."

By a quarter past eight, when she arrived at Cadogan Place, Lucinda's brain was exhausted with dwelling on uncertainties. In the afternoon at the Red Cross she had tried to distract her mind from its whirling speculation, and to think of the men for whom she tied up the parcels. She found it less disturbing to contemplate unhappiness than cheerfulness, and she closed her ears to the gossip of Miss Lanfranc and the other women at her table. One could be, she thought, the prisoner of circumstances, as much confined as behind barbed-wire, or in some grim castle in Silesia or Württemberg. If Hugo persisted in refusing a divorce, which was only too likely, she was no more free to do what she wanted than the men for whom she had tied up these parcels. In the mood she was in at present all the privileges she enjoyed seemed nothing to her, compared with the freedom to accept Pat's love. The uncertainty of her own life at the moment was unbearable. If Pat were to persuade her to break with Hugo and herself be divorced, nearly every tie she had formed would be broken, and her life would arrange itself in an entirely new pattern. She did not even know whether Pat would want her to do this, but if he did not he would hardly have asked her to go to his rooms. He might want her to make the break at once. Perhaps this night the whole future course of her life was to be decided, even the kind of person she was to become. It was as if her whole character and even physical appearance were in the melting-pot. In thirty years' time, if she were to be divorced and to marry Pat, when she came into a room the people there would see in that Mrs Lanfranc someone very different, both physically and in every tract of her emotional nature, from the woman she would be if she were then still Mrs Brayford. She saw herself in this problematical future as she had seen a certain type of woman in society, women whose husbands were notoriously unfaithful, thin, erect, a hard smile on their mouths, trying to conceal the wretchedness behind pale expressionless eyes. This decision as to her whole future life and being would probably be made this evening.

Now, when she rang the bell at Cadogan Place, she thought that this was probably the last time she would dine with Arthur and

Marian. She hated the idea of losing such good friends for whom she had so strong an affection. The sense of a disintegration of her life, which, though primarily caused by the crisis in her marriage, had also been helped by worrying trivialities such as the luncheon with Mrs Galway and Julie's cables, had become overpowering. She felt on the verge of some kind of collapse, and when she came into the drawing-room and was greeted with ordinary natural affection by Arthur and Marian, she was surprised that they did not read the signs of her moral confusion in her face.

Marian's other guests were Lord and Lady Bassingbourne, and Paul, now convalescent and limping with the aid of a stick. The Bassingbournes were what Marian called "nice" people, and were the sort she invited most to Cadogan Place. They were retiring and very conventional. Lady Bassingbourne had dark lively eyes and a faint moustache.

Lucinda went down with Paul. His wound made him walk slowly, and the little procession which moved with cramped dignity down the rather narrow staircase left them behind.

"How are you, my dear?" said Paul. "You look *un peu épuisée*."

"How are you?" said Lucinda. "That's much more important."

"Not at all. But I'm very well, my wound has at last brought me the respect and consideration to which I am naturally entitled."

"You are lucky if your misfortune brings you respect," said Lucinda.

At the beginning of dinner they talked about what was to happen to Baa. His father had been killed, and the death duties had crippled the estate.

"He'll have to earn his living," said Marian.

"How can an earl earn his living?" demanded Paul indignantly. "It would be highly improper."

"Dolly Wendale had better come back from that hospital of hers on the Riviera and look after him, or the boy will go to the dogs."

"As long as they're hounds it doesn't matter," said Arthur, very pleased at his own wit.

Another item of Crittenden gossip was that Fitzauncell Castle had been sold. Old Miss Fitzauncell had died early in the year.

"Your countryman has bought the castle," Marian said to Lucinda.

"Oh, who is that?"

"Mr Straker."

"Good Heavens!" exclaimed Paul, horrified.

"My sister-in-law is an Australian," Marian explained to Lady Bassingbourne.

"Of course, I know," said Lady Bassingbourne, and she smiled at Lucinda with an expression of admiration and envy, as if nothing in the world could be nicer than to be an Australian.

"Do you know Mr Straker?" asked Lord Bassingbourne.

"No. I don't think I have ever seen him," said Lucinda, "but I saw a picture of him in a newspaper the other day and his face did seem vaguely familiar. I'm sure I've never met him. He's not . . . He's not . . ."

"She's trying to say he's not a gentleman," said Paul.

"Oh!" said Lady Bassingbourne, but very kindly, as if Mr Straker had measles.

"I don't see that that matters," said Marian, "if he is able to get rid of Asquith."

"I think Mr Lloyd George has quite made up for the dreadful things he used to say," said Lady Bassingbourne.

"It matters a great deal," said Paul to Marian. "Our sort understands Europe. The other sort don't. Compare Talleyrand and Napoleon."

"Talleyrand!" exclaimed Marian. "That evil little rat."

"How odd that you should mention Talleyrand," said Lady Bassingbourne. "Once he lived in Kensington Square, only a few doors from our house."

"The idea nowadays," said her husband mildly, "seems to be to bring business men into the government."

"High time too," said Marian.

"England isn't a business," said Paul. "It's a cultural growth— at least all of it that matters—and it would be as unsuitable to have a business man at the head of the country as to have one as Archbishop of Canterbury or conducting the orchestra at Covent Garden."

"Talleyrand's house in Kensington Square has a charming old doorway," said Lady Bassingbourne.

"We must win the war," said Marian.

"*Je ne vois pas la nécessité*," said Paul. "It would be better to stop it, than to win it for the ideas of Harmsworth and Straker. Lord Lansdowne understands that, which shows the importance of being governed by the aristocracy."

Arthur was uneasy and began to talk to Lady Bassingbourne about Rome, where they had met in 1909.

"When are you coming for another drive with me?" he asked, chuckling.

Arthur's drive with Lady Bassingbourne in Rome in 1909 had become a perennial joke, a legend in both their families. Actually what had happened was not sensational. A party from the Embassy had gone for a drive in three or four carriages. Arthur and Lady Bassingbourne had found themselves together in the last one. The coachman, thinking to oblige them, had deliberately lost his way, and they were back late for a big dinner party.

It was discovered that Lucinda had never heard the story of the drive, and did not even know that it had happened.

"Good gracious!" said Arthur. "We can't have one of the family not knowing the story of the drive. You must tell her, Gertrude."

"Oh, I couldn't," said Lady Bassingbourne. "You would do it much better." Her reluctance was easily overcome, and with sparkling eyes she began: "Well, you see, I was late coming down, and there was only one carriage left . . ."

Lucinda listened with a bleak smile to the recital of this incredibly innocent escapade. As the story was being told for her benefit, the others watched either herself or the teller. Arthur and Lord Bassingbourne chuckled at the proper places, while Paul eyed her quizzically. Marian was tolerantly amused. All these people seemed so kind, so blameless, that she felt she was obtaining their kindness under false pretenses, that if they knew what was in her mind they would not sit at the same table with her. Marian's righteousness disturbed her less than the others' friendliness. If Marian knew her intentions she would express herself so viciously that Lucinda would feel justified in retaliation, but Lady Bassingbourne would only say "Oh!" in the same way that she had commented on Mr Straker's not being a gentleman, and would regret perhaps that she had told her the story of the drive.

When she returned to the drawing-room with Marian and Lady Bassingbourne, the respectability of her company and her connections overpowered her. When she remembered that she was to be in Pat's rooms in an hour she felt like someone in a dream, who, while half his conscience slept, has planned some crime which his waking mind repudiates, as if, in fact, she were waking from a dream to normal life. But this did not prevent her from keeping an eye on the clock. Then she realized with dismay that she could not leave before the Bassingbournes. She had been guilty of a similar solecism once already this week, and Marian would be even more shocked than Mrs Galway.

The men seemed to be ages in coming up from the dining-room and the whole tempo of the evening was slow. The Bassingbournes were above all things leisurely. At twenty-past ten Lord Bassingbourne was still talking to Arthur about agriculture, and there was no sign of movement. Lucinda wondered whether she should make the excuse of a headache to get away. She caught sight of herself in a mirror, and was surprised and also relieved to see how unwell she looked. She was sitting beside Lady Bassingbourne who was telling her tales of Hugo's boyhood. She asked her quietly:

"Would you think it dreadfully rude of me if I were to go now. I'm awfully sorry. I don't feel very well."

"My dear, of course not," said Lady Bassingbourne. "Marian, your sister-in-law is unwell."

At once everyone stood up and looked with concern at Lucinda, who smiled deprecatingly. This concentration of attention on herself made her feel openly guilty.

"You're as white as a ghost," said Marian. "You'd better go to bed here and be looked after properly for a few days." Marian always imagined that no one's house was as comfortable as her own.

"Oh no, thank you *very* much, but I'm really all right," said Lucinda. "It's nothing really."

Lucinda gave an appealing glance at Paul.

"I'll come with you," said Paul.

"Oh no," said Lucinda. "I'm making much too much fuss."

At last, at twenty-five minutes past ten, she got away. Marian practically pushed Paul out of the house with her. This meant that if they could not get a taxi they would have to walk slowly because of his limp. Fortunately they found a taxi at once.

"I'll drop you at Knightsbridge," said Paul, "and take the taxi on."

However when they arrived at Wellington Court, he wanted to get out and see her into the house. He was eager to see the gray boiseries.

"No," said Lucinda, putting her hand firmly on his arm, "you've done enough for tonight." She shut the taxi door. She knew that he would think, as she intended him to, that she would not let him come in because of his wound. She was using the wounds of a soldier, as a few minutes earlier she had used the possible danger to her little boy, to conceal her meeting with Pat. A kind of ruthless excitement possessed her, now that at last she was on the verge of a decision. Things which normally would have disturbed her she dismissed from her mind. She waited until Paul's taxi turned into Knightsbridge, and then was about to set out in search of another, when she thought that the servants might have heard the taxi stop at the door and her voice talking to Paul, and wonder why she had not come in. Paul meanwhile was driving up Knightsbridge, reflecting moodily on the fact that twice this evening he had been bossed and pushed by otherwise well-bred women, and wondering why so

182

many women destroyed their attractiveness by behaving like governesses.

Lucinda let herself into the house and found Kate waiting in the hall.

"Oh, madam," she said. "I'm so glad you've come in. Master Stephen's not well."

"What's the matter with him?" Lucinda's exasperation at this fresh trouble made her snap at the young woman.

"He's ate something what upset him," said Kate sulkily.

Lucinda went up to the night-nursery. Nannie met her on the landing.

"He only had a little pain, but he's been sick and he's better now. He was asking for you, so I told Kate to let you know when you came in."

"Oh, is that all?" said Lucinda, and to explain her manner she added, "She gave me a fright."

Stephen was flushed and sleepy. He held out his hand to Lucinda and asked her to stay with him till he went to sleep.

"If you go to sleep quickly, darling," said Lucinda.

"Sing to me," he demanded.

She put her hand gently on his shoulder and sang one of the lullabies which Julie had taught her as a child. She stopped to look at the nursery clock which said ten to eleven.

"Is that clock right?" she asked Nannie.

"It's about right. It may be a minute or two slow."

"Go on singing," said Stephen, but he was nearly asleep, and he did not notice when she took her hand from his shoulder and left the room.

She was now afraid that Pat would think she was not coming. Her five minutes in the nursery had relaxed the tension she had felt all day, but it had not resolved its cause. Her mind was still a tangle but the strings were no longer stretched taut. They had fallen in limp confusion. The impulse she had had to see Pat remained and carried her forward. She had to see him and discuss their relationship and arrive at some certainty, but she felt that the conclusion was no longer likely to be that they would make their lives together. She went into the drawing-room to ring him up and tell him she had been delayed. While she waited to be put through she contemplated the gray and yellow room. Its French elegance, its engravings of Lancret and Fragonard, struck her as over-sophisticated, almost immoral, after the simplicity of the nursery, and even after the nondescript good taste of the Cadogan Place house.

When Pat came to the telephone she said that she was awfully sorry but she had been delayed. She was leaving now, as soon as she could get a taxi.

"Stephen was unwell," she explained.

The mention of Stephen's name made both of them pause. She was aware of its effect in him, even across the telephone. It was almost as if she had committed an error of taste in mentioning it, though it was hardly sensible to think so. This made her feel more dispirited by the time she arrived at Pat's rooms in a cul-de-sac off St James's Street.

Pat opened the door, and led her into his sitting-room, a very masculine-looking room with a tobacco-brown carpet and brownish paintings of race-horses on the parchment-colored walls. She glanced about the room and then gave him a wan smile. Her lifelessness disturbed him.

"You aren't well," he said. He put his arm round her and drew her down beside him on a red leather sofa. He had intended tonight to seal their relationship, to make her feel committed to him for good. He kissed her warmly, but she only received his kisses as a tired person accepts some grateful comfort. He sat back and looked at her curiously.

"We must decide what to do," she said.

"I thought the decision was made—when you agreed to come here."

"I wasn't sure whether you thought that. I thought it was possible, then I wasn't sure. I've been thinking round and round everything and I'm awfully tired. I'm sorry I'm so tired, Pat."

"There's only one thing to do—to make a clean break."

"But the trouble is, it can't be a clean break. There'll be a lot of untidy adhesions hanging loose."

"Better to have 'em loose than tied up to Hugo," he said.

"Hugo would be the clean break, not one of the loose adhesions."

"H'm! Did you come to tell me you can't make the break after all?"

"I came to ask you to sort out my mind for me, and because I wanted to see you dreadfully."

"That answers everything—doesn't it? You know how I would sort out your mind."

"Up to this evening I was prepared to let you do it, and I'm awfully glad that you want to sort it out that way. But that's only being a sort of dog-in-the-manger about you. Up to this evening I was only certain of one thing, that I wanted to be with you, and all the obstacles only made a confusion in my mind, but now, since I became tired, my mind seems clearer."

184

"You're hardly likely to make sound judgments when you're tired."

"You are when your brain is cool, not when it's heated."

"What is in your cool brain?" He smiled and took her hand.

"It's hard not to make other considerations sound not only cool-brained but cool-blooded, but they do exist."

"What considerations? Tell me some."

"The family," said Lucinda. "You see my father has been very generous to us, and my mother was so pleased at my marrying Hugo. It would be an awful blow to them if I were divorced."

"Yes. You don't want to hurt them, but you can't sacrifice your whole life's happiness to avoid a slight wound to their pride."

"Then there are Arthur and Marian. They've been awfully kind to me. I felt awful when I was dining there tonight, as if I were there on false pretenses. I shall hate losing all the associations with Crittenden."

"You prefer Crittenden to me?"

"Oh, no. You know I don't. It's only that I'm putting forward *everything*. I'm really putting all these things forward so that you can brush them aside."

"I can brush 'em aside all right. What else is there?"

"Well then," said Lucinda, "there's Mrs Galway."

"What in the deuce has she got to do with it?"

"I lunched with her yesterday and the conversation was horrible. If I were to be divorced everyone would be talking about me like that."

"I don't think you'd better go out to any more meals," said Pat. He laughed quietly, and she thought how extraordinarily kind he was and how much she loved him. She had never had this feeling of being understood by Hugo. She put her hand up and pushed his hair away from his forehead. He put his arm round her and they sat quietly for some minutes.

"So, you see," he said, "your 'other considerations' don't count. I've swept them aside."

"Those may not count for very much, but there's Stephen."

Again the mention of Stephen's name made them pause. It was, she knew, the real insurmountable difficulty which she kept to the last, postponing the moment when it had to be faced and acknowledged. Pat did not make any comment, and she went on:

"It's odd but I'd forgotten him until I came home from Marian's dinner an hour ago. There was a sort of hiatus in my mind. I don't mean that I'd forgotten his existence, but I'd forgotten that if I were divorced I'd have to give him up. The Brayfords wouldn't dream of letting him go. If Paul doesn't marry he'll inherit. Hugo already calls him 'the fifteenth viscount.' I can't give him up."

"I'd give you another Stephen," said Pat very gently.

"Ah, Pat!" She smiled, protesting and put her hand on his arm.

Again they sank into a silence which seemed tireless. It was long after midnight when she freed herself from his arms and said, " must go."

He went with her. They could not find a taxi, and they walked all the way to Wellington Court. He only left her at the door of her house.

"We haven't decided anything," he said.

"Perhaps I shall be able to make Hugo change his mind." But she spoke without conviction. She thought, and so did Pat, that she would soon become his mistress. She needed a little time to make up her mind, or rather to accustom it to the idea of this. She felt more tranquil as she went up to bed.

The next afternoon, when she came in from the Red Cross she found yet another cable waiting for her. She frowned impatiently as she opened it, but as she read it the mist which had seemed to surround her during past weeks, in which had lurked vague premonitions of a disintegration of her life, was suddenly swept away revealing starkly one of the causes of her fear.

At that moment Stephen came in from his walk in the park. He had been stung by some insect.

"Mummy, why does God make us and then make things to bite us?" he demanded indignantly.

Lucinda, holding the cable in her hand, gave a grim distracted laugh at the appositeness of this question.

"Don't, mummy," said Stephen, "don't laugh."

Lucinda at once sent a reply-paid telegram to Mrs Maitland asking if she might come down to see her tomorrow. She had an affirmative answer.

Mrs Maitland had guessed that Lucinda had some important communication to make, and she had arranged to be at home alone. As soon as Lucinda arrived she said, with the expression of someone who had braced themselves to face a difficulty:

"I suppose it is about Bill and Anne. Please tell me at once what it is."

Lucinda was more agitated than Mrs Maitland.

"Bill and Anne must not marry," she said bluntly. "There are reasons which make it impossible."

Mrs Maitland's expression hardened.

"I think I am entitled to know the reasons," she said with dignity

"Yes. I know you are. I'm most awfully sorry, but please don't ask me to tell you. It's something to do with our family."

"Do you mean that Bill has an hereditary taint of some kind?"

"No—not exactly."

"If it's anything of that nature I think I should be told. You may be sure it would go no further. I think I should be allowed to judge whether it's necessary that this blow should fall on my daughter. Also I am rather curious as to why you should suddenly come to this decision."

"I had a cable from my mother. She told me I must stop the marriage."

"Does Bill know of your visit here?"

"No. He mustn't be told."

"You may not realize how much you are asking of me."

"Oh, I do realize it. The whole thing must sound outrageous to you. It is outrageous," exclaimed Lucinda.

"Why wasn't the cable sent to Bill or to me?"

"Because of the thing I can't tell you. My mother cabled to me three times to stop the marriage. I ignored the first cable. I replied to the second that it was impossible to interfere and that Anne was delightful in every way. It was only in the third cable which came yesterday that she told me the real reason."

Lucinda hoped that this information would modify Mrs Maitland's hostility, but although she behaved with outward decorum her rather small eyes remained cold and suspicious.

"May I see these cables?"

Lucinda realized with disgust that Mrs Maitland doubted the truth of what she was telling her. Possibly she thought that she wanted to stop the marriage for some reason of her own. She had wanted to avoid showing the cable to Mrs Maitland, as she thought it would also be painful to her individually, but now she took it from her bag and handed it to the older woman. Mrs Maitland read it once or twice as if trying to understand its contents. Up to now they had been standing. Mrs Maitland turned to Lucinda, and in a more friendly manner asked her to sit down.

"I don't think it will be possible," she said, "to make Bill give up Anne without telling him that he is her half-brother."

"But I *can't* tell him," said Lucinda. "It would ruin his life, and break up our whole family. My father thinks he is his son. It would be terrible for him and for all of us. Ever since yesterday afternoon I have had to force myself to believe that it is true."

"This could break up my family too. Anne would not speak to me again if I stopped her marrying Bill for no good reason."

187

"You could tell Anne."

"That would put all the burden on Anne of breaking with Bill without telling him why."

"I'm so terribly sorry," said Lucinda impulsively.

"It's not your fault," said Mrs Maitland, almost kindly. "I suppose it is my husband's fault really."

Lucinda thought of Hugo.

"Are all mean beasts?" she exclaimed.

"My husband was not a beast. He was kind to me in many ways."

"Oh no. That was a dreadful thing for me to say. I wasn't really thinking of him when I said it."

"Bill must have been born before I met my husband," said Mrs Maitland reflectively. There was a silence in which she appeared to be considering either her late husband's fidelity or the future of her daughter.

"What can I say to Anne?" she said at last. "It will be worse for her than if Bill were killed in the war. She would have to accept that as a finality. This of course is a finality too. I think Bill should have to bear his share of it."

"If Bill is told it will ruin his whole life. It would ruin my mother's life irretrievably. I can't imagine what she would do. Of course she is to blame in a way, but we don't all get our deserts."

Lucinda spoke so feelingly that Mrs Maitland glanced at her curiously, wondering why anyone so young should speak with so much tolerance. After a little further discussion she agreed that the only thing to do was to tell Anne, and to take her away from Oxford for some months.

"My husband's cousin, Dolly Wendale, is running a hospital for convalescent officers at Mentone," said Lucinda. "I'm sure she would be glad to have Anne to help her there, and it would be a complete change of scene."

"I don't think it would be very suitable," said Mrs Maitland.

"No, perhaps it wouldn't." Lucinda was wondering how much longer she would be justified in asking any favor of any of the Brayford connections. Mrs Maitland was thinking of Anne's position in relation to Bill's relatives. Continuing this train of thought she did not even ask Lucinda to stay to tea, but this was partly because she was expecting Anne to be home by then; but she went to the door with her and said good-bye with an air of finality, though without apparent ill will.

Lucinda on her way back to the station went into Buohl's for tea. The place was full of young officers, cadets and what girls they could muster. An artillery captain sitting alone, kept glancing with a half smile in her direction. She began to think that there must be something in her appearance which suggested that she might be "picked up" in a teashop. It could not be in her clothes as she thought her clothes were obviously those of a respectable woman, and today she had not put any dubious brooch in her hat. This disclosure of Julie's had destroyed her confidence in her respectability. The glances of the artillery captain, coming just at this moment, were intolerable to her. She drank her tea hurriedly and left the place, and felt at the same time that it already showed some moral deterioration for her to be disturbed by them.

Until she saw Mrs Maitland she had been concerned solely with the coming interview, but now the glances of this man awoke in her brain the realization that Julie's disclosure deeply affected herself as well as Bill. All the way back in the train to London, fresh and painful considerations presented themselves to her. Was she herself Fred's daughter? She thought she must be as there was a distinct family likeness between herself and one of the aunts at The Pines. Lydia too was obviously Fred's daughter, while Bill had always seemed to be less one of the family. She had put this down, as much as she had thought of it, to his being a boy. She thought of her childhood and youth at The Pines and at Flinders, so decent, so secure, so intensely respectable, and all the time this rotten thing had been built into its foundations, to bring about, years afterwards, this collapse, and to make it impossible to look back tranquilly on that happy past. But even as she thought of this to the accompaniment of the even rhythm of the train, she evoked memories of that past, of a hot morning at Flinders, when Bill and Blake IX made turbans of their towels and put oranges on them, and she and Tony sat in the shade of the Tarpeian Rock.

The train was full of subalterns, but Lucinda had found a compartment in which there were only two women. Their polite chatter was at first only a background to her thoughts, like the noise of the train. The elder and more austerely dressed was probably a person of some importance in her country. The younger, who was more feminine and frilly, was evidently pleased at traveling in her company, and eagerly agreed with the great lady's judgments, of which, like Marian whom in some ways she resembled, she gave many.

Gradually the tone of this conversation impinged on Lucinda's mind. It seemed, by contrast with her reveries of Flinders, intensely English. She began to feel that she hated the English, and when she thought of the people she really liked in England, Susannah and Paul and Pat, she found that they were Irish or half French or something. She almost wished she had stayed in Australia and had married Tony. She remembered his kindness, his restraint, his infinite patience with her, and for the first time since her marriage she recalled vividly that morning on the Tarpeian Rock, and the afternoon below the cliff at Cape Furze. If she had never come to England Bill would not have met Anne Maitland, and this situation would not have arisen. She felt a gush of tenderness for Tony and her adolescence, and wished she could penetrate back into that untroubled past.

When she arrived back at Wellington Court she found that Marian had called, and had left a message asking her to ring up when she came in.

"My dear, I wanted to find out how you were," said Marian over the telephone. "You looked so groggy on Wednesday evening. I would have called yesterday, but I had to go down to Crittenden to make sure that Edwards was bottling the raspberries, and to inspect the Girl Guides."

"I'm quite well, thank you."

"You don't sound very cheerful."

"I've just come back from Oxford. It was awfully good of you to call."

"Nonsense. Did you see that nice young couple?"

"No. I only saw Mrs Maitland."

"Is something the matter?" asked Marian with her swift nose for a mystery.

"Well, yes, it is. I'm afraid the engagement will be broken off."

"How absurd!" exclaimed Marian indignantly. "I shouldn't hear of it. You should box their ears and tell them not to be ridiculous. I never saw a couple more suited to each other."

"I'm afraid that I can't do anything about it," said Lucinda.

"Then what did you go down there for? You want to be more strong-minded. Well, good-night, my dear. I'm glad you're fit again. Go to bed early with a glass of hot milk."

Marian's friendliness in calling, her slight rudeness on the telephone were a tonic to Lucinda. Brooding on Julie's lapse, sin, indiscretion—what was the word for it—she had begun to think of herself as a social outcast. Marian's conversation had told her that she need not be except by her own choice. Her position with regard to the outside world was unchanged.

But she had intended to change it, or rather to give the world cause to change its attitude to her, and not only the outside world, but her closest friends, like Marian and Paul and Miss Lanfranc, who would blame her for leading her cousins astray. It was the fact that she had contemplated doing the same thing that made her discovery of Julie's behavior and of its tragic result so shocking to her. She went up to see Stephen have his bath, and, as she watched him playing happily with the soap and with some floating celluloid animals, she felt that it would be wickedly impossible to do anything which might in another twenty years affect him as disastrously as Julie's conduct had affected Bill.

After dinner she sat down and wrote a long letter to Pat. She did not deny that she loved him, but she said that if they met it must only be as friends. They had had a happy friendly relationship before. There was no reason why it should not continue. She played Stephen as her trump card in this game which she was not anxious to win, knowing from the effect that the mention of his name had had on Pat that he did regard him as a serious obstacle. She went out late herself to post this letter, so that he would receive it in the morning.

The next day was Saturday, when she did not go to the Red Cross, and she had no other engagements. By the evening she was longing to see Pat. If she had even an appointment ahead with him, something to look forward to, she would not have felt so lonely. Of all the other people she knew, Paul was the only one she felt inclined to see at present. She rang up the rooms where he was staying but could get no reply.

At about ten o'clock she was sitting reading, when she heard Kate answer the front door and a man's voice. For a wild moment she hoped it was Pat, and then thought that it might be Paul, who would be less disturbing.

She put down her book and turned with a look of eager welcome to the door, but it was neither Pat nor Paul, but Bill who burst into the room. It was as if a ray of light had been switched away from her, so suddenly did her expression change. She felt the guilt showing in her face, although she knew she was not to blame for his tragedy, and she saw that Bill recognized it. His hair clung damply to his forehead. His eyes were dark, wretched and accusing. There had always been such friendly relations between them that it was difficult for him to break through the habit of a lifetime and speak to her angrily. He was impelled towards her house by the tortured bewilderment which had followed his scene with Anne that afternoon. He had forced himself past Kate, and dashed up the stairs so that his impulse should not be weakened by polite forms. When he saw Lucinda's look of guilt, an expression she had never before shown him, it made her seem a different person from his sister he had known and admired all his life, and he was able to blurt out:

"What the hell d'you want to ruin my life for?"

"I don't," said Lucinda, but still guiltily, unprepared for this attack.

"Then why the hell d'you go down and persuade Anne to break our engagement?"

"I didn't see Anne."

"Don't quibble. You saw Mrs Maitland. The result's the same. I want to know what's behind it all." His voice was high and angry, and yet all the time suggesting that any moment he might burst into sobs. "I am not going to leave this house till I know what it is."

Lucinda could think of nothing plausible to say. She was dismayed that Mrs Maitland had let Bill know that she had intervened, and yet, if he had carried on to her in this threatening and semi-hysterical manner, she had probably been obliged to disclaim some of the responsibility to get him out of the house.

"What reason did Anne give you?" she said.

"Don't you mention her name," shouted Bill, but went on: "She said it was unsuitable. That's all she would say. I only found out by accident that you'd been down there. Thank God I did, because now I know Anne wouldn't have chucked me of my own accord. I suppose they're not grand enough for you. I suppose you want me to be all mixed up with dukes like you, and hanging on to their coat-tails. They don't think anything of you. You're only a colonial to them."

"That's nonsense," said Lucinda. "I have no illusions about dukes, as you call them. It was Mum who was pleased at Hugo's connections."

"Mum!" exclaimed Bill, slapping his thigh. "She's behind it. Mrs Maitland hinted it wasn't your fault when I said I was coming up here. Then why the hell did they send that bloody lying cable, and why the hell do you want to do their dirty work. I suppose she has to keep it secret from Dad. Thank God I've got a decent father at any rate."

"Oh my God!" said Lucinda wearily. She was sick that she had mentioned Julie. It was as if Bill in his fury had developed some hypnotic power and had made her involuntarily put him on the right track. If she spoke denying Julie's responsibility she knew that in his heightened condition he would detect the false note in her voice.

"How could you do it? I can't understand it," he said, running his hand through his damp hair.

"Bill," said Lucinda, trying to speak with persuasive reasonableness, "you will never understand it. Try to accept that."

"Christ Almighty!" He almost laughed. "Try to accept that. Try to accept that I've just lost the girl I'd rather be dead than live without—who—who—" his voice choked with emotion and for a minute he did not speak. "Shall I tell you something?" he asked when he began again, but more as if he were speaking to himself than to Lucinda. He did not look at her, but sat with his head in his hands. "This afternoon when I was biking into Oxford I thought I knew why I was alive. It was still and sunny and there were lots of flowers in the gardens—those tall, yellow flowers that used to be down by the stables at The Pines. And I thought that if you're going to hear some music or see a play, or to read a book you've wanted to read for a long time, you feel excited that something pleasant is going to happen. Well, if you love someone, you love them because in them more than in anyone else is the thing you are looking for in music and books. It's like your god walking about. And when you're going to see the person you love, it's as if you were not only going to see your god walking about, but all the music and poetry and everything you love concentrated into one living thing, and you're able to speak to it and touch it. When I was riding into Oxford this afternoon, I thought this wonderful thing was going to happen to me in ten minutes. But it didn't."

"I know," said Lucinda, almost in tears. "I do know only too well what you felt."

"You!" said Bill, raising his head and staring at her with loathing. "What's the good of talking to you? You don't understand love. You think it's something you sell for a title. Try to accept that! It's nothing of course. I'll get over it like the toothache. But I do understand it—see! I understand that my family are absolutely mad with snobbery, and they've got nothing to be snobbish about. They're nobody. They only stink of money. I won't touch their filthy money. I'll live on my pay and I hope I get killed. The Maitlands are much better than us anyhow. Mrs Maitland used to dine at Government House when Mum was boiling the jackeroos' mutton at Noorilla. Watteau has told me all about that. It was bloody good of the Maitlands to have me there at all. Anne's far too good . . . Oh, what the hell!"

At the end of this confused harangue, childish and yet terrible, his voice sank down into the flatness of utter resignation. He wiped the damp hair from his forehead, and also possibly was wiping tears from his eyes. He picked up his stick and his khaki cap and turned to the door.

"D'you want a bed made up?" she asked.

"I'd rather sleep with an honest prostitute than sleep in your house," he said, still in the same flat voice; "and that's what I'm going to do."

She heard him let himself out at the front door. For a while she did not move. The feeling she had had in Buohl's returned to her—that she was in some way a tainted and potentially disreputable person. She longed for some sane and decent companionship for reassurance. She thought of ringing up Marian again, just to hear her brusque and friendly voice after Bill's raving insults, but she could find no excuse to do so at this hour. She tried to think of someone else who would come round and give her sound advice, or at least a little comfort, but though she had many acquaintances she had no close woman friend of her own age. Paul, more than anyone else in her life, filled this place of intimate confidant. She could say things to him which she would not dream of saying to Marian or Miss Lanfranc, and he appeared to understand and not to judge.

She rang him up but he had not yet returned. Her sense of loneliness became intolerable. She could not go to bed, and she began to think about Pat. She saw him in this little gray and yellow room, where he had so often been. She relived the moment when he handed her that first note, and her heart beat quickly with excitement. Hardly knowing what she was doing, she went to the telephone and rang him up. He answered at once.

"Oh, Pat," she said, "I had to hear your voice. You didn't answer my letter."

"No. It seemed pretty final."

"Can't you think of any answer?"

There was a silence and she thought for a frightened moment that he was shocked and had rung off, but then he said quietly:

"Yes. Come round here."

"What, now?"

"Yes."

"Very well."

Again she stood in the brown room with the red leather chairs and the race-horses. He took her in his arms and a marvelous ease and comfort returned to her. She had found the certainty which she had been looking for.

She returned to Wellington Court towards four in the morning and crept quietly up to her room. She was almost too tired to undress but she was contented. All her difficulties at last were resolved. She had only been unhappy because she had not had the courage to face them. Tomorrow, after a good sleep, she would be able to sort them out and to order her own life. She would be able to face anything with Pat by her side.

In the morning when Kate came in with the tea, she said sleepily: "Don't call me yet. I'll ring when I want to get up."

"Her ladyship from Cadogan Place is here, madam," said Kate.

"Good gracious! Whatever is the time?" Lucinda thought she must have overslept after all.

"It's going on for nine, madam."

In a flood the memory of last night's happenings came over her, and she recalled her final resolution as she went to bed, that with and for Pat she would face anything. Thoughts flew through her mind too quickly for them to find words. She imagined that Marian had already discovered her visit to Pat. How could she so soon? In the morning light her courage was less flushed with confidence, but she was still determined to follow the course she had chosen and to face what it entailed. But she had hardly expected the necessity to come so soon. It was like being confronted with a cold bath before one has braced oneself to enter it. Her voice trembled slightly as she said to Kate:

"Show her ladyship into the drawing-room, and tell her I'll be down almost immediately. Give me my dressing gown before you go."

Lucinda with a shaky hand poured herself out a cup of tea, but before she could drink it Marian was at her bedroom door.

"May I come in, Lucinda, my dear?" Her voice was grave and kind, and Lucinda, without time to think what this friendliness might mean, answered instinctively on the same note:

"Oh yes, do! I'm sorry I'm not up yet."

"I didn't expect you to be. I came early as I thought it better that you should hear my news in your room."

"Your news? Is it bad news?"

"Yes, my dear."

"Tell it to me, then."

"Hugo is wounded, rather seriously. Arthur heard late last night, direct from France. I came to tell you before you received the official communication."

"How terrible!" said Lucinda. Her voice sounded absolutely flat. "Is it very serious?" she asked.

"We are not certain."

"Do you mean he is not likely to live?"

"It may not be as bad as that. We must hope for the best until we have more details. General Fraser only said it was serious. We shall probably hear more tomorrow."

"I can't take it in properly. It's extraordinary, coming just now. It's incredible."

"You must have known it was likely to happen, my dear."

"Yes, I know, but I didn't expect it to."

"We can't all escape scot free."

"Oh, no! Of course not." Lucinda gave a distracted laugh.

Marian watched her with an expression of stern kindness. She thought Lucinda's reaction unusual, but that was only to be expected, seeing that she had just woken up.

All day long Lucinda felt as if she were trapped, body and soul in steel bands. She could not put out a tendril of thought in any direction, not even towards Stephen, as last night she had put her own desires and her own longing for certainty before her duty as a mother. She had set out on a course which might lead to his being taken from her, and when he came down on his way to walk in the park and greeted her with noisy cheerfulness, she felt guilty towards him. She would not ring up Pat as she felt partly that it would be an ill omen if her first conversation with him after all the beauty and tenderness of last night were to convey these tidings, and also that it would be a kind of vulgarity or brutality to tell him a thing, so horrible in itself, which must affect vitally the course of their love.

She told Kate that she was at home to no one, and that she would speak to no one on the telephone but Marian. She spent the day imprisoned in herself. In the afternoon she walked round the park, avoiding the parts where there was any likelihood of her meeting an acquaintance.

In the evening she sat down to write to Julie, to tell her that Bill's engagement was broken off and that Hugo was wounded. But neither in this direction could her thoughts unfold. She sat with her pen in her hand, staring at the girl in the engraving of Fragonard's "Swing" which hung above the writing table. She could almost feel the bands about her head.

In the morning Pat rang her up. As soon as she recognized his voice she told him that Hugo was wounded. He said "Oh!" and then, after a pause, "Seriously?"

"Yes, but I don't know yet how seriously."

"I'll see you tonight?" This was the arrangement they had made when they parted in the small hours of Sunday morning. Lucinda hesitated.

"Well, yes. The only thing is Marian's about a lot. It may be difficult. If I can't get away tonight, will you be free tomorrow? Or shall we fix it definitely for tomorrow?"

"I'm longing to see you."

"So am I—longing to see you."

"Tomorrow for certain, then?"

"Yes, tomorrow."

She put down the receiver reluctantly. She could tell from Pat's voice that he had at once taken in all the implications of her news, and that he realized it was not only because of Marian that she postponed their meeting, but that also she was influenced by a feeling of superstition about the sequence of events. More than ever she wanted to see him to explain, which she could not do on the telephone, that she would allow nothing to form a real barrier between them.

Marian came in at lunch-time looking extremely pleased with herself. Lucinda at once thought that Hugo's wound was not serious after all, and was bitterly ashamed to find that her first sensation was one of disappointment, because she had not been able to ignore the fact that if Hugo died she would be free to marry Pat. It is difficult for a person of intelligence not to see where his advantage lies, though it may be in a shameful direction which he will not take. At first Lucinda thought that Hugo's being wounded would tie her to him more closely, at least for some months, and in the present state of her feelings for Pat any postponement was unbearable. But gradually, throughout the night, she had been convinced, with a sinister optimism, that his wounds would be fatal and she would be free.

However, Marian said, "We've no further news of Hugo, except that he is in a hospital near Boulogne. But I have *some* good news for you. I've just come from the War Office. General Fraser has managed to arrange for you to cross over tomorrow to see him."

Marian had that satisfied smile which she always wore when she had achieved a successful piece of management. Her eye was fixed on Lucinda, awaiting her delighted response.

CHAPTER SEVEN

THERE WAS a small silver-gray airship, called a "blimp," flying behind the cross-channel steamer. It was on the look-out for submarines. There was also a destroyer as escort. General Fraser had reserved a cabin for Lucinda but she preferred to sit on the open deck, though it was crowded with officers returning from leave, mostly subalterns, wearing "British-warms," life-belts and wrist-watches. The sea was choppy and there was a cold wind.

This was the first time since she had left the school-room that Lucinda had gone anywhere not of her own volition. It was also the first time since before the war that she had seen the sea, which had been so much part of her early life, at Flinders, and even in Melbourne where one was always conscious of Port Phillip Bay close at hand, and in the garden of Tourella on the hottest afternoons, one waited for the sea breeze which brought its daily cool relief at tea-time. To feel the spray and to smell the sea again brought her a physical refreshment which had its effect on her mind. There was something bracing, too, in the slight danger of the crossing. The dreadful emotional paralysis which she had felt on Sunday left her. At any rate, movement both of mind and of body was restored to her, even if it was in a direction she would not willingly have chosen.

This train of thought was stimulated by a chance encounter on the steamer. Lucinda became conscious that someone was watching her, and she turned to meet the eyes of a subaltern who was standing by the gunwale. She did not immediately recognize him as the young man who had been at Mrs Galway's luncheon party. He smiled and made his way to her across the crowded deck. She was not very pleased as she was not in the mood to talk to strangers, but his pleasure and surprise at meeting her was so obvious that she could not help feeling touched, especially when he said that he had waited at Miss Lanfranc's till half-past six on Sunday, hoping that she would come.

They talked about Melbourne, and he asked her if she intended to go back there.

"I hope you do," he said.

"It's not possible in war-time, but of course I want to—to smell the violets and boronia in Collins Street."

"But you're traveling to France in war-time?" He was evidently curious to know what she was doing on this boat, where the only other women were half a dozen nurses.

"I'm going to see my husband who is wounded."

"I say, I'm awfully sorry. Am I butting in?"

"No, not at all."

She found his simplicity as refreshing as the open sea. She asked him questions about Melbourne. It turned out that he had been to Flinders.

"Do you know the beach below Strathallan, the boarding-house?"

"Yes, rather, with a big rock we used to dive from."

"Yes, my brother and a friend of his used to call it the Tarpeian Rock."

They talked of the people they knew. Most of his friends were the younger brothers of the men she used to meet at dances. By the time they reached Boulogne, his slight drawl and his unsuspicious friendliness, both marked Australian traits, as well as the subject of their talk, had awakened vividly in her mind that earlier part of her life, and had somehow given her a sense of balance. She said good-bye to him warmly, and hoped they might meet again in Toorak. She also invited him to call at Wellington Court when he was on leave.

"It was good-o meeting you," he said. "It's sort of made my leave an hour longer."

Lucinda was met by a staff captain, who looked at the subaltern as if he were unclean. To compensate this she shook hands with him again and said:

"Don't forget to come and see me."

He did not call, and long afterwards, suddenly remembering this crossing, she asked Miss Lanfranc what had happened to him.

"I'm afraid I don't know," said Miss Lanfranc. "So many subalterns came to tea during the war."

The staff captain led her through the jostling khaki crowd, through the fishy smell of the docks mixed with the smell of "caporal" cigarettes and fried omelettes from the buffet, to a waiting army car. His manner was one of restrained and formal sympathy. As they drove out through the town they passed some platoons of infantry, burdened with rifles and packs and gasmasks, marching with heavy nailed boots on the cobbled streets. They had the air of cheerful endurance of an uncomprehended fate. The whole town looked incredibly gray and dreary. A fine rain drizzled on the windscreen.

"We've taken a room for you at 'The Folkestone,'" said the staff captain, "but the general thought you would rather go to the hospital first. It's in a casino."

She was taken by an orderly to the matron, who gave her an absolutely unsmiling welcome, which counteracted the effect of the warm, light room. The matron disapproved of "society women" using government transport and the time of government employees like herself, in exercising a privilege which would be disallowed to those in a humbler position, and she showed her disapproval in her manner.

A nurse, who must have been informed of Lucinda's arrival, came in.

"Major Brayford is conscious and is asking for Stella, it sounds like. I expect that is you," she said, smiling at Lucinda. Stella was Mrs Fabian Parker's name, but Lucinda did not disillusion the nurse. "He is unable to speak very coherently."

"Then you had better take Mrs Brayford to him now," said the matron. She shook hands and allowed herself the grim flicker of a smile.

The nurse led Lucinda down a passage smelling of ether and iodoform, into what had been the baccarat room. The walls were decorated with tawdry chipped plaster, and the blazing chandelier hung from a painted ceiling which was a debased echo of the saloon ceiling at Crittenden. Along the floor, instead of green baize tables were now arranged rows of beds. At the far end a bed was hidden behind one of those red screens, which are used to conceal intimate functions and to give sketchy privacy to the dying. In this bed lay Hugo, only recognizable by his hair and by his left hand which lay on the coverlet. His face was covered with bandages. The bedclothes rose in a hump over his legs, which were protected from their weight by a cage.

The memories of Melbourne, which had been stirred by her conversation with the subaltern on the boat, still hung about Lucinda. It was against that background that she saw the present scene, which made it seem more unjust to her. Hugo, she told herself bitterly, had taken her out of that happy life, and even now he did not want to see her but the woman for whom he had neglected her. The matron's manner, and the disclosure that he had asked for "Stella," roused her to a cold hostility which increased as she followed the nurse along the ward. But when she saw him lying there all these feelings, which were the result of purely mental processes, were engulfed by a surge of human feeling. Since the early days of their marriage she had been oppressed by the feeling of his power over her, against which she might beat without making the faintest impression. To see him lying here powerless, and in a sense at her mercy, caused a revulsion of feeling, and speechless with pity she took the hand which was lying on the coverlet.

"It's Lucie," she said.

He murmured unintelligibly through the bandages.

She felt her sympathy pouring out to him through her hand. This physical contact through their clasped hands seemed to renew all the ties of friendliness they had for one another, and to revive not their deeper passions, but a tenderness which would not have been possible if those passions had never existed. She stayed until the nurse came and said that now he had better be left to sleep.

When she returned to the hotel it was time for dinner. The restaurant was full of officers on their way either to or from the Front. They all had bottles of expensive wine on their tables, champagnes or very good burgundies. They apparently enjoyed themselves against their background of death. Many of them in a few weeks might be in the condition of Hugo. One or two of them certainly would. What had seemed to her the overwhelming proportions of her own tragedy shrank to a smaller place in the scheme of things.

After dinner she sat down to write to Pat. She had tried to telephone to him several times yesterday to tell him she would be unable to come this evening, but had been unable to catch him in. She had written instead, a letter full of ardent expressions, saying that she would let nothing come between them.

She found it extremely difficult to write again so soon contradicting the sense of her previous letter. There were some things it was too much to expect anyone to understand, or rather they had to be understood without explanation or not at all. She wrote two long letters and tore them both up. At last, in desperation, she wrote a short note saying she could not leave Hugo in his present condition. She hoped that Pat would understand all the things which were beyond explanation, but she had no reply to this letter. She had closed the windows to be quiet and warm while she wrote. When she had finished writing she opened them to take a breath of fresh air, but the fishy smell from the harbor was now so appalling that she had to close them, and try to sleep with her windows closed.

She had troubled and fitful dreams from which she was awakened by an insistent knocking on her door.

"What is it?" she asked. It took her a moment to realize that she was not in bed at Wellington Court.

"Un jeune homme—un soldat veut vous parler," shouted an irascible concierge.

"Pas moi," said Lucinda, thinking the concierge had mistaken the room. "Je suis Mrs Brayford."

"Si, si. Madame Brayfor'."

"Bien. Je viens."

Feeling stiff and bleak, she dressed in the stuffy room. She could not imagine what young man would want to see her. Possibly someone she knew passing through Boulogne had seen her name in the hotel book, but then he would not call on her at—she looked at her watch—two o'clock in the morning. She had brought no warm clothes as it had been hot when she left London. Putting on a light coat, and feeling chilly and a little apprehensive, she went down to the entrance, where the young man turned out to be an orderly from the hospital.

"The matron says that Major Brayford has taken a turn for the worse. She expects you will want to see him. I have a car here." He spoke in a pleasantly cultivated voice which seemed incongruous with his orderly's uniform.

They drove down the smelly quay and along the cobbled streets back to the casino. A different nurse conducted her to Hugo's bed. On the way she explained that he was unconscious and that his condition was serious. The glittering chandelier now hung dead from the ceiling. This frivolous place, put to tragic uses, appeared even more bizarre in the dim light from a solitary lamp, which stood near the red screen by Hugo's bed. When Lucinda came round this screen she could feel as much as see the change in his condition. The triangle of his forehead, all of his face that showed between the bandage and his crisp hair, was flushed and he was breathing heavily. His left hand still lay on the coverlet, and instinctively she took it in her own. The nurse made a movement to stop her, but then nodded as Lucinda held the hand quietly and still. The nurse brought a chair, and placed it so that she could sit comfortably. She asked her to sit like that as long as possible without moving. From this Lucinda gathered that they were not certain that he would die. She tried to renew through her hand the contact she had felt in the afternoon. She tried with all her being to pour her life into him through her hand. After a while she felt as it were a faint pulse or response in his hand, and she was filled with an extraordinary happiness, of a kind she had not known before. This lasted for about half an hour, but then the numbness of her body, due partly to fatigue and cold, and partly to the strain of keeping in one position, brought a numbness to her mind. She knew she must not move, and still rigid she fell into a half-sleep, in which she had what were only half-dreams. She was still in a large room and holding Hugo's hand, but the room with its painted ceiling and ghostly chandelier had become the saloon at Crittenden, vulgarized and distorted, and Hugo's hand like a vice was holding her there against her will.

She came out of this half-sleep to find the nurse offering her a cup of tea, which she drank, holding the cup awkwardly in her left hand. This woke her up thoroughly, and now actual scenes from the past awoke vividly in her tired and stimulated brain—a day at Flinders when Grandpapa Chapman had insisted on the boys going with him for a tramp; Tony bending over a plan in the drawing-room at The Pines; Melba singing *Home, Sweet Home* at Tourella on the afternoon of the garden party; the night of the Radcliffes' dance and the scene with Tony in the library; her conversation with Paul in Susannah's drawing-room on the night she arrived in England; an evening at Crowborough when Paul came to dine—they flashed as clearly in her mind as if they had happened only this week, and now she seemed to realize their meaning in a way she had not done at the time. She remembered that it was said that people at the moment of death saw revived in this fashion the scenes of their lives. It suddenly occurred to her that Hugo might be dying and also reviewing the scenes of his life, and that some strange sympathy had caused her mind to act in the same way. She looked at him anxiously, but he was breathing quietly.

Soon the nurse appeared again. She looked intently at Hugo, then she smiled at Lucinda and disengaged her hand. When Lucinda saw her smile she knew that Hugo was out of danger, or at any rate had passed this crisis.

"You had better come away now," said the nurse softly.

She took Lucinda along to a large bare sitting-room and gave her more tea, while a car was being fetched to take her back to the hotel.

"You have saved your husband's life," she said in a matter-of-fact tone. "If you had not come I expect he would have died."

"His injuries are very bad?"

"They are rather."

For the first time Lucinda thought of what Hugo's face might be like under those bandages.

"Will he be very disfigured?" she asked.

"We have a marvelous surgeon here," said the nurse. "He's a genius at plastic surgery. If anything can be done he'll do it. He's not an Englishman though," she added, in much the same tone that Lady Bassingbourne might have observed that Mr Straker was not a gentleman.

The same orderly who had brought her here was waiting with a car outside the casino. When they arrived at 'The Folkestone' she offered him a ten shilling note, which he refused in his pleasantly cultivated voice. She saw that he was not the kind of man who takes tips and she apologized.

"Why haven't you a commission?" she asked, to make up for her gaff by showing a friendly interest, and with the vague idea in her head, put there by Marian, that it was "absurd for people of our class" not to have commissions.

"I'm a conscientious objector."

"Oh!" She thought of the young Melbourne boy on the boat, of all those subalterns at dinner, so cheerful against their hideous background, of Hugo lying behind the red screen. She looked at the orderly with instinctive hostility, but there was something intelligent and kind in his face, an expression which matched his voice.

"Well, thank you for driving me," she said, and turned and went into the hotel. Her head ached. As soon as she was in bed she fell asleep, but she still had confused dreams—that she was back in the casino, that Hugo held her hand in an iron grip, while she stared up at the dead chandelier.

Part Three
1919–1923
THE LEAVES ON THE FALLEN TREE
We blossom and flourish as leaves on the tree.

W. CHALMERS SMITH.

CHAPTER ONE

JULIE gave a ball at Tourella to welcome Bill and his wife back from the war. Bill in a mood of savage repudiation of Lucinda and all that he imagined she stood for, had married the daughter of Watteau's cousin at Richmond. She was a strong-minded young woman whose rather limited outlook Bill mistook for simple kindness. Her name was Muriel, and she was a year older than himself and the same height. In the time of his distress she mothered him in a brusque and bossy fashion, laughing at him occasionally, but showing an apparent sympathy. After the break with Anne he spent all his free week-ends with the Watsons. In their unpretentious suburban house he felt more at home than anywhere else he had been in England, for he had hardly felt at home at the Maitlands, but more as if he were in a kind of paradise. Although the Watsons gave him a sense of healing comfort, he also expected and hoped that his marriage to Muriel would humiliate his family. He did not want to ask Lucinda to the wedding, but neither Muriel nor her mother intended to throw away the advantage of upper-class connections, and they invited not only Lucinda, but also Marian and Arthur. After the war Bill and his bride, before they returned to Australia, spent a week at Crittenden.

Bill found that his situation *vis-à-vis* Lucinda had not changed, while the family did not show the dismay he had expected. Julie, whom he thought would be most annoyed, wrote him a long and affectionate letter. Fred was the only one who disapproved of this sudden marriage to his housekeeper's cousin, but he said nothing beyond, "I hope my son is not unstable." Paul, when he saw Muriel at Crittenden, called her "one of Nature's mayoresses."

It was with this outward manner of the born mayoress, but with some inward trepidation, that she stood, clad in cream satin, at the entrance to the Tourella ballroom, shaking hands with a stream of about four hundred people who all seemed to know each other. In a line with her stood Bill and Fred and Julie, who passed on the guests to her, saying to more intimate friends, "This is Bill's wife," or "This is the new member of the family." Julie was wearing a pearl necklace for which everyone knew Fred had recently paid £5000, but she did not wear it with her former aplomb. The gray was more noticeable in her hair, and her shoulders no longer had the fullness and swagger of the social pugilist. Her face now had more or less permanently that look of wisdom and kindness which Tony had noticed years ago at Flinders, when she tolerated the children's pranks, but she had also an air of resignation. There were two lines down her cheeks, and sometimes she gave that sort of nervous twitch which had afflicted Bill as a small boy. Her lively manner seemed more a habit than to spring from a natural gusto for living, stimulated by success. In the occasional lull in the announcement of guests, it fell from her and she appeared absorbed in her own anxious thoughts.

Those who knew Julie attributed this change to the war, to the four dreary years of waiting, consciously or unconsciously braced to hear bad news. She had missed Bill more than she had expected to. When he was at Trinity College he sometimes came out for a meal, and his things were about the house, which gave him an invisible presence there, but when he left for the front they were put away, and in his room the bed was stripped and the blinds drawn. That here they were so far from the scene of tragic activity did not make it easier to bear. Those whose menfolk were wounded could not go to them, and if they were killed it was not even possible to stand at their graves. Nor was it pleasant to know that when they went on leave, other unknown women entertained them, possibly nice sensible women of whom it was difficult not to be jealous, but possibly also harpies and whores. Mothers, who had been given only a few short months in which to realize that their sons were no longer schoolboys, would at best receive them back as experienced men, partial strangers, and looking into those hardened eyes would seek the spirit of the boy who had gone away. Here, unlike at Miss Lanfranc's house in Trevor Square, few subalterns had come to tea during the war, and those who did were badly wounded.

Julie gave an unconsciously appraising glance at Muriel and thought, "Thank Heaven she looks like a lady." In fact, she looked rather more than a lady, the eternal type of public wife born to stand at the head of a staircase. Standing beyond her, modestly apart from the family group, was Watteau, a symphony in mauve and gray, with her frizzy hair and her amethysts. It was Watteau who now had the appearance of the cat which has eaten the cream. She held a secret which, if she cared to use it, would blow the Vanes' pretensions sky-high and disintegrate their family life. She had of course no intention of using it, but, seeing that for so many years she had been patronized as a dependent, she could not help enjoying its possession. The slightly malicious glint in her eyes had become more marked, and, as she watched all "the best people" shaking hands so amiably with her cousin Thomas's daughter, her smile was tight and satisfied.

Julie noticed with faint wonder Watteau's smug expression. She thought it was caused by her pleasure at once more being at a party at Tourella, and by the fact that Bill had married her cousin. She would have been startled had she known its true origin. Watteau had supported and sheltered her through the whole agonizing process of the death of her pride, and her gratitude to her had become one of Julie's strongest feelings. Actually Julie cared little now for social pretensions or the correct thing. The war had in some unexplained fashion established the Vanes' position beyond question. They were no longer thought to have any tinge of the parvenu, partly because of more recent and more surprising arrivals in "society," and partly because so many of the older families like the Lanfrancs were becoming poorer and dispersed, and the large gardens of their old houses cut up into sites for red-brick villas.

The lull in the stream of guests had been caused by the arrival of Canon Chapman, now eighty years old and walking with a stick. People stood back to let him pass. His staccato voice had become more querulous, and he behaved as if he were the guest of honor.

"Are your clothes warm enough, papa?" said Julie, looking at his black silk evening waistcoat.

"I am perfectly warm, perfectly warm," replied the canon, who had adopted what he conceived to be a courtly and jovial manner, suited to the occasion, and was annoyed at this domestic inquiry. "And how is my favorite granddaughter?" This had become Lucinda's designation since her marriage.

"She doesn't write very often now. I expect Stephen takes up most of her time. Hugo, too, of course."

"Ah yes—the wounded hero. Still, we must all make our sacrifices, and war is a great mystery. I am sure she will prove a dutiful wife. And you too, young woman," he said with a genial but twisted smile, taking Muriel by the hand. "I see you have already undertaken your social obligations—very great obligations, I may say, to which you will doubtless prove adequate."

The band struck up a wailing and syncopated tune.

"Good gracious!" exclaimed the canon. "What a hideous din! Are they unable to compose melodious tunes nowadays?"

"Watteau," said Julie, "would you take papa to his chair?"

Watteau took the arm which the canon gallantly offered, and she led him to where an armchair had been placed whence he could watch the dancing. He sat in his chair with the agreeable smile of someone receiving homage, but few came to pay it.

"Hell of a mystery to have half your face blown away," said Bill.

"Hush!" said Muriel.

Colman announced Mrs Galway, who had come out for a few months to look after her Australian interests.

"And how is your beautiful daughter?" she asked as she shook hands with Julie. "And her splendid young husband? Is he on the road to recovery? I hope so, as I count them among my best friends."

"I think Hugo is as well as can be expected," said Julie.

"You should make them come out here. I'm sure he would recover in our good Australian air. I like everything in England except the climate," said Mrs Galway, laughing.

"I wish they would come out," said Julie, but she spoke without conviction. She did not feel that she could meet Lucinda again, and it was this which was the chief cause of the unhappy and anxious look in her eyes, and which made her indifferent to social aspirations. Lucinda had always been the special bloom of the family, something fastidious and delicate, to be sheltered from every rough and sordid contact. Her marriage to Hugo and her enshrinement in the life of Crittenden, imagined by untraveled Australians and even by Julie as the crystallized perfection of aristocratic culture, was to the Vanes absolutely right and inevitable, so that it was far worse for Julie to be forced to make her shameful disclosure to Lucinda than if it had been to Lydia with her blowsy good-nature, and her obsessions with her increasing family and her horses. Lucinda too had been the justification of Julie's social efforts, which was perhaps another reason why she had abandoned them, and only continued going to parties and giving entertainments like this ball because it had become a habit and because it was expected of her.

Nearly all the people who had been going about in Melbourne before the war knew of this peculiar position of Lucinda in the Vane family, and as they greeted Julie they asked after her and Hugo. It was tiring enough to have to shake hands with over four hundred people in half an hour, but when about a third of those people asked a kindly meant question which jabbed at an unhealed wound, it became an intolerable strain. At last Colman's pompous announcements became more desultory. Julie said, "I think we may move from here now," but instead of following the others into the ballroom she slipped along to the dining-room and poured herself out a whisky and soda.

The ballroom where Canon Chapman's chair had been placed for him to watch the dancing was not the ballroom where the guests had been received, but a new and much larger room of wood and asbestos, built especially and solely for this evening. It had cost Fred £1000, but a few weeks later he sold it for £1500 to a country town as a war memorial, so that the most brilliant ball of the year cost the host practically nothing. The decorations were by Tony. The walls were covered with yellow hessian painted like tapestry. At intervals facing each other across the room were large mirrors. In the center of each mirror was fixed a bouquet of sprays of yellow roses. When the dancers came opposite these mirrors they looked down a vista in which these bouquets, suspended in a golden haze, repeated themselves endlessly. The ceiling was covered with a vast expanse of dull blue net on which was somehow stuck an arabesque of autumn leaves.

Tony came up to speak to Canon Chapman.

"Ah, the *arbiter elegantiarum*," said the canon. "I believe that you had some hand in this Arabian Nights effect."

"It was entirely Mr Duff's scheme to the last detail," said Watteau.

"Well, it's very pretty," said the canon, "but I could wish the music more in keeping. It sounds to me like the howling of mating beasts in the jungle."

Watteau compressed her lips.

"I believe that is what it is meant to represent," said Tony, smiling amiably.

"Indeed," said the canon. "I don't suppose," he went on, "that there are many men of eighty who go to dances."

"It would be extremely awkward if there were," said Watteau.

The canon ignored this and turned to Tony.

"If you wish to see really beautiful scenes," he said, "you should go to England. In my long life I have seen nothing more inspiring than the court of Clare, my old college, by moonlight, with the turrets of King's rising beyond. There indeed you have an effect which the French, with their apt choice of words, would describe as *féerique*. I hope that my great-grandson, the heir presumptive to the viscounty of Crittenden, will go to Clare."

"I believe Clare bridge is very beautiful," said Tony, tactfully as he thought.

"Yes, yes," said the canon testily.

Fred came up to say a few words to his father-in-law, and Tony moved away, saying, "I must go and pay my respects to Lady Edwards."

He was now nearly forty and the hair was receding from his forehead. Since the unhappy end to the one emotional experience of his life, he had adopted an attitude of cynicism to save himself from appearing pathetic. He was often witty, except with the matrons who employed him to decorate their parties. To them he was flattering and deferential. A note of earnest sympathy came into his voice when he discussed with one of them whether a buffet could be arranged in the dining-room, or whether it would be advisable to enclose the verandah with an awning. As his living came from them, to him their importance was real, and he was able to make as nice distinctions between them as Paul would make between a twentieth baron and a third marquis. All his romanticism he put into transforming a town hall or an enclosed verandah into an ephemeral and lovely bower, which he did superlatively well.

He was generally contented with his lot, but the canon's reference to Lucinda's son gave him a twinge. He thought that the old man must have said it on purpose to impress on Tony that Lucinda and her milieu were now far beyond him. He wished that he had made some sharp retort, little dreaming that he had made the sharpest possible, but even now he was wounded less in his love than in his pride. The sight of all these young dancing couples, gay and rich, who would make successful marriages, accentuated his hurt. He went to talk to Lady Edwards, who had known him from childhood, to afford himself a kind of protection.

Muriel and Bill, followed by Lydia, who had arrived late, came into the ballroom. Bill turned to dance with Lydia, whom he had hardly seen since his arrival in Melbourne a week earlier, but Muriel tapped him on the shoulder and said, "First with me." He scowled and took her in his arms.

"May I dance with my sister now?" he asked when the music stopped.

He found Lydia talking to the Master of the Yarra Glen and Lilydale hounds, and led her back to the ballroom.

"How's your enormous family?" he asked.

"They're flourishing," growled Lydia. "How's Lucie?"

"She's all right as far as I know."

"Did you see *him*?"

"God, yes!"

"What's he look like?"

"Worse than I thought any human could look. When they patched him up they took one part of his face to mend another and hair grows in the wrong places. They mucked up the muscles of his mouth too, and it's hard to understand what he says."

"Doesn't he see anybody?"

"Only Lucie and a male nurse. For God's sake don't let's talk about it."

"Lucie has to look at him every day."

"I know. It must be hell for her."

"Why don't they put him in a home? She could visit him now and then."

"He made her promise never to leave him. Sorry!"

Bill and Lydia were more interested in their conversation than in dancing. Their feet were out of time with the music and they did not look where they were going, so that Bill was obliged to exclaim "Sorry!" at intervals to some couple with whom they had collided.

"That's blackmail," said Lydia.

"Lady Crittenden says how bloody marvelous Lucie is about it, and you feel she means that all Australians haven't got the instincts of convicts."

"She must be a bitch," said Lydia laconically.

"She's not bad really. Sorry! Lord Crittenden's by far the best of 'em, though Paul's not bad. He's a bit of a devil, I should say."

"If I hadn't so many kids I'd go to England to have a look at 'em. As a matter of fact I want to go to Ireland to buy some horses, but it's not a good time to go. They say you get shot. Europe seems to be in a bit of a mess. By the way, back Artilleryman for tomorrow."

After his dance with Lydia Bill went out into the garden. The windows of the temporary ballroom opened onto a wide lawn which was enclosed in festoons of orange-colored lights. These filled all that part of the garden with a curious warm twilight. When the music began again he did not go in, but stood, with a puckered forehead, watching the dancers as in changing patterns of color they went by the open window. Many of them were old school friends and the sisters of those friends. With a start of wistful pleasure he saw Blake IX, brown and lean from Gallipoli, and some lovely girls he had known as a schoolboy. The sight of them made him more depressed. He hated being bossed by Muriel. His conversation about Lucinda had brought the whole business of Anne Maitland back to his mind. In a way he felt that Hugo's fate was a judgment on Lucinda for her "worldliness," but he was confused when he thought of it, and hated to do so. Now the sight of all these friends made him feel that he was back in the security of his natural associations. Anne seemed like a dream, while the girls dancing beneath Tony's blue net and autumn leaves were real. Muriel . . . He dared not yet follow his train of thought to its logical conclusion.

Mrs Galway found him standing alone and said:

"Are you contemplating your good fortune?"

"Good fortune!" exclaimed Bill.

"You have everything a young man can want. They say your

213

father is nearly a millionaire. You have come back from the war intact, at least as far as one can see." She laughed mischievously. "And you have a young and pretty wife. What more can you want?"

"It isn't what you've got that makes you happy," said Bill. "It's what you haven't got stops you from being happy."

"And what does young Mr Vane of Tourella *not* possess? Is your fortune inadequate to your tastes?" She laughed again.

"Money!" Bill snorted. "I hate it. It's ruined our family."

"What an astonishing remark to hear in Melbourne! I'm afraid I don't agree with you. Without money one doesn't exist."

"A good many people exist without it."

"You're not a Socialist, are you?"

"I'm not particularly interested in politics."

"Then don't despise wealth. While you have money you can attract all the people you want. They come to you like flies round a honey-pot. I know from experience. No one could say they came to me for my blue eyes." She laughed.

"I don't want people to hang round me for my money. What good has money done to my sister Lucinda?"

"You don't want to be prevented from knowing people because you have no money. You have the means to follow your heart—that's the important thing."

Bill ruminated on this.

"I'm married," he said thoughtfully.

"Oh, of course, but I still think you are a fortunate young man. Will you lunch with me at Menzies'? But I must ask your wife."

She went into the ballroom. Bill followed her and crossed to where Blake IX was standing by the girl with whom he had just been dancing.

"Hullo, Nine," he said.

Blake's eyes shone with pleasure and he gripped Bill's hand. When these two had met after they went to different schools they had been rather constrained with each other. Now that the purely artificial barriers of arbitrarily fixed different interests had fallen away, their friendship, having skipped the years of later adolescence, seemed to spring back to full life in a few moments.

"Come and have a drink," said Bill.

"D'you mind?" Blake asked his partner. "It's a reunion."

The girl smiled and turned away.

"Let's get out of this racket," said Bill. He led Blake along to the pantry where there were some opened cases of champagne. He took a bottle and they went up to his dressing-room. They had brought no glasses so Bill used his toothglass and fetched Muriel's from the bedroom for Blake.

"What did you do in the Great War?" he asked.

"Went to Gallipoli, worse luck," said Blake.

"Hell!" exclaimed Bill, popping the cork.

"Damned lucky to be back, though."

"I hardly saw a gun fired in anger. Well, here's to the Tarpeian Rock."

Blake grinned and they clinked glasses.

They finished the bottle very quickly and Bill went down for another. Over this they exchanged war experiences.

"England's a hell of a country," said Bill. "I hate the English. I wish I'd gone with the Aussies. I wish I'd been with you. We'd have had some fun in Egypt, eh?"

"Didn't you have any fun in England?"

"Fun in England, my God! D'you know what the English are like? They're like washing that's hung out on a line and gets frozen stiff. They're like wet blankets frozen stiff. Here, hold out your glass. My poor bloody sister has to spend the rest of her life nursing an Englishman who looks like a gorilla that's had its face lifted. They're beauty and the beast, back to front, b'God. She married the fairy prince and he turned into the beast. That's the way things work."

"Poor old Lucie. Rotten luck," said Blake.

"She's changed. She's not what she was. She played me a dirty trick that I'll never forgive—all through her marrying one of the bloody English."

He stared broodingly at his toothglass.

"Still," he said thoughtfully, "I have the means to follow my heart—and I'm damned well going to do it. Come on. We'd better go down. I must have cut half a dozen dances."

Muriel had come up to make sure that her hair was tidy. The light was on in Bill's dressing room. Through the open door she heard Blake IX ask, "Didn't you have any fun in England?"

She listened with increasing dismay to the rest of their conversation until she heard them go out of the room, or rather heard them no longer there, as their footsteps in their light shoes were soundless on the thick carpets. When she judged that they were lost in that hum of voices and music which rose from the distant part of the house, she switched on the light and sat before her mirror. She could not believe that such a terrible thing had happened to her. She had not loved Bill, but she had liked him well enough, and it was a rather marvelous match with which to impress her school friends.

She did not consider whether she had "played fair," but she had as much concern as Marian about "fair play" by other people.

At first she thought of leaving the house immediately, but she had nowhere to go unless she persuaded Watteau, her one relative within a thousand miles, to take her up to her house in "the valley" until she could book a passage back to England. This anti-climax would be a greater humiliation than she could bear. She felt terribly lonely. When she thought of that crowd of laughing people down below, amongst whom she was almost an alien, she felt towards the Australians much as Bill had expressed himself about the English. Then she thought of Tourella and this whole new society in which she found herself. There was a lavishness about Tourella such as she had not experienced before, but, since Watteau had gone away and Julie had lost her ambition, there was a want of order. Muriel saw that here was a job to be done. She saw a way in which she could impress herself upon this society which at present was un-aware of her potentialities. When she rose from the chair by her dressing table to go downstairs again she did not appear happy, but on her face was a look of the strongest resolution.

As she came onto the landing she suddenly wondered what was the dirty trick which Lucinda had played on Bill.

Towards midnight, when the older married people began to leave the ball, Fred took Major Amherst, the Military Secretary, and Mr Lanfranc, a K.C. and nephew of the late judge, into his study to sample some Napolean brandy which Lucinda had sent him for Christmas. In this room everything was brown and solid, and of enduring quality. On the bookshelves which contained detective stories and stud books were photographs of racehorses, prize rams and Fred's grandchildren.

"I wonder when the supply of Napolean brandy will run out," said Mr Lanfranc.

"They fill up the casks," said Major Amherst.

"My daughter would not send me brandy from a filled-up cask," said Fred with dignity.

"How is poor Lucinda?" asked Mr Lanfranc.

"My daughter is not poor. Neither of my daughters is poor. I allow them three thousand a year each, with five hundred extra for every child."

"Wish I'd married one of 'em," murmured Major Amherst into his brandy glass.

Mr Lanfranc to change the subject asked Major Amherst what he thought of the situation in Europe.

"My daughter's brother-in-law, the Honorable Paul Brayford,

says that the Germans are dying like flies of starvation," said Fred. "That'll teach 'em to make wars."

"The children who are dying did not make the war," observed Major Amherst.

"They're Germans, aren't they?" demanded Fred.

"Doubtless," said Major Amherst, "but it is unusual to make war on children, especially after an armistice, which we are doing by keeping up the blockade."

"I should like your authority for that statement," said Fred.

"It is generally known," said Mr Lanfranc, who did not like to see Fred making a fool of himself before an Englishman.

"It was a mistake to bring business men into the government," said Major Amherst.

"I cannot agree with you. It is our business men who have built up the empire."

"I thought it was our army," said Major Amherst dryly.

"Our army is the instrument used by our business men. Several business men, but only two or three field marshals, have recently been elevated to the House of Lords. I do not think that His Majesty the King would make noblemen of men of inferior status or character, nor would Mr Lloyd George recommend them for that honor. One of my own countrymen, Mr Straker, has recently been created a baron."

"What is he called?" asked Mr Lanfranc. "Lord Straker of Woolloomalloo?"

"He is not. He has taken the title of Lord Fitzauncell of Fitzauncell Castle, which he has purchased. It is near my daughter's place in the country."

He poured some more brandy into his guests' glasses, and said:

"I give you a toast—our gallant boys who have returned from the war, and also"—his voice sank to a deep and solemn note—"those who have not returned. Also the health of my daughter, the Honorable Mrs Brayford, who sent me this brandy."

Major Amherst, whose expressionless face did not hide his discomfort, lifted his glass.

CHAPTER TWO

LUCINDA said, "Are you all right, darling? I think I'll go out for a walk." She could now look at Hugo without first having to com-

217

pose the muscles of her face to give so sign of flinching. It had taken her a year or two to achieve this. Hugo, with that difficult enunciation which she had also had to learn to understand, replied:

"Yes, if you will put my chair by the window before you go."

It was the male nurse's afternoon off, and she had the impression that he resented being left alone, but there were times when the atmosphere of the End House, where they had returned as soon as Hugo came out of the hospital, oppressed her so much that she felt she must get away from it to breathe. This oppression was strongest in the library, where Hugo had his being, sleeping in a small room which opened off it, beyond which another had been fitted up as a bathroom. He never came out of this self-imposed prison, except to have his chair wheeled into the little high-walled garden outside the library windows. The gate to this garden was always locked. He wanted never to experience again the involuntary look of horror and pity in the eyes of people who formerly had looked at him with equally involuntary admiration. Apart from Lucinda and the nurse, he saw only Arthur and Paul. Paul's sardonic and subversive comments on society in general, which formerly had irritated him, he now appeared to enjoy. Oddly enough he would not see Marian, though she could view his distorted features with more composure than any of the others.

Sometimes he seemed to be worried that Lucinda spent so much time in attendance on him. These moods generally came after he had been particularly exacting. He was aware that he had first shewn resentment at Lucinda's wanting to go for a walk, and when she had wheeled his chair to the window he said:

"You ought to go away from here for a holiday. Why don't you go up to London for a week? Ask Pat Lanfranc to see some shows with you. I'll write to him."

"Oh no, don't!" said Lucinda.

"Why not? Do you good."

"Perhaps, but don't—don't write and ask him to take me out. I'll think about it while I'm out. I shan't be long." She left the room and went up to put on a hat. She was hardly able to think what she was doing. She found that she was putting on a hat which was quite unsuitable for a country walk. She laughed nervously at her stupidity and changed it.

When she came down she found Baa waiting in the hall. At first she did not recognize him. Not only had he grown, but he had developed a tremendous bloom of youth. He had just left Eton and was going up to Christ Church at Michaelmas. He was standing near an eighteenth-century engraving of the Viscount Castlebar, who had been created first Earl of Wendale, the common ancestor of himself and Susannah, Hugo and Stephen. It was his resemblance to this engraving—he had the same air of absolute well-being—which startled her into recognition.

"Good afternoon, Cousin Lucinda," he said, "how are you? And how is Cousin Hugo?"

"He's as well as can be expected," said Lucinda. "You look such a fine young man, I hardly recognized you. I don't think that you need call me 'cousin' any more."

"Very well, my dear Lucinda," said Baa with perfect composure. "You look very blooming, if I may say so."

"I was just thinking the same about you." They laughed together. "Are you staying with Marian?"

"Yes. It's a relief to be in a comparatively decent house again."

"Is Crittenden only comparatively decent? Then what must you think of this little hovel."

Baa did not blush. "Oh," he said, "you make everything charming, but Crittenden wants a lot of money spent on it. But how to get it—that's the snag, isn't it? That is the major problem of my life. We're absolutely broke, you know. Shall I suck up to Lord Fitzauncell and become an editor, or would it be better to sell motor cars? Then I might have a decent one for myself. It would be nicer of course to marry some really enormously rich girl, but I can't do that till I'm twenty-one, or twenty at the earliest. Could you find me one in Australia? Haven't you any nieces?"

"I have one of two years old, and one of six months," said Lucinda, referring to Lydia's children. "They're not rich at all. No Australians are enormously rich."

"Isn't your father?"

"He appears to be comfortable," said Lucinda, "but I think you'd do better in America."

"Life's a very serious problem for fellows like me," said Baa. "It would be hideous not to have the best of everything. It would be simply bestial not to have a Rolls or a Hispano."

"Paul says that money has nothing to do either with your social position or your happiness."

"Paul! He's awfully decent but he's a bit old-world. Thank God he hasn't made up to me," Baa added inconsequently. "But do consider my problems, won't you, dear Lucinda? My guardians apparently want me to starve, and Mummy only thinks of saving money by going by bus. When I protested, she said she got into a bus with three marchionesses outside the House of Lords on Tuesday—as if that made it all right! Think if it had overturned! My mother in a bus accident! It would have been too bestial. I should have died of shame."

"Wouldn't the marchionesses have lent it tone?"

"Oh no, marchionesses are not what they were."

"I should think that Susannah would be of more help to you than I can be. She understands the importance of pleasure."

"Aunt Susannah! Good Heavens, no! She only understands old ladies' pleasure. She expects me to live austerely and carve out a career in politics or some bestial thing, so that she can have the pleasure of talking about her distinguished nephew. My young pleasure would be sacrificed to her old ladies' pleasure."

"You seem to be terribly clear-sighted," said Lucinda.

"Do you think I am? Then perhaps I may be a success. I expect I shall be a social success, anyhow," he said complacently.

"Well," said Lucinda, "I am just going for a walk. I can only leave Hugo for a short time. Would you like to come with me?" she asked politely, though she wanted to be alone.

"I'd do anything else in the world to be with you, my dear Lucinda, but I simply can't bear walking, even to get anywhere."

"Then I am very flattered that you walked across to see me."

"But I didn't. I borrowed the new footman's bicycle."

They went out to the front of the house. Baa took the bicycle from against the warm red brick wall.

"Consider my humiliation," he said, "at paying an afternoon call on this bestial instrument, when I ought to have a vermilion Hispano-Suiza."

"Still, it was nice of Harry to lend you his bicycle."

"Am I reduced to the necessity of gratitude to a footman? Well, good-bye, my dear Lucinda. I hope I see you at Christmas. Do ask me to lunch if you're in London. I have so few attractive relatives. I think we ought to get together."

Lucinda watched him as he mounted the bicycle and pedaled slowly away. On the right was a clump of chestnuts, drowsy in the afternoon sun, and beyond them the pale gold of the summer grass stretched across the park to where the smokeless chimneys of Crittenden showed above the farther trees. The scene was almost as beautiful as it is possible for an English summer landscape to be, and Baa on the footman's bicycle, wobbling as he turned to wave at the bend in the drive, gave it a human touch. He had amused Lucinda, but when he was out of sight she felt slightly uncomfortable. Surely the hungry generations should not be quite so ravenous?

Before setting out on her walk she went back into the hall, to look again with fresh interest at the engraving of the first Earl of Wendale in his ermine, furbelows and wig. He had been known as "silver-tongued Boyne," and had been largely instrumental in bringing about the Union, which was now in process of being bloodily dissolved. Baa was very like him, but in spite of his youth his expression had less animation. The first earl looked both arrogant and benevolent. Baa might be less arrogant, but in him the benevolence seemed to have degenerated to self-indulgence. This portrait suggested more than anything else a resplendent life, a superb acceptance of every aspect of life. She did not know any man today who would dare to have his portrait painted so arrayed and so standing, the bright sagacity of his eye declaring, "my mind is noble, my body splendid, and my circumstances, by God, are magnificent!"

When she started on her walk she had an impulse to get away from the influences of Crittenden, to walk on land which did not belong to Arthur. She went out of the park gates and crossed the road on to a common, where the gorse was in bloom. When she came to the highest point of the common, where the air was a little cooler, she sat down on the grass, with the whole estate of Crittenden sleeping in the afternoon sun spread out before her.

She was excited at the idea of writing to Pat, and considered its advisability and what was likely to come of it, but every now and then her mind wandered back to her conversation with Baa and the engraving of his ancestor. She saw so few people nowadays that almost any encounter left a vivid impression, and she could hear the tones of someone's voice, and see the texture of his skin, an hour or so after he had left her. Now, her outer vision of the landscape was distracted by an inner vision of Baa's neck. How charming he had been at twelve, really lovely, like a seraph—and even at sixteen, *l'âge du seraphim*. He had still struck her with his look of perfect bloom, just now, in the hall at the End House, but when he came out into the sunlight she had thought that his neck looked too thick, and that under the smooth skin of his cheeks was forming a layer of fat, coarsening its texture. In ten years time he might not even be good-looking.

She was sure, though, that if she were now seventeen she would think him wonderful, as she had thought Hugo wonderful seven years ago. Yet Hugo had not changed essentially in the years of their marriage, at any rate not until he was wounded, only her eyes had opened wider to notice things which a young girl ignored. When one was young one was enchanted by a trick of speech, a gesture, the curve of a lip or an ear, and one did not take in the full significance of a moment's dullness of response, a hardness in the eye, the protective fat growing under the skin. But later, as she had met more and more people and extended her understanding of her fellows, so there were fewer people she could love, just as in cultivating her taste she found that there were fewer things she could appreciate. Paul said that it was sensible only for the very rich to cultivate their taste, and complained that whenever he saw in a shop something that pleased him, a needlework chair or an old mirror, and went in to ask the price, the man always replied, "Yes, that is a fine piece, the price is £500." It was all too dear for his possessing. Was Pat also too dear for her possessing? What would she have to pay in subterfuges, in anxiety, in jealousy if she renewed contact with him?

The charm of the scene before her again attracted her full attention. Thinking of the cultivation of taste, she realized she was now able to give it a far deeper and more subtle appreciation than she could when first she came to Crittenden. Then she thought it beautiful in the same way as the view from the Christmas Hills across the valley of the Yarra to Lilydale. In one sense the beauty was the same, the golden afternoon light on distant trees, the pale dry grass of summer and the purple shadow of woods, but here the landscape had a more antique quality. Australia was supposed to be geologically the most ancient country in the world, and in certain moods its hot, savage, wistful landscape of arid earth and stark trees suggested primeval time, but humanly it was new, so that even its most pleasing prospects, like the view from the Christmas Hills, did not drench one in the past as did the English scene spread below her. A man of the eighteenth century or even earlier standing here would have seen it little different. The rose-red front of Crittenden House would have faced the western sun, the square tower of the church would have appeared above the elms, and away to the south he would have seen the thin spire of the cathedral. The knowledge that normally, when at Crittenden with Arthur and Marian, and even at the End House, not only did she sit on chairs and eat with spoons which had been used by many generations now dead, but that even the view she admired had not changed since it was painted by Gainsborough in his early days, gave her life a richer but a sadder and, in some ways, more limited quality. The Australian artist was free to paint the scene as it appeared fresh to his eyes. Here if one did not see everything through the eyes of the eighteenth century, the result was thought to be in bad taste. Paul thought any furniture later than 1793 which Marian perversely kept in the public rooms at Crittenden as sacrilegiously grotesque as if the dean were to put lavatory basins in place of the piscinas in the sanctuary of the cathedral.

It was this oppressiveness of the past which she had come up on to the common to escape. Here, breathing cooler air, she could look down on it, and viewing the setting of her life from above, view her life itself with more detachment, and see herself as one of the figures in the landscape. As from this distance any visible figures had shrunk to the proportion of ants, she had the illusion that their tragedies were unimportant, as if an ant were crushed on a brick path. She found that she could, under these tranquil influences, apply a detached view to most people and things, except when she thought of Stephen. He was not a distant ant. He was the one living thing, the one life with a future in the whole world of Crittenden. The rest of them—Arthur, Marian, Hugo, herself—they had only the past. To Paul, though he was still a youngish man, this applied even more strongly. He chose to identify himself with the past so that his sympathies were buried in it. He did not seem to realize that this *fadeur exquise* which he loved had been vigorously alive in its time. The first Lord Wendale, for example, had approved not only of houses mellowed with the patina of three centuries, he had built his own palaces and furnished them with new gilt and brilliant colored stuffs. So these very men of the past to whom Paul appealed on almost every issue of taste and conduct, would repudiate him as one who denied their own full-blooded acceptance of life as it was.

Lucinda was fond of Paul, and often listened to him with great pleasure and interest, but she felt an urgent need to save herself and Stephen from the things that had died. Nor did she want Stephen to become like Baa, a poor, anachronistic replica of his ancestor. She wanted him to live in his own right and to live for the future. For a long time she had hoped, though she had been secretly ashamed of this hope, that Paul would not marry and that Stephen would inherit Crittenden. Now, seated on this grassy knoll and looking down at the splendid estate, seeing not only the slopes and hollows of the park, the woods and the farm-lands, but in her mind's eye the stately rooms of the house, the faded damask which hung down the long line of windows, the portraits of dead viscounts and their wives, the soft English gilt of the mirrors, and exquisite worn needlework of the chairs and carpets, everywhere this rare, mellow beauty of fine workmanship tempered by the years, which acted almost as a drug on the senses, she rejected the inheritance for her son, as a godmother at baptism renounces for the whimpering baby temptations to which she herself continues to succumb.

As she descended from the common and re-entered the park gates she made two resolutions. One was not to send Stephen to

Eton, nor to any English public school. The other was to write to Pat Lanfranc.

CHAPTER THREE

Paul came down on a visit, and on his first night there Lucinda went, as she often did since it was reopened, to dine at Crittenden House. At dinner Marian said:

"Arthur, you must call on Lord Fitzauncell."

"Good Heavens!" exclaimed Paul, "you can't possibly do that."

"Why not?" asked Marian sharply. "He's our neighbor and Lucinda's countryman."

"Lucinda has never heard of him. If our family dies out and some guttersnipe buys this place and gets himself called Viscount Crittenden, d'you think Willy Greene-James should call on him—not that it matters much who Willy Greene-James calls on."

Paul normally had those good manners which take into account the implication of everything that is said. Only with Marian he failed to observe them. He was liable at any moment to remind her that she had failed to produce an heir, that she had no clear moral perceptions, or that she came from the middle classes. As his impulses were kind to the point of sentimentality, and he would be horrified to think he had shown ill-breeding, the fact that Marian provoked him into unkind and unintended rudeness, made him perpetually on edge with her.

"If you call on him," said Paul, "you'll have to ask him to dine. Imagine him sitting here. I'd rather ask the footman to sit down with me." When he had said this he appeared slightly confused, though the dessert was on the table and no servants were in the room.

"If you marry," said Marian calmly, "the family is not likely to die out. Why don't you find a job?"

"Because I happen to have been born a gentleman and intend to remain one."

"A loafer, you mean," said Marian.

"You mean a loafer because you don't understand the function of a gentleman."

"Is it to go to concerts and poke about in auction rooms?" asked Marian acidly.

"Partly," said Paul. "It is to keep alive certain appreciations which can only be done with leisure."

"Too much leisure rots the character."

"And too much activity rots the intelligence," said Paul, who at other times had told Marian that she suffered from *la malédiction de n'être jamais lasse*.

"I'd rather have character than intelligence."

"Doubtless. A late Duke of Devonshire," he went on, "said that his cousin who took 'a job,' as you call it, was no longer a gentleman."

"Then the Duke of Devonshire was a fool," declared Marian.

"He understood what our class stands for. No one understands it nowadays. In spite of that I am not going to turn myself into something different from what I was born. What you don't understand is that we are all leaves on a fallen tree. I shall continue to flourish while there is still some sap in the branch, though I may be turning a little yellow at the edges."

"Well, I do belong to the Primrose League," said Marian.

"Your wretched little primroses don't even know that the tree is fallen. They only know that there is still shade from the branches and the horizontal trunk. I at least know what I am doing. I may even be mistletoe—a parasite on the tree, but if I were to attempt to leave the branch and put my root directly in the ground I should die at once. That is what you are asking me to do—to please those who have cut down the tree."

"I have not cut down the tree," retorted Marian.

"You ask Arthur to call on Lord so-called Fitzauncell, which is giving a pretty good hack at it. You approve the fusion of business people with the aristocracy, which has rotted the trunk so that it fell easily. You confuse the tradition of aristocracy with nineteenth-century public school manners, and the aristocracy itself with the vast herd of synthetic gentlemen which these schools have spawned. There are people so ill-informed that they talk of the public schools as one of the homes of privilege. They are the most poisonously democratic institutions we have. They enable the sons of any East End pawnbroker who can pay the fees to be classed as equals with the descendants of Charlemagne."

Arthur, who generally enjoyed the scraps between Paul and Marian, looked a little uneasy, and passed the port round again to interrupt what he thought had gone too far.

"Do you think," Lucinda asked Paul, "that it would be a good idea not to send Stephen to Eton?"

"It would be idiotic," said Marian, who had no idea that Lucinda's question had any other motive than that of a *reductio ad absurdum*.

"On the contrary it would be very sensible, if you can find him sufficiently civilized tutors."

"It would be chopping down the tree with a vengeance," said Marian. She caught Lucinda's eye, and Paul limped to open the door for them. He would have been annoyed if Arthur had forestalled him.

When they were alone together Arthur asked Paul, "Do you really think that I shouldn't call on Fitzauncell, or were you pulling Marian's leg?" For some reason, perhaps because he thought Marian capable of giving as good as she took, or because Paul said things which he sometimes thought himself when Marian became over-bossy, but was too polite to say, and maybe from a faint sense of guilt towards Paul that he had not made a match that would uphold the distinction of the family, or at least bolster up its finances, he allowed Paul to speak to Marian in a way he would not have tolerated from anyone else. This aggravated Marian's bitterness towards Paul, as he was a living witness that there was a weak point in her husband's regard for her.

"Yes, I do think it would be better not," said Paul, who with Arthur dropped his pompous hyperbole of idiom.

"After all, he is my neighbor," said Arthur. He took a less mystical view than Paul of the nature of aristocracy, and if a man was a peer and owned a fine country estate he found it hard to believe that he was not respectable.

"His papers are doing a great deal of harm," said Paul.

"Well, I'll think about it. I expect Marian will give me no peace till I do call, now that you've put your face against it." He smiled slowly, and as Paul did not want any more port he pushed back his chair, and they went up to the Peacock Room, where Marian preferred to sit in the evenings when they were only a family party.

This evening they played bridge. Marian had an embroidery frame on her lap, at which she stitched when she was dummy. Except for Arthur, who enjoyed a rubber after dinner, the bridge was only a background to other preoccupations. Lucinda was wondering whether Pat would reply to the letter which she had written over a week ago. She had a dull sense of frustration, which lasted an hour or more after each post came in without a letter from him. Then she thought, "Perhaps it's as well. It would only be painful to wake it all up again." She could not see how they could achieve a satisfactory relationship while she had to look after Hugo. Paul was enjoying the sound of his own voice. Arthur, with an air of resignation, waited for Marian to put down her needlework and bid, for Lucinda to come out of her reverie and sort her cards, and for Paul, who was giving a scurrilous psychological analysis of Winnie Greene-James, to stop talking and lead. Much of Marian's conversation dealt with the idiosyncrasies of inanimate objects. Any references to the less obvious peculiarities of human beings worried her. There was an aubusson mat which the pile of the carpet worked gradually away from the fireplace. She put down her needlework and, mumbling through the cigarette in her mouth, she pulled it straight, saying, "It walks down the room, this mat."

At ten o'clock Harry, a new footman, whose face was rosy and candid above his white tie, brought in the tray with the drinks. Paul, instead of following Marian's lead, followed Harry with his eyes, from the door to the table, where he put down the heavy silver tray. In his aquiline and bony face his eyes were bright and gentle, like those of a young girl.

"Paul, do lead," said Marian, "and don't ogle the drinks like that."

Paul started and played a reckless card.

"I'm most extraordinarily thirsty this evening," he said. "I can't understand it."

"I suppose it's due to talking so much," said Arthur, and chuckled.

"It's not that at all. There was too much salt in the soufflé."

"There was not," said Marian, but Paul continued to argue that there was until the end of the hand, when it was discovered that he had revoked, and the conversation took a different turn. At bedtime Paul again mentioned his thirst, and poured himself out a large glass of water, which he drank with distaste. He went out with Lucinda to her car. When she dined here she left it at that side door which had impressed her so vividly on the day she first arrived at Crittenden with Hugo, but which now she hardly noticed. He told her that he wanted a new manservant for the flat he had just taken in Ebury Street.

"You might look out for one for me," he said. "I'd prefer someone from Crittenden. I don't suppose Marian would let me have one of her footmen. He'd be sure to be well trained. That younger one who waited at dinner seemed efficient. I think his name is Harry."

"D'you mean the one who brought in the drinks?"

"Did he? I didn't notice. I was so thirsty."

The next day Lucinda spoke to Marian about a servant for Paul, and suggested Harry.

"He's too young," said Marian, who nevertheless was pleased that Paul should acknowledge her efficiency in training servants. "He'd better have William. It's a nuisance, as he's an excellant valet and quite reliable, but he's getting rather old to be a footman."

She went to Paul and offered him William, but he did not appear at all grateful, and said that he had changed his mind. After this he irritated Marian more than ever. A few weeks later Harry gave notice, just before the Bassingbournes and the Frasers were coming to stay for the beginning of the partridge shooting, which was very inconvenient for Marian.

There was a shoot on the second day of their visit. Lucinda drove out with Marian, Lady Bassingbourne and Mrs Fraser to lunch with the men at a farmhouse. It was gray and inclined to be raining. Lucinda, who at first had thought the English autumn so lovely, had begun to dread it because of the close-following winter. Nor did she care much for the outdoor pleasures of this season. The farmhouse where they lunched seemed from its smell to be haunted by the ghosts of a thousand hams and cheeses. Arthur took the greatest satisfaction in this sort of thing, like a plant thrusting its roots even deeper into its native soil, while Marian enjoyed any excursion into the simple and primitive. Lucinda had hunted in Australia, largely because Fred had insisted on it, but during her first winter in England Stephen was born, and she had not taken it up again. She had never had any taste for shooting, and when they left the farmhouse after luncheon, and Lady Bassingbourne appeared to find even the mud outside the door delightful, she was ashamed that she had become so urban.

Lucinda walked with General Fraser down to the field where the shoot was to be resumed. He was rather a gallant old boy and he amused her. Suddenly he said:

"By the way, wasn't Pat Lanfranc a great friend of your husband's?"

"Yes," said Lucinda. "We did know him very well, but we've not seen anything of him lately." She thought General Fraser must be going to say that Pat was dead, otherwise why did he use the past tense?

As before, in moments of sudden tension, the scene where she experienced it was flashed indelibly on to her brain—the dark polished guns, the ruts in the lane, and Lady Bassingbourne's voluminous gray hair bulging over the tweed collar of her coat. She thought that she was about to advance into a further stage of emptiness in her life. The damp autumnal countryside accentuated the bleakness of her heart. She felt that the English country was becoming a prison, and in the second before General Fraser spoke again she half formed a resolution to leave it, and to take Hugo and Stephen to Australia. After all Hugo might as well be shut up in a room and a garden at Yarra Glen or Flinders as at the End House.

"Didn't you know he'd been with Allenby in Palestine? Odd thing was I met him at the station yesterday as we were coming down here. He had just arrived back."

"Did you tell him that you were coming to stay at Crittenden?" asked Lucinda, trying to sound casual.

"Yes, I did, as a matter of fact."

"Did he say anything?" asked Lucinda tentatively.

"He said there'd be plenty of birds, and he wasn't far wrong," said the general with satisfaction.

They came to a wooden gate into a stubble field, where Arthur and Lady Bassingbourne were waiting for the rest of the party to catch them up.

"We're going to walk up this field," said Arthur. "If you ladies are coming with us, you must keep behind the guns and come quietly." He beamed at Lady Bassingbourne and Mrs Fraser, but his speech was directed at Marian, who replied:

"We'll watch you from this gate."

They stood and watched the men walk down the field in a slowly moving line, which was reminiscent of war-time pictures in the *Illustrated London News* of troops moving across No-man's-land. There was a sudden whir, a succession of bangs, a few floating feathers and drifting smell of gunpowder as they put up a covey of partridge.

"We should have a nice dinner," said Lady Bassingbourne.

Lucinda watched the shooting carefully, as she knew that when she returned Hugo would question her about every detail. He was so avid for gossip about the activities of his fellows that she had formed the habit of making mental notes of all that she saw and heard when she was away from home, as the basis of her report to him, particularly if it had to do with any field-sport.

When the women arrived back at Crittenden House, Lucinda did not go in with the others, explaining that she must get back to Hugo. As she said good-bye and turned to go, Lady Bassingbourne came with her a few paces.

"Lucinda, my dear," she said, "I have not had an opportunity before to say how dreadfully sorry we are about Hugo, and how much we admire your devotion to him." In addition to her moustache she had a protruding upper lip, which gave her an expression of pity.

"Oh, thank you," said Lucinda awkwardly.

Lady Bassingbourne gave her a wistful smile and patted her arm. Lucinda walked on across the park.

If Pat had arrived back in London yesterday he would have found her letter waiting for him at his club, unless it had been forwarded to him to Egypt or somewhere. If he wanted to meet her again, if he still had any feeling for her, he might have written last night, and there would be a letter waiting for her at the End House, come by the afternoon post. This, and not Hugo, was the reason why she had made her excuses to Marian and had come straight home. She remembered dining at Cadogan Place on that evening two years ago, when she had arranged to meet Pat, and feeling guilty and ashamed that she had used the danger and misfortune of other people as an excuse to get away. It was then Lady Bassingbourne's kindness which had increased her sense of guilt. It no longer had that effect. It seemed to her now only a form of blackmail. If she left Hugo, Lady Bassingbourne would refuse to meet her. She was kind as long as Lucinda endured the living death of her bondage to Hugo. When she remembered her early efforts to become used to the horrors of his face, his endless exactions, his irritability which sometimes reached such a point of spite that she felt she would be justified in leaving him to the care of paid attendants, and then, almost worst of all, his apologies which she knew must have cost him an inward agony and which both softened and strengthened the tie between them, she felt that Lady Bassingbourne's kindness, and Marian's too, was little more than insolence. She preferred the attitude of Su-sannah, who hardly ever came to Crittenden, but wrote plaintively in answer to invitations, "I know that I am a bad mother and a heartless and worldly old woman, but I simply cannot *bear* to contemplate what has happened to Hugo. It is shocking and I expect I shall go to Hell. Please forgive me. All my love to both of you."

When she was about a hundred yards from the End House she looked at her watch and saw that the postman would have been. She found it hard not to run. As it was, she walked so quickly that she could hear her heart beating when she came in the hall, and looked at the letter table. On its dark mahogany surface, beneath the engraving of the first Lord Wendale, was one white square envelope. Before she could distinguish the handwriting she was certain that it was from Pat. Her heart beat violently and she took the letter up to her room to read it in private. It was as friendly and non-committal as her own letter had been. He apologized for not writing before, explained that had just returned from Egypt, and suggested that they should meet soon in London as they must have "a ton of things to talk about." Lucinda thought over this short note as she changed from her tweeds, and read it twice again before going down to Hugo. She tried to find in it some indication of his attitude towards her. There was none except in the reference to the "tons of things to talk about." That suggested many possibilities, and when, having concealed the letter, she went down to Hugo, there was a new light of hope in her eyes, and she felt as if that hidden letter was a passport to far and beautiful countries.

Hugo catechized her about the lunch and the shooting she had seen. He asked what everyone had said. She told him that yesterday in London General Fraser had met Pat who had just returned from abroad.

"You must write to him," said Hugo in his thick and stammering voice.

"I did write."

"You didn't tell me. What did you say?"

"What you told me to. I suggested we should lunch together one day."

"I told you to tell him to take you out to a show. Well, I suppose he'll reply, now he's back."

"I suppose so," said Lucinda.

"If he doesn't reply I'll write to him myself."

Hugo hated writing letters as his right hand had been injured and he could only use his left hand, that hand by which Lucinda had recognized him as he lay in the casino at Boulogne. His handwriting had always been juvenile and this made it childish, but he wanted Lucinda to see Pat occasionally, not only because of the qualms which he sometimes felt about her, but also because through this contact he was likely to hear news of his former army friends.

Every morning, for two or three days after this, Hugo asked her if she had heard from Pat, and she wished that she had not concealed his letter. She had already written a second time to him to suggest a day for meeting in London, and fortunately the reply to this could be shown to Hugo, as Pat merely wrote:

"DEAR LUCINDA,
Many thanks for your note. You must lunch with me. Will Tuesday next at the Berkeley at 1.30 suit you? Don't bother to reply if this is all right. Till then.

PAT."

"That's pretty curt," grumbled Hugo, "from someone you haven't seen for two years. I suppose he wants to drop us now. I wouldn't have expected Pat to behave like that. You'd better not go if he doesn't feel more friendly than that. It's undignified."

He brooded over this note and mentioned it several times, and told Lucinda that as far as he was concerned she need not go. She said that anyhow she had intended to go up next week for two days.

"Very well. Don't say that I forced you into an undignified position."

"I've never suggested anything of the kind."

"Not to my face perhaps."

She looked at him and wondered in what dark and poisonous atmosphere his imagination, only awakened by tragedy, had begun to work. He sometimes said things which imputed to her so much sly malice that she wished she had not practiced even the slight deception of concealing Pat's first letter. And yet this unconsidered impulse had resulted in the advantage of Hugo's believing that there was only a cold and formal relationship between Pat and herself.

She had been in the habit of going up every now and then to London to do some shopping. She stayed either at Brown's Hotel or with Susannah, whose finances had forced her to move to Bayswater, where she rented half a mansion, of which the drawing-room had been redecorated by a Dutch diamond merchant in a perfect reproduction of Louis Seize plaster-work.

"It is all right once I am indoors," she said, "and I prefer the suggestion of space on this side of the park to a bed-sitting room in Mount Street—and it's nice to look out onto the trees."

On Monday Lucinda went up to Brown's Hotel. In the evening she dined with Susannah in her palatial maisonette. The other guests were an old admiral—one of Susannah's former beaux whom Paul grouped together as "The Elders"—and a very young man with longish yellow hair who was interested in interior decoration. For the rest of her life Susannah generally had one or two of these ephebes about her. She found their flattery soothing, while their sensitive intuition of her wants added to her comfort and dispelled the sense of frustration which threatened her advancing years. In return she introduced them to princesses, and if she had a lucky day at Ascot or Goodwood she gave them presents she could ill afford, a piece of brocade or a papier-mâché table inlaid with pearl.

Lucinda herself found this society soothing. The excitement and anxiety which she felt on the eve of meeting Pat died down a little in the company of these two old people in whom all passion was spent, and of this young man who, she imagined, had no passions. She gave him a lift back in her taxi to his rooms in Shepherd's Market, and on the way he told her what a dear Susannah was, and what a treat it was to meet nowadays a real *grande dame* of the old school.

In the morning the world seemed more matter-of-fact, and by the time Lucinda arrived at the Berkeley, wearing a cheap but rather amusing necklace which she had bought that morning to celebrate the occasion, she was blaming herself for having wasted so much nervous tissue yesterday.

Pat was waiting for her. Except that he was a good deal browner from the suns of Palestine, he had not changed at all since she had seen him last. He greeted her with that affectionate assurance, that entire absence of any sense of embarrassment which he had always shown. His appearance of well-being, of abundant life, at once recalled the pleasure of their former meetings, but also awoke some other association which she could not place at once.

Over their lunch she asked him what he had been doing, but he said:

"Oh, nothing much—tell me about yourself. You look radiant. That's a pretty necklace you're wearing."

"You don't think it's vulgar? My clothes are always inclined to become vulgar when I'm happy."

"And are you happy?" He looked a little serious, as if he were not entirely pleased to hear this.

"Well, today I am."

They looked at each other and laughed.

Everything went easily. They stayed on talking until they were the last people in the restaurant.

When they came out into Piccadilly Lucinda held out her hand to say good-bye. Pat took it but he said, "Are you doing anything now? I have a free afternoon."

They decided to go to some place where they could talk, and they fixed on the Wallace Collection. Here they sat opposite the "Laughing Cavalier" and talked about the last time they had met, and about Lucinda's trip to Boulogne when Hugo was wounded.

"You didn't answer my letter," she said.

"No. It was a bit of a facer. I couldn't think what to say. Perhaps there wasn't anything to say. A fews days later I had a chance to go to the Near East, so I took it."

Lucinda looked up at the picture opposite them and smiled.

"What are you smiling at?"

"Nothing. I just remembered something." She had remembered that it was the engraving of the first Lord Wendale which Pat had recalled when she met him at lunch-time.

When they were turned out of the Wallace Collection at closing time, they went into an arty little restaurant in Duke Street for tea. They stayed here until the waitress told them crossly that she had to lay the table for dinner. They walked back through the early autumn evening to Brown's Hotel. In Oxford Street the shop windows were dazzling, and in Grosvenor Square the trees, looming through a blue-gray mist, were beginning to turn yellow.

"It's good to see the lights of London again," said Pat. "Till last week I hadn't seen 'em for five years."

"Did they seem very marvelous?"

"Yes. I had just found your letter waiting for me. Then I went out into the illuminated streets. That was the evening when I realized the war was over."

"Yes. It seems to me now, too, that the darkness is past."

At the entrance to Brown's Hotel Lucinda again held out her hand.

"I'm free this evening," said Pat. "Are you doing anything?"

They arranged to dine at the Savoy and dance there afterwards. Lucinda sang quietly to herself as she changed. This was the first time for years that she had dressed for anything more exciting than a dinner-party at Crittenden with the Greene-Jameses and the Bassingbournes, or in Bayswater with Susannah and her "Elders."

Not expecting to wear it, but saying to herself "one never knows," she had brought with her a gold colored evening dress for which there had not hitherto been a suitable occasion. She was surprised how well it became the warm tones of her skin, and it was not too gay for the brightness of her eyes.

All the evening pleasure and happiness combined to create a condition so different from that of her usual life at the End House that she felt the latter was only a bad dream, from which she had returned to the life of her girlhood with its ballrooms and its pretty clothes, and, above all, with its hope.

When she traveled down the next day to Crittenden, this feeling, particularly the feeling of returned hope, remained with her. She thought all the time about Pat, and what made him so attractive to her. She thought that it was the generosity of his thought and feeling, and that noble abundance of life in him, which expressed itself in his deep laughter, and although he was an efficient soldier and conventional in his outward behavior, though not so as to be easily labeled "army man," he was capable in private of tenderness, of subtle understandings and of gestures which she felt belonged rightly to a poet. For example, when they parted and he turned away he trailed his hand behind him, as if it were drawn back by the magnetism of Lucinda.

When she came into the hall of the End House she felt more able to cope with Hugo and the general life of Crittenden than ever before. She glanced at the engraving of the first Lord Wendale, and she turned away from it smiling. Stephen came running down the stairs calling, "Mummy! Mummy!" He flung himself into her arms more confidently than usual because she was smiling so happily.

She had asked Pat about various men who had been in the regiment at Crowborough, and she made notes of what news he was able to give her to pass on to Hugo. She decided also to tell Hugo that she had dined with Pat at the Savoy, and this seemed to please him, as he took it as a vicarious attention to himself. When she had finished her account of her two days in London, he said, "You must go again soon. It does you good to have a change and I like to hear what's going on."

She went up a fortnight later, and again they dined at the Savoy, but instead of dancing they went back to Pat's rooms, where she stayed till the early hours of the morning. After this they planned that she should take a small flat, where they could meet without risk of discovery or disturbance. She was not sure how Hugo would receive this plan, and was also afraid that it might awaken Marian's suspicions. According to Marian "nice people" did not live in flats. They discussed the possibility of keeping it secret.

In King Charles's Court, a huge block of flats overlooking the river, was a literary club to which Pat had been elected on his writing a monograph on Arab horses. He could enter this building as frequently as he chose without causing comment. It was here they decided that Lucinda should take a small flat. It was better, they thought, to avoid all unnecessary secrecy. After all, it was not unreasonable that she should want a *pied-à-terre* in London. If Hugo was angry she would have to endure it, while Marian could only silently disapprove.

However, before she revealed her intention a contretemps happened, also connected with flats, which made her feel that it was advisable to say nothing about it at present.

CHAPTER FOUR

ARTHUR AND MARIAN came up to London for a few days. One afternoon Marian, who had been to see a friend in Chester Square, finding herself in the neighborhood called also at Paul's new flat in Ebury Street. She had never called at his rooms before, and he had not foreseen such a possibility, but she was moved by curiosity about the reputed *chinoiserie* of his decorations, and also she wanted an address which he could probably give her. Paul was away for the day, and the door was opened by Harry, her ex-footman who had left at such inconvenient notice. When Paul came in at nine o'clock in the evening, Harry said in that tone of relish which servants use to announce some misfortune:

"Her ladyship called this afternoon."

"The devil she did," exclaimed Paul. "Did she see you?"

"Yes; I opened the door. She didn't half look annoyed."

"What did she say?"

"She said, ''Arry, I didn't know you was 'ere,' and walked straight away without asking if you was in or anything."

Paul whistled and then laughed.

"Now the fat's in the fire," he said.

"It was very disagreeable for me," said Harry indignantly. "What'll they say when I go back to Crittenden?"

"You needn't go back to Crittenden. The country's a horrible place. At least the English country is, especially in winter. It smells of sheep and cabbages."

They were interrupted by the electric stab of the front door bell.

"Go and see who it is," said Paul, "and if it's old or ugly send it away."

Harry went out. There was a brief murmur of voices and he returned, his erstwhile rosy face rather pale.

"His lordship, sir," he said, and retired to the kitchen.

"Oh, hullo Arthur," said Paul. "Have you come to inspect my new abode?"

"More or less." Arthur looked about the room with its pale green walls and vermilion lacquer chairs. "M'm, very pretty. Influence of *Chu-Chin-Chow*, eh?"

"Good God, no!" Paul exclaimed. "It's pure eighteenth century. It's the same period as the Chinese room at Crittenden."

"Oh, I see. I should have recognized it, I suppose. Is the whole flat à la Pekinese?"

"The dining-room is Chinese Chippendale, but not the rest. Like to see it?"

The dining-room had black linen curtains with a design of little Chinamen, suspended in swings from ivory-colored branches.

"Very chic," said Arthur. "D'you eat with chop-sticks?" He chuckled and they went back to the other room.

"Have a drink?" said Paul.

"I wouldn't mind a whisky."

Paul rang and told Harry to bring the drinks. When Harry, looking furious with embarrassment, had put down the tray and left the room, Arthur said:

"By the way, isn't that Marian's footman?"

"He was," said Paul.

"She's not too pleased about it. Says you pinched him from her. As a matter of fact she sent me down here to have it out with you. But I don't know what the devil she expected me to say." Arthur chuckled and lifted his glass.

"Lucinda asked Marian if I might have this boy," said Paul, "and she replied that I might have William who was more valuable to her. So why should she object if I took Harry?"

"She says that you did it in an underhand way."

"I could not help it if he came to me for a job. He had given Marian notice."

"That's what I told her," said Arthur.

"Certainly, I had said to him that if ever he was in need of employment to come to me. He struck me as an exceptional boy."

They talked of other things, both aware that they had avoided the realities of the situation. When Arthur gave Marian Paul's excuse she said he was shifty, and hoped he would not come to Crittenden for some time, adding, "I'm not going to have my servants filched away and debauched by my brother-in-law."

On one or two occasions in their married life Marian had expressed herself beyond the point which Arthur found tolerable. When this happened she was forced to recognize that she had married not only an easy-going English country gentleman, which was Arthur's normal aspect, but a man who was half French, and whose natural amiability could be frozen by an implacable pride.

"Crittenden is not only my private house," he said. "It is the home of my family, whom I regard more highly than my servants, and who are at liberty to come there when they choose."

This did not lessen Marian's indignation, though she said no more to Arthur, of whom in these moods she was afraid. She nagged at him and bossed him with the subconscious desire to provoke from him something more hot-blooded than his prevailing courteous tolerance, but when she succeeded in disturbing this, it resulted not in the satisfaction of a good row and reconciliation, but in the recognition that there were some things which her husband valued more highly than herself, and that he had a closer resemblance to Paul than appeared on the surface.

As soon as they returned to Crittenden she came over to the End House to release her feelings to Lucinda. She told her what had happened, and said that if he were not Arthur's brother she would not have Paul at Crittenden again, adding, "He's a shifty little rat."

"Oh, I don't think he meant to annoy you," said Lucinda feebly. Paul had shown her more intelligent kindness than any of her other in-laws.

"The whole thing is monstrous," said Marian. "Apparently he has furnished that flat like a joss-house. I shouldn't be surprised if he burned incense. The fact is he's decadent. I have an instinct for that sort of thing. I knew that Willy Greene-James's first wife wasn't straight long before he divorced her."

"How could you tell?" asked Lucinda, wondering if she herself were beginning to develop the marks of the unfaithful wife.

"From the general look of her," said Marian.

"Oh dear!" said Lucinda reflectively, and Marian gave her a sharp glance.

Lucinda had that morning received the signed and completed agreement for her flat. She had been going to announce the fact to the family, now that it was too late for her to be influenced by their disapproval, but after this conversation with Marian she thought it better to keep it secret until a more propitious occasion.

Fred had sent her one of those occasional bonuses which he bestowed on his daughters, particularly on Lucinda, and she spent it in furnishing the flat, which contained only a sitting-room overlooking the Embankment, a bedroom and a bathroom. All meals were sent up from the restaurant, but when Pat was coming Lucinda bought her own fruit and wine. It gave her intense pleasure to arrange the flat and to prepare the accessories for their *dîners à deux.*

All that autumn she was intensely happy. She enjoyed even the secrecy of her meetings with Pat, which later became such a burden to her. Sometimes she caught sight of herself accidentally in a glass, and was surprised at her look of recovered youth and the light in her eyes. She wondered if Marian's instinct would attribute her bloom to its proper cause. She was almost afraid of it, and wished that when she returned to Crittenden she could manage to look more jaded. However, Marian, commenting on her looks, merely said, "The cold weather's much healthier."

One evening in particular she remembered for a long time afterwards, when she returned to the End House from meeting Pat in London. Everything was frosty and still. The servants greeted her with friendly deference, and Hugo was less exacting than usual. She went into the drawing-room to tea, so that Stephen could be brought to her. She was struck afresh by the charm of the room with its cream paneling and wood fire. The curtains had not yet been drawn, and each window was a square of blue-gray mist, broken with the tracery of bare trees, against which the reflection of the lights hung like luminous yellow fruit. Kate, who had come with her when she left Wellington Court, wheeled the tea-table up to the fire, and drawing the curtains shut out the blue squares of mist, so that she was enclosed in the soft color and warmth of the room. Lucinda had always taken for granted her circumstances of comfort and even luxury, but coming into this pleasant room after the cold journey, it occurred to her that as far as material things were concerned, she probably lived the most civilized kind of life that had yet been evolved. Now that her emotions had again found release she could enjoy, perhaps more fully than ever owing to the increased cultivation of her taste, all the good things which came to her so easily. She had never harbored these thoughts before, and she was a little puzzled by the sensations which they produced in her. The firelight clothed everything with cheerfulness, the silver tea things, the chintzes and the deep reds and blues of the rugs, but when Stephen came in he looked like an angel in the dancing light. Lucinda took him up and hugged him, but in that moment of happiness the cold thought came to her that her good things were unrelated and even in conflict with each other, and she wondered, if Marian were to come into the room at that moment, whether she would see in the uneasiness of her expression the signs of guilt which she was so apt to detect.

There were times when she actually did have a sense of guilt. Nearly every time she met Marian the latter had something derogatory to say about Paul and his "joss-house." The sinister orgies supposed to happen there probably existed only in Marian's imagination. Lucinda had been to a rather austere but elegantly appointed dinner with Paul and there was no smell of incense. What lust was indulged seemed to be wholly of the eyes, as Paul had spent so much on his lacquer chairs, which were far from comfortable, let alone viciously luxurious, that he had hardly enough left to buy food and drink. Even so, the fact that he had a flat which was supposed to be a haunt of vice, and that she had a flat for secret meetings with a lover, though these meetings brought her so much health and happiness that she could not possibly think them vicious, did give her at times a feeling of disintegration, that the solid, reputable tree of Crittenden had, as Paul said, fallen, and they were useless leaves on the branches.

Paul's settled income from the estate had shrunk since the war, he no longer had his army pay, and owing to his breach with Marian he did not care to resume his long periods of financial recuperation at Crittenden. He certainly could not take Harry there. In the new year he gave up the flat in Ebury Street, for which he was able to charge a high premium, and with that and the money from the sale of his chinoiseries he bought a tiny villa in Provence, whither he departed with Harry.

"I had achieved the frame for a civilized life," he told Lucinda, "but I couldn't afford the picture."

A few weeks after Paul's departure Lucinda, finding the difficulty of explaining her whereabouts when in London increasing, told Marian that she had taken a flat in King Charles's Court.

"What do you go down there for?" asked Marian. "If you want a *pied-à-terre* why don't you find one in Knightsbridge?"

"This is so convenient. It's a service flat. It's really more like a hotel."

"Then why not go to a hotel?"

"I like to have my own furniture."

"Certainly hotel beds do give me the creeps," conceded Marian.

Hugo did not object as much as she had thought he would. His gaze seemed now to be focused inwards, and the light of intelligence was more dull in his pale and distorted eyes.

After Lucinda had told Marian about the flat, she had a bolt put on the door thinking it possible that Marian might call one evening when Pat was there, and that if her strange instinct were aroused, the ordinary lock might prove inadequate against her curiosity, which would then discover something far more startling than a runaway footman. When Pat saw this bolt he was very amused at her extreme caution, and he made jokes about it during the evening. This happened about five months after their first reunion, and Lucinda found to her slight consternation that she was grateful for the extra topic of conversation. It was this that made her first aware of the disadvantage of the nature of their meetings, that they shared none of the ordinary activities of life, nor met outside the close and often wanton atmosphere of her flat, so that a thing so commonplace as a new bolt on the door made an important and refreshing contrast to their luxurious routine.

She seldom met Pat elsewhere. Susannah, who felt both guilty and grateful to Lucinda for bearing the exclusive care of Hugo, asked her friends to send her invitation cards. Lucinda did not very much enjoy dances and receptions, as her life so far had not made her acquainted with many people in these circles, and she either had to sit out with one of Susannah's elders, or to dance with one of her too young interior decorators. But she accepted the invitations as they gave her an excuse for coming more often to London, and Hugo had told her that she should "get about a bit," and also, at one or two parties she met Pat in the outside world. When this happened, and she was able to dance with him, perhaps twice in an evening, she was intensely happy. Like all lovers, she was proud of her love, and although at first its secrecy had been an added excitement, now it was a frustration which was released for the few minutes when Pat held her in his arms in a crowded ballroom.

She was unaware of her changed appearance as she danced with him, but Pat noticed it, and although he was touched by it, he was also embarrassed, and anxious lest it should harm her reputation. She always told him beforehand, when she had the opportunity, what dances she was going to. He began to reply that he had not been invited.

"Susannah would get you a card," said Lucinda.

"Good Heavens! you mustn't ask her," protested Pat. "Besides, I don't like going to the houses of people I don't know. If I get invitations of that kind I always send 'em back."

Lucinda told Hugo that she had met Pat at various dances. He told her, next time they met, to ask him what had happened to a former friend in their regiment. Lucinda asked him this, but was unable to tell Hugo the reply until she and Pat had met again at a public function, which was not for some weeks. Still, at times, Hugo filled her with horror and repulsion, but she hated practicing these deceptions on him in his defenseless condition.

Also at some of the parties she attended she saw Mrs Fabian Parker. Once she was introduced to her and they chatted together for a minute or two. Lucinda's faint, ironical smile as she spoke to her made this sophisticated woman of the world feel like an awkward schoolgirl, and either because of this or some deeper emotion she left the house a few minutes later. Lucinda, thinking it might please him, and even be accepted as a kind of forgiveness, told Hugo of this meeting. His twisted face gave a convulsion which horrified her, and for the rest of the day made her ill at ease that she had been so tactless.

At first, when she began to go out again in society, he was pleased. It appeared to ease his conscience. Later, when she returned to the End House from London, looking so radiant, he would watch her suspiciously and make sullen replies when she spoke to him, but he never complained, as he had formerly when she was devoting her whole attention to him. Brooding here, in this enclosed world, he had begun to live entirely in the imagination, and she felt that this faculty, over-developed, absorbing every other, was able to seize on the most trivial detail, the inflection of a word, or the way she held her gloves or put down her bag, and read back from that slight sound or gesture the whole sequence of events which had led up to it. Before the summer was over she was sure that he knew that she had a lover. He did not seem actively to resent it, but merely to take it as a further morsel for his voracious imagination to seize and digest into part of the design of his ruined life.

He did not appear to know who was her lover, as when she mentioned that she had seen Pat he was always unreservedly pleased, and told her she should see more of him. She had the idea that he would, if she told him of it, have agreed to their liaison, that his imagination would have fed on it in a way too horrible to contemplate, so that to preserve her sense of decency she had, in addition to being unfaithful, to practice little deceptions on him.

She could not help acknowledging to herself that all her difficulties would vanish if Hugo were to die. She tried to put from her the thought that she was a woman who wished for her husband's death, but in tired and lonely moments it came to her as a dark weight on her mind. It put into her eyes an expression which made people say, "That woman looks as if she had a past," whereas it was the present which troubled her. The occasional shadow, the tragic hint behind her eyes, went strangely with the youthful contours of her face, and going about with Susannah, who was so much a figure in the great world, she came herself to be known in society as something of a beauty.

At the end of July Susannah shut up her palatial maisonette and went off on a round of visits. Ten days later Pat left London for Scotland, and would not return till early October. There was now no object in Lucinda's going up to London. Stephen had stopped his lessons with Miss Wallace, his governess, who was shortly going on her annual holiday, and Lucinda had him on her hands. As he became older he became more curious to know what was behind the double doors into the library. Lucinda said it was "a poor, sick man" whom she looked after. She hoped that the necessity would never arise of explaining to Stephen that the man was his father, too hideous to be seen by a child, or by the unaccustomed eye.

Soon Lucinda began to be attacked by depressing fits of jealousy. Stuck here at the End House, she imagined Pat going from one cheerful house-party to another, where he must inevitably meet a great many delightful women, whose attractions would be enhanced by freedom and propinquity. She read his letters anxiously, searching for any sign of coolness. At last she could not bear her rôle of patiently waiting any longer. She felt she must do something, move somewhere, and when Miss Wallace went off for her holiday Lucinda announced that she was going to accept Paul's invitation to visit him in Provence.

Marian was shocked at her associating with the prodigal before his repentance, and said that Stephen would be sure to catch some kind of fever. Lucinda for once stood up to Marian.

"I was brought up in the sun," she said, "and I've hardly seen it for eight years."

"All the sun does in the South of France," said Marian, "is to make the drains smell worse."

They took a night train from the Gare du Lyon and woke up next morning in the brilliant light of the south. Stephen was excited. He kept drawing Lucinda's attention to the passing landscape—the hot white rocks and the sparse trees.

"Look, Mummy! It's all light, it's all light!" he exclaimed.

Paul met them at Marseilles with a small and rattly Citroën. Although he had been accustomed to ride with indifference in the coroneted Daimlers of Crittenden, he was extremely proud of this shabby little car, which he owned and drove himself. They collected Harry with several parcels, and he perched himself on a dickey seat which opened out of the back of the car.

They drove eastward over those wild and arid hills, which look as if they could only be haunted by robbers, savage cats and anchorites, though they were daily traversed by the motor cars of commercial travelers. Paul's villa was at St Saturnin-sur-mer. It was pink-washed with green shutters, perched on a stony hillside and overlooking the tiny port where yachts and tramp steamers called. There was a fig tree at the end of the house and across the rough drive were two eucalyptuses. The scent from their hot leaves and from the surrounding pines filled the noonday air. Under the eucalyptus the ground was hard and dry, with little broken twigs on it, as she had so often seen it in the country near Melbourne. The bright aromatic air awoke and at the same time satisfied a powerful nostalgia in Lucinda.

"Oh, I feel I can breath again!" she exclaimed, as she stood looking about her. There was a vine-covered terrace in front of the house.

"Look, darling!" she said to Stephen, "grapes growing out of doors, just as Mummy used to see them when she was a little girl."

"Is this Australia, Mummy?" asked Stephen.

They had lunch at a table laid under the vines, and the greeny-purple grapes, just beginning to ripen, hung down above their heads. Harry, wearing only a blue shirt, flannel trousers and espadrilles, brought the food from the kitchen, where it was cooked by a young woman called Assomption, who, judging by the sounds from that direction, was giving him a French lesson. The sunlight filtered through the vine and made dazzling spots on the tablecloth, and little yellow jewels in the glasses of local wine. Paul appeared more satisfied with life than Lucinda had ever known him to be before. He talked about St Saturnin as if it were unique, and the people who lived there as if they were the most entertaining in the world. His enthusiasm was infectious, and Stephen, who even for a child was inclined to be too much the mirror of his environment, said:

"Let us live here always with Uncle Paul, Mummy. It's nicer than the End House."

After luncheon Paul showed them the garden which he was making himself. He had already grown some huge tomatoes and zinnias.

"You don't seem like a leaf on a fallen tree," said Lucinda.

"I'm not," said Paul, "I was mistaken. I'm not a leaf on an oak, fallen in an English park, but a leaf on the eternal olive, the sacred tree of Athena, the ever-green tree of humanity and civilization. The olive gives oil for our health and its flavor improves our cookery, whereas with the acorn we can only feed pigs."

In the morning they went down to bathe. Harry came with them.

"You won't mind," said Paul. "I can't ask him to go without his swim."

Paul introduced her to one or two groups of people who were lying about sunning themselves. They seemed to be mostly writers or painters or some kind of intelligentsia. Paul was proud of his acquaintance with them, and also of Lucinda as he introduced her. They looked far more interesting than the Greene-Jameses and the people she knew at Crittenden. Later in the morning they went up to dive from a rock underneath the lighthouse at the end of the plage. Paul gave brief histories of the people to whom they had been talking.

"I liked that woman you called Freda," said Lucinda. "I didn't catch her surname. Her husband has an interesting face."

"That's not her husband," said Paul. "He's married to a Roman Catholic who won't divorce him."

"Does he live with Freda?"

"Of course."

"Oh!" Lucinda smiled.

"What are you laughing at?" demanded Paul.

"I was only smiling at being introduced to them. I don't mind."

"Mind? Why should you mind? They are the most intelligent couple in St Saturnin. They have a charming villa and it is an honor to be invited there."

"Don't be cross, Paul. I've never been introduced to an unmarried couple before and I had to accustom myself to the idea. You must admit it is not usual to find them in Marian's drawing-room, or even Susannah's."

244

"We have a better sense of values here."

"Doesn't it matter then, here, having that sort of relationship?"

"It's your own affair."

"I see."

Harry came up with Stephen, whom he had been teaching to swim.

"Do you like this place, darling?" asked Lucinda.

"Yes, I do," said Stephen.

"I used to bathe from a place like this in Australia," said Lucinda, "only the rock was red, not white, but the sea was the same color. My brother used to call it the Tarpeian Rock."

"Is the bathing good in Australia, madam?" asked Harry.

"Oh yes, it's marvelous. I shouldn't think there is any better—except for the sharks."

"I reckon I'd like to go there," said Harry, "but I wouldn't like to have my leg bitten off."

"It doesn't happen very often," said Lucinda.

She remembered the only time there had been the scare of a shark while they were bathing at Flinders. She could see again the dark triangular fin, shewing above the water about a hundred yards out. From that remembered fin the whole scene spread out again in her mind, particularly a morning when she had felt the soft wind on her arms and her hair. Her present physical sensations were so like those of ten years earlier that she was taken more powerfully back in time. Yet, she thought, in a brief reflective moment in which she seemed almost to grasp an elusive formula which could explain the pattern of her life, it was not so much as if she had traveled backwards but as if the past had moved to the present. She sometimes had dreams in which the landscape of her childhood appeared, but bathed in a supernatural radiance, and the face of some half-forgotten playmate who was with her in the dream had acquired the beauty and tenderness of a seraph. Her present condition resembled one of these dreams. Perhaps the dreams revealed what life could and should become. Perhaps as one penetrated the different layers of experience, the pattern of one's life was repeated in richer colors.

She felt this strongly as they climbed a stony path in the hot noonday, and hung their bathing-dresses on an olive tree to dry, as they had hung them on the verandah rail at Flinders. Then, she had taken these pleasures for granted, but now, after eight English winters and eight tepid summers, after the social elaboration and emotional complexity of her life, their simplicity gave her an intense pleasure and sense of freedom, which was not diminished by the fact that she had spent the morning bathing in the company of one of the Crittenden footmen, whose manner was neither familiar nor subservient, but only showed that friendly respect which every man and woman has the right to demand.

As they sat down again under the vines to a dish of mussels cooked with saffron and garlic, with a tall bottle of local wine in the middle of the table, Lucinda felt that a past far more remote than that of Flinders had moved to the present, and that the kind of life still existed where all things were in proportion and where true human relationships were allowed their natural expression.

In the evening Paul explained that he usually dined with Harry at a restaurant on the quay. Assomption did not generally come in the evening.

"You mean, do I mind dining with Harry," said Lucinda, and anxious to atone for her priggishness of the morning, which she had only realized later was, when expressed by herself, ludicrous hypocrisy, she added, "Not at all."

"I can't send him off by himself every evening," said Paul gratefully.

Stephen was put to bed, and Assomption's grandmother came to sit in the villa while they went out. As they passed the end of the villa on their way down to the port the wall gave out the heat it had accumulated during the day, and the pines and the fig tree filled the air with their scent. They sat at a table at the edge of the quay, with the rows of fishing boats close beside them. The lights of a small tramp steamer and a few yachts were reflected in the oily water.

One or two of the people whom they had met in the morning greeted them and exchanged a few words as they passed, including the unmarried couple. Lucinda was particularly nice to them, not only to please Paul but because it gave her a sense of liberation to be on friendly terms with these people. No one seemed to think it odd that Harry was dining with them and they all greeted him pleasantly. However, he did not linger on with them over their coffee and brandy, but said:

"I reckon I'll go to the dance now, sir—if you'll excuse me, madam?"

They were watching Harry depart along the quay, when a voice said:

"Paul, my dear, where have you been? I have not seen you for three days."

Elspeth Roberts was standing by their table. She lived with her husband in a château about two miles inland where they grew the local wine. They had a boy of about Stephen's age.

"I have been entertaining my guests," said Paul, and introduced Lucinda.

"I've heard a great deal about you," said Mrs Roberts. "Paul has been terrified that you would turn up your nose at his villa and go back by the next train."

"Me!" exclaimed Lucinda, astonished. "Why, I thought you knew me, Paul."

"No one knows anybody till he's seen him in half a dozen environments," said Mrs Roberts.

"Oh, I hope that is not true," said Lucinda. Slowly, throughout the day, there had been forming in her mind the plan of persuading Pat to come to St Saturnin. She was not clear as yet how this was to be done, or how much open acknowledgment of their relationship there might be. This remark of Mrs Roberts made her hopes sink a little.

"I shouldn't think it at all true," said Paul. "The peasant may only see his wife in one environment for seventy years, but I should think he knows her pretty well."

Paul offered Mrs Roberts a drink and they sat for half an hour or so, talking lightly of serious things. Lucinda found this a refreshing contrast to Crittenden where so often there was portentous conversation about triviality, as when Willy Greene-James and Marian discussed a cricket match. They went along to the dance, which was held in a public square. Sailors from the port, peasant girls, holiday-makers from Marseille and the sprinkling of English intelligentsia, shuffled about raising more dust beneath the Chinese lanterns suspended from the dusty plane trees. On the high wooden supports of the band platform half a dozen children had climbed, and they hung there like lazy, graceful monkeys, watching with sleepy wonder or remote derision the antics of their elders.

Paul danced with Elspeth Roberts. Lucinda found Harry standing near her. She smiled at him and he came and stood beside her.

"Do you like living here?" she asked him.

"I should say I do, madam," he said. "I never thought I'd have such a life."

"D'you find enough to do?"

"Oh, yes, there's plenty to do, though it's not like Crittenden where you were on your feet all day, with her ladyship round the corner waiting to pounce on you, if you'll excuse me saying so, madam."

Lucinda laughed. "What d'you do here?" she asked.

"Well, there's the house and the garden, and there's Mr Paul to look after. I have to keep an eye on him, I can tell you, madam, or he'd wear himself to a shred. Then there'll be the vintage soon, and we'll all go and help pick grapes at the château. Mrs Roberts gives a big dinner on the terrace afterwards. Everybody's a human being here. You don't have to give up your self-respect. That's what I like."

"It seems to agree with you, and with Mr Paul, too. I've never known him so well and cheerful."

Paul and Elspeth came back, and Harry went off to look for Assomption. Paul's brown face above his blue shirt was glowing with pleasure. They stood watching the dancing for a while and then returned to the café on the quay. Paul began one of his perorations in praise of St Saturnin, its climate, its wine, its human freedom, its cookery, its links with the golden age and its significant name. It seemed as if some acid in his composition had been dissolved, or, Lucinda thought, as if he had at last found a part that suited him. Because Paul, she realized, was not satisfied unless his life had a dramatic quality. At Crittenden he dramatized himself as the last aristocrat, and his eyes were always turned to the past, and he suffered miseries in trying to drag its dead relics into the foreground of his present life. But here he only used the past to reflect a deeper light on the present, which was the focus of his attention. When Elspeth had left them she said something of this kind to him.

"At last I have what I want," he said.

"You're the first person I've known to admit that."

"I only obtained it by giving up what I didn't want."

"That doesn't sound very difficult."

"The difficulty is in knowing what you don't want."

"What is it you don't want?"

"Crittenden. The thought of it weighs me down—nauseates me. The way I behaved there makes me shudder—like an old maid who, having no human contact, becomes obsessed with her family. The Greene-Jameses as neighbors, my God! And now that appalling Straker. It astonishes me to think that kind of life still goes on, that there's any sap left to nourish the leaves."

"It certainly seems remote from this," said Lucinda, looking at the reflections in the oily harbor, feeling the warm air with its mingled smells of fishing boats and Caporal cigarettes, of Coty perfumes and garlic, and hearing the very French sound of the dance band. "Do you think I would be wise to come and live here?"

"If you know what you don't want."

"I know what I do want," said Lucinda. She wanted above all things to have Pat with her. She imagined him seated with them at this table, and she persuaded herself that he might like the life of the place. He was not, she thought, the conventional army type—not nearly so much as Hugo. He noticed things which Hugo would ignore. He was interested in ideas and altogether more sensitive.

When she left a fortnight later this tentative idea of living at St Saturnin, at any rate for part of the year, had become a definite plan. The place satisfied her nostalgia for a warm climate, she enjoyed that kind of life, and liked the people and the way they talked. It was becoming increasingly undesirable that Stephen should be at the End House with its sinister mystery of the closed door, and as soon as he had made the break of leaving for his preparatory school, she did not intend to bring him back for the holidays. In fact, everything seemed to combine to make it appear reasonable that she should have a house here. She even thought it might be possible to give up the End House altogether and for Hugo to have apartments in Crittenden itself, where a few shut-off rooms would not be noticed. All these plausible arguments were, she felt, sufficient to conceal her main purpose, that of having Pat with her to share at least a part of her daily life. If Paul could do anything so extraordinary as carrying off one of Marian's footmen, and set up a ménage with him without undue comment or retribution, surely her own more ordinary project was not impossible. She did not realize that the very peculiarity of Paul's behavior put it beyond the bounds of conventional disapproval, nor that his ability to dramatize himself enabled him to carry off situations which would fill the more realistic with dismay, nor that there are some people to whom eccentricity is allowed, and who have earned this privilege through a childhood of loneliness and humiliation.

When Paul was being "the last aristocrat" he saw Crittenden as a palace of sublime and fading splendor. Now he only grudgingly allowed its singular charm, and discussed it as a cumbersome white elephant of a house standing for all that was most tedious, and he turned on to St Saturnin where, as he thought, he had discovered his true nature, the rosy light which formerly he had shed on Crittenden.

Lucinda was back at the End House for a fortnight before Pat returned from the north. Hugo appeared neither pleased nor resentful at her return. He asked her about Paul's villa, which she described enthusiastically. He replied that it sounded "damned dirty and uncomfortable," the only ill-natured thing he said.

She also gave a glowing account of St Saturnin to Arthur and Marian. She said how much she had enjoyed the holiday, and how much good it had done Stephen, who was a golden brown all over.

"Gosh!" said Marian. "The child looks like a half-caste."

When Lucinda said that she would take him there again next summer neither Arthur nor Marian looked pleased, Arthur because he liked to have the boy at Crittenden and thought he should spend his summers in the place it now seemed more than ever likely that he would inherit.

Lucinda had not been back for three days before she felt the ties and duties of the End House and Crittenden to be an intolerable frustration. She was having tea with Marian and Arthur one afternoon when Willy Greene-James walked in. He at once began to talk to Marian with earnest indignation about the trivial misdemeanor of a gamekeeper. The matter could have been settled and dismissed in two minutes, but they kept it going for half an hour, and Lucinda could not help comparing it with the lively talk at St Saturnin and she heard Paul's exclamation, "Willy Greene-James as a neighbor, my God!"

She then began to worry about Pat. She had only had a brief note from him giving the date of his return. Again she was seized by fits of jealousy. These combined with the frustrations of Crittenden made her feel desperate to break through into a sphere where she could control her own life, and where her affections, if they were defeated, would suffer that defeat from something inherent in herself and not from arbitrary external circumstances.

At last the day arrived when she was to go up to London to meet him. She bought a single ticket, and a return ticket when she came back. She made a childish superstition of this, that she would never be at Crittenden without a return ticket to London in her bag.

She was so excited when she arrived at the flat that she had to go out again, and she spent the rest of the afternoon buying luxuries for their dinner. She had brought a case of St Saturnin wine back with her, and two bottles stood on the side table with their bright labels of the Roberts' château.

As soon as he came into the flat and their eyes met she knew that all her anxieties had been self-inflicted. When he took her in his arms she felt like some shriveled plant, when the wind changes to the south-west and brings the rain. The only reference she made to St Saturnin was when he opened the wine. She asked him how he liked it.

"It's very potent," he said; "not at all bad."

"You don't really like it though?"

"To be quite honest, darling, it's not up to the Hermitage you gave me."

She looked a little disappointed. He came round and hugged her and said:

"Any wine is nectar when I have you."

"One can easily get Hermitage at St Saturnin," she said, with apparent irrelevance.

She did not mention her plan more explicitly, but she felt that on this first night he would agree to anything she asked. Secure in this belief she gave herself up to the present. She stayed three days in London, and each night Pat came to King Charles's Court. She still did not mention her plan, partly because, although Pat was still an ardent lover, she sensed in him less malleability than he had shown on the first night and she was waiting for a return of that condition to disclose it.

Back at Crittenden, even with the talisman of the return ticket, her former frustrations and anxieties once more oppressed her, increasing in intensity until dispelled for a while by her next meeting with Pat in London. One day she said with an affectation of carelessness to Marian:

"St Saturnin did Stephen so much good that I thought I might take him there at Christmas."

Marian said "Gosh!" with so much emphasis that she did not dare mention it again. The first thing, Lucinda decided, was to gain Pat's approval of the idea. With that she could brave the others. But Christmas was nearly upon them, and she had still not mentioned St Saturnin to him, except in indirect allusion.

Pat was going to spend Christmas with his cousins at the family seat in Mayo. Lucinda begged him not to go, owing to the danger of being shot by Sinn Feiners.

"I'm used to bullets," he said.

"The house may be burned down over your heads."

"Well, we can sleep in the stables," said Pat, grinning amiably. "Mild climate, plenty of straw. I've always spent Christmas at Drumkene, except when I was in Palestine, and I'm not going to be stopped by a few potato-fed thugs."

"Look, listen Pat!" said Lucinda in desperation. "I have an idea. I could take a villa at St Saturnin, and you could come to stay there. It's a heavenly place, and you needn't drink the local wine." She smiled, trying to treat the subject lightly.

"I couldn't do that—for your sake," said Pat seriously. "Doesn't your brother-in-law live there? We must be careful, Lucie."

"Yes, but Paul wouldn't mind. Everything is much freer there. Paul dines in public with his footman."

As soon as she said this she saw that she had made a mistake. Pat said:

"I've heard he was a bit eccentric, but I daresay he's all right.

Still, you don't want to get mixed up with that cheap Riviera crowd, darling. You'd better go to Crittenden and have a good time with your boy and your decent country neighbors, and we'll meet here again early in January. It's only three weeks from now."

"I can't have a good time anywhere without you," said Lucinda foolishly. "And St Saturnin isn't the Riviera."

"You said you enjoyed your holiday there in the summer, so you can have a good time without me."

She saw that it was hopeless to try to persuade him, but she did not give up her plan. When she was with him she did not doubt that he loved her. Therefore, she argued, he must be prepared to make sacrifices for her, if it was a sacrifice to spend a month or two every year with her in one of the most attractive places she had ever seen. She was prepared to make almost any sacrifice for him.

There was a small family party at Crittenden for Christmas. Baa was there with his mother, Dolly Wendale, and Lucinda and Stephen spent most of the time at Crittenden House. They had a family dinner on Christmas night, but on Boxing Day Marian gave an afternoon birthday party for Stephen, to which all the neighbors and their children were invited. Lord Fitzauncell was at this party. He arrived late with one or two of his guests. Just as he came into the dining-room the lights went out, so that the candles on Stephen's birthday cake might make an impressive and symbolic entrance. This cake was carried by the butler past where Lord Fitzauncell was standing, and its faint light briefly revealed his face in the darkness. It was at this moment that Lucinda first saw him, and she gave a start, not exactly of fear, but more the feeling one has when something startling happens on the stage. This powerful head with its heavy chin and thick nostrils, suddenly looming from the darkness in which the children tittered with excitement, was almost too sinister to be real. It made a stronger impression on Lucinda because it was vaguely familiar, and she thought this familiarity must be due to some reminiscence of the ogres in the fairy tales of her childhood.

The cake was now in front of Stephen, and the candles illuminated his golden curls and smiling angelic face, making a contrast with Lord Fitzauncell even more reminiscent of magic and ancient legend.

Stephen gazed in wonder at his cake. Marian said:

"Blow out the candles, my dear, in one puff if you can."

"I like them alight," said Stephen.

"Still, you must blow them out," said Marian.

Stephen reluctantly puffed until the last candle was out, at which the room was again filled with an electric blaze, and the children rubbed their eyes.

Lucinda turned to look at Lord Fitzauncell, who was shaking hands with Marian and smiling with a sort of evil benignity. She was sure now she had seen him before and not only his photograph in a newspaper, but she could not think where. It must have been at some party in Melbourne.

After tea they all moved into the saloon, where Marian organized children's games. In the saloon the electricity only extended to reading lamps and picture lights, and the huge room with its gilding, its yellow damask and the softly glowing colors of its painted ceiling, was only lighted by the many candles in the row of crystal chandeliers, which gave it a rather eerie beauty.

Lucinda found herself, in an interval between games, standing near Lord Fitzauncell, and again she gave him a glance of puzzled recognition. He saw her looking at him, and was about to speak to her when Baa accosted him in a manner in which Wendale assurance had become simple effrontery. After a few conventional politenesses he said:

"You don't have any Oxford news in your papers. The universities are very important, you know."

Lord Fitzauncell grinned.

"They aren't important to the public," he said. "They only have museum value."

"English people like to read about them."

"English people are going to like to read what I want 'em to read," said Lord Fitzauncell confidently. "All that sort of thing's finished—statesmen quoting Latin in the House of Commons. I want to interest my public in the people who matter—business men, men of ability and power. You're an earl, aren't you?"

"Yes," said Baa, for once slightly embarrassed.

"You've no business to be," said Lord Fitzauncell. "Still, earls have social value. Who d'you know?"

Baa mentioned some of his more exalted acquaintance.

"Well," said Lord Fitzauncell, "as you're a relation of my neighbor, Lord Crittenden, come and see me when you leave your High School, and I might give you a social column. I can't promise, mind you, and you'll have to be able to write. I don't like university men on my papers. They're too damned accurate, but I might make an exception to oblige a neighbor."

Lucinda was half amused at this conversation, but she was also a little humiliated, and she moved away. She had, too, enough belief in the dignity of titles like those of Wendale and Crittenden, to be shocked that a man of Lord Fitzauncell's origins—whatever they might be, his appearance declared them low—should speak in such a fashion to Baa.

Baa, however, was elated and a few minutes later he came up to her, and said:

"I've got my foot on the ladder."

"To descend it I suppose," said Lucinda.

Baa looked hurt, and she felt mean at having pricked his youthful iridescent bubble.

Before he left, Lord Fitzauncell came over to speak to her.

"You are my countrywoman, I believe," he said. "An Aussie, eh?"

Lucinda smiled and said "Yes," though it had never occurred to her that she might be labeled "An Aussie."

"I feel that I've met you before somewhere," she said. "Perhaps it was at a party in Melbourne."

"I come from Sydney."

"Yes, I know. But I suppose you came over sometimes for the races. It might have been at a Cup Week ball."

"I don't dance," said Lord Fitzauncell, and laughed.

"I believe it was in a train," said Lucinda, a glimmer of memory waking in her mind. Lord Fitzauncell gave her a glance of suspicion and of such extraordinary malevolence that this time she really had a sense of fear, unlike the mere reflection of fear she had felt on seeing his face in the dim light of the cake candles. There was nothing theatrical in the look of black power in his eyes, in which the pupils were indistinguishable from the irises.

"I can't remember distinctly," she said nervously.

Lord Fitzauncell's expression became normal again.

"Well, we all travel by train," he said. "As we're compatriots we must stick together, eh?" He lowered his voice and added confidentially, "These nobs may treat us civilly enough because we've got money, but what do they really think of us Aussies? Not much, I can tell you."

He left, accompanied by an extremely common-looking young man in a frock coat and spats, also an Australian whom he had brought with him, and whom he was sponsoring as a Conservative candidate for Parliament.

Lucinda stood smiling, but a little disconcerted. Marian, who had noticed with approval that she was talking to her fellow-countryman, said:

"His lordship seems to have amused you."

"Yes," said Lucinda, and was about to tell Marian as a joke what he had said, but she suddenly realized that Marian would not see it in the same light. "He said that as we were both Australians we should stick together."

"That was nice of him," said Marian.

"I don't find him prepossessing," said Lucinda. She felt angry and turned away. This was the second time this evening that she had retorted sharply to her "in-laws"—first to Baa and now to Marian. She had never done this before; but had always acquiesced more or less amiably in whatever they chose to say. She was surprised at herself, but realized that it was an expression of her wish to detach herself from the family.

The butler, carrying a large brown paper parcel, came up to her and said:

"Lord Fitzauncell left this, madam, for Master Stephen."

Lucinda called Stephen and he came running up and excitedly helped her cut the string and pull the wrappings from the parcel. It revealed a large mechanical, mud-colored toy tank. Lucinda wound it up and set it in motion. The children formed a circle and watched it. Above them glittered the fairy-like chandeliers, and behind them was the soft splendor of the lovely room. Their faces were rosy and eager. In the middle of the circle, the focus of all this beauty and attention, the tank whirred and waddled like some huge obscene slug.

Stephen looked up at Lucinda and wrinkled his nose.

CHAPTER FIVE

WHEN LUCINDA met Pat again in London in the middle of January, she described to him all that had happened at Christmas time. He listened attentively enough but she did not feel that he was really interested, even in her description of Lord Fitzauncell, though he did laugh when she told him about the "nobs" and the "Aussies." She seized on his appreciation of this as evidence that they saw things from the same point of view, and it made her even more convinced that if they could share the ordinary round of life together they would be truly happy, though when she asked him about his own doings at Christmas he merely said:

"Oh, the usual thing—turkey, plum pudding, paper caps and a bullet through the dining-room window."

She tried to make him give her further details, but he preferred to make love.

All through the spring and early summer she planned ways by which she and Pat might be together in places other than King Charles's Court. The Misses Lanfranc had not cared for post-war Melbourne, and they had returned to take another little house in Trevor Square. Whenever she could, she went there to tea on Sundays, and if possible she let Pat know beforehand that she would be there, but he never turned up. She accepted all the invitations which Susannah obtained for her, but although nowadays it was permitted to dance far more often than formerly with one partner, Pat, when he was present at these functions, seldom asked her for more than one dance.

She mentioned this one evening at the flat.

"You know," he said, "that I would love to dance with you the whole evening. It's only for your sake that I don't."

"But if I don't mind——" she protested.

"I mind if people talk about you."

She was not absolutely sure that it was solely care for her reputation that made him avoid her on public occasions. Some punctiliousness, she thought, might make him think it unsuitable to meet his mistress in the house of his relatives, especially of such fastidious maiden ladies as the Misses Lanfranc. Lucinda on the other hand was proud of her love. She would have liked to flaunt it, and, in certain moods, was prepared to sacrifice everything for it. Even the privileges she enjoyed of reputability, of being a Brayford of Crittenden, she came to dislike as they came between her and a completely shared life with Pat. When the spring arrived, and after the short break at Christmas, they had continued for some months so that it became almost a routine, their meetings at King Charles's Court, Lucinda was more than ever anxious to carry out her St Saturnin plan. These exclusively nocturnal meetings, the very luxury of their little intimate dinners, made her feel like a courtesan, and her pride in her love had become tinged and confused with shame. She was desperate to keep this pride alive, because she knew that when once it had gone the whole situation would become sordid and impossible. But she knew, too, that even if it did, it was unlikely that she would end it.

The most difficult obstacle in carrying out her plan was Pat himself. It only needed exercise of strength of will to oppose Marian, who, after all, could not stop her doing what she chose. She began by dealing with these minor obstacles. She told Marian flatly, that as St Saturnin had agreed so well with Stephen she was taking a villa there for August and September, and she wrote to Paul asking him to find her one. Again she was ashamed of using Stephen's welfare as camouflage for meeting with a lover.

Before she had a reply from Paul, she had a letter from Lydia who announced that, having weaned her latest child, a boy whom they had christened David, she and Roger were coming to England and would arrive in July. This letter, which at any other time would have delighted Lucinda, increased her sense of frustration, of being held back and entangled by innumerable threads, any one of which she could have snapped singly. However she could not possibly leave at once for the South of France as soon as Lydia, whom she had not seen for nearly ten years, arrived in England. She wrote to Paul not to bother about the villa for this summer, but would he look about for one for next year. To compensate and convince herself that the plan was only postponed, she gave elaborate details of the kind of house she would require. For a moment, before sending this letter, she considered still taking the villa this year and asking Lydia and Roger to join her there, but she knew that no Australian on three months' holiday in Europe would care to spend any large part of it in an out-of-the-way village where the climate and the amusements, apart from the incidental details of Provencal life, were very little different from those of Flinders and of Portsea. She posted the letter and tried to stifle her quite unreasonable feeling of resentment at the Blakes' coming to Europe at this time.

Lucinda came up to meet Lydia and Roger at Victoria, but she came the day before they arrived so that she could include a meeting with Pat. She told him that while Lydia was over it might be more difficult to arrange meetings, but anyhow he would be away in August and September.

"She has chosen the right time to come," said Pat.

"Yes," said Lucinda, "but I had thought of taking a villa at St Saturnin for those months. I thought you might have come there for a week in September. It would have been heavenly."

Now that there was no occasion for his refusal, and she did not have to face that risk, she felt safe in mentioning her plan. Pat only said "H'm." It was something that he had not declared it impossible.

When Lucinda saw Lydia stepping from the boat train she experienced painful emotions, or perhaps only unpleasant sensations. Naturally she had expected Lydia to have changed in the ten years since they had last met, but she had not expected a change so great as to produce these feelings of affection disturbed by pity, and, she had to admit it, of dismay that her sister should look like this. She had a photograph of Lydia taken only two years ago, but it had been taken in a fashionable twilight, touched up, and it did not show her figure. This, after bearing seven children, had become heavy in the breast and enormous at the hips. The dark blue coat and skirt, in which she had traveled from Marseilles, was put on carelessly and wrinkled under the arms. Her fair hair hung in wisps about her sunburnt, unpowdered face. She wore a string of pearls.

Lucinda, confronted by an actuality so different from her imagination, moved forward in a dazed condition of feeling herself unreal. She kissed Lydia, and at the contact all the associations of her youth returned to overwhelm her, as if her umbilical cord had been reunited. Although she had come to feel at home at Crittenden, and had settled naturally into an English way of living, from time to time she had envied those about her, whose adult life was spent in the scenes of their childhood, and who had witnessed the changes in their friends, the lines and the idiosyncracies come so gradually that they also became part of old association, and increased the comfortable security of affection. People who had grown up in this fashion did not receive such abrupt reminders of change and decay from the persons of those they loved. The moisture in Lucinda's eyes was not only due to the emotion of reunion, but to a feeling of pity for her sister, of which she was half ashamed, because the Blakes showed in every line of their faces and in every gesture that natural good will which comes to those whose lives are based on wholesome and plentiful affection. Lucinda was ashamed of her arrogance in pitying them. This feeling was to recur more acutely later on.

Lydia rather gruffly told Roger to go and look after the luggage. When they were getting into the taxi she said, with a kind of defensive apology:

"'Fraid I'm getting a bit broad in the beam."

Roger laughed and said to Lucinda, "She's worth her weight in gold." It was years since Lucinda had heard a man say anything nice to his wife in public, and she found it very moving.

They drove to a large hotel in Northumberland Avenue, having chosen it, they explained, as it was near her flat. Always having a sense of guilt about the flat, she thought they might be hurt because she had not asked them to stay there.

"Oh, my flat is nothing," she explained, "just two tiny rooms. I never stay there for more than a day or two, but it was inconvenient having no corner of one's own in London."

The hotel was not of the kind Lucinda had ever stayed in before. It was frequented by foreigners and rich business men. Lydia and Roger were suddenly transporting her into a different atmosphere. They could not, of course, be expected to know the things that were done, and the places frequented in London by what Marian called "nice people." This increased her feeling of pity which awoke its accompanying feeling of shame. She began to realize that her pity for them was only concerned with such superficial and trivial things, while in all the real things of life she, if they knew her circumstances in detail, would be a profound object of pity to them. She hated to feel that with her comparative youth and her beauty she was an object of pity to anyone, and now and then she had to restrain a gust of irritation with the simplicity of Roger and Lydia.

After tea Roger went down to try to book seats for a musical comedy. He came back and said that the seats for this were all taken but that he had, by a stroke of luck, obtained three stalls for the revue at the Little Theatre.

"I gather it's just round the corner," he said.

"Oh, you can't go there," exclaimed Lucinda.

"Isn't it respectable?" asked Roger, amused.

"Yes. It's quite respectable, but—but I don't think you'd like it."

Pat had told her last night that this evening he was going to the Little Theatre. He would think she had gone there so that she might meet him. It would be humiliating. There would be another cause of humiliation which she hardly liked to admit to herself. Lydia, in spite of her different coloring and different build, had sufficient family likeness to Lucinda to be recognizable as her sister. She knew that Pat, although he was naturally kind, did not care to be associated with what was provincial or inelegant. If he saw her with Lydia he might place her in his mind against a background very different from that of Crittenden.

"Have you seen it?" asked Lydia.

Lucinda was obliged to admit that she had not.

"Well, I don't mind a bit of a shock," said Lydia.

Lucinda could not offer any other objections, and she went back to her flat to dress, which she did with the greatest care. Her first dismay was succeeded by a feeling of excitement, even of defiance. It was ridiculous of Pat to expect her to hamper her own movements and to keep away from ordinary public resorts, simply because he happened to be going there.

They had seats next to the gangway. Lydia sat on the outside and Roger between the two sisters. Pat came in after them, just before the curtain went up. He was with a man whom Lucinda did not know. She had been wondering with whom he would be, and she was surprised at the intensity of her relief that it was not a woman. He did not see her when he came in, nor at the interval when he went out with his companion for a drink. He sat three rows in

259

front of them, on the same side of the theatre. Lucinda was conscious of his presence during the whole performance. She kept glancing towards the back of his head. Her awareness of him was so strong that she wondered that he did not turn round and look at her.

Roger and Lydia thought the revue very amusing, but at the end Lydia said in her gruff, very audible voice:

"If my dogs behaved like that I'd whip 'em."

At that moment Pat and his friend, wedged in the slowly moving stream of people, passed the end of their row, and Lydia's remark drew attention to them. He smiled faintly and then he saw Lucinda. She smiled with the nervous, anxious, friendly smile of a child who is caught in some activity which it hopes is not wrong. Pat bowed gravely and passed on.

Lucinda was so miserable and angry that he had not returned her smile, that the sight of her had removed the smile from his own face, that she could hardly speak for the next few minutes. Fortunately there was not much occasion to do so in the crush of the exit, and in the taxi on the way to Quaglino's for supper, where she prayed Pat might not be, she managed to control the tones of her voice, while Lydia and Roger were unable to see her expression. Lydia asked who the man was who had bowed to her. She told her that he was a relative of the Misses Lanfranc.

"He looked at you in an odd fashion," said Lydia.

When next she met Pat at King Charles's Court she tried to explain convincingly why they had come to the Little Theatre. His only comment was:

"I imagined you had not gone there from choice."

This made her angry with him, but she suppressed her anger as this was their last meeting before he went north for the grouse-shooting, and she would not see him again till October. She returned to Crittenden in a state of absolute dejection. On the way from the Halt to the End House the car stopped in a lane to allow a lorry to pass. Close to the lane was a thatched cottage. In the wire of the roof a tiny yellow-green leaf was caught. It fluttered and blew in frantic circles in the wind. Her nervous tension was so great that she felt that if the car waited much longer she would have to get out and let it blow away. When the car moved on she turned her head to see if it was yet free. In the hall of the End House she looked with a new misgiving at the print of the first Lord Wendale. She found it intolerably smug, but she did not remove it from where it hung.

A few days later, when she had thrown off some of her depression, she renewed her determination to break through all the webs of frustration and to achieve freedom in her love. The happy contentment of Roger and Lydia was an illustration that it was possible. She nursed more tenaciously the St Saturnin plan.

The Blakes made their headquarters at the End House while they were in England. They both went occasionally to Hugo, who made no objections to seeing them. Lydia was not oversensitive to grim sights, and she said, "I'll try to cheer the old boy up a bit." Roger was interested in him, both as Lucinda's husband and as a case. He told Lydia that he did not think there was much hope for him and that he had the look of a man about to die. Roger was one of the most successful young surgeons in Melbourne, and he had discovered a new way of performing a certain operation which had caused the British Medical Association to invite him to come to England, but he was also good at diagnosis. Lydia did not pass his opinion on to Lucinda, but she let her infer that before very long she would be free, which was yet another incentive to Lucinda not to let Pat drift away from her.

From the family point of view the Blakes' visit was a success. Lydia was only too free of that slight over-sensitiveness which Marian was apt to associate with Australian women. She was almost a recognizable type—the blowsy, horsy country gentlewoman, like the Greene-Jameses, only with worse clothes and better manners— and Marian above all things liked recognizable types. Arthur was not very interested in her as he liked women to be pretty and feminine, but he liked Roger as he liked most men who were well informed on their own subject, and on the nights when they all dined at Crittenden House he sat with him for a long time over the port.

This was the first real human association between Lucinda's relatives and her "in-laws," as Julie, the lively and opulent "Baroness Wombidgee," had treated the Brayfords too much as social and genealogical phenomena for them to return more than superficial friendliness. Lucinda realized with dismay that this rapprochement, which formerly would have delighted her, was yet another fine thread binding her to Crittenden.

One hot afternoon when Roger was in London for the day she was having tea alone with Lydia in the drawing-room at the End House. The windows were open, and the exhaust fumes of a car, passing up the drive to Crittenden House, were wafted faintly in, and mingled with the fragrance of the bowls of roses and of *Formosa Oolong* tea.

"This house has its disadvantages," said Lucinda, shutting the windows too late.

"It is very posh inside," said Lydia, "but as a matter of fact I wouldn't care to live bang on somebody else's drive. You put up with things over here that we wouldn't stand in Melbourne."

"They're legacies from the past," exclaimed Lucinda, smiling.

"Are you ever coming out again?" asked Lydia. "Dad wants to see you. He's always talking about you. So does Mum."

"I'd like to go, but of course I can't leave here at present."

"No, but later on, perhaps." Here again was the implication that Hugo would not last long. "I want to show you my kids." Lydia went on to talk about the family, giving more detailed information than she had given in reply to Lucinda's questions on her first arrival. Muriel apparently took her social duties with extreme seriousness, and became more consciously grand every day, while the rest of the family in the longer security of their position became more careless and common. Old Mrs Talbot had died and Muriel wanted to buy Cape Furze and rehabilitate it as a country house, but Fred, concerned primarily with its bare, rabbit-ridden acres, was haggling tenaciously over the price.

"Cape Furze," exclaimed Lucinda.

"You sound surprised."

"No, not exactly, but I can't see Muriel there."

"She has all kinds of plans for modernizing it. She is going to build a sun-parlor overlooking the bay. Tony designed it."

"For Muriel's blue eyes?" Lucinda wondered at Tony's doing any more plans for the Vanes. The thought of it stirred all kinds of memories.

"No fear. For hard cash."

"How is Tony?" Lucinda asked with natural kindness.

"He's flourishing. He did nearly all the balls for the prince's visit."

"Do he and Mum see much of each other?"

"A bit, but Muriel arranges most of the parties at Tourella."

Lucinda braced herself to ask a question which she had been wanting to ask, ever since her arrival.

"Has Mum changed much?"

"She gets tired easily. She has to take a nip now and then to buck herself up."

"Oh! D'you mean whisky?"

"Yes. What's wrong with that?" growled Lydia. "She doesn't take too much."

"No, of course not," said Lucinda with a touch of indignation. Lydia went on talking laconically about their friends and relatives in Melbourne, and was a little reminiscent about Flinders. In reaction from Julie's florid style, she had developed a habit of under-statement. She had a talent for giving dingy touches to any picture, and as she spoke, Lucinda, half amused, half irritated, remembered details of their holidays there which had since become obscured in a golden haze—such as the sticky varnish on the church pews, the flies in the paddock, the rather sordid bathroom at Strathallan, the family joint of roast mutton at midday, with the temperature 108 degrees in the shade, and, worse than these, a bullying pom-posity in Fred's manner, which, as it was not directed towards her-self, she had then accepted with indifference.

She was relieved when Arthur called after tea to take Lydia over to view one of Willy Greene-James's prize rams, which she was thinking of buying for her station in the Riverina.

When they had gone Lucinda opened the windows again. She took from a drawer in a bureau her album of photographs, snap-shots taken from the earliest days at The Pines until the tennis party at Macedon, at which she had become engaged to Hugo. She tried through these gray and glossy squares to capture the reality of the past, but she had looked at them too often, and they evoked it less clearly than the smell of the hot fig tree at St Saturnin, or of boronia in a London florist's. The photographs, though less than Lydia's conversation, made her think that she might have idealized the past, but the effect of these sudden perfumes convinced her that she had not. As she sat in the quiet summer evening, looking through the open windows across the park, with her finger still stuck in the album at the photograph of Hugo in tennis flannels, she knew that her girlhood had been an unusually happy one, perhaps only because it had been easy and full of hope.

However she was more disturbed about the present. Lydia had given her the feeling that all her associations were sordid. Because of her secret relationship with Pat, though their mutual fidelity and Hugo's condition she believed made it pardonable, she was anxious that all her other circumstances should be graceful and above criticism. She could not bear to think of Julie with clouded eyes and drenched in scent to cover the fumes of whisky. Her affection for her mother and her own *amour-propre* made the suggestion intolerable. It could only be Lydia's exaggeration. Doubtless she would go back and say that Lucinda was living in a tumbledown old place on a public highway which her brother-in-law let her have for nothing. All the same, she was unable to throw off the depression which Lydia had left with her, the feeling that everywhere was a pervading disintegration. She found herself again making one of those recurrent resolutions, those desperate acts of will to carry through her purpose at all costs, which are made by people who, in their innermost hearts, know that their intention is different from what their nature will allow.

Paul was in England for a fortnight, and he came down to Crittenden for two or three days. Lucinda and the Blakes dined there on the night of his arrival. The Greene-Jameses were also invited, partly to ease over his reconciliation with Marian, as this was their first meeting since the abduction of Harry. Talking to Lucinda before dinner Paul said:

"I'm staggered to find this place still functioning. It's an incredible anachronism. Marian would be much happier with £500 a year in a suburban villa."

Paul imagined that under the influence of St Saturnin he had discarded his concern with aristocratic tradition, but the very gusto with which he attacked what formerly he had upheld proved that it still obsessed him, and he could not resist a jibe at Marian's bourgeois proclivities. Nor could Marian, at dinner, resist chipping Paul about Provence.

"I can't think what you do there all day," she said. "There's no hunting and no shooting. I once saw a man go out in the morning at Mentone, all dressed up in bandoliers and cartridge belts as if he were going after brigands, and he came back in the evening with two sparrows."

Willy Greene-James roared with laughter.

"We cultivate our minds," said Paul.

"It pays better to cultivate sheep," said Lydia.

"We don't do it for profit," Paul explained with a rather undergraduate superciliousness.

"Then why do you do it?" asked Lydia.

"In civilized periods it was considered a sufficient end in itself."

"That's true enough," agreed Marian, "but it wasn't done amongst a lot of rackety beachcombers on the Riviera. One can hardly imagine Dr Arnold or any of the great Victorian scholars loafing on the beach at St Saturnin." She went on to praise the austere and high-minded divines of the last century, concluding, "They don't produce men like that nowadays."

"They are no longer necessary," said Paul. "The virtue of all that puritan discipline is not in the lives of those who practice it, but in the art which springs from the inevitable neurosis of their descendants—just as a ploughman may take pride in the straight lines of his furrows, ignoring that they are only the preliminary to the wheat which will grow from the rich soil he has turned over. In the same way medical science, by keeping alive sickly children which in the ordinary course of nature would die, is furthering aims very different from its declared purpose of maintaining the health of mankind. For these children, preserved against nature, grow up ill-adjusted to life, and their hypersensitiveness and their sufferings in human contact create a hightened spiritual appre-hension, which may discern truths far beyond the materialistic dogmas of medicine, and may ultimately show them to be ludicrous."

"Healthy stock produces healthy stock," growled Lydia.

"Yes, but it is a mistake to imagine that Victorian deans were healthy stock. Still, unhealthy stock is necessary, at any rate in the human race. It's only from disintegration that new life springs."

"That's decadent rot," said Marian.

"On the contrary, it is decadent to cling to outmoded ways of living and thinking," said Paul. "The further one goes with the process of decay the nearer one is to the new life."

Lydia looked at him uneasily. Although she only half understood what he said, she knew that it was against everything she valued, the reproduction of young Blakes and of young race-horses, and having enough money to feed them.

When they were going to bed she came into Lucinda's room.

"If I saw much of that brother-in-law of yours, I'd take a meat chopper to him before long," she said.

Lucinda too had been thinking about Paul's observations. They threw a different light on those ideas which had been awakened by her conversations with Lydia. In the saloon after dinner she asked him if he really meant what he said, and he had enlarged on his theories.

"You don't want to take Paul too seriously," she said. "At least what he says is serious, but he puts it in an exaggerated way to provoke Marian. They don't get on very well."

"That's one up to her," said Lydia.

"Not entirely. I had a long talk with Paul after dinner. He says it's no good trying to cling to a way of life that's finished. What he is really anxious to do is to achieve living human relationships."

"Then why doesn't he marry?"

"That doesn't always succeed. I don't think that he would marry until he had first achieved complete understanding with the other person. He says the spirit should come first."

"Is he religious?" asked Lydia suspiciously.

"Oh no, I don't think so, but he believes the body should follow the spirit."

"The spirit might lead the body into some queer places. You don't want to listen to all that stuff. It seems to me there's something gone wrong with this country. You don't know where you are. You all want a few kids to occupy your time." Feeling that this was a cruel thing to have said to Lucinda, Lydia added, "Don't get down in the mouth, Lucie, old girl. Things will change for you soon. You must come out to Australia soon and we'll buck you up —plenty of sunshine and parties and no cranky degenerates."

Lucinda smiled bleakly. Lydia gave her a good-natured pat and went back to her room. Her simple heartiness emphasized the gap between them. With Marian, and particularly with Susannah, she still felt herself sometimes to be an Australian, but with Lydia she felt herself absolutely an Englishwoman, and one of a definite type. Her knowledge of the world had given her a tolerance which would shock Lydia if she knew of its breadth, and although she was in no way "high-brow," it was impossible for a woman of moderate intelligence and taste, having money and leisure and living more or less at the center of the civilized world, not to have a wide if shallow cultural awareness, which made difficult a prolonged intimacy with some one whose horizons were bounded by her nurseries and her stables.

She was sad and relieved, sad that she was relieved, when at last she saw Lydia and Roger off to Paris on their way home. Pat had that same day returned to London from the north, and was to come to King Charles's Court in the evening. She spent the afternoon buying flowers and peaches and a new evening dress.

Their meeting was rapturous, and the next day Lucinda bought her return ticket to Crittenden in a happier and more hopeful frame of mind than she had been in for months past. She was also contemptuous of herself that she had allowed the trivial incident at the Little Theatre to cloud all the time till their next meeting. Last night had shown that it was a foolish weakness on her part to worry about Pat's passing moods. She would know better in future.

The winter was very much like the previous one. The intense happiness became modified by custom and anxiety. Pat again went to Ireland for Christmas, and at their reunion in mid-January, after the short break, there was a slight revival of the feeling that the world would be well lost for their love, though neither of them, especially Pat, wanted to lose it if avoidable. Even so, Lucinda sometimes thought that an open loss of reputation would be preferable to these furtive hothouse meetings. Theirs was not a complete human relationship, and what might be the true fulfilment of their lives was becoming like the subject of a music-hall song. She was haunted at times by the vision of Julie at odd hours of the day slipping along to the dining-room at Tourella for a hurried glass of whisky. She began to fear that later on she might come to the same thing. She wondered if there were some inherent moral weakness in their blood, and she had forcibly to rouse herself from morbid imagination. She would not allow all that fresh hope, all the delight of her girlhood to fade into a sordid middle-age. She had a passion for what was light and clearcut. Until recently she had thought that the candid innocence of her life was in the past and that she was retreating from it, but after talking to Paul she thought that it might lie ahead in an open rejection of all that was false and deathly. Meanwhile the furtive routine at King Charles's Court continued.

At Easter she wrote to Paul and asked him to find her a villa for August and September, and if possible to engage one or two servants. They could have their principal meals at the restaurant on the port. When he replied that he had found one which he thought suitable, she told Arthur and Marian that she was taking Stephen to St Saturnin for the summer holidays. It was the first time that she had done anything to displease Arthur. He said little, but his face was heavy and unsmiling. Lucinda was less disturbed by Marian, who said all that she had expected. Stephen had been at a preparatory school since the autumn. He had spent the Christmas and Easter holidays at Crittenden House, which was now considered his home. He would have a week there at the end of July before they left for St Saturnin. Lucinda mildly pointed this out to Marian, who sniffed in reply.

She delayed to tell Pat until the perfect moment of mutual rapport should arrive. When, by mid-July, this had not happened she could not risk postponing it any longer. One night at dinner she said, as casually as possible:

"I have taken a villa at St Saturnin for August and September."

"Oh, that's good," said Pat. "You like being there, don't you?"

"Yes." Making a greater effort to speak naturally, she added, "I thought you might join me there for a week or two."

"But, Lucie darling, that's impossible. I always go north in August."

"Couldn't you come for the first week? You could still be in Scotland for the twelfth."

"Anyhow I can't stay with you at St Saturnin—under the very nose of your brother-in-law."

"He wouldn't mind. He wouldn't say anything about it."

"I'd mind if he wouldn't," said Pat tersely. "Why didn't you take a house somewhere else abroad, in Italy, or somewhere? Then it might have been managed." He felt that it was safe to say this now that she was committed to St Saturnin.

"Arthur and Marian would have thought that too extraordinary. Paul's being at St Saturnin gives me some reason to go there."

"Naturally I'd love to come," said Pat, "but it is impossible for your own sake as well as mine."

Lucinda picked up her wine glass, but as she sipped at it she gulped, and began to weep. Pat was astonished. He had never known Lucinda other than perfectly controlled and reasonable. That she was never ruffled nor made the slightest scene was for him one of her chief attractions. He did not realize how often she felt inclined to, nor that when alone she acted in her own imagination the scene which she might have made, which left her nervous and tired but which spared him. He rose from his place and put his arm round her shoulder.

"What's the matter, Lucie?" he asked. His voice became a little Irish and soothing.

"This bloody flat," she sobbed.

"But it's a very nice flat. At least I've always thought so."

"It's like a prison."

He had a moment of acute discomfort, thinking he had inflicted himself on Lucinda against her will.

"Good God!" he said, and sat down again. Lucinda went on sobbing.

"If you didn't like coming here, why didn't you say so?" he asked accusingly, when she had calmed herself a little.

"I did like it, I do," she affirmed, "but it's so furtive. I want to see you somewhere else—in the daylight—in the sun—not always by pink-shaded candles. I'm not old enough yet to need that," she added, trying to smile. She went on to pour out all her grievances. They sounded trivial when aired, but they made Pat realize that he had as a matter of course accepted a good deal from Lucinda. He was very nice about it, and agreed with much that she said.

"Why didn't you tell me this before, Lucie darling?" he asked, "then we might have made some better arrangement. You see, it isn't really possible—well, it's possible, I suppose, but it would be most unwise—for me to visit you at St Saturnin."

"We could go to some other place on the Continent, you mean."

"Well, yes," he said, doubtfully.

"Italy?"

"I suppose Italy's as good as any other place."

"Could you come then in September to Italy?"

"What would you do with your villa?"

"I'd shut it up. I could leave Stephen with Paul."

"I'd miss the partridge shooting," said Pat. He was disconcerted

268

by the swiftness with which she had seized on his agreement to make a definite arrangement.

She said nothing, but her silence implied that he thought more of his routine pleasures than of her, or even that she was one of them, and there was no need for her to interfere with the other. This was the suggestion he had most strongly repudiated, so he added, "Not that that would matter for once. We'd be back in October, I suppose."

At last the arrangement was made. They would spend the third week of September together in Italy. She had some Australian friends who lived in Florence. They would provide the excuse for her to leave Stephen with Paul and go away for that time on a visit. When finally all this was amicably settled, Lucinda was so emotionally exhausted that Pat did not stay the night at the flat. She lay awake for a long time thinking about the whole situation. She had at one time imagined their excitedly planning a holiday together, surrounded by maps and railway guides, but this week had only been wrung from Pat with tears, and as a concession.

CHAPTER SIX

LUCINDA wrote to tell Stephen that she had taken a house at St Saturnin for the holidays. Stephen was thrilled—it showed even in his laboriously written duty letters from school. He mentioned it every week, and when at last she met him in London to take him down to Crittenden, the first thing he said was, "When are we going to St Saturnin?"

He told the chauffeur at the station, and everyone he met at Crittenden, "We've got a house at St Saturnin, just for Mummy and me." His delight made him beautiful to watch, particularly as it expressed not only his own pleasure, but that touching pride that children show when a good thing happens to their family. It seemed, too, that he must have been aware that he had not hitherto had a complete home of his own with his mother. At the End House there was the large shut-off slice of the house and garden occupied by Hugo, while Crittenden, which was now his home and where he was happy enough, nevertheless clearly belonged to Arthur, or rather, seen from Stephen's angle, to Marian.

Lucinda felt that Arthur and Marian were hurt at Stephen's obvious jubilation about the villa, and she told him to modify it in their presence. Next time he saw them he said, "It's only for

Mummy and me, but you may come and stay there for a week."

"Only for a week?" said Lucinda reproachfully.

"Well, for a year," said Stephen.

Lucinda was almost as impatient as Stephen to leave for St Saturnin, but when they arrived there she was still impatient for the time to come when she was to join Pat in Italy. Nor did she find St Saturnin as attractive as on her last visit, as now she had no hopes of it, but was only using it as a stepping-off place to another destination. Stephen enjoyed it more than ever, which made her feel that her time there was not wasted. His pride in their primitive pink villa, and his assumption that she had taken it so that she might be there alone with him in their own house made her uncomfortable.

Paul was cheerful, but not radiating that naïve happiness which had been almost indecent in a man of forty. Harry had married Assomption in the spring, and although Paul was apparently quite pleased at this, it made him more lonely, by reducing Harry to the ranks, as it were, and leaving him more vulnerable to outside contacts.

"Harry," he said, "has provided me with all the advantages of married life, and relieved me of its tiresome responsibilities. I have a woman about the house who cooks perfectly and mends my linen, while Harry has all the fatigue of her tantrums."

His first enthusiasm for his new friends was becoming tempered with criticism. He said rather plaintively:

"When I'm with the county families I think how deadly they are, and these arty, intellectual people appear in comparison free and enlightened, but after a long stretch with the intelligentsia, I find they have their own snobberies which are just as ludicrous and often more meaningless than Lady Bassingbourne's or Willy Greene-James's, which after all do reflect a real social pattern."

One morning Lucinda had taken Stephen down to bathe. He had gone with Jack, the Roberts's boy, to dive from the rock, and she was lying sleepily in the sun when she became aware that a group of people near her were discussing Paul. Someone said:

"What does he do?"

"He lives with a ploughboy and paints like Conder. He's too ninetyish for words."

"The ploughboy has married."

"Oh, bad luck!" There was a ripple of laughter.

"What does he do now, then?"

Various ribald suggestions were made. The first speaker said, "Isn't he an honorable or something?"

"He has no money," was the reply made by a woman novelist who affected to be a Communist, but from the contempt with which she spoke she might, thought Lucinda, be the most recently rich of Toorak matrons. Later, she heard her frequently complain of the difficulty of living on two thousand a year.

Paul was not unaware that he was spoken of in this fashion, and to defend himself against it he began to fall back on his old weapon, pride of birth, which, however, was only occasionally effective. Most of these "Left" intellectuals who could afford to dawdle round the Riviera came from the class he disliked most, the prosperous bourgeoisie, and he did not always conceal his feelings.

The woman novelist had offended him by sending a note inviting him to dine, adding, "I don't know if you have a wife, but if you have, do bring her." The idea that a woman who, if she existed, would be a grand-daughter-in-law of Prince de Mireval and a future Viscountess Crittenden, should be invited in this casual fashion by a woman whom she would, if she existed, probably refuse to know, affronted him unspeakably.

"She insulted my wife," he told Lucinda.

"But you haven't got one," objected Lucinda, amused.

"She didn't know that," said Paul.

The Roberts gave a dinner party on the terrace of their château. The whole evening glowed in sunset colors—the dark pines, the olives, the golden vines, the white rocks and the sea. On the terrace were great bowls of peaches and figs, and wooden tubs filled with bottles of local wine, which, Paul remarked, suggested a vintage festival painted by Brangwyn.

"Why Brangwyn?" asked one of the young men who had discussed Paul on the beach.

"Because that is what it suggests to me."

The young man began to chip Paul, and point him out as a museum piece to the Communist novelist.

"You may buy a copy of the *New Statesman*," said Paul, "and a pair of suede shoes, and a Picasso print, and a Freudian textbook, and imagine that you are the *dernier cri* of culture, when you are only its last gasp."

As he spoke his face became rigid with archaic lines, and his eyes, which could be so gentle as he watched an adolescent footman bring in the drinks, were drawn and glittering, as if he were jabbing a dagger into the young man's vitals. He seemed to bring to the surface some latent force, as if those ancient princes, his forebears, had through centuries of use of their authority to kill, bred and distilled a daemonic power in their descendant. Although

Paul's retort was undoubtedly witty, it was too savage for people to laugh. The young man giggled and turned away, but he looked a little pale.

It was not until they sat down at the long table and a certain amount of wine had been drunk that the effect of this incident wore off. It had pleased Lucinda. That Paul was able to express in his own person the spirit of that past which had so obsessed him was aesthetically satisfying. He was like an antique masque come to life. There was a kind of antique richness about the whole scene, very different from that of Crittenden. The people, if they had not all perfect manners—and had Willy Greene-James as far as that went?—were far more interesting in their conversation. Intelligent talk in this lovely setting, with the plane trees above their heads, and the seventeenth century façade of the château behind them breathing out the warmth it had absorbed during the day, and with this informal profusion of fruit and wine before them, was a new experience for Lucinda, and she recaptured the feeling she had on her first visit to St Saturnin, that the kind of life still existed where all things were in proportion. One of the men sang to a plaintive melody a ballad describing the woes of a cabin boy. It was both sad and amusing. As she listened she remembered that in a week's time she was to meet her lover in Genoa. All the dusty fabric of English drawing-rooms had fallen away from her. Her mind was full of picturesque images, of voyages by sea and vintage festivals, and lovers in Italian cities.

Another slight incident occurred while Lucinda was at St Saturnin which she remembered long afterwards. She had taken Stephen and Roland, the Roberts's boy with whom he had become great friends, to the cinema. There was a moment in the film when a flock of white doves descended from a church tower on to the cobbled square of an old northern town. The scene was so charming that there was a hush in the cinema. Roland, who, being brought up in France, was bi-lingual, said, "Comme ils sont gentils, ces petits pigeons."

Stephen looked up at her, and in the light from the screen, where the white wings of the doves were still fluttering, she could see his smile, which was not only one of pleasure at the scene, but of pride and amusement at Roland, as if he were saying, "Aren't they funny, Mum, these kids?"

The day before she left for Italy, Lucinda took Stephen down to bathe early in the afternoon. There were few people on the plage, but they were joined soon by Elspeth Roberts and Roland, who went off with Stephen to dive from the rock. After a while Lucinda and Elspeth began to talk confidentially about the difficulties of marriage. Lucinda knew that Elspeth had had Freda and the man with the Roman Catholic wife to stay with her, so that she must be tolerant of other people's irregularities. She told her about Pat.

"I thought there must be someone," said Elspeth.

"Why?"

"You don't look as martyred as·you would otherwise."

"It isn't all *soulagement*," said Lucinda.

"It never is. I have a row now and then even with Bob, who is an angel really. It clears the air."

"Oh, I've never had a row with Pat, thank Heaven. I couldn't bear it."

"Then why isn't it all *soulagement*?"

Lucinda went on to tell her the whole story from the beginning, before Hugo was wounded, and of how she now feared it might degenerate into a routine. That was why she had persuaded Pat to join her in Italy. This was the first time she had spoken of the affair to anyone. It was a tremendous relief, and helped her to see it all in a truer light, and to sort out what was foolish in her own attitude, as when she began to state in words her more idiotic fears she found she was ashamed to give them expression.

"People may be able to combine perfect urbanity with deep emotion," said Elspeth. "I don't know. I'm sure I couldn't. Life isn't all oiled wheels. It's full of tensions, and they must snap occasionally or they'll atrophy. This sounds a bit mixed, but you understand what I mean. If I were always absolutely courteous to anyone, it would mean that I wanted him at a distance, that I didn't want to be emotionally involved with him. Still perhaps you're more of a lady than I am. D'you think you're too much of a lady for him?"

"Good gracious, no. I should think it was impossible. He is awfully guarded—though not stiff nor stupid."

"He might like a contrast."

"I do wear vulgar brooches sometimes," said Lucinda. Elspeth laughed.

"That's not enough," she said. "Do something to startle him. Make him feel you don't care twopence for him."

"But I do," Lucinda protested.

"Pretend you don't."

"I can't pretend with him. It would be horrible. I hate making a game of it."

"For all your Mayfair appearance, you're very unsophisticated," said Elspeth. "You want to retain your respectability and have a love affair. No, it isn't even that. You want to have an irregular love affair and to clothe it with a kind of lofty moral beauty. That is very difficult. It's impossible when you're over sixteen. There must be moral crudities. The fighting man demands it."

"But I'm not a fighting man," said Lucinda plaintively.

"Your colonel is. I expect he would enjoy an occasional thunderstorm. Then you can have the reconciliations and rainbows afterwards."

"Is that a condition of life—that one must fight with what one loves?"

"If one loves in the flesh, and there's no complete love otherwise."

"The idea is hideous to me. I'd rather be dead than fight at intervals with what I love."

"Then there is something odd about your glands. I rather enjoy it. It increases our knowledge of each other. You can't really know anyone until you have had a good row with them. I once had a friend I was very fond of, but when the time came for our bust-up we did it all by letter, so that the vital contact of anger was insulated as it were, and though we became reconciled the friendship died of inanition. The sparks hadn't made contact, or whatever it is that happens in a motor car. I don't understand machinery. I hate it."

"But I have friends and I have never had a bust-up with any of them except my brother, and that was through a misunderstanding."

"Then I don't think you can know your friends properly. If you take your colonel in certain charming moods and pretend that he's perfect, and when he is in other moods say he is not being himself, sooner or later you'll have to face a hopeless dawn."

The two boys came back from the rock and the conversation ended. Lucinda tried to reopen it as they walked up to tea at Paul's villa, but it was difficult with the boys chattering behind them and every now and then interrupting with some question.

Lucinda had originally arranged to meet Pat at Genoa, but she found that the trains were awkward from St Saturnin and that she would have to spend the best part of a day there waiting for him. She telegraphed that she would meet him instead at Turin. Her train arrived there shortly before Pat's. It was pouring with rain and the water came in chutes through the leaky roof of the railway station. She went out to buy him an umbrella and arrived back at the station just as his train came in.

He made a grimace at her from the window of his carriage, and looked up at the sky. His smile was so kind and affectionate that she thought her whole conversation with Elspeth Roberts had been based on false assumptions.

"Is this your sunny Italy?" he said, as he stepped from the train.

"I've brought you an umbrella."

"You think of everything. You even bring an umbrella to Italy in September."

"I've only just bought it," she explained.

"It looks a bit dago, but it keeps out the rain."

When they had seen about the luggage—she was surprised how much he had for a week's holiday—he tucked her arm under his, and sheltered by the one umbrella, they hurried under the cascades from the roof along to the waiting taxi which drove them about a hundred yards to the hotel.

"I'm most awfully sorry," said Lucinda.

"You can't help the weather, darling."

"No, but I persuaded you to come here." As soon as she had spoken she wished she had not said that. She did not want to emphasize that the holiday was her idea. She wanted to feel that it was arranged between them for their mutual delight. Pat's behavior, although it was charming, had this emphasis sufficiently. He was like someone taking an indulgent interest in a child's game. He was amused at the baroque wardrobe in her room and said, "Looks as if they'd robbed a church." His manner stirred some uneasy memory, but it was not till later that she was able to recognize it as like Hugo's at the bungalow at Sandringham on the first day of their honeymoon —faint amusement combined with absolute aplomb.

Pat did not seem to mind the weather which was such a disappointment to herself. He had a hot bath and changed after the journey, criticized amiably the Italian dinner and waited with composure for bedtime. Lucinda thought that perhaps he did not mind the weather as, unlike herself, he had really come for the nights and not primarily that they might spend their days together. During the night there was a horrible scream beneath the bedroom window, where some Fascist or Communist was being murdered.

The next day the sky had cleared and there was brilliant sunshine. They took the train to Pisa. The railway from Genoa was not yet electrified and the smoke in the numerous tunnels was suffocating, but between the tunnels there were charming vignettes of rocky coves and palm trees. Lucinda, to distract Pat's attention from the discomforts of the journey, rather too often drew his attention to the picturesque coast. Pisa, in the evening light, gave her the same sense of liberation into a freer, more colorful world that she experienced at the al fresco dinner on the Roberts's terrace. They walked along to the Campo Santo. The faded marble of the three exquisite buildings, the cathedral, the baptistry and the leaning tower, was golden in the evening light. Beyond the far wall the hills were of that serene and luminous blue which she had seen on the evenings of her childhood when looking across to the Dandenang Ranges. To have Pat with her in this beautiful scene gave her a momentary happiness greater than she had experienced for years, and she gave a faint emotional exclamation. Pat, who had had enough of what he called "beauty talk" for the day, said, "I can't make out why it doesn't fall over."

There were mosquitoes and inadequate nets in the hotel at Pisa. Pat found them more disturbing than a murder beneath the window. In the morning they went on to Florence. In the evening they drove up to San Miniato, and standing on the terrace near Michelangelo's *David* they looked down over the city. Lucinda quoted a few lines of poetry—Swinburne and Oscar Wilde. The towers and domes slowly lost their sculptured shape and became lost in a network of twinkling lights. The smell of frying oil drifted out from the monastery. Pat lighted his pipe.

He fell in with every suggestion she made for excursions and sightseeing, except that he liked to retire with the English newspapers for two hours after lunch. Lucinda also was glad to rest then during the hottest part of the day. She soon found his ready agreement with her plans dispiriting. The implication was that he had made this sacrifice of over a week's shooting to please her, and he was prepared to do it handsomely. If only he had demurred over one of her suggestions and had said, "I'd rather drive out to Settignano, this afternoon, if you don't mind, darling," when she had arranged to go to Certosa, she would have been delighted, but he followed her round like a good-tempered and dutiful schoolboy, and to her decreasingly emotional appreciations he responded with an automatic "Yes, magnificent!" Sometimes he was facetious about a piece of primitive drawing or a sculptured impropriety in the Bargello. There was none of the tension of which Elspeth Roberts had spoken. At least there appeared to be none in Pat. It was beginning to grow in Lucinda. At times, even in his close embrace, she felt that he was far away from her. This sense of loneliness when she was with him was a new and chilling experience. She had never known it at King Charles's Court.

Lucinda bought some reproduction Benvenuto Cellini silverwork, and a Florentine lace table-cloth. In the Pitti Palace she collected some beautiful pieces of eighteenth-century brocade. Her idea was to do up the flat in an Italian style to keep the memory of this holiday vivid for them, but after a day or two she felt her shopping becoming pointless. The holiday did not seem to be drawing them completely together, but only to be revealing an unsuspected gulf between them. One morning she asked him to come to the Ponte Vecchio with her to choose a little jeweled clock, something like that which used to be in the drawing-room at Wellington Court. She half hoped that he would offer to give her this clock. He gave her very few presents. She had been glad of this as it made her feel less like a courtesan. She excused him to herself by thinking, "After all, as the son of an Irish landowner he can't be very well off." He would know that she realized this, and she felt that her understanding made closer the bond between them. All the same, she could not help seeing that all his own things, his clothes, his guns, his boots, were of the very best quality, and his rooms in St James's could not be cheap.

He did not offer to buy the clock. His only comment was:

"Are you sure these things work all right? After all you want a clock to tell the time. It looks to me as if all the effort has gone into the chrysoprase and chalcedony."

When they left the Ponte Vecchio she was far more disappointed than she had expected to be. The whole trip seemed to be an effort on her part, to which he made no response. Her tension was reaching breaking point. She wanted either to burst into tears or to exclaim viciously, "Must you always be so idiotically amiable?"

Suppressing her tears she walked with him along the Lung Arno. Her whole life, for the past two years or more, had been focused on Pat. She could not admit that it had been a mistake. It was a mistake to have brought him to Italy. She could admit that. But if she could be with him in his natural setting, an English country house where she too would be at home, then she was sure that all would go well and they would know without question that they were made for each other.

They had intended to walk back to the hotel along the arcades of the Uffizzi and through the Piazza Signoria. Pat, the evening before, had happened to read Cellini's account of the casting of his *Perseus* and he wanted to have another look at it.

They were just about to turn left when Lucinda saw coming towards them a figure which she recognized as familiar, even before she saw that it was Lady Bassingbourne's. She was seized by a mad and desperate impulse to end all this careful planning and anxiety, to throw her hat over the windmill, to explode the whole situation and force Pat to take the responsibility of her. In that moment she forgot Stephen, and Hugo and all the complications of her life which made this almost impossible.

"Not that way," she said, "let us walk further along by the river."

"But I want to see the *Perseus*," said Pat.

"We can see it tomorrow."

They walked on. As they came up to Lady Bassingbourne Lucinda looked at her steadily lest they should pass unnoticed.

"Lucinda, my dear," exclaimed Lady Bassingbourne, "I had no idea that you were in Florence."

"I am only here for a week."

"It's terribly hot," said Lady Bassingbourne. "I had to come to see a dear friend, who has been ill, and who was so kind to me when we were in Rome." She looked inquiringly at Pat.

"This is Colonel Lanfranc," said Lucinda. "Lady Bassingbourne."

"Weren't you a great friend of poor Hugo's?" asked Lady Bassingbourne. "Won't you come to tea with me this afternoon?"

"I am sorry. We're staying with friends," said Lucinda. They exchanged a few conventional remarks about Florence.

"Well, I'll see you at Crittenden next month, I suppose. We'll be down as usual for a week. We're looking forward to it immensely." She smiled, shook hands and walked on.

Pat was silent until she was out of earshot. Then he said, "That was unfortunate." As he glanced at Lucinda his eyes held a kind of opaque repudiation. He knew that she had deliberately encountered Lady Bassingbourne. She had even stood so that he could not stroll on and avoid the introduction. He imagined that she had done it from sheer stupidity. He had no idea of the exasperated, destructive impulse which had seized her.

Lucinda did not reply. She was bewildered at herself, ashamed and yet defiant. She did not really know what she had expected to come of the incident. She had supposed that Lady Bassingbourne would tell Marian that she had been in Florence with Pat, and that Hugo might then be incited to use what consciousness was left to him to divorce her. Or perhaps she only wanted one of Elspeth Robert's thunderstorms and rainbow reconciliations.

Lady Bassingbourne did tell Marian, simply as an item of news, that she had met them together, but Marian only said:

"Oh yes, she told me that she was staying with some Australian friends in Florence. I suppose they were Colonel Lanfranc's cousins of whom I've heard, but I haven't met them. I believe they are very nice women."

It occurred to neither of them that any suspicion could be attached to Lucinda's conduct. Also Marian, when convenient, could always anaesthetize her sensitive nose for misbehavior.

Lucinda and Pat hardly spoke on their way back to the hotel for lunch, at which they were still monosyllabic, and their eyes avoided meeting. As he took the papers to go up to his room, he said, "Well, it can't be helped. Nothing may come of it."

His manner was no longer that of a schoolboy, but of a schoolmaster who has considered a fault and dismissed it as troublesome but pardonable. Lucinda found it intolerable.

Generally when they parted after lunch they arranged what they would do when they met for tea. Pat had said that he wanted to have another look at the *Perseus,* but neither of them mentioned this because of its association with the incident of the morning. Without making any arrangement they went to their separate rooms. In Lucinda's room the shutters were closed against the afternoon sun and the room was filled with a stifling green twilight. She could not face spending the next two hours imprisoned here with her thoughts. She almost laughed in her misery. Elspeth's thunderstorms and rainbows! This was more like a severe frost, and when it thawed, if ever it did, she would be as lifeless as one of those half-hardy plants which have not been pulled up in the autumn.

She put on a shady hat, and opening and closing her door quietly so that Pat would not hear her, she left the hotel and walked to a part of the city, where she had not been before, to help herself to view the situation more objectively. She sat under the awning of a deserted café. Everything was dusty and across the street was a shop full of cheap shoes. She remembered the party on the Roberts's terrace, and her romantic vision of lovers in an Italian city. She had thought that she and Pat were to be like Paola and Francesca or somebody. She smiled bitterly.

Revolving the scene of the morning in her mind for an hour or more, without coming to any conclusion as to whether she regretted it or what she should do next, she decided to call on the Misses Gear, the Australian friends with whom she was supposed to be staying. She took a cab to their apartment, which was on the first floor of a sixteenth-century palazzo. In the vaulted salon, a fitting setting for enthroned renaissance cardinals, water-colors of Warrandyte and Healesville hung above painted bombé chests-of-drawers. These ladies were nieces of Mrs Talbot and there was also a large painting of Cape Furze House. They were delighted to see Lucinda. Although they could not tear themselves away from the distinguished society and the beauty of Florence, they often felt themselves *dépaysées,* and when they met anyone who had known them in Toorak, they were almost tearful in their joy. For that hour their lives were given continuity, and they were provided with their own legitimate background. They showed Lucinda their Australian pictures and souvenirs.

"And this is dear Cape Furze," said Miss Nellie Gear.

"Oh yes, I've been there," said Lucinda. "I spent one of the happiest days of my life there. We drove out from Flinders."

"You knew that Aunt Emma had died. She was a wonderful woman. She would have been a hundred in three years' time. When she was a little girl she was kissed by Lord Melbourne, and do you know that not one of the Melbourne papers gave her an obituary notice, but there was a charming paragraph in *The Times*. We felt we couldn't go on living in Victoria after that."

Lucinda did not like to say that Muriel wanted to buy Cape Furze, especially as Fred was haggling over the price. They gave her an excellent tea, and even a cake with a passion-fruit filling which they had sent in tins from Melbourne.

Lucinda's effect on the Misses Gear was mutual. When she left them she felt that she too had her own background and that she was not so defenseless against Pat's moods. All kinds of people appreciated her and showed pleasure in her company. It was ridiculous that with Pat she should all the time be on tenterhooks lest she should fail to come up to his expectations. This freedom of mind was increased by the beginnings of a bad headache. The throbbing physical pain distracted her attention from her emotional sufferings.

As she put the key in the door of her room Pat come out of his. "Hullo Lucie," he said, quietly but amiably, "I wondered where you'd got to."

"I went for a walk. I had a slight headache and I had tea out. It is worse now. I think I'll lie down for a bit."

"That's wise. Have you any aspirins?"

"Yes, thank you."

She was irritated with him and with herself that she had been afraid to tell him that she had been to see the Misses Gear, thinking it might provoke the same reaction as the encounter with Lady Bassingbourne.

"I'll go for a stroll," he said. She nodded and went into her room, and after taking two aspirins, in water that she hoped would not give her typhoid, she lay down on the bed.

The aspirin eased her headache very little, but it stimulated her mental activity. She believed that she saw with extreme clarity the whole course of the relationship with Pat from the beginning. She remembered Hugo saying chaffingly and rather enviously to Pat, one evening when he was dining with them at Crowborough, "You'll always make yourself comfortable." She now realized how true it was. During the war Pat had always had exactly the sort of job he wanted, interesting and for the most part safe—not that he was wanting in physical courage. And when he did go to the Front it was to join Allenby's staff in Egypt. She was a further extension of his comfortable environment.

She felt too sick and tired and indifferent to rise from her bed. In spite of all her resentment she was still half prepared for him to come in and be tenderly solicitous, and to have a rainbow reconciliation. At about dinner-time she heard him in his room, but he went out again without coming to see her. She rang for a bottle of mineral water and some coffee, and then went to bed. The coffee with the aspirins stimulated her brain more than ever. She could not understand how she had been so senseless as to take it. It was one of those stupid impulses, like deliberately running into Lady Bassingbourne.

At about eleven o'clock she heard Pat return. She expected that he would come into her room to ask how she was, and whether there was anything she wanted. He did not come at once and she lay with her body taut, waiting for the moment when he would knock gently at the door between their rooms. She had decided by this time to pretend that no "situation" had arisen, beyond the fact that she had a headache.

His light jerked out. "Now," she thought, "he is coming," and she braced herself to make her voice sound natural and affectionate. To her astonishment, instead of his gentle knock, she heard his bed creak as he settled into it. She waited for ten minutes or so, simmering with indignation. She felt as if a heavy weight were being pressed on her head, and as if her eyes were being stretched like those of a Chinese. Then she crept from her bed, and putting a towel along the bottom of the door between their rooms, so that he would not see the light when, very quietly, she switched it on, she fetched her fountain pen and a writing pad. Sitting up in bed she wrote him a long letter, recapitulating their whole relationship with many quotations of what he had said on certain dates, and how these sayings had affected her. The burden of the letter was, "As far as I am concerned I love you still, but I must know where I stand." There were a great many smudges and corrections, and when she had finished she made a fresh copy. She switched out the light, removed the towel from the door, and slipped the letter under it. At last the whirling activity of her brain slowed down, and as soon as she returned to her bed she fell asleep. It was three o'clock.

Pat awoke in the morning feeling more than usually pleased with life. This was the last day of their holiday, and tomorrow he returned to England. He did not think that it had been a great success, but at least he hoped that it had satisfied Lucinda. The only unfortunate incident had been the meeting with Lady Bassingbourne, and nothing might come of that, at any rate nothing that could not be explained away, as the old girl had looked quite unsuspicious. Having been alone practically since lunch time yesterday, he was quite looking forward to Lucinda's society. He hoped her headache was gone. He had not gone into her last night as her light was out, and he thought she would prefer not to be disturbed.

He put on a dressing-gown and was about to knock at her door when he saw the envelope addressed "Pat" at his feet.

"Good Lord, what's this?" he muttered, taking out four closely written sheets of thin notepaper. At first he thought that she must have gone away, and that this was a letter of explanation. He opened the door, but in the greenish twilight he could see the glinting tops of the bottles from her dressing-case, and her dark head still lying in exhausted sleep. He closed the door, and sitting on a hard chair by the window, he frowned at the letter and began to read it. At intervals he murmured, "Great Scott!" and "Good God!" and when he had finished it he threw the letter on to the dressing-table and said, "Well, I'm damned!"

At first he was simply surprised. "Who'd have thought all that was going on in her head?" he asked himself. "Imagine remembering what I said two years ago. Damned if I can remember myself." He lit a cigarette, and glowering with displeasure he brooded on the thought that all this time, when he had believed his relationship with Lucinda to be so satisfactory, that she was sensible as well as charming, and that they had understood each other perfectly, he had been fooling himself, and all this stuff—he picked the letter up and flicked it impatiently—had been seething in her mind. He shaved, had his bath, and went down to breakfast in the empty hotel dining-room.

Pat had problems of his own. Like Lucinda, he found that being in some unaccustomed place did enable him to view them more objectively, and he took advantage of his solitary breakfast to do so. His father was nearly eighty. When he died Pat would inherit Drumkene. His father was continually urging him to marry, but he could not do this while his father was alive without changing his style of living, which he was unwilling to do. He would like to marry Lucinda, especially as she had some money. He would do so at once if Hugo were to die, which at one time he had expected to happen fairly soon, but poor old Hugo, whose life was not much use to him, was apparently a creaking door. If, on the other hand, Pat were to be a corespondent, especially with Hugo as petitioner, it would mean he would have to sever his connection with his regiment, which would be extremely repugnant to him, and was partly the cause of his concern for Lucinda's reputation. But after all Lucinda was not the only eligible party. He was getting on. It was true he ought to marry soon, or his own eligibility might become a bit tarnished. Perhaps this affair was drawing to its natural close. Perhaps this was a let out. He took Lucinda's envelope from his pocket and once more read its contents.

They appeared to him even more fantastic at a second reading. Still, there was no doubt that it had been a very satisfactory arrangement. It had saved him from having to marry before he could afford it, and from intrigues with second-rate women. He felt grateful to her, and affectionate as, having finished his breakfast, he went up and knocked gently at her door.

She called to him to come in. The shutters were open, and she was sitting up in bed with a tray of coffee beside her. Holding her letter he came over to the bed, and looking down at her with his noble, heavy-lidded eyes, he asked how was her headache.

"It is gone, thank you," she said, smiling a little stiffly.

"I've read your letter."

"Oh yes." She had exhausted her emotional capacity in the small hours of the morning. She could only sit back and watch the effect of the stone she had flung into the pond. At any rate she might now have some idea of what was in the pond. It would be better than merely seeing it disturbed by surface gusts of irritation.

"It was a surprise to me," said Pat. She did not reply. "I did not know that things had gone in that direction. I thought you were quite happy with me."

"So I was."

"Was?"

"Am, or rather, could be."

"What do you want me to do?"

"I don't know really." She smiled faintly.

"That's not very helpful."

"No, I suppose it isn't."

"Couldn't you try to be a little helpful?" There was a touch of impatience in his voice. This irritated her.

"Well," she said, "am I wrong in my review of the situation?"

"I didn't know until this morning that there was a situation."

"When you first knew me, if I had been unwell, I don't think that you would have walked out and left me from tea till breakfast time."

"I thought you didn't want to be disturbed. You were asleep when I came in."

"Still, when you first knew me you would have hung about a bit, wouldn't you? I don't want you to do that sort of thing if you don't feel inclined to. I only want to know whether you feel inclined to or not."

"When you get to know people, naturally you don't fuss so much, because you're more at ease with them. It doesn't mean you think less of them."

"It's not only that," Lucinda went on. "Yesterday, when I introduced you to Lady Bassingbourne, you looked at me with absolute dislike. You couldn't have looked at me like that when you first knew me, even if I had been stupid. Everybody is stupid sometimes. Probably people can gauge their feelings for each other by the way they regard each other's stupidities. While they're still in love the stupidities remain endearing traits. When love is dead they appear—well—stupid."

Lucinda was so pleased to be free of the emotional strain of the night, and to be at last discussing the thing with Pat, that she smiled faintly as she spoke. To Pat she appeared extraordinarily cold. She went on with the objectivity of a lawyer, enlarging the points of her letter and emphasizing the deterioration of their love. She was hoping that Pat would with horror repudiate her arguments, would tell her that she was entirely mistaken, that he would embrace her and rid her of this deathly logic in which she was taking a perverse and frozen enjoyment, but all the time she was creating an atmosphere in which it was impossible that this should happen. The arguments that she put forward for him to destroy were much too convincing. In a way she knew this, and she heard in her voice a staccato echo of her grandfather Chapman's, and yet she could not stop herself. For the time her mind was functioning without relation to emotions which were dormant in the morning light, and she also wanted to say, now, while she had the opportunity, all the things she had thought but not dared to say in the past two or three years. "It's as well to clear the ground," she thought, "then we can begin afresh." She did not realize she was clearing it too thoroughly, and uprooting the flowers with the weeds.

"I suppose," said Pat at last, "that some day we'll understand each other again, but at present it seems pretty hopeless."

She had a moment of fright.

"I never thought we could speak to each other like this," she said.

"I can't say that it was my wish."

"Nor was it mine, but I must know where I am."

"Under present conditions it's a bit difficult for either of us to know that. Our situation is rather complicated."

She was about to remind him that he had said that he was unaware that there was a situation, but she had suddenly become afraid of scoring points. She was silent. He stood looking out of the window. He was wondering whether this would be a good opportunity to tackle the whole subject, to explain, very reasonably and gently, his position to her, that he had to marry, that he could not wait very much longer, that they had had some marvelous times together, but that this week had seemed to show that it was time they cooled off. He could put the onus of cooling off onto her. It would be more agreeable and it would save her self-respect. And to tell the truth she did seem infernally cold. He would not care to marry a woman capable of such icy logic. However at the moment it was opportune.

"Perhaps you're right," said Lucinda, quietly and a little wearily, "and there isn't a situation after all. I took too much coffee and aspirin. I'll get up now."

He was disconcerted, and murmuring some agreement he left the room. Perhaps it was as well, though, not to have a break when they had still to spend another day in each other's exclusive company.

When Lucinda came down they went to look at the *Perseus*. She took this as a sign that the incident was closed. Their manner to each other was quite friendly, and only a little constrained. It was a beautiful, still, sunny day, not too hot, and in the afternoon they drove out along the river bank to Bagno da Ripoli. They passed a platoon of youths wearing black shirts. Lucinda asked if they were Italian Boy Scouts.

"No," said Pat; "I think they belong to some new organization to put down Bolshevism. Good idea."

By the roadside were silver-green olive trees, festooned with the darker green of vines, and hung with bunches of purple grapes. At Bagno da Ripoli there was not much to see beyond an uninteresting chapel, but it was pleasant there. They left the carriage and Lucinda went over to the chapel, while Pat walked farther along the road. She enjoyed the peaceful empty feeling of the afternoon. She could not pretend to herself that the trip had been a success. It had not resembled in any way those visions she had conjured up with the words "Lovers in an Italian city." Still, it had made them know each other a little better. They had advanced a stage in intimacy, and as they sat side by side in the carriage they were like people who were related.

The next morning they left Florence, traveling together as far as Genoa, where they parted. They had the compartment to themselves and he kissed her good-bye. His eyes had that affectionate, protective twinkle, his voice that deep, kind, well-bred tone which had first attracted her to him. As she continued alone, looking out, thoughtful and unseeing, at the steep, scrubby cliffs and the baroque churches of the Italian Riviera, she was contented in a sort of minor-key fashion. She began to make plans for the future.

CHAPTER SEVEN

LUCINDA collected Stephen at St Saturnin, spending only a day there, and traveled straight through to Crittenden. She did not care to take Stephen to King Charles's Court. Paul was coming to England for a few weeks, and he asked her to wait and go with him, but she had to get Stephen back to school. She arrived at Crittenden Halt at ten o'clock at night. Stephen was fast asleep, and she had to lift him out of the train and hold him on his feet till he woke up.

Marian had driven to meet them, partly because the chauffeur had had a busy day and her own energy was not nearly used up, but also from friendliness. When she saw how tired they were she demanded, "Why on earth didn't you break the journey?"

"I wanted to get back," said Lucinda. "I feel like Cardinal Wolsey arriving at Leicester Abbey."

"You want a hot bath and some soup," said Marian.

She drove them to the End House. While Lucinda was having her bath she put Stephen to bed. She had already been there to see that the boiler was stoked up, and to order a meal for Lucinda, which she made her take in bed.

"This is marvelous soup," said Lucinda.

"I made it myself," said Marian, sitting by the bedside like a benevolent gaoler and watching her eat. "It's quite easy. You fry some onions in butter in a saucepan. When they're nearly cooked you put with them some patent barley and some salt. The secret of good cooking is to fry salt with everything. Then you pour in milk, keeping stirring it like with a *béchamel,* then beat in the yolk of an egg, and there you are."

"You're a *chef manqué.*"

"I'm a good many things *manqués,*" said Marian grimly.

Lucinda had a glass of burgundy with her supper. She was so tired that the wine immediately went to her head. This, combined with the perfect relaxed comfort of her bed after days in trains, made her begin to giggle. While she was in this state the words "lovers in an Italian city" came into her mind. She laughed until she was helpless. Marian, amused, but telling her not to be idiotic, tucked her up and turned out the lights. She immediately fell asleep, and did not wake up till lunch time on the following day.

She went in to see Hugo. He did not look up, either when she came in or when she spoke to him. His response to what she told him was duller than usual. She beckoned the male nurse out of the room.

"The major's worse," she said.

"He's not so bright as he was."

"Has the doctor been?"

"No, madam, not since you left. He says there's nothing he can do, really."

She wanted to ask if Hugo was likely to live long, but realized that her motive in asking the question would make it improper.

Pat was on a visit in Norfolk, but was to return to London in the middle of October. At the same time the Bassingbournes were coming on their annual visit to Crittenden. Lucinda decided to be away for that week, lest Lady Bassingbourne should question her too closely about her stay in Florence. She would spend the week at her flat. This would enable her, she hoped, to see a fair amount of Pat, and as Paul would be in London at that time, she might see some paintings and plays in his company.

She wrote to Pat, saying that she would be at King Charles's Court for a week from the fifteenth of October. Her letter was more friendly and confident in tone than her former notes to him. She thought that the real benefit of the Italian trip would be felt afterwards. She enjoyed being back at Crittenden, but as the fifteenth of October approached she felt a quickening excitement. Marian said:

"Surely you're not going away while the Bassingbournes are here?"

"I'm awfully sorry," said Lucinda. "Do apologize for me. But I must do some shopping and Paul will be in London for that week, and I like going about with him. I don't suppose you want him down here with the Bassingbournes."

"No, I don't," said Marian definitely.

"I'll write Lady Bassingbourne a little note," said Lucinda. "Mrs Galway once advised me to write little notes whenever possible. She arrived in England with almost no social assets, but through writing little notes she came to be admitted to the highest circles."

Lucinda took to London with her a suitcase containing all the Florentiana which she had bought for the flat, and a separate parcel containing two heavy rolls of brocade. She had intended to wait until the chairs had been re-covered with this to bring about the general transformation, but she could not resist putting the little jeweled clock on the writing table, and washing the reproduction Benvenuto Cellini silver so that it could be used at dinner. She had not brought any flowers up from Crittenden as she had so much luggage, and she went out to buy some. When she returned with a large bunch of *longiflorum* lilies, flowers which had a slightly Florentine association, she found a letter had been slipped through her door.

Her surprise, as she had little correspondence at the flat, was succeeded by the immediate certainty that it was from Pat, although the envelope was lying address downwards. She also knew at once that he could not be coming tonight or he would not have written, but she had greater unadmitted fears than that, and she sat in a low chair before she opened the envelope, as her heart was beating violently and she felt faint.

The letter was long for one from Pat. She read it through the first time in a dazed condition, hardly taking in its full meaning. Clothed in language full of solicitude for her welfare, he said all the things which he had contemplated saying on that morning in her room in Florence. He explained that he had to marry and he wanted to have children before he was too old to enjoy them. He had hoped all along to be able to marry her if she would have him, but this possibility seemed to become more and more remote. Also, to put it bluntly, it was not very agreeable to have to wait for another man's death to marry. Then, too, they did seem to be cooling off a little. Latterly, things did not seem so easy between them. In support of this he quoted from her own letter which she had slipped under his door in Florence. Was it not better to end now, as good friends, rather than to go on and part later, possibly with acrimony? He reiterated his deep gratitude to her and signed himself, "Ever your affectionate, Pat."

In a postscript he said that if she would like him to he would come round to say good-bye, but he thought it better not, and they could later meet more naturally in the world.

Lucinda sat for a long time without stirring. She was like someone who lies ill and dare not move for fear of realizing the pain which at the moment is numbed. She had again that curious feeling that her eyes were being stretched. After a while she went to the writing table and drew some sheets of notepaper towards her. She began to write rapidly, referring every now and then to Pat's letter. She had filled three sheets when an intense weariness came over her. It all seemed stale. She thrust the letter aside and sat staring at the little clock from the Ponte Vecchio. She wondered how she was to get through the long evening ahead of her. She thought of ringing up Pat and making him come round to say good-bye, but her longing for him was mixed with so much contempt and distaste that she felt that there would only be a dreadful scene, in which she would appear maudlin and undignified. But the flat was like a prison. She could not spend the evening alone here, in this place where the air was thick with associations, and surrounded by her laughably pathetic souvenirs of Florence, which she could not even bring herself to put away.

Of all her friends the only one of whose society she would be glad just now was Paul. She was thankful that he was in London, and she rang him up at his rooms in Half Moon Street and asked him to dine with her. Paul sounded a little embarrassed.

"I'm awfully sorry, my dear," he said, "I'm dining with Sir Alexander Portshead, and we're going to the ballet. I'm afraid we've only two stalls or I'd ask you to come."

This name, as Paul hoped it would, suggested a corpulent shipping magnate, but Lucinda knew very well that it belonged to a boy at Eton, whose large and ravishing photograph, signed "with love from Alex," was on Paul's bookcase at St Saturnin.

"Oh, very well," she said rather coldly, but with a break in her voice.

She put on a coat and went down to dine in the restaurant. She had never been here before, as she always had her meals sent up. She was not hungry, but she had to be free for a while of the atmosphere of the flat and she did not know where else to go, and when she had dawdled as long as possible over the dinner which she barely tasted, she had to return there.

She did not bother to turn on a light nor to draw the curtains, but she sat on in the darkness, again like a sick person whose pain is numb till he moves. The only light in the room came from the Embankment, broken by the intervening pattern of autumnal trees. When a tram clattered by the light became brighter, and the shadow of a particular branch on which a few leaves hung traveled slowly across the room, and when it passed over the mirror above the mantelpiece it was like a tree reflected in water. This was the only thing external to herself which she noticed as she sat there, unable to put out a tendril of thought in any direction from which it would not recoil shriveled with pain.

At last she moved and saw that it was eleven o'clock. She knew that if she went to bed she would not sleep. She put on a hat and a light coat and set out to walk in some unaccustomed place where she might be less conscious of her identity. When she came to the Strand she felt cold and disinclined to walk far, and she turned in to one of those huge restaurants where marble pillars and thick carpets give, at a moderate price, the illusion of luxury.

She sat at a table at the edge of a balcony, from which she could look down on the people on the ground floor. She had never been in one of these places before, and later it had for her the quality of a dream, as people remember those improbable occasions which happen at rare intervals in life, as when some peculiar combination of circumstances may lead one to have a conversation with a film star in a potting-shed or, turning suddenly in a bar, to jolt the brandy glass in the hand of a national hero.

This feeling of unreality was intensified when she saw Paul sitting at a table in the restaurant below. Opposite to him was a youth with a rather coarse rosy face, and the expression of a cow chewing the cud. Paul was producing for his benefit all the wit and eclectic reference of which he was capable, and bending towards him with the extreme courtesy which normally he would only show to a Bourbon princess. The only response was a very slow half-derisive smile expanding the youth's already expansive red cheeks, when one of Paul's sallies descended to the range of his comprehension. Lucinda, not intending to spy, watched them curiously. In this spectacle she already found some distraction from her own troubles. The youth, who was facing in her direction, became conscious of her fixed attention. He nodded laconically towards her and spoke to Paul. His actual words were, "That's not a bad tart up there."

Paul turned and saw Lucinda. He was too disturbed to take in the vulgarity of the boy's remark. He gave a preoccupied bow and said, "Excuse me for a moment." In a minute or less he was standing beside Lucinda's table.

"What on earth are you doing here?" he asked. "This is no place for you to come." He half thought she must have seen him going in with the boy, and followed him from curiosity, yet he could not credit her with behavior so out of keeping with her character.

"I wanted a little privacy," said Lucinda smiling.

Paul looked doubtfully at the marble pillars, the clattering tables, the orchestra.

"Am I disturbing you?" he asked.

"No, not at all."

"Would you mind if I were to come and sit here?" He saw that she was in an overwrought condition. That she had already done

290

something so extraordinary as to come alone to this place at eleven o'clock at night made him fear what she might do next.

"I'd be delighted—but what about Sir Alexander Portshead?" Paul snorted.

"That's not Alex," he said. "He couldn't get away. I rang you up, but there was no answer. I found that boy in a bar. It seemed a pity to waste the ticket and I thought the ballet might widen his outlook."

He went downstairs again and spoke to the boy, who received his explanation with a suspicious and sullen leer. However, when Paul gave him a note he seemed to be placated, and as he left he looked up at Lucinda and waved his hand in a gesture which he had learned from American gangster films, and which conveyed clearly, "You can have him, sister."

"Shall we leave this place?" said Paul when he returned. "It's very noisy."

Lucinda suggested that they should return to her flat. She had been dreading going back there alone. It was not so depressing to go in with Paul. The bunch of lilies still lay wrapped in their tissue paper on the corner of the table. Their scent filled the room.

"Someone has left you some flowers," said Paul.

"No. I bought them. Like you I was expecting a friend who didn't turn up."

"It's a hellish feeling," said Paul. "Shall I arrange the flowers for you?"

"Yes, please do."

The fire had died down, but she turned on an electric heater. While Paul arranged the flowers she opened one of the bottles of St Saturnin wine which she had brought for Pat, but which he had not cared for. Paul came in with the lilies and asked, "Where shall I put these?"

"Oh, on the writing table will do," said Lucinda, busy with the corkscrew and forgetting that it was strewn with the closely written pages of her abortive reply to Pat. Paul, clearing a space to put down the vase, involuntarily read part of a sentence, ". . . never for one moment meant to suggest in Florence that I didn't love you, or even . . ."

Lucinda suddenly remembered the letter and turned, but Paul was examining the Benvenuto Cellini silverware, which she had put out on the table she used for meals. She took the letter and tore the sheets in half and threw them on to the smouldering fire, where they smoked and slowly turned brown but did not burst into flames.

All these circumstances enabled Paul to guess with rough accuracy what had happened. Lucinda handed him a glass of wine.

"Here's to more cheerful evenings," she said.

"It's very pleasant here," said Paul, and she too began to feel that the ghosts were being dispelled. "How long are you up for?"

"A week," said Lucinda. "Then I think I shall give up this flat."

"Won't you feel buried at Crittenden without it?"

"I'm half dead. I may as well be buried."

"One always feels like that after the failure of a friendship. Half one's life seems to be gone, but it revives with another attachment."

"I don't want another attachment," said Lucinda, careless of what she said, as she knew that Paul had guessed a good deal correctly.

"But that is the only way of living. One must always have an attachment, or one is half dead. To avoid it is to avoid life itself."

"Do you think there is something about me that alienates men? That it gradually shows through, like the copper under Sheffield plate as it wears thin? Am I too naïve or too adhesive, or too provincial or something? Like a non-alcoholic drink?"

"I shouldn't think so at all, though that might have been true with Hugo. You don't mind my saying this?"

"No, go on."

"You were too good for him. In that way he's like me, I'm not attracted towards the simply kind and good. I like those who have a bit of the devil in them, but I hate it when they display the nature of the devil. I want the devil redeemed, as it were, which is a rare phenomenon. I want the soul of a Dostoevsky character in the body of a Greek athlete. My taste in people is as difficult and expensive to gratify as my taste in furniture."

"I don't want people to gratify my taste," said Lucinda. "I want them to be pleasant companions, I want to live at peace with someone I love."

"It's impossible to live at peace with anyone you love," said Paul. "You can only live at peace with those to whom you are indifferent."

"That's what Elspeth Roberts says. If it's true I can't see any use in love."

"Use!" exclaimed Paul. "No important things are useful. Art and love are useless and without one the other cannot exist. The sufferings of lovers produce great music and painting and writing, and in people of no creative ability a refinement of soul which is pleasing to Almighty God."

"I don't think that Marian's archdeacon would agree with you."

"Archdeacons have no conception of the nature of God. God is a kind of super gourmet, a horrible connoisseur sniffing the fragrance of souls. We are tortured and twisted to wring from us cries of agony, exquisite notes of submission and sacrifice, so that this divine monster may enjoy their music. We are like Strasbourg geese whose livers are diseased to make a delicacy."

"And what is the use of it all?"

"It's no use, I tell you."

Lucinda opened another bottle of St Saturnin wine. The smell of Paul's *caporal bleu* cigarettes mingled with the heavy scent of lilies. As he drank more wine the theories he elaborated became more fantastic, but every now and then he would give a diagnosis of Lucinda's symptoms so accurate that it surprised her, and helped her to understand and accept her situation more easily. He stayed talking till nearly four o'clock in the morning. When he had gone Lucinda found it hard to realize that she had been talking all this time to a man, and yet she felt that no conversation with a woman could have had that curious mixture of intimacy and impersonality. Many of his ideas she rejected, but one thing he said she unwillingly accepted as true, "When love is dead, it is as dead as a doornail and you can't wake it up again." She also realized, this evening, what she had never noticed before, that Pat was exactly the same type as Hugo, more sympathetic in manner perhaps, but less direct.

The resignation which came to her from the midnight conversation with Paul did not last when she was back at Crittenden. She had been sustained through the empty days of her life by the thought of her next meeting with Pat. Always she had something to look forward to, little arrangements to make and wider plans and dreams for the future. Now these were taken from her. Stephen's being away at school, or spending his holidays at Crittenden House, made the End House more lifeless than ever. The pain of her loss, like a toothache, was intermittent. It was strongest when she could not reconcile herself to the fact that the parting was inevitable, that it was due not to outside circumstances, but to something inherent in the characters of Pat and herself. At these times she felt an actual pain in her heart, and the left side of her body felt heavier than the right. Sometimes she felt as if the left side of her face were becoming screwed up, and she examined it in the glass. She could see nothing but some minute red veins which showed in the middle of her left cheek. After some weeks this disappeared, but where they had been there remained a tiny spot, which did not go away for a year.

In the spring Pat's engagement was announced. There was a photograph of the girl in the *Tatler*, to which Marian drew Lucinda's attention.

"Isn't Colonel Lanfranc a relative of those two nice Australians you know?" she said.

"Yes," said Lucinda. She took the photograph to the window to examine it, but also to hide her expression from Marian. Again she felt that heaviness in her body and that screwing up of the muscles of her face. The girl, whose name was Sullivan, was rather florid-looking, round-faced, with fine eyes. The simple animal health which the photograph suggested made Lucinda feel that her own life had already begun to fade, and even more, for some reason, that there was no place where she truly belonged.

"Do you know who this Sullivan girl is?" she asked.

"She looks like a dairymaid to me," said Marian. "Will they like her in Australia?"

Lucinda did not bother to explain that Pat had never been to Australia. When she returned to the End House she removed the engraving of the first Lord Wendale to the back staircase, and hung it by the housemaids' cupboard.

In the summer Hugo died. In his coffin he was again able to receive the recognition of society, and the filial attention of Stephen, who came from school for the funeral. All the county and old friends from his regiment sent wreaths. The most beautiful of these, of white and purple zinnias, bore only a card with the initials "S.P." Lucinda knew that Mrs Fabian Parker's name was Stella. She had the wreath put on the center of the grave.

Feeling like the man from whom all the devils had been cast out, she returned to the End House. The house itself, empty, swept and garnished, where she walked freely through the library and garden, where there were now no forbidden joys, where she did not have to brace herself to meet Hugo, nor flinch when she saw him, was the symbol of her own condition. The morning after the funeral, she woke up saying to herself "I'm free, free!" but it was a freedom she did not know how to use. She was like a child who sees in a shop some marvelous and expensive toy, which at last he persuades his parents to give him the money to buy, only to return to the shop and find it is sold.

In a month, when the feelings stirred by Hugo's death had become dormant, she had a batch of letters of condolence from Australia. One of these was from Tony, extraordinarily friendly and kind. Fred wrote that she should now come out to Australia, at least on a visit. She thought of doing this but not until after Stephen's summer holidays, which they were going to spend at St Saturnin. She also hesitated, wondering if it would be embarrassing for Julie to meet her. She knew that Julie had a capacity for ignoring unpleasant facts, even for deceiving herself that they did not exist. It was possible that someone whose presence would remind her of them might bring her more unhappiness than pleasure.

However, Lucinda had almost decided to go to Australia for six months, leaving in the autumn. She would then only miss Stephen's short Christmas holidays which he would spend at Crittenden, and she would miss an English winter. She was giving up the End House. It had too many grim associations, and anyhow she did not want to live in the English country. There was always Crittenden available for Stephen or for a visit.

Then she had a letter from Tony. He would be arriving in England in December. It was an odd time to come, but he had to wait until after the Cup Weeks balls, and to be back again before the parties began in the Melbourne autumn. Lucinda felt that she could not possibly miss Tony. It might be his only trip to Europe in his lifetime. She was sure he would be disappointed if she were not here, while she would be disappointed if he were not in Melbourne. She put off her Australian journey till the following year.

When she returned from St Saturnin and had packed Stephen off to school, she came up to London on a house-hunt. She found a charming little restored Georgian house in Catherine Street, behind Buckingham Gate. This was a new neighborhood for her to frequent. She chose it deliberately to be away from all stale associations, and she did her household shopping at the Army and Navy Stores instead of Harrods. The End House furniture was too big for Catherine Street and she stored most of it. While she was buying her new furniture she had Tony in mind, and chose things which she thought would please or startle him. She asked Marian if she might bring him down for Christmas at Crittenden. She was sure that the country house festivities, the carols and the candle-lit saloon would please him enormously. The feeling of hope, of being able to do something to please someone, which she had lost a year ago, began to return to her. Marian reluctantly had to admit that London agreed with her.

As the time of Tony's visit drew near she found herself thinking more and more about him. At times a look of great happiness lighted her face, and Susannah, with whom she dined once a week, thought she must be going to marry again, but this happiness was caused by some sudden memory of her girlhood, and by the thought it was being brought back to her by someone who had known her then, and whose affection for her was untouched by the sordid tragedies of the intervening years. Faintly, but enough to make her heart beat more quickly, she recaptured the emotions of the day at Cape Furze and the mornings on the Tarpeian Rock. She remembered too, vaguely, the night of the Ratcliffes' dance, and believed that she had treated Tony badly then. She was determined to make up for it now. She did not really know what she expected to come of his visit. She only knew that at last she had found a direction in which her natural affection could be released, without shame or subterfuge.

Delighting in this new freedom, she went to meet him at the ship. She went by underground to Fenchurch Street where she arrived late, having taken an Inner Circle train by mistake. She arrived on the platform just as the train was starting. She ran to catch it. The guard said, "In here, miss," and taking her by the elbow helped her into the van. Lucinda thanked him breathlessly and sat down on a packing case. Gradually she was aware of a pervading and peculiar smell, which she soon located as coming from a heap of dead rabbits in the corner beside her. Having had little breakfast and having hurried from the underground station, she found this smell unbearable. Also it tinged with a different color, much as Lydia's conversation had done, her golden visions of her Australian childhood. She remembered the rabbit skins at Noorilla nailed out to dry in the sun, the clouds of black flies, and the bare brown honeycomb of the paddocks on the way to Cape Furze.

It was gray and beginning to drizzle when she left the train at Tilbury, and there was some fuss about allowing her onto the ship, which was already alongside the quay. At last she found herself in a lounge at the head of the companionway. Everywhere there was a faint sour smell, almost as trying as that of the rabbits. There were heaps of luggage lying about and hurrying stewards, somewhat harassed, but smiling and eager for their tips. The ship suggested one vast bedroom which has not yet received the attention of the housemaids. The passengers in their smartest clothes, though these were not very smart as they were all intending to buy new garments in London and Paris, were mostly either looking for some piece of luggage or a friend who had escaped them. Lucinda looked about for Tony but could not see him. At last she was about to ask a steward if he could find Mr Duff for her, when she noticed a slight, middle-aged man in a dark-blue suit talking to a large, important-looking woman, who was giving him her earnest attention. His skin was brown and wrinkled, and he was bald on top and at the temples. She stared at him for half a minute before she could grasp that he was Tony. Then a curious feeling possessed her. It was a wave of affection for him, which was more than half pity, something of the same feeling she had when she met Lydia but less complicated. In that moment it was revealed to her that she had hitherto expected life to be something that it was not. She had a tremendous sense of relief, as if she had taken off a pair of green spectacles which she had insisted were rose-colored. She approached Tony, to wait good-humoredly until he had finished talking to the opulent matron, before making herself known.

"I told Mrs Anderson," he was saying, "that she should place a chair in the hall for people who are not entitled to be asked into the drawing-room."

Part Four
1933-1942
IN ADOLESCENTIS FLORE

In ipso adolescentis flore periit inimicorum insidiis circumventus.

BOYD OF TROCHRIG ON THE MURDER OF JAMES, LORD BOYD, AT THE AGE OF FIFTEEN BY A MONTGOMERY, A.D. 1484.

CHAPTER ONE

ON AN EVENING of the Easter term in his second year at Cambridge, Stephen sat in his rooms at the south-west corner of Clare. These rooms as well as being spacious and sunny, with a pleasant outlook over lawns and trees and the river, had two additional advantages. They provided mild entertainment, to the south with the spectacle of the King's choristers in large top-hats and diminutive gowns, hurrying in a straggling procession to and from their daily service, and to the west with the number of people crossing the bridge, who stopped to feel which of the stone balls had a segment cut out of it. These entertainments had ceased for the day. The choristers had long since disappeared over King's Bridge into the unknown region from which they daily emerged, and the only people on Clare Bridge were one or two undergraduates returning from hall to their rooms in the new building.

Stephen very much liked being up at Cambridge. Contrary to his expectation, he enjoyed the traditional academic atmosphere, and the companionship of young men of his own kind, although his impulsiveness had not brought him the friendships he had expected. Also, having been trained by Paul in the use of his eyes, this town with its fine buildings, its lawns and gardens, was a continual pleasure to him. When he was in his fourteenth year he had a mysterious illness, of which the chief symptom was a trance-like inertia, following violent headaches. Because of this Lucinda had been able to carry out her intention not to send him to an English public school—stronger than ever after Pat had left her—which would otherwise have been impossible against the influence of Arthur and Marian, though Paul would have supported her with his view that the public schools were simply channels through which the commercial classes could rise to flood, rot and destroy the aristocracy. When he recovered from his illness he had a tutor for a year, and then was sent to a school in Switzerland. Every August he spent at St Saturnin, where Lucinda took a villa. He had remained friendly with Roland Roberts, who was now up at Jesus and was still his closest friend, though he was a Communist and often said things which Stephen instinctively disliked, not that he had given them any previous thought. At the moment Roland was infatuated with a girl at Newnham, whom he had taken out to dinner and to a play at the Arts Theatre.

Stephen realized with pleasure that it was now light enough to go for a stroll after hall. He took up his gown again and went downstairs. When he came out into the court he thought he might instead go to a cinema, but Lucinda had impressed on him so often how poor they were that he never spent any money if he could avoid it. At the slump Fred had deducted a third of her allowance. He had no need to do this, but he was hurt because she would not go out to Australia. The new exchange rate took away a fifth of the remainder. Like many people who had been rich and then have to economize, Stephen would show the same concern over three shillings as over fifty pounds—in fact more, as one could more easily control the expenditure of fifty pounds than of three shillings.

He turned towards the Backs. Over the bridge the delicate tracery of the wrought-iron gates made a kind of humanized prelude to the tracery of the avenue beyond them, down which a window of the new building looked like an architectural eye. As he dawdled on the bridge to enjoy this scene, in which there was so much drawing with pale washes of color, a pair of duck rose from the river by Trinity Hall, whirred close over his head, and settled on the water on the other side of the bridge. With some dim idea of "two for mirth" he took this as a cheerful omen, and strolled on down the avenue.

He did not want to go for a very long walk, so he turned into King's, thinking perhaps he might after all go to the cinema. He could not go indoors again and read, as this spring weather with its longer daylight made him restless. The grass was thick with daffodils. When he came to the bend in the path he stopped suddenly and made a faint exclamation. All the westward facing windows of Gibb's building appeared to be splashed with green diamonds. The evening sun was behind a film of cloud. Either from this or because its rays were filtered through the topmost branches of the trees, its light was a pale, cool green. It may also have been partly due to the quality of the old glass in the windows, uneven in its surface, so that in one window would appear four or five bright points of light, and in another only two. The semi-circular window over the pediment was a solid blaze. The light did not seem to be reflected externally, but to come from within the building, as if some supernatural assembly were there and the rooms were filled with Christmas stars.

Coming across the bridge was a man he knew slightly, an undergraduate named Hayman. He was at Queen's and was reading for Holy Orders.

"Look at that," said Stephen.

Hayman turned and said, "Yes, very effective."

They stood a moment, looking at the bright windows. Hayman was carrying a flat paper bag containing gramophone records. It seemed a little curt to part immediately after sharing this experience.

"I'm just going to try some new records," he said.

"Are they dance music?" asked Stephen, looking at the bag.

"Good Heavens, no! They're Palestrina."

"Oh!" said Stephen eagerly. "Are they? I didn't know they made Palestrina records. My uncle, who lives near Marseilles, once made me get out of the train at Dijon to hear them singing Palestrina in the cathedral. They're supposed to do it better there than anywhere. It was fairly marvelous."

"Would you like to hear these?" asked Hayman.

"I would, very much. Would you like to play them on my radiogram? It's quite close." He nodded in the direction of his rooms.

"Perhaps that would be more convenient," said Hayman, who had not a very good gramophone.

Stephen's rooms were furnished not only with a radiogram and a grand piano, but with some very good furniture of the more solid variety and thick carpets from Crittenden. The only embellishments by Stephen were an oil-painting of St Saturnin by Duncan Grant, and a bowl in which some super-decorative goldfish trailed their silky fins. Hayman looked about appreciatively.

"You have good rooms. How did you manage to secure them?" he asked.

"I don't know. My aunt arranged it," said Stephen with the faintly surprised smile with which he awoke to any privilege he enjoyed.

Marian, who frequently declared that the young man of today needed above all things a Spartan discipline, fussed indulgently over Stephen, sending him weekly parcels of cake and cream, as if he were a soldier at the front.

Hayman took out the records and Stephen put the chosen one on the radiogram. There were high seats in the two windows overlooking the river, and they sat in these with their backs to each other, so that they could enjoy the music without embarrassment. The disembodied sound floated and filled the darkening room like a river flowing through a land of souls at rest. Stephen closed his eyes. When he opened them at the end of the record he said:

"That music melts my spine."

They played all four records and one of them again. Then

Stephen switched on the lights, and brought out a Crittenden plum cake and a bottle of St Saturnin wine, of which Paul sent him a case at the beginning of every term. Hayman interested and amused him. His conversation was entirely about sixteenth and seventeenth century church music, interspersed with occasional contemptuous references to Protestants.

"I'm afraid I don't often go to church," said Stephen apologetically. "My mother doesn't go in London, and I stay a good deal with my uncle in France, and there's no English church there. I only go at Crittenden. That's my other uncle's place in the country. We have to go to the village church. It's pretty frightful, though sometimes we ring up for seats in the cathedral, which is a bit better."

"Do you book seats?"

"My aunt knows the dean," explained Stephen.

"Is it as good as King's?" asked Hayman.

"I don't know. I've never been there."

"Never been to King's, with it on your doorsteps? Good Heavens! Great Scott!"

"I hear the organ sometimes from the window here. It's rather nice."

"You like Palestrina—you get out of the train at Dijon—and you've never been to King's! They don't do a great deal of Palestrina, but they do some, and Byrd and Vittorio, and more modern stuff, which I don't care for. Still, it's the most perfect Anglican choir in the world, not a hundred yards from your rooms. Gosh! I haven't missed one evensong since I've been up."

Before he left, just in time to get back to his rooms without being fined, Hayman made Stephen promise to accompany him to King's Chapel the following afternoon. Stephen had enjoyed the evening. It had been very pleasant from the moment on the bridge when the duck flew over his head. He liked Hayman, and found his conversation more interesting than Roland's, who at present could only talk about Karl Marx and girls.

He had only once been into King's Chapel, on a gray November evening in his first term. It had been very cold and deserted, and he had found its soaring mystery rather oppressive. On this afternoon, when with Hayman he entered the chapel for the second time, the sunlight was slanting through the magnificent windows, and here and there were lighted candles. When the choir came in, the boys in scarlet cassocks as it was Eastertide, he felt a kind of cheerful anticipation.

Suddenly, without any warning from the organ, the boys burst out singing, *Eya, resurrexit*. The lovely noise rose and quivered high overhead in the glorious vaulted roof. Stephen found he had to blink back the tears which sometimes came to his eyes at unexpected beauty. He was hardly conscious of what followed until the singing began again. When he left the chapel with Hayman the music seemed to remain in him, heightening his whole condition and filling him with tranquil love.

"What d'you think of it?" asked Hayman, as they strolled round the end of the chapel towards Clare.

"It's fairly marvelous," said Stephen. "I think I'll come again."

"Right. I'll collect you tomorrow at a quarter to five."

"Won't you come to tea?"

"Thanks. I will," said Hayman.

This developed into a routine. Hayman came to tea with Stephen, they went to King's together, and afterwards they generally walked through Clare, across the river, along into Trinity, and back again to Clare where they parted. In a few weeks a friendship was established between them, though it was not so close nor intimate as Stephen's friendship with Roland, whom he had known since he was seven years old, and from whom he had no secrets. Hayman was more coldly intellectual and more gentlemanly than Roland, and any emotion in his relationship with Stephen was provided by the music to which they listened together.

In the chapel they sat in the sub-stalls on the cantoris side, between the choir and the high altar. Towards the end of the choir, nearly opposite Stephen, was a boy with eyes set wide apart, and straight, untidy hair, who gave to his singing that absorbed attention which children give to work or play that interests them. On high notes his body became taut and he flung back his head. He was like a singing bird. Stephen, watching the choir, involuntarily rested his eyes most often on this boy.

One day this boy sang a solo. Stephen felt as if his soul were being uplifted by this voice into some heavenly region, where his emotions were purified and made impersonal. When the choir rose to file out the boy gave Stephen a glance, as if aware that he had attracted his interest.

After the service he excused himself to Hayman, as he did not feel inclined for one of the theological expositions to which Hayman was beginning to treat him on their walks, hoping to make him an orthodox Anglo-Catholic. He sat in the window seat looking down at Clare Bridge. He felt extraordinary happy.

Roland burst into the room. He had dark, lively eyes, which would have been passionate if they were not so good-humored.

"There you are, you filthy capitalist!" he cried. "Where have you been? I've come up here a dozen times looking for you, and the place was like the tomb."

"I thought you'd be at Newnham."

"Oh, that's all over. I'm having an interim. God! I believe you're in love."

"What d'you mean?" said Stephen, blushing simply at having attention drawn to himself.

"You've got the look in your eye. Oh my darling boy, I'm so glad. Eros has touched the icy ventricles of your heart. I thought you were becoming a sissy. Tell me all about it. What is she— Newnham, Girton, Town or Tart?"

"She's not anybody," said Stephen.

"Oh, God! What a blow! You're not lying to me. Or is it myself that has brought that tenderness, that illumination, that slumbering fire to your candid eye? My dearest chum, my heart bursts with joy to see you again." He hugged Stephen till his ribs cracked. "Moira had abandoned me for a bloody blue, and you weren't at hand to tell all about it. Where the hell have you been? Come and have a drink."

"I don't want to have a drink," said Stephen.

"Then you are in love, and it's successful. If it wasn't successful you'd want a drink. You've got a sort of pure look in your eye. I don't like it. It's most mystifying."

"I'll dine with you in the town if you like," said Stephen. "I've signed off hall. You can have a drink with your dinner if you like, but you mustn't get tight—and we'll go to a flick afterwards."

"Vicarious passion at a flick. How sombre! You can pay as you're a capitalist and you invited me."

A few days later Roland met Hayman in Stephen's rooms. They eyed each other curiously and seemed incapable of exchanging a word. It was not so much instinctive dislike, as the mutual realization that their tastes and interests were so divergent that they were almost of different species. Roland waited for Hayman to leave, and when this did not happen he left himself. Hayman made no comment on Roland, but his manner suggested he was much too hearty and vulgar to be a suitable friend for Stephen.

Roland, when next he saw Stephen, asked him where on earth he had picked up Hayman.

"If you put him in a parson's collar and he walked onto the stage he'd bring the house down. You wouldn't need to make him up. He's a born music-hall parson."

"He's reading for Orders," said Stephen.

"Good heavens!" exclaimed Roland, really shocked that a young man in these days should read for Orders, and that Stephen should know him. After this Stephen tried to avoid their meeting in his rooms. He had no close friend other than Roland. He was shy, and not having been to school in England he did not fall in very easily with the young men of his own class. Much of their pleasure seemed to be connected with killing animals, which he did not really enjoy. He had hunted as a boy at Crittenden, and still occasionally rode to hounds to please Arthur. But when he had been blooded he was sick over Willy Greene-James's immaculate white breeches. This incident immediately preceded his mysterious illness. He valued this new friendship with Hayman and he did not want Roland to drive him away. He continued to go with him to King's, but he did not tell Roland about this, and he had some difficulty in explaining why he was never in his rooms between five and six o'clock in the evening. Roland thought that this was due to the mythical girl, and was hurt that Stephen would not tell him about it, as he was far from reticent in his own affairs.

Meanwhile Stephen continued to attend King's, where he had become increasingly aware of the chorister who was generally at the end of the row, but was sometimes moved two or three places nearer the organ. This boy, when he arrived at his place, always glanced at Stephen, as if to make sure that he was present, and sometimes at the end of the service, before he rose to leave, he gave him a longer look.

Stephen could not help returning these glances, but after about a week he thought it was hardly sensible to continue this inarticulate recognition, partly because he thought the boy might get into trouble if he were to attract the attention of members of the congregation.

On the afternoon following this decision he sat on the decani side of the chapel, where he could only see the back of the boy's head. He saw him when he came in with the choir, look across at Stephen's usual place. Hayman thought that Stephen had moved for acoustic reasons. During the service the boy turned to take a music book from the seat behind him. He saw Stephen. Their eyes met and he looked hurt. Stephen felt that he had played a mean and silly trick, and had given too much significance to something harmless and amusing. He had a sense of discomfort for the rest of the day.

On the next afternoon he returned to his original place. When the choir came in under the screen, Stephen, without definitely focusing his eyes on him, knew that the boy saw him there and was pleased. The next day was Sunday and the chapel was crowded with ordinary churchgoers and a proportion of sightseers. Although the music was as beautiful as ever, that other quality he had found in the chapel, that peculiar intimate tranquillity, was missing. He decided not to go on Sundays in future, especially as it made him late for tea at Mrs Cranborne's where he very often went on that day. When this lady, who was his tutor's wife, heard his name mentioned, she at once wrote asking him to tea, and when she met him told him he might come whenever he liked. Her mother had been an Australian, a Miss Jameson of Melbourne, who had married an Oxford professor named Maitland. They had known the Vanes, and Mrs Cranborne had questioned Stephen closely about his Australian relatives, and particularly his Uncle Bill. He did not think this at all remarkable as he was used to people being kind to him, and interested in his relatives.

On Thursday the service was unaccompanied, and the psalms, so sensitively pointed, were as beautiful in their words as in their melody. The verse "For one day in Thy courts is better than a thousand" fell to the decani side. The face of the end chorister as he sang this was touched by a sudden rosy flush. Just after this Stephen turned to look at the boy and found his eyes fixed on him. They were wide and dark, and seemed open to his soul. Some piercing current passed between them. Stephen felt a leap in his heart and a compassion that was almost intolerable. Afterwards he wondered at the strength of this feeling of compassion, as the boy appeared in no way to be an object of pity. And yet it had seemed as if from the depth of those wide-open eyes he had implored Stephen's help. Later he was inclined to dismiss the incident as a trick of his imagination, but he could not shed the belief that there existed some singular bond between himself and this chorister.

Hayman, although he was so orthodox, spoke of the services in King's as if they were only a musical performance, whereas for Stephen they held far greater significance. From the condition they produced in him he was sure that they were acts of worship, although he was intellectually uncertain about the existence of God.

The choristers occasionally had secret sources of amusement among themselves. One afternoon Stephen looked up and intercepted a laughing glance exchanged between the end chorister and another facing him across the aisle. The boy, sensitive to Stephen's movements, turned to him an open, smiling face. This was the first time Stephen had seen him smile. He nearly laughed and quickly turned away. Though at times he was amused, this in nowise detracted from the pure intensity of emotion which Stephen felt at certain phrases of music, and at certain words of the service, or, best of all, when words and music combined to make him feel that there was some region where life might be transfigured into another dimension of experience, and that here he was at its threshold. He knew, too, that the faint recognition which had grown between himself and the end chorister enhanced the quality of these things, without which they would have been lacking in humanity. He mentioned this to Hayman, who said, "Of course, theological charity is a necessary ingredient of any act of worship."

He wished afterwards that he had not done so, as Hayman then took an undue interest in the chorister. A few days later he said:

"Why don't you get to know that boy?"

"I don't want to," said Stephen. He would have been disappointed if the boy had been absent from the choir, but he was satisfied for the relationship, if it could be called that, to remain as it was. Hayman, with a levity which surprised Stephen in so earnest a theologian, chaffed him about the boy and called him "The Sweetie." Stephen, who was always slow to take offense, grinned good-humoredly, but he said:

"I don't understand you. You're reading for Orders. I shouldn't have thought you would have approved of—well—the way you talk."

"That is because you don't understand Catholic Theology," said Hayman. "It includes, explains and justifies every good thing in life."

On another day as they came through the screen, some of the choristers were standing there chewing, and there was a strong smell of throat lozenge.

"Good Lord!" muttered Hayman. "Do all those golden Alleluias rise to Heaven stinking of menthol and creosote?"

The next day Stephen was walking up the ante-chapel when he saw the boy, in his Eton suit and black gown, chatting to two companions near the screen. He saw Stephen coming and a smile spread over his face. He gave an involuntary skip of pleasure, and then, slightly embarrassed, went off into the vestry.

"Why don't you find out his name?" asked Hayman. "Then you could ask him out to tea."

"I don't want to, and I don't supppose he'd be allowed to come," said Stephen. He was beginning to find Hayman's interest excessive, and there was a note of envy in his chaff which Stephen disliked.

It seemed to him that his attachment, if it could be called that, should remain one of the spirit, best expressed without words, which were but clumsy symbols, and could only coarsen or obscure those feelings which so far had been clearly and truthfully revealed to the exact degree in which they were valid. There must be people, he thought, with whom one's spirit was in complete accord. One often saw in the street, or in a train or theatre, a face which stirred feelings of friendship which could never be fulfilled, not only because there was no chance of acquaintance, but because, even if there were, there might be impassable gulfs of taste or material interest between that person and oneself. Only the spirit was in harmony. So he thought it must be with this boy. It was conceivable that all his interests would be not even Stephen's at the same age, but would lie in an opposite direction. But he did not doubt that there was a spiritual harmony between them, and that its adequate expression lay in the shared experience of these beautiful services. He was sure that their relationship should remain on this serene level, and that the delicate sense of love which the boy awakened in him could find its right and sufficient expression in the cadences of Palestrina and Orlando Gibbons.

However, on one occasion he did speak to the boy. Early one afternoon he was in the grounds of King's, walking up from the river under the south wall of Clare. It seemed to him that the clouds above King's Chapel always had more significant form, that the sky when it was clear was higher and more majestic than over other places. Today white cumulus clouds were in low bands above the chestnut tree between the chapel and the old library. To the south was another pile of white cloud, but the four pinnacles stood up in their soft gray-gold stone against a vivid blue sky. Gradually Stephen was aware that the afternoon air was full of the clear babel of young voices, which grew steadily louder. He could not imagine where they came from as there were no children in sight. The pleasant noise seemed to be descending from above. Then he realized it was coming from inside the corner turret of the chapel, and that a flock of boys must be descending the stone stairs, their voices echoing in the high narrow space and coming out through the loopholes.

He walked on round the chapel. As he turned the corner by the Gibb building, some boys began to trail out from the porch. Suddenly, before he quite realized how it happened or where he had come from, there beside him, smiling and holding out his hand, was the end chorister.

Stephen at first could think of nothing to say. He shook hands and asked some question about a holiday.

"Only a half-holiday," said the boy. "We've been up on the roof. We could see for miles. We could see Ely Cathedral."

"It's a clear day," said Stephen.

They looked at each other, curious at seeing closely in the sunlight the faces which hitherto they had only seen under constraint in the dim light of the chapel. The boy was in shorts, a blazer and sandshoes. He looked very slight and small.

"Would you tell me your name?" asked Stephen diffidently.

"Brian Wes . . ." He dropped his voice at his surname, and looked round apprehensively at one of his masters who had appeared in the porch. Stephen thought there must be some rule or etiquette which forbade their telling their names to strangers. He did not quite catch the name but did not like to ask the boy to repeat it. It sounded like Westleigh.

"Mine is Stephen Brayford," he said. "I'm at Clare."

The boy smiled. He looked round at his companions who were about to move away.

"Cheerio!" he said and went over to the schoolmaster, who gave Stephen an inquisitive glance. The party moved off, straggling towards the river.

Stephen went back to his rooms. He found that he was affected by this meeting, by speaking to someone with whom he had a sense of close affinity, but with whom the discipline of circumstances had hitherto prohibited any contact. The contrast between Brian's simple boyhood, his ordinary conversation and the aspirations with which he was associated in Stephen's mind, did not make the latter seem more commonplace, but rather the details of the former infinitely touching, his bare untidy head, a scratch on his knee, and his sandshoes, one of which was worn thin at the toe.

Paul was in England for a fortnight, having come to be overhauled by the dentist and to see an exhibition of Chinese art. He arranged to come up one day with Susannah and Lucinda to see Stephen. Stephen spent the morning buying embellishments for his lunch party. He was worried about the wine. If he gave Paul some of his own St Saturnin it might appear mean, while if he did not it might look as if he did not think much of it. He decided it would be better to produce it but to supplement it with some very good dry sherry before the meal and some old brandy afterwards. He bought the best that the wine merchant could produce, which cost him pounds. He then economized, saving sixpence on the flowers he bought for his rooms, and went off to the station to meet his relatives.

Susannah had not come as she was tired after a court ball the previous night. She sent Stephen loving messages and a five-pound note, which Lucinda smuggled to him when Paul was not looking, as she was afraid that Paul might follow Susannah's example. Her precaution was wasted as Paul, when Lucinda was not looking, gave Stephen a ten-pound note, which meant his traveling third class back to St Saturnin.

Paul was full of good spirits and enjoyed himself enormously. He was now becoming rather distinguished in appearance. His nose was more beaky than ever. His clothes, which were very good in the fashion of ten years earlier, with the trousers rather narrow, and his tanned face gave the impression of a retired Indian Army man, but it was belied by the look in his eyes and by his longish gray hair, which was brushed back from his forehead like wings.

Stephen took them a short walk along the Backs before luncheon, first into Queen's to see the old brick and half-timbered cloisters, along into King's, over the bridge into Queen's Road, and back over Clare Bridge to Stephen's rooms. It was a beautiful sunlit day, and the chestnuts, the pink may, the lilac and the laburnum were in bloom. Oddly enough Paul had never been to Cambridge before.

"It is a city of palaces!" he exclaimed.

In Stephen's rooms Roland, whom he had invited to meet them, was waiting.

"Ha, you young Bolshevik!" said Paul. "What devilries have you been up to, eh?" He was bubbling with laughter. "Or have the influences of this city of palaces changed your black, or rather red heart?"

"It's only pink," said Roland, grinning. He liked Paul very much and they spent half their time at St Saturnin in violent political argument.

Paul looked out of all the four windows.

"Every prospect pleases," he said, "and man, judging by the specimens I have seen, is both comely and intelligent, except you, you young blackguard," he said to Roland. Lucinda watched him surprised that this crusty old bachelor could so easily amuse these young men. Her figure was a little heavier than it had been ten years ago, as she enjoyed eating and the pleasures of life, but her face was thinner. Her general expression was one of amusement tempered by something between irony and sadness.

"I should think," said Paul, "that Oxford and Cambridge would be admirable places to live, if in each there was a grand ducal court. It would give life more the quality of an oil-painting and less that of a line-drawing. Also I imagine it would give them a truer social perspective."

Roland turned on him with the furious ridicule which he had expected and which he enjoyed.

"Great Scott!" he spluttered. "The one excuse for these palaces, is you call them, is that they were not built for some stuffy old duke but for people with brains."

"An aristocracy doesn't need brains," said Paul.

"That is why it never has them," retorted Roland.

"It has something better. It has taste. It is the filter of taste. If you have brains you can only be really well-informed on one subject. If you have taste you intuitively select what is best from every kind of creative effort."

"You mean you skim off everyone else's cream."

"Willy Greene-James doesn't filter much except whisky," said Lucinda.

"You skim off a fair amount of cream yourself," said Paul to Roland.

"I shan't when I'm older."

"No, I suppose you'll put dynamite in the cow," said Paul. "Still," he went on, "you'll return to reason later. Every young man is a socialist at your age. I was myself."

"Oh, Paul," protested Lucinda, "you were a most violent reactionary. You didn't go Left till after the war, and then it only lasted two years."

"That is because all the finer types develop slowly. I was in a sense the same age as Roland—as a cat of seven is the same age as a man of thirty."

"You're always saying you're a leaf on a tree—now you're a cat," said Roland.

"It is you who are a cat, my boy, or rather a puppy."

"And you're always on the side of the over-dog," said Roland.

"Only when it shows greater intelligence."

"Anyhow, I'd rather be a live puppy than a museum piece."

"You have your wish," said Paul. "A museum piece nowadays is anyone who has retained his taste and his principles. Even so, I'm not dead yet. I belong to a social organism that has some relation to natural life and order. As you have pointed out I am a leaf, I might almost say a flower, on that tree, but there's not much sap left in the trunk and I'm beginning to turn yellow. I refuse scientific injections to keep myself alive, nor shall I be transplanted as a cutting into the sordid clay of business."

"You're a funny old flower," Roland interjected.

Lucinda laughed.

"I am unable to practice hypocrisy," said Paul, "and so am the victim of many slanders."

"You refuse to move with the times," said Roland. "There's no room for useless things in the future."

"Then God help the future," exclaimed Paul. "Only the useless things have permanent value. What are the useful things? Trams, drains and motor buses. In a few years they are all out of date and forgotten rubbish. What are the useless things? Poems, paintings and buildings like this college and the chapel which you will see, if, first apologizing to Lucinda for leaving the table, you walk over to that window. These things we cherish and preserve against the teeth of time. You dislike them because they are creations of the spirit, and you are trying to kill your spirit in a test-tube. You know secretly that the spirit is stronger than matter, but you have yielded your spirit to matter and you hate these buildings because they remind you of your defeat; because here spirit has controlled matter, forcing hard stone and glass and lead to shape themselves into sublime and eloquent forms. Pure intellect may control matter, but without spirit it cannot shape a building like that chapel. The cleverest architect in the world without a God could not have built it. And in twenty years' time your concrete and chromium-plate abortions will appear as laughable as the *art nouveau* of the 1900's. Remember that, the hungry generations tread even you down."

"Paul, dear, aren't you too devastating?" said Lucinda. "Never mind, Roland, I think that young men who are conservatives are simply horrible. They smell of camphor."

"I don't mind," said Roland, "I revel in being recent."

"You may," declared Paul, "but in spite of yourself you are eternal. You are a leaf on the tree yourself, and thank God a green one. For where does your sympathy for the injustices of the poor come from except from the Christian religion, and your indignant championship of their wrongs except from the chivalry of your ancestors, and where is the archetype of your generous and loyal affections except in the golden annals of Greece?"

"I don't . . . I don't," stammered Roland, and then exclaimed, "Oh, shut up!" and drained his wine-glass. Everybody laughed.

When at the end Stephen brought out the brandy, Lucinda said: "Darling, I hope you're not taking to drink."

"No fear, Mrs Brayford," said Roland. "He's always trying to make me drink milk. This orgy is in your honor, and for Paul, who naturally would want to be as drunk as a lord."

Paul allowed, and seemed even to invite from young men these impertinences, which he would not for a moment have tolerated from people of his own age. He thought that Lucinda would like to be left with Stephen for a while, so he asked Roland if he had the leisure to take him round the colleges.

"I'd like to see them," he said, "before you blow 'em up."

Their animated voices faded down the stairs, and then floated up again through the open windows from the bridge, where Roland was laying Paul a bet on the number of stone balls on the balustrade.

"Darling, you're not being very extravagant, are you?" asked Lucinda. "This must have been a very expensive lunch—the sherry and the brandy."

"The tulips only cost one and sixpence," said Stephen, "and I had to give Paul a bit of a do."

"He's enjoying himself, poor dear, but we have to be careful. Granny really shouldn't have sent you that five pounds. She has to get her meals at Lyons."

"Oh, Mum, take it back to her," exclaimed Stephen, fishing the notes, rather crumpled, out of his pocket.

"No. She'd be dreadfully offended." Stephen was so upset that Lucinda thought she had better explain what had happened. Susannah had let her maisonette and had been staying with some ducal cousins in Upper Brook Street. They had gone away, allowing her to stay on in their mansion, but without meals, as they had taken their chef with them; so Susannah went out and bought ready-cooked food at the Marble Arch Maison Lyons, which she took back and ate privately in her gilded bed.

Stephen took Lucinda down into the Fellows' garden. He led her diagonally across the lawn, and then turning, said, "I think this is the most beautiful place in Cambridge. I come here when I feel particularly happy."

The west front of Clare was partly hidden by the great copper beech, of which the leaves were still only a smoky pinkish color. In the foreground was some darker evergreen foliage and a kind of golden cypress. The sky was a vivid blue, and against it, dominating everything in view, rose the turrets of King's. Stephen had noticed before how the chapel seemed to change its quality, almost its mood, with the weather and in different lights. Today the turrets were at their most light and serene, their most aerial.

"It is lovely," said Lucinda. "It's hardly like an English scene, there's so much variety and richness of color. It's that sky and the copper beech, I suppose. Those turrets are superb. They're like singing stone."

Stephen was delighted that she was so appreciative.

"And are you often particularly happy, darling?" she asked.

"Yes, I am, very often," said Stephen. "Sometimes I'm so happy I can hardly bear it."

"You're not in love, are you?"

"No."

"It's odd being so happy when you're not in love. But perhaps being in love only makes people moody and irritable." She laughed.

"No. I don't think that at all," objected Stephen. "The funny thing is that sometimes I feel as if I were in love, but it has no focus. I almost feel as if I were in love with that tree and those turrets."

"Isn't that rather Freudian, darling?" asked Lucinda.

When Lucinda fell into this kind of banter it froze Stephen's confidence. She was disappointed and annoyed with herself, but she thought, "He really is too sensitive."

"Well, I expect that you'll soon find a focus," she said, "and I hope she'll be a nice one."

They strolled round through Trinity and back to Stephen's rooms for tea. Paul and Roland had not returned. It was after four o'clock and Stephen began to lay out the tea things.

"Won't you wait for Paul?" asked Lucinda.

"I may as well have everything ready," said Stephen. He sat in one of the south windows, where he could see the clock over the King's porter's lodge. At half-past four he made the tea. He was so anxious not to miss the service, and was afraid that some of his duties as host would oblige him to, that he had not yet mentioned it to Lucinda; but when she expressed surprise at his making the tea before Paul's return, he said, "I thought you might like to go to evensong in King's Chapel. It's the best choir in England."

"That would be nice," said Lucinda, "but what about Paul and Roland?"

"I'll leave a note for Roland to give him tea."

Stephen was now anxious that they should not return before he went out with Lucinda, especially as he had not yet let Roland know that he attended the chapel. They did not come, and he gave almost a sigh of relief as he led Lucinda into the chapel at ten minutes to five. Stephen did not mind sitting with Hayman, but otherwise he preferred to be alone. The verger gave Lucinda a stall, but when Stephen did not follow her she turned and said, "Where are you going?"

"Undergraduates mayn't sit up there," Stephen explained.

"Shan't I sit with you?"

"No. That is more comfortable." He went to his usual place.

Sometimes the services at King's were inspired with a kind of divine hilarity. All the music was loud and joyful. Today was one of those days. The anthem was Handel's "Let the bright seraphim in burning row, their loud uplifted angel trumpets blow." Brian seemed to be caught up in this glorious noise, every taut muscle of his body, like the "golden wires" of which he sang, to quiver and respond to it.

316

Stephen experienced that intense happiness of which he had spoken earlier in the day to Lucinda. He was filled with that impersonal love, stimulated by Brian, but not focused on him. It was not a yearning love, but lively and complete in itself.

At the end of the anthem Brian turned to him with an open, rather breathless smile, as much as to say, "What d'you think of that?"

Lucinda saw this, and its frankness puzzled her slightly, but it did not occur to her that they could in any way be acquainted. When they left the chapel and turned the corner towards Clare, Stephen asked:

"Did you like it, Mum?"

"Well, darling," said Lucinda, "*C'est magnifique, mais ce n'est pas la prière.*"

"Oh, Mum," said Stephen, "must you be funny about everything?"

Lucinda was surprised.

"I thought you liked me to be funny," she said plaintively.

"I'm sorry, Mum, I do, but not about—well, things like that."

"But surely, darling, all those cathedral kind of services are admittedly only musical performances. Not that I'm qualified to judge, of course."

"I don't think so at all."

"Perhaps it's because I'm lifeless myself. *Partir, c'est mourir un peu*, and I have parted from so many things."

"I'm sorry, Mum. It was horrid of me to say that. I love your being funny, really." He put his hand on her arm.

In Stephen's rooms Paul and Roland were tucking in to the Crittenden plum cake. They were still in high good humor. Roland had taken Paul to see his rooms in Jesus, which had a fine beamed ceiling and were haunted by the ghosts of eight Regency rake-hells. They all went in a taxi to the station, where Paul surreptitiously gave Stephen his ten-pound note, and Stephen and Roland then returned to dine in their respective halls.

After hall Stephen took a book and went to sit and read on the river bank in King's, but when there he put down his book and watched, though only half seeing them, a duck followed by a brood of fluffy ducklings, darting about the surface of the stream, or the ponies as they grazed on the other side. The events of the day were still too vivid for him to concentrate on reading. Bits of the conversation at lunch, the wonderful exhilaration of the chapel singing and Lucinda's criticism returned to him. He tried to resolve all these things into a harmony. Just before it was dusk and he had to leave the precincts of King's, some verses slowly formed in his mind. He took out a pencil and wrote them down inside the cover of his book, a copy of the poems of Thomas Traherne, which he had bought on Hayman's recommendation.

A few days after this it was raining when Stephen and Hayman came out of King's. Instead of going for a walk they went up to Stephen's rooms, where they found Roland, scribbling a note.

"Oh, there you are," he said, as Stephen came in. "Where the devil d'you get to these days?" He nodded coolly to Hayman.

"I've been to King's Chapel."

"What on earth d'you go there for?"

"The music's very good," said Stephen defensively.

"Have you been before?" asked Roland suspiciously.

"He goes every day," said Hayman curtly. He was irritated by Roland's manner.

"Will you please not talk about it?" said Stephen.

"I jolly well will talk about it." Roland proceeded to do so with extreme volubility, and a good deal of witty but obscene allusion.

"Will you please not talk about it?" Stephen repeated.

Roland was much too engrossed to notice or care about the effect he was having on Stephen, who was deathly pale and seemed to speak with difficulty.

"If you do not stop," Stephen said, "I shall throw this bowl of goldfish over you."

Roland did not stop, and Stephen picked up the bowl and launched its contents in Roland's face. Roland spluttered out a mouthful of dirty water, and wiped his dark and dripping hair from his eyes. He was so astonished that for a moment he forgot to be angry. There were dark wet patches on his tweed jacket and his flannel trousers. Then he gave Stephen one furious glance and walked out of the room. The fish lay in a pool of water on the carpet, gasping and flapping their long silky fins, like fainting ladies in ball dresses.

Stephen picked them up and put them back into the bowl, and took it into his gyp room where he refilled it. He left the pool of water on the carpet.

"I have a headache," said Stephen, putting his hand to his forehead. "I don't think that I can talk any more." He crossed to his bedroom door, and taking no further notice of Hayman he went in and lay down on the bed.

Hayman looked in and said, "Is there anything I can get for you?"

"No, thank you. I'll be all right. I'm sorry."

"Cheer up," said Hayman, with a thin but kindly smile, and closing the door quietly he went away.

The trance-like inertia and the pain in his head, which had come upon Stephen, were the symptoms which had accompanied the illness which attacked him in his fourteenth year. While he lay in this condition processes, independent of his will, worked in his mind. He hated Roland, who had been his closest friend for fourteen years, and this hatred rose from that tranquil, unfocused love which had recently brought a new illumination to his life, and it destroyed the thing from which it arose. He felt as if his hatred and his love had formed a cross on which he was stretched, and he had to reconcile the two things in his own body.

He lay motionless while the processes revolved in his mind. He would remember Roland in some affectionate or amusing mood, and with a stab of pain would put the image from him. Then his mind dwelt on moments in the chapel, and on that afternoon when he had heard the babel of voices descending the turret, and had come upon Brian standing in the sunlight. The longer he contemplated these images the more impossible his hatred became, because he knew that if he allowed it to continue they would no longer have any meaning for him. Contemplating them, his love strengthened and fused with his hatred so that it too became love, and he was released from the cross which the two things had made for him.

This happened in the small hours of the morning. His headache had left him. He rose stiffly from his bed and went to the next room to find something to drink. He undressed and immediately fell asleep.

The next morning Roland was in his room before he was properly awake. He behaved as if nothing had happened, but his good spirits had an underlying note of anxiety. Stephen tried to say he was sorry about the goldfish.

"Oh, I don't mind what you do," said Roland. "It's that fellow Hayman I can't stand. He's like an iced drink of sulphuric acid. Come on, get up. It's a marvelous day."

The next week was May Week, and Stephen's time was occupied with various entertainments. On Friday afternoon he went to King's for his last evensong for the term. He was going down next morning for the long vacation. There were very few people in the chapel, and this was one of the days when the service achieved a peculiar intimate serenity. The moment the choir appeared under the screen Stephen felt this influence. For him there was a living spirit in the chapel. He hardly thought of it in conventional religious terms but more as a *genius loci*. Brian, with wide and serious eyes, glanced at him as he took his place, and Stephen felt that he too was sensitive to the mood of the day. The silence broke into the silvery pattern of a Vittorio antiphon. To Stephen it seemed that this heavenly sound passed through him, and gathering every good thing in his mind and nature bore it up to the perfect witness of all-judging Jove.

He would have liked to have seen Brian after the service to say good-bye, but as this could only have been brief and formal he did not attempt it. He went back to his rooms and sat in one of the windows. Soon he saw the small top-hatted procession, a little hurried and straggling, as it was beginning to rain, walk past Gibb's building down over the bridge, and disappear along the avenue. He tried to pick out Brian, but he could not see at that distance which he was.

He never saw him again in certain recognition, except once, and then the circumstances were such that they could only exchange a few words.

CHAPTER TWO

LUCINDA, although she impressed on Stephen the need for economy, also wanted him to enjoy with reasonable sophistication the pleasures of his class. She felt guilty towards him, as apart from their annual visit to St Saturnin she had put herself out very little on his behalf. She was afraid that she might now be about to reap the reward of this neglect, in having a son who was too simple for his environment. He did not even make the right kinds of friends. In fact, apart from Roland, who was a dear, but hardly a civilizing influence, he appeared to have no close friends at all.

Lucinda also had a sense of guilt towards Fred and Julie, as she had never been out to see them, making from time to time various excuses to put off the trip, until at last she had formed an inhibition about going to Australia, which she found it impossible to break. She had dreams in which she returned to Melbourne and discovered with horror that she had been there two or three months and had not yet been to see her parents. When she set out for Tourella she would be unable to find her way there, or else, having arrived at the house, distorted and unfamiliar in her dream, she would be unable to gain admittance.

With Arthur and Marian, too, she felt that she had been ungrateful. They were so extraordinarily kind and so pleased whenever she appeared at Crittenden for a few days, where she might stay as long as she liked. They had made it more of a home for Stephen than Catherine Street. He kept most of his things there, and it was Marian who, perhaps not unintentionally, had undertaken the supervision of his clothes and his needs at Cambridge, and so relieved Lucinda of much of her maternal responsibility.

When she did go to Crittenden she was always surprised to find that it was still the same, and Marian and Arthur said things which assumed that their way of living was normal and permanent. They spoke as if the only natural life was in a shabby palace, with a number of old and devoted servants and villagers, whose interests were as important to one as if they were blood relations. If Lucinda expressed the tolerances and fears which were a commonplace of London conversation, they imagined that these views were due to her own whimsical originality, or Arthur would say:

"You've been listening to some of these mischievous writer chaps."

To ease her sense of guilt Lucinda took Stephen to a play, where he laughed till the tears streamed down his face, and afterwards to supper at the Savoy, where he watched some exhibition dancers with a look almost of dismay, as he thought their contortions made the girls look so ugly.

When they arrived back at Catherine Street he said:

"It's been fairly marvelous, Mum. Thanks awfully. But I'm afraid you've spent an awful lot—more than I spent on your lunch at Cambridge."

"Darling, I'm glad you enjoyed yourself," said Lucinda; "but don't be too grateful. You're not twelve any longer."

"You don't want me to pretend to be bored, do you?"

"No, but you're so non-alcoholic."

"I drank half a bottle of champagne."

Lucinda laughed. "I don't mean that. You're sweet, really. I'm only afraid some harpy will stick her claws into you."

"You needn't worry. I can't bear those over-sophisticated types."

"Can you recognize them when you see them?" said Lucinda.

Usually Lucinda stayed in London till the middle of July, when she went to Crittenden for a fortnight, and then to St Saturnin for six weeks, where she took the same villa every year. However, now that Stephen was at Cambridge and came down for the Long Vac in June, she went earlier to Crittenden. They were waiting now to see Bill and Muriel, who with their daughter Heather were due in London in a few days. Muriel had brought Heather over to have her "finished" in Paris, and then presented at court. She had hoped that Lucinda or one of the Brayfords would do this for her, but Lucinda had not been presented on her marriage and could not, and she did not care to ask Susannah or Marian, who had put themselves out sufficiently for her Australian relatives. Muriel was obliged to fall back on Australia House and the last of the courts. She had gone out to Australia as a simple suburban young woman, but returned as a *grande dame*. Dining frequently at Government House she had rather oddly acquired her knowledge of English "high life" in Melbourne. When she arrived in London she knew the good shops, the right addresses, and social usages of which she had been ignorant when she left.

On the day after he had gone to the Savoy with Lucinda, Stephen went off alone to the cinema to see a film about Schubert. The plot centered round his romance with the young Countess Esterhazy. The actress who took this part was a delightful fresh-faced girl. The whole film had a spring-like quality. It was full of woodlands, of sunlit trees in blossom and of summer cornfields, also of charming songs.

Stephen returned to Catherine Street and sang in his bath. He came down, bright-eyed and smiling.

"Darling, you look *éblouissant*," said Lucinda. "If Granny brings one of her interior decorators, I'm sure he'll want to acquire you as an ornament." They were dining with Susannah who, through eating ready-cooked food in her bedroom, had saved up enough to take them to Claridges. But the other guest was one of "the elders," a general with whom Susannah had danced in Dublin in the 'eighties. They were both very attentive to Stephen, as if the party was in his honor. Lucinda remembered, with a twinge of envy, how older people used to treat her with this smiling deference, and she supposed that she too must have had that limpid look of youth which was now so evident in Stephen.

The general asked him which regiment he was joining. Stephen looked surprised, laughed inquiringly at Lucinda and said he was not joining any.

The next morning he went off to buy a flute, and after lunch he sat in the drawing-room making erratic noises which dimly resembled Schubert's songs and the religious melodies of the seventeenth century.

After tea they walked along to Victoria to meet the Vanes. Stephen knew Bill and Muriel who had paid three or four visits to England since their marriage, but he had not hitherto seen his cousin Heather, who stepped shyly from the boat train. She was behind Muriel, who looked as if she expected at least a prime minister to meet her, and though Stephen noticed her at once, he did not immediately realize that she belonged to the party. When Bill pulled her forward and said, "Here, I've brought you a cousin," he felt an intense pleasure. She was exactly like the girl who had been Countess Esterhazy in the film. Today was Heather's eighteenth birthday.

Bill grinned amiably at everybody. He had a pleasant expression but his face was marked by lines of dissipation. The Vanes traveled with a maid, a chauffeur and a valet. Lucinda had never seen so much fuss as Muriel made over their departure from the station. Bill winked at Stephen and shrugged his shoulders.

Lucinda and Stephen spent the next week more or less in the company of the Vanes. The older people talked together and Stephen and Heather were thrown into each other's company. Lucinda wanted to hear as much as possible about the family. Since Julie had died Muriel ran Tourella, though it was still Fred's home. Fred was remarkably strong and fit for his age, but his memory was not clear. Hart, his chauffeur, was now sixty, and became very tired after the long motor tours which Fred made between his stations. Fred slept most of the time and would come in from a three-hundred-mile run quite fresh and complaining of the exhausted Hart, "That young feller's getting slack." Muriel's chief worry was that he would not let her move the two huge cloisonné vases from the hall at Tourella.

Both Muriel and Lucinda imagined that as Stephen and Heather were first cousins, no complications would arise from their being left so much together, and that his attitude towards her would be purely fraternal.

Stephen had often wished that he had brothers and sisters. Roland had to some extent taken the place of a brother, but Stephen had almost no experience of girls. He could not make Roland's impudent approaches to complete strangers, and the only girls he had known at all well were Willy Greene-James's daughters, who, as Paul said, were like hilarious draft horses. He was thrilled at having a girl confided to his care. Her physical texture, the fineness of her skin and the way her hair grew behind her ears filled him with a delighted wonder.

Heather, on her way to Europe, had been more excited at the prospect of seeing Stephen than any historic buildings or the shops of the Rue de la Paix. Lucinda had always been regarded by the Vanes as a unique member of the family. Stephen, as her son, had inherited some of this regard, but it was enhanced by the fact that he would also inherit a peerage. Whenever his name was mentioned at Tourella his Australian cousins at once looked interested and rather proud. Heather had thought it improbable that such a grand young man would notice her. When she found that he did, with obvious admiration and with the most charming simple friendliness, she was elated beyond measure. Her letter to her younger sister, describing her arrival in London, was merely a description of Stephen.

One afternoon Bill and Muriel were going to an Australian reception. Muriel was very particular that Heather should not appear at any social function before she was "out," so Lucinda and Stephen took her to Hampton Court for the afternoon. Lucinda went to call on an old Lady Daubeney in the palace, but Stephen and Heather said that they would rather take a boat on the river. They arranged to meet her on the railway station at six o'clock, but they did not turn up till nearly half-past. They were too happy to make adequate apologies. Their eyes were full of the summer afternoon, and she remembered dimly Bill and Anne coming into Mrs Maitland's drawing-room at Oxford, after they had been on the river. If she had known it, Heather even more closely resembled herself, when she had driven back with Tony from Cape Furze, twenty-five years ago.

They had a first-class carriage to themselves. Lucinda would have traveled third, but she thought Muriel would be shocked. She had some misgivings as she sat opposite Stephen and his cousin. She knew, of course, that it was not unusual for Stephen to have that illuminated expression. It could be evoked by a young beech tree or a Schubert song, or an effect of light on King's Chapel. But Heather too was starry-eyed. Lucinda disliked people who interfered and fussed about the attractions of their children. It was only natural that they should find each other amusing and stimulating. It was the proper experience of their age and almost certain to be transitory. When they arrived at Waterloo she put it out of her head.

They were dining with the Vanes and going to a play. When Lucinda and Stephen were shown into Muriel's sitting-room in the Hyde Park Hotel, Stephen's eyes at once caught Heather's, and as soon as he had greeted his aunt and uncle he moved over to her. Muriel gave them a speculative glance and they went down to dinner.

Stephen and Heather sat together in the theatre. They shared a program and when they bent to look at it her hair brushed his temples. Several times, during the evening their hands and their shoulders touched. When they were leaving the theatre, Stephen said to Lucinda:

"Couldn't we go and dance somewhere?"

"It's Aunt Muriel's party," said Lucinda doubtfully.

"Yes, Mummy, do let us go and dance," said Heather.

"You mustn't go to dances till you're out," said Muriel.

"No one will know who we are," said Stephen. Muriel looked shocked. The idea that no one would know Mrs William Vane of Tourella, Noorilla, Wombidgee, Mathieson, Churt and Cape Furze was a novel and displeasing one to her. In Melbourne it would have been unthinkable. Bill said, "Come along," and took them to the *Hungaria*.

Lucinda was pleased that Stephen wanted to go and dance. She sat with Bill and Muriel, watching him dance with Heather while she drank Tokay and listened to Muriel's plans for her Cup Week parties when she returned to Melbourne in November.

She and Stephen were both silent in the taxi returning to Catherine Street, Stephen because of his condition of dazed delight, Lucinda because she wondered whether she ought to warn him about Heather. She was afraid that by speaking she might bring the whole thing surging up into his conscious mind, whereas if she said nothing it might gradually fade out when they parted. Tomorrow they were going down to Crittenden. The Vanes were coming down for a week after Heather's presentation, and after that Stephen and Heather might not meet again for years. It would of course be an impossible union. To begin with they were first cousins, though not as closely related as was generally believed. None of the Brayfords would be pleased. Paul would be disgusted, as he evidently expected Stephen to marry into the higher aristocracy, to recover the slight loss of prestige which the family had suffered from the middle-class alliances of Arthur and Hugo. Though Paul, of course, where his affections were concerned, would throw all his genealogical snobberies overboard. How complicated it all was, thought Lucinda, as she paid the taxi-driver, while Stephen opened the front door at Catherine Street.

"Stephen, you ought to pay the taxi," she said, when they came into the lighted hall.

"Oh, I'm sorry, mum. How much was it?" He took some half-crowns from his pocket.

"I don't mean because of the money, darling," she said, laughing but irritated. "It's only that I want you to behave like a man."

"I would with anyone else, but I'm so used to your doing it."

"With Heather, I suppose?" The words slipped out before she had time to think what she was saying.

"Yes." His face was suddenly suffused with a happy light. Lucinda could not help kissing him, but she went up to bed a little worried.

The next morning he played his flute in the bath, a new and

tiresome habit, and he came down full of health and high spirits to breakfast.

"Would it be all right, mum, if I stayed in London a few days longer?" he asked.

"I can't leave you alone in the house with the maids," said Lucinda. She had two young maids, one of them very pretty.

"I don't see why not," said Stephen.

Lucinda looked at him in a puzzled fashion. She was often at a loss with the new generation. She did not know why Stephen thought he should be left alone with the maids, whether because it was natural that he should be allowed to seduce them, or whether he was so high-minded that the idea would not occur to him. She thought the latter, which in a way made him more difficult to deal with. Life was awkward when the conventions were not followed. One had to apply spontaneous good taste and judgement to every situation, which was very wearing.

"Marian and Arthur will be very disappointed if you don't come today," she said.

"Yes, I suppose they will be," he agreed soberly.

She was thankful that he did not seem unduly depressed at accompanying her. At dinner at Crittenden he was lively and amusing, in the way he could only be in the company of people who knew him intimately, and who he was sure were fond of him. Arthur opened a bottle of champagne, as always on the night of their arrival. The only exception that Marian and he allowed to the rule of rigid economy which they practiced was in the entertainment of their friends. Otherwise they spent almost nothing on themselves, if this exception could be called self-indulgence. The people they entertained were not those they met in society, but old friends like the Bassingbournes and the Frasers. In fact they had few merely social acquaintances as their only excursion away from Crittenden was an annual fortnight at Brown's Hotel in May. They allotted part of their income to charity that their donations might be adequate to their position, and the rest was spent on the upkeep of the estate. The Daimler, built high with wire wheels, which had met Lucinda and Stephen that afternoon, was the same that had met her nearly fifteen years ago after her reunion with Pat. It was as gleaming and glossy as ever. Paul sometimes said that Marian was a country skinflint and that she ought to let Arthur enjoy himself occasionally. He did not know that it was Arthur who insisted on this economy, nor until some years later the reason for it.

A characteristic of Stephen's which worried Lucinda, and Marian even more, was that he seemed to be happy doing nothing. At

Crittenden, until the Vanes arrived, his only noticeable activity was, on being pestered by Marian, to go over to the Greene-Jameses for tennis. Otherwise he played the organ in the chapel in the mornings, and his flute anywhere about the house and gardens in the afternoon. Marian was contemptuous of this instrument and said, "If you must be a musician why don't you get a bassoon?"

The day before the Vanes arrived Lucinda watched Stephen to see if he were looking dreamy or excited, but she noticed little change in him. She hated her prying attitude, but after all it was for his welfare. She thought with wry amusement what a time Julie must have had with herself and Tony. It gave her a slight shock, and made her feel her years, to realize that her rôle had changed.

The Vanes arrived at tea-time in a large new Bentley. Their luggage and their domestics were sent by train. They had tea in the saloon. Muriel sat in the most throne-like chair to hand, and looked as if she were having her portrait painted by Lavery, while she talked to Marian about Buckingham Palace.

"I haven't been to a court for years," said Marian. "The last time I went a woman's dress fell off just in front of me, and the King sent an equerry to tell some minister's wife not to talk so loudly."

Muriel looked grieved and changed the subject.

"I think it so nice Stephen's being at Clare," she said. "Two of his great-grandfathers were there. They were great friends, and when Canon Chapman had to go to Australia for his asthma Mr Vane went with him."

"Oh, I didn't know that," said Lucinda. "I had a vague idea that they didn't get on very well."

"If that were so they would hardly have gone to Australia together."

"No, I suppose not," said Lucinda indifferently. She was sitting where she could see both Stephen and Heather, and felt herself slightly contemptible in doing so. Heather was shy and did not say much. Stephen was gentle and pleased in his manner, but then he was often like that. They looked at each other as two people do who are very well acquainted, but it might have been the look of a brother and sister, or simply of any two young people in the company of their elders. After tea Stephen said:

"Aunt Marian, may I show Heather over the house?"

"Of course," said Marian. "You may as well begin in here."

"This is the saloon," said Stephen.

Heather looked surprise and asked if there were a cocktail bar. Everyone laughed and Arthur said, "I wish there were."

"That's the second viscount over the mantelpiece," said Stephen.

327

"It's painted by Lely. He was a bit of a rip, wasn't he, Uncle Arthur?"

"Not half such a rip as the twelfth," said Arthur, chuckling. It amused him to talk like this to pretty young girls.

"This table," said Stephen, "belonged to Monsieur, the brother of Louis Quatorze. Uncle Paul thinks it's the finest thing in Crittenden."

"Oh yes. We met him at Marseilles. He came to the boat to see daddy."

Paul had befriended Bill when he was a young subaltern in London, and on the few occasions when the latter came to England he would go into Marseilles to meet him. Muriel was very pleased at this friendship, and a few days later at a tennis party she said in a loud clear voice to Willy Greene-James, "Of course Paul Brayford is devoted to my husband." Willy Greene-James raised his eyebrows and nearly whistled.

Stephen led Heather out of the saloon. In the hall he took her hand and they strolled through the lofty rooms, looking more at each other than at the pictures and the Grinling Gibbons mantelpieces. At last they came to the Peacock room. The sunlight was streaming in the south-west windows, giving a golden tinge to the soft gray-greens of the walls.

"My grandfather painted this room," said Stephen.

"He painted it!" exclaimed Heather. "What, himself?" She seemed shocked.

"Don't you like it?"

"Oh yes. It's very pretty."

"How would you like to live here?"

She looked at him in shy curiosity and did not reply.

"I'd like you to live here," he said. He held both her hands and looked into her eyes. Their eyes drew them together and he kissed her on the cheek. They were both so overcome by this that they sat on the sofa. They were startled by voices from the terrace below. They heard Muriel, who talked almost exclusively of her own affairs, say, "I am having a terrace overlooking the sea built at my house at Cape Furze."

Stephen pulled Heather to her feet.

"We haven't seen all the house yet," he said.

He took her along to the chapel. Heather looked at it with misgiving.

"Is it Roman Catholic?" she asked.

"No. My grandfather's first wife was Roman Catholic. It was done up for her, but Aunt Marian made it Church of England again. Would you like me to play the organ?"

328

"Oh yes! Can you play?"

"Yes. You'll have to blow for me. I generally get the gardener's boy."

Heather did not exactly expect dance music, but she thought he would play something cheerful. She was not merely indifferent to, but she actively disliked the remote plainsong melodies with which he filled the chapel. At first the chapel had just seemed like an odd museum to her, but this music gave it a ghostly life, a secret life of its own. The crucifix, the empty yet forbidding face of the Virgin, the tall pale candles acquired a sinister meaning, and revived in her mind dim stories of girls ill-treated in convents. She had an urgent longing to leave the place, and she felt her job of organ-blower, usually performed by the gardener's boy, to be humiliating.

When at last Stephen stopped playing and they left the chapel, he smiled at her, but he seemed to have gone away from her, to have been carried by the music into some remote and, to her, deathly region. Lucinda was a little anxious that they were away together for so long, but when they joined the others on the terrace the different expressions on their faces reassured her.

In the park at Crittenden, in the opposite direction to the End House which was now let to a Major Boothby, was a small lake. It was inclined to be muddy and cluttered with reeds and water lilies. Stephen bathed there in the hot weather.

The next morning at breakfast he asked Heather if she would come and bathe with him.

"You can't take a girl to bathe in that disgusting pond," said Marian.

"I want to go," said Heather.

"Heather, you must do what Lady Crittenden says," said Muriel primly.

"If she likes to flounder in the mud, I don't mind," observed Marian, who did not care for Muriel's support.

Stephen and Heather were at the lake all the morning, from ten o'clock till lunch-time. Stephen bathed two or three times but Heather only once as she did not think much of the lake. He showed off tricks in the water for her. It was one of those days when there are large white clouds which stay on the horizon, while overhead there is an unbroken expanse of blue. Stephen lay on his back and kicked hard, sending fountains of white spray into the air for the pleasure of seeing it against the sky.

"Look, isn't it lovely?" he shouted.

When she bathed he led her about the lake, through channels between the banks of reeds and the floating carpets of lilies. There was no sound except the splashing of water as they swam, and the whirring of a horse-drawn machine with which a boy was turning hay in a near-by meadow. The smell of hay mingled with the smell of the water and its weeds. Clumps of basket willow made patches of cool shadow at the edge of the lake, and at one end there was a thicket of brambles and briar, flecked with pale roses.

"I'm a pilot," he said. "You must follow me closely or you'll get tangled in the weeds and drowned like Ophelia. You must always follow me closely." He turned and grinned at her. He offered to pick her some water-lilies. They were rather far in on the carpet of flat leaves, and he said:

"It's very reckless of me to do this, because I'm the last Brayford, and it's most important for me to marry and have masses of children, like August the Strong of Saxony." He again gave her that impudent grin. She looked away without smiling. He grappled with the water-lilies in silence.

"I say, I haven't offended you, have I?" he asked anxiously as he swam back to her, trailing three of the yellow flowers by their long slimy stalks.

"Of course not." He puzzled her. She was prepared to admire him and everything about him. She was beginning to think him a bit mad, but pleasantly so. She thought this madness part of his distinction and inseparable from the aristocracy. It put him a little beyond her and increased her admiration. The only time this feeling that he was beyond her brought discomfort was when he played the organ in the chapel.

He had brought his flute down to the lake. When he came out of the water he sat on the grassy bank and played Elizabethan madrigals and Schubert's songs. His hair was wet, and the flat locks stuck against his temples. He wore only the briefest slip, and the slowly trickling water glistened on his body. He played the melody of the song:

"Once a boy a wild rose spied
In the heather lying . . ."

Stephen, sitting wet and naked in the sunlight, playing his flute by the reedy bank, awoke some dim recognition in Heather. She was contemptuous of anything she thought "high-brow," but this moment stirred in her a longing wonder. She felt about Stephen, though she could hardly have made this feeling articulate, that he was real, that he did nothing for effect but only what he naturally enjoyed. She looked at him almost with worship.

When he had finished his song Stephen turned to her. At the

look in his eyes her heart turned over. He flung down his flute and took her hands.

Returning to the house they entered the garden by an old wrought-iron gate, set in an arch in the wall. Nearby some of the plant known as heliotrope or cherry pie had been bedded out. Stephen picked some of the sweet-smelling bloom and gave it to her. Then he picked a bud from a climbing rose on the wall, and stuck that too in her dress with the cherry pie.

"Rosebud in the heather," he said.

Lucinda was dismayed when she saw them come in to luncheon. Marian appeared to notice nothing, but she thought that Muriel gave them a brief scrutiny which was not without a trace of satisfaction.

The dean of the cathedral had come to see Marian on some business, and had stayed to luncheon. He had that geniality of manner which well-bred clergymen display in the houses of the nobility. He shook hands with Stephen and Heather with charming deference, as if he sensed in them some singular quality, a flowering innocence. Marian rebuked Stephen for coming to the table in a blue open-necked shirt, which certainly made an odd contrast with the attire of the spruce, starched footman who poured out his lager beer.

In the afternoon, as a result of the dean's conversation, they all went into the country town to look at the cathedral. Lucinda pretended to misunderstand a rather incoherent verger to say that Queen Elizabeth had slept in the cloisters.

"Aunt Lucinda's awfully amusing," said Heather to Stephen as they dawdled behind the others.

"Yes, she is. Poor Mum!" said Stephen.

"Why poor? We think a tremendous lot of her at home. Grand-papa's very proud of her."

"Mum's marvelous, of course," Stephen agreed warmly, "seeing what she has had to put up with. She's had a terrible life."

"Terrible? But she's in the thick of everything, isn't she? She knows all the celebrities."

"No fear. She has a friend who writes plays. Once he had one acted. I think he's not very nice to her. And she knows a few painters. We met them at St Saturnin. She has never been happy, I should think, and now she tries to make up for it by knowing clever people. But she doesn't know the real ones. I know a lot more about Mum than she thinks I do. Uncle Paul told me. He shouldn't have really, I suppose, but he did it so that I would make allowances for her."

They had tea at the deanery. Muriel talked a great deal about, "When my husband's cousin lived here." The dean with a twinkle in his eye said, "I expect you young people would like to see what you can find on my raspberry canes, but don't let the gardener catch you."

"I'm sure they've eaten enough," said Lucinda weakly, but no one took any notice of her, and Stephen and Heather went out into the garden.

In the evening, when Lucinda had gone up to her room and was just beginning to undress, there was a knock at the door and Stephen came in.

"Mum, I'm going to marry Heather," he said.

"Oh, my God!" exclaimed Lucinda.

"What d'you mean by that?" he asked.

"Well, darling, I mean about a dozen things. One, that she's your first cousin. Two, that you hardly know her. Three, that you're still an undergraduate. Four, that you haven't the money to marry on. I could go on indefinitely."

"Aren't you glad then?"

"Did you really expect me to be glad?" Lucinda laughed.

"You always say you want me to be happy."

"You've hardly known her a month. When did you come to this arrangement—among the dean's raspberries?"

"I haven't told her yet."

"Thank Heaven!" said Lucinda.

"But I'm sure she knows. It's only that we haven't put it into words. There are some people who, you know instinctively, as soon as you see them, are meant to be your friends. You don't always have a chance to get to know them. If you did there'd be far more good friendships. I felt it with Heather as soon as I saw her at Victoria. Every day the feeling has grown stronger."

Lucinda sat down on the stool at her dressing table, and indicated an armchair to Stephen.

"Sit down," she said patiently, "and listen to me, darling. You can't marry your first cousin."

"It's not forbidden."

"No; but it's hardly ever done nowadays."

"Paul says it's impossible to marry anyone who isn't a cousin unless you marry beneath you."

"Paul calls any two people cousins who are descended from Charlemagne. He's a dear, but he lives in a quite unreal world— a sort of mixture of the middle ages and ancient Greece. He could only do it by hiding himself down in Provence. None of his theories fit life as it is. He feels that he has achieved nothing in life, so he says that the conditions of life are wrong, and he looks back to other centuries when he pretends they were perfect, though he knows quite well that they were hideous. He's always acting a little. You must allow for that."

"I think he sees the conditions of life as they are more truly than anyone I know. He sees that the only valuable things are those that are human."

"Oh dear, I wish I hadn't let you spend so much time with him," said Lucinda. "Anyhow, what would he think of this match? He'd be horrified. What would happen to the *seize quartiers* of your children? He expects you to make *un beau mariage dans le monde*."

"Mum," said Stephen, "can you really see me marrying a May-fair beauty?"

Lucinda looked at him speculatively.

"To tell the truth, darling, I can't," she said, "but you'll grow up. There are hundreds and hundreds of lovely girls in the world, not all of them over-sophisticated. Do wait and look round a little."

"That sounds beastly."

"Stephen, you must realize that you are born to a certain position in the world, and you must pay for it by accepting the limitations of your responsibilities. I don't want you to marry someone you don't love. That would be beastly. But you haven't yet discovered how many people there are that it is easy to love. One is really attracted more by types than individuals. You more or less admitted that just now when you spoke of the possibility of far more good friendships."

"I thought that one of my responsibilities," said Stephen, "was to marry and have several children, so that the family won't die out. There may be a war soon. Paul says it's certain because none of the business men in the Government understand foreign affairs. Supposing I'm killed and have no children. It would be pretty grim."

"Even business men won't be so stupid as to go to war. It would destroy their business. They might go to war with Russia but there's Hitler between us and Russia. But we're not discussing the next war. Darling, you'll be awfully unhappy if you don't face the realities of life. It's no good living in the clouds. I did it until I was nearly thirty. Then, suddenly, one morning I met a friend whom I hadn't seen for years, and who had, in the meantime, become one of the unreal inhabitants of my illusionary world. He was short and bald and full of ridiculous snobberies. I saw that in spite of this he was still likeable and a true friend. But all my rosy mists blew away, and since then I have tried to see people and things as they really

333

are. Do try and see Heather as she really is. She is a charming little thing, but her character is not yet developed. You don't know what she'll be in five years. The rosy mists you wrap round her are not her true element. I really am anxious for your happiness. I'm worried about the bust-up this engagement would make, with Marian and Paul and everyone. They've been so awfully good to all our Australian relatives, having them here to stay and treating them with every kindness. Then, if one of them grabs the heir to Crittenden, it would seem so mean, like stealing from someone who has been exceptionally generous. After all, the Brayfords don't want to be swamped with Vanes."

"How can you talk of Heather 'grabbing' me?" exclaimed Stephen. "You might as well say a flower you pick in the garden grabs you." His face was suffused with emotion.

"I don't mean Heather personally grabs you. I mean the family. But you're in your rosy mists again. You see something gleaming like the Holy Grail. You fling away all your defenses and go after it with outstretched arms. Either it doesn't exist, or it is unobtainable or else it turns round and gives you a crack on the jaw. Do you remember when you wanted me to take you to live in Peru when you were sixteen, and wouldn't admit that it was impracticable? Then a year later you wanted to stay and live with the monks of Assisi. When you found you couldn't do these things, you didn't exactly sulk, but you went about as if your world had collapsed, and I thought you would be ill. You cannot find in the modern world any place where you can live in that sort of golden age of physical and spiritual freedom. You've got the idea from lying on the rocks at St Saturnin and talking to Paul."

"I got it at Cambridge," said Stephen, "if anywhere. You seem to suggest that if a thing is beautiful it's impossible, or rather that a beautiful thing can't exist, but is only the result of a rosy myopia. I believe that when you see a thing like that you see its true nature, as it's meant to be. Your love for it gives you the power to see it truly. We all know that we could be different from what we are, but we can't make the effort. No one has any faith in us. Then someone comes along and sees us in a rosy mist. They see the real self that we know we should be, and while they see us like that we become it. We can't help ourselves, partly because we're so grateful to them, and partly because we're ashamed not to be what they see. You have to be in what you call a rosy mist to see the real significance of whatever you look at, whether it's a tree or a building or a person. If you only concentrate on its material substance like a so-called scientist, you're not seeing it at all. You have to be

334

in a rosy mist to create anything worth while, as Paul said that day when you came up to Cambridge and he told Roland to look out of the window at King's. I think you'd be much happier, Mum, if you went back to your way of looking at things before you were thirty, and wrapped your bald-headed friend up in his rosy mist again." He smiled up at her from the armchair.

"Oh, Stephen, you're so young!" cried Lucinda. She turned and fiddled with a gilt bottle on her dressing table. "Do you know if Uncle Bill has gone to bed?" she said at last. "I'll go down and talk to him."

"You'll make him agree," exclaimed Stephen, leaping up from the chair. "If you and he agree, no one else can do anything. But what about Aunt Muriel?" he added thoughtfully. "She might put her foot down. She seems so ambitious."

"You're *too* simple, Stephen! Don't you realize that in spite of your funny little ways you're a very eligible *parti?* Muriel would be cock-a-hoop to catch you for Heather."

"Please don't talk like that, Mum," begged Stephen.

"I only give that as an example. I don't want you to be like those smug young men who are only too conscious of their worth, and on the defensive against every respectable girl they meet, but you are capable of kissing the shoes of some Cambridge barmaid, as if she had condescended to you from the gold bar of Heaven. Switch out the lights."

"I'll wait here till you come back."

"You'd better not."

"How do you think I can possibly sleep while my whole future happiness is being decided?" he demanded indignantly.

"O God!" said Lucinda with resignation. Her room opened on to the gallery above the main staircase. Two lights still glowed economically in the chandelier, which hung suspended above the hall, so she knew that some of the family were still up. As she went down the magnificent staircase beneath the high painted ceiling, of which the splendors were enhanced by the dim light, she tried to see Heather as the mistress of this house. She was quite unable to visualize this. It was hard enough to see Stephen as its future owner, but if he married the right girl, a sort of Marian, only not so bossy, he might manage well enough.

Her feelings of guilt towards the Brayfords returned. It was mixed with feelings of responsibility towards Crittenden itself. Although she was now sometimes bored here, she could never forget the impression that this place had first made on her, and she loved the beautiful house, so much a "stately home" and yet so quiet and mellow.

335

Sometimes when she returned after a longish interval it made her catch her breath. Perhaps that rosy mist was not yet dispelled.

It seemed to her that the Vanes had made a gradual assault on Crittenden, reconnoitring on the day when Dean Chapman had brought them out to luncheon. Then Julie had snatched Hugo as a hostage, and sent Lucinda as a vanguard into the coveted territory. Her metaphor became a little confused, but after that the Vanes had come over in successive waves, retiring but each time leaving the defenses weakened. Now, apparently, they were going to take the citadel. Lucinda, in twenty-one years, had become too much a Brayford to enjoy the prospect. She would prefer Stephen to marry one of his twenty thousand cousins in the English aristocracy.

Nevertheless she was more moved by Stephen's harangue than she cared to admit, even to herself. At the foot of the stairs she paused, wondering if, at Stephen's age, for a year or two of rosy mists it was not worth while to mortgage the future. At long after Stephen's age she had been prepared to do it herself. She remembered now, though she had denied it in the intervening years, the intense happiness of her first year of marriage to Hugo.

She went to look for Bill and found him in the library with Arthur, where they had been discussing the future of the land, both in England and Australia.

"Ah, Lucinda," said Arthur. "We were just going to turn in."

"I came to look for Bill," said Lucinda.

"Then I expect I'm *de trop*," said Arthur. "Help yourself to drinks, Vane. Good-night. Good-night, Lucinda." He smiled at them kindly and went up to bed.

Bill looked inquiringly at Lucinda.

"Something up?" he said.

"Yes, there is." She gave a nervous laugh. "Stephen wants to marry Heather."

"They're first cousins."

"I know. That was my first reaction. It will be everybody's. But it's not the only objection."

"What others are there?"

She was surprised that he asked this, when to her there appeared dozens of obvious objections. She saw with a further start of surprise that Bill was looking at her suspiciously. He was absolutely unsmiling and the lines in his face showed only as marks of dissipation. Accepting Arthur's invitation, he went over to the tray and poured himself out a stiff whisky. He could drink a great deal without any outward effect.

"Well, they're so young," said Lucinda lamely.

"You married young yourself."

"Not quite so young. Anyhow, Hugo was much older than Stephen."

"I approve of young marriages," said Bill. "I know you don't, of course, for other people."

She ignored this. She could not believe at first that he was harking back to her interference between himself and Anne Maitland. She imagined that that had been forgiven and forgotten long ago, and she thought he was reasonably happy with Muriel, and as fond of her as most middle-aged men were of their wives, even when they were a little stupid.

"Stephen can't afford to marry," she said. "Hugo's income just keeps him at Cambridge and I can't allow him much."

"That isn't a serious difficulty," said Bill. At Julie's death Fred had settled half his estate on Bill. He could probably give Heather a handsome *dot*.

"I want them to be happy," said Lucinda, looking worried, "but I can't somehow think it's desirable."

Bill gulped down his whisky.

"Heather's not good enough for you, I suppose," he said. He smiled but his mouth was twisted, and his eyes were dark with malevolence.

"It's not that at all," said Lucinda with some heat, because she knew in a sense that it was so, but not as simply as Bill meant it. It was not that Heather was not "born." This was not why she did not want her to marry Stephen. It was because she was a Vane. She did not want the Brayfords to be bought any further by the Vanes. The repetition would emphasize the fact that Hugo had been bought for her, though she was hardly conscious that this was one of the reasons for her objection.

"I'm not as much a snob as you think," she went on, trying to recover a degree of friendliness. "I prefer a witty duchess to a dull charwoman, but I also prefer a witty charwoman to a dull duchess. If they're both witty I'm afraid I prefer the duchess. The real snob is the person who prefers a dull duchess to a witty charwoman."

Bill did not smile. He poured himself out another whisky. Although the drink showed no outward effect beyond a darkening of the eyes, it stirred up in him old resentments, dating much farther back than Lucinda's trip to Oxford—back to his childhood, resentments of which she was completely unaware. Always at The Pines and at Tourella his sisters had dominated the scene. All the talk had been, in that household of women, of their clothes, their parties, their future. He had been made to feel small, unimportant, a troublesome boy about the place. It was true that Fred bought him expensive saddles, but his own tastes and wishes were never consulted. His affection for his sisters did not smother his internal criticism, and he disliked the pervading atmosphere, created by Julie, of social striving. This had reached its climax in Lucinda's marriage. He associated that with the frustration of his own romance. On the other hand he had come to admire his wife more, though he was systematically unfaithful to her, because she now bossed all the Vanes. Someone in Melbourne was reported to have said, "Of course Muriel has made the Vanes." That pleased him. But he knew that by Lucinda's standards Muriel was slightly ridiculous. An incident had occurred to illustrate it only this afternoon. Muriel, explaining the economies they had made at Tourella as the result of the slump, said, "We have shut up the ballroom unless, of course, we are giving a dance." Lucinda, to lighten a conversation which was becoming too obsessed with opulent *ménage*, said, "I always shut up my dining-room unless, of course, I'm having dinner." This had annoyed Bill and he remembered it now. Lucinda with her cool wit, her good taste which did not entirely depend upon wealth, still retained her childhood's ascendancy. She was wearing an apricot dress and a little coat which looked as if it were made of lacquer. There was something in the chic simplicity of her clothing and the composure of her manner, which was unruffled even by her slight indignation, which maddened him.

"Oh, and what is it then?" he asked. "You might also tell me what was your objection to Anne Maitland."

"I hadn't any."

"You interfered from pure malice?"

"I did not."

"Then you had some damned silly objection. I suppose you had discovered that Professor Maitland's grandfather was a pork-butcher or a postman or something."

"It's no good discussing that now," said Lucinda, distressed.

"You have some shame."

"It's not that at all," she repeated.

"So you say. Well, you're not going to do it a second time." He had the malevolent obstinacy of a drunken man who yet remains articulate, and in apparent control of himself.

"I don't want to. I only came down to ask you what you thought of it. It seemed to me undesirable as they are first cousins, but I am quite open to persuasion." She spoke with careful enunciation as if she were talking to a foreigner, or explaining a lesson to a child. She felt that the whole scene was shameful, and although she spoke with such an air of candor she was not being honest. She knew, and she alone, as Watteau had died in her home in the valley a few months after Julie, that Stephen and Heather were not full cousins, and that she was using their supposed relationship to support her other less defensible objections. She was perhaps most ashamed that Bill showed so little pride and delicacy. If he knew, or even suspected that Arthur, whose hospitality he had so freely enjoyed and of whose whisky he was even now pouring out a third glass, would not welcome the match, surely he ought not to be prepared to advance it. There was a kind of aggressive greed in his manner which made her, for the first time, glad to think that he was only her half-brother, though it was true that this could easily have been inherited from Fred.

"I see no objection," he said.

"I'll talk to Arthur about it in the morning," said Lucinda, but she disliked the prospect. She said good night and left the library. As she went upstairs she heard a faint eerie sound floating down from above. For a moment she had the feeling that the house was haunted, before she recognized it as Stephen's flute coming from her bedroom.

CHAPTER THREE

THE NEXT MORNING when Lucinda went to find Arthur, she found that he had gone out riding. Last night Stephen, on hearing that no decision had been arrived at, said, "I'm going to marry Heather, whatever you say, Mum, but, of course, it's nicer to have it all agreeable." He took Heather off to the pond immediately after breakfast and they stayed there till lunchtime. Lucinda had to spend the morning with the whole situation bottled up inside herself. She did not want to tell Marian about it until she had spoken to Arthur, as Marian would probably blurt out a decided opinion one way or another before the entire household.

At about twelve o'clock Lucinda went into the Peacock room and found Muriel there talking to Marian, who was working on an embroidery frame. The butler came in just after Lucinda and said that Baa had rung up from Fitzauncell Castle, where he was staying for a few days, asking if he might bring Lord Fitzauncell over to luncheon.

"Yes, of course," said Marian. "I must go and see if there's anything to eat." She told him to send the cook to the library and went out of the room.

"That will be delightful," said Muriel. "I have so wanted to meet Lord Fitzauncell." The fact that he was both an Australian and a peer seemed to her to raise the level of Melbourne society.

"He's a curious man," said Lucinda. "Did Bill tell you about Stephen?"

"No. Is anything the matter."

"He wants to marry Heather."

"Heather?"

"Yes. He's sure that she would have him—though she hasn't told him so."

Muriel looked reflective, but not displeased. Her large smooth face seemed to have brightened a little. Lucinda wondered why Bill had not mentioned it to her, and thought he must have some motive in concealing it—that he was playing his cards.

"They are first cousins," said Muriel. "It's a very close relationship. Would people think it at all peculiar?"

"Villagers and royalties marry their cousins," said Lucinda. "Only a proportion of their children are imbecile."

"Oh! That would never do," said Muriel. "What do Lord and Lady Crittenden think? Lady Crittenden did not mention it just now."

"They don't know yet. Stephen told me last night and I've only told Bill so far—and now you."

"I was alseep when Bill came up and I've hardly seen him this morning. Does he approve?"

"I think he does."

"It's a puzzling situation," said Muriel. "What do you think?"

"I don't know. I'd rather they didn't marry, but Stephen seems to be desperately in love with her."

"We must wait and see what Lord Crittenden says," said Muriel. "If he thinks it unwise, of course it will be out of the question."

"That is sensible," said Lucinda gratefully, and she listened to an account of Muriel's last Cup Week ball, until Baa and Lord Fitzauncell arrived for lunch. Just before this Marian met Stephen and Heather in the hall carrying towels and wet bathing things.

"Stephen, you must go and tidy yourself," she said. "Lord Fitzauncell's coming to luncheon. Baa's bringing him over."

Heather, who was looking dreamy, suddenly brightened.

"Is Lord Wendale coming?" she asked. "I'm longing to meet him. He's famous, isn't he?"

"He writes housemaids' gossip in the gutter press," said Marian, "if that's fame."

Heather looked at her blankly, as if this simple statement were beyond her understanding, and hurried off to her room.

She was the last to arrive in the saloon, where everyone was waiting for lunch to be announced. She was wearing a very smart dress which was a little too old for her. She had made up her face, not much, as Muriel would not allow it, but enough to dispel that look of the summer morning which she had brought back from her bathe. Marian introduced Baa and Lord Fitzauncell and at lunch she put Heather between them. Stephen faced them across the table.

Heather exchanged a glance with him as they sat down, and then looked quickly away and hardly seemed aware of his presence until they left the dining-room.

Baa set himself out to entertain everybody. His conversation was just like his column in the Sunday newspaper, where some of it would appear. Heather kept her eyes fixed on him with obvious admiration. He was so eupeptic, so masculine and clean, if a little fat. He called Greek royalties by their Christian names and he had met everybody, even Hitler.

"We could learn a few useful lessons from Hitler," said Lord Fitzauncell.

"That purge was a bit grim," said Arthur.

"You have to be ruthless in a difficult situation."

"I can't understand," said Lucinda, "why Roehm, when he was offered the gun, didn't shoot Hitler. He can't have been a very sensible man. Paul thinks Hitler ought to be shot as he has abandoned *la moralité classique*."

"What do you think of Mr Baldwin?" Bill asked him. "Is he alive to the Russian menace?"

"I shouldn't care to see a world governed by Paul," said Marian.

"It would be very simple. There would be only two classes of society—the upper class consisting of Paul and the Duc de Guise, and the rest of us eating below the salt."

Arthur was the only one who smiled at this.

"Mum, that's not fair," said Stephen. "Paul's the kindest person," he explained to Muriel. "He talks to all the sailors at St Saturnin, just as if they were his equals."

Arthur's expression was severe.

"I wish I knew what they were up to in Europe," he said.

"There's only one problem in Europe," said Lord Fitzauncell, "that is to check Russia."

"I'm sure we're all agreed on that," said Muriel.

"Hitler's the man to do it," said Baa. "I was most impressed by him, most impressed. As long as we have the magnificent bulwark of Germany between ourselves and Bolshevism we may sleep securely in our beds."

"Rocked in the cradle of the Nazis," said Lucinda.

Lord Fitzauncell looked at her suspiciously.

"Yes, but he's not beyond criticism, not my criticism—no one is beyond that." Lord Fitzauncell gave a malignant smile.

"I won't have Mr Baldwin criticized," said Marian, "though when I sat next to him at a memorial service last month he gave me the creeps."

"I do admire Mr Baldwin tremendously," said Muriel. "He's such an Englishman."

The conversation divided. Bill and Lord Fitzauncell explained to Marian the need for a "White Australia." Baa entertained the other end of the table with gossip about the great. He was always a little nervous of Lucinda and anxious to placate her. He addressed himself to Muriel who absorbed his words with reverent attention, but every now and then his eyes flickered across to Lucinda to see how she was taking it. Sometimes he turned to Heather who was gazing at him entranced. Stephen sat with a faint frown wishing that this excellent but to him, deathly meal would soon end.

When they returned to the saloon, Muriel graciously invited Baa to sit beside her. Stephen tried to lure Heather apart, but she sat on the arm of Muriel's chair and continued to listen to Baa. There was something about the combination of her childish attitude and her over-smart dress which Stephen could not bear. He touched her hand to make her come away, but she turned impatiently and signed to him not to interrupt. A most terrible feeling passed through Stephen's body. His face went white and he turned away and stood looking out of one of the tall windows, across to where the chimneys of the End House just showed above the trees. Lucinda saw this incident and thought, "That girl's a little bitch." She was more inclined to prevent the marriage if possible.

Lord Fitzauncell thought himself to be too important to stay long in any private house, especially one belonging to the people he most despised, the impoverished aristocracy who had not accommodated themselves to the business world. He left as soon as he had had his coffee.

He turned to Baa and curtly told him to "come along," as if he were an office boy or something less. Arthur who till that moment had been most affable, and was walking with him out to his car, suddenly became very stiff, bowed and said, "Good-bye."

When they had left, Marian asked Bill if he had known what Lord Fitzauncell did in Australia. She always asked this question of any Australian she met and forgot the answers as they were indefinite.

"I don't know what he did," said Bill. "He is said to be the son of Hooley, a former Labor premier, and a Creole woman."

"I didn't know he was so respectable," said Lucinda.

"Actually, Hooley was a very decent old boy," Bill observed.

Muriel listened to this conversation with the same expression with which Heather had heard Marian's comment on Baa's "fame," a look of deliberate mystification.

Stephen turned from the window and stood near Heather, but not close to her.

"I think Lord Wendale is awfully interesting," said Heather. Her voice was a little high. It might have been due to excitement at meeting Baa, or to a rather frightened realization that she had ignored Stephen for nearly two hours.

"Lord Fitzauncell has asked us to go over this afternoon to see the castle," said Muriel, turning to Marian. "I do hope you won't mind, but I should so much like to see it. I believe very few Australians are invited there."

Marian said she did not mind at all. Stephen looked worried. He had arranged to play singles with Heather this afternoon. He was afraid to mention it and so make certain what he could already feel, that she wanted to go to Fitzauncell Castle. When at last he mentioned it diffidently, Muriel said:

"You had better rest for a while, Heather."

"I could play for an hour before we start," said Heather.

"I think not, dear." Muriel gave a majestic smile of apology to Stephen and sent Heather up to her room. Stephen went alone down to the tennis courts and practiced services. He felt that impalpable hostile powers were forming against him. When the Vanes' car was brought round for them to go to Fitzauncell he hung about the drive. He did not know whether he was supposed to go with them or not. He was untidily dressed in an old tweed coat and flannel trousers.

The Vanes came out to the car and Muriel said cheerfully, "Good-bye, Stephen, we'll see you at dinner-time."

Bill saw Stephen's wretched expression and said curtly, "I thought Stephen was coming with us."

"I'd like to if I may," said Stephen, his whole face lighting up.

Heather stood waiting for them to get into the car, and seemed neither pleased nor displeased that Stephen had come with them.

She had changed her dress again and looked as if she was going to a garden-party.

Lucinda was glad to be relieved of Muriel for the afternoon. She had gone up to the peacock room to write letters. She was sitting, wondering what to write next, when she heard the car brought round and in idle curiosity she went to the window. She saw the Vanes come out, and although she could not hear what was said, the meaning of the incident was as clear to her as a silent film. She was angry at Muriel's daring to treat Stephen in that fashion in what was practically his own home. She had seen at luncheon that she was impressed by Baa, and that she had stopped Heather playing singles with Stephen, not from regard for her health but because she had suddenly seen bigger game.

Lucinda thought it possible that Stephen might escape with only a slight wound, and that perhaps after all it might prove unnecessary to mention the affair to Arthur. She felt grateful to Bill for his intervention, although it hardly furthered her wishes, and this modified her attitude of the previous night towards her half-brother.

Heather was excited, but she was not really happy. It was not her fault that her highest good was wealth and social prominence. Regard for these things had been instilled into her from childhood. She came to England naïvely prepared to love the highest when seen. She had also the wholesome dislike of young people for what was not robust, on the up-grade, positive and even predatory. Stephen, a kind of legendary figure in the family, she certainly thought of as one of the highest, and when she met him she did not change her opinion. His kindness and lack of affectation, when she had expected him to be rather aloof, had completely disarmed her, and she imagined that she was in love with him. Certain simplicities in his behavior puzzled her occasionally, as did also a poetic quality she sensed in him as when he played his flute by the lake, but this made her feel protective towards him, which she liked.

However, when she saw Baa, she thought she really had come face to face with the highest. He looked as if it were impossible that he could be anything but an earl, whereas Stephen had the appearance of any ordinary nice-looking undergraduate. There was nothing puzzling about Baa. There he was, resplendent, assured, affable, the twentieth-century replica of his ancestor the first Earl of Wendale, whose engraving, removed from the back staircase of the End House, was now stored in a warehouse at Balham. She did not know that his prospects were much less secure than Stephen's, and that his income, beyond the four thousand a year that Lord Fitzauncell paid him for his weekly gossip, was negligible for his position, so

344

that when Lord Fitzauncell beckoned him away he went like a dog. Muriel may have known this, but she probably thought him more immediately spectacular.

Even if Heather had known it she would not have felt differently. She was not mercenary. What Baa was, not what he owned, excited her. He opened the door on glittering scenes. In listening to him she had no thought beyond the pleasure of the moment. She certainly had no idea of cooling towards Stephen, and had wanted to play singles with him. But she did want to talk to Baa and to hear his intimate stories of the great. She could not reconcile the two things, so she did not look at Stephen as he stood by the car, and she would have felt more comfortable if he had not come to Fitzauncell. She gave him one or two quick restless smiles on the way there. Only Muriel thought of securing Baa for Heather. Lucinda knew that Baa could not resist turning his charm on to any pretty girl, and that when he did marry he would choose someone infinitely more *mondaine* than Heather, but she had no objection to Muriel's dropping the bone for the shadow.

Fitzauncell Castle was now three times the size it had been in Miss Fitzauncell's time when it had consisted of one habitable wing. Lord Fitzauncell had restored the other two wings and had built a fourth to enclose the courtyard, into which the Vanes drove between two massive round towers. This new wing was externally medieval, but inside it was like the entrance to a block of ultra-modern flats. They were shown into a vast glittering hall. In a few minutes Baa appeared and offered to take them over the castle. He explained that a member of the Government had called on Lord Fitzauncell, who would be engaged for some time.

They began their tour. Baa walked ahead between Muriel and Heather. He explained which was restored work, and showed them the room where a thirteenth-century Lord Fitzauncell had murdered his wife.

"Sensible man," said Bill.

"Haven't you a castle of your own in Ireland?" Muriel asked.

"Burnt down by the Sinn Feiners," said Baa.

"But it could be restored, I suppose."

"Yes, it *could* be," said Baa smiling.

Muriel thought this conversation delicately allusive.

"I think it was horrid of him to murder his wife," said Heather.

"You don't know what she was like," said Bill.

"She might have been like me."

"Then I'm sure he wouldn't have murdered her," said Baa.

Stephen hovered disconsolately behind them. He disliked Fitzauncell Castle. Where it was new it was vulgar, and where it was old it was oppressive. He hated this facetious sort of conversation about husbands and wives.

He could not understand why Heather did not walk beside him, holding hands when the others weren't looking, or even if they were. That would be the natural, normal thing. He thought Heather so perfect, so beautiful, that, far from it's being improbable, Baa must fall in love with her. Only himself and Muriel considered this possible. Bill was annoyed with Muriel for showing it. She was like a Brisbane woman, who, when the Prince of Wales danced with her daughter, said, "It's only a boy and girl affair. Rita won't be Queen of England." Bill was obstinately determined to bring about the marriage of Stephen and Heather.

The minister, who was anxious to obtain Lord Fitzauncell's support for the betrayal of Abyssinia, stayed on to dinner at the castle. He did not want to have Baa present at their conversation, so Lord Fitzauncell sent him over to dine at Crittenden. Muriel, who had been disappointed and a little offended at not meeting the minister—neither he nor Lord Fitzauncell had appeared during the afternoon—was amply compensated by this. She was sure that Heather was the reason for Baa's second visit in one day. Everyone else thought the same. He often stayed at Fitzauncell without coming near Crittenden. Even Lucinda viewed Baa less cynically, but not for long.

"Tell me, Lucinda," he said in a disinterested manner, "is your brother very gilt-edged?"

"You mean—is my niece?"

"One follows from the other, doesn't it?"

"Well, she has a younger sister and two brothers. She may have a nice *dot* for someone with modest tastes, but for you it would be useless. It is very good of me to tell you this."

"Yes, it is. I'm grateful."

"You don't see what I mean," said Lucinda.

When after dinner the men came into the saloon Marian said: "It's a good thing you came, Baa. Now we can have two tables of bridge."

Stephen sat at a table with Lucinda, Arthur, and Muriel. The other table was far more lively. Marian and Baa squabbled amusingly and there was a good deal of laughter. From time to time Stephen darted suffering, indignant glances at Lucinda. He did not look at the other table. It was as much as he could bear to hear Heather laughing at Baa's sallies, or talking to Marian with an equability he could not possibly have achieved himself.

Baa left early. Muriel, as he said good-bye, invited him to dine with them one night in London. Baa said he would be delighted, but when she began to fix a night he looked a little vague. However, they finally arranged the Wednesday of the following week. Heather stood eagerly beside them.

When Baa had left she felt a little frightened again. She was puzzled at herself, but hardly consciously. She only knew that somehow she had put herself in an awkward situation. When Stephen came up to her she said in that rather high voice, "It's been a marvelous day." She looked at him directly, but her eyes were bright and hard. She hated the suffering look in his eyes. It gave her the same feeling as the music he had played in the chapel.

"You'd better go to bed now, darling," said Muriel, who saw Stephen's expression and thought it wisest to separate them.

Heather shook hands with Marian and Arthur. Her manner had suddenly become affected. When she shook hands with Stephen she held out her arm stiff and straight in front of her. Her smile was intended to be comradely, but it made Stephen feel as if his heart were shriveling.

He followed Lucinda up to her room. She turned to him with a rueful smile.

"Have you said anything to anyone?" he demanded.

"Not since last night."

"Why didn't you? You said you'd talk to Uncle Arthur this morning."

"He was out all the morning. I couldn't find him."

"If you had, we'd have been engaged by now."

"But I thought you were practically engaged."

"I hadn't said anything, but I felt . . . oh, damn! Why does Baa want to come over here twice in one day? He doesn't generally come near the place."

"Darling," said Lucinda, "I may be able to pay for your taxis, but I can't conduct your love affairs. If, to come into the open, you don't like Baa's civilities to Heather—they are not much more— why don't you tell him that if he doesn't keep way you'll dot him one on the nose. It's odd how the word dot keeps coming into this affair."

"And what would Aunt Marian say?"

"I think she'd be pleased and amused. She often complains that you haven't enough punch in you."

Stephen stuck his hands into the pockets of his black, braided trousers.

"Shall I ring him up now and tell him?" he asked.

347

"I wasn't being very serious, darling."

"It's serious enough, isn't it? My life will be ruined if this goes wrong, and it looks as if it's going wrong."

"Listen, Stephen, I know this sort of thing can be dreadfully painful, but you'll get over it. In six months you'll hardly remember it. Neither of you have any experience. Baa is much more Heather's type than you are. Not that he would think of marrying her. She's not nearly rich enough for him, and he wouldn't be able to endure Muriel's social pretentions. He can only stand the finished article of its kind, a film star who is world famous, a politician who is in the Government. The only second-rate thing he tolerates is himself."

"D'you mean to say he doesn't want Heather? He must be mad. Why does he go on like that, then?"

"I don't think he has 'gone on' in any particular way. You always knew that he had kissed the Blarney Stone. It is Muriel who has behaved as if he were 'going on.' She's a bit of a bitch." To herself she added, "So is her daughter."

"Mum, I wish you wouldn't talk like that," said Stephen. "It doesn't suit you."

This annoyed Lucinda and for a few minutes they wrangled about her choice of words. Stephen exclaimed·

"You see everything is done to side-track it. Now we're not even talking about it."

"You led the conversation on to bitches, darling," said Lucinda. "Anyhow, what do you want me to do?"

"Do you agree to it? You said last night that you did."

"I didn't say that I agreed. I only said that I would discuss it with Bill. I've told you that he approves."

"Then if both you and he agree what is there to wait for?"

"I might ask you that."

Stephen went over and leaned against the mantelpiece. He was forcing himself to realize that his mother and his uncles were not the serious obstacle to his engagement to Heather. He said goodnight in a preoccupied manner.

Lucinda said, "I'm awfully sorry about it, darling."

"It isn't usually a thing to be sorry about," said Stephen.

"No. I suppose not. I mean I am sorry there are all these difficulties."

Lucinda found that she could not sleep. Although she tried to keep her poise during any scene in which the emotions were involved, she found that they upset her afterwards. She felt that for his future happiness she ought to do everything she could to prevent Stephen from marrying Heather, and yet, because of the feeling of guilt she had towards him, she always tried to give him the things he wanted. After she had been in bed for half an hour or more she switched on the light and began to read a novel. She heard a rumbling sound and thought it must be lorries away on the road to London.

Stephen, having left Lucinda, went moodily up to his room, which was on the floor above. He did not know how he could wait till morning, when he intended to ask Heather to marry him. He did not want to go to bed and he thought of setting out for a long walk round the countryside. Then, on the landing, he saw the second footman about to turn off the lights. He asked him to come and blow the organ for him. The youth looked a little sulky, as he was tired, and although it was likely that Stephen would reward him, it was also possible that he would forget, and merely thank him with absent-minded politeness.

They went down to the chapel. For some time Stephen played quietly, with brooding melancholy, but after a time he began to release his feelings in a Bach fugue. The chapel rocked and the rooms near it trembled. One of these was Marian's bedroom. She was a light sleeper, and she awoke from a dream that she was out in a thunderstorm to find the springs of her mattress quivering beneath her. As soon as she realized what was happening she put on her dressing-gown and went down to the chapel. She ran her hand down all the switches by the door, flooding the place with light. Stephen stopped playing and looked round.

"Go to bed, Thomas," said Marian. "You should have been in bed two hours ago."

The footman, his stiff white collar limp with sweat, sheepishly left the chapel. As he had feared, Stephen did not pay him, and all he had gained was her ladyship's displeasure.

"Are you out of your senses?" Marian asked crossly, when he had gone. "You must have awakened the entire household with that din."

Stephen looked dazed and ran his hand across his forehead.

"I'm sorry, Aunt Marian," he said. "I forgot the time."

"Well, go up to bed now," said Marian. "You look absolutely exhausted yourself, and that wretched footman won't be fit for his work tomorrow. You're not ill, are you? Have you any biscuits in your room?"

If Marian had found anyone else at the organ she would probably have sent him packing first thing in the morning, but all the solicitude she should have spent on half a dozen children, she concentrated on Stephen. However, she still harbored some unexpressed annoyance, and seeing a light in Lucinda's window in the other wing, and transferring the blame to her for setting Stephen the example of late hours, she went along to release it. When Marian knocked, Lucinda thought it must be Stephen back again, and she was extremely surprised to see her sister-in-law.

"Stephen must have gone off his head," said Marian bluntly. "He has just been playing the organ loud enough to wake the dead, let alone everyone sleeping within a mile."

"Oh, I thought it was lorries," said Lucinda.

"I suppose he learns from these rackety artists you meet in London that it doesn't matter deafening a respectable household in the small hours of the morning."

"I'm awfully sorry. He's very thoughtless. But it's not due to the rackety artists. He's very upset. He wants to marry Heather."

"Gosh!" exclaimed Marian.

"I thought so too," said Lucinda.

Stephen still could not go to sleep. Twice he left his bed to drink glasses of water, and he sat for a long time on the window-ledge in his pyjamas, looking out into the dark summer night, and trying to find a rational explanation of everything that had happened. His mind wandered after a while and his position on the window-ledge reminded him of sitting in the window of his rooms in Clare. He imagined the view from those rooms, the bridge with the stone balls, and the procession of choristers walking alone by the Gibb building in King's. The music he had just been playing reminded him of the services in King's Chapel, and he thought about the chorister whose name was Brian something. When he returned to the problems of the present they did not seem so difficult. A kind of tranquillity possessed him. Heather had shown clearly, when she was alone with him, that she loved him. She had shown a sensitive living response to his love for her. That was only this morning, or rather yesterday morning. She could not have changed so suddenly for no reason. And yet how could someone who had shown that sensitive response, who had seemed aware of the pleasure of simple things, of the lake and the trees, be impressed by the vulgarity of Fitzauncell Castle, or excited by the conversation of Baa. That was what puzzled him.

In the morning everyone knew that Stephen wanted to marry Heather. Marian had told Arthur as soon as he was awake. She announced abruptly that Stephen wanted to marry "that little creature red in tooth and claw." She referred to the matching vermilion of Heather's lipstick and finger-nails. Although everyone knew about it, no one mentioned it.

Stephen was the last down to breakfast. As he came into the dining-room he felt that everyone had been talking about him. This was not so, partly because Heather was there but also because of the size of the stone he had thrown into the Crittenden pond. Everyone was afraid to move for fear of being upset. Marian did not even refer to his playing the organ till one o'clock in the morning, as this had some association with Stephen's emotions. Only Muriel appeared to be in accord with her surroundings. The beautiful room with its simpering portraits, the Georgian tea and coffee pots on the sidetable, the fine Chippendale chairs, all bright and gleaming in the morning sun, seemed far too cheerful and urbane for the mood of those who sat round the table, glancing through their letters and eating grilled kidneys or omelettes.

Stephen murmured an inclusive good-morning and went to pour himself out a cup of coffee. He could not sit beside Heather as she was between Muriel and Arthur. When he saw this, at once he had a sinking feeling, but it was possible that Muriel had come down after Heather and had fenced her in, in this way. Going to his place he walked behind her chair, so that he could see if her tea-cup were empty. For breakfast she only had tea, toast and an orange. When he saw that it was, he said gently:

"Shall I bring you some more tea?"

"Oh, thank you, Stephen." She smiled up at him over her shoulder. Her smile was bright and friendly, her voice imperceptibly surprised, as if a stranger had offered her a courtesy.

Muriel opened her letters, mostly from expensive shops, and talked of her plans.

"They've reserved our suite at the Beau-Site from the first of August," she said to Bill, "with an extra room for Heather. That's satisfactory. We're only going to be there a fortnight," she explained to Marian, "as we're going to Gleneagles for the latter part of August. I want Heather to see Scotland. Then we have a fortnight in Paris before we leave for Melbourne. Heather, darling, you must have your hair done as soon as we get back tomorrow. I've made an appointment for you with No. 5."

"You'll have seen a great deal of our life over here by the time you go home," said Marian to Heather. "You'll have something to remember."

Stephen looked furiously at Lucinda, who raised her eyebrows helplessly.

"I expect she'll be back again soon," said Bill.

"It looks as if Mussolini's going to grab Abyssinia," said Arthur, laying aside his *Times*.

"I admire him tremendously," said Muriel. "It's wonderful the way he has made the trains run punctually in Italy, and he's cleared up the *Mafia*."

"I hate everything tidied up," said Lucinda. "All this modern regimentation is only tolerable when it's leavened by a few out-laws. Stephen, darling, bring me another kidney, with a very small piece of bacon, well frizzled, and a cup of coffee too, darling, strong, with not much milk but plenty of cream. Since the slump the only decent meals I get are at Crittenden. In fact I might as well shut up my dining-room." She laughed, but every word of her apparently inconsequent and airy conversation was directed at Muriel and Heather, who, she calculated though these calculations were more instinctive than conscious, would not care for a mother-in-law who complained openly of poverty.

Throughout the whole affair Lucinda acted in this way, half-heartedly trying to help Stephen, but at the same time, whenever an opportunity occurred, doing what she could to discourage the engagement.

Arthur was the first to leave the breakfast table. On Marian's instructions he waited for Bill in the hall, and when he came out, asked if he could spare him a moment, and they went into the library. Lucinda went out onto the terrace to smoke a cigarette. Marian always stayed on in the dining-room after breakfast to give orders to the butler, and to interview the cook. She also held there, when there had been any misdemeanors among the servants, a kind of orderly-room.

Stephen did not eat much breakfast, but he dawdled on, hoping to catch Heather by leaving the dining-room at the same time. Muriel seemed to be mounting guard over her. At last she gathered up her letters and they went out together. Stephen followed them. He was extremely nervous and when at the door of the saloon, he asked Heather to come to bathe, the tone of his voice invited her to refuse, if she had not already intended to do so.

"There won't be time to bathe before we leave for Glastonbury," Muriel intervened.

"For Glastonbury!" exclaimed Stephen.

"Yes, didn't you know? Lady Crittenden has suggested that we should drive over to Glastonbury for the day. We'll have lunch at the inn there. We should be back in time for tea." Marian could not resist inviting people to Crittenden, but as soon as they arrived she wished that they were out of her way, and whenever possible she packed them off on some excursion. So that, thought Stephen, was why there had been an air of conspiracy when he came into the dining-room.

"You must write to grandpapa before we start," Muriel said to Heather, who even acquiesced in this as she was afraid to be alone with Stephen.

Lucinda decided to go with them, partly because she always enjoyed going to look at something, but also to see that Stephen had fair play. Bill was driving and Muriel said to Stephen that he had better sit in front with his uncle.

"Oh, Muriel," said Lucinda, "do you mind if I sit in front? I'm always sick if I sit in the back on a long drive, especially if the car is very well sprung."

Bill looked quizzically at Lucinda as she took her seat beside him. He was almost as puzzled by the situation as Stephen. Arthur had just explained to him, very courteously, that, until Stephen inherited Crittenden, he would not be able to keep a wife in any comfort. He imagined that Lucinda was behind this, and yet now Lucinda appeared to have changed sides.

They arrived at Glastonbury at one o'clock and had lunch at the historic inn. Lucinda ordered the most expensive claret as Bill would pay for the lunch. She could not help reflecting that, if all the facts were known, Bill's wealth would have been divided between herself and Lydia, except for a few hundred pounds which Canon Chapman had left to each of them, and so she felt entitled to some entertainment from him, especially when Muriel was being particularly opulent and patronizing. She was a little startled when Bill asked her suddenly:

"What d'you mean by that Mona Lisa smile?"

After lunch they went to look at the abbey. It was impossible for Heather to keep under her mother's wings all the time, as Bill and Lucinda combined to prevent it. Lucinda did not know why she did this. She certainly did not want the attachment to be strengthened, but she disliked the way that Muriel and Heather were treating Stephen, and her instinct was to oppose it.

The sunlight flooded the abbey grounds and the shadows repeated, on the smooth lawns between them, the patterns of the broken arches. They came into that part of the ruins which had been the choir of the church. When the others went on, Stephen stayed here alone. The atmosphere of the place was so extraordinarily peaceful that he felt it as a positive influence, not merely as the absence of discord. It was something of the same feeling that he had in King's Chapel, the sense of being in love, but not anxiously or jealously, nor with the desire to possess. There had been a moment in the services in King's when the end chorister, at the head of the procession entering the choir, had appeared under the shadow of the screen, as if for that brief second alone in the vast noble building. This moment had expressed in some way for Stephen the link between what was human and what was mysterious and unseen. In all his appreciation of gothic buildings and plainsong, and the later music of Palestrina and Byrd, there was a strong human element. These things expressed for him not something disembodied, but human love lifted on to an eternal plane. He wanted to have Heather with him in this quiet place, and he went to find her. The others had gone to look at the abbey kitchen. As he came up to them Lucinda was saying, "There's a monastery in Italy which is only open to the *bon vivant* of noble birth. When he feels the approach of age he pays a sum of money and takes his vows. He then spends his declining years with his fellow gourmets in the enjoyment of good *cuisine*. It must be like a perpetual dinner with 'The Wine and Food Society.' I wish there were one for women."

Stephen said to Heather, "Come over here."

She looked at him with faint surprise that he spoke with such assurance. She had avoided being alone with him, not only because she had behaved badly but also because his nervous manner had made her feel nervous. She went with him across the wide stretch of lawn back to the ruins of the church. When they were standing again in the choir she looked at him expectantly, but without fear of anything he might say.

"I wanted to be alone with you here," he explained.

She thought he was going on to make an explicit reconciliation, and she moved towards him with a youthful confiding movement. The effect of Baa's "brilliance," to which she had succumbed in spite of herself, was wearing off. She had a recurrence of the feeling of some particular goodness in Stephen, even if it was a little "mad." It made her feel that she was outside some sphere which, through him, she could enter and understand. She thought that the moment had come when this was to happen. But although he had brought her here, he seemed to be absorbed in some reflection which did not include her. Having no response to her gentle confiding movement she felt slighted and irritated. However, after a minute or so Stephen turned to her with a slow smile. He was about to speak when Muriel's voice startled them both. Redolent of Bond Street and Toorak, she stood in a shaft of sunlight, a sudden mundane vision in this holy place.

"We're leaving now, dear," she said. "We'll just have time to do Wells on the way back."

Heather gave way to her irritation. She knew that something had gone wrong, and although she was annoyed with her mother for her interrupting them at that moment, her true instinct made her blame Stephen. She expected a man to be bold and resourceful in these matters. She continued to avoid being alone with him until the Vanes left Crittenden the following morning.

"It was all a damp squib," Lucinda said to Marian when they had gone. "Poor Stephen! But I think he's well out of it."

As Heather was Lucinda's niece Marian did not openly state her agreement.

CHAPTER FOUR

LUCINDA AND STEPHEN arrived at St Saturnin a few days after the Vanes had gone to Cannes. They found two letters awaiting them at the villa, one from Muriel to herself, the other from Heather to Stephen, and both containing a pressing invitation for him to stay as their guest for a fortnight at the Beau-Site. Lucinda was annoyed but Stephen's delight was so intense that she did not tell him what she thought was the reason for the Vane's sudden amiability. He at once believed that all the misunderstanding at Crittenden had been due to his own over-sensitiveness. The only objection Lucinda made was that he had not the clothes for Cannes. His wardrobe at St Saturnin was mostly blue cotton shirts and flannel trousers.

"We can telegraph to Aunt Marian to post out my clothes," said Stephen. They did this and he left as soon as the clothes arrived. When she saw him off at the station he was so confident and full of joy that she felt this must precede a disillusionment.

Paul had invited her to lunch and she strolled from the station, through the hot clear morning, down to his villa. When she arrived he was fussing round the lunch table, which was laid out on the terrace. He was disappointed at Stephen's going away so soon, and he was not as immediately voluble as usual.

"It seems to me," said Lucinda, as she stood watching Paul arranging figs and greengages in a green pottery bowl, "that all young life is like a crocus, that springs up so fragile and trusting, and then is trodden on or nipped off by a sparrow."

"I don't think either of us have been very badly trodden on," said Paul.

"I'm not so sure. Anyhow, I was thinking of Stephen."

355

"He is much less trodden on than an unemployed Welsh miner, for example."

"Oh, Paul," said Lucinda, "you always think of some extreme contrast that knocks the conversation silly."

"Will you ruin your inside with gin now," asked Paul, "or will you wait and drink some wholesome wine with your luncheon?"

"If I have to wait for more than ten minutes I'll ruin my inside with gin," said Lucinda, "without prejudice to the wholesome wine later."

Harry, accompanied by his eldest child Pierre, a boy of twelve, came out with a tray of *hors d'oeuvres*. Lucinda said a few pleasant words to them, and sat down to the table.

"Why has Stephen gone to Cannes?" asked Paul, when they were alone again. "He doesn't like that kind of life. Is he going to be nipped off by a sparrow, or a vampire?"

"I was going to tell you, but I'm rather ashamed about it and I was putting it off until I was fortified by your lovely food. These artichokes are delicious. How does Assomption make this sauce?"

"What are you ashamed about?"

"Did you see Heather, my niece, when you met Bill in Marseilles?"

"Yes."

"Stephen wants to marry her."

Paul gave a start. He put down his fork.

"What do you think of it?" he asked after a pause.

"I think she's a little bitch," said Lucinda.

"They're first cousins."

"I know. Stephen quoted you in support of the marriage of cousins. You do say the most irresponsible things sometimes. Anyhow she set her cap for him as soon as she landed, and Stephen, who believes that all life is beautiful and innocent, and who would walk straight into the embrace of a man-eating orchid in the jungle, fell at once. Then Baa brought Lord Fitzauncell over to lunch at Crittenden."

"Good God!" exclaimed Paul.

"Yes, but that's beside the point. The sight of a young unmarried earl simply made Muriel's mouth water. She kept Stephen away from Heather as if he were the most unprincipled libertine on earth. Heather, too, dropped Stephen for the juicier bone, though she seemed to do it less deliberately. I did something of the same kind when I was her age. Stephen came every night to my room and harangued me as if it were my fault. I talked it over with Bill. This is the part I'm ashamed about. I think he wants them to marry. Stephen tried to drown his misery or to express it by blaring away on the chapel organ in the small hours of the morning. To excuse this, I let the cat out of the bag to Marian, who of course exclaimed "Gosh" and set poor Arthur on to Bill. Arthur told Bill that Stephen had not enough money to marry on, not a girl of Heather's up-bringing. Bill gave her fifty pounds when they arrived in London and a week later she only had a pair of stockings to show for it. Bill said he would settle a thousand a year on her. Arthur said if they married he would make Stephen's income up to a thousand a year, which means trebling it. He can't possibly afford it but feels that my relatives are too inclined to pay cash down for a Brayford, and that it's up to him to meet them on the same financial level. It was hardly what Marian wished. I saw him as he came out of the library after his talk with Bill. He had that look of bearing internal burdens which puzzle him. Then Marian packed us all off to Glastonbury for the day."

"Was it an enjoyable excursion?" asked Paul.

"Stephen told me in the bedtime harangue that he had just been going to propose to Heather, when Muriel appeared among the ruins like Medusa or someone—"

"Ox-eyed Hera, I should think," said Paul.

"Well, anyhow, she appeared, and there was no return of favorable conditions before they left Crittenden the next morning. Stephen seemed to think it was my fault."

"What has happened since then?"

"Not a great deal. On the way through London I looked in on Susannah and found Baa there. I imagined he had come more in search of gossip than from cousinly affections. Anyhow, Muriel had invited him to dine with them in London, and I asked him how he had enjoyed his dinner. He looked sheepish and said, 'Well, as a matter of fact, I was unable to go. I was very sorry.' He had sounded me at Crittenden on Heather's prospects. He must have been a little attracted by her. Then, when we arrived here, we found letters from Muriel and Heather begging Stephen to go to Cannes for a fortnight. He had no idea that they were only written because Baa hadn't turned up to dine, and this morning he went off all radiant and I suppose he'll come back all bound and doomed—not that the poor girl is as bad as all that. I'm really terribly sorry, Paul. I can't imagine that you will like it."

Paul looked at her. His eyes appeared blue and penetrating, and very close to his beaky nose. She had a strong sense of his separateness, almost as if he belonged to another race. From time to time Paul revealed himself as a living expression of antiquity, as if in him dry bones really had been made alive. When this happened he was a little intimidating. Harry came out onto the terrace and Paul turned to speak to him. His profile had a bleak look of ancient suffering, most noticeable in the line of his mouth. Then Pierre came out bearing a large bowl of salad. The whole expression of Paul's face changed. Its stern lines broke into a lively smile as he moved a bottle on the table for the boy to put down the bowl. When they were alone again Paul said:

"Let us sit comfortably." He took the brandy bottle, the cigarettes and the coffee tray and put them on a small table between two cane chairs, just at the edge of the terrace. They were still in the shadow of the vines, but here and there a spot of sunlight was dazzling on a glass, or a cup, or on Lucinda's pale yellow dress. St Saturnin with its green shuttered houses was drowsy below them, and beyond the port the shimmering sea stretched towards Africa.

"I don't quite understand you," said Lucinda. "I thought you would be dreadfully upset, but conceal it out of consideration for my feelings. But I don't mind. You may say what you like."

"Why did you think I would be upset?"

"Well, it's not a grand alliance. You go on about Marian's coming from the middle classes."

"Why I go on about Marian is not really because she comes from the middle classes, but because she is the last sterile expression of puritanism, which is mostly found in the middle classes. Puritanism is earnestness without an objective. The major task of the Anglo-Saxon peoples is to sweat it out of their souls. Marian believes that culture is a voracious capacity for information, but she does not know what the information is for, as she repudiates a life of leisure which is necessary to find its meaning. She believes that leisure should only come at the end of a lifetime of hard work, when a man's brain is exhausted, just as she believes that a man should not marry until he has spent years consolidating his position. That is why the middle classes are superior to us. They have to strive before they can marry, and their children are born after the first fine careless rapture is past, so they too are earnest and striving. But the aristocracy and peasantry can marry young. We are closer to life at the source. That is where we are superior to the middle classes. Marian would like to see the country governed by a horde of officials who had passed the appropriate examinations. I would prefer to have my head cut off by my cousin the King of England than to be bossed about by a *petit bourgeois* prig who had acquired his authority by damned merit. That is illogical perhaps, but it's in my blood. Every man, however fair and candid he may think himself, has a closed corner in his mind where he will not allow the light.

If a ray penetrates this dark place his agony is extreme and he cries out in fury and attacks the man who has directed the light. Because of these dark corners all the fine conceptions we build up must ultimately fall. Marian is always illuminating my dark corner."

"I'm surprised that you admit that," said Lucinda.

"I illuminate hers more painfully," said Paul with satisfaction, "and she has so many of them."

"She'll be very annoyed if you don't declare yourself for or against," said Lucinda, "as she might find herself in agreement with you. Haven't you really any stronger feelings about it? You don't seem quite yourself today."

"I like to see young people happy," said Paul. "That's the most important thing of all to me. If I over-emphasize the feudal grandeur of Crittenden and the Mirevals, it is only a form of self-protection. I have no particular qualifications and very little money. Few men can stand alone. We have to fit ourselves into some group, some religious or political system. With the power of that group behind us we feel that we are strong men, when really we are only plants nailed to a wall. I had to choose the only wall available. Down here in Provence I can stand more easily without it, which is why I have so much more sense of life here. When I return to England long habit makes the wall irresistible to me, and I flatten myself against it for a week or two. On that day we visited Stephen at Cambridge I suffered badly from nostalgia, and felt that I had chosen the wrong life, but I think it was only a momentary aberration. However, what I am trying to say is that I don't want to see Stephen nailed to the wall, just as he is about to flower. Your niece looked to me a golden creature. If they are Aucassin and Nicolette, I'm not going to be the Comte de Beaucaire. If they're crocuses I'm not going to stamp on them."

"I see," said Lucinda, but she added after a pause, "but I'm astonished, all the same. You make me feel a hard, worldly old woman. It is rather shattering when someone, who, one had imagined, was far more wicked and cynical than oneself, proves to be less so."

"Surely my way of living is not that of a worldly cynic?" said Paul.

"Isn't *il faut cultiver notre jardin* the last despairing cry of the cynic?"

"Not at all. That's a shocking interpretation. It's the first gleam of faith."

Lucinda did not quite know in what sense Paul used this word "faith." She looked at him curiously. Although she had heard some peculiar gossip about his morals, which was given color by the photographs of Sir Alexander Portshead and a dozen other engaging lads on his dressing table, she felt that he was in some way protected by the goodness of ancient things, that there was strong in him some natural honor and virtue. At any rate he was kind. He would not hurt a fly, though he would stamp heartily on a slug or a scorpion. Harry, who must know Paul better than anyone, allowed Pierre to spend his time almost exclusively in his company, which was some testimonial to his character.

When they had rested an hour or so they went down to bathe, and Pierre went with them. Lucinda was a little vexed that Paul seemed more to enjoy talking to Pierre than to herself. When she succeeded in engaging his attention Pierre crept down into the water and swam alone to the rocks on the other side of the small bay, which was forbidden. When he arrived he climbed up and danced there, waving triumphantly like a tiny golden monkey in the distance. Paul signed to him to stay there, and he and Lucinda swam across to fetch him back.

"J'ai traversé la baie tout seul," cried Pierre.

"Tu es méchant," said Paul, "reviens à la maison."

"Ah non, monsieur," pleaded Pierre, "tu ne veux pas gâter mon plaisir."

"Je te chasse."

Pierre gave a shriek and jumped into the water where he pretended to be a sinking ship, calling:

"Suis un navire. Je coule! Je coule! Au secours!"

Paul dived in and said he was a submarine. It occurred to Lucinda, as she watched them, that Paul played so naturally with children, not from any conscious impulse of kindness but because he had the nature of a child himself. He was furious at a slight to a wife who didn't exist, and yet he allowed the son of a former Crittenden footman to call him "tu."

At first, when Lucinda came to St Saturnin she had been reminded of Flinders. She continued to come there partly because of this, but then the memories of Flinders became overlaid with memories of her early days at St Saturnin, of Stephen as a boy learning to dive, and of Roland in the cinema saying: "Comme ils sont gentils, ces petits pigeons." However, as she sat on the hot rock, watching Paul and Pierre splashing and fooling in the sea, a memory, like the original writing on a palimpsest to which some chemical has been applied, did show very faintly through the more recent Provençal memories. It was of Bill and Blake IX splashing and fooling below the Tarpeian Rock. Oddly enough Tony had faded out of the picture, and she had one of these moments which she had come to recognize as she grew older, when the recurrence of a condition taught her to accept it as a part of what nowadays was called her "life-style." It seemed to her that it was her fate to sit apart, watching men who were less interested in her than in themselves and their own preoccupations.

In three days she had a telegram from Stephen, and the following morning a letter. Both announced his engagement to Heather.

"Dear Mum," he wrote. "I am engaged to Heather at last. Isn't it marvelous? I really can hardly write intelligibly as I'm so happy. Uncle Bill is quite pleased about it and Aunt Muriel doesn't seem to mind at all, as I was afraid she might. Uncle Bill told me that he and Uncle Arthur had talked about the possibility when he was at Crittenden and they had agreed about it. So that's all right. Will you break the glorious tidings to Paul? But it doesn't matter because I'm sure that when he sees Heather, he'll be delighted. We are coming over, just Heather and I, on Saturday. Heather will stay with us for a week and join Uncle Bill and Aunt Muriel at Marseilles on their way back. That's all right, isn't it? We both send all our love. We've such masses of it. Your loving son, Stephen."

Enclosed with this was a rather stilted little note from Heather. Stephen, when Lucinda met them at the St Saturnin station looked magnificent. He had completely lost his fretful adolescent despondency, and even (the first time she had noticed it in him) had a touch of the noble male assurance of the first Lord Wendale. She thought, "If Heather can bring out this in him, it's well worth it," and she was able to put more affectionate warmth than she had expected into her greeting of her niece, who although she did look extremely pretty, had also the smug but wary look of a cat which has just stolen the cream.

In the evening they dined with Paul. Heather had heard so much about him, that she was prepared to be impressed. No one had mentioned to her how he lived and she thought they were setting out for some Provençal château. She was astonished when they arrived at the tiny villa, which was not unlike places she had visited in Australia, to buy fruit or to obtain hot water for tea when they were on a motor trip. There was a loquat tree growing on a stretch of hard baked earth, a rake, left by Pierre, lay across the path, a piece of old hose trailed bath water on to a bed of brilliant zinnias, and the place had an air of amiable, careless poverty. The dinner table, set under the vines, was colorful with its pottery, fruit and winebottles, but it was a peasant's dinner table, not sparkling with silver and crystal like those to which she was accustomed. Pierre saw them walking up the stony path between the eucalyptus and the hot aromatic fig-tree. He ran into the house calling:

"Monsieur! Monsieur! Ici Monsieur Stephen avec Madame et une très jolie mademoiselle."

Paul imagined that he was able to keep his face like a mask, but however successful he might think himself, his eyes always remained expressive. He was very courteous to Heather, but the temperature when he turned to her fell as rapidly as after a Riviera sunset, so that Lucinda felt sorry for her. His cordiality towards her was almost a form of arrogance, as it completely ignored her inadequate response. Heather was too astonished that such an extraordinary old man should be Stephen's uncle, to be sensitive to these nuances. The affinity which Paul declared existed between the aristocrat and the peasant was very evident in himself. She found him faintly repellent. She had a different impression of him in the few minutes she had seen him talking to Bill on the ship at Marseilles. She had visualized him against an entirely different background. Also, subconsciously she knew that he was not interested in her as a woman, but only as a future member of his family. This she could read in his expressive eyes, which in some moods were like Stephen's, but with a dark unhappy knowledge which Stephen did not possess.

When she had an opportunity after dinner, she suggested to Stephen that they should go for a walk in the garden.

"Shall we all walk down to the port and have drinks at the café?" asked Stephen. "Would you mind, Paul?"

"Not at all," said Paul, who did mind a little. "But I shan't come. It's too much of a climb back again."

"Then, of course, we shan't go," said Stephen.

"Yes, you go. It will be amusing for you."

Stephen apologized again, but went off with Heather.

"How d'you like Paul?" he asked as they went down the hill.

"He's a funny kind of 'honorable,' isn't he?" said Heather.

Stephen puckered his forehead. He didn't know what she meant. Somehow the conversation touched on Lord Fitzauncell.

"Paul doesn't approve of Lord Fitzauncell," said Stephen.

Heather laughed incredulously. It was unmistakable what she thought, that it was ridiculous impertinence of a man like Paul not to approve of anyone so rich, so successful, so famous as Lord Fitzauncell.

Stephen could not face the implication of this laugh. He hurried to embrace her. They were at that stage when physical contact could swamp any merely intellectual disagreement.

Lucinda stayed a little longer, but as Paul seemed tired, she soon went back to her villa.

CHAPTER FIVE

BILL AND MURIEL gave Stephen a further invitation to stay with them at Gleneagles, and with Heather he joined them at Marseilles at the end of the week. There had been no mention yet as to when they were to be married, and Lucinda asked Muriel not to fix any date until she had discussed it with Arthur. She thought Stephen should certainly take his degree first. She was afraid that Bill would interpret this as a part of a scheme to postpone and then break the engagement. When Stephen had left, Lucinda invited her playwright friend, who was at Antibes and short of money, to come and stay at the villa. He accepted with the same suggestion of granting a favor which Hugo had shown them when he dined at home, and Pat when he had agreed to come to Italy. This treatment from men she had also come to accept as part of her "life-style," and all she asked from Wentworth Fox, the playwright, was that he should treat her with the outward forms of civility. He had once failed in these and Lucinda had given him a fright. As she was extremely useful to him, in future he observed more carefully the conditions of their friendship. She knew that Paul disliked him, and his presence at St Saturnin caused a slight discomfort, but this, too, she endured with resignation.

When she returned to London she stayed one night at Catherine Street and left the next morning for Crittenden. In the taxi, on the way to Paddington, she saw Susannah, very festively dressed, but carrying a large basket, walking down a Bayswater side-street, through which the taximan was taking a short-cut. She knocked on the window for him to stop. She left the taxi and ran back to Susannah. From the basket protruded the legs of a roasted chicken, loosely wrapped in grease-proof paper, and the top of a bottle of rum. It also contained some bags of fruit.

"Susannah darling," said Lucinda, "are you going for a picnic? You look terribly *surréaliste*."

Susannah had been unable to let her palatial maisonette and had stayed in London all the summer, as it was cheaper than going away, even on visits. She was apologetic about the basket.

"My charwoman is ill," she said. "I was just taking her a few things."

"But why do you dress for Ascot to take a fowl to your char-woman?"

"I'm going on to luncheon at Windsor."

"I'm going to Crittenden. Can I give you a lift to Paddington?"

"I've plenty of time, thank you, my dear."

"Have you heard the rumor about Stephen?" asked Lucinda.

"And your niece?"

"Oh, you have heard? I hoped you hadn't. I was going to tell you when it was all settled. They are engaged. He's in Scotland with them now."

"I hope they'll be very happy. Is she a pretty girl?"

"Yes, she is. I didn't encourage it, of course," said Lucinda. She did not expect Susannah, any more than Paul, to be pleased at the engagement. She imagined that Susannah, having accepted her as a daughter-in-law, would consider that sufficient exogamy, and would expect Stephen to marry back into one of the historic families.

"Tell me, my dear," said Susannah, wistfully, "has she any money?"

"A bit, I expect," said Lucinda smiling.

Susannah was perceptibly relieved.

"Give them my best love," she said, "and bring her to see me when they are in London."

When the Vanes came back from Scotland, Stephen left them to do more shopping—it was very difficult to know how Muriel and Heather could wear all the clothes they bought—and came down to Crittenden. As a result of the engagement the Vanes were to come there for another week at the very end of September, before they returned to Australia, and Stephen to Cambridge.

Marian was cheerful but chilly in her congratulations to Stephen. After dinner, when they rose to join the ladies, Arthur said to him, "Just come in here a minute, will you, Stephen?" and led the way into the little yellow drawing-room beyond the saloon, avoiding the suggestion of the headmaster's study which the library might convey. He took a cigarette case from the pocket of his purple velvet dinner jacket, and offered Stephen a cigarette, which he refused.

"Your mother, your aunt and myself have been holding a council of war," said Arthur, "well, not of war, rather the opposite, and I have been deputed to deliver to you the findings."

"What are they, sir?" asked Stephen, his face suddenly suffused with emotion.

"Unpalatable, I'm afraid, but reasonable," said Arthur. "We think you should, of course, finish your terms at Cambridge. The engagement should not be announced until you come down, and the marriage take place when Heather returns to England with her parents in two years' time. Your mother thinks Mr Vane will agree with us."

"Oh, I couldn't possibly wait as long at that," exclaimed Stephen. Arthur's eyes twinkled, but he looked grave.

"Well, you must talk to your mother and Aunt Marian. I am only the envoy of greater powers." He rose from the spindly Adam chair on which he had been sitting, put his hand kindly on Stephen's shoulder, and they went up to the peacock room to play bridge. Stephen sat silent and glowering, and twice revoked. Lucinda played with bland efficiency and Arthur with visible patience, as Marian talked all the time about the wickedness of the Labor Party, and of a village woman who had been taken in adultery, and whom Arthur was reluctant to evict from her cottage.

As Lucinda expected, Stephen came to release his indignation upon her at bedtime.

"We couldn't possibly wait two years," he said. "It's madness."

"It won't be two full years," said Lucinda. "It's the autumn now and they'll return the spring after next. It will only be eighteen months. Besides there are other people to consider, darling."

"Who? I'm the one who's being married, aren't I?"

"Yes—and Heather," said Lucinda. "But you have to think of Bill and Muriel. They won't want to rush back to England again next spring."

"I could go out there and be married."

"That's impossible," said Lucinda, curtly. "Arthur and Marian wouldn't like it. Arthur is making your income up to a thousand a year, to balance the amount Bill is settling on Heather. You don't want to put that burden on him too soon."

"He didn't mention it to me," said Stephen.

"He wouldn't. He'd just pay it into your account, and when you thanked him he'd say, 'Oh yes,' as if he'd forgotten it. He might add, 'I hope you'll be able to manage all right.'"

"It's awfully kind of him," said Stephen, wrinkling his forehead, "but I don't want all that money. We'll marry on what I've got, and live at St Saturnin, and if it's not enough I'll earn some money."

"How, darling?"

"I can play the flute jolly well," said Stephen. "I might get a job in an orchestra."

"But there's no orchestra at St Saturnin."

"I could write. Paul writes articles that are published sometimes."

"I don't suppose he makes five pounds a year from them. They are all for cranky papers that don't pay. Paul said to me only the other day, excusing some vulgarity in a man's writing. 'Still, I suppose the poor devil has to earn his living. Thank God I've never had to do that.' He said that at the time of the slump he had lain awake at night sweating to think he might come to it, but that now he hoped the Almighty would preserve him from humiliation to the end. You are too like Paul. Although you appear so plastic you've absorbed all his ultramontane ideas, which cannot possibly be held by anyone who is not economically independent. They are the last aristocratic privilege. You'd never fit into a machine, which is necessary to earn one's living nowadays. With Paul it's pride, but with you, darling, it would be utter incompetence."

"You think I'm no use for anything then?"

"Not at all. What I've just said is to your credit."

"Ever since this began, I've felt as if I were surrounded by cob-webs," said Stephen. "Every conceivable thing is dragged in to hinder me. We're cousins, we're too young, Paul won't approve, and now it's money, of all things."

"Yes, money—of all things," said Lucinda smiling.

"If no one gave us anything, we'd still have about ten times as much as a farm laborer."

"Yes, and Heather spends on one flimsy frock as much as would keep a farm laborer for a year. I'm not a Socialist, but it seems to me indecent to buy five hats in a morning, and to decide in the afternoon that only one of them is fit to wear."

"Heather has seen through that shallow kind of life. She told me that she would like to live simply."

"She hasn't tried it yet," said Lucinda. "Well, darling, if you howl for the moon loud enough perhaps you'll get it. But why go on at me? Aunt Marian fixed the terms. I'll agree to anything for the sake of peace. If I were a good mother I would have packed you off to Mount Athos for the Long Vac, as soon as I saw how the wind lay." She kissed him good-night.

"By the way, Mum," said Stephen, hesitating at the door, "could you lend me a hundred pounds to buy the engagement ring?"

"As a preliminary to the simple life, I suppose," said Lucinda.

Stephen's importunity resulted in the date of the wedding being put forward to July of the following year—after he came down from Cambridge. Marian said:

"I have never known anyone so apparently weak-minded as Stephen to be so successful in getting his own way."

"Nor anyone so mild," added Lucinda, "to cause so much trouble."

Marian endured Muriel for another week at Crittenden, and then they all went up to London. Stephen left for Cambridge two days before the Vanes caught the boat train at Victoria. Lucinda and Heather went to Liverpool Street to see him off. In the taxi on the way back Heather was white-faced and looked as if she had been stricken lifeless. She refused to eat any tea and she stayed in this condition, refusing to eat, for her remaining two days in London. Lucinda thought that after all the marriage might not prove such a mistake.

CHAPTER SIX

STEPHEN, as he came into his rooms in Clare, felt that he had returned to a prison. Everything about them suggested to him a way of life to which, he thought, he would never be able to readjust himself. It was as if he had suddenly moved into air of a different density, and breathing was painful. He flung himself into a chair and sat there for a long time motionless, trying to accustom himself to the idea that Heather was about to leave for the other side of the world, and that it would be more than a year before he saw her again. His whole mind and being were so full of the thought of her that he did not see how he could possibly in that time fill it with the other ideas and facts, which was necessary for him to take his degree. After a while he roused himself and opened his bureau, preparatory to writing to Heather. First he took from his suitcase an enormous leather-framed photograph of her, at which he stared for a long time, and then put away in a drawer, where it would be safe from vulgar scrutiny.

Before sitting down to write he stood for a while, absently looking out of the window towards King's. At that moment the small top-hatted procession came scurrying across King's Bridge. A sudden pain throbbed in Stephen's temples. He watched the procession as it came up past the Provost's Lodge, along by the Gibb building, and disappeared into the chapel. He vaguely tried to distinguish individual choristers but his head hurt him too much. He went back to his bedroom and lay down. He lay there inert, icy, almost as if paralyzed, for two days. A college servant brought a doctor who could make nothing of his condition and said it must be due to concussion. Roland happened to arrive while the doctor was there. He explained that Stephen had suffered before from similar attacks, and that they passed off without ill effects. The doctor was relieved.

He recommended hot bottles and a tonic, for which he left a prescription.

Early on Monday afternoon Roland came in again and found Stephen sitting up, looking rather as if he had just emerged from a chrysalis, but quite articulate and cheerful.

"What brought it on this time?" he asked.

"I'm not sure," said Stephen. "It begins in my head, generally when I am confronted with two ideas which both seem true but which I can't reconcile."

"It would take more than an idea to knock me flat," said Roland.

"Communism is an idea and it's knocked you flat," said Stephen. "Anyhow," he added more seriously, "perhaps it is more than ideas. It's more like two irreconcilable emotions."

By the next day he was quite well again. He wrote to Heather a letter which was far less incoherent with passion than it would have been if he had written it at the hour when he was attacked by his headache.

Hayman came in at tea-time. After an exchange of notes on their vacations, Stephen said, "I'm engaged, you know."

"Really?" said Hayman. "Ah, well, you're that type. Congratulations." Later he asked:

"Are you coming to King's?"

"I may as well." Stephen moved the kettle away from the fire and they went out, clattering down the wooden stairs. He had a mild sense of pleasure at falling back into the routine of his Cambridge life.

As soon as they came in to the huge cool vault of the ante-chapel Stephen felt himself susceptible to the ghosts of the place. The very smell of the building, a faintly acrid mixture of the smell of old stone and possibly some chemical, a polish, or perhaps a protection against destructive insects, made his heart beat more quickly. The great expanses of stained glass were richer in the evening light, and beyond the dark mass of the screen the candles twinkled in the choir-stalls, and the cassocks of two or three choristers arranging books made vivid spots of scarlet.

When he took his former seat beside Hayman, the influences were even more potent, and he felt himself to be an instrument on which they played. He knew, perhaps subconsciously, that if he had come in here on Saturday, before the recurrence of his brief, strange illness, he would have been far more impervious to these influences.

He saw a movement of surplices in the ante-chapel and he turned with a touch of excitement to watch the choir come under the screen. Brian was not anywhere in the procession. The disappoint-

nent which this caused Stephen heightened his emotion. There was
a hush and then the silence was broken by the rising and falling
melody of the antiphon. Stephen had a curious sensation in his skin,
as if it had been stretched too tight and now was returning to its
normal tension. The spirit which informed these soaring arches,
the spirit which had moved to Palestrina and Byrd, seemed to possess
him too. Although Brian was not there, the faces of the other boys
were known to him and he recognized the intonation of their different voices. It was this combination of the familiar with the beautiful
that moved him so strongly, as if in this chapel the things of every-
day life were transfigured.

That absolute tranquillity, that sense of impersonal love which
he had not felt since he went down in June, except on that night
when he sat at his window at Crittenden, returned to him and remained with him long after he had left the chapel. While he was
up at Cambridge he never lost it entirely, but was always able as
it were to tap it, especially by attending King's. Always on entering the chapel he felt that more rapid beating of his heart, as if he
were being adjusted to a different atmosphere.

On the way out he stopped a chorister and asked him where
Brian was. The boy said he had left for his public school. Stephen
asked which house he was in.

"I don't know. I could find out if you like," said the boy, who
seemed anxious to be helpful.

"Oh, thank you," said Stephen, but he never made any attempt
to learn the result of the inquiry.

When Roland had heard by letter that Stephen was engaged he
was astonished. He was now inclined to treat him with envious
respect. They had not met as usual at St Saturnin during the Long
Vac. For the short time when Stephen was there Roland had been
away in Switzerland.

Stephen had a long letter from Heather full of indignation and
love, written shakily in the train between Paris and Marseilles. It
was more emotional in tone than the letter he had written to her,
which puzzled him, as always when they were together it was she
who had been the less demonstrative. He heard from her again
from Port Said, a kind of serial letter written on the ship. A second
letter from Colombo was more sketchy.

Stephen, on the second Sunday of the term, went to tea with
Mrs Cranborne. As she was always so interested in the Vanes and
had also been so kind to him personally, he told her of his engagement to Heather, adding that it was not to be announced till the
following summer.

369

He was surprised at the effect that his news had on her, but attributed it only to a high degree of that sentimental interest which older people sometimes take in the love affairs of the young. She asked him, diffidently, almost as if it were a great favor, to bring Heather to see her if she should come to Cambridge.

The Misses Lanfranc were on the same ship as the Vanes. Lucinda still kept up a desultory correspondence with them and saw them when they came to England. One of them wrote to her on the way out, just before they reached Adelaide. She had no idea that Heather was engaged to Stephen.

"Your niece," she wrote, "is very pretty and very popular, especially with a major in the Ghurkas, who left the ship at Bombay. However, it could not have been as serious as we thought, as since then she has danced a great deal with Tommy Bumpus, who is nearer her own age and I should think a better match."

Lucinda was worried, but then told herself that old maids always interpreted the most trivial gestures as declarations of passion. When Stephen came down for the Christmas vacation she asked him if he had heard from Heather. He replied indifferently:

"Yes, about ten days ago."

Paul came to England for Christmas and they all went down to Crittenden together.

"There was no point in staying at St Saturnin this year," he said, "as they are not going to do the Miracle Play. The Virgin Mary, the sweetest imaginable creature, has had to go for his military service."

At Paddington the train was crowded with school-children returning for the holidays, and even the first-class carriages were rather full. At last they found one with three empty seats together. As she was entering the train, Lucinda noticed a "reserved" label on the next carriage, and she glanced at it in brief curiosity. She was surprised to see through the window Lord Fitzauncell and a secretary. She had imagined that he would always travel down by car. Their eyes met and she smiled and bowed. When they were settled in their seats he appeared at the door into the corridor, and asked if they would like to come into his carriage where there was more room. Lucinda knew that Paul would rather travel in the dog-box than with Lord Fitzauncell, and she said:

"Oh, thank you. It's awfully kind of you, but we are settled comfortably now, I think." She was embarrassed, as Paul was looking stonily out of the window, and it made her voice sound stilted. Lord Fitzauncell said nothing but returned to his own compartment. There was something in his expression and attitude as he

moved away from the door that made her feel that this had happened before. In a train . . . a man by a door. . . .

"It's incredible!" she exclaimed quietly.

"What is?" asked Stephen.

"I've just remembered something. I've been trying to remember
it for years." She began to laugh.

"What is it?" said Paul.

"I can't possibly tell you. You'd tell everybody and let me in for
an action for slander. I've no proof—only my memory, but I think
it is accurate this time."

"If you weren't going to tell us, you shouldn't have mentioned
it," said Paul.

"I know, but I can't possibly tell you here," she replied.

The Christmas at Crittenden was much the same as usual, a little
enlivened by Paul. Lucinda was thankful that Stephen did not seem
to be moping unduly for Heather, and rather wished that she had
insisted on the marriage being postponed for another year. She
had the power to do so as under Hugo's will she could withhold
his income from Stephen until he was twenty-five. But she knew
very well that she had a strain of levity which made her incapable
of solemnly using any power she held, especially financial power,
unless it were to protect herself from discomfort.

In the Lent term Stephen began to work hard for his tripos. He
wrote once a week to Heather, and went more often to King's,
but not every day. He had returned to the feeling which he had
had before last summer, that his Cambridge life was his normal
life, and he took part in undergraduate activities which in the autumn
term he had looked upon as transitory and adolescent. As the spring
advanced, the crocuses in Trinity were followed in the Easter term
by the daffodils in King's, and then by the flowering cherries, the
lilac and the chestnut bloom, until the river, under its successive
gray bridges, flowed through one long garden from Silver Street
to Magdalen. Stephen felt a growing excitement. Sometimes, as he
lay reading on the river bank, he would come across a passage which
condensed for him the emotions awakened by the advancing spring,
and by the now more insistent awareness that he was to be married
in a few months. In King's Chapel, when the boys' voices rose in
some clear and perfect cadence, he felt that this too was linked
with the beauty of the outside world and with his love for Heather,
and in these moments the joy of living was almost more than he
could bear.

On his last night up at Cambridge he dined with Roland in the
town. Roland, whose intensity of affection for his friends made him

sulky when he believed that it was not fully returned, was inclined to be silent and moody. He seemed annoyed that Stephen was not more depressed at this end of a phase in their lives.

"We'll often meet at St Saturnin," said Stephen. Roland did not reply.

After dinner they went to listen to the madrigals sung under King's Bridge. They had a brief discussion as to where they should go. Stephen wanted to listen from Clare Bridge, as he said that sound traveled over water.

They heard the first madrigal from there, but the sound was very faint. The river banks between the two bridges were crowded, and it was difficult to tell where the water began as the crowd spread from the banks down into the punts which lined them. Stephen and Roland walked round by Queens' Road into King's, and inserted themselves into the crowd as close as possible to the bridge.

It was growing dusk. The turrets of the chapel had turned from pale gold to an aerial gray. The sky above them was remote and clear. The crowd was hushed except for a woman just behind Roland, who talked to her friend all through the singing, saying:

"Isn't it a nice evening for it? I'm so glad that it's fine. It would have been dreadful if it had rained."

Stephen edged away so that he would not hear her voice. This movement gave Roland an opportunity to express his general discontent. He said, "I'll see you at the station tomorrow," and went off to a drinking party to which Stephen had not been invited.

When the singers came to their last madrigal, their interlocked punts were released and poled slowly down the stream. As they floated between the darkening trees and the dreaming chapel they sang into the cool evening air "Draw on sweet night."

There was a movement as the crowd began to follow the singers downstream. Suddenly on the opposite bank, in the dim light of a lantern, Stephen had a glimpse of a boy's face. He was certain that it was Brian, though he did not see how Brian, if he were at a public school, could be in Cambridge in the middle of term. Stephen hurried across the river, pushing his way through the crowd on the bridge, but when he arrived at the spot where he had seen the boy there was no sign of him, and though he walked about among the people for some time he did not find him.

He went back to his rooms in Clare. He did not turn on a light, but sat in the window seat, watching the last of the crowd disappear from the grounds of King's. He sat there for a long time until the place was deserted, save for an occasional dark figure passing the Provost's lodge. The great lawn was tranquil in a twilight which came not only from an afterglow in the western sky and from the brilliant stars, but from the more friendly lights in college windows. Then the moon rose and caught first of all the finials on the chapel turrets. The warm silver light crept down the side of each turret so that it shone softly as if of a different substance from the dark shadowed stone. That feeling which Stephen had so often experienced, that the chapel had a spiritual life of its own, independent of the people who came to it, returned to him more strongly than ever before. He watched the light descend on this place which to him seemed built to express and receive light. As the moon rose higher it caught the buildings opposite, touching their Victorian gothic with faint magic, until at last a slowly moving tide of light advanced across the lawn below him. As he watched, he found it difficult and painful to realize that this was the last night he would sit in these windows. He crossed the room and looked out at the bridge. The moonlight made a sharp pattern of the balustrade on the path across it. In their shadow the stone balls were elongated to ovals. Whenever he remembered Cambridge he thought the two things which would at once flash into his mind would be Clare Bridge and King's Chapel.

Before going to bed he went to have one more look at the chapel. In his mind's eye he saw the small black procession come out, pass Gibb's building, and go across the bridge. He would never see it again, at any rate not from these windows, and yet it would go on for years, perhaps centuries, a different procession yet appearing the same—never wholly changed at once, a few boys leaving each summer, a few new ones taking their places. That was like the whole life of Cambridge. New blood passed constantly through its veins.

He was part of the receding tide. He knew many undergraduates who spoke impatiently of their life here, and longed for the day when they would go down. They wanted to be recognized as full-grown men, no longer pupils haunted by examinations. At times when he thought of Heather he had shared their feeling, but tonight this impatience had entirely left him.

When he first came up, Cambridge had made such a strong impression on him that he had almost anywhere in the colleges that feeling which was strongest in King's Chapel, that the influences of the place were radiated from the stones of the buildings, as the stored heat was radiated from a garden wall in the evening at St Saturnin. In this city of palaces, built not for the aggrandizement of individuals but as centers of learning, the pervading spirit was more sympathetic to him than that of any place he knew, even more than that of Crittenden. It was not an arrogant claim but a simple fact that here and to Oxford for seven centuries had come the greater number of the imaginative and intelligent youth of the country to spend its most ardent years. There had been a proportion of brutes and fools amongst them, as there must be in any large gathering of men. Yet it seemed to him as if this eternally renewed flow of youth, all these bright spirits passing unceasingly through these courts and halls and chapels, had left in them the echo of their hopes, so that they were not like places sacred because there the dead were buried, but sacred because there the spirit lived.

CHAPTER SEVEN

STEPHEN AND HEATHER were married at St. Mark's, North Audley Street, at the end of July. For the six weeks between the Vanes' arrival and the marriage Stephen went about almost laughing with delight. He followed Heather with docility into dress shops, theatres and restaurants, and when they were alone together he made love to her. He agreed to everything everyone suggested and only asserted his own will when it came to choosing the best man. He insisted on having Roland.

"Oh, I thought Lord Wendale would be best man," said Muriel.

"Why?" asked Stephen.

"He's your nearest male relative of about your own age."

"Baa's years older than I am," said Stephen, "and I hardly ever see him. Roland has been my closest friend since we were seven."

"Who are his people?"

"They live at St Saturnin. They grow jolly good wine."

"Perhaps Roland won't have the clothes, darling," said Lucinda, "and he won't want to have them made just for one occasion."

"He's going to hire them from Moss Brothers," said Stephen, grinning.

"But how dreadful if anyone should find out!" exclaimed Muriel. "Are his people known in society?"

"He got a first in Natural Science," said Stephen.

"We could hardly put that in *The Times*," said Muriel. She wondered why Lucinda laughed, as she had not intended to be amusing. Lucinda, faintly smiling, hovered on the outskirts of all the preparations. Muriel spoke as solemnly of the details of the wedding as if they had as much hierarchical significance as the coronation of a King of France or Hungary.

The wife of an ex-governor of Victoria had lent her house in Park Street for the reception. Stephen and Heather were to spend a month's honeymoon on the Continent and then return to Crittenden, where they were to live at the End House, which was being vacated by Major Boothby. Stephen was to learn to be Arthur's agent, so that when he inherited the estate he would understand its workings. All of Lucinda's furniture which would not go into the Catherine Street house, which was the larger part of it, was taken out of storage at Balham and sent back to the End House. Muriel and Heather had bought some reproduction Queen Anne pieces at Harrods to supplement it, and new curtains and covers in off-white and beige. Muriel went down there after the wedding and bickered urbanely with Marian over the arrangement. As Marian grew older she grew more Old Testament in her idiom, and even less sensitive about other people's feelings. She said that the off-white satin made the drawing-room look like "a harlot's boudoir." The engraving of the first Lord Wendale was hung over the dining-room mantelpiece. Lucinda when she came down to inspect the result had a slight shock when she saw it there.

Stephen and Heather returned from the Continent simply bursting with life and good spirits. Lucinda could not help laughing when she saw them, particularly Stephen, who had quite lost his airy diffidence, and had developed a likeness to the first Lord Wendale, that look of benevolent arrogance, which conveyed that life was full of pleasures, and that it was in the natural order that he should enjoy the larger part of them. He no longer hesitated to express his opinion nor did things he disliked simply to please other people, and when he refused he did so with amiable courtesy, not, as when formerly he had screwed himself up to resist an imposition, with uneasy and too abject apology. An example of this was when Arthur said something to him about buying a hunter. Before his marriage he would either have unwillingly followed Arthur's suggestion, or, if he had refused, have gone about for days feeling guilty and depressed at having displeased his uncle. Now he said blandly, "I don't intend to hunt, sir."

Arthur told Marian. "What utter nonsense!" she said.

The next night they all dined at Crittenden House, and the Greene-Jameses were there.

"What is this idiocy about your not hunting, Stephen?" Marian asked loudly, before everybody.

At one time Stephen would have trembled and swayed like a daffodil before this strong breeze of opinion.

"I don't want to," he said calmly.

"What are you going to do with yourself in the winter?"

"I shall play my flute."

"Gosh!" exclaimed Marian, and Willy Greene-James, whose little elephant-eyes had not forgotten the incident of his hunting breeches, gave a suppressed snort which, Lucinda gathered, was meant to convey that Stephen was failing in his duty to the country.

"*Chacun à son goût*," she said. "After all, Willy, Stephen doesn't expect you to play the flute with him."

She was delighted at Stephen's self-assurance, and thought that if Heather could do this for him he could not have made a better match.

Heather smoothed things over with Arthur and Marian, not intentionally, but because she enjoyed it, by herself riding to hounds. They became more than reconciled to the marriage and praised Heather to their friends. Marian said that she was "straight as a die" and that "as long as she rides to hounds she'll keep out of mischief." When the Bassingbournes came on their autumn visit, she took them over to tea at the End House, and Lady Bassingbourne said when she was leaving, "I shall tell all the young men I know to marry Australians."

Towards Christmas Stephen became worried about money. He had imagined that with two thousand a year between them, he and Heather would be very well off, after the few hundreds which were his undergraduate's income, but he found that he had less to spend on himself than ever before. Apparently it simply did not occur to Heather not to buy anything which caught her eye. After a few days in London she had overdrawn her account and had nothing to show for it except a slight increase in her already enormous wardrobe. Stephen had to lend her something to go on with, and to pay what he could of the household bills from his personal allowance. Heather said carelessly:

"I'll write to daddy. Can't you borrow something from Lord Crittenden?"

Stephen was worried, not only at his inability to meet all his bills, but at Heather's not being able to see the impossibility of asking Arthur for a loan. Heather was cross with him because he would not do this, and because his Christmas presents were almost childishly inexpensive.

In spite of this Stephen very much enjoyed Marian's Christmas party. It was as usual on Boxing Day and was also his birthday party. It was no longer a children's party, but a dinner in the evening. The younger neighbors were invited, including some boys and girls of seventeen and eighteen. With the dessert a large cake was brought in, decorated with twenty-two lighted candles. Mussolini, with the approval of Marian, Lord Fitzauncell and his other English admirers had this year administered the antidote of poison gas to the Abyssinian slave-trade.

After dinner they did charades. Marian took part in these with gusto and gave them an amusingly academic flavor. In one scene he was that Countess of Salisbury who refused to kneel down to have her head cut off. Heather stood apart, looking on as if these pastimes were too unspeakably adolescent. She and Stephen were invited to a party at Fitzauncell Castle and she was impatient to go there. It was barely ten o'clock when she said to Stephen:

"Let's go to Fitzauncell now."

"We can't possibly leave yet, darling," said Stephen, giving her as he had done once or twice since their marriage, a glance of puzzled scrutiny. The look in his eyes on these occasions gave her an unpleasantly empty feeling. She made a half-hearted effort to join the charades.

At eleven o'clock Marian began to pack up the party. Stephen, in gratitude for Heather's joining in the games, hurried off with her to Fitzauncell, driving the four miles in five minutes. Even this did not quite dispel Heather's bleak expression.

The courtyard of the castle was flood-lit and full of polished expensive cars, so that it looked something like a motor show.

At one end of the enormous modern hall was a giant Christmas tree, covered with tinsel and electric candles. At the other end a London band was playing dance music. Heather's eyes brightened and she almost seemed to sniff the air. The crowd of guests was composed of politicians and journalists staying in the castle, and of country neighbors like the Greene-Jameses, whose attitude to Lord Fitzauncell was a mixture of contempt for his origins and respect for someone whose name was known to every child above the age of ten in the Empire, and who had done more than any other living man to corrupt the decent instincts of the English people, including themselves.

Baa saw them arrive and greeted them genially. He asked Heather to dance with him and led her away. Stephen went to shake hands with his host. Lord Fitzauncell was most affable. He put his arm across Stephen's shoulder and brought him up to a cabinet minister, who had arrived at his position by methods as doubtful as Lord Fitzauncell's own. Stephen found it hard not to shudder at this embrace. The cabinet minister was impressively patronizing. Stephen had absorbed most of Paul's social and political ideas. He was also like Paul in that he unconsciously revealed through his eyes far more than he knew. He imagined that he was giving the minister a proper polite attention, but he appeared the very embodiment of aloof aristocratic distaste, which was aggravated by his youth. The minister felt as if he were addressing an empty hall. He suddenly grunted and turned away. Afterwards he asked Lord Fitzauncell, "Who is that damned boy?"

Baa introduced Heather to a man named Maurice Ablett. He was reputed to hold a number of shares in the Straker newspapers and often came down to Fitzauncell. Heather had already met him once or twice in the hunting field. He was dark, stockily built, with a sanguine complexion and cheerful manner. They had spoken to each other while waiting for hounds to draw a covert, but they had not hitherto been introduced.

"Now I know your name," said Heather, as Baa left them.

"I knew yours already," said Ablett. "I asked Fitz. Are you alone?"

"My husband's here. He's gone off with Lord Fitzauncell."

"Then you come off with me."

"Where to?" asked Heather, laughing and feeling excited.

"Come and look at the baronial pile."

In the furnishing of the old part of the castle Lord Fitzauncell had given way to his ideas of the mediaeval. It was like an American film of the reign of Henri Quatre. There were Renaissance chairs, Cromwellian tables and Empire beds. Ablett led Heather along mysterious corridors and up stone flights of stairs into a vaulted chamber with iron wall-lights and Flemish tapestries. He arranged some velvet cushions on a gothic chest and sat beside her.

"What have you been doing with yourself since I saw you last?" he asked.

"Nothing," said Heather. "There's not much to do at Crittenden."

"What a waste of you—to be doing nothing."

"You're frightfully impudent," she said, smiling.

"That's my technique."

"What d'you mean?"

"One must have a technique of getting to know people. What's yours?"

"I haven't one."

"I expect it's subconscious."

"Are you terribly clever?"

"I am rather. Don't you admire cleverness?"

"No."

"D'you admire stupidity?"

"Of course not. But one of Stephen's uncles is clever. He lives

378

in a poky little house in France and is depressing about everything."

"I don't suppose he's clever—sounds merely high-brow."

"Does your technique always work?" she asked casually.

"Generally. When my verbal impudence has come off I try other sorts of impudence."

"Oh!"

"My technique is like Hitler's. Tell people what you intend to do. They become so frightened that they put up with it. Good man, Hitler."

He asked her when she was coming up to London, and they talked about that and general subjects for a while. Baa came into the room with an extraordinary sophisticated looking woman with an aquiline nose, bleached hair, a white dress and emeralds.

"Hullo," he said, amused but not altogether pleased at finding Heather with Ablett. He was annoyed with himself for having introduced them. Wherever he might stray himself he did not care for the circle of his relatives to be tarnished by similar associations, in the same way that Louis XIV would not allow an illegitimate provincial cousin to marry one of his richest and most powerful ministers, who had risen from the people.

"Stephen is looking for you," he said untruthfully to Heather.

"We'd better go and find him," said Ablett, but he did not go back to the ballroom. He opened a door at the end of a long passage and they were immediately transported from the middle ages into a room glittering with tubular chromium furniture and with telephones. On a long desk in the middle of the room stood a large signed photograph of Hitler.

"This," he said, "is where Fitz decides who shall be the next prime minister but three. And here," he said, indicating the photograph, "is the other man who knows how to treat the masses—the model of my technique."

"But I'm not the masses," said Heather.

"By Jove, you're not," said Ablett and turning his back on the desk with the photograph, he took her in his arms and kissed her violently on the lips. She lay in his arms for a moment and then said:

"Wouldn't Lord Fitzauncell mind if he found us in here?"

When Stephen saw Heather come into the crowded, lighted room, his heart gave a jump, she looked so lovely and radiant. It was worth while going to parties, he thought, if it brought this expression back to her face. He made his way across the floor and asked her to dance with him, which she did, but as he put his arm round her she lost her radiant expression, and looked as she had when she was taking part in the charades at Crittenden.

"We won't dance if you don't want to," said Stephen wretchedly.

"I don't mind," said Heather.

They went on till the music stopped.

"Shall we go home?" asked Stephen, as she did not seem any longer to be enjoying the party.

"We've only just arrived," snapped Heather. "We don't often go to a real dance."

She did not want to go home till she had danced again with Ablett. She achieved this and after the dance he took her to a more secluded sitting-out place, where they stayed, cutting the next two dances. They returned separately to the ballroom.

Stephen and Heather left the castle at four o'clock in the morning. He was utterly dispirited. She had the excuse of fatigue not to speak on the way home. Actually, her body was not over-tired, while her mind was buzzing with excitement. Not only Maurice Ablett, but Fitzauncell Castle, with its atmosphere of power and wealth, excited her. Dimly she felt that to be embraced by a man not her husband, while leaning against the very desk at which policies were formed and from which governments were threatened, was seeing life. Ablett had a look in his eye to which something in herself, the world and the flesh, immediately responded. That look of innocence in Stephen, which had begun to irritate her, was entirely lacking in him. She found at Fitzauncell and in Ablett what she had expected but failed to find at Crittenden and in Stephen. She had expected Crittenden to be a super-Tourella, a place where wealth was evident and where there was a continual bustle of parties, with numbers of very good cars waiting in the drive, but in these respects it was dull compared with her own home.

As she lay awake thinking over the events of the night, she felt that her marriage instead of improving her lot, was smothering the promise of her life, and that the Brayfords were trying to turn her into a kind of country vicar's wife. She felt that they demanded of her some renunciation, a clipping of her life to fit their obsolete patterns, a dimming of her bright color so that she should be unconspicuous among their faded legacies. She had not married to practice renunciation and she was furious at the demand. She began to plan to get Stephen away from Crittenden, to live in London. She fell asleep imagining Maurice Ablett's arms around her.

In the new year he came down more often to Fitzauncell, and Heather met him out hunting. Twice they lost the hunt and spent an hour or two together over tea in a farmhouse.

Stephen sensed a change in Heather's attitude towards him. One morning, before she rode off to a meet on the Greene-Jameses' lawn, she was particularly cold in her manner, not angry, but faintly contemptuous. Stephen was angry, and Mr Digby, the agent, with whom he spent the morning, was depressed at his lack of intelligence. Stephen felt that he must be to blame for Heather's attitude, that he must have done something to offend her, or perhaps had been too possessive. In the afternoon he went for a walk up on the common, where Lucinda had gone to resolve her problem sixteen years or more earlier. Now the distant landscape faded into gray mist, but the buildings of Crittenden were more visible behind the bare trees. It was very still up on the common and tiny specks of moisture clung to the gorse bushes. The rhythm of walking and the peace of the countryside restored his equability. He thought that lately he had only loved Heather for the pleasure she could give him, that he had wanted to drag her beauty into himself and own it, instead of worshipping it as a separate creation, existing in its own right. He thought that perhaps he had not sufficiently respected her individuality and that she resented this. He was so relieved at having found the cause of their misunderstanding that he bounded down the hill back to the End House.

Heather came in late. She was going straight up to her room but Stephen intercepted her in the hall. This was the second afternoon when with Maurice she had lost the hunt. Her eyes were sparkling and she had that look of intense vitality which he had noticed on his birthday, when she had returned to the ballroom at Fitzauncell Castle. This, coming immediately on top of his new resolutions, his own recovered and purified love, filled him with unspeakable joy.

"For God's sake don't gape at me like that," snapped Heather, and she went upstairs.

In the evening she made an effort to atone for this. She had no deliberate intention of quarreling with him, but she could not control the direction in which her passionately aroused emotions were leading her. She tried to talk to him of his interests, but she was uncertain what they were. Hitherto they had been drawn together by love-making and by the arbitrary fusion of interests which comes to two people who settle in the same house.

A few days after this King George V died. Heather had a note from Maurice inviting her and Stephen to see the funeral procession from his windows at the top of Park Lane. Stephen was reluctant to go. He had always disliked occasions of mass emotion, and he had a prejudice against accepting invitations from people he hardly knew, a prejudice strengthened by the fact that he had met Ablett at Fitzauncell. This was not merely Pauline snobbery, but a dislike of accepting favors from people who he had been to led to believe were unprincipled and vulgar, while a too easy friend-liness with strangers, unless there was some evident common in-terest or attraction, seemed to him to diminish the quality of one's tried and enduring affections. It was only when his reluctance to go to Ablett's flat had brought himself and Heather to the verge of an open quarrel, that he agreed to accept the invitation.

The experience was even more disagreeable than he had antic-ipated. Ablett appeared to be very rich. There were a dozen people invited to his spacious rooms, none of whom the Brayfords knew. Cocktails were served discreetly to fortify them against the depress-ing sight of the cortège. Stephen was used to the society of old rich people, but with young rich people he was embarrassed as he could not afford, nor did he want to share their tastes and pastimes. Heather expanded in this society.

Everyone chattered cheerfully, and although the party was free from the sentimentality of the lower orders, as the procession passed below, some of the mass emotion rose to moisten the eyes of one or two of the smart women at Ablett's windows. Stephen hated it. He felt that grief, if it were real, demanded privacy. Perhaps in the crowd below there was some element of genuine sympathy, but in these rooms, filled with cigarette smoke and the smell of gin and Paris perfumes, the touch of feeling, real or assumed, was nauseat-ing. Heather, in her smart black dress, was affected by it. She sensed that Stephen was aloof from it and, with a quiet viciousness that surprised herself, told him that he was cold-blooded. In this ac-cusation was contained far more than a criticism of his attitude to the late king. It struck at the root of their life together.

Ablett took her to the end window, from which they could see the funeral procession, with its escort of scarlet troops, crawl through the dense black crowds into the gray winter dreariness of the Edgware Road.

"Now that you've found your way here," he said, "I'll expect you to come again."

"When?" asked Heather.

Two weeks after this, when they were back at Crittenden, Stephen went into the county town one afternoon on business connected with the estate. Heather was out hunting.

There was a place about three miles from Crittenden where the road turned a sharp corner. Just here a ride was cut into the wood which flanked the road. It was getting dusk and Stephen had switched on his headlights. As he turned the corner the beams shot up the ride. Amid the gray-green and brown of the winter wood he had a brief glimpse of a vivid pink coat. He pretended to himself to think that someone had had an accident, but he knew that a deeper curiosity was aroused. He stopped the car and walked up the ride. Two horses were tethered to trees. One was Heather's hunter Pollyanna. A few yards away Heather and Ablett were closely embraced, too engrossed with each other to notice Stephen's approach until he cracked a dry stick with his foot, when they turned quickly to face him. For a moment no one spoke. Then Heather said in a strained voice, defiant with fright:

"Well—now you know."

Stephen was stunned by the situation. It was too much for him to take in immediately, and his body acted conventionally and independently of his real feelings.

"It's too late to keep the horses out," he said. He turned and walked back to his car. He was like someone who has been badly wounded, who sees the gash in his side and knows that soon it will begin to hurt, but at the moment his nerves are numbed by the shock. In this respite before his suffering began, it occurred to him that he was behaving as Arthur might, and he had almost a sense of satisfaction at doing so.

He drove the rest of the way home in this numb condition, but when he had put the car away and come into the drawing-room, and a maid came in to put more wood on the fire, to draw the curtains and to ask him if he would wait for tea till Heather came in, he began to realize the implications of what had happened.

He said that he did not want any tea. The maid looked surprised and left the room. Stephen walked up and down. He wondered if this was an isolated incident, the result of their finding themselves alone together. Even so it was dreadful—extraordinary. He could not imagine himself wanting to kiss anyone but Heather. If it was that, a single incident, he would try to get over it, to forgive it. He would have to, to save their life together. But Heather had said, "Well, now you know." What did she mean by that? He waited with increasing anger, misery and impatience for her return. Anyhow she would have to give up hunting. It was a disgusting pastime for a woman. He still remembered the day when Willy Greene-James had rubbed part of the fox's hot, stinking corpse on his face.

Heather kept her two hunters in the Crittenden stables, where they were fed and tended by Arthur's grooms. On hunting days she left her car there and in the evening drove back the short distance to the End House. Normally she put her car in the old coach house which they used as a garage and came in at the side door, but this evening she drove to the front door and left it there. Stephen's heart beat violently as he waited for her to come into the drawing-room, but instead she ran upstairs. When he felt that he would be able to speak coherently he followed her up. He went to his dressing-room and knocked on the communicating door into the bedroom. There was no reply. He turned the handle but the door was locked. He heard a movement in the bedroom.

"Heather!" he said. There was no reply. He called again.

"What d'you want?" Her voice was distant and impatient.

"Let me in."

"I'm changing."

"How long will you be?"

"I don't know."

He stood irresolute and then sat down on the bed. He heard her opening and closing drawers. After a while the sounds of move-ment stopped. He went out on to the landing and found her quietly closing the bedroom door behind her. She had changed into a coat and skirt and was wearing a hat, and she was carrying a small suit-case. When she saw him the expression in her eyes was repellent. Shame, fear, hostility, repudiation were all fused into a determina-tion to go her own way.

"Where are you going?" he asked.

"It doesn't matter to you."

"Of course it does. There's a good deal to be explained."

When he was alone, thinking about her, he was upset and ap-prehensive, but as soon as he began to talk with her he found that he was calm and almost matter-of-fact.

"You had your explanation—this afternoon."

"You can't be so childish."

"Me? Childish?" She was astonished and contemptuous.

"You've no idea what you're doing," said Stephen.

The parlormaid came out into the hall below.

"You can't make a scene here," said Heather in a low voice, and taking her suitcase she went downstairs.

"Oh, madam," said the maid, "shall I bring in the tea?"

"I don't want any tea," said Heather. "I have to go to London."

The maid came forward to take her suitcase, but Stephen said, "I will take it," and he followed Heather out to her car. The whole situation struck him as fantastic. He could hardly believe that it was serious, and he muttered angrily:

"This is quite idiotic."

She opened the door of her car and sat, waiting for him to put in her suitcase.

"I shan't give it to you," he said.

"Very well. I shall go without it." She pulled the starter and pressed the accelerator to drown any further conversation. Stephen leaned into the car and switched off the engine.

"Listen, Heather," he said. "You can't wreck your life because of one incident. It was pretty awful for me, but I know these things do happen. Everyone isn't made the same. It can be explained away. Can't you see I'm simply longing for you to explain it away? You're like a child that's broken a tea-cup and runs away from home in fright."

The tone of his voice, the look in his eyes, produced in her a softening of determination, a division which she found intolerable.

"You madden me," she said viciously, and, turning the key, she tugged the starter again. There was the same note in her voice as when, at King George's funeral, she had told him that he was cold-blooded. This time the blow struck home. He felt far worse than when he had found her with Ablett in the wood. He was forced to recognize that she had some deep-seated antipathy to him, and his nerves were not, as then, partially deadened by shock.

He put her suitcase on the seat beside her. Heather slammed the door and started the car with a jolt. Stephen stood watching it until he could only see the tail-light disappearing like a red glow-worm towards the London road.

He spent the evening writing her a long letter, putting, as he thought, every aspect of the case before her, but when he had finished it he realized that he did not know where to send it. He went to bed alone, for the first time for seven months. The room was full of Heather's presence and he found it hard to realize that she would not return in a few minutes.

When he had been engaged to her, in the few weeks just before their marriage, if he awoke in the night and thought of her he was so conscious of her individuality that she seemed almost to be there with him. Sometimes during the day, it might be in Catherine Street just before dinner, when he was bathed and dressed, waiting to go out with her, for a moment he would feel her presence which seemed to touch him and then be gone, leaving him with an intensified awareness of his happiness. An odd thing was that different parts of his body felt this presence, as if it were just now his arm or his shoulder where she had been. One night this feeling had been so strong that it had been as if a soft light, a living flame of love, had been burning in his heart. It had been so intense that he was sure that this flame was also in Heather, burning in him and in her at the same time, divine and eternal, so that they were one person, their hearts beating with one pulse.

When they were married this feeling became not perhaps more intense but more tangible, as if the fibres of her being ran through his own body. He still felt as if she possessed him in this way, but as if the fibres of her being which had given him strength and peace, which from time to time had quickened his life to sheer ecstasy, had now become corrosive and remained to torment him.

He cried aloud in the night, "O God, draw out her fibres from my body! O God, release my body from her dead spirit!"

CHAPTER EIGHT

Lucinda was rather pleased with herself and with life. It was one of those February mornings which make one think that the spring is much closer than it really is. She was going to lunch with Wentworth Fox at l'Ecu de France, and for once he had invited her and she would not have to pay. He had just had a short story accepted and a play read on the wireless. It was reassuring to know that he would pay when he could, and that their association was not only due to the fact that she could provide free meals. She did not mind so much now about the actual money, as when Arthur had made such a generous settlement on Stephen Fred had been rather piqued, and to assert himself as Grand Financier he had restored Lucinda's income to its pre-slump level. Altogether Stephen's marriage had not been so unsatisfactory.

As it was such a bright morning she set out to walk across the Green Park to Jermyn Street, but she had just come out of the house when she saw Stephen carrying the suitcase, coming towards her.

"Darling," she said, "I didn't know you were coming up. Couldn't you find a taxi?"

"I came by underground to Victoria."

"Where's Heather?"

"I don't know."

"You don't know! Is she in London?"

"She's left me, Mum."

His woebegone face, his untidy hair, the intonation of his voice as he said "Mum" and somehow the fact that he had carried his suitcase from the underground made her feel towards him as she had a few years earlier, when he had become involved in some boyish scrape or difficulty which had appeared to him insuperable, but which she had been able to smooth out with a little diplomacy.

"Oh, nonsense!" she said. "Come and tell me what's happened."

She opened her bag, took out her latch-key and they went up to her tiny drawing-room. Stephen put his suitcase on a petit-point chair.

"Darling, do put that on the landing," said Lucinda. "When did it happen and how?"

Stephen told her that since Christmas Heather had seemed different in her manner towards him, and of the events of last night.

"If she has gone to this Ablett," asked Lucinda, "would you have her back, that is, if she'd come?" She felt that this question sounded cynical and immoral, but if Stephen and Heather were divorced Stephen would become a problem again. She was sure that he would not go on living at the End House and learning to be Arthur's agent if he were demarried, as she called it. She would be given the awkward job of breaking the news to Arthur and Marian. The End House would once more be evacuated. Stephen would have to find something to do. Even her own income might be reduced again by Fred, not that she would take these things into account if it were a question of Stephen's happiness. But it really would be a complete and widespread mess-up. And only eighteen months ago he was giving her bedtime harangues at Crittenden, demanding that she should bring about this marriage. Sometimes she felt that Stephen was like a weight she had to carry, and just as she thought she had handed it to someone else, back it came, heavier than before. However, she was coming to accept it with resignation, and even to handle it with efficiency.

"You know I would," said Stephen in reply to her question.

"Well, we'd better find out where she is," said Lucinda. "Where does this man Ablett live?"

"In Park Lane. We went there to watch King George's funeral."

Lucinda pulled the blue volume of the telephone book from under her writing table and ran her finger down the A's.

"Is he Maurice Ablett?" she asked.

"Yes, I think so."

She took up her pale green telephone and dialed a number.

"May I speak to Mr Ablett?" she said to a manservant who answered the telephone. "It is Mrs Brayford speaking."

In a very short time a voice said, "Hullo, darling."

"It is Mrs Hugo Brayford speaking," said Lucinda coldly. "Perhaps you could tell me the whereabouts of my daughter-in-law."

Ablett was too taken aback to do anything but give the name of an hotel off Sloane Street.

"Thank you," said Lucinda, and with a rather feline smile she put down the receiver.

"Apparently she hasn't thrown her hat over the windmill yet," she said. "You'd better go and fetch her." She told Stephen the name of the hotel.

"You're marvelous, Mum," said Stephen, his eyes moist with gratitude. "D'you think she'll come?"

"Darling, that depends on you. I can't do everything," said Lucinda irritably.

"When will you be back from your lunch party?"

"I don't know." She had hoped to spend the afternoon with Wentworth Fox.

"By three o'clock?" he asked anxiously.

"Oh, very well." She rang up for a taxi as now it was too late to walk.

She was distrait during lunch and could not give her attention to the very good food. Wentworth, for once her host, was being manly and impressive in a way which she would have found touching if she had been able to give him her full attention. So much depended on whether Stephen could persuade Heather to return to him that she was glad now that she had said she would be back early. When she was younger, during the years of her association with Pat, she had not let her duty to Stephen interfere much with her desires and pleasures. Now, apparently, she had to compensate for this by having her equanimity and her nice little arrangements upset by his demands for help.

Someone had said that if we did not get what we liked we came to like what we got. As she turned into Catherine Street just after three o'clock, she found, to her surprise, that the faint weight of anxiety which she felt about Stephen, though far from pleasurable, was tolerable in its familiarity.

He was waiting in the drawing-room. His shoes were dusty, his hair more untidy than ever and he looked almost haggard.

"What's happened?" she asked

"She wouldn't see me," said Stephen, "but I knew she was in. The hall porter telephoned up to her. So I waited outside the hotel."

"How dreadful!" said Lucinda, shocked at the idea of Stephen hanging about outside the hotel like some kind of tout or detective. "Well, it doesn't matter. Go on."

"At last she came out. She was furious when she saw me. She wouldn't listen to anything I had to say. She got into a taxi and slammed the door. I couldn't do anything. She must hate me."

He sat down and put his head in his hands.

"Have you had lunch?" asked Lucinda.

He shook his head.

"How idiotic! You can't have it in here, it would upset the maids. There's a little foreign restaurant in Wilton Road where they might produce something at this hour."

He said that he was not hungry but she persuaded him to come with her. She sat with him in the dingy little restaurant while he ate an omelette.

"You should have got into the taxi with her and told the man to drive to Catherine Street," she said.

"There was a policeman watching us."

"It's not illegal to drive with your wife."

He repeated that Heather hated him.

"If you arouse any kind of emotion in her there's hope."

"An original hatred may turn to love," said Stephen, "but a love that has turned to hatred isn't likely to turn back again."

Lucinda looked at him, surprised at the truth of his observation. When they returned to Catherine Street he asked if he might stay there indefinitely. He said he would not go back to the End House.

"But Mr Digby and Uncle Arthur?" she asked, her heart sinking a little farther beneath the weight of Stephen's problems. "You can't just walk out on them."

"I can't go back there, Mum. It's absolute hell to be in the house alone."

"Would you live at Crittenden, then, and go on with your agent's work?"

"I don't know. I think I'd rather not."

"I suppose I'd better go down tomorrow and talk it over with Arthur and Marian."

Again his face was suffused with gratitude. She began to understand a little why Heather had left him.

"You know, if you'd beaten Heather occasionally she would have worshipped you," she said.

"Oh, Mum!" exclaimed Stephen, tolerant and faintly smiling. "You don't understand love."

Lucinda laughed weakly and went up to her room. She thought of her attempts to grapple Pat to her soul, and wondered whether it was a good thing she had not succeeded. Pat now lived in Ireland

and spent his time hunting. She heard that he had five robust sons, as horsy as himself. She would have hated that. Again, liking what she got, she liked her well-ordered London life, her bijou house and her little parties. Wentworth Fox, with all his failings, was rather a dear, and provided as much intimate male element in her life as she required. As she thought over Stephen's affair she felt a humbug at expressing any moral indignation towards Heather. After all, she was only in the same position as herself fifteen years earlier. Lucinda did not care to realize this and began to look for differences. After all, Hugo had been unfaithful to her. But when she had thought all round it, she had to admit that the essential fact was the same. Undoubtedly Heather was violently attracted by Ablett in the same way that she had been violently attracted by Pat, and Stephen's boyish "non-alcoholic quality" must be as maddening to her as Hugo's polite imperturbability had been to herself.

In the evening, without telling Stephen, she went round to see Heather. She outwitted the porter by saying firmly that she was Mrs Brayford's mother-in-law, and went up to Heather's room, where she found her just as she was changing to dine, presumably with Ablett. Heather looked frightened and very young when she saw Lucinda, who suddenly felt sorry for her. She tried to imagine how she would have felt if Marian had appeared at King's Charles's Court one night, just as she was preparing to dine with Pat.

"My dear," she said, "I've only come to talk reasonably to you." She proceeded to do this to the best of her ability, but Heather was not responsive. She seemed suspicious of Lucinda's deliberate impartiality, or even to consider her visit a breach of propriety. In one moment of confidence she declared that she was prepared to sacrifice everything for Ablett. Lucinda saw that further discussion was useless, and she rose to leave.

"You would have been furious," she said, "if I had tried to prevent your marrying Stephen. As a matter of fact I did make a feeble effort. Now you're annoyed because I ask you to be faithful to him. I do think the young are difficult."

Back at Catherine Street she told Stephen of the interview.

"She may get tired of him soon," said Stephen.

"You might take her back now, while no one knows about it, but you couldn't take her back in three months' time. It would be indecent."

"If you love anyone, you can't suddenly stop, because of the things they do."

"I can," said Lucinda.

After dinner she rang up Crittenden to ask if she might come

390

down the next day. She then spent a depressing evening with Stephen. They both went to bed early, but not to sleep. Lucinda thought of all the refuse of the marriage to be cleaned up. She was not looking forward to tomorrow's talk with Arthur and Marian. She felt terribly ashamed of her family. She wondered whether Fred would side with his real grandson, the future Viscount Crittenden, or with his supposed granddaughter. She hoped to heaven she would not be financially docked again. Towards midnight faint and mournful sounds of music stole across the landing. Stephen was playing his flute. She really did feel some sympathy for Heather.

CHAPTER NINE

LOOKING BACK in after years, particularly during the Second Great War, it seemed to Lucinda that the last time she had had any sense of security was on that morning when she had come out of her house and seen Stephen walking along the street, carrying his suitcase. She often enjoyed life very much after that, but in the intervals between her enjoyment, when she had time for reflection, she was never quite free from the apprehension, to use Paul's metaphor, that the fallen tree was about to crack up, and that it would be a bad look-out for the remaining green leaves.

In the train, going down to Crittenden, she tried to think out ways of announcing her news to Marian and Arthur. She wondered whether Marian, who boasted that like the Curé d'Ars she could "smell sin," had any previous suspicion of what had now happened.

The car stopped at the side door at Crittenden, that door of which Lucinda long ago had noticed the delicate classic proportions, but which she had entered unseeing a thousand times since, just as Marian with a basket of polyanthus came up from the garden. She greeted Lucinda in a friendly but slightly reserved fashion. She had smelt that something unusual, and possibly troublesome, was in the wind. Heather and Stephen had cleared off to London without telling anyone, and it was unlike Lucinda, whose life was full of little engagements planned ahead, to come down to Crittenden at a moment's notice, especially at this time of year, as she hated the cold. Marian thought that probably Heather had run into debt.

This was the first time for years that Marian had received Lucinda without complete open friendliness, and she was a little hurt, but she accepted that too as just an addition to the weight that Stephen's problems put on her. Because of this she gave up the idea of trying to be tactful, and as soon as the car had driven away and a man had taken in her suitcase, she said:

"I'm awfully sorry, Marian, to descend on you so suddenly, but Heather has left Stephen."

"D'you mean to say she's cleared out?"

"Yes."

"Gosh!" exclaimed Marian. "Already!" They went into the house. The footman with Lucinda's suitcase was waiting to ask which room he should take it to.

"Where's his lordship?" asked Marian.

"In the library with Mr Digby, my lady."

"Let me know when Mr Digby goes," she said. "I'll be in the Peacock room. Take Mrs Brayford's things to the rose room." Lucinda was relieved that she was being given one of the best rooms. From Marian's manner she half expected to be put in an attic.

In the Peacock room Marian took a cigarette and offered one to Lucinda, who preferred her own.

"Where is Heather now?" asked Marian.

"In a Sloane Street hotel."

"She hasn't gone with anyone? Thank God for that. Why doesn't Stephen go and drag her back by the ears?"

"He tried to," said Lucinda.

"Tried to!" Marian almost spat. "That's what comes of not hunting. D'you mean to say that she's sitting alone in an hotel and he can't bring her home?"

"She's not exactly alone. There's someone else."

"Who?"

"One of Straker's friends, a man called Ablett."

"That greasy stockbroker!"

"She met him in the hunting field," said Lucinda with satisfaction. Marian was slightly deflated, especially as it was she who had insisted on Arthur's calling on Lord Fitzauncell.

"Is Ablett at the hotel?" she asked brusquely.

"No, but she sees him."

Arthur came into the room. He greeted Lucinda with that faintly bantering courtesy which he showed to all women whom he liked.

"I heard you were here," he said, "and I walked out on Digby."

"Heather has walked out on Stephen," said Marian brutally.

Arthur looked at her incredulously and with a touch of anger.

"You're not serious " he said, and turned to Lucinda for confirmation.

"I'm awfully sorry, Arthur," said Lucinda. "It's true. You must be sick of my family."

"She's gone with Ablett, one of Fitzauncell's stockbrokers," said Marian. She poked with her toe at a hole in the aubusson mat, in a way which would have maddened her if anyone else had done it. Lucinda was watching Arthur to see how he took the news. He had the same expression as on that morning of his interview with Bill, when he had first learned that Stephen wanted to marry Heather, but if anything he was now more perturbed.

"Where is Stephen?" he asked, after a moment in which he tried to grasp what had happened.

"He went to London to fetch her back," said Marian, "but she wouldn't come." She answered partly from the impulse to express her feelings, but also to spare Lucinda the task of explanation.

"Is that definite?" Arthur asked Lucinda.

"I'm afraid it is. I went myself to see her last night."

A gong sounded distantly and they went down to luncheon, which was one of the most uncomfortable meals Lucinda had ever sat through at Crittenden. Marian was like a champagne bottle which has been uncorked, but is expected not to fizz, but she knew, when she saw Arthur's face at the other end of the table, how his eyelids were heavy and the muscles of his cheeks sagged, that she had come to one of those times which recurred at intervals in her married life, when it was revealed that her apparent ascendency was only a game which he allowed her to play, and that there was in him a real seriousness, far deeper than her mere common sense.

Lucinda did not tell them immediately the full extent of the dislocation which the new situation involved, that Stephen refused to return to the End House and that he did not want to go on with his agent's work. Although Arthur would be more truly upset by this than Marian, she preferred to break the news to him, and waited until she had the opportunity to tell him alone. Arthur, like Paul, accepted that people must act according to their own natures, but unlike Paul, he was tolerant when they did so. She felt that Arthur had accepted Stephen as a bit of a misfit and that although it might worry and disappoint him, any erratic conduct or any failure of Stephen's would not surprise him. He would only feel, as she did, that faint added heaviness.

Fortunately Marian had some charitable committee to attend in that evening, and Lucinda and Arthur were able to put all the cards on the table and sort them dispassionately, without the confusing ingredient of moral indignation. By the time Marian returned they had settled what they thought best to be done, that the End

House should be let, and what financial adjustments should be made.

Lucinda felt so much gratitude to Arthur that she was unable to express it. When he heard Marian's returning car pass the library windows, he said with the familiar twinkle in his eye:

"Don't tell Marian yet. I'll have to make her think it's all her idea."

There was no need for this precaution, as Marian, when she came in, was full of indignation at the archdeacon, who had openly disagreed with her on the committee.

The next afternoon Lucinda returned to Catherine Street and found Stephen moping disconsolately about the house. After dinner she tried to read a book, while Stephen sat writing a long letter to Heather asking her to come back. Sometimes he would read out a sentence for her correction.

The reply to this letter came within three days from Heather's lawyers and conveyed a hint that Stephen might allow her to divorce him.

"What bloody cheek!" exclaimed Lucinda. She was even more indignant when, later in the day, Stephen said he thought he would agree to do so.

"You see, Mum," he said, in reply to Lucinda's expostulations, "it doesn't matter to me which way it happens. People won't treat me any differently. But if Heather is divorced it will crab her whole life. She couldn't go into the Royal Enclosure and all those places, and that's the sort of thing she lives for."

"Apparently Ablett's very rich," said Lucinda. "He'll be able to smooth out her crumpled rose-leaves. Besides, if you liked to go for damages, you'd be set up for life."

"Mum, please don't talk like that."

"I wasn't terribly serious, darling. Still, I don't see that you are called upon to ruin your reputation to let Heather into the Royal Enclosure."

"I love her," said Stephen.

"You are exasperating," said Lucinda, but not unkindly. She sensed that Stephen believed that he had failed Heather in some way, had proved inadequate; and she could imagine that his lack of reasonable self-interest and normal vindictiveness would exasperate a wife even more than a mother. After all, she thought, apparent injustices were often more fair beneath the surface than one could see. She let him have his own way, and when even Arthur was upset and Marian was on the verge of frenzy at this development, she only shrugged her shoulders.

Soon the repercussions came from Tourella. Muriel wrote a letter

394

in which the word "appalling" occurred eleven times. She said that she had always been opposed to the marriage, and suggested that it must really be Stephen's fault. The fact that he was allowing Heather to divorce him showed that he considered himself guilty.

Lucinda would have been amused by Muriel's letter if it were not for the account of the effect of the news on Fred. As he had been equally proud of both Stephen and Heather, he could not make up his mind which of them to champion, and which to visit with his patriarchal curse and consequent stoppage of funds. This impediment to an immediate gesture of power brought on a slight stroke. His heart beat as strongly as ever, but his mind lost its grip. Before long he remained just a body with a heart which a man half his age might have envied, but with a brain which had ceased to function. Sometimes at the sight of a company report or a share prospectus, a faint look of recognition would dawn in his eyes. He would mutter unintelligibly, but almost immediately the brief cerebral action would cease, and he would sink back into his armchair, his hands idly fiddling with the uncomprehended paper. Muriel took advantage of his condition to remove the two *cloisonné* vases from the hall. She sent them to an auction room where they fetched six pounds each.

Lucinda thought that this 1936 summer was one of the most disagreeable she had ever spent, though not as acutely unhappy as when she had parted from Pat. The disturbance and the contempt for human values, which were changing Europe, seemed to be reflected dimly in her own life. She had to go down to the End House for a week to supervise the packing up, and to sort out her own possessions which she had lent to Stephen and Heather. As she looked at the things which had been chosen by Heather, she was struck by a sort of hard opulence in their design, and she wondered how anyone with this taste could ever have come to marry Stephen, and thought that after all she was more suitably matched with Ablett, who, on the one occasion when she had seen him, seemed to personify big business and fascism and blatant manifestations of power.

She did not go to St Saturnin as early as usual, as she stayed to support Stephen through the hearing of the divorce case. Stephen had spent a week-end at Folkestone with a plump young woman whom he had taken to the cinema, but he paid her no more intimate attention beyond taking breakfast in her room. This was all made to appear sufficiently sordid in the Divorce Court.

Paul wrote to say that Roland Roberts had gone to Spain to fight for the Government against Franco. This was just after Heather had got her decree, and it added to Stephen's depression.

Wentworth Fox, now that he was beginning to earn a little money, asked Lucinda to marry him. A few years earlier she might have agreed, but now she felt that to do so would be to increase the disintegration which appeared to be settling on the world in general and on her own family in particular.

A man in Hyde Park had fired a revolver or attempted to fire one in the vicinity of King Edward VIII as he rode past. Just after this Lucinda paid a Sunday afternoon call in Kensington Square, as she did occasionally, on Lady Bassingbourne, who was now a widow.

"The crowd should have lynched him," said Lady Bassingbourne, her fine sentimental eyes flashing with indignation.

Everyone at Lady Bassingbourne's was pro-Franco, and about Mussolini's Abyssinian adventure they said it would never have done for Europeans to be defeated by natives. A woman who was a great admirer of Hitler's came over and sang his praises to Lucinda, who asked:

"But hasn't he done the most awful things? One hears stories about the concentration camps."

"And who invented concentration camps?" said the lady with a vicious smile. "The British in South Africa! And for women and children."

"Yes, but that doesn't mean they're desirable. A German general, a friend of my mother-in-law's, has just arrived in England, having escaped after a year in one of these camps. He looks dreadful. He can't speak of the awful things that happened to him. His only offense was to cross into Holland to dine with the Kaiser on his birthday. And they say the Jews——"

"The Jews!" exclaimed the lady. "You've no idea what they've done in Germany. At the time of the inflation they swept down from Poland and bought up everything, increasing enormously the sufferings of the country."

"Possibly," said Lucinda, and added smiling, "still, they oughtn't to beat up old gentlemen whom one knows."

"My husband and I always go to Germany for our holidays. You ought to come and see the wonderful things Hitler has done for his country. You have to be ruthless to restore order."

"I'm sorry," said Lucinda apologetically, "but I don't really like brutality."

The lady laughed and rose to go. She shook hands warmly with Lucinda and told her she must visit Germany.

At last, with a sense of relief, Lucinda arrived at St Saturnin. As usual, she went down at once to see Paul. He did not seem particularly concerned about Stephen's divorce, probably because of his subconscious belief that no married man could possibly be happy, but he looked older and was almost weeping about Roland. At first he had been indignant at the disorders tolerated or uncontrolled by the Spanish Republican Government. Now his fury was directed against Franco.

"The blackguard," he said, "to release civil war on his country. By the time this is finished every Velasquez and El Greco in Spain may be a piece of blistered ash." He pretended that his main concern was for the art treasures, but really he could not bear the thought of the thousands of young men who must die in agony, possibly Roland amongst them. He cursed the fascists and communists indiscriminately.

"Hitler and Mussolini are only the counterpart of Bolshevism," he said. "They're all the same, secret police, purges and a denial of the human values. We're witnessing the suicide of civilization."

"Certainly," said Lucinda, "the world doesn't seem to be quite what I was led to expect when I was a little girl at The Pines."

"It isn't the same world. Look at these young men who lounge here on the plage. They shelter from their complete ignorance of everything that has made Western civilization behind something they call 'dialectic materialism,' so pleased with this atrocious phrase, like a waitress who calls a slop-basin a residue-vase, and indeed dialectic materialism is the slop-basin of European culture."

"I'm afraid I never know what it means," said Lucinda.

"It means the liquidation of you and me."

"That wouldn't be very agreeable. Though probably Willy Greene-James would prefer it to dehydration."

"Tell me," said Paul, "who is this Mrs Simpson who has gone to the Adriatic with the King of England? Is he going to appoint her *maîtresse en titre*? I hope so. It would show a proper discrimination and bring a little liveliness into Court circles. Duchess of Belvedere would be a suitable title, and would bring an echo of more civilized times to this hideous age."

"They say he wants to marry her."

"People talk a lot of irresponsible nonsense," said Paul.

In the autumn Stephen announced that he was going to study at the Royal School of Music. Lucinda was rather pleased at his becoming a pupil again. It made her feel younger and she had at least been spared from so soon becoming a grandmother. She was also pleased that Stephen did not want to live in Catherine Street, but took a mews flat off Queen's Gate.

In the autumn the king abdicated. Paul wrote furious letters from St Saturnin, mostly to Arthur. They were full of denunciation of business men and references to precedent, and redolent of the Divine Right of Kings. He telegraphed that Arthur should denounce the Government in the House of Lords, and refuse the oath of allegiance to the new king. Arthur was extremely worried and did not at all consider Paul's attitude ridiculous, as Marian did, and of course said so. He even went up to London with the intention of making a speech, but found he would have no support, except from a small group of extreme Tories, who, Paul declared, alone in political circles had retained any glimmerings of honor. Fortunately, King Edward, making the path as smooth as possible for his opponents, released the members of Parliament and the peers from their oaths of allegiance, otherwise the country would have had the singular spectacle of the bench of bishops perjuring themselves.

Paul came over for Christmas, but as he was still almost hysterical about the abdication, and Marian did not restrain her criticism of the Duke of Windsor, there was not much peace and goodwill at Crittenden. Lady Bassingbourne was there and was very shocked at the things Paul said.

"You don't understand," he told Marian, "you are destroying the authority on which your own position rests. The wanton removal of a king is always followed by a period of disaster. The last time it happened we had the rule of that infamous blackguard Cromwell, the prototype of your friend Hitler."

"I'm so sorry for dear Mr Baldwin," said Lady Bassingbourne.

There was such an atmosphere of tension in the household that Lucinda wished she had not come to Crittenden, but this would have hurt the feelings of Arthur and Marian. Paul, who usually added to the liveliness of the party, appeared to have laid aside his sense of humor and only brought discord. Muriel wrote a letter even more full of dismay than that on Heather's divorce, as in 1920, the king, when Prince of Wales, had attended a dance at Tourella. Since last Christmas, when everything had appeared so satisfactory with Stephen and Heather a happy young couple, there had been a rapid spread of the general malaise. Stephen's divorce, the war in Spain involving Roland, the abdication and Paul's hysterical denunciations all combined to make Lucinda feel that the leaves on the tree were at last beginning to crackle and turn brown. Arthur, she thought, looked worried and ill. Stephen spent a large part of the visit in his room playing the flute, at which he was becoming quite professional.

Before the coronation Arthur and Marian had photographers out at Crittenden to take them in their coronets and robes. They gave a tea-party on the same afternoon to show themselves off to their more intimate neighbors. The photographs were taken in the saloon. Marian treated the whole thing as a joke and said: "I feel like the White Queen in *Alice in Wonderland*."

They gave Lucinda a pair of these photographs, in silver frames with miniature viscount's coronets on them. She put them on the drawing-room mantelpiece at Catherine Street, where she thought they looked nice and grand, but Wentworth Fox said they were pretentious, so she put them away, unless Marian was likely to call.

Marian and Arthur stayed for the coronation at Lady Bassingbourne's house in Kensington Square. They went to the Abbey by a special underground from Kensington High Street. They found themselves near Lord Fitzauncell, and Arthur, who felt that he would like to know what he really thought of the international situation, and to have some reassurance about Hitler, invited him to dine at Crittenden. Arthur looked exhausted when they returned to Kensington Square, and on the night when Lord Fitzauncell dined at Crittenden he had not recovered from the strain of the day in the Abbey.

When he came upstairs, after Lord Fitzauncell had left, he said to Marian: "I don't understand these people. They seem to have power without principles, and even without responsibility."

"Don't fuss about them now," said Marian. "You oughtn't to have stayed up so late. You'll be tired in the morning."

But in the morning Arthur did not awake. He had died in his sleep.

When Lucinda heard that Arthur had died she could not help weeping. She did not go out for two days, except alone into St James's Park, as whenever she thought of Arthur she could not stop floods of tears pouring down her cheeks. She was surprised as she had not thought he meant so much to her. It was perhaps because he was the only man she had known who had treated her, for more than twenty years, with disinterested affection and with unchanging kindness.

It was discovered that the reason why, apart from the upkeep of Crittenden as nearly as possible in its former style, Arthur and Marian had lived so carefully, for which Paul had often accused them of being skinflints, was that Arthur had been paying enormous insurance premiums to cover the death-duties, so that Paul should not have to part with any of the estate.

Paul was so affected by this that he invited Marian to stay at Crittenden and continue to run the house, though the prospect filled him with gloom, as he felt himself quite capable of being "the master-mistress" of his inheritance. Marian was too sensible to accept this offer, and she contended herself with the End House which she furnished with all the Victorian furniture from Crittenden, which Paul almost flung out of the windows.

After a lifetime of floating among various social groups, frustrated and uncertain, misunderstood and often snubbed by people who mistook his courtesy for humility, and who had not till then felt the edge of his tongue, Paul suddenly found himself with adequate means in an established position. This did not change his attitude in any way, as he had always known it was likely to happen, and like Arthur, he did not regard Crittenden as his personal possession, but only as something of which he had charge for a while. This attitude perhaps was the real difference between himself and the rich business men for whom he expressed so forcibly his contempt. Also he would not allow that any amount of wealth, or its complete absence, could affect the importance of a man of his blood.

He took his seat in the House of Lords, and after Munich, made a speech there in which his reference was to such a high standard of political morality that no one took it seriously, and the new Lord Crittenden became a day's joke in the cheap press. Paul did not go to Westminster again, except once, after the fall of France when the Fitzauncell papers came out with the headline, "Lock up Lord Crittenden."

He devoted himself to his life of a *grand seigneur* in the country. He brought Harry to Crittenden as butler and Assomption as cook. Pierre had entered the French Navy and was on the *Richelieu*. Marian took three or four of the old Crittenden servants with her to the End House. Paul dismissed the rest, and engaged all the new ones personally, choosing them solely for their looks. He said, "I don't like meeting ugly housemaids in the passages," but he was, of course, even more fastidious in his choice of footmen. Crittenden became an aviary of beautiful but incompetent domestics presided over by the lazily indulgent Harry, who had not the faintest idea how to control a large staff. The disorders did not affect Paul, as Harry saw to his comfort, but in the servants' wing they were extreme, where the lovely occupants filled the air with romance and jealous passions.

In the autumn the house seemed in perfect accord with the season, like some enormous perfect bloom before the petals fall. Paul had removed from the public rooms all the furniture later than 1793, the year of the execution of Marie-Antoinette, the latest date at which aristocratic influence remained pure and uncorrupted. Some of the fabrics, exquisite in their faded colors, were almost threadbare. When Marian pointed this out, Paul retorted contemptuously, "Only the middle-classes have new carpets." To come into the house on an afternoon when it was flooded with pale sunlight was a startling experience. It gave one the sensation of having passed the grave into a dead, yet deathless, world. There was nothing within sight that was made by living men. Then suddenly against the deathly beauty would flash the living face of a footman like Hyacinth or Daphnis, and the visitor, going up early to change, might find a twentieth-century Chloe arranging the towels over a hot-water can, and turning, as he entered, with a shy and vivid glance.

Harry not only failed to keep the servants in order. He had so long lived on easy terms with Paul and his visitors that his manner when the county called was far too casual, and people were beginning to talk of Crittenden House as a place where it was hardly suitable to take their daughters. An incident with Lord Fitzauncell aggravated this talk. He called at Crittenden and came into the hall just as Paul was crossing from the saloon to the library. When Harry announced him, Paul said:

"Lord Fitzauncell died in 1872."

What Paul said was so improbable that Lord Fitzauncell did not take it in. He came forward genially with outstretched hand. Paul ignored his hand.

"Sir," he said, "your newspapers have for two decades been engaged in the degradation of the proper feelings of our people. What is vile they offer to gloating eyes, what is vindictive they applaud. You have done more harm to this country than any of its external enemies. In addition to this, one of your friends has seduced my niece, my elder brother died of disgust after entertaining you at dinner, and you tried to sell filthy postcards to my younger brother when he was on his honeymoon. In my opinion, and I am given to understatement, you are the scum of the earth, so much of which has recently risen to the surface. I beg you will leave before my butler throws you down the steps."

Harry looked a little disconcerted. Lord Fitzauncell had worn a contemptuous smile until Paul mentioned the postcards. Then he became livid.

Paul turned and limped across to the library door.

"Everyone knows what you are, you old——!" shouted Lord Fitzauncell.

"If you're not careful I'll do what his lordship says," said Harry threateningly.

The story spread about that Paul had encouraged his butler to insult Lord Fitzauncell, who had paid a civil call. He became more unpopular in the county. Paul in turn was hurt and angry that people of his own should side with Straker against a Brayford of Crittenden.

"There are nowadays," he said, "two prevalent phenomena. One is to make words meaningless, the other is disloyalty to the thing you belong to. They both originate with the Nazis and the Communists."

Paul was aware of Harry's shortcomings and of the state of his servants' hall, and he did not like these things. His idea was to live like a civilized nobleman. Nothing could have persuaded him to dismiss Harry, but after a year Assomption, who had been growing steadily angrier at life in England and the fuss of a large household, not to mention Harry's obvious enjoyment of the society of so many ravishing young creatures, staged a furious scene one night in the middle of dinner, and hauled Harry back to St Saturnin next day. Paul said he would return there for the *vendange* if Pierre came on leave then, as he was longing to see him with a red pom-pom on his cap.

He was very depressed after Harry had left, as he had been accustomed to rely on him for advice, given in a daily confidential chat while he was laying out his clothes in the morning. In these talks Harry retained his early attitude towards Paul, saying, "I wouldn't do that, Boss, if I were you," or "That wouldn't be very sensible, Boss." Paul hated the word "Boss," but he would have been hurt if Harry had given up its use in these sessions.

Paul engaged a new butler, and the household at Crittenden became more conventional, but still it remained a curious oasis in the county. Paul, who thought he understood himself so clearly, did not see that really he disliked the aristocracy in its practical manifestation, at least the English provincial variety. He hated pomposity without grace, and the restriction of human kindness by artificial barriers. When he had been associating mostly with bourgeois and bohemians, he had idealized aristocratic life, and like Watteau, who avoided the Court, he peopled the parks and palaces of his nostalgia with graceful imagined creatures, rather than with actual fat Bourbons or with fox-hunting English peeresses. Finding himself different from his associates, he came to believe that all his own characteristics were the marks of aristocracy, even his strong powers of invective and his taste for dishes cooked with wine and garlic.

He gave parties at Crittenden in which he tried to express his idea of civilized entertainment. At one the music of Scarlatti was played on a harpsichord in the saloon, which was lighted only by candles. At another Stephen brought some fellow students down from London, who played Beethoven's last Quartets in the chapel. At yet another party, actors impersonated the poets whose works they recited.

Paul knew that these subtleties were beyond the taste of the county neighbors, and would even bring him further discredit, but his neighbors were the only people to whom he could send invitations. He was more lonely than he had ever been in his life. Lucinda did not often come to Crittenden, as she was too involved with Wentworth Fox, though she was sorry for Paul, who had to search among the highways and hedges of the landed gentry for his guests. She thought that he was like that Duke Carl in Pater's *Imaginary Portraits*, in whom people had "the spectacle, under those superficial braveries, of a really heroic effort of mind at a disadvantage."

Paul did not think it suitable that he should continue to make acquaintances in bars. He still sought occasionally in different social groups for the perfect platonic friendship, but found that his wealth and rank, which he had thought would be a help, were more of a hindrance to him. Finding that in spite of himself he was leading an irreproachable life, he gave more thought to the moral law governing the universe, and would now and then refer brusquely to "Almighty God."

He did not go to St Saturnin in the autumn as he waited to see the result of the Munich crisis. He would not have a wireless at Crittenden, except in the servants' hall, and that only because he was obliged to, and he walked down to the End House at the height of the crisis to hear the news on Marian's wireless. He was almost in a frenzy when Chamberlain sold the Czechs to Hitler.

"You can't expect Mr Chamberlain to deal successfully with people like Hitler," said Marian. "He's a Christian and a gentleman."

"Nonsense," said Paul. "He's a Unitarian and an ironmonger."

"It is dreadful to say such things of dear Mr Chamberlain," said Lady Bassingbourne, who was staying at the End House. "You're just like that horrible Mr Churchill."

"You are mistaken," said Paul coldly.

After this, Paul bought a wireless, as his visitors complained when they could not hear the news, but he kept it in a lavatory off the gun-room, and told people if they wanted to hear smug voices announcing treachery and brutality, they could go and listen in a suitable place. He was not going to have his state apartments defiled by the Nonconformist-cum-Fascist emanations of the B.B.C.

Roland escaped from Spain after the fall of Barcelona. He was wounded and spent the summer convalescing at St Saturnin. He was also bitter and disillusioned and had come, like Paul, to hate the

Communists as much as the Fascists. He had joined them imagining that he was following an ideal of world-wide brotherly love.

CHAPTER TEN

LUCINDA AND PAUL came to St Saturnin for August. Stephen came for the first week to see Roland, but after that he returned to England to play in his quartet at a series of concerts. In the third week in August Paul said that war was now inevitable, and that they had better return to England. He wanted Harry to bring Assomption to England and offered them a cottage at Crittenden.

"We're all right here, Boss," said Harry. "There's the Maginot Line."

"The Maginot Line doesn't go to the coast," said Paul. Harry refused to believe this.

"Why, it wouldn't be any use," he said, "if it didn't go all the way."

Paul tried, too, to persuade the Roberts to come to England. He said they could have a wing of Crittenden to live in. They were grateful, but refused, and Elspeth said:

"The south is too much in my blood. We must stay and see it out. Nothing may happen. Still perhaps we were foolish not to settle in some warm British possession—Cyprus or somewhere."

"Cyprus!" exclaimed Paul. "Chamberlain is almost certain to give it to Mussolini for a submarine base."

Paul did not speak on the drive to Marseilles. Lucinda, seated beside him, knew that he was silently weeping. He felt that he was parting from the people and the place he loved most, the place where he had been most happy, and that he was ending the sunlit period of his life. He was disappointed that he had not seen Pierre *en marin* with the red pom-pom on his cap.

Lucinda went down to Crittenden at the beginning of September. On the first Sunday Paul refused to sit in the lavatory or the servants' hall listening to the wireless, and said they might as well go to church. The church at Crittenden was just behind the End House, but they drove as it was too far for Paul to walk with his limp. When they pulled up by the End House, Marian put her head out of the drawing-room window and called:

"Hurry up. You're just in time to hear war declared."

"We are going to church," said Paul. They walked round the high wall of the End House garden and through the churchyard.

There were a few people standing talking by the porch. The vicar came round the corner.

"Ah, good-morning, Mrs Brayford. Good-morning, Lord Crittenden," he said hurriedly. "There is no service this morning, as we all want to hear Mr Chamberlain's speech."

"It has, I suppose, more immediate interest than the word of God," said Paul. The vicar went into the church, the bell stopped ringing, and immediately from the distant town came the hideous crescendo of the siren, filling the sunny morning with the moan of death. They went back to Marian.

"Now we'll have to pull up our socks," she said, with grim satisfaction. "I wonder if they'll bomb London tonight."

"I hope not," said Lucinda. "I wish I'd brought down my Picasso." She talked in this fashion from habit, but a weight of despair was beginning to settle on her. In the same way at Lady Bassingbourne's she had spoken lightly about "beating up people one knows," but she had been horrified when she met old General von S—— at Susannah's and saw what he must have been through. The thought of the concentration camp remained with her for days afterwards. In a way it was a relief that at last we were standing up to Hitler, but neither she nor Paul could share Marian's enjoyment at the prospect, and they soon left. On the doorstep they met the vicar and his wife who had come round to discuss the situation with Marian.

"It's one man's war—one man's war," said Mrs Throssel.

"Mr Baldwin's, I suppose you mean," said Paul.

She glared at him and was only deterred from an insulting retort by the fact that he was patron of the living. Five years later she said that the German children who were now in their cradles were equally responsible with Hitler for the obliteration of their towns by American bombers, and should be punished accordingly.

Lucinda and Paul sat almost in silence over luncheon, as Paul felt that his views, if he were to express them, would be misunderstood by the servants.

In the saloon, when the butler and the younger footman had taken out the coffee trays—the hyacinthine footman had already been taken in the first conscription—Paul said, "I wonder how much longer I shall be able to go on living like this." He laughed. "A short but glorious reign! So they're going to butcher another generation. God, how Marian will enjoy it."

"It's the cold people who are wicked," said Lucinda impulsively. "I read somewhere that the devil is not hot but cold. It's the cold people who are evil and horrible. Or am I wrong? Are they simply unimaginative?"

They were both too moved to remain together, and Lucinda went up to her room.

Later in the day Paul asked where Stephen was. Lucinda replied that he was in Warwickshire with the quartet. She, Paul and Marian were agreed in expecting Stephen to call on General Fraser or some family friend at the War Office and get a commission. That was what young men of good family had done in their day. As the war, after all, had not broken out with great violence, and as all hope of the survival of the family and the title rested in Stephen, they thought that it would be permissible for him to have some kind of safe job in England.

Stephen, however, took very little interest in the outbreak of war, and went on playing the flute in his quartet. If anyone spoke much about the war, particularly if they referred in a matter-of-fact way to casualties, he would fidget and go out of the room. At first so few people were enthusiastic about the war—some of their neighbors even said that they would not be at all surprised if in six months' time we were fighting with Germany against Russia—that Stephen's behavior did not provoke much criticism. Paul, throughout his life, had slowly forced his associates to accept his eccentricities, and Stephen reaped some of the benefit from this.

Early in 1940, Roland, who had now recovered from his wound, but was left unfit for military service, came to England to find something to do. He was given scientific work at Cambridge, which he described as "testing the psychology of wire-worms" and added that it was of national importance. He sometimes stayed at Crittenden, where Marian viewed him with disfavor as he was not in khaki, and he had fought against Franco. There was some confusion in her mind on this issue, and as she disliked confusion she disliked anyone who provoked it in herself.

On the day that the Nazis invaded the Low Countries Paul entirely reversed his attitude to the war. He was aflame with patriotism. The insolence of the attack affronted him even more than its brutality. It flouted every lingering trace of chivalry, and was a complete and final repudiation of the idea of a gentleman's war, which was the only kind of war Paul could tolerate. He wrote to *The Times* and the War Office, saying that every man in the country should be provided with firearms, and offered to arm the men on his estate at his own expense and to form them into a drilled company. He saw himself fulfilling his proper rôle as a feudal landowner. He hurried up to London to see General Fraser, who kept him waiting for half an hour and then informed him that the idea had already occurred to the War Minister, and that the Home Guard was being formed. When Paul discovered that people were being enrolled in this as privates, irrespective of rank, military or noble, he said it was bolshevism, and refused to have anything to do with it. But he still thought out ingenious ways of repelling an invader, and wrote again to the War Office saying that in the event of a landing of tanks all garage proprietors should be instructed to put sugar in their petrol supplies.

At the time of the collapse of Belgium, Lucinda and Stephen came to stay at Crittenden. Marian came up to see them and abruptly asked Stephen what he was going to do. Stephen gave a non-committal reply. For once Paul had nothing to say. He disliked Marian's manner to Stephen, but he was himself upset that he did not appear to feel the danger to his country. When they were alone Lucinda said to Stephen:

"Darling, couldn't you put yourself into some kind of khaki, even if it's only the Y.M.C.A.?"

"What for?" asked Stephen.

"Well, people do rather expect you to, and it's better to do it before you're called up."

The same evening, just before they were going to bed, a footman came into the Peacock room and said:

"Mr Stephen, sir, you're wanted on the telephone. It's Mr Roberts."

"They must have come to England!" exclaimed Paul, but it was Roland, not his father, at the other end of the line.

He was excited, incoherent and a little mysterious. He wanted Stephen to come back to London immediately. He had a motor cruiser and was going over to help in the evacuation of the British Army. He was leaving at once. He wanted Stephen for his crew. Stephen dashed back from the telephone to the peacock room.

"Mum, I'm going to London. I'm going tonight."

His eyes were more lively than they had been since the outbreak of war. "Paul, could I have the little car? I don't think there's another train. Roland has a motor boat. We're going to take off some of the army that's trapped on the coast of France. At least I think that's what it is. Roland wouldn't be explicit. He kept saying, 'Can't you understand, you bloody fool.'" Stephen laughed. "Isn't it marvelous?"

"I thought you weren't interested in the war, darling," said Lucinda, mystified, but a little pleased and a little apprehensive.

"Oh, but Mum, don't you see, this is different. If we don't go, those men will be killed or imprisoned. It's a marvelous chance to do something worth while. I may have the little car, mayn't I, Paul?"

He kissed Lucinda, patted Paul on the shoulder and, with shining eyes, hurried from the room.

"Take some warm things," called Lucinda plaintively.

"I'll get them at Catherine Street," he shouted from the head of the stairs.

When Marian, still on the warpath against Stephen, called the next morning, she was taken aback to hear that he had gone off with the undesirable Roland to help rescue the British Army from France. Paul and Lucinda, as they told her, looked amused but anxious. When she had gone, Lucinda said to Paul:

"I've been thinking over what Stephen said last night. It's curious, but I had no idea that he ever had any ambition to do something worth while."

CHAPTER ELEVEN

ALL THE WAY over to France, sleepless and excited in the chugging motor boat, from the first hours when the Thames banks become remote and mysterious and finally were lost in the darkness, from the time when they first heard the booming of the distant guns until they penetrated into the inferno of explosion, Stephen felt intensely happy. For the first time since the war began, or even perhaps since Heather had left him, he felt himself to be reunited to the majority of his fellow-men. Of recent years he had felt himself in some way to be cut off from their sympathy, and the war had aggravated this condition. When he tried to adjust himself rationally to it, his brain became numbed and he could not think clearly.

Now all these feelings had gone. A rush of life had flooded his body and mind. He had the joy of being reunited to his fellows, not only in physical companionship but, he imagined, in belief and purpose.

Roland and himself had been detailed to tow the lifeboats from the Channel packet, tugs and pleasure steamers which had come over to evacuate the troops. They would tow a lifeboat as near to the shores as it would go, to where the long dark queue of exhausted men, some of them wounded, standing up to their waists, in places up to their necks, in the water, waited in their orderly turn for rescue.

At first he had been nervous but elated. Every man he had pulled into the lifeboat he had been aware of as a life saved. He felt that

408

he really was engaged in the conflict between good and evil, that he was snatching life from death and virtue from hell. This mood did not last long. His muscles began to ache and he fell into a routine of cursing, frenzied effort.

Out here on the water they were only on the fringe of hell, though its stench spread around them—the smell of high explosive, of the burning town of Dunkirk, which gave an angry red light for their work, and silhouetted the line of men who waited, like a trail of black ants, on the Mole; and the actual stench of dead bodies, which came in gusts from the beach. In the daytime the dive-bombers screeched and roared, machine-gun bullets spat about them, and hot fragments of shell whined and fizzed into the sea.

He saw a group of doll-like figures on the beach blown up by a bomb. It did not mean much at this distance, nor had he now any feeling but anger when men were machine-gunned, standing in the water, on the very verge of safety, nor when steamers were blown up and sunk. In the eyes of the men whom he pulled aboard he saw vaguely all the horrors that can happen to a defeated and fugitive army, and were still happening in the country that stretched inland from these flat and bloody beaches. But again, after the first hour or so his imagination ceased to function.

Roland and he took it in turns, one to steer the motor boat, the other to go in the lifeboat and help the sailors pull the troops aboard. As his sensibilities became deadened Stephen caught the attitude of the sailors, cursing and shouting at the men whom they rescued, because of their weight, their wounds, their failing energies. These curses were the only way to make them spend that last ounce of strength which was over from all they had spent in the past weeks. Not until they were on the decks of the steamer was it safe to show them any kindness.

When the machine-gun bullets hit the motor boat, when a bomb exploded, it seemed a few yards from him, Stephen was furious with the soldiers, as if they were responsible. It was now approaching dawn when the dive-bombers would come, and it was his turn in the lifeboat. In their few breathing spaces rumors were exchanged. Someone said the evacuation was nearly at an end. Astonishingly, through all this choas there appeared to be order, a plan of movement. Telephones still worked. These queues, which stretched in dark, tense, patient lines into the sea, had not come out at random, but were obeying a direction to the point where certain ships had been detailed to pick them up.

Now that it was nearly over, the slowness of the men was exasperating. Stephen, aching in every muscle, began to be nervous about his own skin. Another boat-load should finish the queue they were taking off, and with the prospect of getting away so close, the explosions seemed more like a danger threatening his own body. As they returned to the queue from the ship, a pleasure steamer with a gimcrack glass superstructure, the dawn, which was only a pale and dirty increase of the glow from the burning town, brought the first of the dive-bombers. The roar seemed to shake Stephen's flesh from his bones, as he might feel if he were holding one of those London steel drills. Bullets spat and fizzed and a bomb fell in the water near the queue they were approaching, but when they reached it the men were still standing in their patient rows.

Stephen leant over the side and lugged at the arms of a man who was too weak to contribute anything to his own rescue.

"Make an effort, you bloody sack of coal!" he shouted.

The young man had lost his tin hat, but he could hardly hold up his head.

"He's wounded, mate," said the man standing beside him in the water.

"Well, push him up then," shouted Stephen.

"I'm wounded too, mate."

"O God's Teeth!"

A sailor came and helped Stephen yank the man into the boat. He groaned and sagged inert on the floorboard. In a few minutes the sailors shouted "Boat's full!" and Roland let in his clutch and they chugged back to the pleasure steamer. Stephen, nearly exhausted, sank down beside the wounded man whom he had pulled aboard. The men's uniforms were dark, sodden and dripping. As Stephen recovered his breath he noticed an even darker patch on the khaki battle-dress of the man beside him, and then saw that on the already sopping floor-boards was spreading a soft dark stain of blood. He looked at the young man's face, and saw that his eyes were fixed on him. He was little more than a boy. He could not have shaved for a week or more, but on his chin was only a faint down, and the grime on his face was creased into no lines. The boy, watching him, had a look of recognition in his eyes, and Stephen had the feeling that he had seen him before somewhere.

"How d'you feel? What is your name?" he asked.

The boy smiled and held out his hand.

"Brian Wes . . ." he began, but as he spoke his smile faded.

"God, the Sweetie!" exclaimed Stephen incredulously, and then added in explanation, "King's. The Easter term."

The boy nodded, but it seemed with very great effort. His eyes opened wider as if imploring Stephen's help. He gave a convulsive grip of his hand. Then his head lolled sideways and he was dead.

Stephen, dazed and numb, sat holding the dead boy's hand for the rest of the journey to the pleasure steamer. He had no feeling much about what had just happened. He thought that it would be as when he had discovered Heather with Ablett, the feeling would come when the shock of surprise was over—not that he expected to have any intense feeling about this poor kid. After all, he had hardly known him, and he was associated with a part of Stephen's life so far removed from this stinking hell of horror that it might be on a different planet. Still, he was glad that through the extraordinary coincidence—or was it so extraordinary?—he had been able to hold his hand at the end.

They began to lift the men out on to the pleasure steamer. A sailor yelled at Stephen:

"Come on! Get a move on!"

"He's dead," said Stephen.

"Well chuck the poor sod overboard. We've only room for the living."

"All right, I'll do it," said Stephen as the sailor moved to help him.

He released Brian's hand, and first lifted his feet over the edge. Then he took his body under the arms and slid it gently into the sea. The heavy clothing dragged it down, and the hair spread out in the water like fine seaweed. He watched it for a moment, and then turned to help the men.

When Stephen returned to Catherine Street, where Lucinda had come up to meet him, he went to bed and slept for thirty-six hours.

When he awoke, had shaved painfully, and eaten a hearty breakfast, he told Lucinda that he was going up to Cambridge to see the University Appointments Board and try to obtain some kind of war job. He seemed prepared to do all that was expected of him. Lucinda was relieved but suggested that he should first go to Crittenden, as Paul would be anxious to see him and hear about Dunkirk. He said he would go there tomorrow.

The University Appointments Board was in the Old Schools. It consisted of three donnish elderly men. They appeared to dislike their work, the direction of young men into danger they could not share, and to be forcing themselves into an unnatural hardness of manner. They asked him questions, and when they learned he could speak fluent French they gave him a large sheet of paper, at the top of which in tiny writing was, "Recommended to be an interpreter."

He took this into another room, where he was told to strip. After he had been medically examined he was sworn in by a solicitor's clerk in lieutenant's uniform, who, noticing Stephen's intense depression, tried to cheer him up by pointing out the sexual references in the Bible. These mild obscenities, and also the full implication of what he was doing, failed to penetrate Stephen's consciousness. He accepted the two shillings offered him with the information that he was now a private soldier and would be notified when he was to report, probably not for some weeks.

As he was so close to King's when he came out, he went round to look at the chapel, and possibly to attend evensong. As he walked round the west end of the chapel, from the gate by Clare, he felt curiously aloof from this place, which once had such a potent influence on him, but as soon as he had entered the building with its cool, faintly acrid smell, its influence returned with overwhelming force, partly perhaps because of the shock of its changed aspect. It was filled, instead of with afternoon sunlight filtered into a thousand bright tints, with a gray twilight. The glass had been removed and the vast windows were black and blind. To anyone who had never seen it before it must still appear a magnificent building, but on himself, who had last seen it a glorious shell of color and light, the effect was intensely depressing. He walked slowly up the chapel and under the screen. When he came to the last seat in the choir on the decani side, he stood there and put his hand on the bookrest. He tried to recall the pure emotion he had felt on those spring evenings when he had first watched Brian singing in this place, but now, instead of those influences which had lifted his soul to the gate of heaven, others seemed to bear down on him from the blackened windows with an indescribable heaviness of grief, so that he could hardly move but stood still with his head bowed, his hand on the bookrest. Two women sightseers who were passing gave him a curious glance.

Stephen felt so oppressed in the chapel that he gave up his intention of staying till evensong, and he went out into the sunlight again. He walked through Clare onto the bridge, and stood there in the sunlight, looking down at the swaying water weed, and at the ducklings which darted about on the surface of the river.

When he arrived back at Catherine Street, Lucinda thought that his experiences at Dunkirk must be having a delayed action, and she sent him straight up to bed. However, the next morning he was quite well again, and he left for Crittenden. Paul was full of fury and anxiety at the Germans over-running France. He dreaded what might happen to the Roberts and to Harry. The thought of the Nazis in Paris was more than he could bear.

"Those fat blackguards in the Luxembourg Gardens!" he exclaimed in despair.

Marian, who had been in London, as soon as she returned, hurried across the park to pick Stephen's brains about Dunkirk. She was eager to grasp and fix every detail of the war in her mind, but he was unable to give much satisfaction in his replies to her avid catechism. He was unable to single out concrete events from that chaotic dream, in which only one incident stood out clearly against the background of burnings and explosions, of drownings and stench, and of that incident he could speak to no one.

"Mrs Fraser told me that we only had 30,000 casualties," said Marian. "Not much more than a tenth of our losses in some of the great battles of the last war. To think that we're kicked out of Europe for that! Gosh! I don't know what's come over the country."

In spite of Paul's snubs and the national disasters, Marian remained in good spirits, as she was able to tell her friends that Stephen had been at Dunkirk, and was now in the Army, waiting to join his regiment. She tried to persuade him to go about with her, but she said things which upset him, as he did not care to believe that Marian, whom he admired and who had been so kind to him, was possessed by a savage indifference to human suffering. He preferred to stay at Crittenden, where he spent his time reading, riding in the park, and listening to Paul's despairing analysis of the news. The wireless had at last been moved from the lavatory to the library.

One day he came in to hear the six-o'clock news. It was the evening when they announced the British attack on the French warships at Oran. One of these ships was the *Richelieu*, Pierre's ship. Paul waited until the end of this item of news, then he said quietly, "O God! O Christ!" and limped from the room.

After dinner it was still light and warm. Stephen felt that Paul would prefer to be alone, and he went out into the garden. As he walked slowly along the terrace with its worn stone balustrade, while the setting sun bathed the house, the clipped hedges of the garden, and the trees in the park beyond with its mellow light, Crittenden appeared the most ordered and peaceful place on earth, and it was hard to believe that these horrors were happening only a day's journey from here. His imagination was helped by remembered scenes from Dunkirk. He could see Pierre on a bombed and sinking ship. First, that King's boy killed by the Germans, and now Pierre probably killed by the British. Soon he himself would be engaged in killing young men. The golden evening seemed only a thin curtain over limitless vistas which were black and hideous. He walked down some wide steps into the garden. Soon he found himself by that gate into the park through which one went down to the lake to bathe. Total warfare affected Crittenden last and perhaps least of the stately homes of England, and as usual the cherry pie had been bedded out here. It was not yet in bloom, but Stephen bent down and picked a leaf off one of the young plants and examined it in idle curiosity.

He stood there smoothing the leaf with his fingers. The snapdragon was in bud on the nearby wall, and there were many scented flowers at hand, but his attention was absorbed by this tiny leaf, by its intricate design, the mystery of its growth and in such a perfect form. Still holding the leaf he went through the gate into the park. A little way off was a lime, and attracted by the scent, he walked over to it. In Cambridge, in the summer, all the Backs were full of the scent of limes. He examined the leaves and the delicate tassels of flowers. Absorbed in these things, he lost the sense that they were only a curtain concealing horror. They became for him the reality of life, its vital substance, against which the evil phantoms beyond might press, but which they could not wholly destroy. This tree obeyed its own law of being. It was defenseless against ax and fire, yet from a tiny seed it had grown to height and strength, and clothed itself with beauty.

As he stood there, examining the tree, it came upon him with rapidly increasing conviction, that there was another law of being than that which men obeyed. For the first time since his return from Dunkirk, that depression that had remained with him in varying degrees, and was at its strongest beneath the blackened windows of King's Chapel, was lifted from him and he felt at peace. As this conviction strengthened he felt more than a sense of peace, almost as if he were in love. It was as if he had renounced the world, but had accepted it again on a different level, so that his renunciation was not a denial, but a deeper affirmation of life. As he went back through the gate, past the bed of cherry-pie, he realized that it would be impossible for him to take up his duties as a soldier. At the moment this appeared to be of no importance.

Marian called the next morning, and Paul burst out in a violent denunciation of the government and the war.

"How the devil do they think they're going to liberate Europe?" he demanded. "It can't be done without inflicting far worse wrongs on the occupied countries than they will suffer under Hitler. It means that you will have to starve their people and ravish their lands in another invasion. No responsible statesman creates a chaos greater than his capacity to restore order."

"You're pro-German," said Marian.

"I detest the Germans," retorted Paul, "They have no taste."

Stephen, having been present at this wrangle, thought that Paul would be sympathetic to his new attitude, and in the afternoon he tried to explain it to him, but it was not easy, as it was due to an experience more of the heart than of the mind, and too subtle, and even as yet, though intensely felt, too dimly understood to put into words.

"People are all acting against their belief," he said, "what they say has no relation to what they do, and they know that what they do is leading them in the very opposite direction from what they wish to go."

"That is very true," said Paul.

"I've decided," said Stephen, "that I must go in what I believe to be the true direction."

"Yes, and how will you begin?"

"I shall refuse military service."

Paul gave a start.

"You can't do that, Stephen."

"But you are against the war."

"Of course I am, because to continue it is only to turn a disaster into a great disaster, nothing less than the destruction of European civilization, and in this country of the last vestiges of the social fabric of which you and I are part."

"Then why shouldn't I refuse to serve?"

"Because the titles you'll inherit, the arms you bear, this place, everything comes to you from the services to their king of your fighting ancestors. What you ought to do is to take a commission, go into Parliament, kick out the business men, impeach the men who've led us into this mess, and do your best to restore legitimacy in government and in international relationships, which the Bolsheviks, the Nazis and our own traitors have made a web of confusion and lies. But you can't refuse to fight. That sort of thing belongs to the middle classes."

"I'm sorry, Paul," said Stephen quietly, "but my mind is made up."

Paul shrugged his shoulders.

In the evening he said to Stephen:

"You may be right. New situations may demand new methods. But I'm afraid it will lead you into difficulties."

"I'm prepared for that."

"I wouldn't tell Marian just yet," said Paul. "Let her find out." He looked very tired.

A few days after this Stephen had orders to report to a regiment stationed near Bedford.

CHAPTER TWELVE

STEPHEN arrived at the barracks with a few raw country recruits. A brusque, fatherly non-commissioned officer handed them out their uniforms and they were allotted to huts. Stephen at once told the N.C.O. that he did not intend to obey any orders. He explained that the refusal would not be intended as a personal slight. The man looked puzzled, but not resentful. He took Stephen to the adjutant to make his explanation.

"Good God!" said the adjutant, looking at Stephen curiously, but also without resentment. "Damned if I know what to do, sergeant. See about it in the morning."

Stephen spent the evening in the hut with the shy country recruits, listening to their slow conversation. He enjoyed the peaceful sense of human brotherhood. After they had been talking for some time, he told them that he intended to resist military discipline. Only one of them was hostile. The others were interested in this different approach to the war.

"How d'you get away with that, mate?" they asked.

"I haven't got away with it yet," said Stephen.

He spent a wretched night on the hard army planks, and lying awake for long stretches, it seemed to him that he would not be able to get away with it, and that he was on the verge of moral annihilation.

In the morning he did not go on parade. The N.C.O., who had appeared to accept his explanation the night before, found the practice of this disobedience less palatable than the theory. He took Stephen to Battalion Orders. Stephen explained his position to the Commanding Officer, who turned to the adjutant and demanded in a high fretful voice:

"What can we do with the feller?"

"Afraid it's beyond my experience, sir," said the adjutant.

"Take him back to his hut. I'll have to look into it," said the colonel. "Give him exercise every day."

The weeks drew on and nothing happened. Stephen became a peculiar institution in the battalion, a kind of mascot, and yet a mascot that was half taboo. At first men who did not know of his case, when they came into the hut and found him sitting reading, would say:

"Hullo, mate! You doing spare?"

Soon everyone knew that he was refusing duty. He was exercised in the square and given odd jobs to do. He was even sent alone into the town on messages. When the adjutant asked what was to be done with him, the colonel would become fretful and his voice more high-pitched, and he would exclaim:

"Damned if I know. What can I do with the feller?"

Stephen read a good deal, and did tasks for the men which they had not time to do for themselves. He sent for his flute and he played it in the hut. The colonel discovered that Stephen was a professional flute-player, also that he was a Cambridge graduate and the nephew of a peer. He was amused by this curious bird having landed in his battalion. He had Stephen to play the flute in the mess on guest night, and when asked repeatedly what was to be done with him, replied:

"I don't know. Give him exercise."

Stephen was popular in the negative way in which he had been popular at Cambridge. The days were warm, and soon he became used to the hard bed and the primitive conditions, but he was worried by his exclusion from complete comradeship with the other men, and at times by the feeling that he had no future and that his identity was lost. The difference of education made it difficult for him to explain himself to them.

He wrote to Lucinda and to Marian trying to explain himself. Marian wrote back saying that she did not intend to try to understand anyone's disobeying orders, and hoped that the army would soon cure him; but she sent him a cake, and a set of impregnated linen garments to wear under his clothes to keep off lice. She imagined that all private soldiers had lice.

Lucinda wrote plaintively, saying she wished he would make some compromise, and again suggested the Y.M.C.A.

The colonel had a private talk with Stephen and said that if he would agree to drill, he would be glad to recommend him for a commission, and receive him into his mess.

"It's devilish hard to get decent subalterns nowadays," he said. "You should see some of the specimens that have been offered to me."

When Stephen refused, he said peevishly, "Well, I suppose you know your own mind. Wish I knew what to do with you. By the way, could you play that Mozart thing tomorrow night?"

Throughout the summer the air attack on England grew in intensity, spreading inland from the south-east. With the increasing national danger, Stephen's tenuous popularity waned. He was avoided by the other soldiers, who spoke to him, if at all, in curt monosyllables. Then the colonel, whom even Paul would have accepted as a gentleman, and who, like him, would have preferred a chivalrous war with battles by appointment, was removed and a man of very different manners and views replaced him. Stephen was warned to prepare himself for trial by court-martial.

Lucinda stayed in London during the early days of the raids, partly because she always liked to appear unruffled, but mostly to be near Wentworth Fox, who had been given an appointment in a government office, and for the first time in his life had a regular and adequate income. Then he had the choice of remaining in London or being evacuated to Bristol. He was nervous of the bombs and chose Bristol, which meant his parting from Lucinda, as it was obvious that if she left London she would have to go to Crittenden. It would have endangered his reputation, and consequently his job, if she had followed him to Bristol, and also would have changed the light and satisfactory nature of their relationship.

Lucinda was hurt that he was going to Bristol. All her pleasant London life, which she had built up so carefully since Pat had left her, was falling to pieces—the life of little dinner-parties and flirtations, of shopping at Harrods and giving little presents, of plays and new books and gossip, and tender inquiries after some friend who might suddenly have found a pea under her twenty feather mattresses. But Wentworth would be the most serious loss. He was not perfect, but he was the only trace of romance left in her life. One Saturday afternoon he rang up to say that he was going away for the week-end, but would be back on Monday. He was leaving for Bristol on Tuesday. They arranged that Lucinda should go round to spend a last evening with him on Monday night. He had a basement flat on the other side of Victoria Street.

On Saturday the sirens had been going at intervals during the day. In the evening there were some sudden loud bangs, quite close. The maids ran down into the basement. Then it was quiet for a while. Lucinda went up onto the roof to see what was happening. To the east the whole sky was a red blaze. Some timber yards down by the docks had been set on fire. Throughout the night there was the intermittent noise of planes, and the sound of guns and exploding bombs. The maids stayed in the basement, but Lucinda went to bed in her room. This was not courage, as she had a dread of being buried under a fallen house.

The next night the raids were worse, but her chief fear was that Wentworth might not return to London to say good-bye to her. At last Monday evening came, and she went round to his rooms in the daylight, before the sirens sounded, as she was afraid that she might otherwise be caught by an A.R.P. man and forced to spend the night in a public shelter.

Wentworth was very nervous. He kept asking her questions about the two previous nights. They had a picnic meal, which they cooked between them. While they were drinking their coffee the noise of the raid began. She tried to draw his attention to herself, but he kept stopping to listen and to ask, "Was that a gun? Was that a bomb?" Lucinda became reproachful.

"I don't mind about the bombs if I'm with you," she told him.

"If you're blown up it doesn't matter who you're with," he said.

"I think it does."

Their conversation became a wrangle. She was beginning to think it would have been better if she had not come, when there was a deafening crash and a moment of blackness. The shutters had cracked and the windows blown open. Lucinda pulled herself to her feet to find she was facing a terrified Negro. It was a minute or more before she realized that a bomb must have fallen in a coal-bin, and that the Negro was Wentworth. She began to laugh, and with shaking fingers she took her mirror from her bag and saw that she too was like a Christy Minstrel. He was furious with her for laughing and she left him. This was her farewell to love, as she had known it of recent years.

The next afternoon Paul met her at Crittenden Halt. He told her that Stephen had been sentenced to one hundred and twelve days' detention.

"Doesn't that mean he mayn't leave the barracks?"

"No, I'm afraid it means the Glasshouse," said Paul.

"What is that?" asked Lucinda apprehensively.

"It's the military prison at Aldershot."

"But Stephen can't go to a place like that!" exclaimed Lucinda. "It's lunacy."

Paul did not reply. On the drive back he told her that they were expecting a number of evacuee children at Crittenden the following day, and that they were clearing all the good furniture out of the dining-room wing to prepare for them. Lucinda helped after they had had tea, during which Marian catechised her about the bombs. There was no further mention of Stephen, but Lucinda, as she helped to carry the priceless Kingwood commodes from the yellow drawing-room, or lifted the disconcerted portraits of past Brayfords from the dining-room walls, for fear the East End children should use them as targets for darts or pats of margarine, was haunted by the thought of him in a military prison, and was more seriously unhappy than she had been in her life before.

Stephen could not have been court-martialed at a worse moment for himself than when the raids had just been released with their full intensity on London. In the week before his trial no one spoke to him except some men who were undergoing punishment in the same hut as himself, and whose conversation was unrelievedly pornographic. These failed to judge him, not from understanding or tolerance but only because they were themselves devoid of any moral standard. Nauseated by their conversation he sat aloof from them, and for this they did judge him.

When his sentence was promulgated it was commuted to eighty-four days. He was taken by an escort of two men from Bedford to Aldershot. It was a dry, windy day and hot for the time of the year. They walked by harsh new-made roads from the station to the prison. Everything was new and angular, and even the young trees planted by the roads suggested soldiers in uniform.

When they came to the huge wall of the prison, and a voice through a grille asked what they wanted, Stephen suddenly felt afraid. He had heard horrible tales of brutality in this place, and he tried to reassure himself by thinking, "After all they're human beings. They're under the government. They won't kill me and they won't ill-treat me if I behave properly."

A little door in a big door was opened and they were admitted. It was the middle of the day, and the staff-sergeants were just coming off duty and going to their dinners. Some of them had to attend to Stephen which put them in a bad mood. He was taken to the reception room, going through a zigzag of concrete barriers to get there. Everything about the place, the walls, the substance of the concrete bulwarks, seemed to threaten efficient violence. He had the feeling that if he made a false move he would be struck, and then thought this fear was fantastic. He tried to remember Dunkirk, with bombs falling and bullets and bits of shell whizzing about, to rid himself of this sense of danger. Here in comparison he was perfectly safe, and yet here he felt more afraid.

He was in civilian clothes and carrying his equipment. A staff-sergeant told him to put on his uniform. Stephen smiled politely, but he could not help his voice from trembling a little.

"I don't refuse out of obstinacy," he said, choosing his words clumsily. "It's simply that I can't let myself obey a military order."

The ring of sergeants, with their peaked caps pulled low over their small expressionless eyes, stared at him. He could not tell from their eyes what they were thinking.

"You don't refuse!" said one of them incredulously, and gave him a clout over the head. "Pick up your kit."

Stephen blinked from the clout and stood still.

"Pick it up!" barked the sergeant.

Still Stephen did not move. The sergeant came up to him and began to tear off his clothes. When Stephen was naked he gave him a blow on the solar plexus and he fell winded to the floor. The sergeant dragged him to his feet and banged his head against the wall. He felt as if his skull would split. He was taken to a barber, who had a huge beaky nose which protruded from under the low peak of his cap, and made him look like part of an anti-Nazi cartoon. This man ran the clippers roughly over his head. Hairless and naked, Stephen was flung into a blanket with his equipment and carried to a cell on the third floor, and left there for the afternoon. He was cold and had to put on the uniform as his clothes had been taken away.

He lay back on the hard, narrow bed and soon fell into an exhausted sleep. When he awoke it took him some moments to remember what had happened. He put his hand to his head, which was aching from the banging against the wall, and gave a start of surprise that he had no hair. He sat up and wanted to go to the lavatory. He did not know what the procedure was, and wondered if there was a bell-push. He found that the door of his cell was not locked. He opened it a little and peered out. There was no one about, so he went to look for a lavatory.

The building had three floors, the bottom one of stone. The upper two floors were iron grilles, so that the huge skylight which gave this place its name of "the Glasshouse" could light the whole building, and orders could be shouted up from below. He heard afterwards that in peace-time these iron grilles were polished like silver. He found a lavatory and his head ached a little less. On the way back to his cell he read some of the charge sheets, hanging up outside the other cells. Some of the prisoners had been at Dunkirk and had escaped from death or German captivity to this. Some had inflicted injuries on themselves to evade the fighting, had chopped off a finger, or shot themselves in the foot. Others had overstayed their leave, or committed acts of indecency in England. He did not see any charge sheets of men who, like himself, disobeyed orders because they would not accept this way of life.

When he had returned to his cell he sat with his shaved head in his hands, brooding over the hideousness of his surroundings, and as the days of his sentence passed he became no more reconciled to his lot. In the morning they had to run with their full jerries to empty them in the lavatory, while the staff, as the various sergeants were all called, shouted and cursed at them. They had to shave, standing only a few inches inside their doors, and facing outwards, so that they could be seen if they tried to kill themselves by cutting their throats. At night he heard the staff prowling, the "pad-pad" of their soft footsteps, the click as they switched on from outside the light in the cells, and looked through the little window in the door to see that the prisoner was not attempting some solitary pleasure, nor arranging a device by which he might kill himself.

Soon he lost sight of the motives that had brought him here. He forgot that he had set out to affirm love against hatred, life against death. He hated all that he saw, and dreamed of how he would in the future work to have this monstrous place destroyed and these brutal men punished. That was all he lived for, to release his hatred.

He was only allowed to write one letter a fortnight, but there was no limit to the number he might receive. Lucinda wrote begging him to obey military orders, and saying if only he would do this they might pull some strings and have his sentence reduced, and then he could be fitted into a noncombatant job. It was unlikely that he would ever have compromised, and his mood was far too bitter for him to do so now.

When his sentence was served he was taken back to Bedford, where he hoped he would be given his discharge. Paul went to see him there, but advised Lucinda not to accompany him as he thought that under these conditions her meeting with Stephen could only be painful. When he saw Stephen he was glad he had done so. Stephen looked well enough, but there was a hard glint in his eye which Paul found almost repellent. They had an embarrassed desultory conversation.

Stephen was disappointed of his hope. Instead of being discharged he was again brought before a court-martial, and this time he was sentenced to six months' imprisonment. His former sentence had been to detention, and by strict regulations he should not have had his hair shaved. In effect he found that the only difference between detention and imprisonment was that prisoners were inspected for lice once a week.

The second time he arrived at the Glasshouse he was not alone, but one of a group of twenty. He was not singled out for individual ill-treatment, but there was the same attempt at complete terrorization on the first day. It seemed to him even more frightening than on his first day, as now it was more impersonal.

The sense of prevailing terrific discipline made every sound like the crack of a whip. His group had to queue up, facing the wall, and at the slightest quiver of movement a blast of voice struck them from behind, while the barber came along and, seeming indifferent whether he took a piece of neck or ear with it, sent the loose festoons of their hair, black, brown and mouse color, and one bright carroty-red, slithering to the floor. That afternoon he was not left alone in his cell. With the nineteen others he was made to drill, always at the double, and always behind the drill was the threat of violence, of the private beating-up.

The night came and he was in his cell. He heard again at intervals the "pad-pad" of the staff's footsteps, the click of the light switch, and felt the brutal watching eye at the window which was no bigger than a half-crown.

With that single-mindedness with which Stephen throughout his life had given himself up to one thing, whether it was friendship, or music or love, he now gave himself up to hatred. He let it run like poison through his veins and infest his brain and vision. He thought of Heather to strengthen his power to hate. Even people like Paul and Lucinda he saw only with cold detachment, and applied criticisms to them which he had not admitted before. Lucinda had never behaved like a normal mother to him. She had always seemed to be half laughing at him in a silly fear of being sentimental, while Paul was a perverted, arrogant old spinster.

In his first weeks back at the Glasshouse, by day and by night he nursed his hatred. One night, when in a review of his life everything was brought up to be condemned as foolish or evil, he remembered the services in King's Chapel and gave a shrug of contempt to think that he had been so affected by them. He could not have been so affected if he had then had any experience of life. It was sickeningly adolescent. Even when he thought of Brian dying at Dunkirk, he did not feel any tenderness or pity but only hatred of the system which had killed him.

When he fell asleep his mind continued its waking processes, but in a confused fashion. In dreams we are the passive mirrors of involuntary imagination, and Stephen no longer had the iron satisfaction of directing his hatred. He was its passive victim. Whatever innocent and happy visions from the past came to him, they were clouded and distorted by it—the plage at St Saturnin, Clare bridge, or those parts of the gardens and woods at Crittenden where he had played as a child, they all became scenes in hell, peopled by inmates of the Glasshouse and by the corpses of Dunkirk. In one of these dreams he was in the Glasshouse, which in his dream was also King's Chapel. Mistily the sergeant who had first stripped and beaten him was also Brian, the end chorister. In his nightmare he tried to divide the two things, the two places, and the two people, the object of his love and the object of his hate. Then it seemed as if they were both in himself, and his body was torn apart by them, as if he were nailed to a cross made of love and hatred, and he had to reconcile the two things in himself. It was the feeling he had on that day at Cambridge after he had thrown the goldfish over Roland, but far more painful and intense, as part of his conscious mind was asleep and could not rationalize it.

In his agony he cried out to some good thing to help him, and it seemed that he was answered. The answer seemed to be in the form of music. He was again under the lime tree in the park at Crittenden, and some touch of the emotion he had then felt returned to him in his dream. The branches overhead became the branching roof of a college chapel which was full of an extraordinary illumination, not dazzling nor glittering but as if everything contained light in itself. In the midst of this light was the transfigured face of the boy whom he had lifted into the sea at Dunkirk, but he had become nameless. He was singing and yet the music was hardly recognizable as sound. It was more like a quivering in the air which was part of the all-pervading light. Stephen knew that there were words to this music, though he could not hear them sung. They were the words of Lovelace's poem:

> If I have freedom in my love,
> And in my soul am free,
> Angels alone that soar above
> Enjoy such liberty.

He wept with happiness in his sleep.

In the morning when the whistles blew and the shouting began, the peace which had come to him in his dream remained with him. The prisoners all stood six inches from their doors, facing inwards. They were holding their jerries and waiting for the whistle at which they would turn and run to empty them in the lavatories.

The whistle blew and Stephen turned and ran with his jerry. One of the staff saw the expression in his eyes as he turned. It was an expression he had never seen before in the eyes of a prisoner in the Glasshouse. Its happiness infuriated him, and as Stephen ran past he shouted at him and tripped him up, so that his urine spilled, dripping down through the iron grille. These incidents often happened, but there was plenty of labor to clean up afterwards.

Stephen picked up himself and his jerry and ran on. The expression in his eyes had not changed. The sergeant determined to make it change. He could only put it down to effeminacy, and, in

424

a muddled way which he did not himself understand, he took it either as dumb insolence or a challenge to his own virility. He set out to force his male will on it, to break it or destroy it, as if it were a physical virginity. Sometimes he had an inkling of the fact that it was a quality of the spirit which it was beyond his power to break. Then he attacked Stephen's body with kicks and jostlings and jabs with his elbow. At times in private he used greater violence. Throughout the six months of Stephen's second imprisonment this conflict went on between the innocence of his spirit and the sergeant's provoked but unacknowledged lust. The conflict could never be resolved because the two things could never meet. The only result was that Stephen's body became steadily weaker under the kicks and blows, but the expression in his eyes did not change, though sometimes it became more dim and clouded. Sometimes the sergeant affected a leering intimacy, but having no response he turned to violence.

The prisoners were allowed to receive parcels containing necessities, but anything more luxurious than a handkerchief had to be kept for them till the end of their sentence. When a parcel arrived a sergeant would call out the name of the recipient and he would double across to get it.

One morning that sergeant whose mind was fixed on Stephen called out his name, and he ran across to get his parcel. The box was open and contained a little bunch of the flowers that children call cherry-pie. Their living scent overcame the pervading carbolic stink of the Glasshouse. By the flowers was a card on which was written, "To Stephen from Heather."

"Shall I keep them for you till your time's up," said the sergeant sneering, but Stephen did not hear him.

"Oh, thank you," he said, "thank you for letting me see them! Now I have no enemy in the world."

At first the sergeant thought that Stephen had the effrontery to mock him, and he raised his arm to strike him across the face, but when he saw Stephen's eyes, almost weeping with joy and gratitude, he was for once bewildered and embarrassed, and he said curtly:

"Get back to your work."

CHAPTER THIRTEEN

AT CRITTENDEN Lucinda and Paul were trying to appear to each other as cheerful as possible. When the raids on London began, Lady Bassingbourne came down to live with Marian at the End House. Half of Crittenden House was given over to the shrieks and stampedes of the evacuated children, but Paul had baize doors put between his own apartments and that wing, and only occasionally was the noise disturbing. He also fenced off part of the garden with barbed wire and resigned it to ruin. At first he had looked forward to having the children, as he prided himself on his ability to understand them and to be naturally friendly with them, but hitherto he had only had to do with individual well-mannered boys like Pierre, and Roland and Stephen when they were young. He found numbers overwhelming, especially when having overcome their shyness they all screamed at him at once, and made demands with a familiarity which was not entirely friendly. They mimicked his voice and his limp, and he returned through the baize doors and gave up all attempt to be a preceptor and friend to these unfortunate waifs. He did not again invite any of them to tea, nor point out to them the beauties of Kingwood commodes and *famille verte* Sèvres.

Marian had made the last war an excuse for a simple ménage. Paul, although the house was cut in half, achieved an increase in grandeur. Having abandoned the dining-room to the children, he dined in state beneath the painted ceiling and the chandeliers of the great gilded saloon. He kept the library for his private use, and Lucinda had the peacock room. Lucinda spent the time of Stephen's imprisonment almost exclusively in Paul's company, though Marian came up every morning to boss the children and the women in charge of them. Lucinda did not like to go about, as the people whom she met were either awkward or clumsily kind in their references to Stephen, and Paul would say the most dreadful things in public, in a shop, in a drawing-room, or in the porch of the cathedral where they sometimes went for Sunday evensong. He now considered himself an orthodox Anglican, though he spoke as if he were a Roman Catholic, but he attacked the clergy because he thought they should make an attempt to preserve moderation in warfare, and also because so many of them were friends of Marian's.

Marian had received the news of Stephen's imprisonment with a tolerance that surprised Lucinda. When Paul told her that he had been sent to the Glasshouse, she said:

"What glasshouse? Is he growing tomatoes?"

"It's the military prison at Aldershot."

"Oh, well," said Marian, "a military prison probably isn't as bad as a civil prison. It sounds more respectable, and I expect the man in charge of it is a gentleman."

"It does not matter how it sounds," snapped Paul, "we don't have to be respectable, like city clerks. I'm concerned with how they'll treat him."

"It'll make him hard as nails, which won't hurt him."

"It's not his body, it's his mind I'm thinking of," said Lucinda.

"Then why did you bring him up to be so soft?"

"I did not know the world was going to be so bloody. I should have, I suppose, as, if we look back at history, we can see that it's been hell all the time. The masses of the people have always been tortured and wretched. We've only lived in a little oasis of bogus civilization, and now that it's thought immoral for people of our sort to live in our oasis, and we're all to be shoved down into the masses, there won't be any civilization at all, and it will be unrelieved hell. I hate the past and I hate the future."

"I hate the present," said Paul.

"Sitting down and hating everything won't get Stephen out of the hot-house," said Marian. "I'll go up to London and see General Fraser."

"But, Marian, the bombs!"

"You don't want to fuss," said Marian.

Marian's attitude was partly due to her affection for Stephen, partly to the satisfaction it would give her to force the county to continue to accept the Brayfords, with Paul reputed a fifth-columnist and Stephen in prison, but mostly to loyalty to Arthur's memory. Without him her life was a desert, and she believed she had failed him when he was alive. Whatever those of his blood might do, she would stand by them at the cost, if necessary, of everything she had to give.

She had two things in common with Paul, an intense loyalty to her own people, and an absolute directness of speech. Though they continued to fight, they were not intolerable to each other.

Lady Bassingbourne, on the other hand, could not bear Paul's company.

"I don't know how we can talk in that way about dear Mr Churchill," she complained. To Lucinda she said:

"I should have thought that Stephen would have wanted to avenge poor Hugo."

"He hardly knew him. In fact he can't even remember him."

"Still," said Lady Bassingbourne with obscure emphasis.

Paul really was against all war, as it displeased him that young men, even those of foreign countries, should be killed in large numbers; but he could not admit this approach to a liberal and nonconformist attitude, so he pretended that the proper patterns of warfare were found in the age of chivalry, and in the eighteenth century. It was only this war which was wrong, because it was conducted by people who had no respect for tradition, and who said that they disapproved of war, but who, once they were in it, went to the extreme of atrocity, like a puritan woman, who, having decided to abandon her virtue, was most likely to descend to the abyss of depravity. Paul told Willy Greene-James that the war "was like a *nouveau riche* pheasant shoot."

An incident happened about this time which made Marian an unqualified champion of Stephen. The Fitzauncell papers came out with a scurrilous article on him. It said that his godfather was a German, the Grand Duke of H——, and recalled Paul's speech in the House of Lords after the fall of France. In the picture paper was a photograph, which like the information about Stephen's godfather, must have been supplied by Baa. Lucinda was more shocked and hurt by this than by the article itself.

"When a peer tries to earn his living, he's like a business man waging war," said Paul. "He doesn't know where to stop."

Marian wrote to Baa saying that if he was unaware of this article, he should now resign his position. If he had anything to do with it he had better not visit Crittenden nor even the neighborhood again. She had no reply. Paul had the satisfaction of learning that after this the Greene-Jameses and the older county families would not visit at the castle, nor receive Lord Fitzauncell in their houses.

Not very long before Stephen came out of the Glasshouse Hitler launched his attack against Russia.

"I hope the brutes kill each other off," said Marian, when she heard the news.

"That would be a very nice solution," said Lady Bassingbourne, smiling in kindly approval. The raids ceased for the time being, and a few days later she returned to her house in Kensington Square which was still standing. The children also departed from Crittenden House, leaving smudges and scribbles on the Grinling Gibbons carving, and the whole wing full of that undefinable smell, partly of lead pencils, which seems inseparable from schools. Paul could not afford to have it redecorated, and he had not the servants to run the whole house. He had that wing scrubbed out with carbolic soap, and then locked it up.

In these weeks after the departure of Lady Bassingbourne from the End House, and the children from Crittenden, there was a curious still emptiness about the place, as if a tension had been released. Lucinda felt as if she were waiting for something to happen, and supposed that it was Stephen's return.

The wireless had been banished back to the lavatory, but Lucinda obtained Paul's permission to have a tiny inconspicuous wireless in the peacock room, and promised not to turn it on when he was sitting there with her. One evening she was alone, doing some sewing for the Women's Volunteer Service. Just before the news she switched on the wireless and heard the end of the preceding part of the program. It was one of a series of the lives of great singers. Tonight's subject was Melba, and it ended with a record of her singing *Home, Sweet Home*. Lucinda was suddenly carried back with almost unbearable vividness to her life in Melbourne, to the ballroom at Tourella on the day of Julie's first big party. That vivid memory extended its focus to include others, the night of the Radcliffes' ball, her first dance with Hugo, the drive out to Cape Furze through the paddocks like brown honeycomb, and sitting with Tony on the Tarpeian Rock, while Bill and Blake IX fooled about with oranges. The record was only a background to the announcer's voice. She bent close to the wireless to hear the pure and limpid notes which were gradually fading away, and she felt as if she were trying to separate and secure all that was happy in her early life from this insistent voice, the voice in whose urbane tones she had heard announced increasing misfortune and horror, behind which all happiness was as fading and elusive as this song.

A few days later she went to meet Stephen at Crittenden Halt. He had been taken from the Glasshouse back to Bedford, where, as a result of Marian's interview with General Fraser, he was given his discharge. In any case he was too ill to remain in the army.

Lucinda had saved enough petrol to go to meet him at the junction, and save him the wait and the extra bit of tiring journey in the local train. He was thin and tired. She had expected this. What she had not foreseen and what did shock her was that he looked like a young man from the working-classes. He was wearing the suit he had worn all the time of his first detention at Bedford, and it had not been pressed. She was afraid that he might have the look of the general whom she had met at Susannah's, the one who had been in a concentration camp, but his eyes were bright and hopeful, though with the brightness one sometimes sees in the eyes of an old man, not with the soft and smouldering flame of a boy's eyes.

Stephen seemed to be shy and dazed to find himself back at Crittenden. When he came down in the evening, bathed and in his dinner clothes which had been laid out for him, he appeared more his normal self, and Lucinda found it easier to talk to him, but he looked even more tired. Marian came across to dinner and Paul opened a bottle of Château Yquem, and it was a pleasant little family reunion, but Stephen, who had had no alcohol for so long, was upset by even one glass of this perfect wine, and he had to go straight from the table to bed.

The next day he sat in the garden with Paul and Lucinda. She asked him tentatively about the Glasshouse, but such a worried look came over his face that she did not persist.

The next day he collapsed. He had suddenly realized that there was no more need to summon every ounce of strength, moral and physical, to endure the conditions of his life, and at the same time he realized that his reserves were all exhausted. The doctor said that all he wanted was rest and feeding up. He regained a little strength under this treatment, but in the middle of November he had a relapse for which there was no apparent explanation. His symptoms resembled those of that first mysterious illness in his fourteenth year. He was always tired after Marian's visits, and it was a problem for Lucinda to keep her away from him without hurting her feelings.

He was better in early December, and about that time he had a letter from Hayman, who was now chaplain to an infantry regiment, and who had been slightly wounded. He was on leave and his home had been bombed. Stephen asked Paul if he might invite him down for Christmas. Paul was agreeable, and said they would have Midnight Mass sung in the chapel. He roped in three gardener's boys and coached them in simple plainsong. This enabled him to avoid the parish church, where he was liable to insult the vicar. Last year Paul had taken part in an agitation to stop night-bombing by mutual agreement, which, as Lady Bassingbourne said, had quite spoiled the Christmas spirit.

However, even the laws of hospitality could not prevent Paul, finding a clergyman at his mercy, telling him what he thought of bombing bishops. His implication was, of course, that his guest must share his attitude, which on the contrary Hayman found extremely shocking, for in his own mind he had extended the doctrine of the Incarnation to include, not only romantic friendship, but mass butchery. He looked with amazement at this waspish old man, who, seated at the head of his table in a dining-room fit for a royal palace, harangued him about the iniquities of his spiritual superiors.

Stephen now looked miserable and deathly ill. His skin was green and glistening. Lucinda was worried, and trying to restrain Paul, she said:

"You only see one side of the question, Paul."

"Yes, the backside, and damned ugly it is," said Paul, forgetting in his excitement that he was speaking before a woman and a clergyman.

The next day was Christmas Eve. Stephen did not get up till midday. He spent the afternoon quietly talking to Hayman, mostly about Cambridge. Hayman did not mention the war, nor Stephen the Glasshouse. He asked Stephen if he was going to communicate at the Midnight Mass. Stephen had not done this since he left school. He looked thoughtful and said he would. Hayman said that he must fast from five o'clock onwards. Neither of them dined.

Lucinda was vexed about this, as Stephen was in no condition to go without a meal, especially if he were going to stay up till one in the morning. Hayman, helped by Marian and the gardeners' boys, sang the service very nicely, and Paul played the organ. The chapel looked beautiful with its golden eighteenth-century brocade, the tall candles, and the forced Madonna lilies. Unfortunately the best chasuble had long ago been worn out on Susannah's grand piano. Lucinda was rather moved by the service. When they came out Stephen was wide-eyed. She did not know whether this was due to fatigue or emotion. He did not seem any the worse for it the next day.

In the evening Marian came to dinner, and seemed determined to make it lively. She almost forced Stephen to eat more turkey, saying he needed feeding up, while Paul, with an unusual lack of perception kept telling the butler to fill his glass with burgundy. Stephen went early to bed and on the next day, his birthday, he was in a worse condition than he had been in since he left the Glasshouse.

A spell of extreme cold came in with the New Year and lasted, with hardly a break, for eight weeks. Crittenden House was difficult to keep warm without using enormous quantities of coal, and Paul, in spite of his claim to be privileged, was conscientious about using an undue share of any scarce commodity. He would not use a car if he could avoid it, as petrol was brought to the country at the cost of men's lives, but those of his neighbors who dubbed him fifth-columnist also boasted how they had wangled extra coupons, and had reserve tins of petrol hidden in their wine-cellars. Even though Stephen was kept in his room with a good fire, the quality of cold seemed to penetrate there and to reduce his vitality. Sometimes he lay motionless for hours and it was impossible to gain his attention.

"What *is* the matter with him?" Lucinda in despair asked the doctor.

"To be perfectly frank," said the doctor, "I don't know. It seems to me like that 'wasting disease' that young people used to have in the eighteenth century. I should think it is largely psychological."

This was borne out by the fact that if any of the more lurid newspapers were left in his room his condition became worse. It was also worse if there had been any prolonged noise of aeroplanes overhead. Sometimes when Lucinda had left him quite cheerful, and apparently on the way to recovery, she would be dismayed on returning a few hours later to find him sweating and haggard.

Paul spent a fair amount of time with him. He saw their ill-effect, and refrained from political harangues. Their conversation was about the simple events of the day at Crittenden, and occasionally more serious.

Towards Easter Stephen's condition became much weaker, and he had to have a professional nurse as well as Lucinda to look after him. In these days a nurse for one private patient was almost impossible to find, but there was a retired nurse called Mrs Dumble living in the village. She was too old for strenuous work, and she offered to help with Stephen. He now saw no one but Paul, Lucinda and Mrs Dumble, and occasionally Marian, who put her head in the door and said, "What you want is a pound of good underdone steak." She was as fond of Stephen as ever, but she was faintly repelled by his lying there with his large eyes and wasted body, refusing to react to normal treatment. His spirit seemed to be consuming his body. She would have preferred Fred, at the same time lying at Tourella, a perfectly sound log, his fine heart still beating stoutly, but unable to animate his blank mind, or to sustain a spirit which had already evaporated.

One evening, shortly after Easter, Paul was sitting with him when Stephen said:

"Harmony can be achieved in many kinds of ways, but its purest expression is in music. I suppose that is at the root of the idea that endless bliss is a state of endless singing. The music of the spheres. What is the music of the spheres? It must be terrific and beyond our comprehension. There are some kinds of music, like Palestrina and

Beethoven's last Quartets, that give me a glimpse of what I think eternal music must be. Do you remember making me get out of the train at Dijon to hear Palestrina? I didn't take it in at the time. I learned to appreciate it later at King's."

They talked about polyphonic singing for a while, and then Stephen said:

"You know how sometimes you see in a train or in the street a face that attracts you, and you feel an instinctive recognition of that person."

"I certainly do," said Paul.

"There must be an affinity between you, and yet if you were to become acquainted with the owner of the face you might be completely put off by his ideas, or voice or something."

"I suppose that is possible," agreed Paul.

"But even so," Stephen continued, "do you think that sort of recognition might apply to something definite, that it might almost be the warning of a common fate? I mean, do you think it could possibly be a scientific fact that this linking of fate could be acknowledged beforehand in an exchanged glance?"

"We can't tell scientifically," said Paul, "what are the recognitions of the soul. The mysteries of the human heart are the mysteries of God. They can't be analyzed and labeled like the contents of a sewer, whatever Herr Freud may say."

"No," Stephen agreed thoughtfully. After a pause he said suddenly, "Paul, I want to be cremated and my ashes scattered in Cambridge."

"Don't talk nonsense," exclaimed Paul.

Mrs Dumble came into the room and said that Stephen must not talk any more this evening.

"Before you go," said Stephen, "just give me that book—Traherne —the third from the end of the top shelf."

Paul handed him the book and left the room.

"Now don't tire yourself," said Mrs Dumble. "You may read for half an hour if it's not a detective story, then I'll come in and settle you down for the night."

When she came back again he was dead.

CHAPTER FOURTEEN

Two DAYS LATER, when Lucinda had recovered a little from the shock, Mrs Dumble brought her a book and said in a kindly, sentimental manner:

"This was the last thing he held in his hands. I thought you would like to keep it specially."

Lucinda thanked her and took the book, which was the copy of Traherne's poems, up to her room, where she put it on her bedside table. Before she went to bed she glanced through it and her eye was caught by some pencil-writing inside the cover. It was some verse in Stephen's hand:

> Within their cage, where glass and stone
> Are frozen in a mystic's dream,
> Behind the pale gold candle gleam
> The scarlet nightingales intone.
>
> And are these flutes for man's delight
> Just quivering down the branching quire,
> Or do they rise by roof and spire
> To echo in the angel height?
>
> The wakened ear is not denied
> To find this house the lodge of heaven,
> But to the quickened heart is given
> To find the gate of heaven wide.

She wondered who had composed them, as she had never known Stephen to write verse. While lying awake thinking about them, she remembered the afternoon when she had gone up with Paul to see Stephen, the reference to King's Chapel at lunch, her attendance with him at evensong, and his extraordinary touchiness when she made some mild criticism. She was sure then that he must have written these verses.

Stephen's body, flanked by six tall candles, had lain in the chapel since his death. Marian had produced some nuns to watch it, and Lucinda herself took a turn, but she found it too upsetting to stay there for long. She had agreed with Paul that he should be cremated, but it was not until the morning after Mrs Dumble had handed her the book that he told her that Stephen had wanted to have his ashes scattered in Cambridge. They discussed the most suitable place, and thought of Clare Fellows' Garden. Paul said that of course they would have to ask permission for this, and he looked doubtful. They did not know, but they both thought it possible that it might be refused, possibly because of some regulation, or because of Stephen's imprisonment in the Glasshouse. Finally they decided that his ashes should be thrown into the Cam from Clare bridge. It would hardly be necessary to ask permission for that.

They telegraphed to Roland, saying which day they would arrive at Cambridge, asking him to engage rooms for them and to meet them.

Roland was at Cambridge Station with a large black Rolls-Royce which he had hired. He had a vague idea that this car was suitable both to Paul's rank and to the occasion. Paul was sombre and irascible, and Lucinda looked very tired. Marian had not come, as her curse of being never weary had begun to take effect, and her doctor had ordered her to stay in bed for a week, and to cancel all engagements for months ahead.

Paul had discovered among the minor antiques of Crittenden a mahogany sheraton tea-caddy, in which, because of its fine workmanship and beautiful design, he had chosen to bring the ashes. He had had it relined by the estate carpenter, and he carried it in a small suitcase. On the drive to the University Arms, where Roland had engaged rooms for them, Paul tried to relieve his state of tension by fussing and by criticism.

"You'll get locked up under 18B," said Roland amiably.

This set Paul off on a tirade which lasted till they reached the hotel.

After luncheon Paul and Lucinda rested. Roland arranged to bring the black Rolls later in the afternoon to collect Paul and the ashes. Lucinda was not to go with them, but she was to meet them after the ceremony at the west end of King's Chapel. They drove round by Queens' Road and entered Clare from that side, so that they would not have to carry the casket through the college buildings. The half-unfolded leaves of the lime trees in the avenue made them like ferns. On their left, down in the Fellows' Garden one or two flowering shrubs were in bloom, but in the long border were only a few patches of yellow leopard's-bane, arabis and purple aubretia. The young leaves on the great copper beech were still only a smoky pink. Everywhere in the sunshine the colors were pale. Even the stone of the buildings seemed washed with the spring freshness.

There was no one about, except for two people lying some distance away on the river bank in King's. Paul rested the casket on the parapet of the bridge. He felt that what he was about to do should have some resemblance to a rite. Subconsciously copying priests with their birettas, he took off his hat and gave it to Roland to hold. He then took a sheet of paper from his pocket and said:

"There has already been a service at Crittenden, and also the ceremony at the cremation, but before I scatter the ashes I should like to read this. It is from Father Zossima's conversations." He held the paper away from him, as he was long-sighted, and began to read:

" 'Of a truth they have more fantastic dreams than we. They aim at justice, but denying Christ they will end by flooding the earth with blood, for blood cries out for blood, and he that taketh up the sword shall perish by the sword. And if it were not for Christ's covenant, they would slaughter one another down to the last two men on earth. And those last two men would not be able to restrain each other in their pride, and the one would slay the other and then himself. And that would come to pass were it not for the promise of Christ, that for the sake of the humble and meek the days shall be shortened.' "

Paul folded the paper and put it away, then, murmuring something inaudible, he unlocked the casket with a small silver key, and, opening it, tipped its contents into the river. The dust, swirling slightly in the breeze, rested on the surface, but the few bones sank into the water-weed and mud. Paul stood watching the gray patch on the surface of the stream, until it disappeared under Garrett Hostel bridge. When there was no trace of it visible, he took his hat from Roland, and, closing the casket, tucked it under his arm and then went on across the bridge into Clare.

Now that the actual ceremony was over, Paul became more at ease, and he commented appreciatively on the architecture of the college. Roland had modified his former views sufficiently to admit that it was dignified and peaceful, but said that it bore no relation to the life of today. By the time they turned round the west end of King's Chapel they were engaged in one of their usual animated discussions. Lucinda was waiting for them by the south porch and was relieved to see Paul more himself. They looked up at the turrets of the chapel, which today were a silvery-gray in the spring sunlight. Paul repeated what he had said before, that this building was a creation of the spirit, that the mind alone could not have achieved it.

"Won't you come in and rest awhile?" said Lucinda, who felt

he could not bear one of Paul's tirades at this moment, and was afraid that, with his already worn nerves, he would make himself ill.

Before Paul could answer, the procession of top-hatted choristers came round the corner of Gibb's building. They looked with curiosity at the flushed and beaky-nosed old gentleman carrying a tea-caddy, who courteously doffed his hat and limped aside to let them pass into the chapel. In return they lifted their top-hats to Paul, which touched him poignantly and provoked a fresh outburst.

"And in three or four years' time," he demanded savagely, "are these boys, who have been trained here to sing the praises of Jesus Christ, to be made to stick bayonets into their fellows' stomachs, or to roast helpless women to death in the ruins of great cities? Only an ogre bred in Hell could conceive such a sequence for his children!"

At that moment a flight of pigeons descended from the chapel roof and alighted on the lawn near by. It reminded Lucinda of something—she could not think what. Then she remembered, it was of the day, long ago, when she had been with Roland and Stephen in the cinema at St Saturnin, and Stephen had looked up at her with amused pride as Roland said, "Comme ils sont gentils, ces petits pigeons!"

Suddenly she could not bear it any more. She could not speak. She made a helpless gesture and turned into the cool gloom of the chapel. As she left them she had a glimpse of Roland, kindly taking Paul's arm, and leading him away.

Almost sobbing she walked up through the screen, and instinctively she went to that stall which she had occupied on the day she came here with Stephen. She sank back and rested her head on her hand. Paul was too convincing a prophet of disintegration. Often he amused her by his assumption that he alone stood upright in a world of moral ruin, but today she could not bear it any longer. It could not be true that good was only in the past. It was true that now men were cruel and dishonorable, but had they been less cruel and dishonorable in the eighteenth century? Paul took the best men of the past and compared them with the worst of the present. Today more than ever she felt the need for some faith in the future, for others if not for herself. Her own contribution to the future had perished, a failure. He had failed in everything, in social life, in marriage, as a soldier, in all those things which give satisfaction to a young man's friends, and he had died more or less in discredit. In the midst of all this failure and loss and death she despaired of finding any basis for hope.

As she sat in the quiet chapel, her agitation subsided. She began to think more calmly about Stephen, not so much of his last months, but of him as a schoolboy, a nice, affectionate duffer. While she thought of him, recollecting all sorts of simple incidents of his childhood and youth, she found she was not thinking of him at all as a failure, but with affection even for his troublesome ways. She remembered diffident boyish gestures, when he was trying to express some tenderness of feeling which he himself only half understood. She remembered his eyes suddenly glowing with pleasure at the arrival of a friend, or at an unexpected revelation of beauty. As this feeling of love for him grew, it dispelled the blight of despair left by Paul's denunciations. For Stephen was a young man of today, and in him was a love of all that was good. He had not been cruel and dishonorable, and he had been a very ordinary young man. There was nothing exceptional about him, except, perhaps, his power of forgiveness. And if one ordinary young man like Stephen could restore her faith in life, how great it should be when there were thousands and thousands of young men in the world, stronger and wiser than Stephen, with an equal love of good, which, when this horror was over, would be released to affirm as great a sense of truth and human value as that of the past which Paul bewailed, and to create beauty as fine as that which he cherished in his exquisite and faded palace at Crittenden. Why, tomorrow there might spring up an art greater than any the world had yet seen. The builders of the Parthenon, she thought, could never have conceived that there would be a building like this chapel, nor could King Henry VI have imagined Fontainebleau or Schönbrunn. Tomorrow the good must return to mankind, for it was as urgent in him as the evil, which at length it must redeem. Tomorrow the creative passion and the need for truth would supplant the destructive lie, to which men had today abandoned themselves.

She was aroused from her reverie by the rhythmical clack-clack of shoes walking on stone, and she looked up to see that a sprinkling of people had come into the chapel, and that the choir was walking in under the screen. She looked at the boys as they took their places and she thought that they must be about the fourth lot in succession from those who had filled those seats when she was last here. Her eyes rested on the chorister directly facing her, and the boy, waiting for the service to begin, looked up at her. He saw a look of kindness in her eyes, and with the unguarded response of youth, he smiled and then turned swiftly away. There was something about that shy movement which recalled vividly the afternoon she had come with Stephen. And as in moments of powerfully awakened

emory we are able almost to feel the presence of someone who
its object, now she felt Stephen's presence, so that he seemed to
with her there in the chapel. Never before had she felt so
rongly the presence of someone who had left her.

Suddenly, without warning from the organ, the whole building
as full of song. Lucinda started with delight. She watched the
y opposite. He was taut, like a singing bird. His clear young
ice floated up to the lofty branches of the roof, which are them-
lves a form of music:

Eya, Resurrexit!